THE LOST ARIA

BOOK THREE OF THE EARTH SONG CYCLE

Mark Wandrey

Theogony Books
Virginia Beach, VA

Chris Kennedy/Theogony Books
2052 Bierce Dr.
Virginia Beach, VA 23454
http://chriskennedypublishing.com/

Ordering Information:
Quantity sales. Special discounts are available on quantity purchases by corporations, associations, and others. For details, contact the "Special Sales Department" at the address above.

The Lost Aria/Mark Wandrey – 2nd ed.
ISBN 978-1948485319

"I've always loved books that go from being a simple story to suddenly become one of epic proportions. You think you have a world understood, and the writer pulls that delicate sleight of hand, and you find yourself on a roller coaster ride of discovery and deadly peril for the characters you love. This novel, The Lost Aria, signals the beginning of things to come for our heroine Minu Alma. Things aren't quite as she was told, and you're all in for a big surprise. Thanks to my friends who told me the best and the worst of these kinds of stories; I hope you'll consider this one of the best.

Also, for my wife, Joy, always my love.

Prologue
April 2nd, 520 AE

Private Conference Room, Capital City, Planet Nexus

Tak'la, supreme leader of the Rasa, skittered down the hallway toward a meeting he wished didn't have to take place. In the vast Concordia, the Rasa were distant third-rate players—some would even suggest fourth-rate. Ever since Tak'la killed Ko'kra, his incompetent predecessor, he had strived to move his species forward into distinction. As he walked, he hissed and spat curses to the fates that stymied his efforts.

Two years ago, they'd been working for the T'Chillen, a powerful species of the highest order, which often employed lower species. The snake-like T'Chillen preferred employing their fellow reptilian species, such as the Rasa. Tak'la secretly detested the T'Chillen, a prejudice his people held against reptilians without legs, but power was everything in the Concordia, and the Rasa specialized in following others to power. So they'd done jobs for the T'Chillen, often without regard for the legality or morality. While transporting a large cache of high-tech weaponry, a Rasa team was ambushed. Most of them were killed, and the goods seized. The species that made the attack were known as Humans, and they were subjects of the Tog, another higher-order species. You couldn't just attack them with impunity. Still, the laws of the Concordia allowed for ways of punishing even perceived offenses. You just needed an excuse.

Some months later, the humans slaughtered a colony of Rasa squatting on an unauthorized world. The Rasa requested a Vendetta, a mini-war against the humans, which was granted by the Concordian War Council. Ko'kra led them during that Vendetta. The devilishly resourceful humans completely defeated the Rasa troops, and the humiliating defeat allowed Tak'la to violently take the leadership.

For Tak'la, none of this was a problem. It was the aftermath of the failed Vendetta that was the problem. It infuriated him even more, because the prosecution of the Vendetta was not his doing. Now the T'Chillen refused to deal with them, as did any other higher-order species offering the sort of work the Rasa preferred. All except one, that is.

Tak'la reached the end of the hall and entered the meeting room, immediately assuming the posture of respect—on his knees, immobile lips centimeters from the floor. "We of the Rasa thank you for coming," he hissed through his translator.

"We will hear your plea," the reply came quickly. The voice couldn't be more different from his own, so full of volume and resonance. Tak'la rose to his feet and faced the Tanam, where it stood with another of its kind. The felinoids were a full two meters tall, even considering their somewhat slouched posture, standing bipedal on two limbs while two arms hung at their sides. Everything about the beings spoke of barely-contained power. Ten-centimeter retractable claws tipped all four limbs, and fangs long enough to protrude below the jaw proclaimed this being as an apex predator of unmatched ability. While the Rasa evolved as predators on a primarily reptilian world, they were ambush hunters and opportunists. The Tanam caused a deep feeling of fear to run along his spine. He knew they hunted by running down, battling, and tearing their foes limb-from-limb. Tak'la felt a moment of panic and considered running for his life. "Speak!" the Tanam ordered, and he did.

"We have asked you here to offer an alliance between our species."

The Tanam snorted, a deep nearly-subsonic sound, and regarded him even closer than before. The other one, though of similar build, remained aloof and without comment. Their ears were large and mobile, able to detect sound from any direction, and were pierced by a variety of bejeweled ornaments. The one who'd remained silent had more ornate decorations. A superior? The first one spoke again. "We know of an offer, as does every other high-order species in the Concordia." It took a step closer, and Tak'la fought to stand his ground. "It speaks of fear and desperation after your defeat." The other one issued a low rumbling growl.

Tak'la shivered, his resolve barely holding. "What we offer is not without merit."

"Then speak of this offer."

"First, may I state what we wish from this alliance?"

"If you desire."

"Very well...we want these human creatures destroyed, utterly annihilated."

The Tanam chuffed and shook its head, a gesture Tak'la couldn't guess the meaning of. "We have met these humans and tasted their flesh. While hominids are rare, these are no different than other chattering primates we've encountered in the past. Timid, feckless children of a species with a dubious claim on the mantle of higher-order intelligence. Deal with them yourselves."

"We cannot. Our claim of Vendetta expired, and the council chose not to give us another attempt at redemption."

"Again, this is none of our concern."

The other spoke for the first time, its voice even lower and more difficult to listen to while suppressing his fear. "We have always thought it wise to allow the lesser species to settle their own squabbles. We have even less desire to meddle in your prattling than the Mok-Tok, and we don't have such a taste for carnage as the T'Chillen. Still, I'm sure the council could be encouraged to hear your pleas, with the proper amount and type of incentive."

"We have exhausted our supplies of capital in such matters. The Vendetta left us severely depleted in war materials, and our prestige badly damaged."

The first one snorted. "No doubt…it was a disgraceful showing."

"These humans are more than they appear," Tak'la said, pressing quickly on. "They show remarkable tenacity in combat, and an almost cruel inventiveness in developing weapons never seen before in the Concordia."

"Ludicrous," said the first. The second just snorted again. "If you're as impoverished as you claim, then what could you possibly offer us as enticement? To get at the humans, we would first need to orphan them."

"Are the Tog any great challenge to the mighty Tanam?"

"Do not patronize us," the second one said in a deep, dangerous growl.

"I would never dream of it, noble one. But wouldn't the fall of the Tog be reward in itself to compensate you for the cleansing of the humans?"

"Perhaps, were you to offer us that destruction. Instead, you would have us do the task ourselves—to work for our own reward, as it were. The Tog have adequate defenses, more than enough resources to call mercenaries to their aid should a protracted war be underway, and many allies on the Concordian Council. Even these humans would be of some modest help in defending their interests."

"And what if we were able to hand you an easy victory?"

"You can't even handle the infant humans! What makes you think you can defeat their patrons, a higher-order species, eons more mature than you? We've wished them out of the way as far back as our history goes, and they persevere. Obnoxious grass-eaters they might be, they are also tough grass-eaters."

"It is true that we are younger and less powerful than either you or the Tog, but what we lack in might, we more than make up for in shrewdness and creativity." The Tanam stared at him. "If we're able to hand the Tog to you, make success all but guaranteed, would you agree to the second part of our deal?"

The first Tanam looked at the second for assurance, confirming Tak'la's guess the second was of higher rank. The barest of nods, and the first turned back to him. "Yes. I see little chance such a thing can be done, so no risk is being assumed on our part."

"Very well," Tak'la said and reached into a pouch hanging from his waist. Those deadly eyes watched his every move, almost hoping he'd produce a weapon. Tak'la placed a single crystalline rod on the table between them, less than half a meter long, with Concordian script running its length. The entire device glowed slightly from an inner light. Concordian script slowly crawled around its width and length in ever changing patterns.

"That cannot be," the second one said, pushing past the lower ranking Tanam and carefully examining the object. "One has not been seen in many lifetimes."

"As I said, we are resourceful. Two more are included in the offer."

"Three?" The first Tanam exclaimed and looked at the second.

Tak'la didn't have to be a Tanam to see the look of greed that flowed between the two like an electrical charge. It tore him in half to offer almost all the devices they'd found, an incredibly rare and valuable thing to a higher-order species, but a treasure beyond measure to the Rasa. Many months of negotiations and deals within the Concordia's innumerable houses and clans gave him confidence that the fall of the Tog was worth anything he could pay.

"Do we have a deal then?" The two Tanam tore their eyes away from the glowing rod to look at him. One glance at their expressions, and he knew the answer. "One now, the other two when it's done."

* * * * *

Part I

The art of war is of vital importance to the state.

– Sun Tzu

Chapter One
April 5th, 520 AE

Fort Jovich, Peninsula Tribe Territory

Fort Jovich stood huge and proud near the end of a jetty of land jutting out into the Equatorial Sea. Hundreds of meters below, massive waves pounded the ancient lava flow that had formed the jetty, the waves driven by the massive tidal power of the world's twin moons, Remus and Romulus. Early explorers commented that the planet's lack of major oceans was a blessing, not a curse. "Try to imagine," they'd said, "the two moons' tidal forces brought to bear on oceans like those from old Earth." Those waves would likely have been a kilometer high, instead of Bellatrix's fifty to a hundred meters at worst. Regardless, long dead surfers from old Earth would have swooned in barely-controlled lust over the breakers. The sport never caught on here, for reasons Darwin would have understood perfectly well.

Late in the rainy season, gale-force winds pounded the dualloy battlements. Near the top of the eastern corner of the fort, a huge moliplas window overlooked the sea below. The molecularly-aligned polymer steadily resisted the wind's assault and would do so for centuries to come. Minu stood at the window watching the storm spend its fury against the man-made structure, ceaselessly pounding hour after hour. Sometimes the rain was even hard enough to hear through the five-centimeter shield. She knew from the engineering study that the structure had an anticipated lifespan of four thousand years. In the end, it wouldn't be the dualloy or moliplas that would succumb; it would be the very land the fort was built on. Pilings were dug deep into the bedrock two hundred meters down, but she knew that in only a few thousand years, those pilings would be exposed by the merciless forces of erosion. The entire fort would one day tumble into the ocean, to roll down into the abyssal trench just below where she stood. The subduction zone there would grind up and melt whatever survived. Somehow that gave her comfort, knowing that even the much-vaunted Concordian technology was no match for the supreme powers of nature. This location had been chosen for a number of reasons, defensibility chief among them. With the sea at its back, the fort was a redoubt that was easy to defend, and almost impossible to assault.

Fort Jovich appeared complete to many, yet inside, much of it was still under construction. Vast areas were nothing more than open beams and supports, ducts incomplete and wiring hanging like severed veins. The outside, though, was a completed structure, tough, and proof against the weather or an attack. They'd finished it just in time to avoid the stormy season. *Is there ever a time this place isn't stormy?* Minu had wondered. Work continued inside at a steady pace, and that included training.

Leaving her office behind, she went outside and down the hallway. At the end was an intersection that led to the left and right, while straight ahead was the largest open area of the huge fort. Five hundred meters long, two hundred wide, and a hundred tall, the primary training field was spread out below her as if she sat in the press box of a massive sports stadium. From far below, the sounds of drilling and exercise drifted up to her. She leaned on the safety rail and watched the work. A thousand newly trained soldiers drilled nearly every day. They ran, jumped, and exerted themselves while being yelled at by Chosen from the training branch. Though impossible to tell from this height, she knew seventy-nine of them were women. A smile cut the smooth lines of her face as she thought about it. Only half of the women who'd gone into the special soldiers' trials passed. Still, it was a start worthy of a smile. She'd met many of them, and they were a tough, hard-looking, steely-eyed crowd. Soldiers weren't cut from the same broad mold as the Chosen. Their profession was much more specific. She thought of the Chosen as handheld whipsaws. Slow to use, gentle, flexible, and able to handle any task. Her new soldiers were chainsaws—direct, to the point, and completely lacking in subtlety. They'd chew through whatever you put in front of them and feel fine afterward.

Minu had initially expressed displeasure at the small number of women. It was her friend Cherise who'd changed her mood. "Three years ago, when we came through the trials together, being made Chosen increased the number of female Chosen by ten percent! There have never been more than twenty women in the Chosen."

"But is that on purpose?" Minu wondered.

"Who cares? Thanks to you, now there are seventy-nine new females in the ranks."

"Only soldiers, not full Chosen."

"The special trials are coming up to replace the hundreds we lost in the Rasa Vendetta last year."

"I know that, Cherise."

"Did you know that the number of girls taking the first-level written test is triple the record number?" She could tell Minu hadn't by the look on her face. "That's what I thought. The success of those women below, and your own, in no small part, has caused a change in our society. In another year, there could be dozens more female Chosen!"

"That change is long overdue."

Of course Cherise knew that; what woman in the elite Chosen didn't? She watched the soldiers practice and shrugged. Change was coming all right. Two thousand soldiers would eventually be stationed in this fort, more than all the Chosen to have served. Fewer than a hundred of those had been women. Cherise was right, of course. It was a good start.

"Commander Minu, may we speak?" Minu turned from the railing at the hissing speech. She'd been so deep in her reflection she hadn't noticed her visitor. Var'at was standing a respectful distance away; the pendant translator Minu always wore round her neck was faithfully translating his words into English.

"For the Rasa Commander, and my friend, any time," she said and gestured toward her office. A moment later the door slid closed, and they were alone. "What can I do for you today?"

"I believe training comes along well."

"I agree!"

"You humans are fast to learn and physically resilient. While I believe my own species to be tougher in basic build, your own has better endurance and raw strength. You're also more tolerant of temperature extremes, a trait I find amazing."

"An excellent assessment," Minu said. Var'at's jaws snapped twice, his version of a smile. "It's part of the reason I believed we'd be good allies. We complement each other."

"We were left with little choice," Var'at reminded her, "after our defeat in the Vendetta; our leaders didn't want us back. If you hadn't offered us a home…"

"Their own short-sightedness, in my opinion."

"I wish we'd never met on that world when you stole our cache of beamcasters, but at least it resulted in our friendship."

"Agreed," Minu said and poured some drinks. Mead for herself, fruit juice for him. Var'at tasted the concoction and smacked his immobile lips with pleasure.

"Not bad," he hissed.

"I'm sure you didn't come for a drink," she prompted.

"I wanted to discuss the living arrangements."

"Is there a problem? If you need more space, I'm sure something can be done."

"No, no, your people are most generous. Our settlement in the hills here is quite nice. A little cool, but pleasurably moist." Moist? Minu wondered what he considered wet. "We're very grateful for all you've done. In taking in your former enemies, you have done an amazing thing no one would have expected."

"It's how we humans are."

"Again, our thanks."

"Okay, so what do you need?"

"We wish to be less of a burden."

"We've had this discussion before, but I don't know what I can do. We can't allow you uncontrolled access to a portal; this was a condition on our alliance set by the Chosen council."

"I hope to one day prove that this precaution is unnecessary, but I fully understand at this point."

"Then how do you propose to do anything more? By agreeing to fight for us and help train our army, you are more than carrying your share of the load."

"We would like to grow some of our own food."

"Oh…I wasn't expecting that. What kind of crops would you grow?"

Var'at smiled, or rather opened his mouth slightly to display rows of needle-sharp teeth. "You misunderstand. Not crops, food."

"Oh, right," Minu said nervously. Watching him sip fruit juice, it was easy to forget the Rasa's nature. She dispelled the image from her mind of the first time she'd run into the Rasa while they'd been eating one of her team. "What animals do you wish to grow?" she asked, cringing against the thought of him suggesting humans.

"We would most prefer Faka, from our own world. But considering our dispossession, we find it unlikely to be able to obtain breeding stock on any legal market. Your native Tuck, while tasty, are too large and prefer the lower plains. So we were thinking of sheep."

"Really?"

"Yes. Your logistics people have provided us some of this meat, but it's always old and tough. We'd like to grow our own, to have it young and tender."

"Well, we primarily raise sheep to harvest their wool for clothing on our world."

"A need we do not have," he pointed out. The Rasa wore only utility straps and body armor. The only time she'd seen them wear anything approaching clothing was for vacuum or very cold climates.

"True, but this is why you've been getting old sheep. They're too old for us to harvest their fur anymore."

"Would we be able to breed our own? We'd even allow them to have their fur cut off before consuming them."

"I think that could be arranged. I'll get with logistics to purchase a breeding stock of twenty or so." The Rasa force of a thousand lived in a settlement just over the ridge from Fort Jovich. It was considered remote enough to be no threat to the neighboring community of Peninsula tribe, not that Minu thought they were a threat. The Rasa had followed every rule the humans had set for them. Even so, their presence remained a carefully kept secret. "Is there anything else?"

"Yesss as a matter of fact. I would like to know if we are to be allowed to train with your new shock rifles."

"Ah, right. Well, that determination hasn't been made yet."

"Very well," Var'at said and turned to skitter out of her office. In a human she'd take that for a hurt response. From the reptilian alien, it was his way of taking his leave. The conversation's over; time to go. She shook her head and dictated an email to Cherise, her friend from the trials and one of only eleven current non-soldier female Chosen. She was in the Logistics branch and in charge of keeping Minu's army supplied. The Rasa fell under that heading. On the end of the message she tacked a post script saying she would be at the Chosen headquarters at Steven's Pass next week and was looking forward to one of their now considerably-less-common knife and martial arts drills. The much-taller black girl from the Desert tribe was a natural and the best teacher Minu could ask for. Without her instruction in knife fighting during the trials, Minu would likely be dead.

Lightning flashed outside as the storm grew in intensity. Minu yawned and considered heading to her billet. Her chronometer said it had been twenty hours since she'd last slept.

Suddenly her phone squealed for attention. "Chosen Alma," she answered.

"This is Portal Operations," the Chosen answered. "We have a scout team coming through!"

Minu was instantly alert. "What?" Their portal code had been relocated from Steven's Pass. That location was still the center of off-world operations until her facility was brought fully on line, but the Fort's portal address was unique. Any scout team coming through here was one that must have left more than six months ago. "Christian," she said quietly, then out loud, "I'll be right there!"

The drop tube deposited her just outside the operations center. The building had a number of the tubes; the Concordian-made hover fields allowed for fast movement of men and equipment. The operations center walls were a meter thick, made of the Concordian metal dualloy. The fantastic ceramic steel was amazingly resistant to all forms of radiation and able to dissipate heat at a miraculous rate. Inside was a space twenty meters square where the portal sat. A meter-thick moliplas viewing window was set in three of the four walls, and all six sides supported emitters for energy shields and force fields. It was the most impregnable portal room they could design.

As she ran through the ready room into the adjacent viewing room, she could see a very travel-weary looking team of five Chosen standing outside the portal, looking around in amazement. This was not where they'd expected to arrive, having dialed the Steven's Pass portal code. Four robotic beamcaster turrets, one in each corner, were trained on them. All the walls shimmered from obvious energy shields.

"What the fuck is this?" she heard one of them yell through the speaker. It was Christian; there was no mistaking his chiseled features and short cut blond hair.

"Clear them through," she said, knowing the portal monitor would hear her from his armored location some hundred meters away (another security precaution). The shields winked out, and the meter-thick vault-like door began to swing inward. Minu jogged around to that side and was standing there when it opened enough for him to see her. "We thought you were dead!" Minu cried, her voice full of relief and concern. She knew her eyes were shining from unshed tears, and it took all her willpower not run into his arms.

He led his team through the huge door, eying the room in wonder. "Who's the Chosen in charge?" he asked, all business, like any Scout coming in from off world.

"You're looking at her."

He started and looked at her sleeve. Three gold stars rode there, similar to his own three black stars. He came to rough attention, obviously confused but doing his job. "Chosen Christian Forsythe reporting. We lost one member, Derick Benedict. Now, can you tell me where the hell we are? What happened to the courtyard?"

"This isn't Steven's Pass," she said and gestured around, "this is Fort Jovich."

"Fort Jovich? Are we at war or something?"

"You better come to debriefing," she said and gestured for his team to follow. "There's a lot for you to catch up on. And the Council will want to know what happened to you over the last six months!"

* * * * *

Chapter Two
Octember 3rd, 520 AE

Fort Jovich, Peninsula Tribe Territory

"We declare Fort Jovich operational!" The fresh bottle of mead exploded against the dualloy structure, drenching several dignitaries in honey wine. There were laughs and smiles all around; no harm done. Minu snorted. As if they'd be offended? Most of the old bastards had made *thousands* of credits during the fort's construction. Operational? Not even close. There were still a dozen problems with major systems, and hundreds of smaller glitches, but when the Chosen Council wanted a party, you threw a party.

"And here's the Chosen in command of the fort," Minu heard Jacob saying and put on her best ass-kissing smile before turning. She recognized several planetary council members and a swarm of buzzing reporters. "Two years of intense work. We're very proud of what she's accomplished here and with the new soldiers."

"Thank you, First Jacob," she said and affected a bow. Cameras clicked and whirled. Several council members shook her hand, some more enthusiastically than others. Then the press shoved forward, and she prepared for battle.

"How does it feel to be the first female Chosen to reach three stars, and in such a short time?" one yelled over the others.

"It was very humbling, a year and a half ago when it happened," she mumbled the last. She needn't have bothered. No sooner had she said humbling than more questions were being yelled.

"Do you attribute your success to your father, First Chriso Alma?"

"Of course I do; my father made me who I am today. He was the greatest First humanity has had so far." Jacob stiffened slightly but said nothing.

"So you wouldn't be where you are today if your father hadn't been First?"

"That's not what I said."

"But it's true no woman has ever made it as far, as fast as you have."

"We've been over that already."

"And you're the first three-star female whose father also happened to have been First…"

It was a typical ploy by the press, trying to corner her into a box. "Don't be an asshole," she growled. Jacob's eyes got big and he stepped forward to intervene.

"What the Chosen was trying to say is that, while her father was indeed a great First, she accomplished all her promotions in the Chosen after he'd disappeared and was declared lost in action."

Minu took the chance and made her escape from the reporters. She'd rather have mud-wrestled a kloth than talk to those bastards. A short distance away, under a bright-yellow pavilion, Dram was drinking from a massive tankard of mead and laughing loudly. She set her course, and he saw her approach, his shining teeth offset starkly against his jet-black skin as he smiled hugely. "Ah, the Chosen of the day."

"Shut the fuck up," she said and snatched up a somewhat smaller mug of mead. It was a good batch, Pip's favorite brand, unless she missed her guess. She took a deep drink and tried not to think about her good friend, still lying in a coma after being critically injured during the vendetta a year and a half ago.

"Now is that any way to talk to your boss?" he asked. She glanced at the two shiny gold stars on his sleeve then the three gold stars on her own.

"Outranking is not the same as boss."

"Technicality," he said with a dismissive shrug and a deep drink of mead.

Her eyes were drawn to his stars again. "When do we get new colored stars?"

"When the job is done."

"At this rate it'll never be done."

"Nonsense."

"Damn it, Dram, don't screw with me. I want to be in the field when my people go out there."

"You will, don't worry."

"Yeah, then how come Terrence has been spending all that time chewing on my ear about how things are run in his branch?" Terrence Pegalio, the two-star Chosen in charge of the training branch, was notorious for his outspoken dislike of the new soldier branch. The animosity originated when it was decided that the training branch would not be directly in charge of training the new soldiers, only assisting. Since then he'd been doing everything he could to get Minu to join the blue-star designated training branch, thereby hopefully bringing her to heel. "If you think I'm putting on blue stars, you've got another think coming."

"Even if it's two blue stars?"

Minu spat and got a fresh tankard. "There's no way in hell the council will let a twenty-one-year-old wear two stars. Besides, there's no way you're shoving me in that closet of a branch. If there is any more of a dead end than training, I don't know what it is."

"Two stars is a dead end? Where can you go after that anyway?" She glanced up from her mead quickly to see him intensely watching her. She cursed under her breath for taking the bait. "What, you planning on being the next First?" She refused to nibble the hook any more. "Be realistic, Minu. You joined to serve."

"Don't give me the speech; I know it by heart. I've been teaching it to a thousand new Chosen Soldiers, remember?"

"Then try thinking about it yourself. You've done such a wonderful job getting this fort operational and training those boys—"

"And girls."

"Yes, and girls. Anyway, you've done such a good job that to many, training is starting to look like what you're best at."

"They said the same thing when I ran a science team. Now I've done this. Maybe I'm just the best at whatever I do." Minu was taken aback by her own bravado and took a drink to cover the bright red of her cheeks. The mead was making her ears buzz. If she didn't break off this conversation soon she'd be too drunk to control herself. She found her mind wandering to where that annoying reporter went. Maybe punching him out would end this bullshit of being in the training branch.

"Maybe you are," he said with a shrug and finished his huge drink, "but this is where the Chosen need you now." He wandered off to talk to someone else, and that's when Minu spotted Christian. He stood a few meters away, talking to a couple civilians she didn't recognize. She smiled and nodded to him. He smiled back, but the smile never reached his eyes. Things hadn't been the same between them. After the debriefing, he'd been shocked to find out she was the savior of Bellatrix and inventor of an entirely new weapon system. Compared to that, his six months of escape and evasion on the frontier against hostile Tanam counted for little in the big picture. He'd even brought back terabytes of data on worlds in the F sector of space and many minor species who lived there and were willing to trade with the young humans. It'd barely been noticed. Then word came down that the scout branch was to be absorbed by the soldier branch. The scouts would get to keep their black stars, but now they'd take orders from the soldier's military commanders, themselves Chosen from command, like Minu, who technically outranked him. Since then, their relationship was technically dead.

An hour later, the civilians were gone, and more Chosen arrived. Minu picked at snacks and nursed her third mead. "What thoughts trouble you?" hissed a voice behind her. Minu turned and smiled at Var'at. The reptilian alien stood with a plate full of various meats in one clawed hand and a flute of fruit juice in the other. With the civilians gone, he no longer needed to stay out of sight. The Rasa didn't care for alcohol, but fruits and juices were very much to their liking. For carnivores, they possessed a surprisingly deep sweet tooth.

"Just wondering about what might have been."

"That's like contemplating an unfertilized egg." The Rasa commander used his long tongue like an extra hand to snap up a piece of turkey. His teeth worked the meat, and his tongue licked juices from his inflexible lips. "Delicious."

"Unfertilized eggs aside, I'm glad you enjoy the food." *I'd rather not have any of my eggs fertilized anyway,* she thought. At the other end of the pavilion, Terrance stood with several others from the Training branch. As her luck held he spotted her looking at him and raised his glass in salute. With little choice she raised hers in return, though it was now empty. He favored her with a huge smile and thankfully returned to his conversation without taking her salute as an invitation to conversation. It was the politics and intrigue of the Chosen that she despised the most. A strong wind shook the pavilion where it was moored against the lee of the fortress. Clouds chased the horizon. The celebration would need to wrap up soon, or the weather would end it for them.

The rainstorm hit three hours later. More like a fall shower for the local weather, it still sent the pavilion out to sea like a huge, brightly-colored kite. The now-departed guests had been shown the interior earlier, in tour groups of a dozen gaping politicians each. They visited the workout rooms, dormitories, firing ranges, tech training rooms, and of course the huge central mustering field. The finale of the tour were the offices and one of the five armories, where she was forced to answer more annoying questions. "Are the other six forts going to be this big?" Unlikely, since two others were already finished and neither was even half the size of Fort Jovich. "Why such a large facility?" Where else do you train, equip and house five thousand soldiers? "Isn't a military installation sending the wrong message to other species?" What kind of a message do you think we were sent by the Rasa's Vendetta?

By the time the questions were done, Minu had considered taking them on a tour of the combat course located near armory three. That was the live-fire range, and classified, so she contented herself with only the thought of it. Now Minu was meeting with other dignitaries for a few more minutes in the command center. These people were in on the Rasa secret, unlike the average civilian. Located many meters below the thick ceramic concrete floor, the CIC was a near-duplicate of the one deep under Steven's Pass. The various council members, politicians, and contractors were dutifully impressed as they were shown the massive wall-sized liquid display, powerful stationary computers, redundant network transmitters, and, of course, the portal, in its own vault-like chamber, separated from the CIC by many meters of living rock.

"So many precautions," one councilman from the meager Peninsula tribe spoke up. They were known for their dislike of war of any kind. Of all the surviving tribes, they'd sent the fewest to the Chosen over the years, and very few to the new Soldier trials. The land had been purchased from them to build Fort Jovich. Later they'd complained vociferously when it was discovered that the anonymous contract was to build a military fort. "It would seem better to show ourselves as harmless and thus no threat to other species."

"If only the galaxy were so simple," Minu said from where she stood at the back of the group, "then we could spend our credits exporting flowers to the Concordia." Minu could see Jacob scowl and look at her darkly. She was known to be even less diplomatic than the former director of the science branch, Bjorn Ganose, who'd once blown out a wall of his own office to demonstrate the need for a new weapons-testing facility. Dram stood next to First Jacob, his rightful place as the Second, and gave her a little smile.

"We'd expect nothing but dire warnings from the infamous Minu Alma," the Peninsula representative said with a sneer. "Already planning to get us into another Vendetta?"

"Not right this moment," she said with a smile. The councilors and dignitaries looked somewhat taken aback, so Minu continued, "But the day is still young."

"It is indeed a dangerous galaxy," Jacob said, jumping in, trying desperately to pull the conversation away from Minu. "These forts are a good defense and can't be taken as aggressive in any way. They're just forts, how can that be threatening?"

"Of all the tribes, ours never went to war against anyone," the representative said to Minu accusingly. "You Plateau people had many wars."

"You didn't go to war because you were conquered five times," Minu pointed out. The man's Asian features burned red with anger. "Until us Plateau people liberated you from the Rusk about a hundred and fifty years ago, you were well known potato pickers, from what I hear." He sputtered and clenched his teeth, looking like he was either struggling to control his temper or having a heart attack. Jacob tried to speak again but Minu smelled blood in the water. "You look angry, sir, are you planning to surrender to someone?"

The Peninsula man, representative of the most pacifistic people on Bellatrix, did a most non-pacifistic thing. He jumped at Minu with a howl of fury, his fingers bent into claws to tear at her throat. Years of combat training had made her ready for anything, and weekly practices with Cherise had made her a dirty fighter. The man was only a couple of meters from Minu; his attack caught everyone except her off guard. She feigned surprise until an instant before he reached her, then sidestepped and snatched one of his arms. His face went from fury to surprise as she twisted the arm in a way it wasn't mean to be twisted. Forced to follow the direction of her spin by the pain she was inflicting, he found himself flipping through the air, and straight into a thick ceramic concrete wall.

Minu chose the wall to avoid damaging any of the valuable equipment. She knew the concrete wall could absorb the impact of a thousand hurtling fools and only require the blood to be scrubbed off later. Luckily for the man, Dram interceded. He caught him with two huge arms, like a child falling off a toy horse. "Here you go," he said in his deep baritone and placed him on his feet again. "It is best to be careful in here; there are a lot of ways to get accidentally hurt."

He gave Dram a glare, shot death at Minu, screamed something in his native language and stormed out. "Knows how to make friends, doesn't she?" one representative from the desert tribe asked another man, a contractor from Tranquility.

The contractor had been working with Minu for more than a year while building Fort Jovich. He looked at the representative with a hearty laugh. "Sir, you have no idea."

A few hours later, Minu sat behind her desk, storm clouds behind her through the window matching the ones behind her eyes. Jacob was pacing back and forth in front of her desk and yelling obscenities while she was forced to listen. Dram leaned against the wall and did his best not to smile. It was a familiar scene that usually played out when Minu interacted with politicians, reporters, or both. He seemed to finally be winding down. "—just incapable of keeping your mouth closed?"

"I think so, yes, sir," she answered in an emotionless voice.

"If you were worthless, or a nobody, it wouldn't make any difference. But for the love of God, Minu, you're important to the Chosen, to Bellatrix, and to the Tog. Not yet three years in the Chosen, and already you've made more discoveries and changes than most do in their entire career. But mark my words, as long as I'm First Among the Chosen, you will go no further unless you can somehow manage to control that hole under your nose. Is that perfectly clear?"

"Crystal clear, sir." Jacob snorted and left. Minu took a deep breath and let it out with a long whistle. "That was fun."

"He has a point, you know." She looked at Dram accusingly. "Well? You have something to add?"

"I never claimed I was a 'people' person."

"Oh, that's been obvious since your early days. Still, you need to learn some control." She shrank deeper into her chair. "Minu, you may well become the first woman to wear one star." She made a rude noise, and he came away from the wall to lean over her desk, his imposing frame looming over her like a stately Portal Spire on an alien world. She silently hoped he wasn't going to lecture her like Jacob. "It's true. You're being advanced far along in your career for this accomplishment, and others, whether you want to or not. It's time to grow up a little." And with no more to say, he turned and left.

"I'd rather he'd yelled at me," she said to her empty office. The thrill she'd felt from tossing the mouthy little prick from Peninsula was gone, replaced with a feeling of shame. Much better if he'd yelled.

* * * * *

Chapter Three
May 25th, 521 AE

Sanctuary Island, Plateau Tribe Territory

Minu woke to warm sunshine flooding through her window. She climbed out of bed and padded naked across the floor to look outside. The sun shone through one of the huge fern trees outside the cabin window with comfortable green hues, warming her skin. As was her habit when staying at the cabin, especially in the summer, she walked outside and sat in the grass. The cool grass was a little chilly against her bare bottom, but the sun caressed her skin, making it tingle. The only thing between her and the sky was the sapphire necklace hanging around her neck on a dualloy chain short enough to be a choker.

Nearly a year had passed since she'd felt a lover's touch. This was almost enough, for now. The hours spent on the quiet, secluded island with its ancient cabin were a sweet comfort to her troubled life. After soaking in as much sun as she could take, she went inside to shower. It was moments like this that she missed Christian the most, not like yesterday with his mirthless smile and accusing looks. "It wasn't my fault you weren't hailed as the returning hero," she said into the hot spray. "Why do you have to hold it against me?"

She missed the companionship of having a boyfriend, but the work involved in finding a new lover was too much for her right now. Now that she wore three stars, the weight of command pulled down on her like never before. She resisted the urge to open up enough to allow another man into her life. *What about Aaron?* a voice whispered deep in the back of her mind. She mercilessly smashed the voice even further into the recesses of her consciousness and continued her shower.

Minu made a simple breakfast of eggs and toast, then carried it into the second bedroom she'd converted into an office. Inside was an array of instruments, computers, and technology very unlike the anachronistic cabin's exterior appearance. She signed onto the Chosen computer network and downloaded her course load through the orbital relays. Munching on an egg sandwich, she began studying. Leadership was one of her responsibilities, learning the other. "We learn our whole lives," her father had said many times, "whether we admit it or not. It's your choice whether what you learn is worth the effort or not."

Today's studies were different. Unlike the last several years, it wasn't just classes taken from other teachers. Now she was beginning preparations for courses she would be teaching herself. The student was finally becoming the teacher, and at only eighteen years old. Well, almost eighteen. Her own degrees were in technology and science, and she didn't fool herself that she was at all worthy to teach those subjects. Instead, she'd be an instructor in a very different course of study. Her first class was labeled, "Military Science 101," and it was the culmination of years of work, both on her own and with the help of others. The course work covered an eclectic collection of military methodology, leading from Roman military training in the third century to Concordian troop deployment protocols only recently uncovered. Of course, that information wasn't available to anyone but herself. This was data pilfered by Pip, before he'd been left a crippled vegetable.

The Tog carefully guarded their data networks, but there were ways around those safeguards. Many years of research would be required just to fully understand the exabytes of data her friend had stolen. The deeper into the data she went, the more Minu found herself missing Pip. Especially now, as she prepared to teach the course he'd co-conceived, and that he should rightfully be co-teaching with her.

Military Science 101 was not really intended to impart information, although it did to some extent. The wide swath of history and species it covered was too broad to be worth much. This class was more of a recruiting tool for future military commanders and strategists. Two hundred had signed up for the first class taught by Chosen Minu Alma, architect of the human victory over the Rasa Vendetta. The fact that she was also behind the creation of the Soldier branch of the Chosen, designer of the new network of forts, and inventor of the shock rifle was less important and less well known to the average human. She knew her fame (or infamy) would bring in the curious; she only hoped the tantalizing taste of information provided would hook the truly brilliant and the naturally talented.

MilSci 101 would be a prerequisite for entry into the Chosen War College, part of a much bigger dream. Realization of that dream would take decades, and perhaps finally make humanity safe. Hopefully more than safe. The galaxy was full of predators, and they were nothing but naked apes running around with their first clubs.

She worked for a few hours, a bevy of computer tablets scattered across the desk. One contained sorted and organized files for the class she was to teach. Another held the data pilfered by Pip, while still another monitored her various email accounts for activity. She worked on the pilfered data, occasionally transferring a file or two to the first computer. The private network in her cabin moved the data seamlessly and required no more thought than putting a clean fork into a drawer. Being so far from another network was part of her motivation in moving her private residence to the cabin. The two-hour flight in her sleek red aerocar was a mild inconvenience, at worst. The privacy she'd had laying outside that morning was another advantage. In the year since she'd moved to the cabin, an inheritance from her father, she'd yet to see another human on the distant shores, or even a craft flying over in the sky above.

Minu picked up a fourth tablet and sorted for more details. This one carried data from the Chosen network, including terabytes of human history. More files were transferred to the first computer. The fifth and final tablet in use just then held far less data. This one was the tablet she was using to build the War College. It was still a work in progress. Minu had admitted to herself months ago that she needed help bringing the War College to life. Originally she'd planned to tap Christian for that, but the fates hadn't worked in her favor. He might still be able to help, he might even be willing to help, but she didn't want the conflict and pain it would bring. She needed to find someone else and somehow draft them into helping her.

There was another tablet resting on a shelf above the desk, seldom used but deeply treasured. That one linked her with the past just as deeply as the sapphire necklace she wore. Her father, Chriso Alma, former First Among the Chosen, was missing somewhere in the galaxy. He'd gone missing on a mission during her trials and never returned. He'd managed to send a message from beyond, relayed mysteriously through a seldom-seen aunt. The chip contained hundreds of files from her father. Files on the Concordia, the planets around the galaxy, technology, and even his own random thoughts. Some files still remained locked. A few tentative clues pointed to answers on distant worlds that would unlock those files…if only she had time.

With command of the soldiers, she now possessed the power to search for him, maybe finally answer the question of whether he was still alive, or how he'd died. As usual, her duty kept her from it. She couldn't abuse the power of her three stars or take advantage of the loyalty of her men in such a baseless personal pursuit. She didn't have time to pursue clues to unlock the hidden files or try and find him.

Like the computer files, the sapphire necklace she never removed was a link to her past, having belonged to the legendary Mindy Harper. Originally hung by a thin silver chain and clasp, it was now draped around her neck with a dualloy rope that had no clasp. The look the jeweler gave her as he used a Concordian-made tool to cold fuse the chain to the gold sapphire mounting permanently around her neck was a memorable one. The computer file delivered by her aunt had remained a mystery for months until she eventually found the password. Typical of her father, the password was linked to that very necklace. Sapphire. Even what she could now read was tantalizing.

Like a theory she'd first heard years ago, it suggested that the all-powerful Concordia was in decay, and maybe even dying. Visiting the thousands of worlds full of thriving cities would make most people scoff at the very notion of a decaying empire, but she'd also seen an equal number of empty planets in the frontier, many with abandoned cities and perfectly habitable atmospheres. That gave the theory credence. What more had her father hidden away from her?

The sun passed its zenith, and eventually her stomach and bladder conspired to call her away from the tablets. She left the office, visited the bathroom, then the kitchen. She saw the freezer was getting empty and made a mental note to stop at the store in Dodge City on her way out next time. The bustling city near Fort Jovich had grown up since its construction began. Built originally to serve as a temporary home to the thousands of workers, now it fit the bill of a classic military town on old Earth, serving the soldiers trained and billeted at the fort. She made herself a mutton sandwich, with potato chips and a tall glass of grape juice. All but the chips were made locally to Fort Jovich. Much closer in fact. They were produced in Lizardville, the Chosen nickname for the Rasa settlement over the hill from the fort (the real name was unpronounceable by human mouths, sounding rather like a leaky steam heater).

Minu had initially found it amusing to have the Rasa raise their own food, but the aliens had taken to it so thoroughly, though, that they made a healthy profit from the surplus. Their tenderly-reared sheep were slaughtered and consumed as soon as they reached adulthood. They considered the killing of young animals cruel, so no true lamb came from Lizardville. Like many, Minu had tasted mutton long ago, before the Rasa started growing them. It was so strong as to be almost inedible outside of a stew or casserole. The Rasa kept only a few beyond maturing, for breeding and other practices. Of course she'd heard of them hunting the rams they turned out wild into the countryside. The first humans to witness the ritual came away white-faced and firmly reminded that the Rasa were *not* human, regardless of how normal they might appear while watching a movie or conducting business in Dodge City. The Rasa presence on Bellatrix was only a thinly-veiled secret now. She wondered if only the politicians weren't aware of them.

When Minu had asked Var'at if they were interested in hunting Kloth, the question was met with shock and disgust. When Minu asked why not, she got a terse reply. "Would you have wished to hunt Neanderthal humans?" Of course the answer was no, but Minu still found the comparison imperfect. The Rasa and the Kloth didn't share a genetic history, unlike humans and their caveman ancestors. Still, she was amazed yet again at how much the Rasa were learning about their human hosts. Amazed, and concerned. It was a good thing they were fierce allies.

The sandwich, with its thick slice of Rasa mutton, was just as savory as always, and it left her licking juice from her fingers. Afterward, she dressed in shorts and a loose-fitting tank top to go for a run. After the rainy season, the island's ground firmed up nicely. In the last year, she'd managed to wear a fairly good path through the small woods of the island as a personal jogging track. Once around the island was exactly one kilometer. Ten laps today, just an easy one-hour run raising a good sweat. "I need to hit the gym at the fort more," she breathed after the run, sitting in the shade of the porch in the afternoon sun. She eyed her car parked on the newly installed ceramic concrete parking pad. Unlike the cabin, it had air conditioning. "You're getting soft," she admonished herself and stubbornly went inside. She opened the windows to let the slight breeze cool the cabin's interior. After a quick shower, it was back to work sorting data and making notes. The syllabus for the class was nearly complete, but there were months' more work to be done before the War College would be ready.

As the sun began to set, she did some casual housework. Dirty clothes and towels went into the Concordian-made laundry machine, and she walked out to the dock. She considered fishing for a minute but decided against it. She dropped her sweat-soaked clothes on the dock and dove into the water. The lake was only a few degrees cooler than the air, but cooler was cooler. She swam with strong strokes, not bothering to check her direction or distance. It was just over a kilometer to the shore, and she'd swam the distance more than once, but not lately. The far shore was a muddy tangle of water plants and reeds. She'd almost clogged the shower trying to clean it off her legs last time. Instead of going all the way, she swam until she felt underwater plants tickling her tummy, a sign that the bottom was rising to meet her.

It was usually when skinny-dipping in her lake that she fantasized about being caught by a curious observer. The idea that some lecherous man might be watching her naked body sliding through the water made warm feelings run up her legs. She teased herself with the idea, and then remembered her never-realized plans of bringing Christian out here and doing very naughty things for days on end. "I need a boyfriend," she admitted to the lake. A howler in a nearby tree barked angrily. "Oh, shut up," she yelled back. It barked even louder and set off another in reply. Soon the woods around the lake were full of barking lizards. "Great, it'll be hours before they calm down."

Serenaded by reptiles, Minu switched to a backstroke and swam back toward the island. *Might as well give my fantasy voyeur a better view*, she thought. She climbed from the water using the ladder on the dock. The shore of the island wasn't muddy like the other shore, but the rocks were often sharp enough to cut your foot. Clear of the water, she used the hose she kept there to give herself a quick rinse. There were no water animals native to Bellatrix larger than a primitive trout species, but there were leeches, though they weren't as aggressive as the Earthly cousins she'd read about. As long as you spent less than an hour in the water and rinsed briskly afterward, they didn't have time to gnaw through your skin. She noted a couple washing off her ankles and took extra care rinsing her groin. None had ever turned up there, but she still shuddered at the thought. She always rinsed outside, because the house's water system was a closed system, and the mud incident had cost her a week of maintenance. This water was pumped from the lake nearby and only used for this purpose. Besides, she didn't like the idea of the leeches ending up in her drinking water. With a shiver, she replaced the hose and headed for the cabin.

She dried her hair as she walked onto the porch and through the door. The cabin interior was as familiar as the back of her hand. The first thing she noticed was the pan on the stove, then a chair in the kitchen that had been moved, then the smell of cooking mutton. She froze and fixed in her mind how far it was to the bedroom, and what was hidden there under her bed. She could see legs in one of living room chairs and her fear turned to hope. *Father?* She wondered silently. But still, the bedroom…

"Is that my friend I hear?" the visitor said. Cherise stood and turned around, slight surprise crossing her face to see Minu standing in the doorway naked but for the towel in her hair. "Do you always run around here naked?"

"Don't you know how to knock?" Minu countered, her voice coarser than she'd intended due to the disappointment and surprise at having her hidden sanctuary penetrated.

"Hard to knock when no one was home." The taller black girl came closer and observed the look on Minu's face. Uncertainty crossed her own. "I'm sorry, was this a mistake?"

"No, it's okay," Minu relented. "You're just the first person to come here since my father died." She looked down at her naked body and giggled a little. "I guess I've become a closet nudist." She gestured to take in the solitude of the cabin and island. "The nearest neighbor is a hundred kilometers away, and it's hot in here during the summer."

"You don't have to tell me," Cherise said and smiled. "I grew up in the desert, remember? Besides, we have a tradition to always follow a house master's customs." Before Minu realized what she was about, the other girl had stripped. She bundled bra and panties inside her Chosen jumpsuit and looked around for a place to put them. Minu took the bundle and placed them in the closet. "That's more like it," Cherise said and embraced her. The feeling of hugging the naked girl was shocking and more than a little pleasurable. Minu blushed and broke the embrace a little quicker than she normally would have.

Cherise was about a year older than Minu, but now that they were both grown women it made little difference. Aside from the closeness of age, there wasn't much else the two had in common. Where Minu was short with flame-red hair, narrow hips, and small breasts, Cherise was tall with long legs, nicely curved hips, and larger breasts that swayed as she walked and drew many a man's attention. "Mind if I get a swim myself?" the other woman asked.

Minu had no objection and said she'd finish getting dinner ready. She sent her friend off with a warning of the post-swim ritual and assurances that the leeches were not aggressive. Then she showered quickly and attended to the stove just in time to save the mutton from burning. Because she'd had the same thing for lunch, she retrieved some chicken from the freezer and started it cooking for her own dinner.

The food was good and the company even better. Minu found having her friend in the secluded spot more fun than she expected. They ate and talked, then played some card games with a five-hundred-year-old deck she'd found in a desk. Then Cherise went out to her aerocar—she'd broken down and bought her own a year ago—and returned with several bottles of Lizardville Wine, their first vintage. "You feeling brave?" she asked.

"Rasa wine?" Minu laughed. The damned lizards would take over the planetary economy if allowed to.

"Sure, why not?"

It turned out to be just as good as any other endeavor the lizards had undertaken. A very sweet wine, not surprising considering their natural preferences, it didn't have as high an alcohol content as some local brews. By the time the sun was down, the two women were making up their own rules for card games and giggling like school girls.

Minu accidentally dropped the nearly-empty bottle and went after it at the same time as Cherise, the two ending up face to face under the table. Like a flash, Cherise pressed her lips against hers, mouth opening slightly and tongue darting out. Minu smashed her head against the bottom of the table in shock.

"Damn, I'm sorry," Cherise said as Minu staggered around the room seeing stars.

"What the hell was that about?" Minu asked, rubbing the growing knot on the back of head.

"I have to admit something to you," Cherise said, crossing her arms under her breasts. It was a natural motion for any woman but the fact that she was naked made it almost comical. "I came out here to seduce you."

"Seduce me? Cherise, are you a lesbian?"

"What? Don't be silly. I just don't have a set preference."

"It's still illegal!"

"Now you're just being crazy, Minu; it's the sixth century for crying out loud! The Concordia came back over a hundred years ago, and you're worried about laws made in the dark times hundreds of years ago!?"

"The law says two of the same sex cannot have—"

"Not where I come from," Cherise cut her off. "Minu, sex is a much more open thing in the desert tribe. You and I talked about this years ago. Our children play at sex from an early age. Most of us have our first experience with the same sex, especially the boys, who are much more…energetic about it, early on. I've only had three male lovers, but I don't know how many girls." All the while she was walking closer, with Minu giving ground just as quickly.

"It-it's just wrong."

"Why, because hundreds of years ago there were more men than women? Because later small pox was set loose by the damn Rusk and still more men survived than women? Not anymore! There are more women than men now, and have been for centuries! Don't you find me attractive?"

"You have a great body, much better than mine."

"I wouldn't say that," she said and smiled as her eyes ran over Minu's curves. Minu felt a thrill at the look of naked lust in her friend's eyes, something she'd never felt directed at her by a woman.

Minu's back came up against the wall, and Cherise moved to within a few centimeters, her large breasts just below Minu's chin. She slowly looked up into those hazel eyes. Cherise reached out and cupped one of Minu's tiny breasts, gently squeezing the nipple. Before Minu could say anything more, their mouths were once again together.

Minu gently disengaged and pushed her back a little, fear making her stronger, but still in careful control of her right arm. "I'm scared," she said, her hands going around Cherise's waist. The other woman's hips were full, but she could feel the muscles in her bottom. Cherise put her arms around Minu and drew her closer. She felt the other girl's pubic hair rub against her belly and the sensation sent goose-bumps climbing her back. "I've never done anything like this before."

"Sure you have," Cherise assured her, and they kissed. "Don't be scared," she said, her hands going down and gently seeking, "You've just never done it with a girl."

"W-what do I do?" Minu asked, the quiver in her voice giving away her fear and excitement.

"I'll show you." Cherise's fingers found what she was looking for and Minu gasped at the ease of it. As the night went on, Cherise showed her just how much she knew as they cried out in passion. The howlers in the woods barked their reply to the strange sounds.

* * * * *

Chapter Four
May 26th, 521 AE

Sanctuary Island, Plateau Tribe Territory

Minu woke and knew she was in the comfy old bed in her cabin, and that she wasn't alone. It was hardly the first time she'd woken up naked next to another person; it was, however, the first time she'd woken to find her hand resting on a supple breast other than her own. She pulled away gently and got up, her head throbbing. "Oh boy," she said and padded to the bathroom, nearly tripping over one of several empty wine bottles. The hot water cleaned her body of the sweat and passion of the night, and got her mind going, but it didn't help her decide why she'd let things get out of hand like that. When she came out a short time later, Cherise was cooking eggs and bacon in the kitchen.

Minu walked over to see if the other girl had found everything she needed and nodded at the progress. "Sleep well?" Cherise asked.

"Hangover," Minu admitted. Cherise handed her some pain killers, and she took them gratefully. "Look, about last night…"

"It was what it was," Cherise said nonchalantly.

"I just wanted to—well…I don't know what I want to say."

Cherise put the skillet aside from the heating element and turned to face her. Even fresh from bed, Minu still found the girl exotic and exciting. She gave Minu a questioning look. "Did you have fun?"

"Yes," was the whispered reply.

"Did I make you do anything you didn't want to do?"

"No, of course not. I could have said no at any time."

"Okay. Well, I had a good time too, and that's that."

"I don't know if I ever…"

"I didn't come looking for a girlfriend," Cherise said and touched Minu's cheek. Something in her friend's voice made Minu wonder at the truth of it, but she still moved against the touch, a tear rolling down onto the other girl's hand, "I came to be with my friend. I thought you needed to feel the love of another human being, even if it wasn't a man's. I know your heart wasn't in it, but it was nice anyway."

"I was there the whole time," Minu said and touched Cherise's face in turn, "and I have no regrets. I'm just not sure if it's something right for me."

"Enough said," Cherise said and went back to making breakfast "I don't want to spoil this awesome bacon!"

Cherise's aerocar lifted off the landing pad after breakfast. Minu cleaned up after breakfast and tried to clear her mind. She didn't know what to think of the night before. The medicine had done its job and the headache was gone, leaving her clear-minded and even more confused with memories of the night before. It was hard to compare Cherise and Christian. How do you compare two things so different, and yet so alike? It was the most intense sexual experience of her short life, and yet it somehow still seemed to be missing something she couldn't put a finger on. The hardest part was trying to figure out how to avoid thinking about that night of hot, sweet sex all during the day ahead of her.

Minu flew back to Fort Jovich a short time later. The two-hour flight put her in the garage just in time for her morning staff meeting.

As she entered the conference room, the department heads all gave her a strange look. "What's wrong?" she asked no one in particular.

"Nothing," Aaron said, "you just look more relaxed than we've seen you in a while." Minu felt her cheeks getting hot and cleared her throat. Aaron's eyes narrowed at her blush, not liking what it might mean. He forced himself to look down at his tablet, muscles working his jaw. Minu cleared her throat and began the meeting.

The first issue was the biggest. The night before, a large group of the newly-graduated soldiers had been celebrating in Dodge City when they met a group of drunken scouts. Much bragging and muscle-flexing ensued, lubricated liberally with still more alcohol. Minu pulled bios on the names beginning to appear across her screen. All male on both sides, of course. When the pissing contest wasn't enough, it degraded into a general free-for-all. Scouts versus soldiers, Chosen versus almost-Chosen. Forty-two soldiers, eleven scouts. The Soldiers possessed general toughness and specialized combat training, the scouts had experience and what her dad would have called pure tenacity. At the top of the list of scouts was the ranking member present during the 'altercation,' Christian Forsythe.

"So what's the final damage?" she asked Ariana. Ariana Beck was, in many things, Minu's right hand. A cute civilian girl in her twenties, she carried an extra twenty pounds with that special dignity only the Asian descendants of the Peninsula tribe could manage. A few centimeters taller than Minu, her sharp eyes never missed a detail. She was reading from a tablet in one hand while toying with her waist-length pony tail with the other. Minu never let her hair get past shoulder length and often wondered how much work that kind of hair required.

"About like a night at the mines after payday," she said. Minu had hired her away from a boring job working for a zinc mining company where her skills were being wasted. One of her most amazing talents was fixing problems before Minu knew they existed. Most who worked in the fort knew that Ariana's word carried the same weight as Minu's. The girl had yet to let her boss down. "We have six scouts in the infirmary, and twenty soldiers. A few broken bones, couple hundred scrapes and bruises."

"No one dead, that's a start. Collateral damage?"

"The bar was the Hungry Howler."

"Yeah, been there," Minu said as heads around the room nodded their familiarity as well. It was well known as a very Chosen-friendly establishment in a region of Bellatrix that barely tolerated them. In fact, many of the places in Dodge City were anything *but* happy with the Chosen, despite owing their living to the fort and its occupants. They preferred civilians to the hard-charging Chosen soldiers or steely-eyed scouts.

"Damage comes to three hundred ninety-five credits."

"They burn the damn place down?" Minu exclaimed.

"Costs are high in Dodge City."

"They're taking advantage of us," Minu grumbled.

"Well, add another two hundred credits in medical bills for the five constables they put in the hospital."

"Crap, you didn't mention that part."

"I was saving the best for last."

"Right. So how many of them are in jail?"

"None. They were all released to the duty officer in charge." Ariana consulted her tablet for the responsible party. "It was Var'at."

"I bet that was an interesting scene."

"Says here he brought an entire squad of his soldiers along to muscle our men home. The soldiers and scouts all looked pretty cowed when I saw them this morning."

"So why wasn't I called last night?" Minu asked, looking specifically at Aaron. Though only a four-star, he was a ranking Chosen in the scout company, below Christian. She dearly wanted to know whose side he came down on in this little fracas.

"We handled it, or rather Var'at did," Aaron explained, shrugging his powerful shoulders. "I knew you were due back this morning..."

"Okay, I can live with that. So, meeting adjourned for a couple hours while I go skin some boys."

"But ma'am," Ariana complained.

"Put a lid on it; this is something I can't let stew. Only a few dozen were involved, but there are a couple *thousand* soldiers in this facility, and by now they're getting ten different accounts of what happened last night. We've known the sentiments between the scouts and the soldiers were...antagonistic...for a while, but I didn't think it would come to blows before I could make some adjustments."

Minu headed for the door before Ariana could stop her. She crooked a finger in Aaron's direction indicating she wanted him to come along, and headed for the detention center. The section was included at the last moment almost as an afterthought, meant to hold possible prisoners of war during a vendetta. She'd never expected to have to lock up her own soldiers, and especially not the much more experienced scouts.

She reached the detention level and knew right away it was the right place; the yells and curses being hurled across the hallway were definitive proof. "What the fuck is going on here?" she bellowed as soon as she was close enough not to be mistaken for a fellow combatant. "I said *what the fuck is going on here?*" Only a meter and a half tall, she already wielded the command voice of an old-Earth Marine Drill Instructor. The effect was almost instantaneous as the yelling abruptly stopped.

"I asked a question, damn you all!" She marched down the hall between the line of cells. Aaron was the one who'd placed the scouts on one side and the soldiers on the other. At the time, it had seemed the logical thing to do. The cells were simple affairs, only three meters wide, five deep, and arranged along both sides of the hall. The side facing the hallway was made of clear moliplas so the jailers could observe their charges; it was also perforated with holes to allow communication, or shouting and insults in this case. Should the need arise, shields and fields could be added if the occupants were more rowdy than mere drunken humans. The scouts and soldiers went from glaring at each other to looking at her. A few hung their heads or refused to meet her gaze, while others returned her glare evenly, especially the scouts, who were almost all older than her.

"Just a disagreement," she heard someone say. She instantly recognized the voice as Christian's.

Minu turned and looked for him, picking his tall frame out of the crowd of torn and bruised scouts. "And here he is, highest-ranking Chosen scout assigned to Fort Jovich, and what a shining example of Chosen prowess he is."

"Very funny," he grumbled.

"What, isn't that what you were doing, showing the soldiers how superior the full Chosen are to them? I have a simpler solution. Let's just put you all in one big room, pass out shock rifles and knives, and let you boys tear the shit out of each other like a bunch of wildcats.

Put it on pay-per-view, maybe we can recoup the costs of the damage you assholes did to the Hungry Howler!"

"Minu," Aaron said from behind her. She put a hand behind her to quiet him.

"Well, is that what we're going to do?" Christian stared her down for a moment then looked away. She cast her laser-like stare around the cells and saw a collection of downcast gazes, frowns, and outright embarrassed looks. "No one likes that idea? I'm glad to hear it, because you're all Chosen. More importantly, we're all humans! I might have understood it if a fight broke out between the Rasa soldiers and the humans, but you've accepted them better than you do each other!

"Okay, you've had your fun, and you'd better have gotten it out of your systems, because that's it. The next Chosen assigned to this fort that takes a poke at another will be reassigned, and *I will make it my personal duty* to see that it's the end of your useful career wherever they assign you. As far as I'm concerned, you can serve out the next twenty years carrying sacks of grain for Logistics or cleaning up after bugs for Training. I hope I've made myself perfectly clear."

Minu didn't wait to hear whether they agreed or disagreed with her decree. She spun on her heel and left, slamming the heavy dualloy door with a resounding bang of metal. Aaron nearly lost a finger trying to keep up with her. "What do you want me to do with them?"

"Let them spend the rest of the day in those cells, but I want them mixed up, scout and soldier, as evenly as possible."

"Damn, are you sure?"

"Absolutely. If they're too stupid to understand what I said and that I mean business, then we don't want them here. More importantly, they're of no use to the Chosen or the Tog." She stopped and punched the wall with her right fist, the cybernetic limb whining with power as she deformed the dualloy panel. She looked down at the torn light gray skin over her metal knuckles and cursed. "I'm trying to build a cohesive fighting force here, the core of our future, and these fucking morons are out slapping each other around after a few drinks!"

"What about Christian? I have a couple reports that indicate he might have started it." Aaron was still walking quickly to keep up.

"I was afraid of that." She thought for a moment, examining the damage to her synthetic skin, then sighed in resignation. She couldn't show him any favoritism. Then again, maybe there was a tactic she could try. "Release him, right away."

"Just him?"

"Yep." Minu headed for her office leaving Aaron staring after her in surprise. In her office she called Dram. The big man smiled at her through the videophone.

"What's the occasion this early?" Minu reported what had happened. As her commander, she needed to report anyway, but she wanted to get his input on how to best deal with Christian. "An eventful night, but not surprising."

"I'm glad *you* weren't surprised."

"You mean you didn't expect this?" She said she hadn't. "Minu, you have a classic example of too many roosters in the henhouse."

"I've never seen a chicken. They only live in specially prepared habitats, because of the howlers."

"You know what I mean. You have about half the scouts assigned to Fort Jovich, along with thousands of new, cocky, young soldiers. While those new soldiers may never rise above the honorary rank of five stars, they are still Chosen. And they're being trained to be a true fighting force. Until now, the scouts were the fighters, and that's probably the biggest reason everyone wanted to be a scout. Even you and your father. It's worse than if we'd disbanded the scouts. Now they're just part of another branch."

"We talked about that. We need the scouts to perform the function they were originally intended for, scouting. They aren't a military force, and that's why we lost so many during the Vendetta."

"Right, but they're part of the soldier branch now. Even the lowest ranking scout outranks the highest-ranking soldier, but they're not the bad asses anymore. I've led the scouts for ten years, ever since Chriso assigned me there, and it gets under *my* skin from time to time thinking about it. Those black stars were the best; you wanted to wear them too, remember? Now along comes the red stars. Little doubt in the meaning there—fire, blood, and glory. The scouts still get to wear their black stars, but they have bright red outlines. The symbolism wasn't intentional, but it's still there."

"Okay, so what do we do? Give up and integrate the scouts?"

"No, it won't solve the problem. And if we reassign or demote Christian, you'll make a martyr out of him. No, I think we need to give him a vested interest in the results."

"And how do we do that?"

* * * * *

Chapter Five
June 7th, 521 AE

Fort Jovich, Peninsula Tribe Territory

Minu leaned on the railing, watching the squads of soldiers working out below. Even from a hundred meters up, it was easy to pick out the dark gray skittering forms of the Rasa where they moved among the humans. She consoled herself that at least *that* part of her plan had gone without incident, here in the fort anyway. The Rasa had been irreplaceable in teaching her how a Concordian fighting force worked. And once the soldiers finished basic training last year, they joined in the second level of training as her integrated combat technique was put to the test. But it wasn't fully integrated yet. At one end of the massive workout field stood several mockups of transports where the soldiers practiced embarking, disembarking, defending an LZ, and extracting casualties from a downed craft. Only it wasn't a real transport.

Minu went back into the office and punched up a call. She was taken aback when Bjorn answered the phone. His aged face and always-wild hair leaned too close to the camera with a look of urgency. "How much longer for the damage control team—" he stopped when he recognized Minu. "Oh. Good to see you girl! But I'm a little busy just now."

"Bjorn, what the hell happened?"

"Just a little, bitty problem…" smoke swirled around his head and Minu heard the unmistakable sound of a small explosion in the background.

"Little problems don't explode, Bjorn," she said. Bjorn tried to smile and then ducked as another, larger explosion boomed behind him. The view tilted and spun wildly as the phone was knocked from the desk. Someone picked up the phone and she saw the somewhat less chaotic features of Dr. Ted Hurt. While he was smoke-smudged and his hair was disheveled, there was no sign of panic on his face. Minu breathed easier.

"Hello Ted, got a minute?"

He looked over his shoulder, and Minu heard many new voices raised in alarm, quickly followed by the hissing of fire suppression gear. "I do now," he said with a little laugh.

"I guess we should start with asking if that was my prototype bursting into flames?"

"No, it was a small part of it." Minu cursed, almost further damaging her knuckles on the desk. "Now don't get overly worked up, it wasn't integrated into the complete system yet. Bjorn had a rather unorthodox idea on how to approach power utilization."

"I saw in the last report the power system was considered operational."

"It was. At least until Bjorn thought he had a better idea. The good news is he dismounted the system from the prototype before experimenting. The bad news is the entire system is now scattered all over the lab."

"Damn it, Ted!" The scientist shrugged helplessly. "I need you to run roughshod over him as much as possible."

"I was, Minu, but I have to sleep sometime. Honestly, I hope I'm half as unstoppable when I'm eighty." Minu sighed. "I've been doing mainly theoretical work for years, Minu. Young Chosen like you have taken over the hard R&D."

"I know, but most of them died or were too seriously injured to continue after the Rasa Vendetta."

"And most of the civilians won't come back to work because a few got killed."

"They were warned."

"I agree, but they're still gone. I hear we have some good prospects in the latest trials graduates just coming into service."

"That's good news."

"Yeah." He got a somewhat evasive look on his face. "I've seen some test results, and I have to say that a dozen or so of those new soldiers of yours might do nicely, too."

"You can't have them."

"Minu, see reason here. We're desperately short on technical and scientific prowess just now. I admire your singular vision and unrelenting zeal, but without tools, you can't build things. And those missing people are the tools we need."

"Send me the list; I'll see who I can part with." Numbers danced in Minu's mind. While the graduates of the first soldiers' trials came through in acceptable numbers, attrition from the training was several percentage points higher than expected. They were dangerously close to the minimum number she wanted to put in service. Every week a couple dropped out, or were washed out. "I can't give you all of them."

"I understand."

"How long for that prototype, Ted? We're going to be all dressed up with no place to go without it."

"Bjorn is just too valuable to cut him out, or I would. He makes amazingly innovative breakthroughs that outweigh his foibles, most of the time."

"How long, Ted?"

"Six weeks, but don't quote me on that."

"Okay, do your best."

"We always do." Ted looked sideways as light gray smoke billowed across the view and the sounds of angry conversation drifted through the speaker. "I really miss Pip right now."

"Don't we all?"

* * * * *

Chapter Six
Julast 27th, 521 AE

Chosen Headquarters, Steven's Pass

As the week wound down, Minu dabbled with the idea of going home to the island, and ultimately discarded it. Perhaps if she'd been on base when the incident with the scouts had occurred on Monday, she could have dealt with it better. Nothing more had happened since then, but the tension was a tangible thing. Even though she'd defused the situation, it didn't solve the underlying problem.

Thursday, she took a quick trip to the Chosen headquarters at Steven's Pass. It was the usual meeting of the council where she presented her quarterly report of progress. Fort Jovich was not quite fully operational, and the soldiers were coming along in their training on schedule. The only glaring problem was the conflict between the scouts and the soldiers. First Among the Chosen Jacob Bentley was not too concerned by this. "Some friction is to be expected," was his comment, delivered without looking up from his tablet. The others on the council shared his opinion, and, before long, Minu was back in her car and rocketing away.

A straight course to Ft. Jovich would have taken four thousand kilometers of travel. She elected for a slightly longer route that took her over her hometown of Tranquility, capital of the Plateau tribe. As the car descended through some clouds, she was gifted with a wonderful view of the five-kilometer-wide plateau from which the tribe derived its name. Here the survivors from the United States arrived five hundred years ago and found themselves on the most defensible real estate on the planet, surrounded by the migration route of the planet's most deadly predators, the Kloth.

What had once been a small village of little more than a hundred was now a thriving city buzzing with three hundred thousand humans and quite a few aliens. The planet's public use off-world portal was located here, along with the planetary council, business center, the largest university, and the best hospital. Minu landed her car in the modern parking facility at the Plateau Mercy Hospital and headed inside. She'd walked the route enough times to know where she was going without consulting the signs. The hoverfield-powered lift deposited her on the lowest level of the hospital. Down the hall, she entered the coma wing.

"Good afternoon Chosen," the elderly nurse smiled as Minu pushed through the doors.

"You too, Helen. Any change in his condition?"

"No, sorry." Minu nodded and moved on.

It was an open ward; dozens of beds ran the length of the room. A year ago, the beds were all filled; now only three patients remained. Minu moved to the last occupied bed and found a visitor already there. A slightly overweight girl a year or two younger than Minu's age, with acne on her face and long brown hair, sat in an uncomfortable chair, her head against her chest, large bosom rising and falling in sleep. Cynthia spent most of her free time sitting with Pip, her boyfriend of a few months before he was critically wounded in the Rasa Vendetta. Minu quietly took the other seat and reached out to take her friend's hand. "I've really been missing you, Pip," she whispered into his ear. Dozens of machines, human and Concordian-made, beeped and displayed a wide range of bio-data on the patient. Since he'd been wounded in the head, nothing at all had changed.

Minu spent an hour holding Pip's hand and talking to him. She talked about the weeks since her visit, how the fort was coming, the problem with her relationship with Christian, and finally of her night with Cherise. She didn't feel it was a betrayal; Cherise would understand. It was with Pip one night more than a year ago that she'd spent many hours talking about boys and girls, drinking mead, and learning about relationships. Call it the blind leading the blind. At the end of that night she'd come within a hair's-breadth of sleeping with Pip. It was only his sense of duty to her as his boss and friend that stopped it from happening. In a way, she'd always regretted her decision to make him chose to not sleep with her. And since his brain was irrevocably damaged, Minu had come to realize that she loved Pip as more than a brother, and maybe as much as a boyfriend.

Her time up, Minu stood and patted his hand one last time. "Nice to see you again, Minu." Cynthia was looking up at her, a sad smile on her face. Minu felt a moment of fear as she wondered how much the other girl had heard. Cynthia rubbed sleep from her eyes and yawned, and Minu decided her sexual peccadilloes were safe for now.

"You too, Cynthia." Minu came around and gave her a hug and a kiss on the cheek. "It's late, you should be getting home."

"You want to spend the night at my apartment? It's small, but I have a comfy couch."

"Thanks, but no. I have to get back to the fort." Cynthia nodded and looked back at Pip. His breathing continued regularly, as it had for months on end; machines made sure of that. "I'm sure he's glad you're here, but he might wish you'd move on at some point."

"Thanks, but I'm where I need to be." Minu nodded and headed out the door.

* * * * *

Chapter Seven
Julast 30th, 521 AE

Fort Jovich, Peninsula Tribe Territory

Dram's solution to Christian was not what she would have done. Christian would now be in command of the scouts, but he stayed at three stars. Minu knew Dram hadn't given him the full promotion for three reasons. One: he hadn't earned it with his actions. Two: he didn't want a two-star in the soldiers' branch yet. And three: if promoted, Christian would outrank Minu, and that was reason enough not to do it. She almost wished he had, if only for the latter reason. Who could argue that the biggest problem was her promotion in his absence? She outranked him in all but fact. She was in charge of the soldiers, at least during this phase of their training, and as such the scouts under them. She wished it could go back to the way it had been. Of course, after her night in the cabin with Cherise, not as much of her wished for it.

The soldiers were ready to go operational. A thousand well-trained men and women, along with two thousand integrated Rasa soldiers, stood ready to answer the call. They were untested, and that was her biggest worry. If she didn't find a way to grind the green out of them before a real fight, her losses would be twice as big when they saw serious combat. Without the new multi-role fighters, they couldn't do much more in the way of real world training, just more boring static drills. Worse still, another thousand soldiers were in the second stage of their training cycle. Give it another two months and the new kids would be competing for training space. Her plans counted on these men and women being able to help the new recruits along. What would they be able to show them that they didn't already know?

Minu took the drop tube down to the lower level, the hoverfield working flawlessly as always to let her gently step onto the ceramic concrete floor. A pair of guards came to attention, hands flat along their sides, slapping against their thighs in salute. Minu nodded as she walked onto the wide-open level of the primary training field. It was much louder down here, with hundreds of humans and Rasa grunting or hissing with exertion, orders being shouted, and cadences called out as platoons marched. She liked to come down and quietly observe, but it wasn't an easy thing to do. There weren't any other young three-star female Chosen around to mistake her for, and certainly none as short or intense in presence as Minu Alma. Add a slightly gray-colored right arm that ended with three fingers and a thumb and, well, never mind. She would stand and watch them work for hours, taking careful note of how her new manuals were being followed, how some things worked or others needed possible changes, and just how the soldiers were shaping up. Every day they looked more like training films from old Earth. United States Navy Seals, Israeli Special Forces, Russian Spetsnaz, and French Foreign Legion had all unknowingly donated training techniques now being used. But she'd also read about techniques in the Concordian data stolen by Pip. How to effectively employ anti-bot tactics, correct use of shields by a mobile military force, and how to take advantage of gravitic impeller technology. Of course, the techniques were also used by the Rasa to good effect. They included much of the Concordian training, with their own particular innovations. The troops were getting used to her showing up, and on cue, they began to perform for their boss. Her vantage point a hundred meters up or the dozens of remote cameras just wasn't the same thing. You couldn't feel the intensity through a camera. You couldn't smell the sweat and sense the accomplishments, or the failures.

The biggest reason she got in as close as possible was one she kept to herself. She'd done all these drills with Dram, Gregg, Aaron, and Cherise, over and over. Her excuse was to make sure they were effective, but the truth was she intended to lead these soldiers into battle herself. After the dedication last week, she'd suffered a mental setback to that plan, but she hadn't given up. Training branch? It would be a cold day in the Christians' Hell when an Alma was in the Training branch!

Several teams had now spotted Minu watching and were doing their best to impress her. Decorum was breaking down, and it was almost time to head back upstairs, when she spotted Christian. He was working with a couple of scout teams, along with several squad-sized soldier units. She smiled slyly and nodded in appreciation of Dram's brilliance. Now that he was in charge of the scouts, their failure would be his own. She turned and headed back up the jump tube, which reversed direction for her ascent. Minu worked in her office for a while until an idea suddenly occurred to her. But was it possible? An hour's work on the fort's network made her decide it was worth the effort, so she put in a call to Cherise.

"What can I do for you, boss?"

"I'm not your boss; you know that. Can you lend me twenty or so of those old capsule transports we used to use on the personnel runs? You remember; they used to shuttle Chosen all over the place before the maglev network was finished."

"Yeah, I remember. We've sold a few off to the civilian market, and use the others for moving cargo around the planet if it's too urgent to wait for a train. But, twenty of them? A lot of them are in questionable shape after so many years at hard labor."

"They're Concordian tech; they should last forever," Minu noted. "If I remember, some guy from Logistics once told me most of them were already thousands of years old before we got them."

"True, but we haven't been able to maintain them properly. Parts are all but impossible to get through the Concordia, and it isn't worth fabricating them ourselves, even if that were possible. We've been cannibalizing the worst-shape units to fix the others for quite a while. It's part of the reason we developed the maglev," she explained. "It's more than ninety percent homemade tech, and the rest of the parts are available in unlimited quantities. You know what's funny? We're in negotiations to build similar maglev networks for a dozen other minor species. They came here to trade and were dumbfounded that we'd built our own system instead of contracting it to a Concordian firm. Cheap, dumb, human tech. Who would have guessed?"

"Several people I know," Minu whispered. A voice echoed in the back of her mind, *The Concordia is in decline, maybe even dying.* Yet another little piece in the construction of a theory that, years ago, had seemed like a house of cards or the ramblings of a madman. Every passing year made that house of cards look more like a dualloy and ceramic concrete bunker. "Well, regardless of the condition, what can you do?"

Cherise consulted a computer out of Minu's view and then turned back. "How soon?"

"Say, a week from today?"

"That long? Then twenty won't be a problem."

"Great. Throw in a couple field logistics teams, whatever repair parts you got. Oh, and make a couple of them in such bad shape that they're barely working, will you?"

Cherise laughed. "What the hell do you have planned?"

"Just some fun."

The next morning at the training briefing down in the main auditorium, several thousand soldiers were stunned to see Minu step onto the stage. They jumped to their feet, hands slapping their thighs. The Rasa were just as fast, but their salute was less pronounced, lacking the flat fleshy hands of the humans. "At ease," she said and waited while they took their seats. They shouldn't have been too surprised; she had, after all, informed the Chosen temporarily in charge of the units that she had an announcement to make.

The soldiers were arrayed in groups based around their smallest units. Each squad was comprised of two five-man fire teams, each lead by a corporal. Two squads joined with an extra command fire team to produce a platoon. Four platoons to a company, and three companies made a battalion. Ranks ranged from private to sergeant major, currently the highest ranking soldier. At that point, a Chosen stood in command of each company, accounting for a lot of the active duty command Chosen four- and five-stars. There were additional command platoons and support personnel with each battalion, bringing the total to one thousand fifty men and women in the three battalions of Red Army. As they progressed, soldiers would assume the command officer ratings from the temporary Chosen pressed into duty. The scouts would retain their own structure.

The Rasa were led by their own officers, their native ranks replaced with the human equivalent for organizational purposes, minus the human Chosen. The six battalions of Rasa were all under Green Army. It was the only color that made sense. The aliens again proved their versatility by quickly adapting to the changes. Var'at even said it made more sense than their strictly birth-ordered ranking system. As Minu took the podium she looked out on the seated multitude. More than a thousand humans and two thousand Rasa soldiers stared back at her. Nine battalions ready to defend Bellatrix. Just over a year ago, they'd stood against five thousand Rasa with only a few hundred scouts. She closed her eyes for a moment and tried to imagine how the Vendetta would play out today. Would Var'at's people here even have survived to surrender? She doubted it.

"Good morning, soldiers."

"Boss!" they all roared. Minu's head jerked around to skewer Aaron where he stood. He blushed and held up his hands like he was helpless to control them. She gave him a 'we'll talk about this later' look and turned back to the assembled troops.

"I am proud of each and every one of you. From the moment we, the Chosen, first conceived of this mighty fighting force until now, I wasn't sure we could accomplish our goals. But here you are, many thousand strong, with more on the way. Do you stand ready?"

"We are ready!" they roared back at her, their raised voices buffeting the air around her.

Minu nodded and smiled. "Very good." She turned to the three Chosen in temporary command of the human battalions: three-star commanders named Daniel Tucker, Alex Dawn, and Samuel Ubuntu. The latter was from the Desert tribe, and a relative of Cherise's. Var'at stood next to them, alert and excited. "We are on alert until further notice," she told them. Then without another word, she turned and walked out. They did their best to remain quiet until she closed the doors behind her, but as she left there was a smile on her face and a dull roar of excited conversation behind her. By the time she reached her office, Aaron was waiting for her. "When did you learn to fly?" she asked him upon seeing he'd beaten her back to her office, despite leaving before he did.

"You gave me this job to drive your crazy training regime. I've found it necessary to develop the skills of flight."

"Good, now teach all of the rest of them as well," she said and cocked a thumb out her door to take in the entire fort.

"Funny, but not as funny as putting the place on alert. We've never even had them march in formation more than a few kilometers. What do you think will happen when they try to maneuver together?"

"Mass hysteria, at the very least. Somewhat disorganized mayhem at best."

"Sounds reasonable," Aaron said and shook his head. "If you know the results, why bother with the attempt?"

"Because you can't succeed until you fail."

"We haven't even begun working with these fighter-hybrids we've been promised."

"The next-best-thing is on the way."

"Okay, whatever you say." A few minutes after he'd left, Var'at came skittering in. Unlike Aaron, he was agitated, his tongue flicking in and out, an obvious sign of excitement.

"We are to fight?"

"It's practice." Var'at seemed a little deflated, but then gave a very human shrug.

"It's better than farming and training all day. What more do you wish of me?"

"I want you to detach First through Third battalions of Green Army as an OPFOR."

"What is this 'OPFOR'?"

"It's short for Opposition Force. I mean to have you act as an enemy unit in the field. Then, after the first round, we'll reverse the players and try again."

"We will do as you ask," he said and bowed low. "But we wait for the chance to truly sink our teeth into your enemies."

She considered her friend for a long moment and recalled how they'd once been bitter enemies. "I can wait for that day, at least a while longer," Minu admitted, "but I'm sure the day will come, and sooner rather than later."

* * *

After her announcement, the fort was buzzing with excitement all that day and the next. Even the section of the fort where the newest soldiers were in basic training held excited conversations, everyone eager to see what was going to happen. But as the time extended into the third day, there were mumbles of discontent and confusion. Had Minu just been kidding? Maybe a test to see how wound up they could get the soldiers before they freaked out? She got inquiry after inquiry on her computer asking when there'd be a drill. Every one she answered the same. "Soon." Eventually, they quit asking.

On the fourth day, in the nearly empty vehicle bays, two dozen capsule-shaped transports were quietly delivered. Minu went down as the last two arrived to meet Cherise, who'd flown the last one herself. It landed somewhat roughly, with a little smoke curling from one of the Venetian vents where the gravitic impellers were housed. "Nice landing," she told Cherise as she got out. There was even more smoke inside. "Glad you made it."

"Had to land twice and do patch jobs on the flight controls," Cherise said. She came over and gave Minu a peck on the cheek in greeting. Minu was at first worried she was going to try and kiss her on the lips, then disappointed when she didn't. But of course, with the bay full of green-star Logistics Chosen and civilians working for logistics, Minu should have known nothing more would happen. Cherise pointed to the craft she'd flown and the other that had landed moments before hers. "Numbers 92-B and 61-A are the junkers you asked for. We managed to get them here, but I doubt they'll make it to Dodge City and back."

"Are they safe?"

"Oh sure. The emergency impellers have their own electroplasma capacitors, or EPCs, that are recharged every time you replace the main, and if they don't check one hundred percent, it won't fly at all. You can override that safety if you're feeling suicidal."

"What happens if the main fails?"

"You drop to about fifty meters in a gut-wrenching descent."

"Scary surprise?"

"Better have a spare pair of undies. At that point, depending on your cargo, you'll either be encouraged repeatedly to land and only be able to go about 50 KPH, or you end up making a rather bumpy emergency landing whether you like it or not."

"Good, thanks for the loan."

"Am I going to get them back?"

Minu smirked and looked innocent. "Can I get back to you on that?"

"Right. Got some time for a swim this weekend?"

Minu knew without a doubt what the other girl meant by that. She felt a little thrill of excitement but suppressed it just as quickly "No, we're going to be playing soldier."

"Suit yourself," she said and headed for the main exit. An overland bus left on the hour for Dodge City, where she could catch a maglev back to Steven's Pass.

"I'll call you when I have some time," she called to the retreating girl. Cherise held up a long thin arm and gave her a backward wave just as she went around a corner and out of sight. Minu turned to the team of specialists who were staying to help her. "Okay gentlemen, I need all of these transports to look identical."

"They won't work identically, Chosen," one man told her. He looked to be in his fifties and had callused hands. He was leaning against a transport with a familiarity that bespoke many years of working on the machines. He was a civilian and, given his age, was probably hired back when the first of the venerable transports came online.

"It's not necessary that they do, but I want to make sure you can't just tell by looking. Let's get rid of the smoke, clean off the carbon scoring, give the seats a good cleaning, and empty the ash trays." The men all laughed in good humor. "Also, on this tablet you'll find some specifications. Please modify the paint job accordingly and add the number schemes."

"Which one with what number?" the same older man asked. Even though he was a civilian, it was obvious he was in charge.

"The list indicates an asterisk next to two of them; those are to be the trashed transports."

The man nodded and took the tablet, scrolling over the instructions. "Shouldn't take more than twelve hours."

"Very good. What's your name, sir?"

"He's just a civilian mechanic," interjected a Chosen showing four green stars. The man who was supposed to be in charge had finally spoken up.

"I know that, but I'd still like his name."

"You can call me Max, ma'am."

"Max it is, then. Max, would you consider working for Fort Jovich here, with my people?"

"Chosen Alma," the four-star barked, "we have a hard time getting trained people in Steven's Pass."

"Not as hard as we do here, I'd wager. Half the adults in the Peninsula Tribe can't use a computer. Dodge City is nothing more than bars and whorehouses."

"And it's my choice where I work and live, with all due respect to the Chosen," Max said to the green-star he'd arrived with, "it would be an honor to work under the daughter of Chriso Alma."

"You knew my father?"

"Who didn't? But yes, I worked under him before. It was at least twenty years ago, when we first got these fliers. Of course, I was just a snot nosed twenty-five-year-old, and your dad younger than me."

"My thanks." Minu shook his hand and gave the Chosen a shrug. "Now as quickly as possible, if you please?" she indicated the computer with its list of modifications and headed from the bay. The Chosen from Logistics glared at her retreating back.

*****

Chapter Eight
September 4th, 521 AE

Fort Jovich, Peninsula Tribe Territory

It was three o'clock in the morning on the fifth day after placing the fort on alert. Minu had returned to her office late the night before on the excuse that there was a meeting she needed to attend via teleconference. What she'd really done was take a good long nap on her office's comfy couch. When the alarm on her chronometer went off at 3 A.M., she'd already been up and showered in the office's small fresher and was just zipping up her clean black jump suit, three golden stars shining on her cuffs and boots polished to a mirror finish. Clipping on her belt, she pulled out one of the three computer tablets that rode in holsters on her hip. The command was already entered; all she had to do was touch the button.

Alarm klaxons blared, almost loud enough to frighten her, despite being ready for them. A supposedly reassuring female voice came over the intercom. "Attention, attention. This is an action alert. Alien forces are attacking the maglev station at Dodge City. Red Army, First Battalion is ordered to prepare for emergency deployment! This is a drill."

Minu really wanted to leave off the last. It was only Aaron reminding her that the fort was full of partially-trained kids that had shaken her resolve. Some accidents were unavoidable in training.

Calling an alert without at least letting them know it was a drill was *begging* for something to go deadly wrong. As it was, she knew thousands of young people would be tumbling from their bunks, bumping into each other, some smashing into walls and cots as they hurried to get ready. There would be excitement, there would be fear, there would be confusion, and there would hopefully be invaluable experience gained. She went to her closet and grabbed her field kit. There was a little dust on it; that really annoyed her. How many months had it been since she'd led a mission, or even been off world? Six months? A year? They were going less than a hundred kilometers, but it was still something.

Var'at and his OPFOR had left late last night, shortly after lights-out. The Rasa commander looked very excited at his chance to test the new soldiers in combat. It was with no small sense of concern that she used the Rasa as the aggressors first. To some, the Vendetta was still fresh in their minds. That also helped her decide to proclaim that this was only a drill.

Down in the ready room, she was the first to arrive, except for the few Chosen who knew what was going on. The ready room was a large chamber attached to several areas of the fort via tunnels, including the vehicle bays, an outside ramp, and the portal chamber one level below. On one side, a pair of stairs entered and angled in either direction to a line of drop and jump tubes. Up the stairs Minu could hear the sound of running feet. She stood by the ramp leading to the vehicle bays, tablet in hand, waiting impatiently. Seven minutes had now elapsed since the alarm sounded.

With a yell, a pair of sergeants raced in, followed closely by their platoons. She recognized the platoons and wasn't surprised. Both the sergeants were Chosen soldiers trained up with the rest. But unlike many, they'd been in an existing military on Bellatrix prior to joining. Minu had been on the lookout for soldiers like these from the beginning and used them extensively to fill NCO slots as much as possible. They would likely be the first full officers, and their showing today backed up her assessment.

As squads continued to arrive in increasingly less organized condition, Minu took copious notes on their readiness rating, from one to five; five being the best, and one the worst. Only six squads earned a five, and that disgusted her. All these months of training, and it had only taken five months of cooling their heels to cause a total lapse of readiness.

Once she got to the last squad she rated with three or above, Minu ordered the door closed. A worker gave her the thumbs up and the doors rumbled closed. The sounds of men yelling on the other side came through as they tried to stop the doors from closing. Chosen Daniel's command squad had earned him a ranking of four, and he stared in surprise at her as she locked almost an entire company out. "I'm sorry, commander, the rest of your battalion is too late to be of any good in this deployment."

He was taken aback but nodded in understanding. "We will work very hard on this issue after the drill."

"I'm sure you will," she said and looked around at the state of readiness for the soldiers that had made it inside, many still trying to finish securing weapons or zipping uniforms, "among other things." Daniel turned red and cleared his throat.

"Shall we move to the exterior ramp?"

"No, Colonel Tucker, down to the vehicle bay ramp."

"As the commander orders," he said and yelled for the battalion to move out by squad up the ramp to the vehicle bay. The ready room was crowded with five hundred men and women, though not as crowded as it should have been. It took more precious minutes to get them moving in an orderly manner. All the time, Minu was taking notes. She'd be the one to command the soldiers if it was the last thing she did. Minu hadn't spent a lot of time wondering why she was so driven to be an old-style military general. Maybe it was all the historical studies she'd been doing in warfare? Maybe it was the Rasa Vendetta? Maybe there was some other, deeper reason. At the moment it didn't really matter. Despite the sloppiness of the deployment, she was leading her soldiers into the field for the first time. As the day wore on, her excitement would give way to a profoundly humbling sense of frustration.

Minu followed Chosen Daniel up the ramp and into the vehicle bay. She didn't know what he and the other soldiers had been expecting, but it wasn't the array of vehicles that awaited them. They'd all worked with the mockups of the future multi-role fighters and been trained on gravitic-style flight controls. The transports had been painted in the same black and red color pattern as the training mockups and were now loaded onto the newly-finished vehicle management system, a complicated array of hydraulic platforms, robotic arms, and hoverfield stabilizers that allowed for the rapid launching of multiple craft through limited exits. Again, old-Earth tactics with Concordian technology. A fort with too many doors was impossible to defend. It was capable of handling hundreds of vehicles and craft, as long as they were equipped with an RF identifier and constructed with enough stability for the magnetic clamps to haul it around. A few of the soldiers gawked, wondering if these were the promised multi-role fighter craft they'd been training to use.

"A much more interesting drill than I expected," Chosen Daniel said. Minu nodded, glad he realized this wasn't a simple readiness test.

Minu took out her computer and held it up to get their attention "Assignment by platoon to the transports." She thumbed the computer, and it transmitted the assignments through the network. The transports were designated Saber One through Twenty-two. It was an accident that only six hundred soldiers made it to deploy. Had they all made the cut, the craft would have been overloaded. Now only the command units would have more than twenty-five in each.

Minu watched the ranking noncoms to see their reactions. Most snatched at their own computers, a few took a moment to realize what was happening. All the time Minu continued observing and making notes in her tablet. A lot more work to do, she thought. "Here we go!" she yelled and gave the loadmaster a wave.

The vehicle management system came alive with a startling roar of machinery. The first transport was snatched off the tall rack on the wall, dangling by two small magnets, and swung out over their heads. A few of the soldiers shouted in surprise as the multi-ton vehicle went by only a few meters overhead. Once in place over the loading ramp with its bright yellow warning lines painted on the floor, klaxons blared and lights flashed as it was lowered to the floor. Hoverfields in the handling arm made sure the transport was level with the floor, then gently sat it down; the ceramic concrete floor reverberated with a *thrum*. Magnets released, the huge robotic arm swung up and away, and the klaxons and lights ceased their warnings as the craft was now ready for boarding.

"Get them going, commander!" Minu ordered.

* * *

The drill was an unmitigated disaster, as Minu had feared it would be from the poor showing of the first minutes. In retrospect she wasn't overly surprised, just profoundly disappointed. There were many tense minutes as the unit commanders and noncoms figured out the order of vehicle assignment. Naturally she made sure the vehicles didn't come off the wall in order. What would have been a well-practiced, neat, and orderly deployment had the whole battalion made it on time was now badly disrupted. As the transports were swung into place time after time, squad loading assignments needed to be revised on the fly, forcing units which were from different platoons to double up. Chaos reared its ugly head.

Taking the better part of an hour longer than it should have, twenty-two transports floated just outside the vehicle bay exit. Minu rode in her own aerocar, accompanied by Aaron, and used the computer built into her car to monitor the war game. The rest of her training team used multiple tablets linked with hers.

The drill was simple. As the alert had explained, aliens were invading Bellatrix from an unspecified point and were assaulting the maglev railhead in Dodge City. On everyone's computers were pregenerated maps showing where the alien invaders were attacking. Of course, it was all simulated. For the drill, Minu hired contractors to erect temporary buildings just outside of Dodge City. Nothing more than big empty metal boxes with less than convincing facades and spray painted names like Computer Center, Food Storage, Civilian Housing, power generation. It would be enough.

At dawn, the recon team led by Sabers One and Two swept in low from the east, and then climbed rapidly into the just-lightening sky in an overflight of the 'city' to get the lay of the land. Naturally

Var'at was waiting, and shot down both transports, scoring verified kills with simulated missile launchers. The four squads in the transport were now 'dead.' The pilots landed the transports in a nearby field designated the 'kill zone' for the drill.

Chosen Daniel complained to Minu over the network that the drill had made no mention of enemy anti-aircraft. She replied that she was certain the next aliens to invade their world would be sure to inform him what weapons and equipment they'd be bringing. He sent no follow-up message; she'd made her point.

The second time Daniel sent only one craft, Saber Eleven, in from the North, flying low and fast, near supersonic and close to the vehicles' maximum velocity, sensors running at full speed. It was fired upon but came through intact, thanks to the different approach vector. Minu watched as the tactical map was filled in showing enemy locations and numbers, and other unknown concentrations of heat signatures or power readings in buildings.

Less than a minute after the overflight, Daniel transmitted his deployment plan. Two platoons were to land on the east side of the town and create a secure LZ; a two-platoon element would also neutralize the anti-aircraft missile battery that had destroyed Sabers One and Two. Four transports swept in low and fast for deployment. It was a practice drill used regularly, if not as dynamically. Of course, in the usual drill, none of the transports ever failed. One of the four transports experienced a primary gravitic impeller failure with a spectacular flare of plasma and trailing smoke. Fire suppression gear kicked in instantly, and the emergency impellers worked to keep the craft from crashing nose-first into the soggy ground, but the heavily-loaded craft slowed to a crawl. Without being ordered to do so, two other transports turned back to check on the damaged craft just as Rasa snipers opened up.

The low-powered laser weapons were designated as crew-served beamcasters. The lead rescue craft's sensors registered a direct hit on the cockpit. The pilot and avionics were 'destroyed,' and the craft was listed as lost with all aboard. The second rescue Saber dodged wildly, and thus avoided the same fate (Minu made note of the pilot's ability), but of course the damaged craft was easily picked off. Four transports down, four platoons dead, and not a boot on the ground.

Daniel was trying desperately to salvage the landing and ordered it to proceed. Minu saw what was about to happen and again was thankful Var'at was on her side. The remaining two transports hadn't landed but circled, waiting for orders. By the time they turned around and came to settle to the ground, their appearance was no longer a surprise. The Rasa waited until the pair was on the ground, wide boarding ramps lowered, and soldiers pouring out before they opened fire. Bright green lasers flashed, and simulated explosive charges were detonated. A small swarm of centipede-bots and crab-bots raced from a nearby building to attack both craft as well.

In less than a minute, the entire force was wiped out. Careful weapons fire disabled their transports so they couldn't make a run for it, allowing Var'at to make the landing a total loss. Minu wondered if he was laughing right then. She wasn't.

Daniel responded quickly this time. Saber Eleven arced in and strafed the Rasa formation, causing a dozen or so 'casualties' and making them fall back from the LZ. It was the first enemy losses of the now five-minute-old engagement.

The LZ was finally established in the growing light of dawn, and two more platoons came in for a landing. Just as he was strengthening his LZ perimeter, the Rasa hit in force, a moving wave of bots attacking the east and west flanks, while the foot soldiers stormed in from the south. Lasers flashed and paint bombs burst as the firefight developed. Minu piloted her car to circle the battle, taking careful note of the tactics on both sides. While she spent most of her attention on the human soldiers and how they responded to the rapidly changing tactics of the enemy, she also watched how the Rasa dealt with their comrades, now temporary enemies.

Var'at knew he had them against the wall and pressed his advantage, but no sooner did he get his first breach in the soldiers' line than the humans deployed one of their new weapons. Like magic, every bot for two hundred meters froze in place. One of the gifts left by Pip, the PUFF (Pip's Universal Frequency Fracturer) disabled all bots with ease. The OPFOR responded with confusion, as they'd been instructed, and the soldiers counterattacked. It was so quickly executed, and to such advantage, that an observer would almost think it was all part of the plan. Minu could see the lengthy casualty counts, along with dozens of soldiers lounging on the ground, as the fight played out around them and knew better. The Rasa fell back, minimizing their losses. Two squads of human soldiers, emboldened by the sudden retreat, pursued the Rasa and paid the price. They were enveloped by hidden Rasa warriors and neutralized moments later without a single additional enemy casualty. The ill-advised pursuit of the retreating forces shifted the advantage back into the Rasa column once more, even after the surprise of the PUFF's deployment.

Daniel landed with the last of his forces. His losses were already approaching thirty percent, though, and his chances of retaking the simulated Dodge City were severely in doubt. As he organized his surviving forces, the pickets set around the LZ perimeter were constantly under harassing fire and probe attacks. Worse, Rasa snipers picked off several more soldiers before their location was pinpointed, and the snipers neutralized. Minu almost laughed at the ease with which Var'at was taking down Daniel's soldiers. Then she remembered they were her soldiers, and thought, *What if this was a real fight?* To be fair, Var'at now knew human tactics much better, and he had the defensive advantage. Still, she'd hoped for a better showing after a year of training.

Finally organized, Daniel prepared to take the town. Two platoons were reloaded into transports and the immobilized enemy bot force was cleaned up so the PUFF could be deactivated and the soldiers' own bots deployed. The soldiers moved out on foot toward the town, while the transports took off to circle overhead and provide fire support. They stayed in careful contact to coordinate their attack. The transports dropped their platoons on the far side of the town at the same time those on the ground hit the near side. They met scattered resistance, which was easily pushed aside, and were about to link up in the middle. The soldiers' bots did their job, flushing out enemy soldiers to be picked off. When Daniel was in sight of the five-star Chosen in charge of the other light company, he figured victory was in hand.

Outside the simulated town, the bulk of the OPFOR attacked in perfect order. The sun was just peaking over the nearby hills as wave after wave of bright green laser fire tore into the stunned soldiers. A dozen soldiers were 'killed' in the first salvos, just as turtle-bots with their shields and fast dodging firefly-bots attacked. The soldiers had deployed with three PUFFs. Two were on Sabers now lost or disabled, and Daniel had left the last one to hold the LZ in what was a 'play it safe' strategy. That proved too conservative. The soldiers hadn't planned to be encircled in the center of town; they were the ones on the attack. The Rasa had their way with them. Daniel's men made a good fight of it, but it was ultimately futile. They were soundly defeated twenty-seven minutes and fifteen seconds after the first shot was fired. A small force of Rasa stormed the LZ, seizing all but two of the remaining transports and the PUFF intact. Christian's team of Scouts held the LZ to the last man as the transports got away, while Daniel fought with them. Of the two that succeeded in getting away, one had its drive fail less than a kilometer away and was subsequently declared captured by enemy action.

"Chosen Daniel," Var'at said as he came out in front of his soldiers, "you are defeated."

Daniel's eyes narrowed, and his face went red with anger and embarrassment, but he bowed his head in acknowledgment. Then the Rasa soldiers bowed to their defeated adversaries. The human soldiers followed in kind. Minu watched through remote cameras high above, smiling so hard her cheeks hurt. It was a bitter failure, and a great success. "Okay folks, let's do it again," she ordered over the radio. "This time the Rasa are on the attack, and the humans are OPFOR. I'm transmitting the details to the soldiers; you have one hour to reset. Aaron, call the mechanics in and get those two transports back in the air and turn all of them over to Var'at. Oh, and be sure to mix the identification number up again so they can't tell…"

* * *

It was early evening before the soldiers and transports limped back to Fort Jovich, both so tired they could scarcely walk or fly. Minu ran them through a total of sixteen engagements. Three each with human and then Rasa as the OPFOR and two with a combined human-Rasa defensive unit being assaulted first by Rasa, then by humans. After that series, it was lunch, and 2nd Battalion was called out and Rasa forces were refreshed with rested troops. Then they did it all again.

The eventual plan was to use the humans and Rasa together as a cohesive fighting force, but that created more logistical problems than she'd expected. One being the Rasa tendency to use a hybrid hand signal/native language communication during intense combat. The translators they used didn't recognize the hand signals, because it wasn't in their language set. Another was the human soldiers' natural aggressiveness. The Rasa were less aggressive in seemingly untenable situations. Simply stated, they tended to give up easier.

"There's no reason to fight if the odds say you'll lose," Var'at explained late that night in Minu's office as they shared a tasty bottle of cherry wine from Lizardville Vineyards.

"But sometimes you can still win," she said after a deep drink of the sweet beverage. "In human history, the greatest victories have been by a force that supposedly had no chance of winning."

Var'at had some more of his own drink and considered. "When we attacked you during the Vendetta, I was confused. You'd suffered bad losses in Steven's Pass. My commander there said they'd penetrated your inner defenses and expected you to surrender at any time."

"But we never did."

"Exactly! You fought, and fought, and fought. I was still waiting for news of your surrender when your team showed up in Tranquility and began ruining my plans there."

"This is our way," she said, finishing her drink. She turned and looked out the dark window overlooking the sea. Far out in the water she should see the bobbing lights of a vessel, probably a fishing ship. There was almost no shipping that took place on the equatorial sea. Why bother? It was less than a thousand kilometers across at its widest. Even in the days before dirigible travel, when the maglev wasn't even a dream, it was simpler to just go around. The sea was on the equator, but only covered one hemisphere. The weather was just too unpredictable for safe navigation. So why did some still brave the hazards of the sea? Because humans live to go where there's danger. "Are there any among your people who live to take risks?"

"Just soldiers."

"No, I mean dangerous pastimes? Say, skydiving, deep sea diving, flying experimental craft…"

Minu waited while Var'at's translator chewed her comments over. After it finished hissing, popping, and clicking her comments, he locked both eyes on her in the Rasa's version of a wide-eyed stare. "We do not encourage behavior contrary to the species' survival."

Minu chuckled and didn't look away from the ocean vista, instead watching the light bob up and down on distant swells, occasionally being lost from view behind tall waves. The craft made steady progress to the east. The city of Gulf was hundreds of kilometers in that direction. She knew that more than a few Chosen living here owned sailing craft in a small private marina a few kilometers away. It was a dangerous pastime, especially since there were no Coast Guard or safety patrols. She told him about sailing.

"And your people do this for fun?"

"And much more," she said. Minu spent a few minutes explaining cave spelunking and mountain climbing. More stares. Then she told him about skydiving.

"I sometimes wonder if your people are entirely healthy in the brain," he said as he refilled his glass with wine.

"We've wondered that about ourselves for most of our history. Earth died without our having a chance to fight for its survival, killed by an anonymous rock from space. We have a grudge to settle against the universe."

"But no one did this to you, it was an accident. Shouldn't you be grateful your species survived at all?"

"We're very grateful to the Tog for saving us, but I feel a deep swell of pity for any species that comes to destroy us. We have no intention of being on the wrong side of fate twice. That's why I had this dream of the soldiers, and why I let you stay and join. You must understand, we will never surrender. It isn't our way. We'll fight in the most impossible situations, with our backs against the wall. And when it looks like there's no chance to survive…that's when we'll attack."

"This is contrary to all logic."

"Who said humans are logical?"

"No one." Var'at sipped his wine and nodded. The longer she knew him, the more human he became. "I understand you better now. We're allied with you humans; our futures are intertwined. We too are no more if you lose. Our numbers are small."

"Your people are all males; have you thought of your long-term future?"

"We have none without females; what can we hope for?"

"Maybe something can be done about that."

"Who knows what the future holds?"

* * * * *

Chapter Nine
September 9th, 521 AE

Planet Coorson, Traaga Leasehold

The world of Coorson would be considered by most species to be the bitter end. To the Traaga, it was home-sweet-home. Not all species were fortunate enough to have powerful, wealthy, or influential masters. The Traaga were a pitiful example of that. The species that had introduced them to the galaxy had gotten embroiled in a catastrophic conflict with a higher-order species a few centuries earlier and were all but eliminated from the stage, leaving the Traaga orphaned. The leasehold on their world reverted to the control of the Concordian Council, and it was worth too much to allow a penniless species like the Traaga to remain. Plus, they themselves were considered of little use. Only three hundred years since coming into the great awareness, they were on their own.

But the Traaga did possess a few useful talents. An arboreal species, they had no fear of heights. Also, their home planet was oxygen-poor and high in natural contaminants, giving the Traaga an ability to filter most dangerous gases from the air they breathed. And they were willing to do anything for a credit. After a century of doing just that, their rulers managed to secure the leasehold on the world of Coorson. The Traaga scratched out a place to live through sheer tenacity and their natural ability to live in places that would kill most oxygen-breathers.

The portal flashed into life, and out came the catlike forms of a trio of Tanam. Their two sets of emerald eyes were set deeply into both sides of their triangular heads. The eyes were ever in motion, scanning all directions for trouble. To say it was impossible to sneak up on a Tanam was an understatement. The rear set of eyes had no lids and were linked to an area of their brain which more closely resembled hearing than vision. Though unsuitable for detailed jobs like reading or shape recognition, the Tanam were aware of their surroundings in three hundred sixty degrees, all the time, even when asleep. The three beings looked around with their long, flexible necks, able to turn their heads more than two hundred degrees from side to side. Long interlocking teeth snapped shut in disgust as they tasted the air. Trace chemicals in the atmosphere were detected and analyzed. In seconds, they knew this was not safe for long-term exposure, but the few hours they planned would be fine. Their bodies metabolized dangerous chemicals much faster than most other species.

"Welcome, noble Tanam," a Traaga said. Its four radial arms lowered the roundish torso in a somewhat conventional posture of respect. Its long neck retracted into its body as the torso lowered. From the notch in its armored torso, the Traaga watched the three Tanam cautiously with black-on-black eyes adapted to a dark world. "May I inquire as to your visit today?"

"You may not," the leader spoke. The Traaga used its limited knowledge of the Tanam to estimate the station of these two mysterious visitors. The incredibly-well-muscled bodies of the Tanam supported six legs; the bottom two were purely for locomotion, but the middle two could be used for fighting or running, while the top two were for fighting or manipulating—mostly fighting, if their species' reputation was to be believed. And with up to four powerful limbs, each wielding ten-centimeter curved and serrated claws, the Tanam could kill a massive Beezer in moments. Were even the Mok-Tok a match for them? They varied in coloration, usually being either black or brown, with only the royal family displaying white. Rank was denoted by shaved fur on the neck and head to display colorful tattoos, further accentuating rank or position. They wore little in the way of clothing, except possibly armor in combat, and belts to hold tools and pouches. The leader, the only one to speak, was mostly white, with vast areas of shaved skin showing intricate tattoos. The Traaga was careful with this one. "Give us access to your local network," she demanded of the Traaga,

"Agreed," came the quick reply. It scuttled sideways, staying low to the ground and showing none of its vulnerable neck. There was no doubt it would die fighting even one of the Tanam. Its body was bony and dense with powerful arms for defense, however the neck was tender and fleshy. He found a computer terminal and keyed in a command. The Tanam used a hand to grab one of its tablets from a utility belt and accessed the now-opened network connection. The Traaga Portal guardian activated a tracer program, just to be safe. Such an action, while not considered polite, was within the planet owners' rights. The Tanam cast a single eye toward the Traaga, making it obvious they knew of the trace, then turned to its work.

The Tanam leader worked with the computer, deadly claws tapping commands with surprising grace and gentleness. The Traaga watched from a respectful distance away, but one of the other Tanams hissed at it. The scuttling being moved farther away. Seela was of royal blood in the grand Tanam line, one of the highest order of species in the Concordia. She'd grown up knowing the power her species wielded, and thanks to her upbringing, she had no qualms about using it to her advantage. She was here this day by order of her mother, matriarch of all the Tanam. It was a small scent trail to follow, but when the matriarch gave an order, it was obeyed. To not do so would risk a challenge. The hair rippled along her flank, a sign of disquiet or even fear.

After a minute with the tablet, she turned it off and replaced the device in its pouch. The Traaga severed the network access. "Will the honorable Tanam require anything more?"

"We are to enter your world to search for contractors to work on a facility in our space."

"Very good," the Traaga said through his translator. "Permission for twenty standard hours is granted. You may find transportation outside." Defense fields were deactivated, and the three Tanam left. The Traaga stayed where it was, grateful it wasn't the one the Tanam were seeking. Its people were becoming known as good traders, but bartering with a Tanam was like trying to deal with a solar flare.

Outside the portal facility, Seela hissed in dismay. It was planetary afternoon, and an intense bluish light flooded down, making it several degrees too warm for the felinoids. A blast-furnace wind blew debris and dust through the air at high velocity as well, and everywhere was the chatter of the Traaga. This wasn't a city, it was a junk pile. She'd never been to the frontier; that was a job for low-stationed sisters, or even better, a client species. But she'd seen images of junkpile worlds, ancient decaying piles of buildings and equipment. This city was little different from those places. The building holding the portal looked like the most permanent, well-built facility in view. Most others appeared to be built of local materials or constructed from castoff Concordian components, temporary buildings, or even cargo containers, all thrown together with no sense of order. It reminded her of a refugee camp she'd raided during a war shortly after beginning her service to the matriarch. Worst of all was the smell that assailed her senses in a relentless wave of putrid odors, many unidentifiable and no doubt rotten. Seela shook her head and mewed, hopelessly trying to clear her nose of the olfactory nightmare. Slowly, she was able to calm the inputs to her brain.

Once she had control of herself, she moved out into the street, following the directions gleaned from the haphazard planetary network. Her sisters followed, close behind. In most cases Seela wouldn't have brought one of her two direct sisters along; there was too much chance they'd try to claim some or all of the credit. This mission had already taken months and wasn't proceeding the way it should. The possibility of failure now outweighed that of being able to personally claim all of the credit. She'd exclusively used those of the warrior caste until now and unfortunately they'd failed her over and over. No matter how many throats she ripped out, they just continued to disappoint. Following this cold trail was taking valuable time, and despite the effort put forth so far, it was quickly running colder. Muscles in her snout unconsciously opened her nostrils wider to allow more scents across her sensitive detection organs. She overrode that and closed her nose as much as possible, but not before sneezing several times.

"The stench of this place," Kelaa moaned behind her. "It makes my brain burn."

"It's horrid," Veka agreed, "but you need to learn control," she admonished. Veka was the eldest among them, but fortune had not favored her in her endeavors. Kelaa snapped her jaws in annoyance at the delay.

The streets, if you could call them that, swarmed with Traaga, but of course what else would you find on Coorson except gamboling, smelly, worthless Traaga. They were everywhere on the ground, climbing walls, swinging from wires strung between buildings. It was horrid watching their disgusting movements, so unnatural, so skittery, and without the natural fluid grace of a sister, or even the clumsier, yet comparatively graceful brothers.

They followed the map until it led to an intersection, and they realized how easy the going had been so far. The computer demanded they follow a road down an alley. The previous thoroughfare, crowded and cluttered, had been a major road compared to this. The alley was paved with mud and rocks, and still more Traaga. Millions of Traaga, like an infestation of fleas. Unlike earlier, there were now children in evidence. Seela's lips pulled back from her long deadly black teeth, and the nearest Traaga young fled in a panic. If it was possible, the young were even more hideous than the mature creatures. Only a completely uncivilized species allowed their children anywhere except the carefully-controlled training grounds where they were made to understand how to act around adults. This was the worst offense of all, and there were many on this world.

"It would all make a disgustingly great feast," Kelaa said from behind her. Veka bobbed her head in agreement. Seela had yet to feast on the flesh of a Traaga, and if the taste was at all like the smell, she prayed it would never happen. A deep secret of the Tanam was that they prided themselves on having tasted almost every sapient species in the Concordia, and rated them in their individual culinary attributes. What true predator would not revel in feasting on the flesh of a defeated adversary? To ignore your nature was to surrender to another's interpretation of civilization.

"We must follow the law here," she reminded her sisters. "We cannot hurt or kill unless they break the law themselves." Her sisters growled their understanding and consent. She didn't worry about Veka, of course; age and wisdom tempered most of her decisions. It was Kelaa that concerned Seela. Young and impetuous, she seldom passed up a chance to try something new, no matter how ill advised. They all carried a formidable armament, far in excess of tooth and claw. Despite the laws, Seela thought that perhaps the three of them could end the lives of every living vermin in this so-called city. She found the mental exercise rather liberating.

Eventually the trail led to an actual structure, in that it had a foundation, walls, and a roof, and wasn't just resting in the mud. A sign over the doorway in three different Concordian scripts described it as a 'guild hall.' "Thank the Lost," Seela said as she clawed at the door. Despite her care, she nearly tore it from its rusty hinges.

"That door was locked," came the first voice on the inside, a series of scrapes and clicks translated by the three Tanams' translators. There in the gloomy interior sat a despondent-looking Veelox, if it were possible to tell the mood of an insectoid. It was perched on a long table covered in old, obsolete computers and a large moliplas jar full to almost overflowing with squirming little grubs. Seela wondered if they were the creature's food or offspring. The insectoid made a halfhearted attempt to clean one antenna with razor-sharp mandibles, then reached for another before remembering it only had the one. The shiny black wing cases rubbed against each other with a high screech.

All three Tanam yowled and rocked back onto their hind legs, making the middle legs ready for combat. The Veelox held up a half dozen limbs and shook its head, the huge multifaceted eyes showed no emotion. "I apologize, great Tanam sisters. The Traaga have only rudimentary hearing, and the songs my wing cases make go unheard by them. I have forgotten myself."

"It is forgiven," Seela said and returned to four legs. Kelaa mouthed "Songs?" incredulously to Veka as Seela continued. "Please forgive me for damaging the doorway; it was so feebly made, I had not realized it was barred."

"It's nothing," the Veelox said with a wide gesture of several arms. "The workmanship is of a very poor quality."

"Indeed," Veka agreed.

Seela cast her a sidelong look and turned back to the Veelox. "You are the master of the guild?"

"I am," the Veelox said, preening its sole antennae again. "The Traaga have difficulty negotiating equitable contracts, so it's left to an outside intermediary like me to handle the deals." Its head cocked sideways, mouth parts moving before it began communicating again. "Three Tanam, of the noblest line, on Coorson just to seek a Traaga contract? Highly unusual."

"We're not here seeking a contract," Seela said.

The Veelox's wing cases made a couple of little chirping sounds, not the cacophonous screeching of earlier, but almost a plaintive question. "What then can this humble guild master do for you?"

"We are interested in a contract the Traaga carried out a year ago."

"The Traaga are very industrious. Don't let the condition of this world fool you; they are in the state they are more as a result of misfortune than anything they did wrong."

"We couldn't care less about the condition of this scuttling minor little species," Kelaa snapped. The Veelox nearly jumped out of its chitin at the threat. The Veelox were just as minor a species as the Traaga, if slightly more cultured and careful in their dealings with higher-order species.

"Very well, highborn daughters. With whom were the contracts that you are interested in?" Seela told the guild master. "Yes, um…let me see." Its sudden movements and jumbling of computers spoke of nervousness. Seela flexed and unflexed her middle arm claws over and over, scraping at the ceramic concrete and making chips pop and fly. "You see, the species you inquire about are very good clients. Young and small, but they pay in advance or barter lucrative food contracts! The Traaga are particularly fond of the later."

"Do you think we care what kind of customers the filthy skittering Traaga like?" Kelaa rumbled, moving closer to the Veelox, her blazing red eyes fixed on it. "Or how much the scrambling trash Traaga like their food?" She spat the word for Traaga, her long teeth flashing in the rooms artificial light.

"You have to understand, noble sister!"

With a flash of motion too fast to follow, Kelaa's right foreleg shot out, black claws slashing. The Veelox's only remaining antennae arced through the air to land on the dirty floor, where it twisted and spasmed as if still attached. The Veelox reeled away, too late to stop the blow. It fell off the table and twitched, wing cases popping open, and four gossamer wings emerged to help it escape.

Seela shook her massive head. Overreacting had always been one of Kelaa's shortcomings. The sister continued, bounding forward and sending the table on which the Veelox had perched crashing across the room with enough force to splinter against the wall. She lunged and caught one of the Veelox's wings in her mouth and crunched the delicate chitinous structure. The sounds the Veelox made were not translated, but none listening would have any doubt they were screams of agony.

"Enough sister," Seela said calmly. Kelaa released the screaming Veelox, backing up slowly and spitting out inedible pieces of wing.

"Is there nothing in these insects that's edible?" she asked her sister. Veka laughed a barking laugh.

"I beg of you, I beg of you," the Veelox said over and over.

"You will answer our questions, or I'll allow my impulsive younger sister to see what parts of you she finds to her taste." Seela leaned close to examine the writhing insect. "You have a lot of parts to sample, and if I understand your physiology, it'll take some time for you to die."

They exited the guild hall back into the brutal heat of the Coorson sun. Kelaa was still trying to clean green and yellow goo from her muzzle and making disgusted retching sounds. Who would think, with so many tender parts, that none of them would be edible? Kelaa emptied her primary stomach into the dirt and used a middle hand to retrieve a nutrient pack from her utility belt. "Disgusting beyond words," she said as she took a bite of the nutrient meat mixture, chewed and spat it out, cleaning her teeth and mouth. She ate the rest of the pack and cast a rueful gaze at Veka. "Next time you eat the alien."

Seela finished entering the data into the computer she held in a front hand as she walked, then put the device away. "We need to exit this world before the dead bug is discovered."

"It's of little concern," Kelaa said, but she still hurried her pace as her senior sister instructed. "Who'll miss one Veelox?"

"These things can be touchy," Veka said. "We had no provocation to kill that being."

"You overreacted," Seela added. "It may not have been necessary to kill that alien, and it might have had more information it would have been willing to give if you hadn't been chewing on its thorax."

"I'm sorry sister," Kelaa said, lowering her head almost to the mud-covered ground. She found another chunk of chitin in her teeth and spat it out. "I've learned a lesson."

Though it was her right to further punish her for killing without permission, Seela let it go. The Veelox had given up some important information before succumbing. Impetuous Kelaa might be, but it often got results. She found herself wishing she wasn't in charge so she could get away with impulsive things like that. Ripping the Veelox's limbs off one at a time reminded her of being a youth and tearing the wings off Kafa living in the trees of her pack mother's compound. The small warm-blooded fliers cried loudly when their wings were torn off and tried gamely to get away. But unlike the Veelox, the Kafa were tasty to eat after the game lost its amusement.

"I look forward to tasting the blood of our true prey," Kelaa said, her teeth flashing in the blue sunlight. They all bobbed their heads in agreement. That would be something to look forward to trying, for many reasons. And with the data she now had, Seela was certain that day was getting closer. "I've never tasted a hominid before," she mused as the portal building approached, "and humans look very tender."

*****

Chapter Ten
Octember 22nd, 521 AE

Training Room, Chosen Headquarters, Steven's Pass

Minu breathed hard and tried to keep the pain from her mind as she slid through the forms, trying desperately to keep her attacker at bay. She barely managed to turn blow after blow aside before it made contact, but as a result, the blocks hurt almost as badly as a full-on hit. A properly-executed defensive block was nearly painless, a simple redirection of force that provided the possibility of counterattack. In her desperate defense, countering was not an option.

Finally a fist scored through her defenses, a solid blow against her chest that sent her sprawling. Minu tried to roll away, but her attacker was on her in a second, a knee landing on the side of her neck with enough force to make her see stars. "Okay!" Minu cried out and the pressure fell away immediately. "Damn it! You trying to kill me?"

"You're going to kill yourself," Cherise said as she got to her feet. There was a thin sheen of sweat on her skin as she stood, breathing easily and offering a hand to Minu, who took it and was pulled to her feet. It was her fourth fall of the sparring session; she was getting mad and losing her concentration. "You're not practicing between our bouts, and you're not working out regularly. Look at yourself; you're almost completely spent after half an hour."

Minu stooped over, hands on knees, and tried to catch her breath. She was beaten, bruised, and pissed at the other girl's comments. But they hurt because they were true. "I'm just so damned busy with the soldiers," she admitted.

"I heard the first drills went…less than optimally?"

"You can say that again." Cherise gave her a sideways look and Minu chuckled. "We're making progress, just slowly."

"Are they bonding as a unit?"

Minu smiled and nodded. "Better than I hoped. You should see their uniforms. We went with those camouflage jump suits, the same design as our Chosen jumpsuits, but with the grey and blue multi-environment camo I found from Earth history. It looks really cool."

"Sounds like it."

"They're finally meshing as a fighting force; I'm very proud. I've seen groups in Dodge City during liberty, all partying together."

"Then why are you still putting in twenty-hour days?"

Minu sighed and finally stood back up, bending over backward to stretch her back and twisting her head to see how her neck was. There'd be a good bruise, but there seemed to be no lasting damage. The punch had landed almost dead center on her left breast though, and it was very tender. "It takes some work to make an army."

"That much is obvious. You should've seen the panic you created on the finance board." Minu knew what her friend was talking about. She'd been informed a year ago that she needed to cease-and-desist with her weekly war games; they were costing a fortune in materiel and scaring the hell out of the timid local farmers. She decreased them to twice-monthly but still got regular grumbles from the bean counters. "I hear Christian is busy."

"He was put in charge of the scouts. Along with overseeing their training of joint operations with the soldiers, he's been using some of our techniques with a couple of scout teams. He says it's to make them all better able to deal with combat situations, but I think he's spoiling to prove that his Chosen scouts can do in small numbers what the soldiers require large units to accomplish."

"Sounds like he's more trouble than he's worth. Sorry you guys haven't worked it out."

"Yeah, me too."

"Let's do some knife drills," Cherise said, "since you can't keep up hand-to-hand." They practiced with rubber knives for a few minutes, but the effects of the beatings Cherise had administered over the first half of the workout had left her too tired to give it a hundred percent, so they broke off early. Later in the showers, Cherise saw the growing bruise on Minu's breast and frowned. "I'm sorry; I didn't mean to hit you that hard."

"More my fault than yours," Minu said and tried not to look at the ugly red and brown spot. Very sexy. She saw how Cherise's eyes lingered on her body and felt a little thrill.

"You want to get together this weekend?"

"That would be fun," Minu said, surprised at her own answer. After she'd said it she realized she meant it. Why should she deny herself some pleasure just because of taboos from ages past?

"We could go get some lunch. The cafeteria has beans!"

Minu laughed and shook her head. "Much as I miss the gourmet fare of the Steven's Pass cafeteria, I have a meeting with Ted." She grabbed a towel and headed for the lockers.

"Oh, hey!"

"Yeah?"

"Happy birthday!"

Minu laughed. "It was yesterday."

"Yeah, well, you didn't answer my call; I tried. A girl doesn't turn eighteen every day, you know."

"It's just another year."

"You're legally an adult now; you can do anything you want!"

"We were legally adults three years ago."

"Good point." One tangible benefit of being Chosen is you were legally emancipated adults as soon as they pinned on the stars. Since you could be as young as fourteen, that was a big deal to many. Only adults could drink or own a vehicle. She'd bought her aerocar when she was sixteen and had her first drink the same year. "Regardless, happy birthday, old girl."

"Who you calling old, you turn nineteen in a few weeks!"

Showered and in a clean uniform, Minu left the gym behind and took a jump tube up to the main floor. The mezzanine never failed to bring back painful memories of the day, two years ago, when she'd taken her science team and fought the desperate defense against the Rasa. The Vendetta was a test none of them had been ready to take, and the cost in blood was enormous. A crowd of young, newly-minted Chosen moved out of her way as she left the tube, a variety of different-colored five-star clusters on their sleeves. They instantly noted her three golden stars, then that she was a woman. She could hear them whispering between them, wondering if she was who they thought she was. Minu's excitement at the number of women who'd made it through the second round of soldier trials (a hundred and twenty-two) was sobered by the fact that the full Chosen trials had only yielded two girls, even fewer than the three that had made it through her own trials three years ago.

She left the group of fourteen- and fifteen-year-old 'kids' behind and headed for the science branch hall. The repair work was long finished. All the weapon damage from the Vendetta was cleaned up, making it look like nothing had happened. The only evidence remaining was the central column in the mezzanine. The ceramic concrete column was scarred by weapons fire, burns from beamcasters, and still had a few Rasa flechette darts embedded in it. The entire column had been encased in moliplas and a plaque embedded in the material. It read:

To all those, Chosen and civilians, who made the ultimate sacrifice to defend our world, our people, and our oath to our Concordian masters. On Julast 21st, 518 AE, in this hall, six Chosen held for six hours against overwhelming Rasa forces. In our darkest hour, the Chosen shall always shine.

Below the dedication were the names of all two hundred thirteen Chosen who'd died in the fighting. She'd stood here more than once, her fingers tracing the names one by one. Missing was Pipson Leata. Though a casualty of the fighting, he was technically still alive. She made a note to visit him again soon in Tranquility. "We take care of our own," she said as she walked by the monument.

The Steven's Pass facility had six wings, each housing a different branch of service, with one empty. Above the arch leading to each branch was inscribed Science, Command, Logistics, Training, or Scout. No one had yet changed the latter to Soldier. She wondered if they ever would. Turning down the science hall, she passed the director's office. As usual, there was a group of people sitting, waiting to speak to the science branch director, Jasmine Osgood. Minu had been working for science when Jasmine had taken over from Bjorn

Ganose. The very old, but brilliant, scientist was forced into semi-retirement as revenge for his faithful defense of Minu's tactics and decisions. That wasn't a good time. Jasmine was the highest-ranking female Chosen, two stars, and very ambitious. A good friend of First Jacob, Minu still believed she'd gotten the assignment because of that friendship. Unlike Bjorn, she was no scientist.

Near the end of the hall, she paused at the door to her old lab. She'd spent a lot of happy hours there working with her team. Alijah Richards and Terry Drake, two young Chosen working in her team during that time, had died in the Vendetta. Mandi Bishop, a civilian who no longer worked for the Chosen, had survived by fleeing the facility before the fighting started. Pip was of course no longer working. She sighed and moved on to the suite of labs at the end of the hall, tapping on the door before opening it.

Inside a dozen scientists and technicians were all bent over apparatuses doing various tasks. A female civilian looked up and made a face. "We don't allow visitors in these labs…" She stepped in further, and the three gold stars on her sleeve came into view. In a now time-honored tradition, she glanced at Minu's breasts, red hair, and the three stars once more before awareness dawned in her eyes. "Chosen Alma, I'm sorry ma'am."

"No problem," Minu said congenially, "you must be new. Can you tell Chosen Hurt that I'm here?"

"You mean Dr. Hurt?"

"Of course." She nodded and left to get him. After decades of service, Ted Hurt had been elevated to honorary Chosen. Many didn't refer to him as Chosen, feeling it nothing more than a bone tossed to an old dog. During Minu's time in the science department, she knew it was real work, dangerous and valuable work. He'd *earned* his status, and she used his title every chance she got. She figured it was nothing more than his due. Ted's distinguished frame came around the corner, his sharp eyes scanning the progress of a dozen projects, and Minu smiled at the knowing way he appraised each project. He stopped and made a suggestion to one man, then looked up and spotted Minu. Instantly he burst into a big leer. "Good grief," she moaned as he put on his lady-killer grin. He never gave up, and probably never would. The old lech had put the moves on her the first day he'd met her, and she'd only been sixteen.

"Minu darling," he said and leaned in to give her a peck on the cheek. She was always careful to remember to turn her head; his intent was a direct frontal assault. Unlike a lot of old men that played at flirting, she knew he meant it. Though in his seventies, Ted was still a vibrantly charismatic man with a strong build, square jaw, and a head of dark black hair shot with silver. He not only hinted at his lust for every attractive woman he met, he'd happily sleep with them all. If only *half* the stories she'd heard were true, he'd probably slept with every woman in Steven's Pass except herself and Cherise. And it wasn't for lack of trying. "When are you going to go out to dinner with me?"

"When you're fifty years younger," she said without missing a beat.

He looked her up and down with a critical eye. "If I wasn't an atheist, I'd sell my soul to do just that." Minu smiled despite herself as his dimples came out. He really was a smooth one. "I'm thrilled you could make it; come back to the patio." He led her through the maze of desks, benches, and cabinet machinery to a doorway. What had once been a solid wall on the other side had been converted to a large sliding moliplas doorway that opened like a garage door. Minu had been the one that made the original opening when she'd blown out the wall to lead the Rasa soldiers attacking Steven's Pass into a trap. On the other side of the transparent door extended a platform like a large balcony. Jasmine called the modification the Vehicle Research Platform, or VRP; Ted and his team just called it the Patio, and true to the title, they often barbecued there on long nights. They'd gone so far as to string garden lights around the edge and added a few lawn chairs. Jasmine wasn't amused, but Minu loved it. As the patio came into view, she saw something she loved even more. The problem was the state it was in.

"What have you done to my prototype?" she screamed

"*Your* prototype?" Ted demanded. "Funny, but I thought I'd been the one spending the last six months working on that beast."

"That beast is one of the biggest parts of what can bring my vision together."

"Your vision has been giving me nightmares." They stopped just inside the Patio where the fighter prototype was in a dozen pieces, scattered all over the place. It didn't look burned or damaged, unlike the last time, when Bjorn had gotten an idea and blown the prototype into junk, thereby setting the program back by months.

"So what did you do? Some of the parts aren't even here! It wasn't Bjorn again, was it?"

"Well, actually, yes." Minu put her hands on her narrow hips and rounded on him, but just then the whine of gravitic impellers came screaming through the Patio. Minu looked over her shoulder in time to see a flier come hovering into view on approach to landing. For a second she got excited, hoping maybe, somehow, they had made a leap ahead, but as she turned she recognized one of the cargo transports of the type she'd used in her war games, down to the paint job and numbering.

The pilot brought it to hover just off the end of the Patio and lowered the side door. Aaron sat with his big frame wedged into the pilot's seat, a huge grin on his square-jawed face. "What are you doing?" she asked, having to yell to be heard over the scream of the impellers.

"Let's go for a ride," Ted said into her ear, his lips almost touching hers, his voice rich and sultry.

The transport door closed, and it climbed away from the buildings of Steven's Pass under smooth acceleration, much more powerful than she'd expected. "What's going on?" she asked Ted, who shared the second row with her just behind Aaron.

"We gave up on the prototype and went another direction. Back to our roots, you could say."

"You retrofitted the transports?" Ted nodded. "Damn it Ted, I said I didn't want to go that way. The fighter needs to be uniquely ours."

"Sure it's a good idea, but making it happen is just impossible right now. Unless you can magically pull a dozen more of those configurable factory modules out of your ass, the kind you used to make the targeting computers for the shock rifles?"

"No, I told you, I only scammed the one."

"Well, there you go. We end up using components forced into service for purposes they weren't intended for, or spending millions on custom-made stuff from aliens."

"And then the higher-order species will figure out what we're up to." Ted shrugged, and she sighed. "But why these clunky old transports?"

"Because they *are* clunky old transports." Minu gave him a dirty look and Ted held up his hands to hold off her wrath. "Who would look twice at these things? They have to be thousands of years old."

"Right, and falling apart."

"Not when we're done with them, they won't be."

"Come up here," Aaron invited her and patted the copilot seat. Ted gestured for her to go and smiled. Minu grumbled but unbuckled and took the seat. She could tell right away the controls were different.

"This is a gunner's station," she said as she examined the controls. Even inactive, she could recognize humanized targeting systems of Concordian design. Hand controls, viewfinders, weapon control computer, and power management systems were all there.

"Right," Aaron agreed. He started to reach over to show her how it worked, but Ted cut him off.

"Let's stick to the plan," he said, and Aaron nodded. "Take it through the modes, if you please."

"Okay," he agreed. "So, you wanted three craft rolled into one. First was the transport."

"Combat transport," she clarified, "and these things don't come close."

"Didn't come close," Ted corrected. "Now be quiet and let him explain."

"Excuse me," she said and affected a hurt tone.

"So, combat transport," Aaron said. While they talked he'd been flying at high speed. She looked outside and realized they were skimming the canyon valley below Steven's Pass at nearly the speed of sound. The gravitic systems inside the craft held them smoothly in place, removing all sensations of motion. "We beefed up the gravitic impellers inside and out. It can pull eleven Gs in any orientation."

"Including acceleration?" she asked.

"Yep," Aaron said. He pulled up slightly and his hand slid forward on the throttle. She felt the first sensation since they took off, a sudden shudder announced their passage through the sound barrier. Her mouth dropped open. "Yeah, we managed to make it supersonic."

"Wasn't very bloody easy, either," Ted admitted. "We couldn't rebuild the damn thing to the superstructure, so we realigned the aerodynamics with field generators.

"Force fields to create a new aerodynamic profile? I didn't know that was possible." He just grinned when she looked at him over her shoulder.

Aaron spent a few moments concentrating on the controls, carefully threading their way down the snaking canyon. Minu got a few brief images of surprised fisherman and hikers along the river as they shot by at more than a thousand kilometers per hour. "We couldn't make it hypersonic, obviously, without reshaping the entire hull. It'll manage Mach six without overheating the fields."

"Damn," she hissed. "What happens if you're supersonic and the fields fail?" Aaron and Ted just looked at each other, then at her. She got the idea. It would be…bad.

A few moments later, he throttled back. A tight bank around a bend in the canyon, and the river was split by the hand of man; two concrete viaducts created an artificial island. Leavenworth came into view, full of skyscrapers and neon signs. Sin City, to many Chosen. It was early afternoon and the city bustled with life, both on the ground and in the air. In the years since Minu had become Chosen, flying vehicles had gone from rare to commonplace, then ubiquitous. Cheap and plentiful Concordian-made imports, like most everything else in their lives.

Aaron worked the controls, and Minu avidly watched it all. He used a map to designate a set of coordinates, then set it on automatic. The transport banked and came around, dropping below the speed of sound as it looped the long narrow artificial island. When they'd come a hundred eighty degrees from where they'd started, the transport dove toward the city and all its traffic.

"Is this a good idea?" Minu wondered aloud as they entered the buzz of other craft. The old transports were known for finicky guidance control systems.

Like the rest of the craft, the avionics weren't original. The vehicle wove and dodged with unerring accuracy even as the other craft swerved wildly to avoid the sudden appearance of the blazing transport. At twice the size of most other vehicles, it maneuvered like it was a tenth the size. True to Aaron's words, 11 Gs of gravitic impellers made for a smooth ride. They dove deep into the afternoon traffic pattern, dodging still more vehicles, while navigating between buildings. One last hard turn, and a small park came into view. Almost before Minu recognized the clearing, the transport flared nose-up and came down with almost no sense of motion.

"We need a little of the sense of motion to get through so the crew knows what's going on," Minu said to Ted, who nodded in agreement.

"Other test pilots have said the same thing."

"It's almost like flying a video game like this," Aaron agreed.

The transport settled, and the doors opened, and kept opening! Each transport had originally come with two doors, one passenger door on the left and a cargo door in the rear. This transport now sported three more doors. One opposite the original left-hand forward, and two more behind those. She turned around and saw the rear cargo door was now the entire width of the craft, allowing the loading of anything as long as it matched the interior dimensions. Aaron flipped a switch and low couches rose from the floor, just as a platoon of soldiers swarmed aboard. It was stunning to watch her training in action for real. The original transport, with only two doors, was difficult to load and egress quickly, taking more than ten seconds no matter what she'd tried. With five doors, the platoon swarmed aboard in less than five.

As the last man's boots cleared the door, all five closed, and the craft threw itself back into the air. Outside in the park Minu caught a glimpse of civilians standing around, jaws hanging down as they watched the spectacle of a military exercise in their midst. But she only had an instant before the transport spun and rocketed back into traffic, following an entirely different extraction route than it had on coming in. A glance at her troops showed a healthy mixture of exhilaration and fear on their faces. A petite blond, Denise, not much taller than Minu, sat in the second squad. That meant this was First Battalion, A Company. Minu looked but couldn't find their Chosen lieutenant, so she asked where he was.

"Didn't make the trip," the Saber sergeant said.

Minu gave Ted a look, and he explained. "This wasn't scheduled. The men volunteered, since they were in town here and wanted a ride home."

"And there just happened to be a full platoon of soldiers from the same unit handy?" Everyone grinned, and a few chuckled. "You guys are a real pain in my ass sometimes." Open laughter was her answer this time. She shook her head and turned back to Aaron, but he was smiling too. They'd cleared the city's traffic and were accelerating past the speed of sound. "Well done," she told her friend and patted him on the shoulder. He didn't turn from the controls, though she saw him wink.

"Yeah?" Aaron said and patted the controls, "Watch this."

They reversed course and rocketed into the city a second time. For a moment it appeared they were going in the same as before. But as they swung around the main avenue, the transport suddenly stopped and ascended like an elevator next to a high-rise hotel. Clearing the roof, it angled sideways and set down just as nicely as the previous time. All five doors swung open and five seconds later the soldiers were gone. Aaron punched the throttle, doors closing as they vaulted off the side of the building. Minu saw the excuse of a ride home disappear as they left the men behind. She'd known it was all a setup when they'd landed, and the soldiers had piled in.

"Very well done," Minu admitted. Aaron and Ted grinned at each other. "It's a transport all right. But then again it already was, just not as well suited for what we wanted. So you've boosted the avionics, improved the propulsion system, and punched a couple holes in the hull. What else can it do?"

"Next," Ted said. Aaron nodded and climbed away from Leavenworth, turning east and heading toward the valley past the city.

"Here we go," Aaron said. He flipped a control, and the transport began to change. It was disconcerting to sit there as the transport's interior narrowed and flattened. Her seat reclined and those that had appeared in the rear sank back into the floor. The window widened and lengthened as well, vastly increasing the pilot's arc of visibility, even though it became shorter. Through the smaller side windows she could see long sleek pods extending from the hull on sturdy thin wings.

"Oh my," she said in amazement.

"You ain't seen nothing yet," Ted said soberly.

Aaron took the controls in both hands and put the now fighter through its paces. He nosed over into an eleven-G dive, pulling out at the last second hard enough that Minu felt the stomach-lurching maneuver even through the powerful compensator. He did barrel rolls, a couple of split Ss, an Immelmann or two, and finished it all off with a vertical ascent where he shoved the throttle as far ahead as it could go. The impellers screamed each time the fighter broke the sound barrier, sending shock waves thumping through the hull. Outside, the blue-green sky turned purple, and slowly continued to darken.

"Better level her out Aaron," Ted warned, "we haven't worked out the program for reentry yet."

"You mean it can go into orbit?" Minu said in awe.

"Oh, certainly," Ted said, "and probably to another planet. Remus or Romulus at least, if you want." Minu looked up as Aaron leveled the flight path. The pale green face of Romulus moved slowly above their heads, tantalizingly close. She'd only recently watched an ancient movie called *The Right Stuff*. Floating at the edge of space sent her mind off on flights of fancy and raised the hair on her arms. She silently chided herself for getting excited about flying into space when she'd traveled thousands of light-years with a single step. "The big problem is the life support. It's really only good for a few hours, and we don't have it worked out; we haven't worked out re-entry without burning up, and I'm not sure how effective the impellers will be with less gravity to push against once you're out of orbit."

"But it *is* possible, right?" Minu asked. He nodded and eyed her. Minu's mind was working overtime, whirling with the possibilities, plans churning, probabilities colliding. She heard a groan of metal fatigue and looked down. She'd been grasping the chairs with her cybernetic right arm so tightly she'd bent the hand rest. "Sorry about that," she told Ted.

"It's just a prototype," he said nonchalantly, but he eyed the damage with a slight frown.

As the ship nosed over, Minu could clearly see the curvature of Bellatrix from the edge of space. There was the great equatorial sea several thousand kilometers away, and the mountains extending away from Steven's Pass below them. Even the view from her aerocar at fifty thousand meters couldn't compare to this. It was exhilarating and addictive. Floating there like that, she felt like one of the old Mercury astronauts on Earth. "How did you do this?" she asked.

"Not telling our secrets yet," Ted said.

"We still haven't shown off her teeth," Aaron said as they raced down as fast as or faster than they'd gone up.

A smooth-as-glass eleven-G pullout brought them out low over the western plains of the great equatorial desert, approximately a thousand kilometers from the distant ocean. The fighter was doing at least twice the speed of sound. Aaron tapped in commands and slid a one-eye reticle visor down over his head. "Now you're going to see some serious shit," he said. He pulled the fighter over hard enough to take the breath from her lungs. Suddenly the empty desert gave way to an encampment. She could see personnel carriers, portable troop barracks, and weapons emplacements. Minu felt a shudder through the fuselage as streaks of light leaped from both wings. Both personnel carriers vaporized as the fighter rocketed over the camp at less than ten meters above the sand. Aaron started banking one way, then reversed his turn. Minu had the impression of a streak of light flying through the space they would have occupied had he not reversed his turn.

"Impressive simulations," Minu said as she felt the Gs.

"What makes you think it's a simulation?" Ted asked.

Halfway through the turn to bring them back in line for another attack, something hit them like a hammer. Outside, the air glowed orange for an instant, and an alarm chirped on the console. "Gregg's too good a shot for his own damn good," Aaron said calmly.

"Tell me that beamcaster was turned down," Minu said. No one answered her, and for the first time, she felt her heart start to race. This was a real-world test she was part of. Might have been nice if they'd warned her beforehand. They'd either meant to show off or were ready to put this craft through its paces.

More beams of energy danced by as somewhere below, Gregg did his best to blow them out of the sky. The cool, calculating part of her brain noted that there were too many shots for one weapon, and she wondered how many Chosen were down there trying to kill them. Did any of them have a vested interest in seeing her die, or this test failing? Had her friends thought that through? They finished their Mach-speed turn and came back on target. Another beamcaster scored a direct hit. The flash of light and wash of reddish colors was a clear statement that these were full-powered weapons. Without the shields, they'd have died instantly, bodies flash-boiled into a cloud of chemicals and water vapor. The chirping alarm became a buzzer.

"How many more can we take?" she asked.

"Shhh," Aaron snapped, the reticle over his eye glowing green as he squinted, trying to find the gunners. Minu held her peace so he could do his job, and Aaron slapped a control. The sound of power relays snapping loudly could be heard somewhere under her feet, and the fighter's beamcasters came alive, pulsing bolt after deadly bolt into the enemy camp. Unlike before, there were no balls of fire or spinning debris (the troop transports must have been loaded with explosives for effect). The beamcasters cut swaths of destruction through the camp like a surgical knife. Both troop barracks were sliced in half, bursting into flames, and the beams continued onward to cut through weapons emplacements. The volume of fire coming at them was halved.

Minu knew that even with the fire lessened, they'd probably score a couple more hits and the shields wouldn't last. Aaron held steady as they raced over the camp, giving Minu a good look at the smoking remnants of the two destroyed weapons emplacements. There was no sign of dead operators. She'd known that must be the case, but the simulated attack was too realistic to allow that kind of assumption.

Another beamcaster hit the shield, which glowed blue this time; the alarm became a loud ringing. It appeared that Aaron had been waiting to be hit, because the instant the shot scored, he pulled back on the controls as hard as he could. Even through the compensator, they felt several Gs push them into their seats, and the hull groaned in protest. He cut the throttle and reversed it. Minu didn't think she'd ever felt herself pulled in more directions at the same time and wondered just how much time Aaron had spent familiarizing himself with the craft.

The maneuver flipped them over and turned them back in a split S, now facing the camp once more at a surprisingly short distance from the center. Aaron flipped a control and stabbed at the joystick.

From underneath the fighter came flashes of laser light and dancing plasma. "Shock rifles!" she said, a laugh in her voice. The chin-mounted side-by-side weapons with their high firing rate raked back and forth across the camp like a buzz saw. Aaron fired the beam-casters a couple times for good measure, sweeping the enemy camp clear of anything man-made and leaving only smoking ruin and mangled debris in his wake. "Very impressive," she said, almost in a whisper. It was like watching a movie unfold.

"Damn fool maneuver," Ted snapped from behind. He looked pale, and she suddenly remembered he was a very old man.

"Are you okay?" Minu asked, reaching over to touch his hand. It was a little clammy.

"He'll be fine," Aaron laughed. "He's just freaking out because a few of the systems were hit and miss in testing."

"Like the structural integrity boosters," Ted said and slapped Aaron in back of the head with the flat of his hand.

"Ow!"

"Okay, explain," Minu ordered them.

Since Aaron was massaging his head, Ted took it up. "That little transformation we did to turn this into a fighter is managed by basically taking the transport apart and not bolting it back together." Minu gave him an open-jawed look of confusion. "Instead of bolts, welds, and such, we use magnetically-powered couplers and force fields."

"Are you telling me the only thing holding this together is magnets?" Aaron looked at Ted and Ted looked back at him.

"Yeah," Aaron said.

"Basically, yes," Ted agreed. Minu looked agog. "The cockpit and a few critical systems are structurally held together by flexible dualloy assemblies, so should the systems fail, there's a small measure of survivability."

"Small measure?" Minu gasped. "So if you turn the power off it just falls apart?"

"No, but it becomes unstable on the various hinge points that allow it to change shape. And considering this smartass was pulling those maneuvers at faster than the speed of sound…"

"If the fields failed we'd have been torn to pieces," Aaron finished for him, "but that wasn't going to happen."

"You seem so sure," Ted said sarcastically, "considering we had a critical failure during testing only a week ago."

"That was a week ago."

"Would you two quit?" Minu snapped. "Is this thing ready or not?"

"Yes," and "Sort of," were their answers. She wasn't sure who'd said which.

"What about the third mode?"

"We're still working on that," Ted admitted.

"Good enough," Minu said. "Let's head home."

"Thanks for the workout," Aaron said into his headset. Minu thought she heard something about asshole and cheater coming from the headset, but Aaron just grinned as he turned and accelerated them toward Steven's Pass. Minu was smiling herself; she wanted to know how and why they'd done it this way, but she had her multi-role fighter/transport.

The flight back took a few minutes, but it was long enough for Ted to explain his methodology. In engineering a new craft from the ground up, they'd run into the same problem Minu had in building her shock rifles. Too many Concordian technologies just didn't work with human-engineered components, and they needed too many things that were hard to come by. The team had taken one of the badly-damaged transports she'd used in her series of war games and started using it as a test bed for various techniques, including the ground-breaking structural integrity fields, an idea Gregg had heard about from an old science fiction television show, of all places. A few weeks ago, they'd realized that all the planned features and components had been built into the test bed transport. It was no longer a transport; it had accidentally been transformed into the intended end product. They'd abandoned the other ship they'd been working on, cannibalized it for parts, the remains of which Minu had despaired over, and finished the first working model.

That model had been recently destroyed by the aforementioned unexpected failure of the structural integrity fields, but the problem was worked out and this subsequent model was perfect. She'd stumbled into the office on the day of the finished product's maiden combat test run. "Pure coincidence," Ted assured her. "The systems integration went flawlessly."

"So what are you calling them?" she asked.

"We thought we'd leave that up to you, boss." Minu looked at Aaron and thought. By the time they were landing back at Steven's Pass, she'd made up her mind.

* * * * *

Chapter Eleven
Octember 22nd, 521 AE

Leavenworth, New Jerusalem Tribe Territory

It was hard to believe it had only been a few hours since she'd flown over this town at Mach Two. It looked different at cruising speed, Minu thought as she approached in her trusty bright red aerocar. The city of Leavenworth was alive with traffic, lights, and sounds as night approached. She marveled at how much the city had grown in the few years since she'd first visited. Fans of old Earth history often made the comparison between Leavenworth and Manhattan. Her happy recollections were brought to an end when she remembered the reason for her first trip to the city. She silently cursed. That first weekend of romance and love with Christian had been a life-changing event, in more ways than one.

Minu handed the car's control over to the city traffic management network, allowing it to guide her into a landing in one of the interface zones around the perimeter of the city. It was illegal to land a flying craft inside the city traffic zone except in a designated parking area. They all charged for the luxury now. She wondered if she would have issues to deal with tomorrow after Ted and Aaron's little display worked its way through the news. It was hard to miss a ten-meter-long fighter flying through your town at the speed of sound.

Once on the ground, she steered through the busy twilight traffic toward a familiar building. It had once been one of the tallest casinos; now it was just average. The Dunes was named after a hotel in the old Earth city of Las Vegas, the city modelled after when Leavenworth was first conceived. The cities even shared the same nickname, Sin City. Lucky for her, she really didn't believe in sin. She didn't believe being a Chosen went well with the theory of sin or most religious doctrines in general. She knew there were some observant religious Chosen but, like the rest of the religious in their world, they were in the minority.

She navigated her car through the thick ground traffic. Designed to ply the skies, it was a tad clunky on the ground. The wheels were half the size of a traditional ground car, and the suspension even more reduced. It added up to a slow-turning, poor-handling ground car. Luckily, it was only a short drive from the landing zone to her destination.

Minu handed her aerocar off to a valet and strode in through the front doors of the Dunes. A huge bar dominated one wall, all glass, polished dualloy, and neon. Few were in attendance this early, mostly Chosen in their night-black jumpsuits. One was a very shapely black woman nursing a beer, who looked up and smiled as Minu entered. "What happened to the island plan?" Cherise asked.

"I have something to celebrate and wanted to enjoy some nightlife." Minu walked over and ordered a mead, downing it in one long, luscious swallow.

"I thought you didn't celebrate your birthday."

"I don't," Minu said and smiled. Cherise gave her a questioning look, her pretty face scrunched up in mock impatience. "It's a 'birthday;' it's just not mine."

"Damn it!"

"All right, all right," Minu laughed and ordered another mead. "We celebrate the birth of our new baby." She raised her drink like a toast. "Happy Birthday, Lancer!"

"New baby? And who the hell is Lancer?" Minu explained the new multi-role fighter, and Cherise smiled, shaking her head. "You know, after your people started transferring all the old, beat-to-shit transports, the same kind you used and abused in the war games, I knew you were up to something."

"Not my idea," she said. Over another pair of meads for herself, and beer for Cherise, she explained the day's events.

"You think it's really that good?"

"Cherise, that was an R&D job; they've only built three so far. Ted and Bjorn might have screamed bloody murder at having to do engineering work, 'getting his fingers dirty' as he called it, but they delivered a top-notch development team." She looked down at her empty glass and sighed, lifting it again. "If I could've figured out how to name them Alijah, Terry, and Pip, I would have."

"Here, here! But Pip isn't dead." Cherise said and downed the last sip of beer. "Let's go have some fun!"

* * *

Leavenworth was nothing if not a twenty-three hour a day, three hundred seven days a year, endless buffet of fun. No matter what your taste, you could find it in bountiful quantities and at affordable prices. Minu and Cherise went from place to place, watching shows, occasionally seeing other Chosen, dancing, and drinking. Always drinking. The dancing was fairly safe; no one really looked at two girls dancing. And the clubs were dark enough to sneak a squeeze or a kiss here and there. Once they found themselves in a mixed group of young non-Chosen men and women. For a few hours, they club-hopped and just enjoyed being young. It was fun for a while, until Minu overheard one of the good-looking young men whisper to his friend that he'd never fucked a Chosen before. At the first opportunity, she hauled Cherise toward the bathroom and at the last second turned to the front door.

It was well toward morning before they made it back to The Dunes. Minu had cut back on the drinking an hour earlier, but as their cab dropped them off, she was *still* drunk. Cherise, on the other hand, was wasted. "I want to get up to that room and have sex with you," she whispered in Minu's ear, her normally accent-free English now thick with her native Desert tribe.

"Okay, shhhh," Minu whispered back with a giggle. A thrill ran up her spine, a thrill of sexual excitement and concern. What they were doing was still illegal, after all. There were probably all kinds of girls doing the same thing all around them, but they weren't Chosen. She realized that danger was an aphrodisiac. The pair passed through the doors of The Dunes, and Cherise almost fell. Minu caught her under one arm and Cherise used the excuse to grab Minu's ass.

"Well isn't this the fucking perfect picture?" Minu looked up after steadying Cherise to see Christian standing there with two of his fellow scouts, all obviously as drunk as Minu and Cherise. But they weren't grabbing each other's asses. "I should have known you were this sick!" He tossed aside a partially drunk beer bottle that smashed on the polished floor, making the bartender look up in annoyance. When the man saw a potential confrontation between Chosen, his expression changed to worry.

"I don't want no trouble here, Chosen, sir."

"Then shut up," one of the other scouts said, "go wash some glasses, boy." The man retreated down the bar.

"She's just drunk," Minu said, straightening her friend up again and trying to let go. Cherise teetered. Minu cursed and grabbed her around the waist.

"What the hell is your problem?" Cherise spat at him.

"Looks like you're the problem," he said, taking her in with a look of disgust.

Minu tried to will her friend quiet, but it wasn't working. "Sorry, you just couldn't get the job done, so Minu upgraded to someone with more manhood." In an instant Christian's face turned from disgust to rage. "Never send a boy to do a woman's job." In an instant his hand flew out, backhanding Cherise across the face hard enough to spin her out of Minu's grasp.

"What do you think you're doing?!" Minu cried and bent over Cherise, who'd landed on hands and knees, shaking her head to clear it, and spitting blood from a split lip.

Christian was suddenly behind her, bending over and grabbing her prostrate form around the waist with one hand and cupping a breast with another. "Come on baby, I can give you more than this Desert bitch ever could." His crotch was pressed into her ass and she felt him getting hard against her. She struggled a little, but that only seemed to encourage him. Christian pressed his growing erection against her buttocks. "Yeah, I always wondered why you wouldn't let me do this to you." He pushed again, his meaning evident. The position behind her, the voice in her ear, his lewd behavior, all added up to the breaking point. The memory of being raped during the trials crashed into her mind with bitter clarity. Something snapped inside her.

In a flash she jerked free of his grip and spun, one foot snapping out. He crashed to the floor, nearly knocking over one of his surprised friends. In an instant he was on his feet and in a fighting position. Minu flipped to her feet and attacked. "You're in deep shit now!" she snarled.

She now had years of fight training under her belt: close combat, knife fighting, bone-breaking, dirty-ass fighting. Cherise had taught her there was no such thing as a fair fight. She was only dimly aware that Christian's two friends were flanking her, and that they were all Chosen. Hadn't she just admonished him a few weeks ago about brawling in Dodge City?

"Men are different adversaries," Cherise's voice came to her as her body flowed around his first clumsy punch, "what you can use against me will lead to quick and bitter defeat against a man." Christian swung hard again, his fist a blur of power. As she would against Cherise, she raised her left forearm to fend off the blow and the impact almost broke her arm. His strength forced her hand back into her face almost as hard as if the punch had connected. It was only her speed that kept his follow-up left from ending it right there. "You can't match a man's raw power." Minu jabbed him once with a stiff arm in the abdomen, and he backed up a half step in surprise. "Speed is your weapon, and their mass is their enemy."

The bartender was yelling now, and Cherise lay moaning on the floor. A dozen guests in the bar exclaimed in surprise as service staff rushed to clear the combat zone. Minu caught a shadow to her right and sidestepped. A fist shot past her head close enough that her hair flowed in its wake. She grabbed the wrist, turned and rolled the surprised Chosen over her hip, her right arm pushed past human limits to send the man like a missile right into Christian, who was coming at her again. The two men collided with a *whump* and crashed to the floor.

Minu's mind was operating on a subconscious level; instinct told her to jump and spin a foot around. It was half a second too late to be perfect, so her ankle caught the third Chosen in the side of the head instead of her. Still, the spin was fast, and the impact solid; the shock on his face was interrupted only by his face smacking into the floor. He was out of it. Minu spun to hopefully put another out while they were off balance, but they were already coming like a flash. She hesitated for an instant, finally settling into a jump to avoid both. Christian's outstretched left caught her foot and she flipped off balance, crying out as she tried to roll. She hit the floor hard on her left shoulder and rolled as best as she could, but the second Chosen had her by the hair and jerked her back.

"Oww!" she cried as she felt hair tear, yanking her neck back farther than it was intended to go. She kept her feet, but barely. Quick as a flash, there was an arm around her neck and mind-blurring force was applied. He meant to choke her out. "Stop," she gasped, but nothing resembling a sound came out. She willed Christian to stop him, and she craned her neck to try and see. He was standing there, holding his ribs, and laughing as his friend choked the life out of her.

"See if *you* can have any luck getting her to behave," Christian laughed.

Spots floated in front of Minu's eyes, and she knew she only had seconds. In that instant she decided she'd had enough. She reached up with her right hand and grasped the wrist around her neck. Again Cherise's voice in her head, "Men have iron-handed strength that only their sex is capable of, no matter how hard a woman tries to match them." She mentally overrode the instincts she'd developed over years, instincts that kept her from hurting people accidentally when shaking hands or sparing with a friend. The cybernetic actuators whined audibly as she took his thumb and twisted his hand from her neck. Air returned in a whoosh, but she didn't release her grip. She continued to bend the hand backward, bearing the man to the floor. His eyes were wide in pained shock, looking at the grayish skin of her artificial hand with dawning realization. Only an alcohol-soaked moron would forget during a hand-to-hand battle that the grayish arm with its four-fingered hand, so normal looking and so alien at the same time, was a Concordian-made cybernetic wonder. Her natural arm had nearly been bitten off by a Kloth in the Chosen trials years ago.

"Bastard gonna choke me?" she snarled and finished the move. His forearm snapped with a sickeningly loud pop, followed by his scream. One on the floor crying, another unconscious, only one left now. "You don't know who you're screwing with." She turned with slow, deliberate intent to Christian, standing a few meters away, only he wasn't laughing anymore. She lowered her head, sweat dripping from her brow, and watched the emotions play over his face. Surprise was followed by anger, then a creeping fear. In all their time together, her arm had never really been a subject of conversation, even though she'd held his most delicate parts with that powerful hand. He gulped as that very thought seemed to occur to him.

"Minu, listen…"

"Oh, no, no, no, lover…it's far too late for that." She dropped into the most aggressive stance she knew, feet spread far apart, one fist raised over her head, the other, her cybernetic right, aimed at his throat. Kung-fu was so unsubtle, and that was just what she wanted now.

"Just who do you think—" he never got a chance to finish, because Cherise's fist slammed into his groin, doubling him over with a strangled scream. Cherise reached up and grabbed his hair in both hands, jerking him down with all her might. His legs went out from under him and his face slammed into the floor with a sickening thud.

"Mother fucker," Cherise said and climbed shakily to her feet.

Minu looked around nervously, suddenly remembering this wasn't the practice floor in the Steven's Pass gymnasium. To her surprise, almost no one was looking. In fact, at this late hour, the majority of the remaining casino goers were more interested in their drinks than the yawning silence following the fracas. The bartender walked over and looked down at the three male Chosen, two of them unconscious and the third holding his broken arm and making mewing sounds. Minu held her breath as he clucked.

"Those boys should learn to be more careful," he said. Minu stared at him, open-mouthed. "Such a shame that they came running in and tripped over a luggage cart." Understanding dawned in her eyes, and he winked at her. "Saw everything, lady Chosen. I'll see they're taken care of, and have a chat with the constable when he arrives." She looked around and saw a couple of the patrons nodding into their drinks in agreement.

"I thank you," Minu said and went to Cherise. "Can you walk okay?"

"Hell yeah," the taller girl said with a weak smile, "I'm ready for more." Then she almost fell over. Minu put her right arm around her waist and steered her toward the lift.

"I just hope I can remember what our room number is…"

* * *

Morning light flooded through the huge moliplas window far earlier than Minu would have liked. Cherise snored loudly next to her, and Minu shook her head. The other girl had tried to get romantic when they got to the room, but Minu resisted with loving gentleness. Not because was she no longer interested, but because she knew better. Once the adrenaline wore off Cherise was out like a light, leaving Minu to lay there staring up at the ceiling. She thought for a while about her relationship with Christian, the things he'd said to her, and how quickly he'd turned against her, and slowly came to the realization that what he'd said about his feelings for her was all lies. It somehow hurt worse than the actual ending of the relationship. A few tears came. Not a lot, just enough to feel like it was an ending. And in her core, she knew that's what it was, an ending. Eventually she found sleep, snuggled against the naked form of her girlfriend, the one person she was certain had never lied to her. Somewhere in the back of her sleeping mind hovered the question, *How much of what you think is really just a lie?*

Minu got up and showered before pulling on a fresh jumpsuit from her seldom-used overnight bag. She had duty that morning but considered calling in sick. She'd never done that, even once, since becoming Chosen, but the sheets pulled back as Cherise slept, and Minu could see a breast exposed seductively. Thoughts passed through the back of her mind that sent shivers up her spine. Then her communicator went off.

"Chosen Alma," she said quietly, heading for the entry area to keep the noise down.

"Minu, where are you?" It was Dram's deep bass voice.

"In Leavenworth, blowing off some steam." She felt a moment of panic. Had the bartender's attempt to keep the fight quiet failed?

"Well, get to Fort Jovich, right away."

"Can I ask what's going on, sir?"

"A Chosen transport team on a Tog world is under attack. They say the enemy is the Tanam."

"I'll be right there."

She let Cherise sleep, grabbed her overnight bag, and sat it by the door. Using the pad and pen the hotel provided, she left a brief note explaining she'd been called to duty, and that she was sorry their date had turned out so poorly. Almost as an afterthought, she added that she wanted to spend an entire weekend with her at the cabin as soon as possible, then drew a little heart and signed it Minu. Fifteen minutes later she was in her aerocar, rocketing into the dawn sky.

* * * * *

Chapter Twelve
Octember 23rd, 521 AE

Fort Jovich, Peninsula Territory

The two-hour flight was just long enough to let her get her thoughts in order. Chosen on a distant world were under attack by a higher-order species. The ROE dictated that humans gave ground or retreated when faced with a higher-order species. In addition, there was a short list of species they all knew were openly hostile to all young species, and/or humanity in particular. The feline Tanam were right at the top of the list. Minu kept the aerocar's throttle against the firewall and ignored the overheat warning for the gravitic impellers. She normally babied the bright red car; this time it could damn well deliver some extra.

Luckily, it didn't let her down, and she dropped below the clouds and into one of the never-ending rain storms. The huge octagonal shape of Fort Jovich was just below her as she angled toward one of the vehicle bays. The doors automatically swung open when her IFF transponder was recognized. The vehicle loadmaster looked up in surprise as her car hummed to a stop. She asked him to find a place for it, left him with the car's valet ID card, and ran for a lift.

The command center in the thick ceramic concrete heart of the fort was busier than she'd ever seen it, even during war games. Only this time it wasn't a game. Somewhere out in the vast galaxy, humans were fighting for their lives. "SITREP!" she yelled as she crossed the threshold. She came up short when she saw Jacob, along with Dram and several other Chosen from the council. "I'm sorry, First," she said and bowed her head. Instead of looking annoyed, he looked worried, and that made her pulse race even faster.

"Thanks for coming so quickly," Dram said and gestured for her to come next to him. He began briefing her before she'd even crossed the room. "A transport team of eleven Chosen and fifty-two civilian contractors were en route to Amber…"

"The Tog experimental farming world we've been working on," she said instantly.

Dram nodded and continued. "We've been trying to duplicate the distribution system we've made here. Amber has an unpredictable harvest cycle that makes our unique harvest and distribution system much more practical."

"That's the downside of the over-automated systems the Concordia tend to use," Minu pointed out, "you'd think they'd never heard of a grain silo."

"Exactly. All the true farming worlds in the galaxy utilize huge distribution networks through portals linked to processing facilities. They work night and day, rotating input from different parts of the planet depending on the growing season and field rotation. Amber is more like Bellatrix, with shorter growing seasons that start at irregular intervals. It's hard to have the Concordia's massive factories getting random shipments, so we've been building networks of silos and storage bins. Aside from a few bots and our teams, there's not much there."

"Low value target," Minu agreed. "Any defenders?"

"A garrison of fifty Beezer." Minu snorted, and he nodded. "So our team comes through with transports and starts to unload their gear. The portal opens again, and Tanam come through. Chosen Bainbridge was in charge. He offered respectful greetings, and they killed him on the spot."

"How many more did we lose?"

"Only Bainbridge; the other Chosen were attendees of one of your little combat readiness camps." Minu smiled, glad she'd made that suggestion a few months back, and even gladder the Chosen Council had listened. All the Chosen who'd taken the class complained unceasingly about the unnecessary imposition, especially the logistics and science branch. "The team fell back and established a strong defense that held the Tanam at bay, even though they only had two shock rifles and a beamcaster stowed in the transport." Minu nodded in appreciation. The combat readiness camp instructed Chosen in how to defend against a superior force by establishing a good defensive position.

"After falling back they retreated in one of the transports to the garrison building. The Tanam are laying siege against them now. They can fall back through the garrison portal, but under Concordian law…"

"If they do, the Tog surrender possession of the world," Minu finished for him.

Dram nodded. "The Beezer are ready to make a run for it, but our people are trying to restrain them. So far, it's worked."

"Okay," Minu said and looked at her tablet. Several images of the Tanam attackers were there, both from cameras in the hardened garrison building and from bots sent out by the Chosen for recon. She figured about three squads of the feline Tanam. Their warriors weighed at least four hundred kilos each, with six legs, four eyes and razor-sharp elongated canines that reminded her of saber-toothed tigers. They were equipped with top-of-the-line Concordian technology and were as fast and deadly a being as could be found. The fact that they were a higher-order species made it that much worse for them. Of all the species to attack the Tog's interests…it was a bad situation. Still, with only three or four squads, it could be worse. She turned to find Gregg standing there, as she knew she would. "Order up Red Army, 1st Battalion," she said with a wry smile, "we'll show these—"

"Hold up," Jacob said a few meters away, "we've already responded."

"You ordered out the soldiers without me?"

"Your soldiers are still here," Jacob said and glanced at Dram who looked a little uncomfortable.

"We sent a scout combat team," Dram told her, glancing between her and Jacob. The meaning was obvious. It was *his* idea, not mine.

"The scouts were reorganized under the soldier branch," Minu complained, "they work for the soldiers, not independently of them."

"This team has been training for just this sort of mission," Jacob said confidently. Minu shot him daggers and he cleared his throat. "Some believe the soldiers are overkill…subtlety is called for."

"Against three squads of a first-order species' warriors?" Minu asked. "Those are well-trained, well-equipped, and capable aliens, and they're there for a reason."

"To take that world from the Tog," Jacob said, smacking the dualloy tactical console for emphasis. "These specially-trained scouts will deal with the situation, and with a minimum of bloodshed."

"Who's in command?" No one answered, and Minu looked around at them. She cocked her head when no one spoke. "Will you at least give me a straight answer?"

Dram looked down and Minu felt control of her anger slipping, but then he answered. "It's a team led by Christian."

"Oh," she said and turned on her heel.

"Where are you going?" Jacob demanded.

"To wait with my soldiers for the inevitable." He called after her for an explanation, but she kept on marching.

Gregg stayed behind for a minute, and the others suddenly noticed he was standing there. "What is it, Chosen?" Jacob asked.

"This is bullshit," he said simply and spat on the floor. "All this time and money, and you just keep on doing the same damn thing. I'm embarrassed to be Chosen." He turned and followed Minu out. No one called after him.

Two levels below in the ready room, the twenty Chosen and noncoms of Red Army, 1st Battalion gathered, listening to her description of the situation. There were shouts of anger and outrage when she explained that a group of only a dozen scouts had been sent instead of them. Minu smiled to see that even the Chosen temporarily in charge all scowled, especially since they wore the black of Chosen instead of the tiger stripe camouflage of the soldiers. Chosen scouts they might have been, but they'd spent months training these new soldiers and wanted to see it through. After so much time and effort, the Chosen didn't leave a job half done. Gregg came in as she was finishing up, a look of satisfaction on his face, and she worried about what he'd done.

A moment later Dram stormed in, slamming the heavy dualloy door behind him and pointing a thick finger at Minu. "You go too far," he said and then pointed it at Gregg, "and he's picking up your bad habits."

"What the hell have you had us doing here all this time?" she demanded and gestured expansively, taking in all the soldiers waiting with stunned looks on their faces. "I know it wasn't just to keep me busy; I've experienced that before. All this time, money, blood, and sweat, and you send a few Chosen, again."

"You think I had a choice?"

"Of course I do, and I think you had a say."

Dram took a deep breath and stopped, letting it out instead of yelling back. "Look, Christian got Jacob's ear a few months back, said he was owed something after all the months he spent marooned on the frontier being chased by Tanam."

"They put him in charge of the scouts; wasn't that enough?"

"Apparently not." He looked around and suddenly seemed to notice the command staff all watching with jaws hanging down. The muscles bunched in his jaw. "Be ready," he told her, "we don't know what the Tanam mean by this crazy attack. There seems to be little to gain, and less to be learned."

Minu watched him leave and returned to her spot at the head of the room. A man she'd once thought she loved was off trying to prove she'd wasted the last year of her life on a fool's errand. "You see?" he'd say when he returned. "Real Chosen can handle anything, given a chance." She ground her teeth and cursed.

"What are your orders, boss?" Gregg asked.

"Stand down, remain on alert." All around the room the officers and noncoms nodded. "This is just the start."

"How do you know?" Chosen Daniel asked.

"I know." They stared at her with wide eyes. "Because it's my job."

The next move was only a few hours later. Word came from Christian's elite strike team that they'd successfully relieved the besieged garrison on Amber, forcing the Tanam back through the portal they'd initially invaded through. He'd only sustained one wounded, and the enemy had suffered no casualties. "Doesn't make any sense," Minu said, back in the command center. Jacob and the others were all slapping each other on the back and laughing. A few cast disparaging glances at Minu, but she refused to bite. Her mind was busy trying to sort it all out. Nearby Dram caught her eye and nodded. He'd heard her comment and agreed. The Tanam were known for their schemes; they were perhaps only second to the T'Chillen for scheming, according to many.

The portal flashed to life, visible through a monitor in the vault, and computers began relaying data. A flash traffic message came from the Beezer on Amber. Minu read the live feed as technicians applied the cipher, and the message decrypted. One of the service portals on Amber had opened and a second force of Tanam were landing, much bigger this time. They were seen by the portal monitoring camera heading off at a high rate of speed straight toward the production facilities. The Beezer were crying for help and asking permission to retreat.

"Do they even know how to fight?" she asked Dram, who shrugged. Minu knew better than to ask that. The Beezer, huge bipedal buffalo with unexpressive faces and powerful bodies, were indomitable fighters, but only when cornered, which they avoided at all costs.

The Chosen councilors, led by Jacob, began to consider their moves. A few minutes' later orders were given to deploy another force of scouts to deal with this second attack. The first squad under Christian would remain at the barracks to guard against a surprise attack.

Jacob cast an angry glance at her, inviting her, daring her to disagree. This time Minu held her temper in check. She was beginning to get the sense of what was going on here. No sooner had the second squad of scouts left through the portal in the vault than another communication came in; two more incursions on Amber, these forces heading to parts unknown. Moments later, communications came from P'ing on Herdhome. "This is a move against our interests," hse said in as certain a tone as the translator was capable of. Thanks to human scientists, the new translator matrix for English was even clearer than the last. P'ing actually sounded somewhat human.

"Have they declared a war or vendetta?" Jacob asked in his capacity as First Among the Chosen.

"No, they haven't. This action is unsanctioned, but because it's a research leasehold, the attack is legal. We've been declining to sell them foodstuffs in response to their attacks against you, our Chosen, over the last year or more." They all knew Concordian law to one degree or another; Minu doubted any one person could know it all. Often contradictory and easily manipulated to the needs or wants of higher-order species, the Law was more an instrument of revenge or oppression against lower-order species such as humanity. The Tog could only do so much to protect humanity as their clients. Minu was glad to be working for a species such as the Tog. From what she'd seen of the Concordia, they had a light-handed approach and even some dependence on their clients for help and technical prowess. Of course that very attitude toward their clients was one of the reasons the Tog weren't the most prominent of the higher orders. "They claim we're using starvation as a weapon, and this is the reason they can attack. Others will support their move, claiming we're greedy and vindictive toward them."

"Then why haven't they attacked Herdhome?" Jacob asked. P'ing spread serpentine arms wide, three-fingered hands splayed in a disconcertingly human gesture. "This is escalating quickly."

"Any sign of other species' involvement?" Jacob asked. Even higher-order species often brought along allies to better spread the risks.

"No, thank our luck for that. We need our Chosen to deploy what forces they can immediately to defend the Amber world until the Beezer can be made ready for battle. If their home world is threatened, their instincts will be to race home and abandoning our holdings." Minu tensed; this was the moment of truth. Jacob would have to send every Chosen able to fight, and they'd still have little hope of defending four worlds at the same time.

"Concordia Master, we have an alternative," Jacob said grudgingly, all eyes turning to watch. "Our new soldiers are ready to serve. Chosen Alma has more than a thousand prepared to deploy at this very moment." He didn't look at Minu, but she could tell he was shaking with anger. She understood a lot better now. Creating the soldiers and these forts had been approved under protest. Jacob had resisted her every move from the day she'd become Chosen, even opposing her being made a Chosen. And still she had no idea why. Maybe her father could answer that question, if only he could talk to her from beyond the grave.

If it were possible for the almost featureless face of a Tog to look surprised, P'ing almost managed it. Hse stared at Jacob through the communications relay for so long, Minu began to wonder if it was a still image. Finally hse moved and spoke with hser flowing gestures and gentle pulses of bioluminescent light. "We hadn't known they were so close to being trained. This is surprising news. Good, but surprising. Please deploy them as quickly as possible."

The Tog's image disappeared and Jacob turned to Minu. "Okay, you have your wish."

"My wish? How arrogant do you think I am?" His eyes narrowed and she continued. "I've fought to do all this for our own sake, not as some self-serving ego trip. And after the soldiers are proven, I'll happily take a battalion command and step aside for you to put whichever of your toadies in charge you want."

"Basking in all the credit, I'm sure," one of the Chosen council members said behind Jacob. Minu couldn't tell who it was, and it didn't really matter.

"Credit? Keep the credit. I'll exchange it for a chance for humanity to survive."

Minu turned slightly toward Dram for his approval. He gave the barest nod, and she quickly left. By the time she reached the ready room, her unit commanders were swarming in. The formal orders were in her tablet, and she shook her head. She was to deploy to Amber in order to assist the Chosen teams already there in repelling the Tanam attack, keeping a third of her forces in reserve should more attacks follow. She nearly stormed back to the command center to tell Jacob what she thought of his plan when a message from Dram came in. It read simply, "Minu, don't try to argue. This is the way it's going to be. If you fight, you'll be relieved, and I'll be forced to assume command. Just like the Vendetta, do your best with the cards you've been dealt."

She didn't like that last; the Rasa Vendetta had cost the lives of three good friends and hundreds of Chosen. She turned to an expectant Gregg. "We're going in," she said and the room was suddenly rocked by cheers. She tried for several seconds to shout over them until Gregg noticed and used his booming voice to obtain silence. Then she told them the plan, and the cheers turned to moans. "We can do it," she said, turning in a circle and taking them all into her view. "We can do anything we want, succeed at any task, and best any adversary. We're humanity's soldiers, the long-lost weapons of Earth!" This cheer made the previous one pale by comparison.

"Well said," Gregg told her and slapped her on the back.

"Thanks. Now put 2nd and 3rd battalion on alert, and Green Army."

"You think it'll get that bad?"

"It could."

Gregg nodded and reached for a communicator. "Var'at will be thrilled. When he heard his army wasn't going on alert, he looked mad enough to chew rock."

"He'll understand," Minu said, "his troops are blooded, these are not. Once he sees the situation, he'll know why I'm leaving Green Army as backup. If things go south, and I yell for help, I don't want more inexperienced troops coming as backup." Gregg nodded and started talking into the device. To her surprise, he hissed and popped in a fair imitation of the Rasa speech. She'd had no idea he was learning the alien language. But now that she thought about it, quite a few of the soldiers were picking up a few sentences in Rasa, and many of the Rasa were able to speak some English, even if it sounded rough and pinched due to their lack of lips. That done, she turned to her commanders. There was finally some work to do.

* * * * *

Chapter Thirteen
Octember 23rd, 521 AE

Planet Amber, Tog Leasehold, Elysium Sector

Visiting Amber could be either a joy or a nightmare, depending on what season you arrived in. Minu studied the planet's details as she uploaded the data to all of her commanders. Its growing capacity was marginal; the seasons were too unusual to be considered economically viable. The Tog had applied for and got a leasehold at a ridiculously low cost. No infrastructure and a marginal growing season—who'd want to live there? It was only thanks to their ingenious human helpers that they were making a profit.

Like most alien worlds, the humans gave it a unique name in their own language. No one from Bellatrix had ever visited the obscure world until the proposal was put forward. It was named based on the plan. "Amber waves of grain," someone suggested. They should have seen the world first. Minu had no doubt that, if not for a shortage of water, it would have been a valuable leasehold for some middle-order species. Amber suffered from a severe axial tilt and an equally extreme solar orbit that took it alternately too close to the sun, then frigidly distant. However, the world's ecosystem was adapted to these yearly extremes, so for two 98-day growing cycles every 406-day year, Amber was a rich, almost lush, growing land.

Minu and her soldiers came through the portal a week after the second growing season ended. The nearly endless fields around the simple portal facility were covered in harvest trash, cuttings and leavings from the reaped plants, ready to be tilled under to help fertilize next years' planting. The air was already frigid as the days grew shorter, and the sun fell more distant.

Minu crouched next to the portal building, a twenty-meter-tall squat ceramic concrete pyramid with doors on all four sides. She'd come through twenty minutes ago with A Company, 1st Battalion, Red Army. Besides the need to perform well on this first mission, she was nervous because the battalion-level command structure was still untested. By forcing her to cut back on drills, the Chosen council had also kept her from doing any full-scale war games that could have projected how entire battalions would operate in the field.

"Perimeter is secured," Gregg told her. He was acting as her aide in this mission, as she'd assumed command of the battalion. The deployment through the portal was precisely executed. The soldiers swept out from where she stood guard with her personal squad, taking the building in minutes. The Tanam offered only token resistance before being thrown back.

"Casualties?" she asked.

"Three casualties, no KIA." Minu nodded. Medics were sprinkled through the ranks evenly, with at least one per squad. She'd encouraged medic training in all those interested and was thusly rewarded with a high levels of takers. According to her files, most Concordian species only deployed medical personnel as separate units, and kept them out of the fight until the coast was clear. She'd much preferred the Earth tradition of the combat medic.

"Once they're stabilized, transport them back to base," she ordered. "Send recon out." There weren't any Chosen scouts with them; they'd all been deployed under Christian and were holed up in the Beezer command bunker many kilometers away. If her mission failed, she was sure the experiment of the soldiers would end just as quickly as it began. She owed it to her men not to allow that happen, while at the same time not spending their lives recklessly in pursuit of quick success. At the back of her mind was the body count she'd incurred the last time she'd led people into battle.

A hastily picked squad of recon troopers mounted their broomsticks, a simple gravitic impeller-powered two-man flying vehicle the Chosen had used for decades, and leaped into the air. They raced away with a high-pitched whine and quickly located the retreating enemy.

"Orders?" Gregg asked.

"Shadow them, do not engage."

The mounted recon unit followed the Tanam from a safe distance, drawing an occasional stray shot or two from the retreating cats. The broomsticks' camera feeds began transmitting to Gregg's tablet an image of the Tanam's armored transport as it rode nap-of-the-earth, weaving among the modest terrain features with computer precision.

"Type eleven, basic transport," Gregg noted on the screen. Minu nodded. They were similar to the ones her people had been modifying into the new Lancers. No tanks or assault transports. This had to be a feint.

Minu moved outside now that the perimeter was secure, and B Company began deploying through the portal. "I'd like some answers from these cats," she told Gregg. "Send Third Platoon in a pair of transports to do a force recon of the garrison. Tell them to stay alert; I don't want them doubling back here and punching through to escape."

"Makes me nervous," Gregg said, pointing to the body of a Tanam lying nearby. The shock rifle had punched through its personal shield and armor like it wasn't there. The alien's chest had exploded like it had swallowed a bomb. "They're a higher-order species," he said as if almost afraid the dead Tanam would hear. "We've spent decades running from their like because of the ROE."

"The Rules of Engagement don't apply in this case," Minu reminded him. "They attacked a Tog holding, and we're legally entitled to fight them and kill them if necessary."

"Still," Gregg said and pulled his eyes away with some effort, "all the same, I'd rather be shooting Kloth. At least they can't declare a vendetta, or worse." Minu shrugged her shoulders. She didn't really care who she shot at, as long as it served humanity.

I thought you were Chosen to serve the Tog? A voice whispered in the back of her head. "We have to serve ourselves eventually," she answered the voice.

"Huh?" Gregg asked.

Minu hadn't known she was speaking aloud. She shook her head and made a dismissive gesture. Gregg gave her a sidelong look but turned back to his tablet. They both carried bulked-up computers serving as tactical interfaces. Eyepieces rested in pockets in case things got hot and they needed both hands.

The garrison was twenty-five kilometers to the east. She watched on a little tactical map as Third Platoon raced around the retreating Tanam, taking advantage of the superior speed of the souped-up transports. The cats were going by the book—the Concordian book on warfare, that is. Never retreat too quickly so you can be fully ready for what lay in your path. Minu had found their rules too cumbersome and inflexible when teaching her soldiers. It didn't take into account such things as home-field advantage, or those times when you must take a chance in desperate situations. Her men easily outdistanced the cautious cats and swept into radio range of the garrison.

"Beezer garrison to the human Chosen," their secure radio link came alive. The translated voice sounded like rocks rolling down hill; the distant speaker was a huge Beezer soldier.

"This is Chosen Minu Alma, in service to the Tog. We're here to assist you."

"We're glad for it. The Chosen already here are keeping us from being overrun. Now can you hold this insufferable lot of screaming cats at bay while we retreat? I fear this world is lost to us."

"We will not retreat."

"Excuse me, I misunderstand?"

"I have a hundred soldiers just outside the Tanam lines. We're here to give these Tanam a much-needed thrashing."

"But you barely match their number."

"That's only a small percentage of my force. Rest assured, we can easily deal with these flea-bitten cats."

"We will hold, for now."

Minu switched tactical channels and spoke. "Chosen scout Christian, come in."

"Chosen Christian." His voice was familiar, and it brought a pang of regret to her heart. Minu could hear the sound of high-energy weapons fire and suspected his squad of scouts was now manning the defenses of the garrison.

"What's your SITREP? We're here to lift the siege."

"We've been hoping to get the Beezer into the fight. Jacob thought that with our help they'd dig in and we could take it to the cats. Didn't work out that way. We've got six squads of Tanam dug in around the garrison working on deploying heavy weapons. They seem to be taking their own sweet time about it. Looks like another five squads are mounted on heavy transports and are probably the breaching team they'll use once the shields are down."

The unspoken part was his hope that her presence wouldn't be necessary at all. At least he'd been professional enough to keep it out of his voice. "Got it, beam me whatever tactical maps you've assembled, and we'll start discussing tactics to take these felines down a peg."

Once the entire battalion was through the portal with the remainder of their vehicles, Minu had them mount up in order. The craft weren't Lancers; the fighters were still several months from completion in more than small numbers, but they also weren't the clunky old models she'd used for drills. These were new-looking units with a little armor, shields temporarily installed, and more powerful impellers. Cherise called them 'light combat transports,' and Minu agreed it was as good a description as any.

In the air she formulated her battle plan. Companies B and C would deploy on opposite sides of the Tanam position, just out of sensor range. They'd move as close as possible and engage the enemy with precision shock rifle fire. Once they began to reposition their forces in response, Minu would bring in Company A and exploit whatever breach was presented to them. Two platoons from 2nd Battalion, B Company were deployed from Bellatrix to guard the portal. It was a simple plan, but she didn't honestly think they could land unopposed.

The Tanam forced to retreat from the portal had alerted the rest of their forces to be on the lookout for an attack, but they were expecting a Concordian-style attack—a flying wedge of combat craft with dueling shields and waves of bots. Instead, she regrouped with Company A and orbited the battlefield for half an hour, briefing her teams and letting the cats stew in their own juices. When the two waves of five transports set their companies down over a kilometer from the garrison, no Tanam moved to intercept.

"I know they're cats," Minu said and scratched her chin, "but they're acting like pussies."

Gregg laughed but quickly shushed the nearest squad of men in the cramped transport. The boss was thinking. "Maybe we have them confused."

"You don't have to think much to use standard Concordian tactics. It's more like a religion to them." She grumbled to herself and thought. *Could this be a trap? Could they possibly be expecting a larger assault? The cats don't know about the soldiers; no one does.* "Have 1st Platoon, Company B swing out an extra five kilometers and perform a full orbit around the combat zone before deploying. Look for any EM radiation or maybe solar screens."

"Think it's an ambush?"

"I don't know."

Another ten minutes passed before the platoon reported. "No sign of additional forces out to seven kilometers, commander."

Gregg noted it, ordered the unit to rejoin the other transports of Company B, and turned to Minu. "Orders?"

"Finish deploying as planned." Minu watched on transport's the tactical screens as the little red arrows numbered B-1 though C-4 moved steadily toward the Tanam's position. She forced herself to breathe against the knowledge that those icons each represented twenty lives. It felt like an eternity before the radio came alive again.

"Company B is in position."

"Company C is in position."

Gregg turned and looked at her, sitting in the command chair, watching the screens, biting her lip, and thinking. "It's just not right," she said aloud, giving voice to her thoughts. She flicked the channel over to the garrison. "Christian, do they have those heavy weapons up yet?"

"Not yet," he replied immediately, "but it has to be very soon. Are you in position?"

"Stand by," she said and changed back to the soldiers' tactical channel. "Company A, Company B, withdraw, I repeat, withdraw to your LZ and stand by for orders."

"What's up?" Gregg asked.

"They're waiting for us."

"How's that possible? No aliens have ever seen the soldiers in action. As far as they know, all we have is a hundred or so Chosen."

"I know, I know, but every ounce of my being is screaming that this is a trap. Somehow they know about the soldiers."

On the monitor the arrows began to creep back from the ambush point. No sooner had they moved a few meters than motion sensors picked up activity at a dozen new points. "Heads-up all platoons!" Gregg warned over the channel. "We show multiple mechanized units coming on line."

The display showed six new units between the retreating soldiers and the dug-in Tanam with their unprepared heavy weapons. She leaned close and watched as the sensor data began to resolve the new units. It took several seconds because the data was relayed from the less-than-ideal sensors on the besieged garrison bunker. "Tanks," Minu said even before the results appeared to confirm her suspicion. "All units, we have Tanam heavy armor deploying, check your tacticals, data is being relayed. Do not attempt to take off; establish defensive lines at your LZ and hold tight!"

"So that's why the heavy weapons aren't done," said Gregg, his eyes wide as one screen showed the model and types of the Tanam tanks. They were beasts of the first order. Seventy tons each, gravitic impeller-powered, heavily armored, with both shields and force fields, sporting dual heavy beamcaster turrets. As if that wasn't bad enough, it could also hold a squad of soldiers.

"Yep," Minu said, "the incomplete heavy weapons were bait."

"Damn good thing we didn't storm over into them. We'd have been pasted."

"We still might get creamed," she reminded him.

"Orders?"

She thought for a second as the monster tanks finished coming to life and emerging from their concealment. "I need to know if those heavy weapons are real."

"We aren't close enough," Gregg told her, "and if we try to get closer, those tanks will tear these tin cans to pieces."

Once again she cursed not having the Lancers operational. The ground-attack mode had been designed with this scenario in mind. Four of them would clean the lumbering tanks from the battlefield with ease. "Order recon in to find out."

He looked at her soberly. "They won't stand a chance against all those soldiers dug in there."

"They'll have surprise on their side. Our survival may depend on the data they gather on the run." She took a breath and let it out, maintaining eye contact with her old friend for a long moment. Finally he sighed and nodded, relaying the order that would send men to die.

"Acknowledged," the improvised recon team replied instantly. "We'll find out."

Six little icons that looked like lightning bolts raced toward the forces surrounding the garrison bunker. They were labeled R-1 to R-6, and they were moving in blurs. "Come on," she urged them. "Fly those things!"

Minu had flown broomsticks from time to time and found them both exhilarating and horribly dangerous. They were the first Bellatrix-manufactured flying vehicle, built decades ago from scavenged parts. Yet they still stayed in the inventory because they were simple, cheap, and effective. A flying bicycle minus wheels, with a wind screen, gravitic impellers, and duel saddles. The original version had lacked even rudimentary avionics. These newer ones were much more sophisticated but were fundamentally the same vehicle. The top speed was effectively unlimited, though most users kept it under two hundred KPH.

"They're insane," Gregg whispered as they watched the readout. All six broomsticks were exceeding three hundred KPH, and as they came within range of the field of combat, they accelerated further to nearly four hundred. Minu blinked, trying to imagine what it was like crouching behind the minimal wind screen of the broomsticks as the screaming wind tore at them.

The Tanam anti-aircraft systems warned them of the approaching craft and instantly engaged them when in range, but the tiny craft were so small, the computer-controlled beamcasters of the anti-aircraft batteries were hard-pressed to score a hit.

With a flash, R-2 disappeared, followed an instant later by R-4. In less than a second, four soldiers were the first human casualties of the battle. The four remaining recon broomsticks split up, each over-flying a different heavy weapons site. At four hundred kilometers per hour, they were over the targets and gone in three seconds. R-5 flashed from existence as the last three surviving units cleared the combat area, and Minu exhaled. The only thing that would have been worse than losing six lives just to get the data would be losing them all and getting no data. "Good job men," she told the broomstick pilots, swallowing the pain she felt at the loss of half their number.

"Checking the data," Gregg said. One of the monitors showed ultra-high-speed images frame by frame, complete with surprised Tanam technicians interrupted in their jobs assembling real working heavy energy weapon field pieces. "They're real, no doubt about it. And by the looks of it, now that the tank trap is sprung, the crews are busting their furry asses to get them on line." Minu looked over his shoulder and nodded. "Companies B and C report contact with the enemy armor in five minutes, max."

"Okay, here's what we're going to do."

* * * * *

Chapter Fourteen
Octember 23rd, 521 AE

Planet Amber, Tog Leasehold, Elysium Sector

The three broomsticks swept in again, from the opposite direction this time, and even faster. The Tanam manning the anti-aircraft battery snarled and licked her lips with a long flexible tongue, unable to believe the foolish humans would come back in such a predictable way. She coordinated with the other anti-air units and opened fire. This time the enemy wasn't trying to evade and all three were quickly destroyed.

"Crazy apes," she laughed and glanced out the shielded enclosure around her portable battery toward the nearby heavy energy weapon where the crew was finishing its setup. Soon they'd crack the garrison bunker open and feast on the skulking Beezer, then the annoying humans. Her second set of motion-sensitive eyes caught movement to her left, and she turned just as five transports came in for a hasty landing and began disgorging a horde of humans! "Where did they come from?" she wondered a second before a shock rifle tore the life from her.

"Hit them hard!" Minu yelled over the radio, and Company A opened up with everything they had. Beamcasters cracked and shock rifles zapped as fast as the soldiers could fire them. In moments the two closest anti-air units and the adjacent heavy energy weapon were overwhelmed. "Gregg, get a team on that thing, quick!"

"You got it boss."

As Gregg cut out a squad of men, she turned back to the transport. The pilot stood in the doorway, a beamcaster cradled in his arms. The weapon was linked by a cable to the craft's substantial power cells, allowing him to fire many more times than a normal beamcaster.

"It worked, good job!" Minu called over the clamor of men running toward the next heavy energy weapon. "I'd have never thought to mess with the shields that way."

"No problem, ma'am," he said, his cheeks turning red under his face shield. "It's from a shield operations manual written by Chosen Pipson Leata. It's tricky, usually jacks up the shield controls, and doesn't make you completely invisible."

"But with those broomsticks on automatic…"

"Exactly," he said and nodded, "who'd notice five transports coming in low and slow when three broomsticks are flying down your throat!"

"How are the shields?"

"Down to forty percent efficiency, but they'll hold up for now."

Minu gave him a thumbs-up and made a mental note to ask Ted if redundant shield generators could be installed to allow this to be a regular tactic. She took shelter just inside the doorway to the transport and flicked down the eyepiece linked to the tablet at her waist. Her personal squad covered the transport as she evaluated the battle's progress.

Second platoon was overrunning the heavy weapons battery to the east, while third platoon had split into two squads to assault the heavy weapons battery to the west and the nearby anti-air unit at the same time. She bared her teeth to see both squads heavily engaged. A man was down in each squad but no KIA marks showed up. "Gregg, send a squad from First Platoon to help Third Platoon take their objective."

"You got it, boss."

Now she had to hope they weren't spread too thin for their own good. Just over a rolling hill were hundreds of Tanam soldiers. None of them had come rushing over the hills, so she knew they were unaware of the battle taking place here. But that wouldn't last, especially with Third Platoon bogged down.

"Gregg, what's the story, man?"

"Five minutes."

"Shit," she snarled and ran toward the gun battery. Her squad jumped in surprise, then raced after her, struggling to keep up. She might have lost her regular martial arts workouts with Cherise, but she still ran every day. By the time she reached the heavy energy weapon, they were twenty meters behind. "Gregg, come on!" she said as she jumped up into the control cab.

Like all Concordian-made equipment, the heavy energy weapons battery was designed to be transported through a portal. In this case it had been moved in three pieces. The main part carried the weapon's focusing barrel and particle beam generator, the second held the massive electro-plasma capacitor, or EPC, and targeting equipment, and the final was the command truck it was aimed and fired from. Three of the soldiers Gregg had brought were desperately trying to figure out the final stage of setup while he was yelling at the computer controls. "I'm trying," he growled at her.

"I'm sorry," she said and none too gently pushed him aside. The displays were configured for a Concordian script she didn't recognize, but like all Concordian equipment, it was designed to be versatile. She found the main computer control screen and isolated the configurations. A couple of quick taps on the screen, and the script changed to the same one the Tog used. "We don't have time to lose."

All the displays went blank for a moment and when they came alive again it was understandable. Tog Concordian script had been taught in the Keeper's Academy where Minu had attended school for ten years. The other Chosen learned as soon as they joined if they weren't already fluent. All the gun batteries' systems were displayed with icons and status displays. She studied them with frenzied intensity. Main system on line, power on line, targeting on line, stabilization offline. "Tell them to get the damn stabilizers working," she yelled over the whine of the machinery.

"Company B to commander," the voice in her radio spoke into Minu's ear. "We've engaged the tanks."

"Shit," she spat, "out of time. Have them clear away!" she barked and activated the battery.

Outside the main transport opened, and the ten-meter-long tube of the weapons barrel was erected by robotic arms. It teetered dangerously without its supporting arms, and Minu gritted her teeth, hoping it held. On one monitor she watched as the crew, heedless of the danger, bravely continued to attach the stabilizers. Minu swallowed and did her part, ignoring them and bringing the weapon online.

In one eye she could see her two companies of soldiers fighting for their lives. They were raining down a steady stream of fire on the advancing tanks, which seemed to take no notice of the attack. Even the shock rifles, which passed straight through the shields, lacked the punch to do more than explode small pieces of heavy armor. The tanks' dual heavy beamcaster turrets spoke, turning one of their transports into a fireball, and ten soldiers flashed to KIA.

"Hold on," Minu told the soldiers. The gun battery status flashed to 'operational' with warning lights. She stabbed the screen, overriding the warnings, and the targeting screen came alive. One of the tanks was only two hundred meters away, just on the other side of a low hill. Tanam soldiers were also dug in over there, waiting for the tanks to do enough damage that the warriors could go in and mop up. She shook her head in disgust at the tactic. The tanks were ideal cover for advancing troops; to just lay low and wait was to leave them vulnerable. The target data scrolled across the screen, colored blue-green with another warning. "Friendly," it advised her. "Thanks, but no thanks..." she mumbled, stabbing the override again, and fired.

Energy weapons employed as artillery had some disadvantages, regardless of the raw devastating damage potential. Principal among their limitations were range, and indirect fire. Atmosphere made the energy beam attenuate rapidly and lose effectiveness, and since the beams couldn't bend, you couldn't fire over obstacles. The robotic holders of the weapon were capable of lifting the gun almost a hundred meters up, but Minu decided surprise was more important than maximum damage.

The gun bucked as mega-joules of energy were pumped into the particle accelerator, then toward the target. The blast tore into the low intervening hill, and through it. Rock and dirt were vaporized, exploding out the other side as the beam slammed into the back of a tank. Its shields flashed through the whole spectrum, but held. Minu snarled and fired again before the crew could react. This time the blast already had a hole to utilize and the entirety of the energy was transferred into the tank's shields.

Like all shields, they dumped incoming energy into the EPCs until they couldn't hold any more. On both sides of the behemoth, plates exploded outward, the shield EPCs detonating like tiny, spectacular lightning storms. The spectacle was only visible for a split second though, because as soon as the shields failed, the beam sliced the tank in two and turned it into a fireball.

When the tank exploded all hell broke loose in the enemy lines. The tanks responded by turning around to face the unexpected attack, while the Tanam warriors abandoned their dug-in position because they were now vulnerable to attack. In response the human soldiers charged at the flanks of the tanks.

Minu targeted the battery again and quickly fired. This tank was close to the peak of the hill; the gun had less dirt to shoot though. The tank exploded, throwing debris high enough for her to see from the command truck. The soldiers working on her battery cheered. She picked another target just as the first tank came into view over the hill. At only a couple dozen meters, the blast took out the shield, cleaved the tank, and kept going high into the chilly sky.

A pair of heavy beamcaster bolts slammed into the batteries' own shields, turning them crimson and setting off yowling alarms. Minu yelped and slapped the 'counter-battery fire' control. The robotic arms spun the weapon, and it fired automatically. The tank that had fired on her met the same fate as the previous three. Then her men screamed and dove for cover as the entire gun battery recoiled sideways and toppled over with a ponderous crash.

"Clear out!" Minu yelled and abandoned the command truck at a dead run. A second later the final two tanks cleared the hills and fired on the battery. When it exploded she was no more than twenty meters away. The shock wave lifted her off her feet and tossed her to the ground, and into unconsciousness.

"Come back to us, boss." Minu heard the familiar voice and struggled out of the darkness. Gregg and her personal squad were all looking down at her in concern. "You okay?"

"Do I look okay?" she croaked and sat up. Nothing seemed to be damaged, so she continued to her feet. She tapped the tablet at her belt, but the eyepiece remained transparent. When she looked down there was a five-centimeter-long fragment of heavy beamcaster battery sticking from the computer. "Oh," she said.

"Here's a backup," her squad sergeant said and handed her a new tablet. In seconds, she'd linked it with the eyepiece, logged into their portable network, and was in command once more. The first thing she did was check for active enemy units. There weren't any.

"We mopped them up," Gregg told her. "Right after our battery blew up, Second and Third Platoons got the other two heavy beamcaster batteries running and took out the last two tanks. Our guys were chewing up their soldiers, and the Beezer finally came out of hiding and neutralized the other three heavy turrets. They surrendered a few minutes later."

Minu continued to use the eyepiece to confirm the field was clear of combatants, eventually nodding and heaving a sigh. They'd won, but twenty-four soldiers were dead, with ten more out of action. Two transports had also been destroyed. It wasn't a small butcher's bill, but the Tanam paid a higher price. Forty dead Tanam warriors, a dozen wounded, and thirty-one captured. Add to that five intact heavy beamcaster batteries that now belonged to the humans, and it hadn't been a bad day.

The Beezer commander appeared a short time later, a huge three-meter-long ballistic weapon cradled in its arms like a toy, wearing combat armor from head to hoof, with gold trim along the helmet rim. "We're grateful for your assistance," he huffed and grumbled like an earthquake, "but we must leave quickly."

"What's wrong?"

"Serengeti is under attack, and we must return home."

"We'll have the Chosen scouts hold the garrison here and go with you."

The Beezer cocked its massive head as the translation came through. "Your Chosen are already on Serengeti; they left as soon as the outcome of the battle here was no longer in doubt."

* * * * *

Chapter Fifteen
Octember 24th, 521 AE

Capital City, Serengeti, Beezer Leasehold

It had been years since Minu last set foot on Serengeti. It was a great world, if you liked endless plains of grass and brutal heat with humidity to match. She'd been there many times in her early day as a Chosen still in training, but not since. The Beezer's leasehold of Serengeti was a hundred thousand years old. It was an unremarkable world, not really suited for large-scale agriculture, despite the endless plains. There was little available water; the majority was either in small streams and lakes or in the air. It also lacked a large skilled population for industry. But it was a Class A environment, sporting one large city of five million, and was home to a species vital to the Tog's survival. For as long as they'd held the leasehold, the Beezer had been the Tog's defenders and muscle. Few would challenge one of the massive grazers unless you knew their true nature. The problem was over the last few centuries the secret was out; the Beezer were all horn and no fury.

Minu's transport slid through the portal and jogged sideways, shields coming on and soldiers ready to jump out. Nothing happened, and the rest of the transports came through one after another.

"Using the transportation hub portal was inspired," Gregg said. Minu gave him an annoyed look, and he laughed.

"It made sense they'd ignore these portals," Minu said. "Big boys don't come in through the back door." The Concordian rules of warfare again, she thought. She'd learned this from the Rasa; attack the weak points.

"No, just loser clients like us." She grunted and nodded. As her forces rolled through the portal, her tablets were already linking with the local network. She supplied the pass codes given by P'ing an hour ago, and they were linked into the city's defensive computer grid. In moments, a virtual battlefield came alive on her display, providing a rich, textured image of the land around the terminal. Minu donned her headset and linked it with the tablet. She knew she might not be able to sit comfortably in the transport for much longer.

"Try and establish a link with Christian," she ordered.

"Here so soon?" was the first thing he asked.

"Might have been nice if you'd told me you were bugging out," she said in her coldest, most level voice. "Now we're here."

The connection was quiet for almost a minute. Minu knew he was weighing the situation, like any good scout. He might be riding an ego trip, but the job came first. As she waited, the radio link with Christian started relaying data from his team. More maps became available to her. The virtual battlefield expanded by leaps and bounds. Christian commanded twenty scouts in the central defensive complex next to the capital's Portal Spire. They, along with about a thousand Beezer soldiers, had the Tanam pinned down inside the spire and were taking only sporadic fire. After all the reading she'd done, Minu knew what was going on in moments. The cats were preparing to execute a textbook breakout maneuver, right out of the Concordian playbook.

"Hold your position, we have this under control," he said finally. "We'll call if we need you."

"Your back is against a wall," she said, "you launched an attack half an hour ago."

"They can't make a move without getting their asses shot off." Minu started to tell him just how much trouble he was in but he cut her off, yelling over her. "Damn it, Minu, you're here under orders to assist me, and that means waiting until I call for you." She considered telling him what an idiot he was being, and trying to explain to him that when the cats broke out, they'd envelop that five story defensive mini-fortress and chop them to pieces. But it wasn't worth the time. Time they just didn't have. With a curse she cut the voice channel, keeping the data coming in to feed the virtual battlefield.

"Orders, boss?" Gregg sat behind her in the command transport, waiting patiently. Of course he'd heard the exchange. Minu wondered if Gregg would take her orders over the First Among the Chosen, then she chastised herself for even thinking it. Of course he would; all her friends would. And she'd do the same for them.

"There are hundreds of warehouses around this distribution portal complex," she said and called up the maps. "Link back home and contact the fort; here's what I want done."

Minutes ticked by rapidly as Minu directed her soldiers in their frantic labors. There continued to be only sporadic combat around the distant Portal Spire, the tallest building on the planet and just five kilometers distant. She kept the virtual battlefield steady in one eye as she gave orders. Every time the eyepiece flashed a warning of weapons fire, she stopped what she was doing and watched, praying that this wasn't it. After each brief exchange wore down, she went back to work. "Every ten minutes or so," Gregg observed.

"Just enough to keep our attention," Minu said.

"You figure the cats are just buying time?"

"Without a doubt. Standard Concordian military procedure when facing a dug-in enemy is to deploy as much force as possible and break out with unopposable numbers." She used a hand on the tablet control at her belt, changing views on the virtual battlefield. The Portal Spire came into view, soaring more than a kilometer above the tallest nearby building.

Gregg turned to watch a trio of transports being frantically loaded before speaking. "The Beezer aren't going to like this."

"They'll like it even less if we fail." Gregg nodded but still looked concerned. "What I wouldn't give for some artillery.'

"The Concordia don't really use it." He glanced back at her, then at his wrist chronometer.

"Well, they have huge high-energy direct-fire cannons, the closest thing to arty, I guess."

"We roll the couple we took intact through this portal, and they'll know it, right away."

"I know," Minu grunted and continued to examine the maps, "that's why they're being moved back to Fort Jovich and not here. Did you confirm what I asked about a few minutes ago?"

Gregg busied himself with a tablet, pretending to ignore her. She punched him in the back, hard. "Ow, damn it!"

"Answer me."

"Yes, he's with Christian." Minu looked down and sighed. She'd expected it all along, but finding out Aaron was fighting a few kilometers away sent a jolt of unexpected fear into the pit of her stomach. "He was ordered to work with the unit because of his experience under you. He didn't do it because he wanted to."

"I never said he did; now get back to work."

"Yes, boss."

Minu turned to her tablet and tried to stop thinking of the powerfully-built Aaron. Handsome Aaron. Aaron who always smiled when he saw her. There was so much more there, and she struggled against allowing it to dominate her mind. She needed all her faculties to concentrate on what she was trying to pull off.

The lack of artillery was a fundamental shortfall in her ability to fight like a human army. "The projection of force beyond the curvature of the horizon," was how it was referenced in old Earth military manuals. The invention of long-range artillery on Earth had fundamentally altered how wars had been fought. In among the thousands of hours of Concordian military doctrine Pip had helped Minu steal years ago, before he was critically injured, was a few minutes showing high-energy cannons in use. The damage they could inflict was beyond description. Brought to bear against an unprotected city, you could carve it up like a pie. Even in the many thousands of years of Concordian history they'd seldom been used except in the deadliest of wars. An enemy would usually surrender once defenses were battered down, or at the mere sight of a battery of high-energy cannon being set up. It was the Concordian way. Better to give up and salvage something. Not to acknowledge the inevitable when you're about to be overwhelmed was considered insane. If it hadn't been for the small primer, she'd have never been able to use the ones back on Amber against the cats.

She again turned to look at the distant Portal Tower. Gregg looked away from the dark expression on her face. Even a few dozen old howitzers would shake things up. She made some notes and turned back to the work at hand. The portal was open again and, one after another, transports were sliding through. They were painted in the same green/brown scheme as her own, but each had a little red outstretched claw on the nose. Green Army was arriving.

"How much longer?' she asked him after a moment.

"Six done, two more to go; maybe an hour?"

"Maybe?" He shrugged, and she grumbled. "Where is Cherise when I need her?"

"Probably drinking mead in Chelan," Gregg said and checked off something on his tablet.

Weapons fire erupted at the Portal Spire. Minu spun her view in the virtual battlefield and watched. After a moment the intensity doubled, then quickly doubled again. "We're out of time," she said and ran for her transport. "Get the logistics people back through the portal and mount up!"

Her transport hummed to life and began lifting off as the last man was boarding and the door still closing. "First and Second Companies, on me!" she called and tapped the computer control. With her other hand she checked her gear to be sure it was ready. Shock rifle over one shoulder, light pack with extra equipment, miniature energy shield on her belt, its switch taped to the back of one hand. They'd trained in the use of the new shields, getting the hang of when to turn them on and off. They covered you out to a little more than half a meter. Turning them on prematurely could spend them against weapons fire that wasn't going to hit you. You only activate them when you're directly exposed and in harm's way. Once you're hit, your training was to fall back behind someone else who was still shielded. Last was the dagger on her waist, an older design made from steel native to Bellatrix instead of dualloy. It dated from her trials and carried a heavy emotional meaning to her.

Satisfied her gear was in place, she checked on the deployment of her forces. Dozens of transports poured out of the factories around the remotely located portal she'd been using. The Tanam weren't monitoring the area; one lone portal out on the periphery of the city was of no concern. The Portal Spire held dozens of portals, and the cats had been making use of them for hours. *How many thousands,* she wondered. *Tens of thousands? Is this a smash and grab, or an army of occupation?*

As they cleared the warehouse complex and began approaching the spire from a circular course, she could see the Tanam in full battle suites working to set up heavy weapons defensive points just outside the spire, under the cover of withering beamcaster fire. Christian, with only a few dozen Chosen and the overly cautious Beezer soldiers, fought furiously to stop them. The sectional shields on the structures protecting the Chosen and Beezer were failing in rapid order, leaving the fighters unprotected. And still there was no call for help. He meant to fight to the death in spite of the help available only a few kilometers away. There was no way he could face the Tanam suites. Their battle suites were a smart suit of armor, the equivalent of an old Earth tank, but much more, with suites of built-in, computer-controlled weaponry and countermeasures.

"You fucking moron," she hissed. "You stupid testosterone-soaked stubborn man."

"Don't indict all men just because of him," Gregg pleaded. She could see the pilot nodding in agreement, but she could also see them both smiling.

"I'll think about it. Var'at, you there?"

"Ready to go," hissed the Rasa from one of his own, more capable, combat transports. When the lizard and his force surrendered and were later taken in by the forgiving Chosen, they'd had dozens of their own transports. It'd made sense for Minu to let them keep the machines. Besides, the interiors were scaled to their own more modest builds.

"Begin your bombing run," she commanded.

"As you order. It's good to work in our profession again. We're not farmers!"

A dozen of the more advanced and heavily-armored Rasa transports broke formation and screamed away in sections of two craft each. They covered the distance to the spire in a minute, hugging the side of the spire and looping around just under the speed of sound, and in a flash they descended on the Tanam massing there. The enemy was intent on their breakout from under the guns of the Beezer and Chosen and didn't notice the new combatants entering the scene until they were on top of them. Chosen and Beezer looked up in surprise as the Rasa transports raced over their position and dropped a line of glittering canisters around the base of the Portal Spire. The Tanam dove for cover as the projectiles began falling among them; even massively powerful battle suites avoided the attack as quickly as they could. Incredible war machines the combat suites might be, with armor, life support, and weaponry, but a bomb could destroy them. The ECM module alone would be beyond Ted's capability at the moment. Once again, she grieved Pip's loss.

The bombs didn't explode. They were covered with razor-sharp spikes that slammed into and stuck onto whatever they hit, be it moliplas, dualloy, or ceramic concrete. Feline faces rose from protection to blink in confusion at the spiny cylinders just as they burst and unleashed a swarm of bots. Minu had all but emptied the bot stores at Fort Jovich before deploying, and Logistics wouldn't be happy. She knew this was a make-or-break mission for the soldiers...and maybe humanity. If the cats took Serengeti, it would only be a matter of time before Herdhome fell. Her soldiers weren't ready for a battle of that magnitude. Bellatrix would be defenseless, and what happened to a client species when their protectors fell was a gray area.

She didn't want to be living under the whiskers of the Tanam while it was all hashed out.

The myriad of bots attacked the Tanam and their equipment in earnest. Crab-bots used pincers to snap weapons and bone with equal ease, while turtle-bots brought lasers and beamcasters to bear. Much rarer and many times more expensive dragonfly-bots zipped among the Tanam using deadly miniature energy weapons to blind, maim, and kill. The Tanam breakout fell into momentary disarray.

"Christian, come in," Minu called over the radio.

"What the hell are you doing?"

"Attacking," she said deadpan. "I would think that's obvious."

"We had the situation—"

"Completely fucked up," she finished for him. Gregg snorted and covered his face. "Yes, I can see how under control it was. I'm sending you coordinates; get the hell out of there. That defensive installation is going to fall in five min—" Minu stared at the dead screen in stunned silence.

"He severed the connection," Gregg told her.

"Stubborn son of a bitch," she snarled.

"Oh, you two were made for each other."

The Tanam followed procedures in dealing with a bot attack and threw out canisters of their own bots to fight the enemy machines. Their canisters popped and scattered arrays of more modern and more deadly bots, which stood there and did nothing. Minu knew their operators would be panicking now, trying to understand what was happening. "So predictable," she said, "and they still haven't figured out what we're doing to their bots."

"Why would they?" Gregg asked. "You don't mess with the bots; you just send them to fight. Isn't that what the Concordian book says?"

"Yep," Minu agreed, "but still, sooner or later they'll figure the PUFF out and come up with a way of countering it."

"Then we'll come up with something new again," Gregg said confidently. Minu wished she shared his confidence. Ted and his crew had improved the PUFF so it only affected enemy bots, but with the inventor of so much of their advantage lying in a coma, it seemed their ability to invent new tricks had been severely diminished.

"Order the four Achilles transports into the air." Gregg spoke into his mike and Minu saw them leave the warehouses. Through the virtual battlefield she watched the Tanam battle the thousands of bots with hand-to-hand weapons and their claws. Battle suite-wearing warriors seized bots in their strength-boosted arms and crushed them or smashed them on the ground by stomping their powerful legs. "B Company and C Company, Green Army, Red Army, hit them from opposite sides." She indicated the locations on her computer, and the information was forwarded. Transports broke formation and darted away. Unlike the bombers, these stayed low and wove through the deserted avenues around the spire. In minutes they were landing to deploy hundreds of soldiers, both human and Rasa. The troops formed up and began moving forward even before they were all on the ground. Hundreds of hours spent doing grueling drills were paying dividends.

"Get in as close as you can," she told them. The Tanam continued to fight the bots without realizing they were being encircled. When the soldiers were within two hundred meters, she gave her order. "Attack!" Hundreds of weapons fired as one.

Beamcasters, flechette, and shock rifles spoke, mowing down hundreds of Tanam before they even realized what was happening. Caught flatfooted, they tried to rally as the humans and Rasa rained death upon them. The human shock rifles went through shields like they weren't there, and the Rasa used beamcasters to disable the shields, then finished off the unprotected soldiers with their deadly streams of flechette darts. The Tanam fell into disarray. Being caught between the marauding bots and the withering fire of the soldiers was like being fed feet first into a wood chipper. The Tanam finally organized enough to begin retreating back into the Portal Spire under unorganized cover fire, taking casualties at every step.

"Push them," she ordered the troops. At her words they broke cover and began to advance, marching in long lines and firing in volley. It was a rolling wave of high energy death. Minu observed the slaughter and swallowed, her mouth suddenly gone dry at the spectacle of destruction. The Tanam had no idea what to do with carnage of this magnitude.

"Now it gets ugly," Minu said. "Achilles ready?"

"Orbiting at one kilometer," Gregg confirmed.

"Okay, send them in."

"Company C command to CIC…"

Minu flipped to the channel immediately. The C Company commander wouldn't call unless something was wrong. "Minu, go."

"The Chosen are abandoning their defensive positions."

"About time, what is their angle of retreat?"

"They aren't retreating," the man told her, "they're attacking the spire."

"No, damn it, no!" Minu roared and tried to reach Christian. Gregg looked over and shook his head. The channel was open but he wasn't responding. "Christian, don't go in there! They're massing for attack! We're going to hit them hard, you don't want to be in there!" Still no answer.

Minu slammed her fist against the transport bulkhead in her fury. She knew Christian had seen a momentary advantage and was going to try and decapitate the Tanam by finding and neutralizing their leader. Kick them while they're down, as one might say. The problem was they weren't down; she'd just managed to screw up the dance by smacking them in the face hard and fast. They were recoiling from a bloody nose, but not defeated. Their disarray wouldn't last. Unable to make room for the thousands more Tanam at their backs, they'd retreated to the relative safety of the Portal Spire. Minu spun her controls on the virtual battlefield until she found them. A dozen brave Chosen leading a few hundred foolhardy Beezer. Too late, they'd already reached the Portal Spire and were flooding in through an auxiliary freight entrance. "Christian, please, stop! I'm begging you?"

"I just bet you are," he finally replied, a laugh in his voice. "Thanks for the opening, now I'm going to finish this."

"You don't understand, there are thou—"

"It's you who don't understand, Chosen can do things your scurrying soldiers can't. We don't use tricks, we use brains and speed. We're a scalpel, compared to that sledge hammer you've made. I'm going to end this with as little bloodletting as possible."

"Christian, there are thousands of Tanam in there. You're going to get yourself and all those Beezer killed!" Only silence answered her. "You moron," she said quietly.

"The Achilles are holding position," Gregg said. Minu was about to yell at him for not following her order, but then she just sighed. The virtual battle field followed the Chosen in to the spire then began to dissolve, but not before the first wave of Tanam began to descend on them.

"We can't just let them die," she said, arguing with herself. "But he knows what he's doing. Damn it, why do men run around like crazed kloth in combat?"

"Comes with the testicles." Minu gave Gregg a veiled look, and he turned away.

"Red Army, Green Army, Companies B and C, hold them in there. Pin the damn cats down and don't let them get a whisker out of that spire. Hold until relieved."

"Done," Gregg said.

"Company A, on me," she ordered, and her own company peeled off toward the spire.

* * * * *

Chapter Sixteen
Octember 24th, 521 AE

Portal Spire, Capital City, Serengeti, Beezer Leasehold

It hadn't been part of the plan, but since when did battles *ever* go as planned? Minu remembered something about a general on old Earth making a statement to that effect. The Tanam in the Portal Spire now knew beyond any reasonable doubt that they were surrounded and desperately wanted to break out. The feint against Amber had failed to distract the Humans long enough. Minu knew the Tanam must have spent hours pouring vast amounts of war materiel through the portals. The inside of the Portal Spire was probably as crowded as a Chelan bar at quitting time. Hundreds of troops with their transports and weapons to be used in the pacification of Serengeti were crammed into the building.

The garrison of Beezer and a handful of Chosen scouts believed they'd been successfully holding the cats inside the spire. The reality was the exact opposite. The Tanam commander was biding her time, letting the humans feed on their own delusions. With a good sense of what little true opposition she was facing, she knew she could easily break out, encircle the defenders, and finish them off piecemeal. Minu's arrival with almost two thousand specially-trained soldiers was tearing that carefully laid plan to pieces.

"Can anyone tell where the scouts are inside the spire?" she asked over the command frequency. There was no answer. If they assaulted through the same entrance Christian had used to penetrate the spire they were all but certain to meet the stiffest opposition. On the other hand, if they forced an entrance elsewhere, it could take a long time to find them, if they were even still alive. The spire was average in size, only half a kilometer across at its circular base and four times that tall. Hundreds of landing pads circled its exterior to ease in the arrival and departure of traffic. The upper levels contained the offices of trading companies and were most often used for foot traffic. It was easier to move people up to the heights than it was cargo. The Tanam would be forced to use the lower levels to bring through and stage their war machines. Likewise, it would be all but impossible to move any heavy equipment or transports up the rapidly-thinning interior and have them exit through those openings. That could work to Minu's advantage.

"Establish a reinforced perimeter," she ordered her platoon commanders. "Up for a little special close-in work?" she asked Var'at on a private channel.

"Always," he hissed. She transmitted the details and knew the alien would be smiling in his open-mouthed manner. It was risky and unplanned, exactly the sort of tactics that Minu had employed to defeat the Rasa during their Vendetta. "We're with you, leader!" She heard the hissing cheer of other Rasa in Var'at's personal transport. Rasa were bred for battle and happy to be back at their trade after long months in exile. Minu felt relief that the question of the Rasa's loyalty was now forever put to bed. She believed they might well fight to the last for her, something they'd been unwilling to do for the leaders of their own species. But would they fight like that for any human commander? She wasn't so sure.

"Take your best platoon and follow me as I break off," she told the Rasa Commander.

"You teach us, Commander, and we'll learn."

"Come, and we'll learn together!"

"Yes, I like that!"

Minu tapped out orders for the rest of Company A on her tablet. "Cover the top of the spire, no matter the cost. If they break out, all is lost." The transport made almost a complete orbit around the spire as the soldiers deployed. Two kilometers below, weapons fire poured into and out of the spire like a holiday fireworks display, beautiful and deadly lances of energy trading back and forth. Every second there was more fire lighting up the sky. Beamcasters and sporadic shock rifle blasts sought out the entrenched enemy Tanam while they fired back with withering volleys of beamcaster and hypervelocity accelerator guns. No signs of the heavier energy weapons, at least not yet. Her people would be keeping a sharp eye out for the first sign of the heavy weapons and be ready at a moment's notice to direct all fire at them. The Tanam would wait as long as possible out of fear of losing the guns.

The city of Serengeti and the spire were taking the worst of it. The pitched battle was tearing the city apart as effectively as a demolition company. Heavy beamcasters sliced and tore at the surrounding structures like wild animals. She could see a hundred buildings in flames, and dozens had collapsed already. Minu just hoped that those buildings had been evacuated before the worst of it started. Christian would have informed the city leaders of the coming battle. Amid the swirling maelstrom, her soldiers fought and died.

The battle was as well in hand as it was going to get. Minu looked the situation over one last time, both out the window, and through her virtual battlefield, then spoke into her radio. "Ready Var'at?" she asked.

"Always for you," he replied.

Minu tapped the driver on his shoulder. "According to the plan," she told him.

"Yes ma'am," he said, and she felt the transport change course toward the Portal Spire. It was hit almost immediately by a beam-caster. Minu could see the first warning light come on. Weapons fire seared the air all around them and the pilot began to maneuver radically.

"Get me there, soldier," she said.

"I will," he assured her, and the transport danced like a fish.

For a short time as they raced toward the spire, they flew unchallenged. Then, at roughly the halfway point, her transport was acquired again, and they started taking fire. The pilot wasn't going to be taken so easily. He dodged with dizzying turns, spins, and pure instinctive flying.

Then suddenly they came up against the spire. The pilot spun them around, and they moved along for a short distance before setting down in the fastest landing Minu had ever experienced. "The soldiers are yours," she told Gregg as she leaped to her feet and raced for the door.

"Don't be long," he told her. She could see how badly he wanted to go with her.

"Hold them, Gregg."

"We will," he assured her, and a second later, she was out the door with her personal squads.

* * *

The change from the relative quiet of the transport to the horrendous roar of battle was stunning. Like all her soldiers, Minu wore high-tech ear plugs that compensated for dangerously loud sound spikes, but the baseline noise was so loud, it was almost like not wearing them at all. The pilot set them down on one of the small upper-level landing pads, on the opposite side from where Christian had made his ill-advised intrusion. Only a few meters below were hundreds of Tanam soldiers, all firing their weapons, and themselves being shot at. The sounds of firing beamcasters, high-powered accelerator guns, big brothers of those the Rasa carried, shields being hit and overloading with a screaming blast, and the building itself being torn to pieces was a serenade straight from hell. Minu understood for the first time the adage of 'no atheists in foxholes.'

"Through here," she called the squad leaders to follow her. Minu chose a maintenance entryway, the hatch sitting slightly ajar, possibly dislodged by a nearby weapon impact. "We need to get out of the fire line before we get tagged by friendly fire."

"Friendly fire, isn't!" intoned her squad as one, making her smile grimly.

The two squads made it safely to the hatch and quickly through to the interior of the Portal Spire. Before going inside, Minu bumped up the power on her radio to maximum. If she lost eyes and her virtual battlefield, she'd lose her ability to command the army. The last man pulled the hatch closed, and they were inside.

"Find us a drop tube," she ordered her men. The interior was a maze of tunnels and crawl ways, little more than a maintenance area. Two men scurried off into the labyrinth. Less than a minute later they'd found something, but not what Minu had hoped for. "You're kidding, right?"

She'd wanted one of the hoverfield lifts common in elevated facilities. A small out-of-the-way drop tube would go unnoticed by the Tanam, who were fully occupied with the rampaging soldiers. Jump and drop tubes used all kinds of sensors and safeties to be sure users were delivered to their destinations unharmed and at a safe speed. They'd found a dedicated light cargo lift, using the same hoverfield principals, minus the bells and whistles. "Damn," said the senior squad sergeant; another man whistled. The hoverfield projectors were a couple meters across and hummed menacingly. They'd all ridden a jump tube; this was more like a moon rocket.

"Any idea where it goes?" Minu asked.

"Down," the man who'd found it said.

The other leaned over the emitter a bit and looked down, the gravitic field causing his short hair to stream upward. "Yep," he agreed.

Something made the hair stand up on the back of Minu's neck. Her hand slid to the grip of her shock rifle and she turned without knowing why. Two Tanam were about twenty meters away, wearing dark colored scout armor, and they were leveling weapons at the unaware humans. Just like at the firing range, Minu raised her weapon to her shoulder, stabbed the energizing button with her left thumb, and swept off the safety in the same action.

Bzzaacrack! Bzaacrack!

Both Tanam crumpled to the floor, dead, as the rest of the soldiers spun. "Always have eyes out," she warned them. And just like that, her legend grew. "Scouts, by the look of their armor. You two," she indicated the ones who'd found the lift, "check the approaches. They probably know we're here."

"Limits our options," the sergeant said. Minu eyed the drop tube and nodded.

"Okay squad, with me," Minu decided.

"With all due respect, Chosen," the sergeant said.

"Don't even say it, Sarge. Form up and follow me." Minu took a good two-handed grip on her shock rifle, one more deep breath, and stepped into the drop tube.

She plummeted downward with no concern for such things as human physiology, cartilage, or blood pressure. It felt like ten G's of acceleration, and she almost blacked out. Luckily, the trip was as short as it was brutal, and she came to a mind-numbing stop at the bottom, stumbling off just before the first of the squad behind her would have slammed into her back. In moments, men and women were tumbling out of the tube, like laundry from a dryer. Minu, still shaken from the trip, found herself at the bottom of a dog pile. "Well, that was fun," she mumbled into someone's boot. A moment later, the two men who'd watched the rear dropped into view and added to the pile.

Once Minu extracted herself from the bottom of the pile, she sent men out to set a perimeter and figure out where they were. Her virtual battlefield filled in quickly as the soldiers' data filtered into her computer. They were almost a kilometer lower, most of the way to the floor. Almost ideal for her plan, if you could call it that.

"Sarge, take your men out to the central landing and prepare for the assault." The man nodded, and the wall exploded.

Minu hadn't expected the Tanam to guard all the landings; it wasn't worth the effort and manpower. She'd thought they'd set up a sensor to watch for an assault of her type, only they'd expect it to land via transports, not drop out of nowhere. There'd probably be a couple to tend the back door. It was just the luck of the draw that one of them was on their floor. The battle suite crashed through the blown-out wall, all weapons firing and middle arms lashing out with scythe-like metallic claws. That the warrior was wearing a battle suite was the worst kind of luck.

Soldiers not immediately killed dove for cover or fired on the suite. The massive war machine couldn't stand up all the way in the three-meter-tall lift space as shock rifles flashed against its fields. The operator dropped to all six legs and charged like a runaway train. Minu just managed to grab her rifle from where she'd leaned it against the wall and roll to one side; the sergeant she'd just ordered wasn't so lucky. The Tanam warrior sliced him nearly in two with a casual gesture, hot blood spraying Minu like a sprinkler as she rolled. The floor was instantly soaked in it, and she went sprawling.

Four soldiers knelt and fired their beamcasters at the suite in volley fire. The overlapping fields and shields of the suite flashed from yellow to red in the second it took to lumber around and kill two of the gunners. It spun once more and went after another group of soldiers organizing an attack. Minu slipped and slid on the floor until she reached one of the downed men and snatched up his beamcaster. One of the other dead was a girl no more than fifteen. She stared up at Minu with glazed eyes wide in surprise.

Minu swallowed and slung her shock rifle, then hefted the beamcaster. Taking careful aim, she thumbed the override on the controls and fired a sustained shot next to the Tanam. The particle beam vaporized a long gouge of floor, pelting the suite's defenses but causing no damage. Another override and another shot, this time the other side. The Tanam turned, finally noticing the attack behind it, and pointed an arm. Minu took an instant to slap the switch on the back of her left hand and her personal shield popped into life. As the enemy fired, she unleashed her final shot.

The Tanam's beamcaster smashed into her shield with enough energy that Minu felt the skin on her left hand blister. Another half second, and her shield would snap off, and she'd cease to exist. Her own shot flashed just behind the Tanam, tearing up more floor. She got a glimpse of the feline warrior, her face partially shaved and covered in tattoos, teeth bared in perceived victory, just as the floor gave an ear splitting screech of failing dualloy, and collapsed.

The warrior began to fall, all six limbs shooting out to grab at something, anything, to arrest its fall. The force field that made it almost invulnerable also made it difficult to grab anything outside the field. Looking for all the world like a cat that's missed a jump, the Tanam dropped through the hole, scrambling and yowling. Minu had no idea what was below them, but the crash of the suite's landing took five long seconds and was immediately followed by an explosion. She looked down at the shield control on her wrist. Five percent remained. Maybe another tenth of a second?

Minu checked her virtual battlefield for the status of her two squads. Ten were down, seven dead for sure. They'd defeated the suite-armed Tanam warrior, but at a catastrophic cost. Rescue was out of the question now; no way with only eleven men. The second squad sergeant was looking down at the unblinking eyes of his first squad counterpart while the lone surviving medic went around quickly checking for anyone that could be saved. There were two. "Stay with them," she ordered the man, who nodded gravely.

The nine soldiers still able to fight followed her through the wreckage from the brief battle to the interior of the spire. The inside was hollow, it's inside walls lined with platforms and jump tubes. She pulled her binoculars from their pouch and began scanning. Below, every square meter of floor was covered with vehicles and formations of troops, just as she'd known it would be. She wasn't out for vindication, she was looking for something.

"Can I help, Chosen?" asked the surviving sergeant.

"No, not unless you've spent a few hundred hours studying Concordian troop deployment procedures." She slowly panned along the groups, finding bot carriers, troop transports, and a squad of tanks in a design she'd never seen before—she pressed the record button on the binoculars—and next to them, four transports carrying the feared heavy energy cannons. They were deployed near the rear, far from the door. Their intention hadn't been to use them here then. They'd be saved for the next target, Herdhome. "Damn it, where are you?" she growled as her gaze moved on. She dialed up the power on the computer magnification all the way, and individual Tanam warriors came into view. There were no other species present, and that was unusual. Most of the elite species preferred bots to do their dirty work. Or even better, lower-order species. You didn't have to pay to have a dead alien repaired or replaced.

Just when she was about to admit defeat, she found what she was looking for. "There," she told the sergeant and clicked a button on her binoculars. The coordinates transferred to the rest of the unit, and soon they were all looking where she was. A few dozen meters of floor far off to one side, protected on three sides by load-bearing walls, were three Tanam females standing in the center of a group of warriors. The warriors were all resplendent in shiny battle armor and kept their eyes trained outward, watching for any threat to their charges. A pair of the nearly unstoppable battle suites also stood guard. "Highborn," she told them, "and likely the assault commanders."

"So what's the plan?" the surviving sergeant asked.

She took a deep breath and considered. While she watched, another warrior would occasionally rush up to the three, bow low and wait, then run back out. No field, she realized. They almost certainly have a shield up, even if we can't see it, so sniping is out of the question. Besides, with the Tanam, taking out the highborn will more than likely drive the rank and file insane, instead of forcing retreat. The last thing we need is a fight-to-the death against thousands of crazy cats. Then as she was watching, the pair of warriors in suites that were guarding the highborn turned and stomped away. It could only mean one thing; another attempt to break out was about to begin. It also meant that the highborn were no longer guarded by the massive suited warriors. It was the chance she was looking for.

"Quick, before they start feeling vulnerable," Minu urged and was up and running. The soldiers were hot on her heels as she ran as fast as she could around the interior of the spire to reach the same side as the highborn. The battle outside was increasing in intensity once more, and Minu could feel the spire vibrating with weapons fire as they ran. Halfway around, they started taking fire.

From opposite them, a team of Tanam warriors was firing beamcasters at the racing humans. The suite-clad warrior she'd disabled had gotten off a call for help after all. Minu dodged between supports and equipment as quickly as possible while doing everything she could to maintain her forward momentum. A glance toward the new arrivals showed still more coming up a jump tube. They were about twenty meters from their destination when another squad of warriors began arriving almost in front of them. Her squad all dove for cover behind a huge machine, all but one man making it.

Beamcasters burned from two directions now. One of her fire teams set up suppression fire as Minu consulted her virtual battlefield. They either had to take out the squad in front of them, or give up on their objective and find a route of retreat. She turned and could see the burned corpse of the soldier who didn't react in time. The sounds of battle outside intensified still more. The breakout was under way. She had to do something, and quick.

"Sergeant, how far is it to the jump tube we were heading for?"

The man used his binoculars and risked popping his head up a couple times to take the needed readings. "About forty meters." Minu's fingers worked on her tablet, manipulating the controls on her virtual battlefield. She chewed her lip for a second and made her decision. It's too far, time to improvise.

"Okay soldiers, we've got one chance to stop this slaughter, and it's a long shot. If we pull it off, we can save Serengeti and the Beezers. Are you ready?"

"Yes sir!" they all barked.

"Okay, let's do it!"

* * * * *

Chapter Seventeen
Octember 24th, 521 AE

Portal Spire, Capital City, Serengeti, Beezer Leasehold

With a hail of fire, the soldiers broke cover. They split their fire between the two groups trying to pin them down. First one man, then another went down from enemy fire. The Tanam near the jump tube began to move to cut them off. And that was when Minu, in the lead, turned and jumped over the railing, followed by the surviving soldiers.

"This is crazy!" one of the men yelled as they plummeted toward the floor.

"Trust the technology," Minu called back. Halfway to the floor, hidden hoverfield generators kicked in and each of them was caught, their descent slowed and controlled. Minu took her binoculars and oriented herself with their target. She dropped the glasses onto their strap and brought her shock rifle up. Firing a scoped weapon while falling in a hoverfield was *not* something she'd trained for. Luckily, she'd practiced regularly for just about every other situation.

Minu acquired her target and fired in rapid order, dropping the three closest Tanam guards before she'd gently set foot on the floor. The safety mechanisms in the spire's inner core had worked as designed, delivering the entire team within meters of their objective.

The other soldiers began firing, and the rest of the Tanam guards nearby died in quick order. As Minu had seen from above, no one was using fields, and the shields were transparent to the shock rifles. The last of the dozen guards went down, tossing a small case of bots on the floor as she fell. One of Minu's squad flipped on their PUFF and the bots went inactive as soon as the case broke open. The Tanam guards had gone down so quickly, the surprise of the attack was still rippling through the formations of warriors nearby.

"On me!" Minu yelled and charged through the opening, her men spread out into a tight spear around and behind her. Ahead in the center of the circle of warriors, the three highborn Tanam turned at the commotion to see Minu and seven soldiers charging toward them.

Veka was so surprised to see the humans, a bare paw-full and unarmored, charging into the center of her invasion force, that she first turned to look at her sisters Kelaa and Seela before responding. Charged with protecting their higher ranking sister, the other two were less surprised. Veka had all six eyes on Kelaa, and she responded to the situation as she would to any other; she activated her personal shield, drew two miniature beamcasters, one in each middle hand, and charged the humans with a roar.

"Wait," came the pleading voice of their older sister, "let the guards—" but she never finished the sentence. Kelaa took two great bounding leaps and her abdomen exploded as if a bomb had been hidden in her food. She gave a hideous screech and crashed to the floor in a bloody heap. "No!" Seela cried and drew a beamcaster of her own.

Less than ten meters away, Minu snarled in frustration as she fired again. The highborn weren't supposed to spend their lives in reckless abandon like this. It was the first time she'd seen a species of the Concordia meaningfully deviate from their rules of warfare. She aimed to wound this time, and her shot shattered the Tanam's left middle shoulder joint, and the newly-drawn weapon fell from now-useless fingers. She looked ready to charge, so Minu added a shot to the hip region. Flesh and bone exploded and the highborn crashed to the floor. The handgrip under her right hand buzzed against her palm. A small part of Minu's mind managed to get her higher brain's attention and told her that was the second warning from her shock rifle. The power pack was almost empty. "Swell."

She and her team passed the first highborn she'd shot. Despite the horrendous damage her shot had done, the female snatched out with her two top arms and grabbed one of the soldiers. He cried out in surprise and pain as razor-sharp claws penetrated skin and started to dig deeper. The soldier next to him fired at point blank range, and the Tanam's head exploded.

Minu finished covering the last few meters, her weapon held high against her shoulder and pointed right at the head of the last standing highborn. "You are my prisoner!" she yelled at her, the translator turning it into the growls and snarls of the Tanam language.

"You've killed two of my sisters," Veka snapped; only her incredible will kept her from snatching up the petulant human and biting its head off. That and the seven other humans now surrounding them. As she expected, none of the hundreds of nearby warriors were doing anything to stop the humans. They'd never dare risk injuring a highborn. Seela mewed miserably and rolled in agony on the floor. Obviously the humans had no such qualms.

"Only one is dead, and she gave me no choice. You're my prisoner."

"I acknowledge," she said and gave the minimum head bow required. "How do you expect to remove your prisoner through all my forces?"

"You'll surrender your forces to the Tog, and us, their human soldiers."

"Soldiers? I believed you were Tog Chosen."

"I'm Chosen; these are soldiers. We have thousands more outside ready to assault this place and kill every one of you if necessary."

"You're a poor liar; the Tog would never engage in such warfare."

"We are not the Tog." Minu used her left hand to flip on her headset, taking a quick glance at her shock rifle as she did. Three, maybe four shots remaining. The only downside of the shock rifles was it took a good five seconds to change power packs. This was getting interesting. "Gregg, you there?"

"On station boss." His transmission was full of static, and she could hear the sounds of combat in the background. She desperately wanted to ask him how it was going out there, but made herself keep to the script.

"Are the Achilles all ready?"

"Ready and standing by."

"Send the first one in, sector three."

"Acknowledged. Are you okay?"

"Fine, we have the Tanam leader prisoner and we're beginning negotiations." Minu turned her attention back to the Tanam highborn. Despite her surrender, Minu hadn't moved her shock rifle a millimeter, and the Tanam hadn't moved either. "You have five minutes to surrender your command."

"You're deranged."

Minu nodded and consulted her chronometer. "Five, four, three, two…" The Portal Spire was rocked by a blast that shook it to the core. Ceramic concrete dust and chunks rained down from high above, and one platform in the distance collapsed a hundred meters to the floor with a thunderous, slow crash. "Now four minutes, highborn."

"You won't destroy this place," she spluttered, "You lack the weapons! The Tog don't own any energy cannons, we know this as fact!" Minu glanced at her chronometer again, and when it reached the right time, counted down once more. "Do you think you can intimidate me, a highborn noble from the highest of the higher-order species?" *Crash!* The building shook even worse this time, and a huge section of wall to one side caved inward, trapping and crushing dozens of warriors, their equipment, and transports. Veka hissed nervously, her two sets of movable eyes darting around to take in the growing panic of her warriors. "You wouldn't destroy this building, no matter how you're doing this damage; the Tog would never allow it."

"I already told you, we are not the Tog!" *Crash, boom!* This time the explosion penetrated to the spire's interior. Flame blossomed through the wall, followed by the bright afternoon sunlight. Above them, the entire spire's immense bulk shivered.

"You'll sacrifice yourselves to defeat us?"

"I'll sacrifice myself, and all my soldiers, to save the Tog, and even the Beezer."

Veka snarled and spat on the floor, then spoke. "All forces retreat immediately. The crazed humans are bringing the Portal Spire down."

Minu nodded and clicked her radio transmitter twice. The fourth blast never came. "You're still my prisoner, even if you will not surrender your forces."

"Yes, what do you want of me? We can buy your entire pathetic world, wherever it is."

"Release any prisoners you hold, and leave here as fast as you can."

"Is that it?"

"Yes." All around them, warriors were beginning a mass exodus through the closest portal.

"Some of the prisoners are of great value to the Tanam, to the Concordian Council itself. We do not—"

"That does not concern me in the least. Those are my terms." Minu held her ground, gun never wavering a millimeter from the highborn's head. All she needed to do was press the transmitter two more times. "Your bargaining position is tenuous at best," Minu said, showing her teeth. Veka was a cat, right? She knew cats showed their teeth as a threat, and hoped it held true in this case. "One or two more, and the building *will* come down."

"Very well, we have an accord! Cease your attack!"

"Very well." Minu activated the radio. "Gregg, stand down the Achilles and have all soldiers cease fire!"

"We're clear, Minu," Gregg's voice announced. Was it her imagination, or was there a slightly hysterical edge to it? "They've stopped firing from inside the spire; do you want us to mount an assault?"

"No, stand down and monitor the situation." Veka showed a small amount of teeth, and Minu quickly spoke. "If you don't hear from me in five minutes, destroy the building."

"How dare you question the honor of a highborn Tanam!" Veka roared.

"I trust you as much as I trust any species of the Concordia," Minu countered and bowed respectfully, though the barrel of the shock rifle never left its target. "Five minutes remain for your evacuation."

"You didn't specify that in our agreement."

"You didn't request a specific time interval."

Veka looked around at all the equipment staged and laughed. "You humans are growing up quickly."

"You'd be surprised at what we're capable of."

"And you have no idea what we're capable of. You have a *real* enemy now, human, not just the scurrying, bug-eating Rasa."

"Oh, are they behind this?"

"Perhaps." Minu nodded and asked no more. She knew there was no chance of getting more information at this point. Besides, she had a friend that knew a lot more about the Rasa than any Tanam ever could. "Four minutes, highborn."

* * *

The last of the Tanam warriors and their larger equipment were being shoved through any portal that was still accessible. Minu's Achilles, transports laden with as much high explosives as they could carry, had done an incredible amount of damage to the spire, and forced the enemy commander to retreat or risk losing everything. Veka stood impatiently with a pair of guards as the last of the heavy equipment she could get out was moved through a portal. In this case, the heavy energy cannons. Minu would've loved to add those to the others captured on Amber.

She glanced around at the vast amount of equipment Veka was abandoning and suppressed a smile.

"Your time's up," Minu told the highborn Tanam, "where are my hostages?"

One of the closest portals deactivated and immediately flashed to life again. Through the shimmering field was visible an advanced Concordian-designed facility, where a group of humans huddled under guard. Eleven men, all nearly naked and most injured, stood dejected and awaiting an unknown fate. Behind them was a crowd of Beezer in similar condition. "You will honor your deal and free me in exchange?"

"I will. Bring them through."

On the mysterious distant world, a pair of armed and armored Tanam warriors watched the unexpected scene on Serengeti. Minu examined the group and quickly spotted both Christian and Aaron's tall frames. One she was exhilarated to see, the other not so much. At a signal from Veka, they were moved forward by the guards and stepped across space to arrive back where they'd started. "Hey boss," Aaron said. He couldn't wave; both arms were immobilized at his sides by bloody bandages. Several of the scouts were helping their brethren, and in more than one case outright carrying them. The Beezer followed next, and behind them…

Minu tried not to gasp in shock as the trio of Squeen came into view. There was no mistaking their appearance, bipedal squirrels no more than a meter tall, with long dexterous fingers, big bright black-on-black eyes, and even a bushy though rather short tail. "We are reluctant to give up these scurrying vermin," Veka snarled.

"What is your quarrel with them?"

"They are *Gracktaag*!" she spat.

Minu glanced down at her translator in confusion. It was rare to come across a word with no English analog. When it did, the device usually still found something, even if it wasn't a good match. "I'm sorry, what is that?"

Veka turned a pair of eyes on one side toward her; the larger third eye in the row was wide angle and could not be consciously controlled. "Nothing; I'd forgotten you're not Awoken."

Minu was about to inquire further when the first of the three Squeen arrived before her. He or she looked up at Minu, head cocking from side to side to give both eyes a good look. The being wore no clothing, only the remnants of a torn equipment belt. No doubt the Tanam had relieved them of whatever else they'd had when captured. "I do not know your species," it said in a very low clicking language that her translator instantly recognized.

"We're humans, in service to the Tog."

"Ah, then I know of you, though we weren't told you were a hominid species." Minu could have sworn the Squeen was trying to put the pieces of a puzzle together as it examined her and her companions. "I am Quick Finder, and these are my companions." The translator added a single beep after the name, and now she knew Quick Finder was male. "Are we now your prisoners?"

"No, you are free to leave."

"Interesting," he said and used a hand to smooth down the fur on his head.

"Your release was an accidental side effect of our victory against the Tanam."

Veka grumbled low in her throat and Quick Finder glanced from her to Minu and back again. "Very interesting," he said and glanced at his two companions. After a quick glance at the unconscious form of Seela he looked right at Veka again. "Bested by a young species of hominids?" The growl turned to a threatening snarl. "This is a story that has never been told before. I will enjoy telling it over dinner!" Christian and his surviving scouts were clear of the portals and gathered nearby as newly-arrived medics rushed over to see to them.

"We've met our side of the accord," Veka said with a tiny bow of her head, though her eyes never left the group of Squeen. Minu burned with curiosity to know what was going on.

Minu turned to her radio and directly linked with Christian. "Are there any unaccounted for Scouts?"

"No," was his monosyllable reply.

She nodded and turned back to Veka. "The deal is complete; you are released."

"Oh that wasn't smart," Quick Finder said and along with his friends took off at a run.

"Huh?"

"Very well," the highborn said and lowered her head. She growled something at the two remaining warriors, then spoke to Minu directly. "I challenge you *personally*!" And fast as a bolt of lightning, jumped at Minu.

Some small part of her must have been expecting it because she fell back at the last second and raised her shock rifle. Before she could fire, Veka's serrated claws hit the outstretched shock rifle front and shattered the foregrip, along with all the important electronics located there. She wasn't hit directly by the claws, but the impact from the strike was enough to turn her backward dodge into a wild spin sideways. Veka's follow up blow, an upper cut that would have disemboweled her, swept through empty air.

"Minu!" Gregg cried, and along with the seven soldiers who'd been guarding her, raised his shock rifle.

"Do not interfere!" Minu screamed at them. Either through luck or training, no one fired. "This is a personal challenge." The Squeen were taking cover behind the injured Chosen and medics, watching the events unfold with their big dark eyes.

"She was your prisoner," Aaron complained, his voice full of confusion and obvious fear for her. Even with both arms crippled, he looked ready to take on the Tanam with his teeth.

"I set her free, then she challenged. It's legal under Concordian law."

"You're not as primitive as I would have believed."

Minu looked down at the shattered weapon and tossed it aside, being sure it went toward her troops and not the other Tanam. Veka circled her a few meters away, down low on all six limbs, appraising her just as she'd seen house cats on Bellatrix do before pouncing on a howler. Minu saw what looked like hesitation or uncertainty. Was she hoping to be shot after the challenge? It would've been a horrible breach of Concordian law and may have allowed the Tanam to declare war directly against the humans. To sacrifice your life for such a goal was an amazing display of selflessness. This was one crazy pissed-off cat.

"Come human, let us dance."

"Do not interfere," Minu warned her men, "no matter what happens. That's a direct order."

"Minu," Aaron almost whispered.

"Yes?"

"Kill the fucking cat."

Minu reached down to her ever-present ankle holster and drew her knife. Twenty-five centimeters of gleaming stainless steel, curved on one side, false edge on the other, and serrated teeth against the back side near the handle. She'd carried it since the trials as a remembrance of the cost of leadership. It had only taken one life, and that was during those very same trials.

"You mean to fight me with *that,*" Veka asked, a huffing laugh in her voice. She held out a paw, and five ten-centimeter-long claws slid out like daggers, making her lone blade look almost pathetic by comparison. "You'll wish you had more knives, little human."

"Are you planning to talk me to death?"

Veka hissed and pounced.

Minu passed the knife from her right hand to her left. She was better with the blade in her right, but she needed that hand free. Veka came in high, the front part of her body raised so all four sets of claws could rake at her, trying to scoop Minu into a meat grinder of a hug. Minu dropped and rolled, flashing out almost blindly with the blade, and feeling it bite flesh. She rolled to her feet and saw the satisfying flash of bright red blood on the weapon. One of Veka's middle legs dripped blood on the debris-cluttered floor.

"You can scratch me all day human, I only need to strike once."

"You'd have to actually touch me first." Again Veka charged, and again Minu's blade tasted flesh. A third try, and she only scratched armor, and on the fourth she almost died. Veka's all-out lunging attack changed with catlike grace into a feint, and in an instant, those massive jaws were reaching for her. Minu tried to turn away, putting out a hand to push against the neck of the Tanam for just a little help moving. The jaws snapped closed on her hand.

"Your game is over," Veka said around her forearm.

"Big mistake," Minu said through teeth bared against the pain. Then she overrode the pain signals. As a doctor had told her years ago, it's not real pain, just mechanical feedback. She moved her hand within the Tanam highborn's mouth, searching, then grabbing. Veka's look of victory turned to surprise, and she bit down as hard as she could, splintering a tooth on the arm's dualloy superstructure. Minu squeezed, overriding the arm's natural safeties and exerting twenty-times more force than a human could hope to muster.

Blood sprayed as the organ was pulverized. Veka screamed and tried to shake her off. Minu refused to let go. The pain was so intense the Tanam never thought to use her formidable claws. With Minu dangling from her mouth it would have been a simple matter to render the human into fish bait. All she could think of was to get the pain out of her mouth. She shook from side to side, howls of agony reverberating from the spire's walls.

Finally she slammed Minu down on the floor. Minu shook the stars from her head, set her feet against the underside of the Tanam's jaw, and pulled with all her being. Veka shook at the same time, and finally the human's hand was out of her mouth, and so was most of the tongue. A gout of blood splashed Minu, the bright red stuff spurting from the Tanam's mouth like a grotesque fountain. Minu jumped up, dropped the severed organ, and switched the knife back to her right hand. She swung with all her cybernetic might at the spot between Veka's eye sets.

The never-closing rear eyes did their job and the still functioning part of Veka's animal brain sensed the attack. Veka rolled her head to one side and Minu's blade slammed into her rearmost left eye instead of where Minu had aimed. The pain took the highborn beyond all reason. She rolled backward, away from the attack, landing with a thud on her back. Minu jumped up, the knife held in both hands, driving toward her enemy's exposed belly for the coup de grâce. Veka screeched and swung wildly with a midarm. The impact was more of a punch than a slashing cut. Hundreds of kilos of force slammed into her legs, sending Minu spinning wildly across the ceramic concrete floor. She crashed down almost five meters away, landing on her left arm as the bones snapped.

Fighting against the pain, Minu rolled over and looked, ready for whatever happened next. She needn't have worried; Veka was racing on all six legs toward the nearest portal. One of her guards had already activated it and, once she was through, they followed. The retreat was so fast Minu didn't have time to get a good look at the destination before the portal closed.

A thousand voices rose in cheers around Minu, many crying out her name and pounding the ground with feet or weapons. A few of the more excited fired their guns in the air, but squad leaders quickly put a stop to that. They didn't want to bring down the critically-damaged Portal Spire around their ears. Gregg and Aaron weren't cheering; they were racing to her side. And despite his injuries, Aaron was the first there. "Medic!" he yelled.

As he came running up, she was examining her cybernetic arm. A few optronic connectors were protruding from the shredded skin, and her pinky finger was twitching uncontrollably. "I'm fine," she growled, "I need a mechanic though." She sat up and checked her left arm, wincing from the pain. The radius or ulna was broken, maybe the elbow, and some torn ligaments. At least she wouldn't have matching arms!

"Minu, don't move!" Aaron gasped as he knelt next to her, fear written on his face like a book.

"Gregg," Minu said to her second in command as he ran up, shock registering on his face too. "Stand down and safe that last Achilles."

"Done, boss," he said, swallowing.

The medics came over, and they looked worried too. Now Minu was getting mad. She tried to get up and her legs wouldn't respond. It was then that she looked down and saw both legs were practically filleted. The floor under her was awash in blood, and she could see the sickening white of bone through both thighs. "I guess she used her claws after all." And then she passed out.

* * * * *

Chapter Eighteen
Octember 24th, 521 AE

Portal Spire, Capital City, Serengeti, Beezer Leasehold

As Minu came to, the medtechs were swirling around her, attaching machines and shouting orders to each other. She did her best to beat them away and speak to her commanders. She hadn't wanted to go over the details until the Tanam were gone for fear of them overhearing; now she was insane with the need to know. Finally she'd had enough.

"If I don't see Gregg over here in the next minute, I'm going to twist the head off the first son of a bitch I can reach! And get me on my feet, damn it."

"Chosen, that would be unwise," a young medtech explained, and Minu made a wide sweeping grab for his closest leg. The man squeaked indignantly and jumped clear. She was sitting on a gurney resting almost on the floor, her back elevated to forty-five degrees and both legs wrapped in complicated trauma pads. Inside, micro-miniature robots were working to stabilize the massive wounds, but the injuries were beyond their ability to fix in the field. Perhaps even in the Chosen hospital. Two burly soldiers roughly shoved the man out of the way and hoisted their fallen leader onto her feet between them. A few meters away was the sizable puddle of blood from her mangled legs. Despite the pads, blood began to dribble over her feet.

"Damn it boss," Gregg swore as he came through the wall of medtechs, "are you stupid or just too damn stubborn?"

"I'm unable to make a clear determination on either opinion at the time," she moaned but refused to allow them to set her back down. "Humans are at a real disadvantage against all the killer beast-ies in the galaxy." She looked down at the dagger back in her belt and sighed. "We need something better. Anyway, give me the num-bers. I want the butcher's bill."

"That can come later." She looked at Gregg hard and long, her resolve obvious even to him. "Okay, we lost about two hundred, maybe half that injured."

Minu set her jaw and nodded. So many young people, gone for-ever. All the months of training, their lives up till then, spent and gone. "Any unaccounted for?"

"Not that we know, no. Christian reports that everyone who went through alive came back with him."

"What about their weapons?" Gregg looked confused. "Shock ri-fles, damn it, what about their shock rifles."

"I didn't ask about that."

"You need to; I want every one of those weapons accounted for and to know how many weapons the cats took, and what shape they were in."

Gregg nodded that he would find out. "We did it boss." Gregg half-grinned. "We really kicked their asses."

Minu whistled. It had been her biggest gamble, that she wouldn't have to actually bring down the spire, and that the four of six she'd managed to get loaded would be enough to do the job if necessary. Luckily for all concerned, she'd been right on both accounts. Her unauthorized appropriation of the transports and the explosives she'd stuffed into them would be a minor infraction next to what she'd done to this Portal Spire.

"Just got word," Gregg said after listening to his radio, "Jacob and Dram are here."

"Oh, goody," she said with a cockeyed smile.

From a nearby working portal she could see an entourage of Chosen escorting Jacob and the towering dark figure of Dram. Even from dozens of meters away she could see the stunned look on their faces as they took in the devastation around them, the random scattering of Tanam bodies, and finally the orderly lines of dead human soldiers. Before he could get to her a medtech got her attention.

"Chosen, please…"

"I said leave me the hell alone."

"It's not about you, it's about the Tanam."

"What Tanam? I thought they were all dead."

"The highborn you shot just before the battle ended is still alive."

It was then she remembered the second of the three highborn Tanam, the one who'd drawn a weapon and charged her after she'd shot the first of them. "They didn't take her with them?"

"Frankly, I think they wrote her off as dead. We did too, until someone heard the breathing."

"Will she live?"

"If you authorize the medical work. We're not normally allowed to render aid to aliens without permission."

"Do it," she said, "a highborn might be worth some ransom." Besides, she admitted to herself, it was the right thing to do. She hoped they'd do the same thing for her in a similar situation, but considering the condition of the Chosen prisoners that'd come back through, she rather doubted it.

"What have you done?" asked Jacob as he came up behind her.

"I told them to save the life of that Tanam highborn."

"Not that, you idiot!" Minu turned slowly, both because there were still two soldiers holding her up, and because her anger was seething just under the surface. "I'm talking about this!" He took in the ruined Portal Spire around them with an over-exaggerated gesture of both arms, like a game show host showing off a particularly impressive prize. "I said relieve the siege on Serengeti, not blow the fucking place up!"

"The Tanam had thousands of warriors here, assault vehicles, support, and heavy energy cannons."

The last brought Jacob up short. "Energy cannons? Why would they bring energy cannon for a target like Serengeti?"

"Because after this they were going to Herdhome, why else? This whole thing was a setup. They knew about the soldiers, that's why they attacked Amber first. They had heavy cannon there, too. I don't think they were expecting a well-trained force, or the shock rifles. If we hadn't acted quickly, Serengeti would have fallen, and then Herdhome."

Jacob looked from her to Dram, then down at her legs. When he saw the trauma pads soaked in blood and more pooling under her feet, he paled. "Good lord, what happened to you?" Minu explained about her duel against the Tanam commander while Dram talked with the head medtech and looked at her nervously.

"We need to evacuate her and the worst injured immediately," Dram told Jacob. "This conversation can happen later."

"You're right," Jacob agreed, and the medtechs swooped in and gently placed Minu back on a hoverfield-equipped gurney. As they moved her, Jacob walked alongside and continued to take in the damage and death. "I just can't believe what you did to this place. What was your plan, anyway?"

"My plan? My plan was to win."

* * * * *

Interlude

The mountain winds blew strongly across the rocky outcropping, making the pair of warriors crouch against the overhang for cover. Their fur was more than enough to keep them warm, but relief was hours overdue and they were becoming concerned. The shields they'd set up kept their presence a secret, but only so long as they had power to operate them.

Just as night was approaching, the nearby portal flashed, and they became instantly alert. The senior of the two snatched her computer and read the communication in dismay.

"Our forces were defeated on the filthy grass eaters' world."

"Impossible," the other growled.

"We're ordered to abort. The third attack is postponed." They both looked at the portal and growled their anger at the storm that raged around them. So much effort gone to waste.

"And this invaluable artifact? We cannot reuse it."

"I know," the senior snapped, making the younger warrior bow her head in supplication. "We'll take our weapon power packs and rig them to keep the shields running. It'll last for years if necessary; the shields will recharge them when summer comes to this matriarch-forsaken place."

"If it ever does."

The senior warrior didn't reply; she just began packing their gear. An hour later, they activated the portal and passed through, leaving no trace of where their camp once was. Under the masking shields waited the portal they'd brought with them, unused and patient as the stars. A kilometer away, a farmer lead his goats up a winding trail toward a nearby mountain meadow, only hours from Steven's Pass.

* * *

The medical bots moved back, and the doctors consulted and discussed options. Their patient was mildly anesthetized and in no immediate danger. The course of treatments would be critical. While they were working, none of them noticed a pair of heavily-armed warriors enter the operating theater, armor gleaming and golden, weapons at the ready. A second later their charge came in, her face shaved to the neck and covered with intricate tattoos telling a long story of battles, conquests, and leadership. When one of the doctors noticed the warriors he started to snarl in complaint. Luckily for him another doctor saw their other visitor and instantly dropped to both sets of knees. A lifetime of learning had taught the first doctor to respond quickly, and he joined all the others on the meticulously-sterilized operating theater floor.

"Matriarch, we beg you for our humble lives," they all mewed in unison.

"You live another day," she replied ritually, her voice aged but still strong. Few Tanam lived long enough to gain gray hairs. The matriarch was almost all gray with only streaks of red and yellow on her flanks. "That is, as long as you can save the life of my daughter." She made a gesture that allowed the doctors to rise to their feet, only both rear sets. No one, not even the eldest daughter of the Matriarch, was allowed to stand on their rear feet in her presence. "Tell me her condition."

"This alien did her serious harm, Matriarch," the senior doctor said, careful not to look her in the forward set of eyes. The two bloodline guards stood behind her, ready to enforce the law for the smallest transgression. "Her left main eye is lost, and can be replaced by a cybernetic one easily. It is her tongue that causes the complication. May the cybernetic specialist address this?"

The Matriarch made a dismissive gesture with a long razor-sharp claw inlaid with delicate scrimshaw. The first doctor bowed back into the group, gratefully abandoning the explanation to the specialist.

"Your daughter's tongue was torn out completely, Matriarch." She examined his face, noting a number of complicated tattoos displayed. Of course, being male, the hair wasn't shaved, but he obviously trimmed it short. It was a stretching of the law the Matriarch had allowed to take place on her watch. Her mother had been brutal in her enforcement of the law, often casting into the pits entire bloodlines of valuable warriors. She'd learned from her mother what worked and what didn't. Allow them a few harmless affectations, and they'd reward it with real faithfulness. Males were a necessary evil in many ways. Few females were interested in the sciences, and why would they be? Abandon glory and combat for science, even lifesaving science? Ridiculous.

"The organ cannot be re-grown?"

"You honor me with your discussion of my meager knowledge. It is not so, Matriarch. There is nothing left of the organ, it is as if it were torn out by a warrior wearing a suite."

"She has lost her speech forever?"

"If it serves you to listen, there is a way."

"It may, inform me."

* * * * *

Part II

It is a mistake to look too far ahead. Only one link of the chain of destiny can be handled at a time.

–Winston Churchill

Chapter One
Octember 29th, 521 AE

Chosen Council Chamber, Stevens Pass, Bellatrix

Sitting in front of the Chosen council was a familiar thing for Minu now. She'd lost track of how many times she'd been here. The table curved toward her where she sat in the middle; on the other side were the seven Chosen council members and a pair of Tog. She was pretty certain one was P'ing, a very high-ranking Tog who oversaw humanity for hser species. Minu was more comfortable than normal. Instead of the brutally hard moliplas chair, she was enjoying a form-fitting hoverfield-equipped chair. Her left leg was elevated, a Concordian-made device clamped where her foot used to be, working to finish the healing process. Sometime in the next week they'd be implanting a prosthetic lower leg and foot. It would be her second artificial limb, much to her chagrin. The left arm, much less injured than she'd feared, was only in a brace now, and was working fine.

"Chosen Alma," spoke the official recorder, who wasn't a member of the council, but a young Chosen man no more than fifteen from the newest group to come through the trials. "The council has just a few more questions."

"Are you well enough to continue?" interrupted Dr. Edward Tasker, chief physician to the Chosen.

"I'm fine," she said, "let's get this over with." In the center of the group, Jacob Bentley, First Among the Chosen, nodded, and the young man continued.

"When did you formulate the plan to use explosive-laden transports as weapons against the Tanam?"

"I didn't use them against the Tanam; I knew that wouldn't work. They were used to directly assault the Portal Spire." A grumble went up from the council. "As for when I 'formulated' the plan, that would be about a minute after I realized a frontal assault was out of the question."

The council spoke quietly among themselves for several moments while Minu waited and ignored the throbbing from her leg. Eventually the young Chosen spoke again. "And what about the decision to attack the interior of the spire with only two squads of soldiers?"

"Two squads were all I was willing to risk."

Jacob dropped the pretense that this grilling was by the entire council and spoke up himself, his dark, chiseled features slightly distorted by anger. "So you were willing to risk twenty lives on what, a hunch?"

"It was good enough for Christian to lead fifteen Chosen scouts and two hundred Beezer into the spire on effectively the same mission. I don't see him sitting here being grilled."

"Chosen Christian Forsythe has faced this council already for his poor decisions during the assault on Serengeti. We're talking to you now."

"Yes, you are." Minu fought her temper back under control and continued in an even voice. "Can we wrap this up?"

"Very well," Jacob said and smiled like a kloth eyeballing a crippled deer. "Does anyone else have anything to add?" Minu looked right at Dram, resplendent in his dress uniform, his skin almost as black as the jumpsuit. He returned her stare without comment, and Minu knew it was done. Two years of around-the-clock work, hours fighting almost everyone in power, enormous amounts of credits pried from the hands of greedy politicians, and more than a few dead friends had brought her here to this moment. And all of this pain, suffering, blood, sweat, and tears was to create the soldiers. The soldiers were to be the weapon to defend the Tog, and mankind on their leasehold of Bellatrix. And now they were going to take it away from her, and maybe her stars, as well.

"I would like to speak." Minu turned and saw the Tog, P'ing, unfolding from where hse rested on a mat, silent for the entire three days of the hearings until now.

Jacob looked stunned, completely dumbfounded. Minu doubted he'd look more surprised if his left arm suddenly jumped off and ran around the room. The whole council shared his shocked expression, all except Dram, who maintained his cool demeanor. "Of...of course, Concordia Master," Jacob said, bowing his head.

"Minu Alma, offspring of Chriso Alma, your actions were not in keeping with the long-established Concordian rules of warfare."

"That's correct," Minu replied, the council gasping at her temerity. Minu just sat and waited. She had no choice—she didn't know how the damned chair worked and couldn't walk out if she'd wanted to. The doctors said a dozen more surgeries were in her future before she'd walk again.

"You took the required classes all our Chosen are submitted to," hse said, not a question. One serpentine hand produced a tablet of the style the Tog preferred, slimmer and easier for them to wrap their long, snakelike fingers around. Hse consulted the tablet for a second before continuing. "Your marks were exceptional in these classes, like every other training opportunity you took. It is noted in your transcripts that your instructors, even Tog instructors, found you 'precocious' and 'obsessed,' not with how the Concordia wage war, but why it's done the way it's been done for time beyond memory." Minu shrugged, not really caring if hse would understand the gesture. "After your training, you began service and continued your learning of unconventional warfare measures. You've taken every class in military matters we provided, as well as any your own world offers, and when that was not enough, you colluded with Chosen Pipson Leata to break into the Concordian Database here on Bellatrix and stole as much information as you could get away with."

"You did that?" Jacob roared in fury. "Have you any idea of the repercussions of your damned action?"

"I don't care," Minu snarled, struggling to get to her feet and almost managing despite the frightened look Dr. Tasker gave her. The posture she was forced to adopt was a half-slouching, half-sitting position, far from comfortable but better than lying back in the mobile chair. "I was given a task, but not the tools needed to complete it. Damn you! I was going to succeed despite your obstructionist attitude!"

"No matter what damage you did, no matter who died, no matter how much *shame* you brought onto the Chosen, and me?"

"Shame? Damage? You egotistical son of a bitch, this isn't about you! It's about our species' survival!" Jacob came to his feet instantly. "You just don't get it, do you? Except for the Tog, and maybe the Rasa, everyone else couldn't care less if we live or die! The ends, in this case, completely justify the means." Jacob took a deep breath, his face bright red with rage. He looked ready to jump across the table at Minu, and part of her wished he would, mangled legs or no mangled legs.

"First Jacob," P'ing said in hser emotionless voice, "you'll cease your transcripts of this proceeding, strike my last comment, and clear the council chamber."

"Concordia Master, please," Jacob begged, the wind instantly going out of his sails, "this is a Chosen situation, and we—"

"Will do as I have ordered."

The council rose and departed, conversations and shouted arguments barely waiting until they were outside. Jacob almost needed to be dragged from the room by Dram, who kept one massive hand on his shoulder at all times as they filed past Minu. As the young Chosen record keeper rose, P'ing reached over and relieved him of the tablet computer used for the transcript. The young Chosen looked confused and reverent at the same time, as he reluctantly gave up the device before walking out. Then the door closed, and Minu was alone with P'ing for the second time in her life.

"Resume your injured conveyance," hse said and gestured at the hoverfield chair, "your wounds are not healed."

Minu sat as gracefully as she could, basically collapsing backward into a heap. She didn't know whether to be excited or afraid, and settled for confused. Besides her legs throbbing, now her casted left arm felt like a missing tooth. The only thing in good shape was her cybernetic arm, which was fully repaired. "How long have you known about the data theft?"

"Since the day it happened. Z'kal realized what was happening only a few moments after you started your intrusion. It's not the first time Pipson made such an attempt."

"Then why were we allowed to take such a vast amount of data?"

"Vast? You have less than you thought." Minu looked down and wondered just how big the Concordian network really was. "I left very specific instructions with Z'kal concerning who was allowed to acquire forbidden information. Pipson was not on that list; however, you were."

"So I was allowed to think we were stealing data?"

"By Concordian law, you *were* stealing data; we simply did not employ our full abilities to stop you." Minu was dumbfounded. P'ing cocked hser head and regarded Minu with unblinking huge eyes, so inhuman, so expressive in indefinable ways.

"Why not just give us the data?"

"That was against Concordian law; we are forbidden at this time to give you that information. You are young, and have not had your Awakening. We could see your genius growing; we could witness the innovations and ideas just under the surface. You needed more information, more tools to begin to truly develop into what we hoped for."

There's the same term the Tanam highborn used, she noted—Awakened. "What do you mean, what you hoped for?"

"There's a lot you don't yet understand."

"Well, maybe you can help me understand? Wouldn't I be a more useful servant to the Tog?"

"More useful, and more dangerous." P'ing consulted the computer, though Minu knew there was nothing there that would affect this conversation. Did hse realize that hser last statement was caught by the translator and relayed? Minu fought against her emotions to stay as open to what she was hearing as possible, some part of her knowing this was a pivotal moment in her life; she didn't want to miss a single nuance. "You must understand I cannot tell you everything you want to know, even should I personally wish it."

"Concordian species never do."

"This is true. We are a thing of secrets, and lies. We have all colluded to create this web of deceit and come to an accord in that." Minu shook her head in stunned silence, then P'ing continued. "Many years ago, we found among your species our best, our brightest, our most inventive Chosen to ever come along. Young Chriso Alma excelled in every test and challenge, much as you have. Rising above disaster in his trials, he quickly rose through the ranks to become First. His ascension to First began a very difficult time for you Chosen. Many died, and more were lost without a trace. Including, to our frustration, Chriso himself. War came to your leasehold for the first time, and noncombatants perished." Hse paused for a full minute, perhaps in thought, before continuing. "I'm ahead of myself.

"The young First Chriso was so driven, he didn't consider his own needs in many ways. He would work until he collapsed from fatigue, sleep a short while, and return to the same task as if he'd never stopped." Sounds familiar, Minu thought. "This is admirable; however, it is by all indications damaging to humans and does not serve our purposes of growing your Chosen. A suitable mate was located, and he was required to reproduce."

Minu blanched, shaking her head again in amazement. "Are you telling me you made him marry my mother and have me?"

"Exactly. It's a shortcoming of your species that you have two sexes." *Speak for yourself,* Minu thought. "So we were unable to directly combine two successful First Among the Chosen lines. Instead, the offspring of a prominent scientist was mated with your father. You are the result. And once you were sired, your father lost interest in more breeding and returned to his duties."

Minu felt like she was going to puke. It took all of her self-will to keep her raging emotions under control and continue to listen carefully as the Tog continued. Her mother and father, an arranged marriage? Inconceivable! And yet, deep in her now-wounded heart, she knew there was truth. Truth she'd seen over her whole life in how her parents acted together before her mother died. And for that matter, even the circumstances surrounding her mother's death. "Naturally your genetic material was exemplary, as we'd planned, though Chriso was disappointed in your sex. Had we fully grasped the implications of your species' natural sexist issues, and that they would interfere with your career, we would have manipulated his seed to assure a male offspring. As it was, we found no problem with you, so we proceeded as planned.

"You were provided all the necessary pushes and opportunity. State-of-the-art Concordian learning tools were made available, and the best education your world could offer was given to you. As you approached sexual maturity, your father was ordered to make you Chosen."

"Make me Chosen? That isn't how it works."

"It works how we say it works. You are our Chosen; we can pick and choose as we wish. Does not every candidate stand before me when the final decision is made? The covenant between our species is simple, but direct. You decide how to pick the candidates who will be Chosen, we make the final decision. Your trials are simply the way you narrow down our choices. A particularly sexist way of doing it that overly favors physical prowess, while neglecting mental fortitude and general inventiveness. Regardless, Chriso defied our desires and refused to simply make you Chosen, even though you wouldn't have been the first one so appointed."

"Really? Who else did you just pick?"

"Another time, perhaps. Chriso insisted you go through the trials like any other candidate, and then no doubt proceeded to try and convince you not to. Luckily, you proved as incorrigible in this as any other task set before you, and here you are now."

"The council wasn't going to make me Chosen," she realized aloud. "After the trials, when you picked me, they were all outraged." *Except Dram,* but she kept that to herself.

"Correct. However, since you'd finished the trials, you were presented to us, as is tradition. They were sure that in your weakened emotional state, and as injured as you were, you would be completely unsuitable." Minu could swear that P'ing was smiling, despite hser complete lack of a mouth.

"You wanted to make me First Among the Chosen right then and there, didn't you?" It was an epiphany that allowed her to see the truth of it. All the times the Tog had interceded in her short career, the arbitrary promotion two years ago when she was on the verge of quitting. Even now, when she'd all but blown up Serengeti, and the council looked ready to have her shot by a firing squad, here hse was to save her. And, most of all, the unmitigated hatred of Jacob from the day of her first arrival. With her father missing, he was the logical choice for the new First, and the Tog had tried to make her First by fiat. It all made terrible sense.

"Intuition and insight are two of the criteria your parents were picked for, and it's bred true."

"Jacob didn't like that, did he?"

"No. He and the entire council threatened to resign. We couldn't accept the losses that would have resulted in. Analysis suggested twenty to twenty-nine percent of the Chosen would quit if a sexually immature female was placed as First Among the Chosen, especially if led by the protest resignation of the current council. So you were placed in service like any other Chosen."

"And they've given me every shitty job they could to slow my progress."

"Indeed, and every time they moved to impede your progress, you've turned it to your advantage." P'ing shook hser head in a very human gesture. "You humans revel in political intrigue of all kinds. So self-important, so obstinate, so intractable. Even after this, in the face of what you've accomplished against all odds, they were on the verge of throwing you from the Chosen because you took too much initiative."

"So here we are again," Minu said with a sigh.

"Indeed. You've exceeded your father in every way but one; his prowess as a scout in the field. We cannot force the council to assign you to a branch—that's their prerogative—but we have some power.

"Your…soldiers, as you call them, are exceptional. As brave as any Chosen we could pick ourselves, but with ten times the tenacity and a hundred times the capacity for violence. In all the years I've lived, never have I seen the Tanam so roundly bested in combat by a numerically inferior force." Now Minu was certain the Tog was smiling. There was history between the Tanam and the Tog; she was certain of that. "The soldiers' willingness to spend their lives in combat and their skills in warfare are unparalleled. The entire Concordia will soon be talking of them in hushed tones."

"And I'm to have them taken away from me, aren't I?"

"Yes." Minu almost screamed in pain and frustration. "Only for now. I'm sure that once they realize I don't intend to let them throw you from the Chosen, they'll shuffle you out of the way somehow, into a job with no exposure to anything useful. You've gained the ire of the council and the Beezer." Minu looked down in defeat. "But Minu Alma, you've gained *my* gratitude."

"I am your servant," she said solemnly. Hse nodded and moved toward the doors. "P'ing, can I ask a question?"

"You may."

"Why won't you tell us more—why are we only allowed limited database access? You said it was the law?"

"One day, when you're ready, and the time is right, will come your Awakening. On that day, all will be open to you, and we will no longer be your masters. It will be a unique Awakening, in many ways. At that time, should it be in your lifetime, we'll talk about many things. You'll thank me, and likely curse, me as well. It's the best I can offer." She sighed and nodded. Hse opened the doors. "Please come back in," hse told the suddenly hushed crowd outside.

Once everyone was back in and at their seats, and the recording device returned to the young Chosen, Jacob addressed P'ing directly. Minu could see he'd spent the intervening minutes composing himself, though stress still showed in the way he ground his teeth. "May we proceed now?"

"Of course, First. Understand this though," hse said, once again bringing Jacob up short. "Our Chosen, Minu Alma, is not to be removed from the Chosen, reduced in rank, or forced to retire. Despite her injuries and unconventional tactics, it is our judgment that she has acted in the true tradition of our Chosen and deserves to be treated as such."

"I see. Well, there's little I can do then, except this. Minu Alma is to be detached to service in the Training branch under Terrence Pegalio—" the dark haired Pegalio smiled, his long-time ambition to get Minu under his control finally realized, "—there to serve in whatever capacity causes the least amount of material damage and abuse to her fellow Chosen. An official statement of displeasure from the Chosen Council will be entered in her file; I have that much control."

"Noted," P'ing said, then hse addressed the council. "Please also note, I've decided that Minu Alma is appointed as the new permanent liaison to the Tog for humanity."

"What?" Jacob choked. "There's an ambassador elected by the planetary council to serve that purpose."

"Ridiculous. We've never taken that low-level bureaucrat seriously. From now on, all matters of communication and protocol between humanity, the Chosen, and the Tog will go through Minu Alma in her new capacity as Ambassador. She'll be assigned such staff as she needs, and office space will be created for her on Herdhome. In her new assignment with Training, due consideration needs to be taken that she can accomplish her new task for us. A fifty-fifty split of time between these new jobs should be sufficient."

Jacob sat with his jaw hanging open, unable to speak. Dram nodded and spoke for him, as the Second Among the Chosen. "It will be as you wish, Concordian Master." Then he gave Minu a small but unmistakable wink. The meeting ended.

* * * * *

Chapter Two
Octember 31st, 521 AE

Portal Spire, Capital City, Serengeti, Beezer Leasehold

Minu was due in surgery in an hour to have more work done on her right leg, the one that was more seriously damaged. She was spending every minute she could sending emails and sorting files. Her transfer wasn't official until she returned to duty. If the soldiers were to continue without her, she wanted to be sure the various unit commanders understood what had happened, knew where she stood, and realized how proud she was of them. The hundreds of emails from her soldiers spoke volumes about how much they thought of her. She had a casualty list from Gregg and vowed to send a letter of condolence to the family of every soldier on it.

Just calling them soldiers no longer felt appropriate. Any person with a gun and a uniform was a soldier. Her men and women had acquitted themselves with guts and aplomb. None of them surrendered. Not a one failed to carry out an order. She'd been thinking about it for some time, and thought she was close to a decision, when a gentle knock came from the hospital room door.

"Are you okay?" She turned to see Christian standing a few meters away, dressed in a hospital robe similar to hers, carrying a portable vital signs monitor.

"I'll be better when I can walk again."

"Did they throw you out of the Chosen?"

"No, but not for lack of trying." He nodded and looked down at the floor nervously.

"I was surprised you weren't there testifying against me."

"They tried to make me."

"Really?"

"Yeah, I told Jacob to shove it up his tight ass." Minu laughed, then gritted her teeth against the pain in her prepped legs.

"I needed to come here and tell you something."

"So talk, it's not like I'm going to walk away." He shared a small laugh with her; Chosen humor.

"Thank you for saving our lives. No, wait, let me have my say. For the last six months I've been a huge asshole."

"Massive," she corrected.

His face looked stormy, but he nodded. "I can accept that. You didn't do anything any other Chosen wouldn't have when faced with a chance to gain advancement and help the organization. I became a jerk, jealous at your success, and did my best to sabotage you every step of the way. For that, I'm truly sorry."

"You forgot how you tried to beat me and Cherise up in Leavenworth."

"We thought you were homosexuals."

"What the fuck does that have to do with anything? You know for a fact there are half a dozen Chosen men who've shared beds for ages; it's the worst-kept secret in the organization. Was it just that you were afraid she could give me something that you couldn't?" The storm clouds returned, and she moved to head them off. "Your male pride is safe. You were my lover for months, Christian; do you really think I prefer girls?"

"Well, no, I suppose not."

"Then let's leave it at that, shall we?" He nodded and looked defeated. "Apology accepted. I hope we can be friends again."

"Maybe something more someday?" She looked skeptical. "Only if I earn it. I know I have a *lot* to make up for."

"Agreed. You can go a long way by helping integrate the scouts into the soldiers' organization. There're more kids on the way soon from the next round of trials, and it looks like I'm going to be training some of them. Take those kids under your wing; don't let them become antagonistic toward the soldiers."

"I promise."

She gestured to him and he came over. She grabbed him and pulled him into a hug, finishing with a light kiss on his lips. "I knew the man I cared for was still in there, somewhere, even during the worst of it."

"Thanks. I wasn't so sure myself."

He left after a few minutes, his departure leaving Minu feeling a deep sense of closure she hadn't felt since their relationship broke up. She didn't think she'd ever be with him again, but at least he wasn't her enemy now, as she'd feared he was before. While she was waiting to go into surgery, she saw a young doctor go by, and saw he had a lot of orange fur and blood on his clothes. "Excuse me, doctor?"

"Yes, ma'am?"

"Chosen will suffice." He looked at her a little surprised, then saw her gray right arm.

"I'm sorry, you must be Minu Alma."

"Correct. I assume you're working on the cat I brought back?"

"That's your handiwork? You made a real mess of that being."

"I'm all broken up over it." He was no more than twenty, relatively short, with square-cut curly dark hair, and a wide nose that spoke of Summit Tribe heritage. His name tag pronounced him as Dr. Julio Rico, and the glare he gave her made it obvious he disapproved of her comments.

"Well, she'll live, no thanks to you. Her name is Seela, highborn to the Tanam ruling family."

"You know a lot about them."

"I'm about the closest we have to a xenophysician, I guess. I've studied under Tog xenophysicians for years now and was lucky enough to read a tablet on the Tanam."

"I didn't figure she was alive after the fight."

"She lost her left mid-arm and left leg to your nasty shocking rifle."

"Shock rifle," Minu corrected and earned another glare. He was quite cute. She suddenly felt like kissing him and shook her head hard to clear it.

"Ready for surgery?" asked a nurse and Minu turned to see her pumping medicine into the IV.

"Ah, now I understand." she said with a slight slur. "Doctor cutie-pie, one more question?"

For the first time, he smiled. "Sure."

"What are they going to do with her?"

"I haven't heard, but she doesn't want to be ransomed back in the shape she's in so we're just going to rehab her as best we can."

"Oh," she said, falling back toward the mattress slowly but steadily. "Night, night," she mumbled.

"Sweet dreams," the doctor said as the lights went out.

* * *

Minu had always loved the vistas from the Steven's Pass facility. Of all the various installations the Chosen owned and operated on Bellatrix, this was by far the most picturesque. The view almost made up for the building's drab ceramic concrete block construction and squat profile. At its peak, it had once held most of the currently serving Chosen; now less than ten percent called the six spokes and central hub home. The room she now occupied was in the busiest section, the medical wing, on the fifth floor recovery ward. Perhaps as a result of the three gold stars she wore, she had an exterior room with an incredible view over the valley below. A beautiful Julast day, she could just see the gleaming little village of Chelan some kilometers distant below. During her early years, it was the most common place to escape to; now it held little appeal.

She spent most of her time in the hospital trying to avoid pain and reading. The reading was her standard fare of college material, some research linked to her recent experiences, and more on what P'ing meant by Awakening. The Concordian database defined Awakening as the time when a client species was given full access to the Concordian computer network. It was one of the most stringent rules of the empire that young species which had yet to Awaken weren't allowed full access. Doing so could bring down swift and horrible retribution, supposedly up to destroying a planet. That was possible? And that was the extent of the information on Awakening she could find. The damned computer just clammed up. And there was nothing further on the subject in her bootlegged data, either.

Minu avoided thinking about her own fate and how she'd ended up where she was as much as possible. A few times, like when she was trying to sleep, the thoughts would come unbidden. Her father had probably never loved her mother. He'd married her only because the Tog demanded he produce an offspring. Her mother had always been the matriarch of the family, telling Minu proudly where her ancestors came from and how important she was. It was her mom who'd first told her that the story of Mindy Harper was about her own ancestor. She'd tried a couple times to remember her mother and father openly showing affection for each other, and failed. A kiss on the cheek and a 'be careful' was all her mother would offer when Chriso left to do his duty. He would nod, smile, pat Minu on the head, and go. Never once had he told his wife that he loved her. Their family was a lie—a deception, or worse. An exercise in eugenics by their Concordian masters. As the days rolled on, her depression settled into a deep funk.

"Good afternoon, Chosen," came a cheery voice from the doorway.

"Nurse Ratchet," Minu grumbled.

"Now, you know my name is Yukiko," she replied, her disgusting saccharine cheeriness undiminished. "I don't know why you insist on calling me that."

Minu smirked; her command of old Earth movies was about her only weapon against the medical staff. "Time for some exercise."

"Come back after lunch," she said and glanced at the stack of tablets sitting on the desk. Did some of them have dust? "I've got too much work to do now."

"You've dodged too many sessions," the ever perky dealer of pain admonished. "Now, up and out of that bed!" Minu tried to complain again, but quick as a flash the nurse was there. She slid an arm expertly under Minu, and had her swung out and onto her feet. And that was the problem. Signals from her nerves met cybernetic linkages, hesitated, complained, and pain shot up her leg and threatened to make her knees buckle.

"Damn it," she gasped and struggled to stand. Unlike most of the time, she succeeded and stood on her wobbly feet. The damage done to her legs was extensive, but not as much as what the kloth had done to her right arm years ago. This time they'd managed to salvage the limbs. The bones were now dualloy, the joints moliplas hybrids, and many of the muscles were synthetic cybernetic actuators (the same as in her arm), but at least the skin was hers. Scars and all. "I'm turning into Frankenstein's monster," she mumbled.

"Okay Frankenstein, let's take a few steps!" Yukiko laughed. Minu put her left arm around her, wishing she was on her right side, but the nurse seemed to know better, and took a tentative step. The pain was just as bad.

"How come it hurts so fucking much?" she demanded for the hundredth time.

"Like your doctor explained," the nurse said for the hundredth time, "the link between your bone and the cybernetics must grow together naturally. If you don't exercise that connection, it won't be as strong. Also, the neural interfaces between the new artificial muscles and your nerves are still healing. Your arm was more straightforward. Instead of the main nerve linkages, in this case, there are hundreds more when living muscles have been grafted to cybernetic ones."

"They should have just taken the whole damned legs," Minu complained. Minu had horrified Dr. Bane by suggesting they simply take the legs off. It was, of course, medically unethical to remove salvageable body parts, even if it would make more sense.

"You're just being stubborn. You Chosen are such babies, sometimes."

"Watch it," she warned the petite Peninsula tribe nurse, who just smiled in reply. "How did you end up all the way on the other side of the planet, anyway? Ouch!" One more step toward recovery.

"Many in my family have become scientists and technicians working for the Chosen, including my only brother. So I came here to be closer to Tranquility, where he serves. Medicine has always been something that interests me."

"And it was only a small step from medicine to torture! I understand now." Yukiko made a little good natured laugh. It had proven impossible to get under the girl's skin; no doubt that was the main reason she'd been assigned to Minu after the first therapeutic nurse left in tears.

"You're doing much better today!" the nurse said. Minu snorted, then realized it was true. After the first few agonizing steps, it was much less painful, with the majority of the hurt coming from the dualloy pins in her upper thighs. They provided additional stability to the new metal/bone joining while it grew stronger. With growing optimism, she took some more steps.

Later that afternoon, while she was gagging down some lime gelatin, there was a knock at the door. Minu looked up to see Cherise with a box in her arms. "Ready for a visitor?" she asked.

"Absolutely." Minu laughed and waved her in. "Pardon me if I don't stand; there's no ass in this damn gown."

"Nothing I haven't seen before," Cherise said with a smile full of meaning.

"Very true," Minu agreed, her cheeks turning hot. "What did you bring me there?"

"Something to make you feel better." Cherise brushed the door closed with a foot as she came in and sat the box on the tray Minu was using to eat in bed. Her friend cleared away the food tray and the offending contents. She took a sniff of the gelatin and dropping it in the trash with a grimace.

"Yeah, doesn't taste any better than it smells." Minu opened the box and inside found a big stuffed rabbit. "Okay, sure."

"What, it doesn't make you feel better?" Minu shrugged, so Cherise took the rabbit and, with a rending tear, pulled its head off.

"That kinda makes me feel better…"

"I've got to get you out of this place," Cherise joked as she stuck a hand into the severed neck and began to pull. Amid a puff of stuffing she produced a bottle of Minu's favorite brand of honey mead.

"Oh, fuck yes!" Two glasses were secreted, one in each leg, and the arms held flatbread-wrapped Rasa mutton sandwiches. Soon they were sipping mead and munching the sumptuous sandwiches. "You're a lifesaver," Minu said around a huge mouthful.

"So I've been told. How're the legs coming?"

Minu stuck one out from under the sheets to show it off, metal pins and all. "It hurts still."

"At least it's not gray."

"Yeah." Minu decided not to mention her trying to talk the doctor into an outright amputation. "Dr. Bane says its insides are from the same stock as the arm. After the Vendetta, they bought a large supply of the same models. Got them pretty cheap, from what I hear." Minu held up her right hand and turned it around, admiring the design. She'd long ago gotten used to it as part of her, despite the color difference and only having four digits. "He said the salvagers that sold them to us don't know the origin, and nothing comes up in the database we have access too. Whatever species they're based on must have come and gone long before we were even cavemen."

"Probably looked a lot like us."

"Except gray," Minu agreed. "Did you know there aren't any other hominids out there in the Concordia?"

"I didn't know that."

"Me neither, until I met the Squeen at the end of the battle on Serengeti. Once I could think straight again I did a search and confirmed it. We hairless apes haven't done well in the Concordia, only two others in the last 100,000 years, and both of the others just up and disappeared."

"How does a species just disappear?"

"Ask the Squeen; they managed to do just that." Minu had also found out when she woke up that the Squeen had been allowed access to a functioning portal by the Beezer and quickly departed for parts unknown. She hadn't pursued the supposedly long-lost species any further yet. Finding a camp of them on a supposedly dead world was coincidence enough; running into a group on Serengeti was like getting hit by lightning twice in a row. She needed to get cleared for duty before she started trying to solve any more mysteries.

The two women sat eating their contraband meal in silence, finishing only a minute before a nurse stuck her head in to be sure everything was okay. The nurse narrowed her eyes suspiciously at the two, both smiling at her in return. She sniffed the air, and Minu hoped it didn't smell like mutton sandwich and mead. "Good grief," Cherise said when the nurse finally left, "when you getting out of here?"

"Next week, but I'm not going to be allowed to return to duty for another two months."

"Excellent!"

"Hardly! I have stuff I want to do, and a lot of it means being on duty."

"You are a certified workaholic, you know that?"

Minu shrugged. "I don't have a family or a love life; what else is there to do?"

"I can take care of one of those two…"

"Shhh," Minu hissed. "They might be monitoring us in here."

"They wouldn't dare," Cherise said, but still let the subject drop. "I have some leave saved up; why don't you come home with me for a few weeks?"

"Sure, I'd rather live in Chelan and not be able to work than spend a week living here again."

"I haven't lived here for months; I bought a house back where I grew up."

"Desert Tribe? I don't even know what city you're from."

"City? Hardly a city. It's a little town called Naomi, about two hundred clicks from Mt. Sahara."

"Oh, well, I don't know…" Minu thought quickly for a reason not to go, then thought again about how selfish she was being. Aside from a small dinner with Pip's family after he'd been critically injured, she'd never been to the homes of any of her best friends. And she knew the least about the Desert Tribe's people.

"Quit making excuses, and just say yes."

"Okay, yes."

"Great, I'll fly you there in your own car when you get out of the asylum."

"Chosen Minu, time for exercise!"

"Yes, Nurse Ratchet."

"How many times…oh, who's this?"

"My friend, Cherise."

"Nice to meet you, Chosen. Do you need rehabilitation too?"

"Not a chance, nurse."

"Okay, then get out now." Cherise lifted an eyebrow, and Minu gave her a 'don't ask' look. Cherise leaned over and gave her friend a hug then got up to leave. "Oh, Chosen Cherise?" She turned around at the nurse's call. "Please don't forget to take the empty mead bottle?"

* * *

Minu was so happy to be out of the hospital ward that she didn't even care she couldn't drive her own car. Oh sure, she could if she tried, but the doctor had specifically forbidden her from operating any vehicles which would have risked damaging her still-healing legs. With the temporary support bars removed, at least she could wear shoes again.

Cherise operated the red sports-model aerocar with a practiced hand. All her friends now owned the flying vehicles, even if none of them were quite as fancy as Minu's. Of course, she was the only one among them who didn't have any other bills to pay, so she'd spent all her savings on the vehicle two years ago. Her account balance was creeping upward again but would still take some time to recover.

To stave off boredom, the friends watched movies on the car's entertainment system, played cards, and napped during the flight. It was two hours from Ft. Jovich to her little island retreat, but it was six hours from Steven's Pass to the town of Naomi in the Desert Tribe territory. "Quite a commute you've got yourself," Minu said when the trip was half over.

"I have regular duties nearby at the harvesting facility on the southern steppes, less than an hour by air, so it works for me."

"No boyfriends?"

"I wasn't impressed with your experiences. A few guys have tried, but it doesn't strike my fancy for now." They hadn't talked about what would happen during their time in Cherise's home town, but there was an unspoken understanding Cherise would be Minu's lover any time she wanted. After long months of training, the brief but bloody battles beating back the Tanam, and then her extended time under the ministrations of Nurse Ratchet, the idea pleased her greatly. Deep in her heart, Minu knew a celibate life didn't appeal to her nature.

As they were beginning their descent from twenty thousand meters, Cherise sighed and turned toward her. "I need to tell you something."

"Uh oh."

"Yeah. You see, I told my father that I was coming home with you, and he told my sister…"

"Oh no, Cherise!" Minu whined.

"Yeah, there's going to be a celebration in our honor. Well, mostly your honor."

"Ugh," Minu spat. "Just tell me no bureaucrats or reporters."

"We don't have reporters, but the tribal elders are sort of like bureaucrats. Don't be that way; I didn't plan this!"

The car dropped below the meager cloud deck, and endless kilometers of brown desert spread out below, broken occasionally by cultivated green zones along streams and intermittent roads. As the car went lower, Minu could see settlements along the green zones, far fewer than would have been expected in other parts of Bellatrix.

Finally the car banked and dropped toward a town no bigger than any of the others she'd seen since they began their descent. "Naomi?"

"Home," Cherise said with a big smile, her beautiful dark features lit by the afternoon light flooding through the canopy. "Remember, it's Julast in the desert."

"I went through the trials; how bad could it be?" Once the car touched down at the town's small landing area, Cherise locked the controls and opened the wide gull-wing doors. Heat washed in as if an oven door had suddenly opened. "Woof," she said simply.

"Don't say I didn't warn you." Cherise climbed out, then came around for Minu, helping her out then handing her the simple dualloy forearm crutches she'd been given by the therapists upon her release. She stood and got her balance as Cherise got their bags and locked the vehicle. Minu looked around through the heat haze and noticed no one was waiting for them. Maybe this gathering would be low key? She examined the nearest town buildings and found them unspectacular. They looked like brick and mortar with wooden roofs and simple shutters. Except for the adaption to local materials, they weren't that different from what you'd find in a Peninsula tribe house, the other less advanced tribe on Bellatrix. But unlike the Peninsula people, the desert tribe wasn't primitive by choice, but by location and circumstances. Civilization had reemerged around Minu's Plateau tribe, nearly on the other side of the planet. Technology was slow to come to this remote location, and the desert was a harsh place with limited resources.

Regardless of their circumstances, the Desert Tribe people were proud and self-reliant survivors. Every year they sent more people to serve in the Chosen, and a disproportionate number of the soldiers called the Desert Tribe home. In the Chaos times, they'd been fierce warriors. They were one of the few tribes to resist being conquered by the warlike Rusk.

Beyond the modest ceramic concrete parking area, the streets were simply hard-packed dirt, easily discernible from yards and other property by the collection of wheel tracks. Minu tried to imagine what the roads were like on the rare times it rained. There was no one else on the road or in sight as Cherise led her around a gradual turn and past dozens of small buildings that had to be homes. Her legs were really beginning to hurt, and she hoped it wasn't much farther. Then the center of the town came into view, and she moaned. The square was full of people of all ages, which accounted for there being no one to meet them when they grounded. Cherise grabbed her arm and unceremoniously hauled her forward.

Once they were in sight, a cry went up from the square, and every face turned toward them. Minu didn't know what she'd expected, but it wasn't a song. All the people's voices joined to form one in verse, directed toward them. Of course Minu couldn't understand the words, but it had a very melodic sing-song quality she found pleasing. Despite the surprise, a smile came to her face.

"It's our people's way," Cherise explained, "a tradition we brought from Africa on old Earth. They sing to welcome a returning daughter and a new member of the tribe." Unbidden, tears joined the smile on her face as they walked.

No one rushed to meet them as they walked. The people waited patiently and sang their song. It didn't seem to repeat and had as many verses as they needed. Finally, as they approached, the people in the crowd slowly moved around them until they were standing in a circle. "What do I do?" Minu asked, afraid to offend anyone.

"Nothing, just wait until they're done."

Minu hoped it wouldn't be too long, her legs were on fire and the good Dr. Bane had warned her against excessive standing for another few days.

Just as quickly as the song began, it ended. A dozen children carried the last rising note past the point of any adult's range. The effect was beautiful and a little haunting. "Thank you," Minu said, because it was all she could come up with. A cheer rose from the people and in a moment they were squeezing in around her. For some reason they all wanted to touch her head, and Minu wondered if that was another tradition. All she could do was nod and smile. Unlike a lot of tribes on Bellatrix, they'd clung to their native language, which she understood to be Ethiopian. Something else she quickly realized was that Cherise was not unusual for her people in many ways. The women were all beautiful, thin-figured with well-shaped breasts, and quite tall. Minu hadn't felt so short since attending Chosen functions with her father as a young child. And the men! They practically *towered* over her. Yet none of them treated her as anything other than a very special person, an honored guest. And more than a few men were casting appraising looks at her thin figure.

Finally some of the English speakers made themselves known, something for which she was very glad, because the Concordian translator didn't handle other human dialects. They all seemed to think she was single-handedly responsible for making Cherise a Chosen. Since she'd been the first to be Chosen from Naomi, that was a big source of pride for their town. They also thought Minu had single-handedly defeated the Rasa and the Tanam. She did her best to dissuade them of this, but to no avail. Finally, and to her immense relief, they were guided to a beautiful grass-covered area a few hundred meters away, where a big bonfire was blazing and dozens of tables were laden with food of all sorts.

At first she was concerned because not a single chair was in sight, then she spotted two Concordian-made office chairs set to one side, and she was guided toward them by Cherise. Minu fell into one with a groan of pleasure. When she turned to Cherise to ask her about the chairs, she found an older man sitting in the other chair instead. Confused, she looked around and found her friend sitting cross-legged on the ground and deep in conversation with a woman who could be her twin sister.

"I am Casan Macubale," the man next to her said. Minu turned back to see him smiling and inclining his head in a bow, "I'm the elected chief of our town, and I am very grateful to meet the great Minu Alma at last!"

"I am hardly great, just Chosen," she said as humbly as she could. "Are you any relation to Cherise?"

"I am proudly her father, Chosen Alma."

"Please, call me Minu." He nodded and smiled broadly. His perfect white teeth flashed in the dimming afternoon light, his skin a rich coffee color as opposed to Cherise, whose skin more resembled milk chocolate.

"I am honored, Minu. I can see you're a little confused. My first wife died when she was very young, in child birth. We do not often miss the technological life you lead, but at times like that the cost of our agrarian lives is very high indeed. While I was recovering from the loss, a Chosen came to help us install our humble computer network and power station. I'd never seen a Chosen, especially not a beautiful white female Chosen. Of course I fell in love with her and spent every waking moment trying to turn her heart to mine.

"I failed to earn her heart, but she did honor me by sharing my bed. Nine months later she honored me again when she brought twin daughters for me and the town to raise. Cherise and Alicia grew up here never knowing their mother."

"Is she still Chosen? I've probably known her!"

He looked down and she saw some of the happiness slip from his face. "She died seven years ago on a mission with your father. He was devastated and told me in person."

Minu was sure she could remember that mission. She always knew when her dad returned and had lost men on a mission, but this time had been worse than most. He hadn't talked to anyone for days, and it was one of the few times she'd ever seen him on the verge of tears. "I'm sorry for the loss." Casan nodded his thanks. "So that's Alicia," she asked, nodding her head toward the girl speaking with Cherise.

"Yes, she's the other shining light in my life. I feared she would race off to be Chosen with her sister, but she decided that teaching the next generation was her calling. She's worked hard to make sure the children here are among the best educated in our tribe."

Minu took a moment to look around. About four hundred men, women, and children were gathered around the fire, all talking animatedly. The sun was beginning to set, and the fire was becoming a welcome relief from the oncoming chill. Every time she made eye contact, the people would smile brightly and bow their heads. Minu decided this is what it must have felt like to have been royalty; to be adored like this. There were a few other lighter-skinned members of the town, but not many. Cherise and her sister Alicia were by far the lightest. It seemed to make little difference here though, and it made Minu feel right at home. In some places on Bellatrix, racism was alive, but not in the Chosen. You couldn't be Chosen and harbor such meaningless bigotry. Now sexism…? Well, that was another matter.

"May I ask you a question?"

"Of course, Casan."

"Your hair is the most amazing color! Do all your siblings share it?"

"I'm an only child. Even in my family it's almost unheard of. I suppose one day there'll be no one left with red hair," Minu explained, then told the story of her hair's origin going back to Mindy Harper and the exodus from Earth.

"Ah, I know that story from Plateau. A truly amazing woman, your matriarch. Our distant ancestors were very patriarchal, but to our credit, here on Bellatrix we've grown past that. My position, that of an elected chief, is about the only traditionally male position which remains. Of course the town council has more power than I do, so I guess it makes little difference."

"Your English is outstanding."

"I attended a Keeper's Academy in New Jerusalem," he explained. "My father sent me there hoping I would escape the poverty of our people. The Concordia had only just returned when he was a young child, and he saw the future wouldn't be here. Once I was educated, I didn't agree with him, and much to his chagrin, I returned here. But I brought with me a hunger for change and growth, and have strived ever since to drag us forward to join the rest of the world. The Concordia has much to teach us, and I believe we have just as much to teach them. But no one will listen to a primitive Stone Age people; we must stand beside them as equals. That's my quest."

"You're a wise man with a beautiful vision, Casan; I'm honored to know you."

"You're too kind. But please, this celebration is for my daughter and her newest sister! Food for the Chosen!" he bellowed and a moment later trays were being paraded before them.

* * *

Hours after dark, the town was still celebrating, singing, talking, and amazingly, eating. How could people so thin eat so much food? And the drink too! She favored mead, but their own alcoholic drink made from a local berry was quite impressive and doubly intoxicating. If not for a timely intervention by Cherise, Minu would likely be sleeping it off instead of taking a walk.

Despite the fun and fondness of the people, it was still a party. And like any other party, not her sort of thing. Minu was becoming an increasingly private person as she became an adult. A bit earlier Casan had gave a small speech praising first his daughter, then Minu. Then, using his admittedly limited power, he officially made Minu an honorary member of the Desert Tribe and a resident of Naomi. Shortly afterward, Minu decided on a private walk. No one tried to stop her or insist on going along, and that was refreshing.

Minu walked along the rough ground carefully, using the forearm crutches for their intended purpose as well as probing ahead to avoid any holes. Behind her the town was alive with light, making her smile, but she was also glad to be out of the middle of it. She decided she was far enough away and looked up at the night sky. The low cloud cover had burned off just before dark, leaving a startling vista of stars twinkling over her head. She'd only seen such a star field years ago during her trials. Ironically it was in a distant part of this very desert that she'd met her fate, and had her destiny brutally foisted upon her by a rapist and an attempted murderer.

At the edge of the eastern horizon, Remus was slowly climbing into the sky. Minu only needed to give it a momentary thought to know that the moon's twin, the tiny ocean moon Romulus, was several hours behind it. The two chased each other across the sky every night, Romulus being roughly twice as fast as its sister moon, but in a similar orbit. The two moons always appeared to be about to collide in their passage. The truth was they were thousands of kilometers apart; Romulus was in a much lower orbit than the more massive Remus. As a little girl she'd read books by Jules Verne and Robert Heinlein, and she had imagined flying to those moons and exploring for aliens. The truth was much more boring. Romulus was covered by a shallow sea brimming with stinking algae and tiny crustaceans. Remus was just a dark obsidian rock, a rogue captured by Bellatrix eons ago.

A sound made Minu turn her head and look. There, under a bush, two kids were sitting. There were no more than eleven or twelve. They hadn't noticed Minu's approach, or simply were indifferent to her presence, and she could see they were both naked from the waist down. Minu turned and quietly walked away, shaking her head. She remembered Cherise telling her that such things weren't uncommon where she came from, and how she'd lost her virginity at just about that age. It was a very different place from the sheltered, overly-civilized city of Tranquility.

Minu wandered the perimeter of the town until her legs started hurting, and eventually ended up sitting on a rock within sight of the town. Somewhere, a dog howled in the dark and was answered by another. There weren't many wild dogs where she came from; the kloth were too hard on them. Here in the deep desert, the kloth seldom ventured, so more Earth species thrived. She knew a couple species of gazelle did well out here, brought by Cherise's ancestors, as did some goats. It was a hard place to live, but there were no large predators, and there were no howlers barking at you. They were like flies around her cabin this time of year. Every time they heard any sound, the blasted lizards would all start their bone-grinding serenade.

The stone was warm and the air quickly cooled as she watched Remus climb into the sky. Three years as Chosen seemed more like a hundred as she thought about it. So many she'd known were dead or lost to her. So much talent, so much hope, so much pain. It sometimes felt like a long, drawn-out drama playing before her eyes, only with more tears. She relived the scene after the battle on Serengeti, with her in the hospital demanding the after-action report and scrolling through the losses of her soldiers. Nearly two hundred were dead and half that number injured. The Rasa had lost twenty as well, with five injured, when the Tanam brought down one of their transports. An entire company of soldiers gone in one battle. Every time she fought, the butcher's bill got bigger.

A few tears rolled down her cheeks, far fewer than she expected, and in moments they were gone, the moisture drunk by the hungry dry desert air. It felt like there was less room for grief and remorse, and less time to indulge in such things. The revelation of how she came to be born and the real relationship, or lack thereof, between her mother and father had done more to harden her heart than she'd realized. And then there were the Weavers, the mysterious entities that appeared to live inside the portals. They'd saved her life during the Vendetta, at least she believed they had, and now they wouldn't talk to her. They insisted on talking to Pip, and he was all but dead. How was she supposed to put a comatose patient in touch with ethereal aliens that may or may not be living inside portals?

She took out one of the tablets she always carried and brought it to life. The screen cast a ghostly shadow on her face. Displayed was an email she'd received a few days ago. A friend in the office of the Dean at the University of Plateau had told Minu that they'd heard about her treatment by the Chosen council. The board of governors at the school had discussed it, and Minu had officially been offered a position as an Associate Professor of History. If things worked out, and she continued her own education, she'd be made full professor in charge of a new Military History department in a few years. They didn't come out and say it, but she was sure they were a little nervous of appointing an eighteen-year-old woman as a professor. Still, it was the most tempting offer she'd had in a very long time. Leave the Chosen behind and teach? Maybe form her own military history department? Very tempting.

Then she found the files from her father. Her birthright, of a sort. An invitation from her dead father to explore the cosmos and find the clues he'd left for her that promised to lead to an even greater mystery. Maybe he was alive out there, waiting for her to find him? It was a tantalizing thought. More tantalizing than the teaching position? She needed to think about it some more.

* * * * *

Chapter Three
April 28th, 522 AE

Village of Naomi, Desert Tribe, Bellatrix

Dawn broke over Naomi on the second week of her rest, and Minu blinked. Already the sounds of children running and playing came through the simple lace screen that served for windows here in the desert. It had only rained once in the two weeks, a pathetic trickle of moisture from the parched skies so meager the shutters weren't even closed. Even though no one closed their windows, Concordian-made moisture locks captured the water from each roof and sequestered it into the residence's individual cistern for later use. Water was more precious than steel in the desert.

Minu yawned and sat up in bed, the scant single sheet falling away from her naked body. Next to her Cherise snored on peacefully. She patted the girl affectionately on her shapely bottom, but she continued to sleep. "Typical," Minu whispered and crawled from bed. More often than not, the two spent their evenings together. Minu admitted to herself that she was glad for the company, and the physical pleasure it brought. It was hard to believe she'd reacted with such fear and negativity the first time Cherise had offered. Now it was a natural thing, a sort of safe love she could share with her best friend.

Her normal morning shower ritual was curtailed here by necessity. Instead, most times she sufficed with a washcloth bath of all the important parts. She'd had a shower a few days ago, so she stuck with the simple cleaning today. Breakfast was leftover biscuits from last night and a package of instant oatmeal, simple yet filling fare. The oatmeal was for her enjoyment. The Desert Tribe preferred a sort of curdled goat milk that just wasn't to her taste. When she was done, Cherise still hadn't stirred, so she went outside.

Walking around naked from the waist up had taken some getting used to, even after the trials and their forced nudity. Now two weeks later it felt normal. She'd found out the next day after her welcome party that near-nakedness or outright-nakedness was commonplace. She'd stuck to the light blouses she'd brought the first two days, but then quickly tired of being sweaty and sticky at the end of each day and had gone topless after that. To her relief, no one even looked twice, not even the men. She admitted to herself it might be because, except for the young girls, she had the smallest breasts in the village.

The only challenge to adapting was her pale skin. Redheads had been known to burst into flames on overcast days. The blast furnace of the sun here was almost unbearable. Luckily, she didn't go far without ample supplies of Concordian-formulated sunscreen. It went on lightly, lasted for days, and had saved her from being burned to a crisp. Not even a swim washed it away.

After the brief rain earlier in the week, she and Cherise had joined the young teenagers of the tribe in a first for her, skinny dipping with others. It was quite an experience to be naked with thirty other young men and women in a shallow stream. That water was cool and refreshing, and the young were completely uninhibited in their behavior. By late in the afternoon she'd watched at least five pairs wander off together into the sparse underbrush, not all opposite sexes, and one couple simply consummated their passion right there in the shallow water. It was so strange to see it on display for everyone to see that it had the natural reaction of driving her into

Cherise's ready arms. They were the sixth couple to find a secluded place that afternoon.

Though she was less well-endowed than normal for the town, that didn't slow the boys down from trying to gain her attentions. She'd lost count of how many had asked her to 'tour the woods,' as Cherise explained was the local euphemism for what Plateau kids called a roll in the hay. It didn't seem to matter that there were no trees more than a meter tall within many kilometers. Most of the potential suitors were somewhat younger than her, with the exception of one man old enough to be her father; that'd had the unexpected result of making her blush spectacularly.

The last few days she'd spent her time shared between mornings with the older women, accompanied by Cherise as translator, listening to them talking about their ancient traditions, and afternoons with the young men, watching and slowly increasing her knowledge of their unique style of martial arts fighting. At first they were amused that a non-Desert woman would want to learn fighting. Then at Cherise's urging she'd picked up a wooden practice knife and pinned a boy to the ground in a couple of seconds. It would have been faster, but her legs were still not a hundred percent. It was the first time she'd straddled a boy, nearly naked herself, and been sure he wasn't more impressed by her breasts than her abilities. After that demonstration, they eagerly awaited her arrival, often seeking her out should she be late or otherwise occupied. They were most interested in the other martial arts moves she'd integrated into her personal style—everything from Bruce Lee, Chuck Norris, and Jackie Chan. Now with her time in the desert running short, she could see bits and pieces of what she'd shown them slowly working its way into their native fighting style. They were integrating what they liked and discarding the rest.

One morning Minu started with a run, something she hadn't felt good enough to do yet. The legs had a strange otherworldly quality about them that the arm never. She thought it might come from the hybrid nature of the limb, compared to the purely cybernetic arm. She'd sent an email a week ago to Dr. Tasker, complaining about that very issue. His reply was that her complaint was common and to get used to it. So with a shrug, she'd set about doing just that. Now that she was finally running, it was fading.

As she ran, she was most grateful for being small-breasted. She couldn't imagine running topless with the large breasts Cherise sported. Even with her lithe build she ran with her arms pulled in, reducing the amount of bounce she experienced. A couple boys in their mid-teens paced her for the first kilometer, hoping she'd be impressed with their endurance and want to sleep with them. Before long, they dropped out, pretending to be interested in something else, though the truth was only Cherise and a few of the oldest boys could keep pace with her. Running had been her favorite way of keeping fit her whole life, and after weeks of sitting on her ass, she'd noticed a little roll of fat on her tummy when she sat up. "That just has to go," she growled and started running that morning.

Today, after only two kilometers, she was forced to slow to a jog, cramps rippling through her abdomen. "That's new," she growled as one hit, strong enough to almost send her face-first into the sand. Reluctantly, she admitted she wasn't well and turned back. By the time she reached Naomi she was walking and holding her stomach.

"What is wrong, young Chosen?" a voice asked in somewhat broken English. An elderly female member of the tribe walked up with a look of concern on her face, and Minu bit back the urge to blow her off.

"Just got some bad cramps while running," Minu admitted, then stumbled from the pain.

"Come to my hut," she invited, "I am a healer in Naomi and would be honored to help our new Chosen daughter."

"I can just get a pill from my kit."

"Pills," she said and made a rude noise. "Your pills can offer nothing that I cannot do." Afraid to offend, Minu agreed. At the worst she could take a muscle relaxant after she'd obliged the old woman and eaten her herbs, or whatever.

Her hut was only a short distance away, for which Minu was glad. The cramps had her almost bent over double as she entered through the fabric screen door and sat on the offered mat. Now that her legs were less of an issue, there was no longer a need for her to sit in a chair. "When did these cramps start?" asked the elderly healer.

"About half an hour ago," Minu grunted as another wave hit, "while I was running."

"I see. Lie back please and remove your pants."

"Excuse me?"

"Minu, I am a healer, like your doctors. Now please remove your pants." Minu nodded and reluctantly shed her shorts before lying back naked on the mat. Her abdomen contracted as she stretched out, making her hiss in pain. Shortly she felt the age-toughened fingers of the woman feeling her stomach, low, just above her pelvis.

"I think it might have been the stew last night," Minu suggested. She could feel the woman pressing on her abdomen and suddenly yelped in pain as the woman nudged something that was the center of the cramps.

"It wasn't the stew," the woman said. Minu was about to ask her what she thought it was when she felt the woman press a cloth between her legs.

"What the?" she yelped and sat up suddenly.

"Minu, you don't know what's happening?"

"I don't know what you're trying to do to me, old lady, but please don't touch me there."

"Look at the cloth." Minu looked down at the cloth. There was a tint of red on the white cloth. "Take it away and look."

Her fingers shaking, she pulled it away from her groin to see it covered with dark red blood. "Am I hurt?"

"It is your moon time, Minu." Minu looked confused, then with a grumble spread her legs wide and against the cramps bent double to look. With a gasp, she replaced the cloth. She was bleeding all over the mat she'd lain on. "You are having a menstrual cycle, Minu, and unless I miss my guess, it's your first."

"Um, yeah, it is. Why, I mean how, uhh, oh shit!"

"You are unusual for starting so late in life, this is sure. You're nineteen, like Cherise?"

"Eighteen."

"I see. Still, not completely unheard of. The cramps are your uterus squeezing out the blood and dead tissue. It's also a way your body practices for having a baby."

"Ugh, stop already, I've had anatomy classes," she said quietly. Of course that was many years ago, back in Plateau, when the other girls all started having their periods. She'd been secretly grateful she didn't share those experiences and, that as the years went by, she'd all but forgotten. The last time it came up was two years ago during a routine physical. The doctor was a Chosen physician who didn't seem overly surprised. He'd explained it was likely due to her very low body fat, and she'd quickly forgotten about the subject. Now she was sitting on a mat in a town thousands of klicks from a modern pharmacy, bleeding like a stuck kloth.

"What's this scar from?" the woman asked, her finger gently tracing the small scar just above her pubic hair. "It's from a knife, right?"

"Yes; long story."

"It may have damaged your uterus; it's in the right place. That could also account for your delayed moon times."

She nodded. What bothered her most was all the times she'd been hurt, even the last time with two mangled legs, and the blood had never really bothered her. Now she felt like she was about to puke. She decided to chalk it up to the period. Then she did puke.

* * *

For some reason, the hardest part was explaining to Cherise what was going on. Her friend was almost in tears before Minu finally told her what was wrong. Cherise got a surprised, then a sad look on her face. Minu started to cry and then they were holding each other just bawling like little girls. Minu hated crying and despised losing control, but despite her best wishes, it just poured out.

Later in the afternoon, her friend showed how her tribe's women dealt with those womanly needs. A simple absorbent cotton pad and a light strap to hold it in place dealt with the blood. It involved checking several times a day to avoid 'accidents' as Cherise informed her. Then the other girl insisted she wear a necklace. A simple piece of twine holding a teardrop shaped piece of hematite. She wouldn't explain why, and it was much later when Minu realized that none of the boys were trying to get her attention. The necklace was a tasteful and simple notice. "I'm having my period, please leave me alone." With the cramps (reduced by an herbal tea from the healer) went a headache and slight moodiness. She found herself very grateful Cherise had insisted on the necklace after all.

The next day her 'situation' hadn't changed, so Minu took a short jog and a stop at the healer's hut. She thanked the older woman, who she finally found out was named Jasaise, and accepted a many months' supply of the tea. Minu assured her she'd use the tea. Later she sat in on a training session with the young male fighters. This time she only watched, and was disappointed she couldn't really participate. One look at the hematite necklace, and she was invited to have a seat.

After an hour of practice they broke for a rest, and Minu chatted with them about styles. They were open to interacting with her; they just wouldn't let her join in the actual practice. After the break, a new man was escorted to the workout area by some older tribesmen. He was easily as old as Ted Hurt, maybe seventy, and had the complete respect of every young man there. To her surprise, as the practice resumed, he skinned down to just a loincloth, the common dress for men fighting here, and joined the much younger boys. By this point Minu wasn't really shocked when he started beating the kids one after another. What did surprise her was that he used only a single long stick.

"He is Ojanbique," explained one of the young men already beaten and sent to the sidelines. "He is a wanderer from our tribe who travels the desert teaching and living off the land."

He came over and smiled when he saw her, his busy and bright eyes quickly noting her build, skin color, flashing copper colored hair, and the necklace she wore. He spoke in the tribe's native language, translated by the same young man who'd told her who he was, and held out a hand. "I'm pleased to meet the tribe's new daughter, Chosen Minu Alma."

Minu laughed and took the offered hard. "A pleasure to meet the great Ojanbique," she replied.

"My legend precedes me?" he asked, and gave the young man a serious look. The boy smiled big, said something in their language and shrugged. Ojanbique chuckled and shook his head. "I understand. You've enjoyed my lessons?"

"Very much, and I'm sorry I wasn't able to participate."

"As am I. Another time, perhaps? Is it true you have fought alien monsters hand to hand?"

"I'm not sure if they're monsters, but aliens, yes. But I have to say, watching you now gives me a bit of a revelation. Would you consider coming to the Steven's Pass facility of the Chosen in a month or so?"

"I have no means of transportation or even getting in touch with you," he admitted. "I'm a simple traveler."

"I could leave word here with Casan with the details when I have them worked out. He could send me a message, and I'll come get you personally."

"I've never left the desert," he admitted and scratched the light beard covering his chin, "but this interests me. After eighty years perhaps it is time."

"You're eighty years old?" she gasped.

He nodded. "It may be months before I'm back here, is that a problem?"

"Not at all. Can you tell me a little about how you use the long stick?"

* * *

The next morning Ojanbique was gone. He'd left her with a promise that he would stop in Naomi regularly for word from Minu. She'd been up late after talking with him, working on yet another idea of how to make the soldiers more effective fighters. It was the first time she could honestly say she'd enjoyed a vacation, even if it was more rehabilitation than relaxation. Her legs no longer bothered her, and she felt nearly a hundred percent. In fact, with her mastery of the new legs came their increased endurance and jumping ability. Not as profound as what her arm could do, but still considerable.

Minu contemplated reporting for duty ahead of schedule, then discarded the thought. She could make use of the final two weeks. She wasn't even overly annoyed at the emergence of her monthly cycles. Cherise was a big reason for that. Part sister, part lover, Minu didn't know what she'd do without her.

Cherise woke up as Minu finished packing, unusual for the typically late-sleeping woman. "It's not noon, sure you don't want to go back to sleep?"

"Very funny," Cherise mumbled as she stumbled into the simple bathroom of her little house. "You didn't think I'd let my new sister leave without saying goodbye, did you?"

"It's not like I'm dying; I'm just going back to Tranquility to get some work done. I love it here, but I need more computer access. It might be possible here, but I'd suck up almost all the bandwidth you have. And there're kids here trying to learn…"

"I know, we've talked about getting another network transceiver; it just hasn't happened yet."

"Casan is a wonderful leader. Naomi is very lucky to have him."

"I agree," she said as she emerged from the bathroom. Minu zipped her bag and turned to face her. A tear was rolling down Cherise's beautiful cheek. "I'll miss my new sister, my lover."

Minu blushed, but she stepped forward, and they embraced, finishing with a kiss. "I've really enjoyed our time here, and I'm glad you were with me when my body suddenly decided to turn on the baby factory."

Cherise laughed and patted her on the cheek. "I've always felt a little like your older sister, even back during the trials."

"Then why did you let me lead?"

"Older does not necessarily mean wiser, Minu." The blush deepened. "You're the smartest person I've ever known, yes including the 'egg heads' as you call them, because you put it all together and do what has to be done, regardless of the price or consequences."

"You sound a little like Jacob."

"Screw him," she said and Minu giggled. "You know what I meant. The difference between what I'm saying and what he says is that from me, it's a compliment."

"Thank you."

A few minutes later she was standing at the center of the town square, just like two weeks before, with the residents of Naomi singing her another song. This one felt more sad than happy, and Minu couldn't help but feel hot tears rolling down her cheeks. In only a few days, these people had become her family, and she was going to miss them profoundly. As the song wound down, they came to her, one at a time with the youngest first, and kissed her gently on the cheek, then whispered a word of their language in her ear. She favored those she knew best with a special smile, a nod, or more tears. Jasaise got a hug and a kiss in return, the young troupe of fighters were offered respectful nods. Cherise received an unashamed kiss and a torrent of still more tears. They'd lived as lovers for two weeks, a pair of women openly sharing affections. She'd never imagined such a place of freedom like Naomi existed.

Casan came last. "Return to us, my daughter, as soon as you can, or when your heart can stand it no longer."

"I will," she said solemnly, and meant it. "One question?" she asked, and he nodded. She inquired as to the word they'd all whispered in her ear.

He smiled and whispered it in her ear as well, then added, "It means friend."

* * * * *

Chapter Four
May 3rd, 522 AE

Coma Care Ward, Plateau Mercy Hospital, Tranquility, Plateau Tribe

The tea was terrible, but what could you expect in a hospital? Minu drank it anyway and tried to enjoy the conversation. Cynthia was sitting next to her in the austere hospital room, also drinking the terrible tea, telling Minu about her job in Tranquility. "The bank is not as interesting as the theater was in Chelan, and this is such a big city, but the pay is good, and I have an apartment a block away so I can see Pip twice a day, at lunch and then after I get off work."

Minu nodded and looked at her old friend where he lay under a light cotton sheet. His face looked older now, and someone obviously shaved him regularly (Cynthia?), but his eyes only intermittently opened, and when they did they stared straight ahead. That phenomenon started a year ago and had caused momentary excitement. Unfortunately, the doctors pronounced it an autonomic response, not a sign of coming wakefulness.

Once Minu had leaned over and looked into those eyes, so familiar yet so empty. But they weren't dead eyes, just vacant. Like a hotel room patiently waiting for the occupant to return. Bed made, covers turned back, a mint on the pillow. The doctors said they knew there were higher brain functions occurring, complex functions, in fact. He might well be completely conscious and aware inside his head, but unable to interact with the outside world. She tried not to think about what that would be like, but couldn't completely avoid the idea. A never-ending nightmare where you were surrounded by friends and family. Did he scream for them to hear him, only to be ignored?

"How're your legs?" Cynthia asked, surprising Minu from her reverie. Cynthia saw her confusion and laughed a little. "Gregg and Aaron were here a week ago, and we talked. I mentioned I hadn't seen you in a while, and they explained you were in rehab and what happened."

"Glad to hear it didn't make it into the press after all."

"They don't like you much, the press. The story they wrote about you saving Serengeti was…sort of a backhanded compliment. I think they're still mad about that bit with the beamcaster years ago."

It was Minu's turn to laugh and smile when she recalled that day. They'd been trying to fund the construction of the HERT, the High Energy Research and Testing facility. Of course the press was against the 'needless waste of money.' Her boss then, Bjorn Ganose, who was in charge of the Chosen science branch, called a press conference to show them how the new beamcasters worked. Under his instructions, she'd fired the weapon at a target only a few meters away, and at full power. The explosion injured several of them and nearly deafened them all. Bjorn had made certain he and Minu were standing behind a shield, safe from the explosion. They'd gotten the funding for the HERT and earned the ire of the press in one fell swoop.

"Yeah, they don't think much of me." She pulled up one leg on the jeans she was wearing. Cynthia leaned over and examined the ugly pink scar gashes running up from mid-calf well past her knee.

"Looks bad," she observed.

"I've had worse," Minu said and flexed her right arm. Cynthia's eyes narrowed when she regarded the four-fingered hand, a nearly universal reaction. "They had to replace most of my leg bones, knees, and muscles." Minu chuckled. "About all that's left there that's me is skin. Dr. Tasker, the cybernetic physician, says that all these replacements came from a big cache the Chosen bought a few years back. After the battle last month, there are quite a few more Chosen with gray limbs."

"I've seen a few in town," Cynthia said. She sighed and looked at Pip, then checked her watch. "It's getting late, but I can't help spending every minute I can here."

Minu nodded then thought about it. "What's wrong?"

"What do you mean?"

"I've seen you on and off enough over the last few years to know you fairly well. Something's wrong, isn't it?"

Without warning the slightly overweight girl started crying and couldn't look away from Pip. Minu leaned over and wrapped an arm around her shoulder, and before she knew it they were holding each other. Minu let her wind down and waited patiently. "The doctors include me in the family meetings," she sputtered, producing a tissue and blowing her nose. "They didn't do that when he was still at Steven's Pass, but his family insisted here. His uncle calls me daughter." Minu smiled and nodded. Bjorn was Pip's uncle, and his kindness to her was in keeping with his gentle nature. There were a few more tears shed before she continued. "The neurologist says we're running out of time. The machines that help keep him alive are slowly killing him. Something about how the machines override his body systems and such, the brain is slowly giving up control. When that happens, the individual organs will start to fail, and soon after, he'll be gone."

Minu remembered some of that from the doctors back when Pip was first injured. There had been a tiny amount of hope for a cure, or his own spontaneous recovery, or even for Concordian tech to heal him. When they'd moved him to Tranquility and the coma care center, she'd known it was because there was no real hope of recovery. It was a warehouse for the living dead. "I'm sorry to hear that," she said as Cynthia used another tissue to dry her face. "How long do they think?"

"Six months, maybe a year. He had a spate of renal failures last month, but they got that under control with drugs. The doctor said it was the first sign that his body was starting to fail." Minu sighed and looked at her fallen friend, thinking it might have been better if he'd died quickly back then instead of slowly wasting away like this.

Minu stayed for a few minutes after Cynthia left, quietly sitting and holding Pip's hand. It might have felt once like he squeezed back, but she knew better. Your imagination sometimes tries to give you what you most hope for.

The trip to her cabin in the trusty red sports aerocar was a familiar one. Minu was sure she could probably fly it with her eyes closed. She knew the car could. As she climbed out of the car on the ceramic concrete landing pad, she breathed the familiar scents of home, but somehow it wasn't as homelike as before. She'd become used to the blast furnace heat of the desert, and none of her new family was there. As she carried her bag in, she found herself thinking of Mindy, a common thing here, and all the years she'd spent alone after her husband and the last of her children died. It was the first time she'd really thought about how her own life might end, or what might happen after she retired. She didn't want to spend it alone.

Once she'd settled into the little cabin, got her dirty clothes into the automated Concordian-made washer, and had some food cooking, Minu settled back in an ancient easy chair and took up her personal tablet. Over the next few days she fell into a routine. Wake up, take a nude swim in the tepid lake, bathe, eat breakfast, work out, blind fight, lunch, relax and read for an hour, work out again, a late afternoon dip in the lake again, another bath, and in bed to read until she fell asleep. Intermingled were orders and follow up reports for the soldiers.

Her reading list was massive and dominated by the thousands of pages from her father's mission logs and the Concordian computer data Pip had stolen years ago. The later were several orders of magnitude larger than the logs, but also infinitely more boring. The realization from P'ing that they'd been 'allowed' to steal the data made it all that much more compelling, and frustrating. What data they'd purposely *not* been allowed to take kept her up nights.

As her time off was running down, Minu loaded her bags and took her car to Plateau. On the east ridge of the huge escarpment sat the overwhelming edifice of Plateau University. Despite collecting two degrees from there over the years, she'd rarely set foot on the campus; an occasional test, the rare in-person lecture, and two award ceremonies for her degrees. Chosen got special consideration for distance learning, even on classes that weren't normally offered as such.

As she flew over the plateau she was again taken by the volume of flying traffic. Every time she came back, the skies were busier. It already sported more flying vehicles than Serengeti; although the Beezer weren't as big on flying as many species. The car descended toward an automatic landing at the university. Far to the west was Chosen Tower, the old headquarters of the Chosen, now a medium-sized building among the ever-growing number of skyscrapers.

* * *

"Dean Shinobu, I'm pleased to meet you in person," Minu said warmly and shook the woman's hand. The Dean's assistant bowed slightly after seeing her in and left, closing the office door behind her.

"And you, Chosen Alma." Minu smiled and looked around the simply-appointed office. The dean was an attractive woman in her forties, obviously of Peninsula ancestry. For some reason, Minu had never realized the Dean of Special Programs was a woman. "Can I assume your visit is in relation to our offer?"

"Correct, and thanks for seeing me on such short notice."

"Not at all, we'd be honored to have you here at the university. Many of us are very proud and impressed with what you've accomplished."

"Don't take this wrong, but you're from Peninsula, right? The Chosen aren't exactly liked there, or me either."

"We're not all quite that ignorant," she said with a wry smile. "I and others completely understand the necessity of bringing us forward from our cocoon." She came from around her desk to look out the long window. From her office on the twentieth floor of the ultra-modern university complex, you could just glimpse the far side of the plateau through the haze, some five kilometers away. "I heard through the grapevine that they took away your fantastic soldiers."

"I've been reassigned to the training branch. However, I've also been elected by the Tog to be their representative to humanity."

"That I hadn't heard. So, are you going to give it up and come teach for us?"

"I'm sorry, but no. There's too much for me to do still, and I can't do it from outside the Chosen."

Shinobu looked obviously disappointed, and resigned at the same time. She turned to Minu and nodded in understanding. "You Chosen are a breed apart. I'm really not shocked. Will you still proceed with your War College at least?"

"If the university is still willing to host it."

"And if I say we aren't?"

"Well, then it will be my turn to be disappointed."

"And I suppose you'll just go ahead and do it somewhere else?"

"Yes, you're right about that."

"I see. Just as well that the board of governors has already agreed to sit a chair for you then, even if not as a fulltime professorship. Congratulations, you're the Dean of the new Plateau University War College. So let's sit down and figure out how this is all going to work."

Minu couldn't help but smile as she pulled out her tablet and powered it up. "I just happen to have a few ideas."

* * *

In her months' absence from Ft. Jovich, construction had been completed. No more open conduits, exposed wiring, or unfinished rooms could be found. She was glad she'd gotten to see it finished before losing her place in command. Gregg had met her in the hanger, resplendent in his new Chosen/Soldier hybrid uniform. The camo tiger stripe pattern fatigues she'd chosen for the soldiers was blended with black stripes down the arms and legs, representing his branch of Scout. Three black stars now rode his sleeves, just like hers. "If I had to lose the soldiers, I'm glad it was to you."

Gregg smiled behind her old desk and looked…in command. "The council wouldn't let Jacob put anyone in charge except someone who'd worked with you in training the soldiers."

"And speaking of soldiers, are you ready for my official last act as Commander?"

"Let's do this." He pushed the intercom button. "Ariana, tell the commanders we're ready." He stood and headed for the door. Minu was glad he'd kept her old assistant, Ariana Beck, when he took over. She was both capable and knew the fort's operations better than anyone except Minu or Gregg.

Down on the main floor of the fort she found every man, woman, and Rasa of the service waiting for her. Eighteen hundred men and woman, and almost two thousand Rasa, were arrayed in order by army, company, platoon and squad, in lines firmly dressed and uniforms crisp as razors. Every one of them had their kits on their backs, and shock rifles slung over their shoulders. That too was one of her last acts as commander. She'd seen to it the Rasa had been issued the weapons. They'd shed the same blood on the battlefield; they deserved it.

Minu led the way, and she and Gregg mounted the address stand to face their troops. As she stopped at the podium, thousands of arms snapped to heads in salute and back down, hands slapping their thighs and left feet stomping the ground making the air reverberate.

"At ease," she said, the invisible microphones catching her voice and sending it out booming over the room. With mechanical precision the host of troops clasped hands behind their backs and changed their stance to a slightly more comfortable one, with feet spread precisely a half meter apart. "It's really good to be back in uniform."

The room exploded into a cheer. "Mi-nu, Mi-nu, Mi-nu!"

She smiled despite herself and shook her head. "Would you please stop that?"

"YES, BOSS!" roared the soldiers, and she laughed despite herself.

"You honor me, one and all. But as you know, I won't be your boss anymore." She bowed her head and recalled the prepared speech, then in a second, she tossed it from her mind and went with her heart. "I've personally helped train every one of you. Fought to get you the best equipment, all the skills you need to be soldiers, and then went into battle with you.

"On the fields of Amber we first showed the Tanam what they were facing." The troops all cheered, and she waited patiently for the yelling to die down. "Then on Serengeti we taught them the meaning of the word defeat!" More cheers, and her name was chanted. This time she cut it short. "And we left lives there. We fought, we bled, and we died on that world. Human and Rasa, Chosen and soldier, we are now a family forged in the heat of battle; we are forever brothers- and sisters-in-arms together.

"Though you might be soldiers, that's not a name, it's simply what you are. Like I am Chosen, I am a Commander. Others are Scouts, Scientists, Logisticians, or Trainers. To name something is part of the human condition. Present company excluded," she smiled and nodded to where Var'at stood with his officers. The Rasa had both eyes fixed on her, giving her his undivided attention. He gave her a brief nod of understanding before she continued. "You needed a name.

"With that decision made, I searched through human history to find a suitable title for you. There are many names of honor throughout that history, many with storied pasts that still ring in our tales. Spartans, Trojans, Special Forces, Spetsnaz, Legionnaires, Vikings, I could go on for hours. But for us I chose something that transcends any one era. I found it first used in middle-ages England, special soldiers who fought in woodlands, able to operate without support and live off the land. It was revived during the Second World War by the Allies for their soldiers trained to go anywhere, anytime, and act behind enemy lines. They continued in use by the United States until Earth was destroyed, and they were one of the most elite fighting forces in the world."

"So from this day forth, you are to be known as Rangers, one and all. The tradition is reborn."

Minu waited while the soldiers received their Ranger patches from their platoon sergeants, who fixed them to the logo adhesive spot on their shoulders. It was a black and red tab, symbolizing their unity with the Chosen scouts, curved slightly, that said in block letters "RANGER." It was a very minor change to the uniform, but she hoped a major change to the fighting force as a whole. They needed an independent identity, not one that was in the shadow of the Chosen. Then it was time to finish.

Gregg came up beside her and saluted. "Chosen Alma, I relieve you."

"Chosen Larsen, I stand relieved." And it was over. There was a short reception afterward, attended by sergeant and above only. She shook hands (and claws), accepted congratulations on her appointment as ambassador, even though everyone knew it wasn't a promotion, and good wishes in her career. She also got to speak to Lieutenant Theodore Bodenson, formerly Sgt. Bodenson. He was the sergeant who'd led the charge to capture the highborn at the end of the Serengeti Campaign, as it was called in the records. He was the first ever officer promoted from the ranks of the Rangers. Minu shook his hand and congratulated him. "I know you won't be the last."

* * * * *

Chapter Five
Octember 2nd, 522 AE

Governing Complex, Capital City, Herdhome, Tog Leasehold

Living on Herdhome every other month was at first a joy, but it quickly became a pain. Minu didn't exactly hate it; her apartment was luxurious, as was the office and budget provided by P'ing. She also appreciated the grudging respect the Beezer now afforded her in such a prestigious position as Humanity's representative to the Tog. The open animosity with which she was treated by the elected officials of her home planet was no real surprise. She'd known her position was formerly one of those cozy jobs given to a fat old political hack nearing retirement. P'ing's arbitrary decision to appoint Minu to the post, and thus force the retirement of the old office holder came as a shock to the bureaucrats of Bellatrix and a wakeup call. The Tog were still in charge, and best you don't forget it.

Minu's real dislike of living on Herdhome came with the bureaucratic dealings, which made up ninety percent of her job, and the environment. While perfectly suited for the Tog, the perpetually overcast world was like walking around a darkened movie theater, even at high noon. The world's atmosphere was warmer than Bellatrix, somewhat more humid, and contained more oxygen as well. The whole effect left her feeling like she was always sleepy, but too full of energy to actually sleep. When her friends Cherise and Gregg came to visit during her second month of duty on the dim world, they'd brought her a gift of light-intensifying 'sunglasses.' Ted Hurt and Bjorn Ganose, aware of her new situation, had personally rigged the common-appearing sunglasses with light intensifying technology. They helped keep her from feeling like she was stumbling around inside a closet when she took to the narrow Tog-crowded streets.

"Damn nice office," Gregg whistled when he saw it. Easily twice the size of Dram's, and nearly equal to Jacob's, it was well-appointed with three walls made from fluid displays, allowing her to make them look like anything she wanted. One usually showed a view from the upper floor of the Steven's Pass facility in the spring, or out the window of her little island cabin; the others were often blank or displayed data files.

"Impressive," Cherise agreed. Minu snorted, and they both took comfortable human-configured seats. There were two of them, along with three of the low couches the Tog preferred. "Don't be that way, it is a nice office!"

"I know, but the job is bullshit. All I do is get emails from P'ing and forward them to either the Bellatrix Council, Jacob, or some businessman. I mean, really?"

Gregg was busy studying some of the files displayed on the one wall. "Military doctrine…The ethics of multi-species command…Civilian casualty mitigation?"

Minu shrugged and waved a hand to wipe the data, replacing it with a second wall matching that of the view from Steven's Pass, creating a huge three-wall panorama. "War College stuff," she admitted.

"So you're going forward with it?" Cherise asked. Minu tried to avoid blushing. "Damn you! Are you going to quit the Chosen?"

"No, we worked out a compromise." They both glared at her so she fished into her desk, one of the small writing desks from her cabin and handed them both a card. On it in nondescript black printing was:

Minu Alma
Chosen – 3SC

Associate Professor - Military Science
Dean, Plateau University War College

"I knew you couldn't resist that offer," Gregg laughed and pocketed the card.

"But you're not quitting?" demanded Cherise.

"No, I'm using most of my spare time working with the university getting the War College off the ground. The first classes start next quarter."

"So you will be teaching?" Cherise asked.

"Yes, I'll be teaching some distance learning classes regularly, and at least one series of lectures a month." They both gave her reproachful looks. "Just think of this as life after Chosen. My father told me to go to school; I'm following his wishes." She wished she didn't feel dirty now every time she mentioned her father.

"What does Dram think of your moonlighting?"

"It's none of his damned business," she said darkly. "What the hell am I supposed to do here most of the time, stare at the wall until a message comes in?" They both shrugged, and she looked at them. "Don't get me wrong, there has to be a reason you came to this dingy corner of the universe, besides bringing me these cool glasses." Gregg stared at the ceiling, and Cherise stared at him. After a minute she leaned over and punched him hard in the arm.

"Ouch, damn!"

"Spill it," she snapped.

"Spill what?" Minu demanded.

Gregg took a deep breath and looked her in the eye. "We're taking the Rangers into the field next week."

Minu sat up straight in her chair. "What! Tanam again?"

"No, not a squeak from the cats. Intel thinks they're still licking their wounds.

"So what's going on? Trouble with the Rasa?"

"Nope."

"Gregg, you might have three stars too, but you're starting to piss me off."

"We've been hired as a garrison unit for the world of Coorson."

"That's not a Tog-aligned world."

"No, it belongs to the Traaga."

"The scary starfish guys who did the structural work on Fort Jovich?"

"Right," Gregg said and snapped his fingers. "They've been doing a lot of high-steel work all over Bellatrix. They can run up the side of a forty-story building and dangle by one arm without blinking an eye. Or several eyes on that periscope head of theirs."

Minu suppressed a shudder. The Traaga were the meekest and the poorest species she'd ever known, but they were the most disgusting one as well. "Are they contracting for the other fort construction as well?"

"Yep," Cherise confirmed. "We're still working on the foundation for Ft. Chandler, but they're putting up the superstructure for Ft. Alma as we speak."

Minu made a face and wished they'd gone back farther in the list of First Among the Chosen when it came to naming the defensive fortresses. "So why do the Traaga want to hire us, and since when are the Rangers for hire?"

"It's Jacob's big idea," Gregg took up the conversation. "We started getting requests left and right to hire the Rangers within weeks of pasting the Tanam. A surprising number of species from small and obscure to huge and powerful. Initially they were disregarded as cranks or possibly a plot to get even, but as the requests got more credible, the Tog came in and told us they had no opinion on the offers and that lent them credibility. Turns out some of the bigger species were trying to move the offers through the Tog, pressuring us to take the contracts. So we're accepting our first contract. Carefully picked for the species' neutrality and our relationship. The Traaga say the Tanam are making hostile overtures toward their interests, but no details why."

Minu nodded and thought for a moment, watching as a fox ran across the recording from Steven's Pass on one wall. Funny, she'd never noticed that in all the hours since installing the recording. "I don't think I'd agree with that decision," she said finally. "Did you voice an opinion?"

"I did," he replied, "at the meeting of the council I went on the record as officially against the move. It was duly noted and disregarded."

"It seems like a slippery slope," Cherise added. "Where do you stop?"

"Right," Minu said, pointing at her with a finger. "So now we're mercenaries. Granted, the Traaga are dirt-poor, and we're getting our own credits back, but it's like Cherise said, once you become a mercenary, where do you stop? Can you even stop?"

"What does Concordian law say about it?" Gregg asked.

Minu considered the question. "I don't know that I've ever read anything on mercenary troops. Alliances and such are common, but not mercenaries. I'm going to have to do some reading. Either way, Jacob has opened a real can of worms."

The three friends spent the afternoon catching up, then had dinner at a Tog restaurant specializing in off-world cuisine. It was one of exactly two restaurants Minu knew of in the galaxy outside Bellatrix that served human food. The other was on Serengeti. During the meal, Cherise told her the one on Serengeti had stopped serving human food. The Beezer were really pissed about the Portal Spire. Such was life.

Early in the evening she saw them off and returned to her apartment. A few hours of seeing her friends had improved her mood, but as she sat in the room watching an old Earth movie (Shogun), her mind was bothered by the thoughts of turning the Rangers into mercenaries. At least the movie was interesting and informative.

That particular turn on Herdhome was even more boring than normal, allowing her to complete quite a bit of research and communication with the other teachers in her new War College. On her last day in her Herdhome office, she got an email she'd been waiting for. When it flashed on her computer, Minu felt her pulse racing, and she read it twice to be sure she got every word. She let her assistant know she was leaving early, grabbed her bag, and left at a run.

"Chosen Alma," the Tog manning the portal controls acknowledged her as she trotted up, "returning to Bellatrix?"

"No, please send me to Serengeti."

The Tog looked up from hser control console to regard Minu with unblinking almond-shaped eyes. "The Beezer are not happy with you, Chosen Alma."

"Do I have to code the portal myself?" Hse stared at her for a moment with huge unblinking eyes, and Minu began to wonder if she'd have to do just that. Finally, almost reluctantly, the Tog leaned over the controls and hser snake-like fingers moved over them. The portal flashed to life, showing the interior of a building, and she stepped through without reservation. Should the Tog have obstinately sent her to Bellatrix, it would be a small matter to go from there to Serengeti. As luck would have it, bright sunlight bathed her as she stepped down from the portal dais. The temporary warehouse was open to the sky on one side, and she could see vast expanses of bright green grass leading away and a scattering of parked transports. This was the temporary portal complex she'd heard about.

"We greet you human," said a chuffing voice that was translated automatically by the device around her neck, and Minu nodded to the Beezer attendant. "Your name, please?"

Minu sighed and spoke clearly. "Chosen Minu Alma, on personal business."

"It's difficult to believe there would be many eager to speak to you, Destroyer."

In normal times, she would have found her new nickname on Serengeti somewhat amusing; today it was just annoying. She took a breath, ready to retort with the question of whether the anonymous Beezer would rather be serving the Tanam, then let it out with a sigh. Instead she just walked past him and out the door. "Try not to blow up the city, Chosen."

Outside there were plains as far as you could see in all directions. Occasional building mounds or ground traffic were the only indication that she was on the edge of the capital and only city of the same name as the world. "How would you tell it was gone?" she mumbled once out of ear shot. Only the downtown of the city, near the spire, had any number of tall buildings. Taking her computer tablet out, she summoned a taxi and waited patiently.

The taxi, an automated aerocar, took her over the city and unfortunately near the Portal Spire. Thousands of heavy vehicles and workers swarmed over the building, working non-stop, as they had for the seven months since the battle. She noted that most of the bigger holes were now patched. Originally they'd browbeat her with the dire diagnosis that the spire was terminally wounded and would have to be replaced, supposedly an unprecedented event in modern Concordian history. She considered the loss of real estate a worthwhile trade for the lives of sentient beings.

The taxi deposited her at the destination she'd programmed, some forty kilometers from the center of Serengeti, next to the office structure of a sprawling warehouse complex. It was not a new location to her. She'd first come here almost four years ago, back on one of her first assignments as a Chosen. This time she wasn't working for the Tog.

The automated computer attendant noted her arrival and inquired what her business was. She told it she was there to meet with another Chosen and was instantly allowed entrance. Why would it not believe her? Once inside, she went to a small office on the third floor where she found a single human Chosen working over a small stack of tablets. "Hey Victor," she said and the man looked up to smile. She'd only met him a few times, but he was a good friend of Cherise. His dark skin shone from the sweat of the warm world as he stood and warmly shook her hand. "I can't thank you enough for this," she said.

"For a friend of Cherise, and a daughter of Naomi, it's nothing."

"Where did you see them?"

Victor nodded and handed her a tablet. On it was displayed a map of the warehouse complex, with one far-away building highlighted. "I don't know how long they'll be there," he warned her.

"Noted, I'm off." They embraced quickly and Minu was running down the stairs.

If the Beezer liked anything, it was wide open spaces. This particular warehouse complex spread out more than five kilometers on a side. It was nearly the size of the entire plateau that Tranquility rested on. As she raced through the doors she'd come in through only a moment before, she wished she'd keyed the taxi to wait. Her destination was two kilometers away, and she didn't how much time she had. Minu leaned into the run with wanton abandon. For the millionth time she was once again glad that running was her favorite form of exercise, and in particular that she'd worked so hard to get her legs back in shape.

The ground fell behind her quickly despite the pronounced heat of Serengeti. The ground was soft and covered with ankle-high grass that made for an almost ideal running surface. She was just getting a little winded when the building she wanted came into view.

Minu took a precious minute after gaining entrance through the automated doorway, which thankfully didn't question the reason for her presence, to catch her breath. It would do her no good to be so winded she couldn't speak. As soon as her breathing slowed, she moved into the warehouse proper and listened for any sounds, hoping she would hear her quarry. Victor could only tell her what building, not where inside. The warehouse was cut into a low hill, like most buildings of its sort on Serengeti, and was probably fifty thousand square meters inside. Luck was with her as she quickly heard a booming Beezer speaking not far off. Minu steeled her resolve and walked purposefully toward the voice.

Coming around a massive stack of crates, Minu saw her objective, a huge Beezer speaking with a group of a dozen Squeen. She walked calmly toward the group and was only a few meters away when she was noticed. One of the Squeen spotted her and tapped the shoulder of another one. That one turned to look at her and an unmistakable flash of recognition crossed the furry face.

"I greet you, Quick Finder," Minu said with a customary bow to an equal.

"I greet you, Chosen Minu Alma." He looked down as he bowed and noted her legs. "I see your injuries have been treated."

"Cybernetic technology," she said and gently pulled up the jumpsuit leg to show the lines of scars, less visible but still obvious, "not the first one I've earned." She waved with her right hand and shrugged.

"Type Zero One cybernetic; I'm not surprised."

"I don't follow you."

"It's not important."

"What are *you* doing here!" roared the Beezer. Minu was amused that it took him this long to notice her arrival, but he'd been deep in discussion with another Squeen.

"Good to see you again, Ki'ki'taan," Minu said with a bow, the same as she'd given Quick Finder. All the Squeen were now watching the human and Beezer, some looking back and forth between them.

"I cannot believe the gall of you, Destroyer, to come here like this. Does your First know you're here bothering me?"

"No, and he doesn't know about the amount of merchandise you're stealing and selling on the black market either. Shall we contact him?" The Beezer took a stomping step backward as if Minu had physically struck him. "Don't be afraid, I'm not here to blow up your warehouses, or to demand any more goods."

"Then gift me with the reason you're here."

"To speak to the Squeen."

"How do you know about them?" Ki'ki'taan asked in hushed tones, as much as a Beezer was capable of anyway.

"I rescued Quick Finder while I was destroying your Portal Spire. Please give me a few minutes alone with him, and you can continue whatever illegal transactions you were trying to complete." He thought about it for a second before stomping off, mumbling to himself and shaking his huge head from side to side.

"You know how to make an entrance," Quick Finder said, his huge buckteeth showing in an obvious smile. "This is my leader, Strong Arm." The Squeen who'd been speaking to Ki'ki'taan came forward and bowed to Minu; she favored him with a slightly deeper bow than she'd given Quick Finder.

"You must know by now that we do not exist."

"Fascinating, talking to a species that doesn't exist." It seems to be a theme of my life, she thought. First the Weavers, then the Squeen.

"How do you know about us, beyond your encounter with Quick Finder months ago? And on that, please accept my thanks for their release."

"You're not my enemy; this is how humans are. We don't make hostages of innocent beings." As she spoke his bright, perceptive eyes were taking in all the details of her. Her cybernetic arm, the Chosen uniform with three gold stars on the cuff, the curve of her hips and breasts. These Squeen were analyzers, this much was obvious. "I'm familiar with your species from a mission on a planet years ago." She quickly described the planet and the mission where she'd seen the seemingly primitive Squeen camping in the desert.

Strong Arm nodded. "The pilgrimage," he said.

"What's that?"

"Once every ten years some of us spend a month on the planet of our birth, a sort of religious pilgrimage. Because of the condition of the world, it's an arduous undertaking and has a spiritual cleansing effect. It's required at least once in your lifetime if you are to lead our people."

"How many times have you done it?"

"Five times," he said proudly.

"We know it wasn't just a leasehold. How was the planet made uninhabitable, and why?"

Strong Arm was quiet for several long moments, studying her. He turned to two other Squeen flanking him, both with considerable amounts of gray in their fur, and they looked at him with obvious nervousness, their movements quick and flighty. "I'm afraid I can't go into any detail with you. You have not had your Awakening yet."

"Damn it," Minu snarled, and she stared at the distant dualloy-supported ceiling. She tried to find another tack to take. "Where do you live now?"

"Here and there."

"You're squatting on another world?"

"No, absolutely not."

"Then you have a leasehold? That isn't possible, there's no record—"

"I didn't say we lived on any world." Minu gawked, and he laughed, almost like a human would have. "Quick Finder said you humans are incredibly curious." The alien looked at her appraisingly, as if comparing her in some unknown way against a standard. "This trait is something you come by honestly."

"I don't understand."

"And I can't help you reach an understanding."

"I see." She looked down at her right hand and thought of something. "Quick Finder recognized this type of cybernetic implant."

"Yes, it's a very specific type not in use for eons."

"Okay, well if a species in ages past used this type of implant, then their physiology must have been much like ours."

"It can be safely assumed you shared nearly identical physiology."

"Wha—"

"Please proceed, time is short."

"Um, okay, well if that ancient species' physiology matched ours, then there must have been a complete biological codex, all the necessary data which took advantage of the full breadth of Concordian technology, right?"

"You're getting close to the limits of what I can say."

"Then just answer the damned question."

"The answer is yes; complete medical technologies exist tailored to your species' basic physiology."

"But why can't I access it through the computer networks?"

"I can't tell you that."

"Then tell me where to find the codex."

"It isn't that easy."

"I don't care how easy it is, I have a friend slowly dying from an injury that could be treated in your species with a simple medical procedure. I'll do whatever it takes to save this friend."

"Whatever it takes? That's a bold claim."

"You have no idea how bold I am."

Strong Arm looked toward Ki'ki'taan and shook his head. "That is the most stubborn Beezer I've ever dealt with, and that's saying something considering their basic nature. The fact that you handled him so easily is a strong testimony in support of your statement." With a tiny delicate hand he removed a tablet from his utility belt and activated it. Instantly Minu jerked her own out and Strong Arm touched his to hers, initiating a private connection unreadable by even the most sophisticated listening device. Her screen flashed, indicating an incoming transmission. It was a simple file holding only the coordinates for a star system. "I can help you no more. I may have gone too far already."

"I can ask no more of you than a chance." Minu bowed low and turned to go.

"Chosen Alma, wait a moment." She turned back in time to see the other two Squeen trying to stop Strong Arm from speaking. He shook them off and spoke a few stern words in their language before approaching her. "You seem to enjoy mysteries; ask yourself this. The Concordia are old, millions of years old. Countless species evolving, interacting, learning, fighting, living, dying over the endless years. So who were the first, the original Concordia? You're correct about one thing. That was the world of our birth."

*****

Chapter Six
Octember 27th, 522 AE

Chosen Training Complex, Stevens Pass, Bellatrix

Terrence Pegalio watched Minu run the young group of prospective scouts through a drill with a critical eye. Having her under his control had been a longtime dream of his, but now that she was actually here, he was forced to admit that she was good, perhaps very good. The group of five scouts she was working with had been considered hopeless by the previous instructor, a hard-working four-star originally from the Rusk territories. With an even mixture of hard work and abuse, he'd turned out some of the best scouts. When Minu showed up, half his age and sporting three golden stars on her sleeve, Eric had decided instantly she was his enemy. Terrence had been forced to order him to work with her.

"I don't like you," he'd told her near the end of their first week, the days spent mostly showing her the training procedures they used.

"No, really? I wasn't sure, what with all the animosity and hateful glares."

"That's why I don't like you," he snarled, his Rusk accent thick. "The Malovich family is friends with my family. They told me what you did to their young boy, such a prospect to the Chosen he was, and I have never trained a better—"

"Prospect? Now you listen to me, you son of a bitch," she snarled, rounding on the man who was easily twice her size, "that little bastard almost got me and my friends killed in the trials. Then when that wasn't enough, he started the Vendetta with the Rasa that almost cost us our leasehold and *did* cost us hundreds of lives." He started to speak while backing away; Minu closed in and jabbed a finger (her cybernetic one) hard into his chest and cut him off, "I don't care what you've heard, that's the truth, and if you mention that fucker's name in front of me again I'll kick your ass up one side and down the other. Do I make myself clear?"

Of course after that Eric wanted nothing to do with the fiery redheaded Chosen, and that made Terrence's job more difficult. So he figured he'd bring her to heel by assigning a group of unruly Scout trainees with poor prospects for redemption. After she failed to turn them around, she'd be at least slightly cowed and maybe more manageable. But now, after two weeks of one-on-one work, the five young Chosen were arguably the best team in the last part of the training cycle, outperforming even Eric's handpicked crowd.

"Come on!" Minu yelled from the front of the group, easily staying ahead of them. Michael, the best runner among them, was making some progress in speed, but not in endurance. Tanya, a very rare female scout, and Orlando were better in endurance, but stuck in a rut and not getting any faster. That left Chris and Derek, her two problem children. She'd quickly realized when taking over the team that they were the reason for the trouble. Naturally Terrence refused to break them up. The two had recruited Michael, Tanya, and Orlando as friends during their trials and, like many such groups, were all but inseparable. They didn't succeed in the trials through teamwork and perseverance like Minu's team, they'd followed the lead of Chris and Derek to lie, cheat, and steal their way to success. The rules allowed for this, as long as no one was 'hurt,' and the scouts needed Chosen with less than stellar character. The problem now was her need to forge them into Chosen, transforming them from the pack of thugs they'd started as.

The job was all the more frustrating to her since the team had real potential. Despite the distraction of a woman, they worked well together in solving problems and helping each other; a synergy her group had also achieved. There was no underlying sexual tension between them, something she was certain the trainers had seen in her own trials group and had thus broken them up for training. Motivating Chris or Derek into being the official leader of the group was not possible; neither of them elected to take responsibility despite the fact that they'd forged the group themselves and led it in all but name. They preferred to keep to the shadows and manipulate, being sure that everyone else followed their subtle lead.

Minu would have given up on them weeks ago if it wasn't for two simple reasons. One, their potential. Two, she needed them for something she was planning. Something she hadn't dared talk to anyone about, not even Cherise.

"Slow down, damn it," Tanya snarled from behind as they rounded the track again. Minu glanced over her shoulder at the young woman; her long black hair was meticulously tied into a single pony tail that flew behind her as she ran. She was tall, like Cherise, but of a much more normal build with an average bust line common to her Summit Tribe.

"Masochist," Orlando agreed, his medium build still keeping pace with Tanya. He liked her, but in a safe way. His looks were the type you couldn't remember five minutes after you'd met him, and he kept his brown hair cut short, like most Chosen scouts. He was only the second person she'd known from the Boglands, besides Gregg.

"Nothing better to do," Derek mumbled between gasps for air. Minu pushed him relentlessly, usually running circles around him saying, "I'm shorter than you; what's your excuse?" He kept his blonde hair a little longer than most men, but that was the style in Plateau, where he'd grown up, just like Minu. Despite his laid-back style, he was a cute guy and quick to smile. Of the five, Minu liked him the most personally.

"Maybe she just wants to run us to death?" Chris barked from the back of the pack, making sure she could hear him.

"Yeah," Michael agreed, as always. They were a sort of Mutt and Jeff pair in many ways. Chris heralded from the Desert Tribe, like Cherise, but his skin was very light brown. He preferred to shave his head, like Dram, instead of cutting it short. Michael, on the other hand, was olive-skinned and native to New Jerusalem. His looks were classically Jewish, down to the slightly curly brown hair. He liked to keep a very thin mustache just on the edge of notice. It made you look closer to see if it was really there, and that seemed to please him.

"You guys are an unbelievable bunch of pussies!" she yelled and suddenly stopped. Tanya and Orlando almost ran her down before they dodged out of the way. Derek came to a smooth stop while Chris and Michael trotted up like there was no particular hurry. "I'll tell you what; if any one of you can take me hand-to-hand, we can be done for the day." She looked from one to the other for any sign of interest. Each had met her more than once in the fighting arena and knew what she could do. No takers today. "Okay, I'll tell you what, how about two, three? Wow, amazing. Fine, all of you at the same time."

"I'll take that bet," Chris said quickly.

"Yeah," Michael agreed. The others slowly nodded their heads, with Tanya being last. Of them all, she was the least accomplished in hand-to-hand combat.

"Great," she said and walked them toward the nearby sand pit. The training center covered forty acres on the back side of the Steven's Pass complex, right against the mountains' base. It was a cool April afternoon, with the sun beating down at an angle only slightly above the peaks. Darkness would fall quickly, just like it always did in the mountains. Minu doffed her light sweatshirt and flexed her shoulder muscles. "You win, and we're done. I win, another ten laps."

"What about the arm?" Chris asked, gesturing at her gray right arm. Dozens of Chosen in and around the complex sported cybernetic limbs just like hers, many of them working for Training. It was often the last stop for a crippled Chosen still hoping to stay in the corps. That wasn't the case for Minu, of course. She was a poster child for adaption to cybernetic enhancements. As part of her duties she did therapy sessions with those who struggled after losing a limb if they had trouble adapting to the alien-made limbs.

"I'll keep it on the level, you have my word."

"And how do we know you won't push it a little."

"Oh, watch it now," Orlando warned. Tanya cringed.

"You ever question my honor again, Chris, and you can go find another team, and do it while I'm kicking your skinny little ass all around this complex."

"Hey, just kidding!" he said, smiling and holding up his hands in mock humor.

"Yeah, no biggie."

"Same goes for you, Michael." His little mustache wiggled as he looked at her, but he held his tongue. This late in the afternoon, the fighting area was deserted. As she led the team toward the Snake Pit, a triangle of sand surrounded by benches, Minu spotted a solitary figure standing up in the bleachers surrounding the training ground. She knew instantly it was Terrence. With most of the last class of Chosen having already completed their training cycle, they were going to other branches already. Only a few dozen potential scouts remained for their more intense physical and field training. Minu's habit of training late into the afternoon with her misfits, long after the other trainers were gone, drew him like a fly to poop. At first her practice drew harsh emails from him demanding to know why she was deviating from established training techniques. Her only replies were test results and physical evaluations of the five candidates previously considered hopeless. He stopped demanding answers and now stood this almost daily watch, often staying for hours. His unusually tall frame never moved, and he never sat down.

"Okay," she said as they reached the soft sand of the Snake Pit, "ready?"

"Rules?" Chris asked as he removed his sweatshirt.

"No bone breaking, no disabling."

"Okay," he said and stepped in with a roundhouse to her face. Minu effortlessly caught his arm, cocked a leg, turned, and threw him over her hip using his own momentum. As she suspected, Michael was there aiming a kick at her back. He tried to check his swing and instead caught one of Chris's out-flung knees in the face just before his friend crashed fully into him, sending the two crumpling to the ground.

Acting on instinct, Minu dropped down and spun on her left foot, the right one lancing out at full length as she spun. It would have hit most people in the knees, but Derek was nearly as short as her, so it hit him in the mid-thigh instead, throwing off the punch he was aiming at her head and causing his fist to slide harmlessly along her shoulder. She cocked the foot back, angled it upward, and kicked him in the solar plexus. He folded and went down, struggling to breathe.

An arm went around her neck, and she was pulled up and back high enough for her feet to clear the ground. Tanya came around from the side and delivered a forearm to her stomach. She'd seen the blow coming and tensed her abdominal muscles. The hit was solid, and she felt her ribs creak more than enough to knock the wind out of her. Of the two, the stranglehold from Orlando was the bigger threat. Minu thrust both arms straight up, making him strain to keep a hold on her, then rammed her elbows back with as much normal force as she had. Years of tough physical training meant it was a lot of force. Her arms were bands of solid muscle, except the one that was a machine. She was careful to keep her word, allowing the mechanical arm to perfectly match the force from the natural one. Orlando cursed and dropped her just as Tanya aimed a spin kick.

The roundhouse kick would have hit her in the side of the head had Orlando not released her. Instead the kick landed squarely on Orlando's face, spinning him and knocking him cold. "Aw crap," Tanya said as Minu moved in. She blocked Minu's first two attacks, but then her pride and joy was her downfall. Minu got hold of her waist-length ponytail, gave a powerful yank, and raised a knee. Tanya's face met Minu's knee with a dull thud and the girl fell back, out cold. The whole fight lasted ten seconds. They'd landed a grand total of one blow between them.

Minu massaged her abdomen, noting a small twinge to one side, but nothing severe. The team was rolling over to shake their heads or massage deep bruises. All except Orlando, who was still out cold. "Pathetic," she said, turning and jogging toward the distant buildings. "Ten laps, kids, and I'll check the recordings."

"Bitch," Chris moaned.

"Yeah," Michael agreed.

* * *

"You called, Terrence?"

"Come in," he said, and Minu walked into the office. Every time she was there she got a little smile realizing it was only half the size of her own office on Herdhome. Of course, offices in Steven's Pass were all on the small side. As a council member, Terrence's was one of the largest, with only Dram's topside office and Jacob's any bigger. "Have a seat," he said and gestured toward the office's couch.

Minu was curious; it was the first time he hadn't insisted she stand while he barked at her, so she went and sat down. As she walked to the couch she could see the track where five lonely figures were still trudging around in circles as night fell. "What can I do for you?"

"I was watching you work with those rejects, and frankly, I'm impressed."

"Really?"

"Sure, how could I not be? Even Eric mumbled something about thinking they would make a good scout team."

"Hard to believe."

"I know. I'm going to go ahead and authorize them to go into operational training. Take them out and get them some experience."

"Sure, whatever you say." He walked over and casually sat on the couch, not as far away as he could, but not as close either. "Is there anything else?"

"You've impressed me a lot more than I expected. I was pissed when your pet soldiers—"

"Rangers," Minu reminded him coldly.

"Right, anyway, I was pissed because they were outside my training control; I still think that's a mistake, but you got results. So to have you here now, it's a good move on your part."

"Really, why would that be?"

"You haven't had anyone on the council on your side. Oh, Dram of course, and Bjorn, but he's been brushed off the table with the rest of the stale crumbs. I'm in a position to move you to the next step."

"I'm listening," she said with no small amount of suspicion. The higher you got in the Chosen, the deeper the plotting and intrigue tended to get. She also knew for a fact that Terrence didn't like her, regardless of how sweetly he was sitting there talking to her.

"I've been considering retirement for a while now; I'm almost forty after all. It's been a tradition of sorts to suggest your own replacement."

"Worked out great for Bjorn."

"He was never a team player; I'm sure you realize that now. With my recommendation, and Dram's support, Jacob would have to take the promotion seriously."

"Wow, I don't know what to say."

"Don't carry on; it's what I want to do, for you." Minu nodded and he smiled slightly. The feeling of suspicion in her belly began to grow into full-fledged paranoia. Suddenly leaving was the best option. "I would only need one small favor."

"Favor?"

"Sure, it's nothing that big for a smart girl like you. And in a few short years you'll have another star off that sleeve!" Minu glanced down at her sleeve and sighed, wishing he'd cut to the chase. "So, I think we have an understanding?"

"I'm not sure I do—" she cut off as she looked up, the words catching in her throat. While he'd been talking, Terrence had been busy. He sat there with his pants down, penis standing up from his waist.

"Not such a big thing to do?" he laughed and gestured with his head, "A smart girl like you has to know how the world works."

Minu realized her jaw was hanging down as she stared at his throbbing member. Suddenly terrified he'd get the wrong idea, her mouth snapped shut. "Is *that* why you called me here?" He shrugged and spread his legs wide, obviously certain of how things would turn out. "It's kind of amazing, isn't it?"

"I'm proud of it," he laughed and slid a little closer, making it bob up and down. Some small part of her noted that age didn't treat men's testicles kindly.

"Well, let's see here," she said and leaned over his waist.

"Absolutely," he said and leaned back confidently. Minu took a good grip with her right hand, way down against his pubic hair, and tugged. "Easy honey, don't want to pull it off, do you?"

"That's an option," she said, low and menacingly. She doubled her grip to her human maximum, that scale built into the cybernetic limb with which she gripped his member. His eyes bugged out, and he gasped. Minu quickly straddled him and grabbed his testicles with her left hand. It wasn't as potentially powerful, but it didn't have to be. He let out a strangled scream and cocked an arm back to punch her. "Touch me, and I'll show you something you've never seen…" he froze and looked at her, panic in his eyes and drool running down his chin, "the roots."

"W-what do you want?"

"I want a world where nasty bastards like you don't try to use their shriveled up, nasty, crusty old dicks as weapons against girls less than half their age!" Her feet slid to the floor and she stood, slowly, without giving up an ounce of pressure. He followed her as if he was connected to overhead wires, an almost comical marionette linked at his genitals. "It's beyond the pale to even *think* that someone of your power would do something like this to get into my pants. And you couldn't even fucking *ask in a civilized manner!*" She squeezed harder with her left hand and his knees almost buckled. "Who knows, maybe I would have entertained the idea. You're not that bad looking. But no, what do you do? You just drop your pants and pull this thing out, waving it in my face with half-veiled promises of 'career guidance.' What do you think Jacob would think of this situation?"

"I, I, ach?"

"Right, hard to say. Maybe I'll just march you down the hall and find out. Not a lot of Chosen in the building right now, being late and all. Still, there should be a few dozen to see me towing you around by this shriveled hunk of meat." She looked down and saw that he'd most definitely lost his erection, but the amount of pressure she was exerting wasn't allowing the blood to flow. The head had a decidedly unhealthy pallor about it,

"I didn't…ugh!"

"Didn't what, think I'd put up much of a fight. Do you even *know* who my father is?" He nodded vigorously, and she shook hers. "Really, it doesn't look that way from where I stand, and what I'm holding. I've got news for you; you're not going to see me naked, touch my body, or get this thing anywhere near any part of me, except this cybernetic hand that could just rip it off, of course."

"No, no," he said. She wasn't sure if it was a plea or an agreement, and it didn't matter.

"But you *are* going to give me that help you promised. You know why? Because I turned on the recorder on my tablet before I walked in here. Every word you said, and probably a few stills of you sitting there with this thing standing up, are now recorded on it. If you so much as say an unkind word about me or look the wrong way at me or any of my friends, I'll see that it not only gets into Jacob's hand, it will find its way into the press."

For just a second she considered ripping his penis off. Dr. Tasker might have a prosthetic that would work for that too. Ultimately she decided against it, because the secret was more useful than having to explain why she'd gelded the man in charge of the Training division. She boosted her right hand past human normal; just enough to make him utter a short visceral scream, then let the horribly mistreated piece of meat drop from her hand.

He dropped to the floor, trembling hands going to cover his abused parts, tears rolling down his cheeks. "Of all the nasty things done to me by men since I've joined the Chosen, all the low-down dirty tricks and attempts to sabotage my career, I thought I'd seen it all. Thanks for proving me wrong, you son of a bitch."

"Sorry," he hissed between his teeth, eyes wide in agony as his hands explored the damage.

"Don't even try, you animal." She pulled the tablet from her pocket and waved it at him, "Just don't forget what I said, ever." And with a purposeful stride she marched from the office, wishing she could slam the door behind her. As she walked down the hall, the sounds of his sobs slowly fell away. She needed to get to her billet in the main building. It would take a gallon of soap to get her hands clean.

*****

Chapter Seven
Octember 27th, 522 AE

Chosen Training Complex, Stevens Pass, Bellatrix

"The most important thing to remember is you're never safe," Minu said as they walked through the ruins of a once massive industrial complex. Tanya, Orlando, Derek, Chris, and Michael were in a rough echelon formation following closely behind her. Their weapons were slung over their backs, kept charged and ready should trouble appear. Minu had picked this world, Deep Blue, because of the low chance of that happening. As advertised, the skies were a bright shade of blue, the system's star riding high in the afternoon sky. The air was clean and crisp, hovering around seventeen degrees with little breeze. A lovely day for some training, and legend-tracking.

"How do you know if you're being watched?" Tanya asked.

"Depends on who's doing the watching."

"Say T'Chillen," Derek suggested.

"You start dying," Chris offered.

"He's probably right," Minu admitted.

"Yeah," Michael added.

"Doesn't do you any good to entertain worst-case scenarios," she told them. "Most species aren't nearly as bloodthirsty, aggressive, or as well-equipped as the T'Chillen. All the better junk piles are staked out by species, some with the ability to enforce their claims, others with less dubious skills. Deep Blue here is about as worthless as you get. I've been here a dozen times over the last year and haven't seen another being. Only backward species like us come here looking for stuff. Not even the Rasa mess with it, although we ran into them here, years ago, during my father's time. Now, it's just a good place to train kiddies like you." Minu didn't have to look to know that Chris was making a face at her back.

"Okay, so I want you to spread out and find something useful."

"Like what?" Orlando asked. "We're not techs or anything."

"You've all been trained in salvage operations, including how to recognize operational Concordian devices that we use. So find something and bring it back. First one back gets bonus points, best find gets more points. Get going." She found an overturned aerocar and perched on a crumpled door panel. Most of the team was off individually; they'd been trained to keep an eye on each other's backs. She could see Chris and Michael staying close together and shook her head. *I wonder if they're homosexuals?* she thought for the first time.

Once they were all out of sight in the ruins, she took out her tablet and tabbed it to life. Deep Blue was indeed a good choice for a quick run to the frontier with her team of misfits, but the data on the computer was a better reason. They were a few kilometers from the usual junk zone, in an area that her salvage maps said held nothing useful. Another map she had, one left for her by her father, told a different story. Her father's secret logs spoke of the dozens of caches he'd left all over the frontier, each containing both rare and valuable goodies, and hints that would eventually allow her to unlock the deepest encrypted files he'd left for her. And beyond that, hopefully a way to reach the unnamed system whose coordinates had been provided by the Squeen.

The Squeen—now that was a mystery. Ted was digging a little deeper for her, trying to find out some more details on the supposedly long-dead species. The hints given to Minu on their last meeting proved enigmatic at best. How could a species have no leasehold and also not be a squatter somewhere? And if GBX49881 was the world they'd evolved on, what had been done to it and how? Maybe they blew the crap out of themselves in a nuclear apocalypse. Judging from the ground water, it was a real possibility.

The system Strong Arm had suggested resided in the Tog database of stars and was noted as dangerous, classification FCZ1011. Minu had named it Enigma in the database, for her own convenience. Sector F of the galaxy was mostly quiet, unlike G, where they were now. Sector G was often called the Frontier and contained only a couple of leaseholds scattered around. Sector F contained no leaseholds, but more than a few valuable resource locations and junk piles considered 'high value,' which meant they were usually claimed by a species. Atmospheric designation C meant it wouldn't be nice to visit. The C worlds were considered 'survivable' by human standards, but only just. And as went along with being in sector F it was a Z ownership designator. An X meant no one wanted it, a Z meant it was in constant contention. Open warfare was not only possible, but common.

Since taking on the misfits, she'd hatched a plan. If those five losers could be formed into a real team, perhaps they'd be the ones for a high-risk mission to Enigma. She justified the danger she'd put them through by rationalizing that they wouldn't have been scouts without her. It was the least they owed her.

"Found something," she heard over the radio in her ear. It sounded like Chris, which would make sense, since it wasn't called in by procedures.

"I'm not listening if you're not doing it right."

"Chris calling team leader, I have something."

"Roger that," she smiled. "Squawk your location; other team members continue your sweep. That includes you, Michael."

"Yeah, okay."

As soon as Minu entered the collapsed building, once a power distribution center, she knew this was it. In each corner of the remaining open space was a small pile of rocks; the topmost rock was different from the rest in the pile. Standard Chosen cache marker. Chris was kneeling next to a corroded control panel sweeping his energy sensor back and forth. If he was following procedures, that would be the last step.

"No EM, no life signs, no flux from a shielded plasma charge, and nothing from the bio sensors."

"Very good, scout, proceed and open the cache." He nodded and carefully began opening the panel. Once the four fasteners were released it swung open easily, final confirmation that it was a cache. Inside were three small standard Concordian packing crates, somewhat flat and thin; they'd hold no more than a cubic meter each.

"What could be of any use in these?" Chris asked as he examined the crates.

"Something small," Minu offered as he looked.

"They're code locked. I'll try the standard code group." Chris typed in a sequence to the script keyboard. A single light flashed white, negative in Concordian tech-speak. He tried four more before giving up. "None of the standard codes work." Minu nodded and leaned over the cache. She typed in a sequence, and the light flashed blue. The case made a pinging sound as the magnetic locks released. "How did you know the code?"

"A little birdie told me," she joked. Actually it was her father. The access code was recorded in his journal next to this location. It was the first time she'd made it out to one of his secret cache locations, and the first proof of what he'd promised. "Let me," she said and nudged him out of the way. "Rank has its privileges."

"Whatever," Chris grumbled and made room for her. "Say, why do you wear that old knife in the field?" he asked and gestured at the blade riding in a thigh holster. "It looks like one of those crappy steel jobs they gave us during the trials."

"It's the very one I used, actually." She shrugged as she prepared to swing open the case. "Call it sentimental reasons." The case lid swung up to reveal three rows of carefully packed dragonfly-bots. Their gossamer dualloy wings were nestled one on top of another, brilliant green visual receptors and sensors glistening in the sunlight shinning in through the shattered walls.

"Woof," Chris said, dumbfounded at the find. "That's a mother lode of D-bots," he said. Minu nodded, a little amused at the younger Chosen's habit of abbreviating everything. She used her code, checked the other two cases, and found them all similarly stocked. Each case held thirty D-bots, as Chris called them, ninety all together. In the last case, one of the bot's wings was not folded precisely. She plucked it from its case and held it in her hand.

"Activate," she said.

"It probably doesn't even have a battery," Chris said, but the bot twitched and stood up on its six tiny legs, wings swirling around and humming audibly. "I'll be damned."

She held up her tablet and the bot touched its antennae to the device. The tablet beeped once, and a secure connection was established. Minu pressed the download button and a single file transferred. It only took a moment to verify that nothing more was in its memory. "Shut down and secure," she told it, and a second later the wings folded back and it nestled into the box with the others. "Go through and check them all for any files or intel," she ordered Chris as she glanced at the file nestled into her tablet.

"What's in the file?" he asked. Minu ignored him and turned to leave. "Keeping secrets from your team? Is that what command is all about?"

"If you survive long enough as a Chosen, you'll understand that the universe is made of secrets." He opened his mouth to give a smarmy reply, then thought about what she said, and thought better of it. "Michael, you might as well come in here and help your buddy check these bots."

"Yeah?" came the voice from outside.

"Sure," she said as she walked by, "and I'm entering your disregard of orders in the report."

"Yeah," he said, shook his head, and went inside. "How the hell?" he asked Chris.

"X-ray vision, I think. Get your ass over here and give me a hand. Can you believe this shit?"

Outside, away from the two misfits' prying eyes, Minu extracted the file and opened it. As she expected, it was a code cypher. Taking it from there she dropped it onto one of Chriso's top secret files after another. On the third and last file, it dropped into place. "One of three complete," the access encryption responded.

"Crap," Minu said dejectedly. "Well, it's a start." Three files, three cypher strings per file, nine total. But there were a hell of a lot more than three 'special caches' in Chriso's journals. Was it just luck that she'd found one on the first try?

An hour later, the team was reassembled at the rally point, Minu with one case over her shoulder, the other two carried by Derek and Orlando (a conscious choice on her part, the bots were very valuable). The team had also found a small pile of power control modules and rare sizes of empty EPCs that could be reused. Deep Blue lived up to its reputation of a safe training ground, and gave Minu her first step toward unlocking the remaining mystery of her father.

* * *

It was a week later during a meeting with the combat readiness sub-council of the Chosen that Dram caught up with her. The meeting was breaking for lunch when he got her alone. "What the fuck did you do to Terrence?" he asked.

"Good to see you, old friend."

"Don't give me that, answer my question."

"Why?"

"Okay, fair enough. He's asked for you to be reassigned. Said you did a great job and suggests you be given command of the scouts."

"Heh," Minu grunted and shook her head. She'd been quietly expecting much worse. After their encounter, Terrence took a medical leave for a week and then completely avoided her after that. She shrugged and told him, in brief, what had happened in the Training department leaders' office.

"That bastard," Dram snarled, and Minu saw real rage for the first time on his face, and it scared her. "What happened? You didn't…"

"Hell no. No, I basically grabbed him, in a very delicate place, and threatened to rip it off if he ever tried that sort of thing again. I also told him I'd recorded everything because I thought he'd try something like that, and if he made trouble I'd give it to Jacob and the press."

"Did you record it?"

"No; wish I'd thought of it, though. Never even considered that someone would do something like that." She chuckled and shook her head. "It's not the first dick I've seen, but to turn around and see the old fart sitting there with his boner pointing at the ceiling…" she blanched, then laughed long and hard. Dram looked shocked, then his facade broke, and he joined in.

"I never told you, but I promised your dad to keep an eye on you."

"You didn't have to tell me," she said and winked. He shook his head again and patted her arm.

"Anyway, after he got me to promise to watch out for you, he laughed and said maybe I should watch out for everyone else around you. I have to say, he had a point."

"No, Terrence had a point, but it might not work as well as before."

After more laughter they continued their conversation over sandwiches. "Those bots you brought back are incredible," he told her, "ninety state of the art dragonfly-bots."

"D-bots?" Minu asked with a smirk.

Dram gave her a queer look. "All the young Chosen have taken to abbreviating like that."

"Oh, gotcha. We must have sent a thousand teams to Deep Blue over the years. EPCs, some other barely useful junk, maybe a rare control panel, that's about it. You take a training mission and come back with a couple million worth of the best bots made in the Concordia. You care to tell me how?"

Minu considered telling him for a moment. Telling him about her father's message from beyond the grave, the talk with P'ing, the Weavers, her plans for the trip to Enigma, everything. Then she let out a long breath and shook her head. Even though this was her father's best friend, she didn't dare take the risk. If he knew she meant to mount up a team and take off into the hinterlands of the empire, he'd have her locked behind a desk, probably chained to it. Especially now that he'd admitted what she'd already known in her heart, that he'd been shepherding her all along.

"Okay, I understand. Secrets make the galaxy go around."

"Ain't that the damn truth?"

"I always thought your dad was the sneakiest, most double-dealing SOB I ever hoped to meet. Now I see you're his kid, through and through." Minu wasn't sure if that was a compliment or not. "Tell me some day?"

"Sure, I promise." He nodded; that was good enough for him. More sandwiches came and they concentrated on refueling their bodies.

After the conference, she got a rare chance to do some cornering herself. In this case, it was Ted Hurt and Bjorn, probably the two smartest people on the planet. She found them both just down the hall from the conference center, hard at work in the lab they jointly operated. As had been the case for the last year, they were still hard at work on the multi-role fighter she'd needed for the Rangers. Most of the fabrication's design work was done, and they were tinkering with the systems integration. The center of the lab was dominated by a large pod holding two seated Chosen, both with helmets covering their entire faces and heads. The pod simulated the interior controls of the fighters; the helmets provided the simulated operating environment. Before the battle with the Tanam, Minu had spent at least one afternoon a week here working with them. The first twenty fighters were already in service, an ingenious hybrid of existing old-fashioned Concordian transports and state-of-the-art fields to help reform the hull and add weaponry.

Bjorn, white hair still wild and unkempt, was typing furiously at a holo-keyboard while Ted watched a projection of the simulation on one wall of liquid display. The pilots were running through a strafing maneuver exercise against an armed target, dodging and weaving through realistic looking hills and valleys. Inside the pod, the pilots jerked and bumped around; the simulation made it as realistic as possible through the use of small hoverfield projectors. Ted was shaking his head from side to side, his long but meticulously-kept graying black hair waving. She noticed the bald spot on top had grown wider. "I was wondering when you'd make an appearance," he said without looking up.

"How?" she asked.

"My dear, that subtle body lotion you use is enough to make me sit up and grin." Minu rolled her eyes. He'd never missed a beat in his attempts to get into her pants. She wondered if she just gave up and let him if he'd give it a rest, or become completely uncontrollable. "Is my massive sex appeal finally getting to you, lass?"

"More like a slight case of nausea," she said and came closer to look at the displays.

"Hi Minu!" Bjorn called without missing a key stroke. "Where the hell have you been? You're supposed to come by once a week, remember?"

"She was reassigned months ago, Bjorn," Ted exclaimed. "Don't *you* remember?"

"Can't say that I do," he replied. Minu observed for a few more minutes as they strafed the ground target over and over.

"What's wrong?" she finally asked.

"Absolutely nothing," Ted grinned. "We just locked down the last control problem, the one that caused the crash last week."

"Crash! No one told me about a crash."

"Aaron must have considered it unimportant. He was the pilot. Now calm down, I said it wasn't bad. They were simulating strafing runs, and the controls developed a feedback wobble. The fighter clipped a hill and nosed into a river. Aaron is an excellent pilot and managed to roll over and level them before they hit."

"Casualties?"

"Three injured; he was the worst with a broken wrist. I hear he's already back in with the training cycle."

Minu made a face and reminded herself to give him a hard time for not telling her. Then she remembered she wasn't in charge of the Rangers any more. Would she have called her friends if the same thing happened? Unlikely, she was forced to admit. "Okay, so you've got it taken care of?"

"Yep, old Bjorn over there just made us go through a full dress-rehearsal. They'll take one out next week to Ft. Jovich and do a live test. It was just software, a skipped digit in the dynamic feedback resistance subroutine."

"If you're done, do you have time to talk?"

The three went and shared a table in the corner of the cafeteria. Minu saw they'd painted the walls, but the food was the same, filling and unspectacular. Over meatloaf, tasting suspiciously like kloth, with potatoes and gravy, she told them why she'd come.

"Original Concordia?" Ted asked, his face at first confused then intrigued.

"Been wondering that for a long time," Bjorn said around a mouthful of potatoes.

"Kloth shit," Ted said.

"No, really. It's kinda like the chicken and the egg, but bigger."

"Eloquent, as usual."

"Whatever. It's part missing link, part creationism versus evolution." Minu always loved when the two got going; it was always amusing, and very often it was educational, too.

"The only advantage of getting our home world blown up is that the fundamentalist view is mostly dead." Ted grinned widely. "The Concordia had to start somewhere, right? All the aliens I've spoken to go every which way. Most don't think there was an original Concordia; they think it just became an alliance of species that grew and grew, maybe beginning a billion years ago."

"I don't buy that," Minu said.

"Me neither," Ted agreed.

"Then we're in consensus. The other two theories are thus. An ancient and powerful species evolved at the beginning of time, and being all alone, seeded the galaxy with a nearly infinite variety of genetic seeds, then died off before any of them matured, leaving behind the portals as a gift to their progeny."

"Poetic," Minu offered.

"And improbable." Bjorn laughed.

"Sure, sure. The last theory, and the one I subscribe to, is of an ancient species, maybe the oldest in the galaxy, maybe from outside our galaxy, was possibly the first to become a space borne species. They then went around helping every species they found bootstrap themselves up and/or rescuing those about to die."

"Much more probable." Bjorn nodded, and Minu did too.

"But what happened to them?" Minu asked.

"Who knows?" Bjorn shrugged and finished his drink with a flourish. "Long gone. What was the first civilization on Earth? No one knows, and there was probably no evidence left."

"Yes," Minu said, then added, "but they weren't a super technologically-advanced species spanning millions of light-years of space and responsible for creating an empire that encompasses an entire galaxy."

"Maybe they pissed someone off," Ted suggested.

"As good an explanation as any other," Bjorn said with a sense of finality.

"What do you call them, Ted?"

"The Lost."

Minu thought that if it didn't matter, then why had Strong Arm brought it up? Were they the Lost, as Ted called them? No, it just didn't feel right. She couldn't believe that a species so powerful, so potentially benevolent, could become nothing more than nameless wanderers. No, they weren't the Lost, but they knew more than they'd told her. The others with Strong Arm had made it obvious they didn't like what little he had said.

"So how comes the War College?" Ted asked.

Minu spent a few minutes talking about the reactions she'd gotten to the first semester of classes as well as the students. A nearly even mixture of the curious and the seriously interested. "I've given a lot of thought to your theories of the Concordia."

Ted nodded and watched her with his perceptive eyes. "And what conclusion have you come to?"

"That you're right, the Concordia are in decline. It's obvious." He nodded to her and smiled; Bjorn scratched his chin and listened. The two had developed their theory long before Minu was born, and had done so with her father, Chriso. "The real question is why."

"Bingo!" Bjorn cheered, gesturing with his drink and sending an arc of fluid across the room. Minu looked confused, and he waved her off with the same hand, forcing her to duck the spray. "How could they begin this contraction, this decline? No signs of major wars, at least for eons, and no evidence of internal decay beyond the typical avarice and hubris you see of egotistical types like these so called higher-order species."

"So what are you going to do about it?" Ted wondered.

"Nothing, now. My field time is limited. But that doesn't mean I've stopped developing for the Rangers and such."

"Oh, really?" Bjorn looked excited. "Please, do tell?"

"Have you ever heard of combined munitions? They were a type of artillery under development before Earth was destroyed. And what about rockets, or missiles, or artillery?"

"The Concordia don't use them," Bjorn told her with authority. "A few youngsters like us employ chemical-powered rounds, and some are big enough to be artillery, but no combined rounds if I'm familiar enough with what you're referring to. And as for missiles, I can't say I've ever seen them anywhere in the Concordia." Ted nodded in agreement and took a sip of his tea.

"Might be worth pursuing. What about nuclear weapons?" Minu asked.

The normally proper Ted spat his tea out, almost choking on it. "What, are you mad?"

"No, just curious."

"I'm sure they wouldn't. I mean, it would be insane, wouldn't it?"

"Really?" Bjorn wondered aloud, annoyed by the tea on his shirt, "I wouldn't be so sure." Ted gave him a look as if the older man had just suggested they go running through the complex naked. "There's ample evidence that the Concordia, at least in the past, had the capability to destroy entire worlds!"

"Exactly, so why bother with nuclear bombs?"

"You can't run, until you walk, or crawl."

"Boys, give it a rest." They both turned to Minu. "My question is, could we build them if we wanted to?"

"This planet is so poor in heavy metals, I doubt it," Ted said.

"We've encountered plenty of radioactive elements on other worlds," Bjorn prompted. "In fact, I recall a sensor survey from the one trip our people took to Romulus that it is lousy with several uranium isotopes! As for building it, the plans are lacking in the Concordian database given to us by the Tog, but I have at least two legacy files from Earth with detailed plans, including how to enrich uranium or make a breeder reactor to produce plutonium..."

"The only real challenge would be building the cyclotrons, or centrifuges," Ted replied. "The rest is just fancy explosives, designs, and some inherently risky engineering work."

"Have either of you heard about progress made with calibrating Concordian high-tech medical devices, like the cerebral nano-bots I read about?"

Ted and Bjorn looked at each other, then around the room. They both knew why she was asking; Pip was not only a friend, he was Bjorn's nephew. "They're continuing to work on it," Ted told her. For a time they all sat quietly, each with their own thoughts.

"What if I said I think I might have a track on a matching physiological codex," she said and held up her right hand.

"I thought Tasker said we have a good-sized stock pile of those cybernetics? I mean, they're not perfect, but they're perfectly attuned to our physiology."

"If you don't mind gray skin," Bjorn added.

"And three fingers," Minu said and flipped them her unique bird. "Arms and legs are nice, but I'm talking about the whole deal."

"A full physiological/biological codex?" She nodded, and he smiled. "That would be something."

"There aren't any other hominids around," Bjorn said. "All we have to work with is leftovers from a species long gone."

"Why aren't there more hominids?" Minu asked. "It doesn't seem to make sense. I mean, look at how many species there are with similar bilateral symmetry!"

"The young lady has a point; even the snakes look a little like us from the chest up." Minu and Bjorn both shivered at Ted's comparison between humanity and arguably the most dangerous species in the galaxy.

"So how come the monkey descendants get such a raw deal?" she renewed the question.

"I don't know," Bjorn said, "but I want to know more about the codex you have a line on."

"It's no guarantee, mind you, but I have some good leads. Good enough that I'm thinking of going off-leash on this one."

They were silent again as it sank in. Taking a team and going without filing a plan, or getting permission, was akin to mutiny. You didn't do that without a good reason. "You know," Bjorn said and pointed at her, "there's no small amount of irony that it's you talking about that."

"Why?"

"Because the only other Chosen to ever do that, and come back, was your dad." She looked at Ted, who nodded.

"Then why wasn't he disciplined, or something? I've never heard about it."

Bjorn gestured to Ted to let him explain. "When you go against orders, you better have a really good reason, or bring back something worth the risk. Chriso didn't have a good reason, but he did manage to bring back something that was worth it. About a thousand medium-sized EPCs, fully loaded. Damned things looked like they were brand new, right out of the box."

"I've never seen an EPC that didn't look like it'd been rolled down at least one flight of stairs," said Minu.

"Neither had I, until that day. He obstinately refused to say where he'd found them."

Bjorn nodded and laughed. "Jovich was fit to be tied."

"That was when Jovich was still First?"

"Yep, in fact your father was only a four-star. The council, myself included, saved his bacon. We were pretty poor in credits and power back then. A good part of our industry and capabilities today are a result of that cache of EPCs he brought back. Of course, now that golden pile would have lasted maybe a month; back then it was years."

Seems every time someone talks about my father, I learn something more. She made a mental note to read through his logs and see where he'd found those capacitors. She leaned back and a pain jabbed in her abdomen. She hissed in pain and bent slightly forward.

"You okay?" Ted asked.

"Yeah, just girl stuff."

"Ah. Well, please keep us in the loop on your plans."

As the meeting broke up, she gave both men hugs and kisses on the cheek, being careful where Ted put his hands. She was walking down the hall toward the garage, doing her best to ignore the stabs of pain in her abdomen from each step, when someone called her name.

"Excuse me?" she answered.

"Are you Chosen Alma?"

"Yes," she said and turned to face the young man wearing five silver stars. "What can I do for you?"

"Dr. Rico sent me to get you; he heard you were in the facility." Dr. Rico, she thought, trying to recall the name. "I've been running all over the building, always a couple steps behind you."

"Did you consider having an operator page me?" He looked crestfallen, then embarrassed. "Never mind, what does this Dr. Rico…" she suddenly remembered him, "the xenophysician, want with me?"

"It's his patient, the Tanam. She wants to see you."

"Me?"

"Yes, she asked for you by name."

"So lead the way."

* * * * *

Chapter Eight
December 16th, 522 AE

Secure Medical Ward, Chosen Headquarters, Steven's Pass, Bellatrix

The young Dr. Julio Rico met her outside the small special needs wing of the Steven's Pass hospital. It was the same place her cybernetic arm had been implanted, the facilities now moved to a new high-tech hospital in Tranquility. Now they were using it as an isolation ward for the amazingly-still-alive Tanam. Just like when she'd first met the doctor more than half a year ago, he wasn't happy with her, only this time she wasn't doped up with mangled legs. "You bellowed for me?" she asked as she walked up.

"You seem to be doing well," he said as he watched how she walked.

"Well enough, what's going on?'

"Seela wants to talk to you."

"Why would the cat I shot up want to talk to me?"

"She wouldn't say."

"Weren't we going to ransom her back?"

"I think that was the council's plan, but we can't reach their leadership through diplomatic channels. I don't think they want to talk to us."

"Maybe not, after we kicked their asses and ended up with a thousand tons of their best gear." The high point of the whole adventure was the goodies list afterward. The two dozen transports abandoned by the Tanam in the hasty retreat she'd forced on them were worth millions. The heavy energy weapons many times that. To rub salt in the wound, Gregg and the Rangers had turned back two raids on Coorson last month. The Traaga were ecstatic and more contract offers came in daily. "Is she restrained?"

"She's lost a mid-arm, and her left hip is pieced together from scraps of that lost leg."

"And that makes a difference, how? These damn cats start at three hundred kilos, and just get bigger. I watched one tear a man's head off without a strain. Now, is she restrained?"

"There's an on-demand hoverfield that would crush her to the floor should she move off the bed without permission, and two of your Rangers are there with those horrendous shocking rifles."

"Shock rifles," she grumbled and slipped by him into the room.

She immediately recognized the two Rangers on guard duty by face if not by name. Both were expert marksmen with the shock rifles and veterans of the Tanam campaign. They each held their rifles across their arms, at rest but able to bring them to bear in a heartbeat. She nodded to them and got the same in reply. On two beds combined into one large one lay the recovering Tanam, and she watched Minu intently with all four front eyes. "You're the human who shot me?"

"I am," Minu said. "Minu Alma, Chosen in service to the Tog."

"I'm Seela, Second Daughter to the Matriarch of Tanam."

"Second Daughter? I'd think your mom would be desperate to get you back."

"Before now I'd have thought the same; though I'm not first born, I am senior among my siblings."

"Who was the one I killed?"

"Kelaa? She was youngest and lowest in status. Her impetuousness and impatience were her downfall, and when she met you in combat, ultimately her undoing." Minu nodded. "The fact that you haven't ransomed me says either you are lawless beasts and mean me ill, unlikely since my injuries are being tended to, or that you cannot contact my government."

"The latter," Minu confirmed for her prisoner.

"Then it would be better were you to simply kill me, though it seems illogical. Can you tell me what transpired after my wounds rendered me unconscious? These very well-disciplined soldiers of yours won't tell me. They're not Chosen, are they?"

"No, they're called Rangers, a new army that I trained. They're the troops you met in combat on Serengeti."

"And likely the reason for my being a prisoner. We didn't expect a young species, not yet Awakened, such as you, to muster a true army. Most unusual. You are to be complimented."

"Thank you. I don't see any reason why you can't know the outcome after our encounter." Minu took an empty chair and told Seela how it had all ended, including a brief but detailed blow-by-blow of the fight with her sister Veka, which ended with Minu ripping her tongue out and almost losing her legs.

"You truly tore her tongue out with your bare hand? I find this dubious at best."

Minu held up her two hands side-by-side for the Tanam to see. "This one is real, this one is cybernetic."

"Unfortunate for my sister. And you stabbed her in the eye with a knife. It's possible she's dead then."

"I'm sorry, but I have no way of knowing."

"Of course. Well, I thank you for treating me as an equal and coming to speak."

"Your actions during combat and afterward prove you're deserving of it." She thought for a second then remembered a question she'd wanted to ask. "When I spoke with Veka before she challenged me, she referred to the freed Squeen as *Gracktaag*." Minu struggled to get her lips around the Tanam word and seemed to manage from the look Seela gave her. "What does that word mean?"

"You are not Awakened; I cannot help you."

Minu nodded and left with another piece of the puzzle. Her translator wouldn't handle the word, and that meant it was part of the language dictionary not uploaded to them through the Concordian database. Like everything else, it was all tangled up with the 'Awakened' subject. "This is getting old," she said as she walked by the doctor on the way out. He looked confused as she addressed him directly. "Will she recover completely?"

"Without access to their codex of medical therapies, I can't fix the lost arm, but I've managed to fix the leg at least well enough that she'll be able to walk."

"Has Jacob said anything about her fate?"

"I think he's ordered her held indefinitely, and he was to be informed when she was well enough to travel."

"Do me a favor?"

He made a face and shrugged, so she took it as a positive. "Let me know when you make that call?"

"I can do that."

"Thanks," she said and turned to leave. Her meeting complete, she planned to spend a long overdue weekend at the island to unwind before going back to the training center.

Throughout her interview with Seela her side hurt her intermittently with random pains of varying intensities. As she walked out to her car, another stab of pain went through her middle. What she'd thought at first was her period starting was obviously something else. The pain was different, and in the wrong place. Hoping it would settle out or just go away, she guided her car from the garage and into the afternoon sky.

An hour into the four-hour flight to her island, the pain was getting to be too much. She'd resisted reaching into the combat pack stashed behind her seat for a pain pill until now, and when another shot of pain hit hard enough to make her yelp, she gave in and reached for the pack. The flexing of her torso to reach over the back seat sent a lance of agony through her stomach and out her back. Lights went off behind her eyes, and then everything went dark.

* * *

Minu came to with the blaring of the aerocar control system so loud it hurt her ears. Even before she was fully conscious she was checking the controls and struggling to concentrate through the stabbing pain in her side. The car was in level flight at ten thousand meters, on the same course, but slowed to two hundred KPH. She'd been cruising at fifty thousand meters and going over five hundred KPH when she'd blacked out. Of course, she'd been on manual control then, too.

With her sight clearing, she checked the log. Once she'd lost control, the craft plummeted four kilometers. As the ground approached the computer took over and saved her life. She thanked whatever god was listening that even basic Concordian technology was so infallible, and then started looking for the nearest city of any size. To her painful amusement, it was Tranquility.

Minu accelerated the car and set the course, carefully programming it into the computer before struggling to find a comfortable way to sit. There didn't seem to be any good way. Reclining the seat slightly, she lifted her shirt and examined herself. There, a few centimeters below her left breast, was an angry blue/black bruise. "Where the hell did that come from?" she wondered. It was in the right place for a broken rib, but no one had laid a hand on her there in at least a week. She probed it with a finger and pain shot deep into her insides. Not a rib, but something more sinister.

The car alerted her as she entered the Tranquility traffic pattern. She coded for a direct approach to the city hospital and waited impatiently through the pain. Flying traffic was limited to two hundred KPH above the city's flight corridor, and one hundred below a thousand meters. The approach and landing were agonizingly slow. As the car came around for an approach on the garage the pain got worse again, reaching a level she didn't think was possible. Minu overrode the controls and altered the approach. Two flying transports blared their horns and were forced to dodge her as she came over the roof of the hospital, around the building, and landed just outside the emergency entrance, crushing a couple of rose bushes.

The landing was gentle, but even that slight bump made her scream in pain. Worse, she felt the uncontrollable urge to cough. She fought it as hard as she could as she fumbled with and eventually found the door control. As it swung outward she lost her battle and a single wracking cough tore through her with ripping pain. Minu wiped moisture from her lips and her eyes went wide when she saw blood on her hand. The first feelings of panic hit her like a lightning bolt.

"What the fuck do you think—" someone yelled at her through the open door, but he cut short when he saw her black Chosen uniform. "Oh, what's—" then he cut off again as she looked up at him with fear in her eyes, blood dripping down her chin and covering her hand. "Are you all right?"

"Do I look all right?" she gasped. He turned and ran, and she silently cursed her sarcastic attitude, how the hell was she going to get out and to the entrance? Every breath was agony now.

Then the man was back, and with medical staff. There were three men and a woman, all in the red of hospital staff, with a gurney in tow. The man who'd first come to her was leaning over and releasing her safety harness. "What's your name, Chosen?"

"Minu Alma," she said, feeling a gurgling in her lungs and fighting another cough.

"Have you been shot? Tell me what's wrong." As he leaned over her she saw a hospital name tag, then they began extracting her from the car and the pain attacked once more. Minu started to scream, and the darkness returned.

*****

Chapter Nine
December 16th, 522 AE

Trauma Center, Mercy Hospital, Tranquility, Plateau Tribe, Bellatrix

Minu fought her way up through the cotton-stuffed fog, slowly making her way to the light above her. It seemed the harder she struggled, the deeper and denser it became. Voices drifted in and out, some sounding concerned, others more businesslike. And through it all she felt pain, numbness, and anger.

"I'm having trouble keeping her under," someone said. Minu took the encouragement and clawed toward the light.

"Watch the arm, watch the arm!" Someone cried out and she heard a crash. "Okay, I got it. Damn!"

"She's almost conscious."

Another voice, this one calm and authoritative, spoke up. "Let her wake up." In moments she opened her eyes, blinking against the bright white light of an operating theater. "Do you know where you are?"

"A hospital, obviously," she said and coughed. At least there was no stab of pain with it now; in fact her whole lower body was numb and a screen blocked her view. "What are you doing to me?"

"We had to open you up to find out what was causing the internal bleeding. We thought first you'd been shot, then maybe some sort of blunt force trauma."

"What was it, why was I bleeding inside?"

"I've been ordered not to tell you."

"Excuse me?" She craned her head and saw that the man who'd first found her was the one speaking. He was older than she'd first thought, and he now wore the typical hospital red scrubs and high-tech Concordian-made filter mask.

"We notified your listed physician, Dr. Tasker, of what we found, and we were ordered to wait for his arrival."

"I want to know what the fuck is going on."

"We can't violate your chief physician's order."

"You can if he's not my physician. What's your name?"

"Dr. Robinson. I'm a trauma doctor here and was just getting off when you almost landed on my head."

"Sorry about that. Dr. Robinson, I officially fire Dr. Tasker, and appoint you my physician."

"You shouldn't do this," another doctor who'd arrived during the exchange said. "You're Chosen and should be attended to by a Chosen physician."

"I'm having details of my condition hidden from me by my old doctor, that isn't what I'd call trust. Dr. Robinson, can you please inform me of my condition?"

The other doctor scowled and left. Dr. Robinson moved closer so she could see him without having to crane her neck. "You were in a fight a short time ago?"

"Fight? I train Chosen in hand-to-hand, but I haven't been in a fight."

"You took a blow to your abdomen, probably less than a week ago."

"Yeah, one of my students got lucky, but it wasn't that bad." She chuckled remembering the sucker punch that Tanya had managed to land. A forearm to her stomach, right near the pain.

"The blow didn't directly cause the damage, this did." He held up a little cylinder, about five centimeters long. It was silver in color, had a slight tinge of red from where blood clung to it, and a short hose ending in a needle from one side. "That impact dislodged this device that was implanted in your abdominal cavity, just below your 2nd anterior intercostal rib muscle. Once it was loose, it started to move around, and eventually pulled out this catheter that was inserted into your interior gonadal vein. As the catheter was treated with an anti-coagulant material, the vein just kept on bleeding. Eventually, you would've died."

"How much longer?"

"Probably less than two hours. The hole wasn't that big, but the bleeding was persistent. Then it looks like your coughing from the pressure caused it to perforate a lung. The pain from the hemorrhaging in your stomach must have been excruciating."

"It didn't feel good, that's for damned sure. What the hell does it do?"

He looked at it and then at her. "So you don't know what this is?"

"I have no idea."

"Nor did you know it was implanted in you?"

"Does it sound like I fucking knew it?"

He took a deep breath before speaking. "It appears to have been inserted though that knife wound over your uterus when you were stitched up."

"Again, what the hell does it do?"

"We found residue of progesterone and estrogen, common ingredients in birth control pills."

Minu looked at the little device, rather like an insulin pump she'd seen years ago in a class, an adaptation of a neutral Concordian technology for injecting steady rates of drugs. "Birth control?"

"I would have to say yes." She laid her head back and stared at the ceiling. "It isn't like any kind I've ever seen, though. We have a type of implant, but it is a soluble tablet inserted under the skin, maybe good for a year. This thing, based on the power cell it has, would probably work for five or six years."

"Would it delay my first period, if it were installed when I was really young?"

"Quite possibly, yes. I would never do that with a young girl; it's always best to wait until puberty is well under way, or even over, before beginning a birth control regime." He looked down at her abdomen, chewed his lower lip, and tossed the device into a specimen tray.

"There's more?"

"Yes. We had to go into you to figure this out. Being as you're a young, attractive, and possibly sexually active woman we used a scope procedure, just a couple little slits below your bikini line that will be almost invisible when they heal."

She looked at her hand and thought about the growing collection of scars, then laughed. "I appreciate the sentiment."

"Right. Well, we found this, removed it, and patched the vein in question. I looked around while I was in there to be sure there was no other damage. Had to drain almost three units of blood." He gestured for a nurse who brought over a small Concordian-made video monitor.

"Doc, I don't want to see home movies of my girl parts, especially from the inside."

"You need to see this one." The video came alive with a somewhat blurry image from an endoscopic camera. It was all red and gooey images of tissue and such, and a lot of dripping blood. "Sorry for the quality, your abdominal cavity was a bloody mess. So, this is your gonadal vein." It was a gray colored tube spurting blood. The image fast-forwarded through the repair. "Okay, here are your reproductive organs, fallopian tube, one of your ovaries, quite healthy looking, and this is your uterus."

"Ugh. You have a point?"

The screen split to another image, obviously another uterus. The two were quite different, and it was obvious the difference was in hers. "The damage was extreme, from the appearance of the repairs. That knife wound extended all the way back to your spine." The camera moved again and she could see another vein, this one huge and pulsing, and what must be ribs. "The knife nearly severed your inferior vena cava. A miracle you didn't bleed to death in minutes. Add to that the damage to your spine," he paused and used a little pointer to show where a white bone was missing a neat chip.

"I was there, I know it was bad." She thought about the images for another moment. "So I can't have babies?"

"Correct. They tried hard to repair the damage, but the knife nearly cut your uterus in half. You must have been pretty young, because the scar tissue is massive. Between the birth control implant, and this damage, there's no doubt why you were late in starting estrus, as you mentioned. Whoever operated on you went out of their way to be sure you wouldn't know."

Minu let it sink in. It took a few minutes. There would be no more Alma family when she was gone. Mindy Harper's line was going to die. It was one more little debt she owed a certain Rusk. A single tear rolled down her cheek, and she sighed. "So I'm all sewed up and good to go?"

"Aside from the blood loss, you're in good shape. I need you to stay for a day to be sure the sutures hold and that your blood volume normalizes."

"Turn the field off?" she asked, referring to the hoverfield immobilizing her on the table. The doctor nodded and she shoved the privacy screen out of the way. Her crotch was modestly covered with a towel, but her abdomen was naked. The knife wound was as light as ever, but the deeper damage rested in the back of her mind like never before. To the side were two new bandages, slightly bloody, the site where the scopes entered her body. She felt remarkably well; the only tubes still connecting her were the ones leading to an IV bag hanging next to her bed.

"Get out of my way, now," she heard a familiar authoritative voice outside and turned her head just in time to see Dr. Tasker enter. His sharp eyes took in the scene quickly. Minu's naked waist, the new bandages and exposed scar, the monitor showing the old damage to her spine, and the specimen tray holding the birth control device. The last thing he saw was the pure, dark, seething rage in Minu's eyes. "Now let me just say—"

Luckily for Minu it was only two steps, because she almost fell when she slid off the table. Tasker's eyes got big as she came at him, and he tried to back out. A nurse was just coming in behind him after failing to exclude the Chosen doctor from the theater, and he backed into her with a bump. Minu managed the two steps with a visceral snarl of anger, and seized Tasker's throat with her right hand.

The two crashed to the floor on top of the unfortunate nurse. He clawed desperately at her fingers as she consciously overrode the safeties and servos whined. His eyes bugged, and his face started to turn purple. "You *mother fucker!*" she snarled in his face as she could hear ligaments starting to pop in his neck. She was bare seconds from snapping his spine when stab of pain hit her bottom and cold flooded through her. She tried one last time to push the arm to finish exacting her revenge, but darkness won, and she slumped onto the good doctor, her hand loosening. He cried out and gasped for breath, blood and spittle flying from his lips.

"Sh-she tried to kill me," he gurgled.

Dr. Robinson looked down at him, the needle he'd used to knock her out held in one hand. "You're lucky I didn't let her finish the job," he said simply and tossed the needle into the same bin that held the birth control pump. "It's to your benefit that I, at least, follow the Hippocratic Oath." Tasker gurgled a curse, then passed out. "Nurse, better intubate him, I think she crushed his wind pipe."

* * *

It was a sick irony that Tasker ended up only a few rooms down from Minu. When she woke up, Dr. Robinson was there explaining to her that he was just down the hall, and no charges were going to be pressed. The latter surprised her as much as his proximity annoyed her. "Why didn't he press charges?"

"Because I told him if he did I'd bring an ethics complaint against him in Plateau, where he holds his license to practice medicine, and I'd demand that all gynecological records for every female Chosen be opened and reviewed by the same ethics board."

"Thanks, doc," she said and managed a smile. "You're doing a lot to redeem your profession in my eyes."

"It shouldn't need redeeming," he said, his mouth set in a thin line of anger. "What they did to you without your knowledge or consent in unconscionable. I only wish you hadn't tried to kill the bastard."

"Why?"

"Because then I wouldn't have to trade away the threat of a complaint to keep you out of a trial."

"Might have been better not to have bothered." He gave her a confused look so she proceeded. "I could have used what you did as evidence for my being cleared of charges. Justifiable homicide, from where I see it."

"I'm not sure the courts would agree, but perhaps. Do I have your promise not to kill him?"

"Absolutely not."

"While you're in this hospital?" She gave him a dirty look. "I like you Minu; I like you a lot. Don't disappoint me by doing something stupid in my wing."

"Fine, I promise." He flashed her a smile of perfect teeth and dimples, and she was compelled to return it, minus the dimples. "Can I get out of here now?"

"In a few hours; we're just finishing up some tests."

She thanked him, and he promised to see her before she left. After a bit a nurse brought her a lunch of the typical gelatin, crackers, and sugar-free soda which she ate grudgingly under her supervision. Then as the time of her release approached, the door opened and there was Dr. Tasker.

"Take one more step into this room, and I'll twist your fucking head off," she snarled. He froze in his tracks and sweat broke out on his face. He was dressed in street clothes, but a support collar encircled his neck and she could see bruising climbing toward his head. "What do you want?"

"A chance to explain myself, to maybe justify my actions." His voice was gruff, and he spoke with some difficulty.

"Impossible."

"Minu, you have to understand—"

"No, you have to understand," she roared and sat up. He took a step back toward the hallway and a pair of nurses stopped to look in the room. "You weren't able to fix the damage that bastard Malovich did to me, yeah don't give me that look, we both know perfectly well that it wasn't a sharp branch like the reports said. I wondered for quite a while why the convenient lies; I can only assume it was to protect that little Rusk shit. So you couldn't fix me properly, but you managed to keep me alive. You slapped my uterus back together, stitched up my stomach, and stuck a damn machine inside me to make sure I couldn't get pregnant, because if I did it would end in disaster. Does that just about cover it?!"

"Sort of."

"What more can you possibly offer to explain why you did this to me, then didn't even bother saying, "Oh, by the way, you can never have babies!" He looked at her, then down at the floor. "How many other women in the Chosen have those hideous things inside them, quietly pumping birth control drugs into their systems?"

"All the non-married ones," he admitted. "That's between the Chosen council and—"

"You unspeakable son of a bitch," she snarled and snatched up the tray. Her right hand crushed the metal plate and hurled it at Tasker. He made a squeaking noise and ran for it, the tray nearly taking out one of growing audience she'd collected before bouncing down the hall with a horrible racket. She pointed at one of the stunned nurses. "Get me out of here, right now, or so help me I'll start tearing out the walls!"

* * * * *

Chapter Ten
December 24th, 522 AE

Meeting Room #12, Chosen Headquarters, Steven's Pass, Bellatrix

Minu sat on the comfortable couch and checked the time again. Fifteen minutes remained, and she fidgeted nervously. She hadn't gone about this course of action brashly, instead agonizing over it for almost a week. The problem was that in two weeks she was due to rotate back to Herdhome, and she had plans before then. Big plans that necessitated her going forward with this little drama now.

As she was about to check the time again, the first of her visitors showed up. Naturally, it was Cherise.

"What's going on?" she asked as Minu rose and embraced her friend. Since they were the only ones present, they shared a quick kiss too, forcing Minu to admit she missed their intimacy. In the last six months they'd only managed to meet a half dozen times, and just two of those had resulted in any romantic encounters. At least each time they'd been able to work out together, and Minu was beginning to work out the basics of a new fighting technique. Getting her ass kicked by the Tanam hadn't sat well with her. Humans were at too severe a disadvantage against many of the Concordian species that had evolved from predators.

"I'll tell everyone once they're here," Minu explained. "It's simpler that way."

"Okay, whatever you say." The small conference room she'd had a friend reserve for her quickly filled after that. By the appointed hour, there were twenty-two female Chosen sitting in chairs, on couches, or standing and talking to each other. "I can't wait to find out now," Cherise whispered to her when the last one came in.

Minu kept careful head count and knew when the last one was there. She'd sent individual emails from her university email account to keep the Chosen leadership out of the loop. To her surprise, they'd all accepted her invitation. Cherise had told her some time ago that her status among the other female Chosen was approaching legendary, even with the older ones, but this was the first tangible proof of that assertion. So here they were, every female Chosen except one. She hadn't bothered inviting Jasmine Osgood. As a member of the Chosen council, she was likely duplicitous in this whole thing anyway.

Minu moved to the far wall of the conference room and cleared her throat. All conversation quickly fell off. "I wanted to thank you all for coming on such a strange and short notice."

"Are we leading a coup against the council?" asked Heather Mansford, a tall blond Chosen scout with more muscles than half the men Minu knew. To her relief there was a ripple of amused laughter. Her piercing brown eyes watched Minu intently. It was no small secret that the woman harbored resentment against the Chosen leadership, resentment spurned by the four black stars she still wore after many years of service.

"Not yet," she replied under her breath, then spoke up. "I know you're all curious what's going on. I recently had a small training accident while working with a group of scouts. One got in a punch on me I wasn't looking for."

"Getting slow?" the only other female scout asked, Tamara Komatsu, and that brought more laughter. Minu smiled at the girl whom she knew from their trials. Tamara was the adopted daughter of a racially Japanese Peninsula tribe family. They'd raised her as one of their own despite her blond haired, blue-eyed ancestry. The Shinto/pacifist upbringing common with their people didn't take, and she'd gone off to join the Chosen. Her parents hadn't spoken to her since. Minu had only seen her occasionally after basic training and thought she'd grown five centimeters over the years. More interestingly, she carried a longsword into the meeting, along with a gym bag. Her long meticulously-braided ponytail was still damp from the shower.

"Probably; I'm nineteen now after all. Anyway, I ended up with some serious internal bleeding and barely made it to the hospital." She saw the fear and concern on Cherise's face and continued anyway. "It turned out the punch didn't do the damage, but something it dislodged." She pulled the birth control pump from her pocket, now cleaned of course, and held it up for them all to see. "This is an implanted medicine pump, like what they're using for diabetics and others needing regular injections. Only this one contained birth control hormones. It was inserted in my body immediately after the trials, without my knowledge, and was dislodged by that hit I took. The vein it was hooked into bled, and I almost died."

There were surprised looks between many of the women there, some twice Minu's age, many younger than her. Some shook their heads, and others spoke up demanding to know why they'd done it to her. "Not just me," she said, loud enough that they could all hear her.

"No!" someone in the back screamed.

"Mother fuckers!" another snapped.

"Wait, that can't be right," one of the oldest among them called out. Faye Martinez from the Summit Tribe was the oldest serving female Chosen and had just celebrated her fiftieth birthday. She proudly wore the three green stars of logistics, like Cherise. Her black hair was attractively streaked with silver, but her face was still line-free. "I've had three children; how could I have had one of those?" Two other women both stood and agreed with Faye.

"But what about me?" A woman in her twenties spoke loudly to be heard. "Me and Bill have been trying to have a baby for two years! The doctor keeps telling us to keep trying…"

"Because you're not married, are you?" Minu asked. She shook her head no. "These are implanted in us when we're made Chosen. Some sort of excuse is made for a medical procedure. In my case an excuse wasn't needed," she said and unzipped her jumpsuit uniform to the crotch. She spread the fabric to show the scar over her uterus. "When they were fixing the wound, they stuck in this damned thing. The wound that caused this also ruined my uterus, so I can't have babies, ever. Something else they didn't tell me."

Despite her desperate wishes, tears were pouring down her cheeks. She easily found Cherise and saw she was crying too, as were most of the women in the room. Some looked stunned, others confused, and more than a few were furious. At least one dangerously so.

"That fucker Jacob," Heather snarled and made fists with both hands. "I ought to—"

"Do nothing," Minu said. They all turned and looked at her again. "That's what I said. He didn't start this program; it goes way back."

"But he sure as hell perpetuated it," Heather pointed out. "I know how you found out you had that in you, since you gave us the whole story. But how did you know most of us have them?"

"I'll only tell you on condition that he doesn't suddenly fall down a malfunctioning jump tube." She looked around the room, making eye contact one after another. It took a full thirty seconds of staring at Heather before she grudgingly nodded. "It was Dr. Tasker."

"Why did he tell you?" Cherise finally broke her silence.

"Guilt, I think. It started long ago, when the first women joined. I'm guessing they quietly did it to be sure they weren't lost from service due to a pregnancy. I think the Tog were involved, but again, I'm not sure."

"You're their liaison," Tamara pointed out the obvious, "ask them!"

"It isn't the kind of thing you just bring up over a latte." There were angry grumbles, and she raised her hands in a calming gesture. "I'll find out, somehow. The important thing is you know, and now you can have them removed." She gave them the specific details of their location and function, reminding them to go to a private physician and inform them of the anti-coagulant function to avoid clotting. Then one at a time, she went around the room with a compact field medical scanner and confirmed their fears. Every woman in the room had one, even the three married women. "When you got married, it was deactivated by remote control," she told those women. "I want you all to understand, I still have faith in the Chosen as an organization," she told them near the end.

"Just not their leadership," Heather barked. Minu reluctantly nodded.

"Maybe it's about time a woman ran things," someone suggested.

"Yeah," said more than a few others.

"And who do you think could do that?" she asked them.

"You, of course," Cherise said, almost knocking Minu over with the audacity of it. She shook her head and looked around for support against the idea, and instead found them all nodding and encouraging each other.

"Don't even think about it," she said, shaking her head. "This isn't a democracy, if you recall." But even Heather was looking at her with a respect the powerful woman had never shown before.

"It would take time," another woman said. "We'd have to plan this out carefully." More head nods and more conversation.

"I'm not going to listen to this," she said and packed up her gear.

"Just as well," Cherise said and took her by the arm. To her surprise she was being shepherded out the door. "We need to talk this over."

"Cherise, don't you dare—" But the door to the small conference room was closed, and then locked. She stood there for more than a minute gawking at the metal door, unable to believe what had just happened. *Exactly what* did *just happen?* she wondered as the sound of conversation drifted, muffled, through the metal.

* * *

Two hours later the group came out. Unlike the way she'd left them they were all smiles, talking to each other and joking. Almost every one of them caught her eye as they went by and either grinned, waved, or winked. Minu felt her stomach sink as the last three, Heather Mansford, Tamara Komatsu, and Cherise, walked up to her. They all shared a big conspiratorial smile. "What did you do?" Minu asked.

"Congratulations," Cherise said.

"For what?'

"We've decided to have you made First Among the Chosen."

Minu heaved a great sigh of relief then burst out in nervous laughter. "Oh, thank goodness, I thought you were going to do something foolish. Crazy is much more acceptable."

"We're not kidding," Heather growled at her, crossing her powerful arms over her small breasts.

"I don't care, you're all still crazy. Twenty-two women, none of us higher than three stars, can't elect a First Among the Chosen. Damn it, we aren't even five percent of the corps!"

"We might be only one percent," Tamara agreed, her strong Peninsula accent at odds with her equally strong Summit tribe looks, "but we represent ninety-five percent of the women Chosen."

"Fat lot of good that'll do us."

"It means something to us," Cherise said. Minu looked at the three and saw their resolve.

"I don't know what you expect this to accomplish."

"We expect you to look out for our interests."

"How am I supposed to do that as a three-star command Chosen marooned in Training branch?"

Tamara smiled, and Minu felt worried again. "We expect you to do that when you're named to the council."

"You're crossing over into foolish now."

"We don't think so," Cherise said, just as gravely as the others. "We might only be twenty-two, but we're assigned all over the Chosen, we have the ears of a lot of powerful movers in the organization, and even more politicians, scientists, academics, etc."

"You all believe it's possible to manipulate the Chosen council so that I end up on it?" They all nodded, and she almost laughed in their faces. Then the conversation with P'ing came rushing back. How she'd come to be born, the way the Tog had manipulated and molded her career, then tried to have her moved way beyond her station much sooner than any would like. Were her friends here being used by the Tog like pawns in a grand chess game? She almost asked them, and then came up short once again. Starting to talk and stopping again must have looked quite comical because the girls all laughed. "Look, I don't know what to say."

"Just say you'll do the best you can to help the other women when you're named First," Cherise said.

"I bet Jasmine would have something to say about that; she's got eyes on the job herself." Minu said, bringing up the head of the science branch who'd taken over from Bjorn.

"Screw her," Heather said, and they all shared a good laugh. "So what's it going to be?"

After it was done, she caught Tamara and pulled her aside. "What can I do for you?"

"I was wondering about the sword."

"Oh, this?" she hefted the sheathed blade. "It's a Bushido thing, picked it up from my adopted dad."

"Shinto pacifists practicing a thousand-year-old warrior philosophy? That's a dichotomy if I ever heard one."

"It's part of the reason I ended up here in the Chosen. They want all the power of Bushido in their lives, but none of the responsibility to community, namely Bellatrix."

Minu nodded, understanding where the other woman was coming from. "So you know the katana fighting style?"

"Sure, I trained under a master in Peninsula."

"I have an idea, and maybe you and a guy from the Desert tribe can make it all work out."

* * * * *

Chapter Eleven
January 3rd, 523 AE

Junk Pile, Deep Blue, Galactic Frontier

"I'm really not going to play this game with you idiots anymore," Minu snapped as she ran up with her weapon out. The bright blue sky blazed above them in the late afternoon, the temperature a comfortable nineteen degrees, just like almost every other day on Deep Blue. What wasn't normal was shooting.

As she ran up, Chris was pumping his fist in the air and whooping as Michael grinned and watched through his shock rifle scope. This was the first training mission they'd been issued live shock rifles for and they'd found something to shoot. She only hoped it wasn't a higher-order species.

"They were sighting us with weapons!" Chris yelled back and pointed from their third-floor vantage point. The afternoon was warm for Deep Blue, and sweat made his light brown skin look shiny in the sunlight.

"They? Who's they? Patch me the recording from your scope." Chris looked surprised and stared at his gun. "Didn't have the recorder on, right?"

"Yeah," Michael grumbled.

Just in case they were telling the truth, Minu dropped to her knees and crept up on the edge of the roof. A small utility building about a kilometer away had three smoking holes in the wall, accounting for the weapons fire she'd heard a minute ago. "Did you at least hit what you were shooting at?" Chris acted like he was about to brag, then seemed to change his mind. "Shit," she shook her head and unslung her own shock rifle from her shoulder.

Hers was one of the new Mark II designs, which incorporated the improved optics and target designator. She ran a quick spectrum scan on the building and detected three heat signatures. "There's something in there alright. What species?"

"I couldn't be sure."

"So just because they checked you out, you opened fire? That's going on your record, mister." Chris grumbled and Minu activated her radio. "All units report in, I have potential hostiles in search sector two." The other three misfits quickly checked in and wanted to know if they should rendezvous with her. "That is negative, circle back to the portal. Do not enter the building. Run a sweep for hostiles and hold position until I say."

Once they'd confirmed the order she returned to her problem children. "So let's wait and see who pops out."

"Let's just go down there," Chris complained, "it was only two bipeds, unarmored; I'm sure of that much. We have them outnumbered."

"Yeah!"

"No. First, because it's an unknown situation. If they have backup, they may be waiting for just that, us to go down there and present our backs. And second, because scouts don't go sticking their dicks into stuff just because they can." Chris glanced down at Minu's waist and grinned, so she smacked him in the forehead with the heel of her hand.

"Ow!"

"Keep your head in it, dipshit. Now quit arguing and take up positions a few meters to either side."

Once they'd repositioned as she'd instructed, Minu picked up her observation again. Depending on how skittish the beings down there were, or how pissed-off at being shot at, it could be hours. She was just thinking about a ration bar in her pack when the signatures began to move. A second later a pasty-skinned little head peeked around the corner of the door.

"I got him," Chris hissed, and he thumbed the safety off on his weapon. He squeezed the trigger nice and slowly. "Bye bye," he said, only nothing happened. "What the fuck?"

"I disabled your guns," Minu told them as she watched. The alien had a flattened head with oversized ears. Red, almost glowing eyes surveyed the area as it crept out, a nicely-made linear accelerator rifle held in its delicate, clawed hands. "Vampires," she said. There might be some validity to Chris's claim. They were known to shoot first and ask questions later. They were also incredibly aggressive fighters and a serious threat.

"Why, damn it?" Chris asked and stabbed the trigger twice more. Minu's special command gun had control over all the others in the team. She could arm or disarm them with the flick of a finger. Should she die, the weapon would automatically release all the other guns. "See, they're Vampires. The crazy bat-faced bastards have killed several Chosen over the years."

"Because we're scouts, not instruments of vengeance. We don't run around the galaxy looking for revenge for every wrong done to a human. We log this incident and go home. The fact that Vampires are on Deep Blue is news. They've never been spotted here before."

A minute later two more pasty-skinned aliens skittered out. Their arms were almost as long as their legs, allowing them to move equally well on four limbs or two. They panned their weapons around, searching for the source of the earlier attack. Minu hoped they didn't have anything sophisticated enough to pick them up through the stealth fields on their combat suits. After a minute they formed up and raced off down the avenue in the opposite direction from the portal.

"Seems like a waste to pass up an opportunity like that," Chris complained, not willing to let it go.

"Yeah," Michael agreed.

"Scouts from most species don't snipe at each other. How would you like it if every small species like us routinely took a shot at you?"

"I'd shoot back!"

"If you survived." Minu stood and slung her weapon. The Vampires were out of sight as she consulted her tablet, noting the location and number of the sighting. "Their weapons aren't energy-based. Our armor is based around energy defense with only light ballistics defense. We can't plan on every scenario." Chris looked annoyed but he stayed quiet. "If you can't learn more restraint, you're going to find yourself with green stars instead of black." Chris made a face and looked down. She'd hit a nerve. "This is Minu," she spoke into her radio, "report on the portal."

"All clear," Tanya came back right away. "The most recent thermal is several hours old."

"Very good, we're on our way back."

As they were lowering themselves down to an adjacent rooftop, Minu caught her new sword belt on a protuberance and almost lost her grip. Michael leaned out and caught her leg, steadying her while she renewed her grip. "Thanks," she said to the young scout who nodded.

Chris hadn't moved a muscle. Maybe he hoped she'd fall to her death. "Why do you wear that stupid thing, anyway?" he asked and pointed.

Minu placed a hand on the sword hilt and grinned. "'There are more things in heaven and Earth, Horatio, than are dreamt of in your philosophy.'"

"Huh?"

"A single cat almost tore off both my legs half a year ago," Minu explained, "because all I had was a knife and no gun. The cat has six limbs with more than a meter-long reach, each holding five razor-sharp claws, and a set of fangs." In a blur she drew the sword and pointed it at Chris, less than a millimeter from his nose. "Call this an equalizer. We don't even have sharp teeth."

Chris swallowed and nodded. "Sure, but it's clumsy."

"I'm still working on the best way to carry it. These training missions are useful for more than just proving you aren't ready to be deployed. We've field-tested a lot of equipment on Deep Blue."

A short time later they linked up with the rest of the misfits and checked the area. There were no other signs of the Vampires. They had an hour before their planned return, so she found a quiet corner and talked to them as a team.

"I'm pleased overall with the way you've come together, and I'm close to making my final recommendation for your readiness for service." Minu saw excitement from each of them.

"When?" Minu wasn't surprised it was Tanya who piped up first. Her tall frame leaned against a wall as she'd listened, her eyes intent on the older Chosen. She was the best in almost all areas, and Minu often wished she'd push hard enough to make herself the leader of the misfits. It was obvious she resented being saddled with the others and believed if she'd found a different group she'd already be assigned as an active scout.

"Soon."

"Why can't we know more precisely?" Orlando asked.

"Scouts don't often have that luxury. You could get called to a mission on only minutes' notice. So self-train; I'll clear range time for you."

* * *

Minu finished logging in her shock rifle, along with the misfits', then checked in with the range officer. As she'd promised, she left an authorization for them to continue using shock rifles for training without having to check with her each time. Afterward, it was to her office in the training branch to write the incident report from her trip to Deep Blue. Coming across Vampires in a formerly 'safe' place was worthy of a high-priority report. She left off the part where her misfits had opened fire on the Vampires without provocation. It was a minor incident, and she decided to skip over it.

"Just being a scout is dangerous," she mumbled as she typed the report. And she was certain they'd have never made scouts without her intervention. While she was typing, her communicator beeped. "Chosen Alma."

"Bored training the brats yet?" asked a familiar voice.

"From Day One, Gregg. How are things with the Rangers?"

"Complicated." She heard him sigh. "This crap with the mercenary contracts is getting crazy."

"How so?"

"The Akala have filed a complaint with the Concordian war council because we refused them a contract."

Minu thought for a moment. The Akala were a senior species, but not high-order. Fairly rich, but not aggressive. And that didn't mesh well with their belligerent nature, so they liked to hire others to do their fighting. "I'm sure they wanted to use us to stomp on someone."

"Oh, without a doubt. Jacob might be greedy, but he's not stupid. It only took a little digging to find out the Akala and the Mok-Tok are having a dustup just now."

"Wow," Minu whistled. "The last thing we want is to get tangled with the Mok-Tok right now."

"Absolutely. But they're still crying to the Concordia. Jacob is thinking about giving in to a limited contract to keep from pissing anyone off."

"We can't play all sides of this thing," Minu replied with a sigh. "He should have known this would happen. What can I do to help?"

"Can you come to the next strategy session?"

"I doubt I'd be welcome," Minu explained.

"I know, but you might be surprised. Several on the council have asked me to invite you."

"Really?" she asked, honestly surprised. She'd been unaware of that development. "Sure, I can do that. I have a couple days before leaving for Herdhome."

"Thanks Minu, I appreciate it."

Later that afternoon, Minu met with her new workout team. Cherise and Tamara Komatsu had been training with her for weeks now, and they were the reason for the sword she carried. What she'd first seen Ojanbique doing in the desert had jelled with the input from Tamara into a new close-combat style incorporating the sword, knife, and a specially reinforced vambrace on both arms.

"You must be kidding," Cherise had said the first time she saw the getup. But after a few minutes of easily holding the much taller woman at bay with a wooden practice sword Tamara called a Bokken, Cherise was forced to admit Minu was onto something.

After weeks of work, the basics were finished, and now Minu was concentrating on learning some real elements of style with the sword from Tamara. The lithe Peninsula tribeswoman could move with almost superhuman speed with a sword in one hand or both. Even with Minu and Cherise both trying to attack her at the same time, the results were consistently a defeat for the two old friends, and Tamara laughing at them.

Once that day's session was finished and Cherise was on her way, Tamara came to Minu with a gift. "What's this?"

Tamara smiled and held out the long thin case. "The results of a friend's brainstorming."

Minu cocked her head but opened the locks on the case. Inside was a katana, obviously brand new and slightly different than what she'd been working with. She carefully removed the scabbarded sword, then drew it with a flourish. The blade was about ten centimeters shorter than a regular katana and with less curve, but the blade itself was very interesting. It had the familiar blue sheen of a dualloy-wrought blade, and it felt as light as a feather.

"The blade is magnetically-forged dualloy, made by the master smith who made my blade," Tamara explained as she braided her waist-length hair. "But the edge is unique." Her hair finished, she fished into a duffel and removed another sword. This one was crude and in poor shape. She drew the blade and held it at point guard, tip aimed at Minu's neck. "Deflect the blade," she told Minu.

Minu shrugged, took a two-handed grip, and swung at an upward angle as instructed, deflecting the other blade away from her neck. There was a high-pitched *CHING!* and half of the other katana blade spun away to embed point first in the wall. "Shit!" Minu barked, taking a step back and reaching for the blade she held.

"No, wait!" Tamara yelled, and Minu's hand recoiled as if stung. "The blade edge is monomolecular. It can cut through a one centimeter bar of dualloy."

"Damn lightsaber!" Minu chuckled. "So how do I keep from cutting my own leg off or beheading the Chosen standing next to me?"

Tamara grinned and took out a little device, handing it to Minu. "Clip it on your belt." Minu did as instructed. "Now try to cut your hand."

"After what that just did to a dualloy sword?"

"Trust me."

Minu swallowed and gently ran the blade along the palm of her hand. It felt kind of sharp, but only in the way a butter knife might. She experimented and put a little more force against it. The edge stung, but still didn't cut. Tamara still held the split sword. She leaned over and used Minu's sword, the same one that wouldn't cut bare skin, to slice off another twenty centimeter chunk off her blade.

"Okay, I'm impressed," Minu said, "how does it work."

"The belt pack is a very low-powered shield. The sword also has a shield in it; the two react to each other like a pair of positive magnets."

"So this won't work against anyone with a shield? That defeats the purpose of the sword."

"No, these shields are of a unique polarity, opposite of the ones we use for energy weapon defense. There's also one in the sheath so the sword doesn't chop that up, as well."

"How long do the batteries last?"

"Months?" Tamara said, cocking her head and thinking. "Maybe years."

"This is amazing," Minu whispered, trying out a few practice moves with the sword.

"I had it made shorter after you bitched about it on deployment." Minu shrugged. "Here's a harness the smith made; it works like a shoulder holster over the back. That should keep it out of the way, and ready for quick access."

"I'm flattered. So how many Peninsula tribe swordsmiths know how to make a monomolecular-edge dualloy blade?"

"None. The smith made the blade, but Bjorn created the edge and the defensive system."

"You've been busy."

"Just trying to help. Try it out, see how it works, and give me feedback. Imagine all the Chosen and Rangers with these!"

"Yeah, I can imagine that." Minu sheathed the sword and let Tamara show her a few features, including how she could flick a control on the box and deactivate the self-protection feature.

"The blade should be good for quite a bit of brutality before needing to be sharpened again, but Bjorn is still working on a way to do that in the field. He's pretty sure he'll figure it out."

"I'm sure he will too." A few hours later she was back on her little island and ready for a couple days off before rotating to Herdhome. Unfortunately, rest wasn't in the cards. Instead she woke the next morning and continued to work on her big plan. Late that afternoon her communicator went off again. "Chosen Alma."

"Miss Alma, this is Dr. Evan Martin at the Tranquility Hospital, coma care wing."

"I remember you, doctor; what can I do for you?"

"Miss Basil requested you be contacted."

"Who?"

"Cynthia Basil."

"Oh, right, Pip's girlfriend."

"As you will. She requested we contact you if Pipson Leata's condition should worsen…"

Minu sat up straight in her chair. "What's happened?"

"He's reached the end of his body's tolerance for the life support systems."

"But you said he had another year or more the last time we talked."

"I know, but the situation has changed." The doctor spent a minute talking about degenerative nerve failure and immune-suppressive drug resistance.

"How long doc?"

"Hours."

"Don't do anything, I'm on my way."

"His family's coming too," the doctor said, but Minu was already running toward the landing flat behind her cabin.

* * *

She pushed the aerocar to the limits and beyond. By the time she dropped from cruising altitude and banked toward a landing at the Tranquility Hospital, there were two warning lights flashing on the car's control boards where she'd never seen them before. 'Impeller Over-Temp' and 'Check EPC Coupling' both glowed bright yellow. Minu ignored them as she landed and jumped from the car. Minutes later she was running from the stairs (too long a wait for a jump-tube) down to the coma wing.

As soon as she turned the corner to the coma unit she saw Dr. Martin, dressed in white hospital fatigues and wearing stylish dualloy-framed glasses, talking with a middle-aged couple who had to be Pip's parents. She only knew they lived far from Tranquility and couldn't afford to travel to visit their son very often. Minu had never met them. The woman was looking at the floor, tears dripping down her cheeks, while the man listened as the doctor talked. For a second, Minu feared she was too late.

"You must be Minu Alma," the man said as she approached. Minu almost tripped at the man's thick Rusk accent. Could this really be Pip's father? "Our boy, Pipson, told us a lot about you before he was hurt."

"Thank you, sir," she said. The woman lifted her head for a moment and spoke a few words Minu didn't understand.

"I'm sorry, Aliana doesn't speak much English. She comes from the Trablinsk region, and there it's a matter of pride the villagers only speak Russian."

"It's not a problem." She chewed her lip for a second before continuing. "Please don't take this wrong, but Pip never said he was Rusk."

"No, I don't imagine he would. Our family was an ally of the Malovich clan, long, long ago. It's a very long story, but suffice it to say our two families had a parting of the ways, and for many years now we've been on the opposite sides of events."

"Pip didn't even have an accent!"

"He spent hours on end learning to speak without an accent. He knew what people would think if they knew his racial heritage before they knew him as a man."

"It wouldn't have mattered to me," Minu said, the lie tasting vile on her tongue, "very much," she softened the statement. She turned to the doctor. "So what's Pip's situation?"

"He's continued to deteriorate since we talked," the doctor explained and gave a quick synopsis. From behind him, Minu saw Cynthia walk out of his room. Her face was red and swollen, and still more tears fell. "The family was about to make a decision."

"Let me ask something first," she said and got all of their attention. "How long does he really have?"

"Two days, maybe a week at the most. One organ after another will shut down until he has a catastrophic episode. At that point it's all over with."

"I need a month, maybe two weeks."

"For what?"

"There might be a way to save him. I'm not a hundred percent sure, but pretty damn sure. Is there no way?"

"Not on basic life support, but we have another way. We have a few Stasis Pods. As long as the patient isn't brain dead, you can toss them in and it holds them at death's door until you can treat them. We used them to good effect during the Tanam war to save quite a few lives."

"Well, there you go! Toss him in that, and I'll be back in a few weeks."

"No so quick. We've never used one for more than thirty-six hours, the time it took to fly in a surgeon from halfway around the world."

"But it *could* last weeks?"

"Theoretically, sure. We don't have our biological codex to load into the pod's computer, but its system is very flexible with most life forms. It's worked flawlessly, except on one of your soldiers. It wasn't the worst injury we've put in one, but the thing just got brain lock and let him die. The techs never figured out why."

"So the odds are the same either way?" she asked and got a curious look from the doctor. "Look, if it keeps him alive until I get back, we could save his life. If not, it doesn't affect the end in any way except maybe he lives a few more days. Am I right?"

The doctor looked from her to the family. Both the Leatas and Cynthia had a look on their face Minu hadn't seen since she arrived—hope. "It would be up to the family," he told her. So Minu left them alone and went down to the waiting room. She didn't have long to wait. Less than ten minutes later a pair of burly orderlies came up the lift with a gurney. On the gurney was a shiny white cylinder covered in computer controls. She followed them down the hall, where the doctor stopped the orderlies to give instructions, and the Leatas met her.

"We appreciate what you're going to try to do," Pip's dad told her. Minu nodded. "Especially since it's probably against the rules." Her head came up, and he saw the twinkle in her eye. "You love him that much, and that's what helped make up our minds. If you bring our son back, that would be wonderful. If not…well, we said our goodbyes years ago." He looked over his shoulder into the room where the orderlies were setting up the pod. Cynthia sat next to Pip, where she'd sat for so many years now, gently stroking his hand. "I only wish they could have married before he was lost. Such a nice girl."

The doctor turned from the work on the pod when she came in the room. "We'll put him in it at the first sign of trouble, before anatomical damage becomes irreversible. Probably a day at the most. At that point, the clock is ticking."

"What kind of power does the pod use?"

"Power? A self-contained EPC, I don't think it uses one recharge for a month of use all added up."

"So it's self-contained?"

"Yes, the built-in computer takes care of all the details, and it transmits on a standard Concordian network that the hospital can read. Why do you want to know all of that?"

"Scientific interest," she said distractedly. He gave her a queer look and went to oversee the final setup. Minu moved over and sat in a chair next to Cynthia.

"I want to believe you," the other girl whispered. "I want to share that hope. I can't remember what his voice sounded like." Minu took the heavyset girl in her arms and let her cry. "Please bring him back to me?"

"If it's possible, I'll do it. I swear."

*****

Chapter Twelve
January 5th, 523 AE

Coma Care Ward, Mercy Hospital, Tranquility, Plateau Tribe, Bellatrix

"Three days," she mumbled to herself as she raced down the hall, medtechs and doctors dodging madly out of her way as she ran. It was only the night-black jumpsuit that kept them from saying anything. If a Chosen ran in a hospital, there was probably a darn good reason.

On the garage roof she jumped into her car and keyed it to life. Immediately it began warning her that she'd likely damaged the gravitic impellers and partially depolarized the EPC coupling. She dutifully noted it, offering an apology to her faithful car, and took the control to leap into the air. In acknowledgement of the damage she'd caused, she kept the speed below normal cruising velocity as she raced toward Steven's Pass. She needed a few hours to work anyway. Her personal tablet was interfaced with the car's more powerful network link, and she went into the Chosen system.

Years of working with the system had given her an in-depth knowledge of the ins and outs of that system. What it could do, what it couldn't do, and most importantly, what it could do if you didn't care how much trouble you got into eventually. She knew through Cherise how the chain of command worked for requisitions. In particular, that for expediency any three-star could order a consignment of goods relocated and the approval signed off prior to the goods' release. She deftly initiated a supply order she'd stored in her tablet months ago.

Twenty field kits, twenty type five EPCs (charged), two field expedition mess kits, enough to feed twenty people for a month, frontier water reclamation system, and a single reserve transport. All these items were low-priority and wouldn't attract immediate attention. The Chosen working in logistics would figure a field operation was in the works, note her three stars, and ship it. She tagged the request as urgent, with a requested delivery date of tomorrow. It was a little risky to increase the priority, but she didn't have time to waste.

Next she jumped over to the armaments subsystem. There she accessed the entire armory records for the Chosen detailing every field and shield generator, beamcaster, ballistic gun, accelerator rifle, and shock rifle in the inventory. Also inventoried were bots considered of tactical use. She didn't initiate an order here; that would draw the attention of the Head Armorer, and then likely the Chosen Council. Instead she used another tablet to take notes on what was held in the meager locker at the Tranquility Portal. To her dismay, there were no shock rifles and pitifully few beamcasters. "I thought we'd learned a lesson," she said in the quiet cockpit. She made some more notes and moved on.

Next she opened her own system at the training branch and created an order. Her misfits were reported as field ready with a note for their scout commander to pay special attention to them for their first few missions, "too willing to use force." And finally, a prepared email was sent to an old friend that she'd be calling in a favor.

By the time all that was finished, her car was descending to a landing at her private island. Even as the car was settling and the impellers spinning down, she was leaping from the driver's seat, tablets in hand, and heading for the door.

Inside she continued her fevered pace, organizing notes, putting together her personal kit, and writing a few emails. The messages were designed with two things in mind. First, they'd cover her tracks and provide potential explanations if her plan worked out and she returned before being listed as MIA. The second part was an admission of guilt, telling the Chosen council what she'd done, and why. It would work with the notes in her personal files, all of which would be unlocked once her plot was discovered. *They can have my fucking stars at that point,* she thought as she finished the disgustingly cordial letter, *this is nothing more than what they should have done years ago.* The medical data codex she was pursuing would save the lives of thousands of humans, and enable millions more to live longer, more productive lives as well. Not to mention saving one really good friend in particular.

The next morning she was up as the early spring sun began to glow through her living room windows. Late last night she'd finished her will, giving her car to Gregg, whose own was a much cheaper model, her home in stewardship to the Plateau Historical Society, since she wasn't allowed to give it to anyone by law, and the rest divided up between her few close friends. Minu took a final look around, then went to a cabinet by the front door. In the cabinet was her field belt and the knife she'd carried on missions since her trials. Also, there were two blades nearly the same length. They all went into her duffel bag and she headed out the door. As the car climbed away, she couldn't help looking back at the rapidly dwindling island and wondering if she'd ever be back.

She flew to Steven's Pass at a leisurely pace, the flight again giving her time to work with the Chosen network and finish setting her plans in motion. Her first assignments in the Chosen had often been working with Logistics to move materiel around Tog worlds, and for that she was now grateful. It was amazing what you could do if you only had to hide it for a couple of days and didn't care if you got caught in the end. As she was flying over Chelan, she got an email informing her that the required shipment of fields kits, etc., were delivered and waiting in warehouse 12-A, only requiring her department heads sign off to be picked up. A transport had been delivered to a nearby warehouse the previous night, having been shepherded there by a Chosen on his way home.

Minu landed and carefully parked her car in a lower level of the lot, under cover, and emailed a service request to the dealer where she'd bought it. "Silly me, I overloaded the drive; can you fix it for me?" The request was additional cover. Her actions didn't suggest any suspicious behavior, after all. If anything went wrong, Gregg wouldn't inherit a torn up car too. An authorization to pay for the repairs from her personal account was included.

Minu left the car behind, casting a last longing look at the sleek red flying machine, before lumbering down the stairs to the building entrance. The load of kit weighed out at nearly fifty kilos.

"Can I help you with that, Chosen?" asked a young intern. They were a new addition to the Chosen, pre-teen boys and girls who hoped to be Chosen someday, who spent vacations and free time working at Chosen facilities, learning their future lives, and deciding if they really wanted to pick that path.

"Thank you," Minu said and handed off the pack. The boy's eyes bugged, and he nearly collapsed under the load. He clearly hadn't expected a girl to be carrying that much weight. "Take that to the jump-off staging area, please." He nodded and headed down the hall, teetering back and forth as he struggled to stay on his feet. Minu was glad there was nothing fragile in the pack. All she'd kept was her own small duffel bag, carrying a few precious items only she would see.

Her next stop was the science wing. In the early morning there were a few techs and young Chosen around working on projects and getting ready for the day. They all knew her; who in the Chosen wouldn't recognize the lithe girl with flaming red hair, a gray arm, and three gold stars on her sleeve? She nodded in acknowledgment. They didn't even get curious when she went into Bjorn and Ted's lab and promptly filled her bag further with test instruments, sensors, spare parts, and anything else she could find that might be useful. Then she saw a case resting on a table and peeked in. There were six guns inside, unmistakable relatives of the ones designed by Gregg and Aaron back before the Rasa Vendetta. Those had been primitive revolver-style projectile guns, simple hand cannons with few refinements. They'd been copied from old Earth weapons. These were of a semi-automatic pedigree, with a number of additional improvements.

Minu picked one up and felt the heft. Milled from a solid block of dualloy, they were half the weight of the earlier design, and fit her small hand rather nicely. Laser rangefinder and scope were integrated into the slide, as well as a tiny digital ammo counter visible only to the wielder. The general shape was similar to one of the old Desert Eagle handguns she'd seen in a New Jerusalem tribe museum. Further investigation found a case of loaded magazines. Each mag held seven massive 18mm cartridges, much better than the old revolvers' five. Unable to resist exacerbating her crimes, she appropriated a hoverfield-powered cart, and loaded the crates.

Minu guided the hovercart loaded with all her gear outside and down to the ground level and maneuvered it across the grass-covered field. The skies were turning gray, and Minu hoped it didn't mean rain, at least until she was done. She knew she was being far more conspicuous than she'd wanted. A young Chosen woman pushing a heavily-laden hovercart was sure to draw someone's attention in the ops center. It turned out she was right, only it wasn't in the ops center that she was noticed.

She reached warehouse 12-A and floated her cart inside. There was the transport she wanted, parked just inside the door. She used her access code to open the craft's doors and stored everything from the cart inside. As long as she didn't fly the transport out the door or take any of the other equipment stored here for her without first logging permission from a higher-up, no alarms would be sounded.

Minu took the hovercart back out into the warehouse and found the consignments she'd requested. Food, kits, equipment, and charged EPCs were all ready and waiting, as promised. One at a time she moved them over next to the waiting transport. The only thing that surprised her was how clearheaded she was. There was no fear of jettisoning of her career, or worse. Theft from the Chosen was not completely unheard of. Chosen themselves stealing equipment, on the other hand, might well be unprecedented.

Finally, after several hours' work, she'd moved all the goods just outside the transport's big rear door and was ready to begin loading. She could have accomplished the entire task in minutes with the rack of bots stored in every warehouse, but again, she needed to avoid notice, and the bots' activation might draw attention from the ops center. Besides, she liked the physical labor. She wanted to know where every piece of equipment was stowed, how many of each was left, and, most importantly, if she'd missed anything they might need.

When everything was cued up in the order it was to be loaded, Minu sat on one of the crates and consulted the chronometer on her wrist. Six hours remained before the others would be geared up in the jump-off room waiting for her. The only thing she wished she'd brought was some water; she was getting thirsty.

"You look tired!" Minu spun to see Cherise leaning against the warehouse's open doorway. "Been busy?"

*****

Chapter Thirteen
January 5th, 523 AE

Warehouse 12-A, Chosen Headquarters, Steven's Pass, Bellatrix

A dozen lies ran through Minu's mind in the time it took her to answer. "Just moving some gear for the training division. No biggie."

"Hours before start of business?" Her dubious look said it all. "I know your boss; he calls a girl in my section for all his dirty work. In more than a year I've never seen any of his people move their own gear."

"Uhm…"

"Don't bother," Cherise said and stepped closer, surveying all the gear laying around the transport in carefully-stacked piles. "You honestly think I wouldn't see an order of this size?"

"Did anyone else?"

"No, I made sure of that. Now, you want to tell me what's going on?"

"It's Pip," Minu started, then explained the entire situation. Cherise listened quietly, the pain and realization slowly dawning on her face as Minu laid it all out.

"I didn't know it was that bad. I don't get to see him often enough, I know, and I hate myself for it. It's just so damned far to travel and all."

"Don't apologize," Minu told her, and the two embraced. "Who wants to spend a few hours holding hands with a man that's been essentially dead for two years?"

Cherise nodded and moved Minu out to arm's length while keeping her hands on the redhead's shoulders. "You really want to take this kind of a risk? I know, just answer the question."

"I might be able to save him," Minu said, "and maybe many more."

"Okay, so when do we leave?"

"Well, my team will be—what?"

"I said when do we leave?"

"I'm leaving, not you."

"I dare you to try and keep me from going," Cherise said, standing up straight to her full nearly-two-meter-height and looking down at Minu.

"I might surprise you," Minu whispered menacingly.

Cherise's demeanor broke, and she laughed, her friend joining her. "You probably would at that, but I'd still beat the shit out of you, and do you want to go out to God-knows-where covered in bruises and miscellaneous bite marks?"

"You'd like to give me some bite marks, I bet!" Cherise laughed even harder. "You're dead set on going along, I suppose?"

"Yep."

Minu glanced at her chronometer and groaned inwardly. She hadn't planned on extra mouths. Cherise saw the look on her face and walked out of the warehouse to return a second later carrying several crates identical to some of those already stacked for loading. "I planned ahead, just like you."

"Traitor."

"Glass houses, young lady."

With Cherise helping her, the final loading and stowing took half the time Minu had expected. "I think you need some more gear, Boss," Cherise said, panting as they finished and wiping sweat from her forehead. Minu smiled at the use of 'Boss.' It brought back both good and painful memories of the trials and missions shared with her closest friends, especially the one she was setting out to save. An old familiar tingle started in her toes and worked its way upward. The game was afoot.

"Let's go collect the rest of the team," Minu said. She shouldered her personal field kit and snapped the belt around her waist.

"Will anyone say anything about me going along?"

"Why would they? Besides, I've been freelancing teams of scout trainees onto the junk piles of the frontier for months."

Cherise took her own pack and belt, then trotted to catch up with Minu. "That's a new sword," she said and tapped the sheath Minu was buckling on her back. "From Tamara?"

"Yes, she gave it to me on Friday. Something she wanted me to try out; I don't think she was expecting an extended field test." Cherise carried one as well, but the more traditional katana fit onto her belt.

They entered through the old ground-level entrance that had once led to the portal chamber, now just another entrance to the building, and then down to the basement level where the new portal chamber was located. Just outside the heavily-armored dualloy vault holding the portal was the control room, and the jump-off room directly adjacent behind redundant force fields. She entered the later without glancing into the control room, and found her team waiting there.

"Was it really necessary to start this early?" Var'at yawned, jaws opening impossibly wide, showing rows of razor-sharp teeth.

"I can't thank you enough for this." Minu put a hand on his shoulder and nodded to the squad of fellow Rasa waiting nearby. They all carried combat gear of their own manufacture and were armed with their flechette dart guns. "You know this isn't sanctioned and we're liable to get in a lot of trouble."

"We aren't concerned. We pay our debts to friends. Good to see you again," he said to Cherise.

"You as well," the tall woman replied.

"Everyone ready?" Minu asked and did a quick once around the room to be sure. "Okay, we're taking a transport, so I need to arrange to have the garage door opened." The massive dualloy door could be opened to admit as large a vehicle as could fit through the portal. Minu left her gear and went across the hall to the control center and her first major setback.

"I have a team ready to go off world," she said as she walked through the door. The duty officer turned around, and Minu felt her heart sink.

"What the hell are you doing here?" Ivan Malovich snapped, looking up from the tablet he'd been reading. The sole satisfaction Minu felt at finding him sitting there was the five gold stars on his cuff. It had been two years since his atrocity caused the Rasa Vendetta and cost the lives of thousands of humans. The Chosen didn't just toss out members, not even a colossal screw up like Ivan. He'd gone from four to five stars, and apparently stayed there. Maybe permanently?

"I'm doing my job," she said as she recovered quickly, "I have a team to go out on a training mission to the frontier."

"There isn't anything on the mission log," he replied. During the trials, Ivan's group of thugs had ambushed her team, injuring many of them and almost killing Minu. One of his friends raped her and forever changed the course of her life. After killing the rapist, she'd done her best to kill Ivan, and he'd tried to kill her as well. Despite all that, his eyes still followed the curve of her hips and breasts like he was sizing up a steak dinner.

"I have authorization to freelance teams on the frontier," she told him.

"According to the records you have unlimited access to Deep Blue on the frontier," he admitted with a disgruntled tone in his voice.

"I want to go to FAX109, and I'll need an unlocked PCR."

"I can't give you an unlocked portal control rod!" he complained. "And why do you want to go there. Nothing's there!"

"Why and where I'm going is not your concern. And as for authority, I am that authority. Now, are you going to do it or not?"

"The day shift duty officer comes on in two hours," he told her, and Minu knew he wasn't going to be intimidated. "You can just wait until then."

"Waste of my time, five-star," she snarled and marched out the door back to the jump-off room. "Mother fucker," she spat once out of earshot.

"Didn't go for it, did he?" Cherise asked. No doubt she'd recognized his voice. Cherise shared a history with Minu.

"Of course not."

"What's going on?" Var'at asked.

"I want to go to a...unique destination," she said. "The little twit in charge won't let me go without authorization."

"You didn't file a mission plan, did you?" Cherise asked.

"Of course not. You think I'm stupid?" Cherise stared at her. "I thought it through as far as I could, but I'm not a criminal at heart.

"Need some help?" a new voice asked. Minu jerked in surprise to see Aaron walking up to her, a big smile on his face.

Minu instantly looked at Cherise, accusation in her eyes. The look she got in reply said it all. "Who else did you call?"

"Uhm," Cherise said and Minu suppressed the urge to slap her in the back of the head. The urge must have at least partially manifested into some movement because Cherise took a half step backward, out of Minu's reach. "I didn't know what you were up to!"

"And just decided to come here and stop me."

"No, decided you might need our help," Aaron said firmly, and suddenly Minu felt like a total asshole. In partial repayment for the accusation she quickly brought Aaron up to date on her plan. "I'm in," he said without even waiting for her to explain further. "Gregg wanted to, but with him in charge of the Rangers, we both agreed it was better he stayed where he was or we'd risk losing them to someone who didn't care, or worse."

"I agree," Minu said and glanced toward the command room, making certain Ivan wasn't eavesdropping. "We can't just kick his ass and go through…"

"I don't see why not," Aaron ventured, making fists with his hands. Minu enjoyed the way his arms flexed when he did that. Aaron had obviously continued his workout regimen, and he'd gone from just muscular to herculean proportions. She was surprised to realize how good it was to have him along.

"I think I know a way out of this," Cherise said and took out her communicator. While she worked on that, Aaron also got his out and made a call of his own.

"What are you guys up to?" Minu asked suspiciously.

"Just getting into the whole conspiracy thing." Aaron chuckled then began talking quietly into his phone. After a minute he looked up and caught Cherise's eye. She nodded at him, and he turned back to Minu. "Let's go."

Minu almost complained, then thought better of it. They were here on their own, risking their careers, to help her. The least she owed them was some trust. She went into the jump-off room and got Var'at's attention. "Let's roll," she said. The Rasa glanced at each other, then all six scurried after her.

In the control room, Ivan watched the Rasa suspiciously. He knew something was going on; he just had no idea what it was. The prim and proper Minu Alma was now far above him in rank through no fault of his own, and his hatred for her burned like a blue-white star. But if he made another misstep, he'd probably spend the rest of his career as a cook's assistant in the cafeteria. Still, his instincts had often proved to be his strongest asset, with one glaringly disastrous exception years ago. With a sigh, he cast the die and picked up his communicator.

* * * * *

Chapter Fourteen
January 5th, 523 AE

Chosen Headquarters, Steven's Pass, Bellatrix

Minu and the Rasa followed Aaron down the hall and up the stairs, his strides full of purpose. In a minute, they were back in the science wing, and Minu felt her pulse quicken. Sure enough, they entered the familiar labs, and there was a whole group of technicians standing around looking at an incriminating empty spot on the floor. She and Aaron slipped by them and found their friends, Bjorn and Ted, standing next to a table, sipping tea and watching their techs. Minu knew who Aaron had called now without a doubt.

"So what's this all about?" Ted asked, smiling broadly when he saw Minu.

"Your missing equipment," Aaron said.

"We figured some idiot just moved it after hours," spoke up Bjorn.

"I've been called worse," Minu said, her face burning.

"What?" Ted stuttered. "Why would you take those prototype guns? All you had to do was ask."

"I would have, if I'd had time." They both looked even more confused. "Pip is dying, and I think I can save him." For the second time that hour, she explained what was happening.

"We wondered what you were on about during the talk we had," Bjorn spoke, nodding his head. Minu recalled the luncheon, and her discussing just such a scenario, and instantly regretted not letting them in on her plans.

"In my defense, I didn't really want to drag you into it at the time."

"He's my friend, and Bjorn's nephew," Ted scolded, and Minu blushed again.

"Well, that's that then," Bjorn said and got up off his stool, "we'll be back in a few minutes." He nodded to Ted and the two went through the rear of the lab into their private offices. Minu wanted desperately to know what they were going to do. Turn her in? Make a call to Jacob and put an end to her stupid plan? Instead they emerged in black field jumpsuits, packs on their shoulders and equipment belts buckled in place. Minu had never seen Ted in a Chosen uniform and it caught her a little off guard. The cluster of five silver stars on the sleeve clashed badly with his many years.

"You can't be serious," both Aaron and Minu said at the same time.

"Deadly so," Ted assured them in his dignified voice. Bjorn nodded as he fussed with his belt, his slight paunch making it difficult to latch. Ted was in perfect shape for his advanced age and had no such difficulty.

"How long has it been since you were last in the field?" Aaron asked, pointing at Bjorn.

"Twenty-six years," he admitted proudly, "but not for lack of trying!"

"And have you even ever been off world to the frontier?" he asked of Ted.

"Nope!" Ted admitted easily, "but I've read every log and manual there is and believe I'm quite well-versed in procedures."

Aaron looked at Minu incredulously and Var'at shook his head, but Minu just sighed. What caught her attention the most was the two gleaming silver stars on Bjorn's cuff. He'd once been on the Chosen council as the head of the science branch, until politics had dethroned him. It wasn't as crazy a plan on the surface as it might appear.

"I don't think we have a choice," Minu admitted.

"We can leave them here!" Aaron snapped, more adamant than she ever remembered seeing him. "Minu, they're old enough to be grandparents, and Ted's never been on a frontier mission; what can they offer us other than their brains?"

"This," Bjorn said and held up his midnight black sleeve with the two shiny silver stars, echoing Minu's thoughts exactly.

"And this," Ted said, pulling a portal control rod from his uniform leg pouch and holding it up.

Minu laughed. "You can't argue with that logic!" Aaron scowled, realizing a lost cause when he saw one.

When they got back downstairs, another two Chosen in tow, Minu found the jump-off room disturbingly empty. There was no sign at all of Ivan or any other Chosen. "Oh, that's just great," she mumbled.

"Is something wrong?" Ted asked, looking around the empty room.

"I don't know," Minu whispered.

"Okay," Aaron said as his communicator beeped loudly, and he nodded toward the huge bay doors just as they began to swing open. A slight gust of cool morning air wafted in as a pair of transports floated down to level with the entrance. Neither was the older surplus model delivered earlier that evening to the warehouse, and to her surprise both were piloted by Rasa. "Our ride is here."

"You sneaky son of a bitch." Minu could see behind one of the pilots Cherise was standing gesturing for them to get aboard.

"You didn't think we'd all fit in that one old flyer do you?" Var'at asked.

As Minu and her friends clambered aboard, Ivan returned to the command room, and his jaw dropped. Where had the two transports come from? What about the ancient two-star who was with the damned Alma girl? And he'd yet to get a call back from the duty officer in the bunker. On his board the portal access display came alive, telling him that an unlocked PCR was programming the portal for a destination. He tried to stop it, but he lacked the access to override the system. The portal came alive with a shimmer and the first transport lined up with the door.

The communicator beeped and he stabbed the activation button. "Chosen Malovich," he said quickly.

"What's going on?" the voice on the other end said. Ivan didn't have to be told it was the First Among the Chosen, everyone in the service knew his voice.

"Alma is here, she has a large team and two transports, and they're about to go through the portal!"

"She has an unlocked control rod?"

"No, an old male Chosen has one, and I can't override!"

"Ted!" snarled the voice. "What the fuck is she doing?"

"She has a team of Rasa with her!"

"Transfer control to my tablet, immediately!"

As Minu jumped through the hatch she turned and caught a clawed hand to help Var'at in.

"I hope you didn't steal these transports," Minu admonished the reptilian.

"No," Cherise called out from the front, "I did."

"With our help," Ted told her. Bjorn grinned hugely and nodded.

"We're all going to jail," Minu moaned.

Ted took out his control rod, and like most Chosen, unnecessarily pointed it toward the portal while entering data. The portal flashed to life and the transport moved into position. Just as they started to move forward the portal swirled and deactivated. "Huh?" Ted said and took the rod back up again.

"Won't respond?" Minu asked.

"No, I can't make it do anything!"

"Jacob," Minu told them. "I was hoping Ivan wouldn't have the balls to make that phone call this early in the morning. I was wrong."

"So what do we do now?" Aaron asked.

"Nothing; we're screwed. By the time we can get to another portal he'll have warned those duty officers and they'll all be shut down."

"Not Fort Jovich," Aaron suggested.

"I won't do that to Gregg," she insisted.

"How long before they shut down the entire network?" Ted asked.

Minu shrugged and thought. "Depends on how thorough they are. Jacob is sure to call the high-use portals first, probably finishing with Tranquility. Call it half an hour?"

"Set course for Tranquility," Ted told the driver.

"Ted, there's no way this thing can go two thousand kilometers in thirty minutes!"

"Not a normal transport," he agreed, "but this isn't a normal transport. Better take a seat."

Inside was the rest of a full squad of Rasa soldiers, bringing the total to ten. Even with all of them, enough seats remained for the new arrivals. As she sat down, Minu noted that her supplies were loaded in the back along with quite a bit more things she didn't remember ordering. The craft spun around and began to climb. No sooner had it leveled off than the interior began to change. The roof descended and the walls widened out.

"This is a Lancer!" Minu cried and clapped her hands. "I thought you'd only finished a few."

"Two, to be precise," Bjorn told her. "These were just turned over to the Rangers. No one has had a chance to pick them up yet…" The second fighter paced them easily just to their side as powerful field generators came on, acceleration continued to build, and in moments they were shuddering through multiples of the sound barrier. "Supersonic is a gas," the aged scientist cackled. Outside the front view port, the energy force field glowed blue-white as the craft rammed through the atmosphere at almost eight thousand kilometers per hour.

The driver hissed in glee as the fighters tore through the early morning sky. "This is a fantastic craft!" she heard him say through her translator. Ten minutes after lifting into the sky they were in a stomach-churning power dive toward the city of her birth, Tranquility, a transit time that would turn her souped-up red aerocar hotrod green with envy. Slowing to less than the speed of sound, they did a slow circle of the sleepy town center.

"If we're doing it this way, we might not have any control of what we find when we get back," she told them. "Have the second fighter loiter near the Temple Plaza, and set us down on the hospital emergency roof pad, the east wing."

"What's the plan?" Aaron asked.

"We need to pick up a friend."

* * *

With less than ten minutes left in her proposed thirty-minute deadline, Minu and Aaron burst through the doors back onto the roof within sight of the waiting transport. Between them they pushed a white capsule suspended on a portable hoverfield generator. Inside lay the body of their friend, held at the edge of death's door by technology no one on the planet really understood. "I hope this works," Aaron said as they pushed the seemingly weightless capsule. "If it doesn't, we're screwed."

"I don't care about myself," she said grimly. "We owe it to him to try."

Rasa soldiers spilled out as they approached and the capsule was quickly manhandled aboard the ship. Almost as an afterthought, Minu snatched up the hoverfield generator and tossed it in then climbed in behind it, the doors humming closed.

The suspended animation capsule took up an inordinate amount of space, and the once large interior was now quite cozy. Unable to quickly secure the load, two Rasa soldiers squatted next to it to be sure it didn't fly around as they climbed away from the roof. Minu took the copilot's seat, Var'at just behind her and her other friends behind him. "A fine adventure," he hissed in her ear, and she shook her head. The Rasa never passed up an opportunity to do something new, even if it was not completely legal.

"Adventure, for sure. Hurry, we've only got about five minutes."

The craft raced the few kilometers to the center of town as Ted programmed the portal from his PCR. Minu knew the officer in charge would be looking at his controls with a very confused look (hopefully) and likely picking up his communicator to get answers. The plan depended on him not being warned yet of what had transpired back at Steven's Pass. They had seconds at best.

"Exterior access doors opening," the driver confirmed, and he brought them down to the deck. Minu got an excellent look at one of the city's ubiquitous pushcart vendors only a meter away as they slid along at street level. The back of the ancient Portal Temple, once home to all Chosen operations, was opening wide to reveal the portal inside. She just got a glimpse of the duty officer standing behind the moliplas window, communicator to his ear, and a look of profound surprise on his face as the two transports shot past and through the portal with only centimeters to spare.

*****

Part III

In all our quest of greatness, like wanton boys, whose pastime is their care, we follow after bubbles, blown in the air.

–John Webster

Chapter One
January 6th, 523 AE

Planet Green Able Three, Galactic Frontier

The two multi-role fighters rested on the ground a few meters from where Minu held a conference with her new ad hoc team. The world where they'd stopped was two jumps after first leaving Bellatrix, to be sure no scouts tried to follow them. This planet was known only as Green Able Three, a nondescript world of rolling hills covered with vines and occasional brackish pools of water. The air was breathable, and the orange-tinted sun gave them sufficient warmth that they didn't have to power the heaters in their field uniforms. The gravity was a little more than normal, but not enough to be uncomfortable.

Everyone stood around listening to Minu describe the mission in detail and why they were risking their careers, and in the case of Var'at and his personnel, their freedom. She worried a little about the Rasa and their role in the rescue she'd planned. Pip still rested in the fighter, his suspension pod safely stowed, suffering from wounds inflicted by one of Var'at's own soldiers. She believed that this was the biggest reason her alien friend had jumped at the opportunity when Aaron had secretly called him a few hours ago.

"So that's it in a nutshell," she said. Except for part of the Rasa contingent, which was on guard duty, all eyes were on her. Minu saw mostly interest, some excitement, and in Ted's case, concern. She'd been over most of it with them before leaving, but it felt good to lay down all the details.

"Hard decision you made," he said with a nod.

"I'm sure Pip would be grateful," Bjorn added. Aaron nodded.

"We don't really care what or why you're doing this," Var'at told her, "I promised when you made us safe on your world that if you ever called, we'd answer."

"And I thank you," Minu said, "I just wanted you to have all the facts."

"Our species is not as unique as yours, so we've had a biological codex since we became clients. I can't imagine how difficult it must be not being able to take advantage of all the Concordian technology. It's a noble quest."

"Well," Bjorn asked as he rubbed his hands together, "where to?"

"I've named the system 'Enigma,'" she explained, careful not to give details on the private log from her father and its corroboration of details of that world's existence. "The Squeen didn't provide any hard details, little more than the world's location."

"Have we ever had scouts there?" Aaron asked.

Minu swallowed and took a breath before speaking. "Yes and no." They all looked confused, and she was forced to continue. "My father was there, once, but never reported it to the Chosen council."

"So you *are* following in his footsteps." Ted laughed. It broke the tension Minu was feeling, and she smiled. "We all knew he was doing a lot of things off the books. He never told anyone what he'd been up to or why. It now seems he shared at least some secrets with you." Minu nodded. "Will you share some of this with those who can use it best?"

"When the time comes."

"And when will that be?"

"You'll have to trust me to make that call."

Ted and Bjorn exchanged looks, and for the first time, Minu fully realized that she'd dragged two men many times her age halfway across the galaxy on a hunch. But after a moment they both nodded to her. "Okay," Ted said simply. "What's our next step?"

Minu smiled at him and picked up her tablet from where she'd laid it on a clump of vines. "Enigma is in a backward area of the frontier, and it won't be easy getting there." She explained one detail that her father had learned many years ago and passed on to her through his logs; many portals were dedicated to only one other destination, and thus couldn't be called up from any other portal.

"So he confirmed the theory of local and long distance portals!" Bjorn crowed, slapping his knee with his hand.

"Yes, he did." Minu nodded. "And what's more, some portals are actually long distance, but still only dedicated to one or two destinations. So that's how this system of Enigma was kept a secret. At some point, an old Concordian species cut it off from the rest of the galaxy and left it hidden."

"Must be quite a treasure trove," Aaron commented.

"And may have once been home to another hominid species like ourselves," Minu agreed. "The important thing to remember is that my father provided no details on the world, only that he highlighted it as 'of interest.'" Once again she felt sick at not telling them the full details. This was one of those clue worlds he'd left her, where there was likely some additional piece of information that would allow her to eventually unlock the last of the encrypted files on his logs. Files so massively encrypted that not even Pip could get in. "The Squeen told me this is where our human-matching cybernetics come from," she said and held up her four-fingered right hand.

"What is the biggest risk?" Var'at asked.

"This is uncontrolled territory, deeper into the frontier than humans have ever gone. As you Rasa know, many of these are prime-choice picking worlds claimed by higher-order species, and they defend them with maximum prejudice. We could be walking into a seemingly worthless junk pile..."

"Or a hornet's nest teaming with T'Chillen," Aaron finished for her. She nodded; they all understood the risk now. It was important to her.

"So, what's the route we need to take to get there?" Bjorn asked, pulling out his own tablet computer and calling up a glowing map of the galaxy as they knew it.

*****

Chapter Two
January 10th, 523 AE

Undesignated World, Galactic Frontier

The plan was a simple one, a controlled mad dash for Enigma, avoiding all contact with alien species, passing through far-flung worlds so quickly they didn't draw attention to themselves. Four days and a dozen jumps into the plan, Minu was forced to admit it wasn't working.

"It was a good plan on the face of it," Bjorn consoled her. The two stood outside underneath one of the fighter's gull-wing side doors, using it as a shield from the world's unceasing rain. Lightning flashes illuminated the endless rain forest that surrounded them. Adding to the misery of unceasing rain, the world's temperature hovered just above freezing.

"History is littered with good plans," Minu said, wiping water from her bright red hair, "and the dead left afterward." Bjorn shrugged, so she bent over and glanced under the fighter. There, lying in the mud and muck, was Ted and one of Var'at's soldiers, a technician, struggling to remove a fickle gravitic impeller. "How's it coming?"

"Faster if you'd leave us alone," Ted said as rain dripped from the underside of the fuselage onto his face in a steady stream.

"I'm thrilled you talked me into this!" Bjorn crowed, stretching under the dry shade of the door. "It's great to get clean unspoiled air into your lungs!" Ted just sputtered and spit out dripping water as he wrenched on the stubborn impeller. Nearby, a temporary shelter had been set up by the Rasa soldiers, and they were roasting some local wildlife they'd caught. It looked far too much like a primitive monkey for Minu's liking. She admired their ability to make the best out of any environment and to always find something to eat. Their resourcefulness was exceeded only by their culinary constitution.

Minu sighed and moved back inside. The interior of the fighter had a musty feel to it now, and even here, water was everywhere. It was a little warmer, but they didn't dare turn up the heaters all the way. Hot and humid was worse in her opinion than cold and wet. Aaron sat in the pilot's seat, snoring loudly, while Var'at sat carrying on an animated conversation with one of his soldiers. Minu took another seat and pulled out her personal tablet.

The galactic holographic map sprang to life, and she projected it in space above her, the better to make three-dimensional connections. She'd been marking worlds with portals and highlighting those with site-specific destinations. She'd spent months before this mission entering data from her father's personal logs, and the map was crisscrossed with hundreds of color-coded lines. To the casual observer, it looked like you could go anywhere you wanted quite easily. The truth was many areas of the galaxy were difficult, if not impossible, to get to. Chriso had never discovered how to unlock a portal that was limited in destinations, but the fact that they could be locked was obvious. Someone, a very long time ago, had purposely isolated vast swaths of space. She accessed her father's logs and read.

"The more I see, the more I learn. I find myself running in circles. Someone obviously did this on purpose, and they must have been very old and very powerful." Minu could sense her father's frustration in his writing as he continued. "Even more tantalizing than the thought that someone knows how to manually program portals, is what they might be protecting."

She put the log down and looked up at the map again, zooming in on their location and spinning the view. Enigma was there, glowing gold, and tantalizingly close. "Only fifteen damn light-years away," she grumbled, "why did the damn Concordia give up ships? Doesn't make any sense."

"I agree," hissed Var'at. He'd finished his conversation and moved to sit next to her. He watched her with one turreted eye while the other studied the rotating map.

"It's a mystery my father never figured out either," she told him. "On one hand, some old species made it difficult to reach certain areas of the galaxy; then around the same time, they abandoned space ships."

"Maybe they did one to enable the other."

"What?"

"I said, what if they isolated those places, and then got rid of the starships so that no one could sneak around their blocks?" Minu was dumbfounded and sat staring at Var'at. "I'm sorry, it's a silly idea."

"No, it's brilliant really." Var'at smiled at her in his species' way by hanging his mouth open and flicking his tongue. "This theory of yours suggests that both events must have been implemented by one species." Var'at shrugged in a noncommittal fashion. "One species with that much power?"

"Who knows how much power the Lost wielded?"

Var'at moved outside, maybe to get some roasted monkey, leaving Minu with her thoughts. Months ago, after the Tanam incident, the Squeen named Strong Arm had told her that she should wonder who the original Concordia were. She could find absolutely no evidence who that might be on the networks. Moreover, there was research by other species that suggested there never was an 'original Concordia' species. To her, it was nothing short of phenomenal that a loosely-formed empire spanning most of a galaxy would have no real memory of who'd started it. The other species, by and large, didn't seem to care or were offended by the idea. Then you added in a fact Pip had discovered years ago, that all Concordian portable-media chips were designed to self-destruct after 100,000 years. She leaned back and rubbed her eyes, feeling wholly inadequate to get her head around the sprawling mystery. In a seat nearby, Cherise gently snored.

"And I can't get any closer than fifteen light-years," she said to the gloomy, dripping interior of the fighter. Every turn they'd made, they ran into obstacle after obstacle. Obstinate portals that wouldn't accept commands from the control rod Ted brought, portals that appeared dead and inactive, hostile aliens more than willing to engage the fleeing humans, and worlds so inhospitable even operating the fighters was challenging were just a few of the problems they'd run into. And now only two paths were left to enter the region of Enigma. "At least the aliens we've encountered don't know who we are." She was relatively certain. The transports her fighters were based on were ubiquitous in the empire. Thousands of them could be had for rock-bottom prices. Of course, thanks to Bjorn and Ted's magic, these were no longer ordinary transports.

As if he'd tuned in on her mental musings, Bjorn appeared in the doorway, looking around with a thoughtful expression. He seemed unhappy about something. She turned farther in her chair and regarded him before speaking. "Something wrong?"

He noticed her there and smiled. Minu had always found him a friendly man who never got angry. Even when he'd been usurped from his old job as head of the Science branch, he'd never raised his voice. "I was just realizing we forgot to add something to the fighter."

"Really? Looks perfect to me; what did you forget?"

"A damn bathroom," he grumbled then laughed at the look on her face. She gestured to the ubiquitous 'field portable relief station' and he laughed all the harder.

"Maybe we can stop by somewhere and use a pay toilet?" Minu asked

"We couldn't even pay them for a candy bar." Minu looked askance so he continued. "We aren't part of the wider Concordian economy. We're nothing more than itinerant farmers, trading what extra food we can."

"So what's the Concordian economy based on? They have credits they use and trade to us for our products and salvage."

"Right! But what are the credits based on? There must be a material base for every economy, right?"

"Unless you're the 20th century United States." Minu just stared at him. "Some powerful nations on earth based their currency on trust that they'd be around and powerful in the future. It was called Fiat Currency."

"Rather foolish to take a simple promise for your worth."

"Isn't it? Anyway, it was your father's belief that the Concordian economy has energy at its base. And we agreed with him."

"Energy? But, but, that's just a…"

"A commodity like any other," he assured her. "In old-world governments on our planet, they valued things like food, and even salt. Just because it's a consumable doesn't mean it isn't valuable. A third of all our off-world trade goes to purchase power in the form of loaded EPCs."

"I remember now; we talked about this a few years ago." Bjorn nodded and grinned. "Pip said they got the power from something called Solar Taps, sucking it up from suns and such."

"Yep, crazy technology. The same kind of stuff that probably let them move our world, more than once, despite its aging star."

"Okay, like you said before, you think this is lost technology, magic from the past and such?" Again Bjorn nodded. "So how are they keeping up with the power needed for a galaxy-spanning empire?" With a twinkle in his eye, Bjorn told her to explain as she saw it. "Well, even though a star is really big and all, it has a finite amount of plasma you can harvest. Won't you eventually destabilize the star?"

"Possibly, but not if you're careful. The plasma is a byproduct of the fusion process in the right type sequence star."

"But what about aging?"

"Aha!"

"These ideal stars, they're young, right?"

"Very young."

"So you only have a limited time you can harvest from them? What, a few million years?"

"About."

"So if that technology is lost…"

"Go on!"

"Then it's a ticking time bomb, a disaster waiting to happen!" Again the smile and a nod. "But is that enough to cause the decline you say is under way?"

"Not by itself," he said with a shake of his head.

"A lot more is going on we don't see," Ted said as he entered. He was dripping wet and covered with mud as he carried in the offending impeller. They could have just ignored the malfunctioning device, but he decided to repair it lest they end up in a combat situation and be down to only backups. The stock impellers were slightly modified to work in the fighters, which was a problem. It was doing double duty and was prone to failure. An upgraded model was on order, but not yet available.

Ted set the impeller, a round flattened housing with two dangling cable harnesses, on a chair and fell into the chair next to it. The Rasa tech was right behind him with a diagnostic tool kit. "This little troublemaker is part of the problem."

"Why is that?"

"Because it's thousands of years old," he said and absently slapped the troublesome machine. "We can't get new ones and couldn't afford them if we wanted to. The Concordia is like one long endless flea market, but where are the factories?" Minu shrugged. "Exactly! Your father found what he thought were dead factories. He called them Ghost Factories, and there are dozens of them all over the place. He also found what looked like abandoned farm worlds, given over to fallow conditions due to a lack of manufacturing base. It's like the whole galaxy is in the grips of some massive malaise!"

"Or decadence?" Bjorn asked.

"Even a decaying, decadent society recognizes the need for production," Ted countered.

"There must be a way to head off our own addiction at the pass," Minu said with more conviction than she felt.

"We used to be independent," Bjorn reminded her. "Up to a few decades ago, we only imported a tiny amount of power. Now, with all those factories, aerocars, other industry?" He shook his head and Minu made a frustrated face.

"If you're done entertaining flights of fantasy," Ted barked, "could you give me a hand with this fickle instrument?" Bjorn gave her a wink and left her with her thoughts.

"Don't you think we'd make some enemies if we became energy independent?"

Minu looked up at Aaron leaning against the fighter's door. During her conversation with Bjorn he'd awakened from his nap and gone to stretch his legs. He seemed indifferent to the rain pouring off the roof and down his back. As a scout he'd been through much worse. "Maybe, but who cares?"

"She dances where angels fear to tread."

"Don't be melodramatic.'

"Perish the thought." He moved over and sat behind her. He looked at the map she'd left hovering with a critical eye. "Someone went out of their way to make it less than obvious that something was hidden there."

"Not subtle enough. Only two ways in, and both are contested worlds. One controlled by the T'Chillen, and the other by the Mok-Tok. The latter was so hot we nearly lost a team of scouts twenty years ago."

"Sas-quad pods can be real antisocial," Aaron agreed. Humanity rarely interacted with the enigmatic species known as the Mok-Tok, and thus very little was known about them. They were a symbiotic species, the visible one being a two-meter-tall quadrupedal furry monster lacking any obvious head or visual organs. Scouts quickly dubbed them Sas-quads because of their resemblance to a disembodied four-legged Sasquatch of old Earth legend. Whatever the other half of their species was like, they hated humans with even more passion than the reptilian T'Chillen.

"Well, sounds to me like the only real option is the T'Chillen route. At least we have a known threat, and previous intel."

"True," Minu agreed as she eyed the map with him.

"Trust these fighters," he advised, "the guys know what they're doing. We can be in and out pretty quickly. The stupid snakes won't know what hit them!"

Behind them, the gravitic impeller went *SNAP* and started to smoke. "Bitch!" Ted screamed and smacked it with a wrench.

* * * * *

Chapter Three
January 11th, 523 AE

Undesignated World, Near Enigma, Galactic Frontier

The fighter slid through the portal and into darkness. As they had since leaving Bellatrix, Minu led in her fighter, Aaron piloting next to her in the front, Ted and Bjorn behind them, a squad of Rasa soldiers farther back, and finally Cherise overseeing the delicate cargo of Pip in his suspension pod. The other fighter would follow in seconds, commanded by Var'at and the remainder of his troops. No sooner had they cleared the portal than a proximity alarm went off and they came to a quick stop.

"What is it?" Minu asked as she looked out through the moliplas viewport.

"Can't see a thing," Aaron said, "but the radar says there's solid wall right in front of us.

"Side slip before Var'at rear-ends us." Aaron nodded and the fighter rode its impellers sideways. A second later the computer told them the other fighter was arriving, and just like them coming to a sudden stop. Another alarm went off, arresting their sideways momentum this time. "What the hell? Damn it, we better have a look. Exterior illumination, half power."

Aaron brought up the lights mounted along the fighter's flanks and they got a look at their surroundings. Nearly featureless walls ran along in a sweeping arc in front of them and away in both directions.

Minu craned her neck to the right and could just make out a huge pile of debris. They hovered over a metallic floor, and above was a similar ceiling.

"Where the hell are we?" Aaron wondered aloud. He was delicately maneuvering the fighter to make more room for Var'at's fighter. The space was only five meters ceiling to floor, and twenty meters wide. Not a lot of space for a three-meter-tall, ten-meter-long refitted transport.

"Some sort of portal facility," Minu guessed. "Maybe an underground bunker, or antechamber of a Portal Spire." She manipulated the fighter's systems and verified there was an atmosphere sufficient to support human and Rasa life. "Land here and let's have a look around."

The air was biting cold and smelled of decaying metal, but it was breathable. Minu pulled a field issue support mask from her kit and slid it on over her head. The device came alive, and instantly the air she breathed was warmer and scrubbed clean. The chamber the fighters rested in did look a bit like some freight handling rooms she'd seen in Portal Spires in the past, but also not. The group spread out to investigate.

"Some automated handling equipment," Cherise announced from the huge pile of debris.

"What happened to it?"

"A little age, and a lot of weapons fire." She held up a charred piece of debris for Minu to see. At the same time, Ted was using their control rod to examine the portal.

"Been inactive for a while, probably months at least. Won't accept programming, just like your father said. We can only go back where we came from."

"The next portal onward must be in another chamber," Minu said. She looked at the only door, currently closed, and whistled through her teeth. The fighters might fit through, but only just.

"My people are getting all kinds of crazy energy signatures," Var'at told her and he gestured around them. "This is a most unusual place you've brought us to."

"Thanks dad," she mumbled under her breath, then directed her attention to Aaron. "See if we can get that door open."

A few minutes later, the big doors were rumbling open. It turned out to be easier than she'd suspected. Someone had overridden the mechanisms long ago, making it no more difficult than flipping a switch. Minu was the first one through the door, two of the new generation hand cannons strapped to her waist, one on either side. Aaron now called them Enforcers, some kind of inside joke he shared with Ted and Bjorn. The weight was substantial, but extra magazines balanced the load well enough. Without shock rifles, it was the best close-range weapon in their arsenal. Aaron wore a pair as well, and Cherise carried the last two.

Outside was a massive hallway running parallel to the doorway. The sweeping slow turn of the hallway made something tickle the back of her mind. Each man carried a powerful electric torch that cast harsh white light in all directions. Despite the power operating the door and apparently cleaning the air, there were no lights.

"Which way?" Var'at asked. A squad of his soldiers backed Aaron and her up as they prepared to explore their surroundings. The rest waited with the fighters and remained on high-alert lest a speedy retreat through the portal became necessary. Minu shrugged and pointed, and they were off.

The hall continued a slow turn to the left as they walked. No other doors were evident, only plenty of dust. The debris cover on the floor was light and well-trampled. This facility was used fairly often. At one point, one of Var'at's team knelt next to a clear track in the thick dust. It was unmistakably a massive snake. "Oh shit," Aaron said.

"We knew the snakes had laid claim to vast areas of space around here," Minu reminded them all. "This isn't a surprise."

"Tell that to my shorts," Aaron said under his breath, which Minu heard clearly. She shot him a nasty look, and he smiled innocently.

The hallway ended in another doorway; this one operated automatically and began to slide open at their approach. They moved through carefully, weapons holstered but with hands on gun butts, ready to respond in a second. Minu instantly realized something was different. Their torches reflected from the wall opposite the door they'd just entered through, as if the wall was a massive sweeping mirror. "Everyone turn off your lights," she told them. One by one the lights went out until they were cast into complete darkness.

It took a moment for their eyes to adjust to the darkness and discern the dim points of light shining through the glass wall. Minu stepped closer and gasped. It was a huge window, and below orbited a planet. "We're on a space station," she said.

"Extraordinary!" Var'at spoke as he came up next to her. Minus the glaring light of their torches, the stars and the world below cast enough light to illuminate the chamber in a dim glow rather like a child's night light. Tearing her eyes away from the window, Minu saw a portal dais at the rear, and then the unmistakable signs of a fight. Here and there the dualloy walls were scored from energy weapons fire, and several pieces of unusual furniture were completely destroyed. This place had seen battle.

"Have you ever been on a space station?" she asked her Rasa friend.

"Once, many years ago when I was young. It was a horrible, dangerous place. There was no atmosphere, and the gravitic systems were down. We used space suits to move from one portal to another as quickly as possible."

"Where did you get space suits?"

"We, our people, had a small supply of them. We ordered them many years ago from some company in the Concordia."

"If the Concordia gave up space ships eons ago, why would anyone bother stocking space suits?"

"That's a good question. And one for which I have no answer."

While they'd been talking, Aaron had examined the portal using the manual controls. Stepping on the dais, the archway came alive, and he used his hands to make the icons appear. All portals were addressable in this manner, even if no one knew how to operate them using the icons. It served as a simple way to query the device's programming and status.

"It's active," he informed her after a moment, "set for only one destination. Hasn't been used in about a month, but it has seen steady traffic over the years."

"Ask it if there are any other portals on the station," she told him.

He tapped icons that rearranged themselves in answer. "There are at least two nearby."

"Okay," she said and turned to Var'at, "let's find them, shall we?"

* * *

Ted and Bjorn stood staring out at the magnificent panorama of the world far below, both babbling about the possibilities of owning such a station for research and such, when Minu returned with the Rasa scouts. As soon as Ted saw her he spoke up. "This particular portal probably only goes to that planet below," he told her.

"What makes you so sure?" she asked.

"Well, look out the window. It's kinda like how you get to watch a dirigible land and take off through a window while waiting for your own flight to leave. Makes sense, in a psychological sort of way."

"You're assuming the aliens who built the station share any psychologically common reference points," Bjorn said, still looking out the window. Ted turned to debate him on the issue so Minu quickly stepped in.

"Lots of snake traffic through the station, so you figure there are goodies down there?"

"Yes," Ted answered, shooting a 'later' look at Bjorn. "Probably a prime find that they've been exploiting for years. We're so far off the beaten path that they're not even blocking the back door."

"Still, we better get out of here ASAP," Minu said more to herself. It wouldn't serve to have a squad of T'Chillen warriors slither through either portal to find a bunch of humans squatting around digging in the dust. Minu had searched the area thoroughly, hoping this would be one of her father's secret caches, but to no avail. It was, however, most certainly the key to reaching Enigma. The question was, which portal? This was where her dad's map ended, and where her instincts would now take over.

There were only three real options. One: go home. She immediately tossed that one out. Two: send scout teams through each portal to see where they went. And three: pick one and go in force. Options two and three each had their pluses and minuses. Two was riskier to the individual scout team, but safer to the expedition as a whole. Three was safer to the individual, but risked the entire team should she guess wrong. After several years of leadership, it still wasn't easy to make decisions where lives were at risk. Minu hoped it would never be easy.

Var'at came over with one of his scouts. "We've located the other two portals," he told her. Together they went with Ted and his control rod to verify what she already knew in her heart. Each portal was only open to one destination. But in a bit of luck, there was evidence to help her make a decision.

"This one hasn't been used in years," Var'at said of the portal dais before them. Dust lay on everything, and the room was piled high with debris. There were a few tracks in the dust, but no snake trails. Wherever this portal went, it wasn't somewhere the T'Chillen frequented.

The decision seemed obvious, and that worried her. "Is it this easy?" she wondered. To make it worse, the hallway was tight, and the fighters would be a difficult fit. They'd have to move them along at a crawl with someone calling out clearances all the way. This portal was obviously meant as a personnel mover, not cargo. They'd been on the station an hour, and every minute they waited increased the risk that a snake patrol would come through.

Everyone was looking at her as she thought. Even the much older Ted waited patiently for her decision. "Okay, this is our target," she told them. "Have Aaron start moving the first fighter ASAP."

* * *

Just as Minu thought, maneuvering the bulky fighters down the hallways was a nightmare. Each one had a person on either side relaying instructions to the pilot every meter of the trip. Even with the guides, the turn was tight enough in two places that the fighters were forced to literally scrape along the wall for several meters. The screech was bone-chilling and reverberated through the entire structure. Instantly the Rasa on guard duty were on alert.

The first fighter was lined up with the exit portal and the second one about half way there when things started to go bad. Minu checked the progress of the last fighter and decided it was time to call in the rear guard. "Var'at, bring them all in, we're going through as soon as we squeeze that beast around the corner and line it up."

Var'at nodded and spoke into his communicator. He cocked his head and spoke again. "There's no response."

"Oh shit," she said, turning from where she'd been watching the slow, plodding progress of the fighter to look back down the hallway. They were at a vulnerable point where the weapons of the fighters would be useless should they come under attack from behind right now…"Var'at, with me!" she yelled and trotted back down the hallway.

"What about us?" Ted asked from the rear cargo door of the fighter.

"Get a weapon and be ready," she tossed over her shoulder. Var'at gave a loud hissing snap as he followed her. Instantly, five of his soldiers fell in behind as a fire team.

If humans possessed any noticeable advantage over the Rasa besides sheer physical size, it was running speed. Despite Minu's diminutive height, she was almost a half meter taller than Var'at, and she quickly began to pull ahead of him as she raced down the hall toward their original portal. She was pretty sure what had happened. A team of some sort came through the original portal and Var'at's team was pinned down or keeping silent to avoid detection. Minu figured a quick distraction would get them clear, then they could all beat it back to the fighters and out of the station. The last thing she expected was to come around a corner next to the room with the huge window and be confronted with a pair of T'Chillen.

Their bodies were at least as big around as a well-built human, and between six to eight meters long from their beak-like mouths to the metallic tail-spike they used as a weapon in close combat. The two Minu encountered flared up, serpentine arms waving at their sides in a threat display. Both had been carrying Concordian standard packing crates. The one on the left dropped the crate and fumbled at its belt for a compact beamcaster. Minu snatched at one of her Enforcers. The snake was a hair faster, but Minu was more accurate.

The 18mm cartridge boomed, and the gun rocked with a familiar slam against her cybernetic hand. The T'Chillen's beamcaster bolt missed her by half a meter, still close enough to raise blisters on her shoulder. The new gun generated less recoil because Ted and Bjorn had redesigned the concept. Instead of packing the casing with power, they'd packed the projectile with propellant. Once clear of the barrel, a tiny computer inside the bullet activated a miniature rocket charge and deployed stabilizer fins. Programmed with data from the gun's sight in the instant Minu pulled the trigger, the bullet corrected for initial recoil and target movement as it accelerated to four times the speed of sound in less than ten meters. The round impacted with more than five thousand kilograms of kinetic force almost instantly. The round was frangible, and after the initial armor penetrating impact, it shattered, spreading the hydrostatic shock.

The T'Chillen's central body mass exploded with a wet resounding *bang*, spraying gore and bone fragments for meters in all directions. The second T'Chillen screeched in a most un-serpent-like fashion and spun back toward the portal. Minu was too surprised at the power of the improved hand cannon to react. A buzz saw grinding sound that set her hair on end came from behind Minu and the second snake fell as a line of discarding sabot projectiles nearly cut it in half. A glance over her shoulder saw Var'at lowering his weapon as he drew alongside her. "We don't have much time," he said as he passed and turned into the portal chamber. The two Rasa scouts had been keeping their heads down, just as they'd thought, and they quickly came out to join them. "It wasn't a combat team," Var'at told her, inspecting the two dead beings, "the one I killed is a scientist; the other you shot was a guard. They'll be missed, and quickly."

Minu snatched up the compact beamcaster and two extra power cells before turning and examining the hallway. "Get your men to set up two fallback positions," she told him, "if they come looking we need to buy time." Without shock rifles they were sorely undergunned against T'Chillen soldiers. Minu moved to help her friend prepare the defenses, all the time hoping they wouldn't be needed.

* * * * *

Chapter Four
January 11th, 523 AE

Space Station, Undesignated Star System, Galactic Frontier

Where the first fighter made the last turn with only a nasty loud scrape, the second one lodged tight as a doorstop. "It won't budge," Aaron told her over the radio.

"What the fuck? They're identical, why would one fit and the other not?"

"I don't have a clue," he admitted, "but the mystery is providing no end of amusement for Bjorn and frustrating the shit out of Ted."

"Well, tell them both to stop screwing around and get that fighter unstuck, or they can explain it to the snakes!" She cut the channel with a final curse and rubbed the bridge of her nose where a headache was threatening to spread backward and engulf her in a sea of pain. This was supposed to be a smash and grab mission. If they ended up in a pitched battle with T'Chillen...

From her vantage point in the doorway to the windowed portal room Minu saw the archway flash into life. They wouldn't make it in time. A pair of T'Chillen slithered through, both much larger than the first two they'd dispatched and wearing articulated body armor covering almost every millimeter of their scaled skin. Both wore a segmented helmet which was rotated back to allow their slitted eyes better visibility. They were investigating an overdue scientist in their own secret corner of the galaxy, not making a combat jump.

"Left," Minu whispered.

"Right," Var'at replied.

She raised her Enforcer, placed the laser designator on target, and pulled the trigger. The left-hand soldier's head exploded in a hail of red mist, while the other was engulfed in a flashing storm of hyper-velocity discarding sabot, several shredding the unprotected head.

Minu was about to rush in and relieve them of their unused beamcasters, but Var'at put a hand on her shoulder. He pointed and she could see the portal was still on, and on the other side was a distant world. A dozen more warriors were there, all of them looking through in surprise at their dead comrades. "Hurry it up!" she yelled at her friends through the radio. Already the squad of T'Chillen soldiers were lowering their helmets and rushing toward the portal. Their bodies were low to the ground and snapping from side to side, a snake rushing to the kill. "Hit them hard," she told Var'at, and the instant the first one came through the portal she opened fire.

Despite their heavy densified dualloy armor the first two fell under their fusillade. The combination of the massive Enforcer's punch and the grinding buzz saw of Var'at's accelerator rifle tore them to pieces before they could clear the portal and activate their fields. But after seeing what had happened to their comrades, the next four dove through together in one huge mass. The booming Enforcer stunned one of them and Var'at chewed him up on the spot. The other three slithered with shocking speed behind the portal dais and began to return fire.

"Beamcaster!" Var'at hissed and a second later the squad's heavy weapons specialist came sliding up, peeking around the corner for a quick look. His head exploded with a crack.

"Son of a bitch," Minu spat and wiped bloody gore from her face. She slapped a fresh magazine of seven shots into the Enforcer in her right hand and added the second one in her left while Var'at dispassionately relieved the dead trooper of his weapon.

"Is this fun yet?" he asked as he safed his accelerator and swung it over his shoulder. The ammo feed track that led from his belt was an additional encumbrance, but it didn't seem to bother him any.

"Getting there," she said. She leaned just far enough forward to put both hands around the door frame and unleashed the two Enforcers, pounding round after booming round in the direction of the portal. Var'at used the distraction to peek around the corner. Finding a target to his liking, he fired several quick snapping shots before Minu's guns ran empty, then quickly pulled back. A fusillade of energy beams clawed at them, all far closer than either of them would have liked. "Fucking snakes are good shots!"

"Yes, they're no Tanam. Where the cats are crazed fighters, the snakes are well-trained, disciplined, and patient." More weapons fire tore at the doorway, the intense energy beams threatening to chew through the wall.

"Really? News to me!" Minu swapped out magazines while he radioed his men. Another flurry of fire from the snakes started, this one more subdued than the last, and Minu was immediately on guard. She sat the two Enforcers on the floor in easy reach and snatched the compact beamcaster she'd taken from the fallen guard just as a lone T'Chillen raced through the door, low and fast, under cover of fire from its comrades.

Minu cycled the small beamcaster over and over, the soldier's shields flashing red, blue, and then white. Var'at turned his own energy weapon on it, and the shields overloaded with a *pop*. A single shot from Minu's gun killed it, easily tearing through the torso armor and vaporizing internal organs. At the same time the hallway reverberated with a monstrous blast back toward the fighters. Minu only gave it a second's thought; it was all she had to spare.

She snapped a quick look through the doorway and cursed. "Run," she said and raced back down the hallway. Var'at was up and behind her in an instant, his pace further slowed by the additional weapon he now carried. Two T'Chillen burst through the doorway they'd just abandoned, closely followed by two more Minu had seen coming through the portal; still more reinforcements were staging, and their situation was quickly becoming untenable.

Shots bracketed Var'at on both sides, and he tried zigzagging as best as he could. Minu slowed her pace a step and slapped the shield control on her belt. Var'at moved a step closer as they ran, close enough to be inside the perimeter of her shield as a beamcaster shot hit square in the center of his back. She heard him hiss in pain as some of the thermal energy penetrated through the shield and the dualloy combat armor they wore. She felt the Faraday grid in her uniform buzz from the stray EM splash. Luckily, they cleared the next corner before any more shots scored a hit. Her shield unit was smaller than the one carried by the T'Chillen, making it much more portable, but it could only survive two hits, where theirs could handle three or four.

"Have the next group fall back right away!" Minu screamed at Var'at as they ran. As they rounded the second corner, the remaining Rasa soldier was already retreating; his partner lay dead back by the portal. The three of them rounded the final corner and fell in behind the three Rasa soldiers already there. Var'at quickly handed off the beamcaster and got his accelerator rifle ready again. Minu nodded toward the squad-sized shield the soldiers had and Var'at reached over to turn it on. Six T'Chillen soldiers slithered around the corner, their speed making Minu gasp. Who would believe a snake could move almost as fast as a running human? "Fire!"

All five Rasa and Minu opened up together, Minu with the captured T'Chillen compact beamcaster and the Rasa with all their most powerful weapons, four accelerator rifles and one beamcaster. The T'Chillen were staggered by the sheer volume of fire; Minu and the Rasa beamcaster gunner concentrated on one soldier who went down under their combined fire. Momentarily taken off guard, the surviving five retreated back under cover.

It won't last, she thought as she looked over her shoulder. The fighter was gone, and she gasped in relief. There was a huge gash in the wall, the result of the massive blast she'd heard a minute ago, and she wondered what cost it came with. What made her do a double take was Bjorn squatting in the middle of the hallway over something and fiddling with a tool kit. "Bjorn, get back!" she yelled. He looked up and, upon spotting her, he smiled and waved casually before going back to his task. "Damn it, Aaron, are we clear? And what the fuck is Bjorn doing messing with a science experiment in the middle of my combat zone?"

"Here they come," Var'at warned. Minu leaned out and let go with the last shots in the compact beamcaster.

"We're right at the edge," Aaron told her, "we had to send the second fighter through first. We're here, door open, just waiting on you!"

"Roger, we'll be there any second, coming in hot as hell!" While she spoke she dropped the beamcaster into a pocket, doing her best to ignore the burn its red-hot emitter gave her thigh, and drew both Enforcers, one in each hand. She opened up, firing one gun then the other, over and over again. Normally kinetic weapons had little effect on the more resistant force fields the T'Chillen used, but the ballistic energy of the Enforcers imparted enough force to stagger the soldiers. If they'd had legs, the one she slapped repeatedly would probably have been driven to the ground. Instead it just brought the snake to a jerking stop, its field glowing red from absorbing the attacks. The furious rate of fire of the Rasa accelerator rifles literally covered them in bright flashes of light, confusing and slowing them down.

"Time to go," Minu said and walked backward, quickly swapping out mags to her final reloads. There were cases of extra ammo in the fighter, if she could get there. The Rasa soldiers skittered past her, all except Var'at, who fell in next to her, shoulder to shoulder.

"We keep finding ourselves in these situations," he said, his jaw hanging open in their typical laugh.

"Lucky us," Minu said. The first T'Chillen head poked around the corner and she double-tapped, the impact shattering armor and sending blood flying. Must have knocked out at least one of their fields, she surmised. The injured soldier tried to back around the corner and Var'at unloaded a hundred rounds into it, tearing the head to pieces and scattering blood, bones and brains all over the walls. They reached the midpoint where Bjorn knelt, working and talking to himself. "Whatever you are doing needs to be done," she said just as a beamcaster bolt flashed past them, her shield glowing slightly from the near miss.

"Oh, sure, just fine tuning the field—"

"Screw it!" she almost screamed, fear coming through in her voice and penetrating through to his nanotech brain.

"Oh, sure," he said and started trotting toward the final doorway. Minu and Var'at paced him, both silently willing him to hurry. Whether it was respect of their weapons, or just plain luck, they made the corner with only sporadic uncoordinated fire coming at them. As soon as they were clear the T'Chillen came fast and hard.

"In the fighter," Minu yelled, but Bjorn was carefully peeking around the corner as the alien soldiers surged toward them. She tried to pull him away but he slapped her hand back.

"Watch, watch!" he cackled. Minu swallowed and peeked around the corner.

The first T'Chillen was just reaching the machine he'd been working on. She saw the soldier regard it as it slithered in its side-to-side race. Its HUD apparently declared it harmless. Just before it reached the box, Minu heard a queer sound, a gravitic impeller spinning up. "What did you—" she didn't have to finish the question; the answer was obvious. Sitting in the middle of the floor was one of their spare impellers, and it was screaming to full power.

The first T'Chillen was grabbed by invisible forces and slammed to the floor with a sickening crunch. As Minu watched she saw the second one in line grabbed by the same widening field. It struggled mightily to pull away but the field wouldn't relent, pulling down and crushing that one against the floor too. The others stopped dead in their tracks and slithered back, unsure what to do. When the growing field grabbed yet another soldier, one of the others made a decision and fired at the impeller. "That's not wise," Bjorn said.

The powerful gravity field being generated did strange things to a contained particle accelerator packet such as the beamcasters fired. The beam splayed, only a portion hitting its target. The impeller jumped, the pitch of the whine changed, and suddenly hull plates gave an ominous groan as the hallway was pulled and bent. "Oh shit," Minu said as they all heard the telltale whoosh of escaping atmosphere. "Run for it!"

The T'Chillen cast a few desultory shots at their adversaries before slithering away for their lives. Minu physically dragged Bjorn toward the door of the waiting fighter as the wind turned from a hiss to a roar, and then a scream as his toy tore the station apart. Worse, the venting was becoming so bad Minu found herself having to lean into the wind as it whipped past her. Her uniform flapped against her skin, and her hair whipped back so violently she began to fear it would be torn out by the roots. It took every bit of her will to put one foot in front of the other. Her cybernetic arm had Bjorn's uniform in such a grip that it would tear to shreds before she lost him. The improved muscles in her legs strained and protested against the power of the wind.

Then it got much worse. The wind began to abate, but as she tried to take a breath, it wasn't there. It was almost like sucking on an empty drink bottle, only a trickle of air, and then nothing. Her vision burned and blurred, forcing her to close her eyes for the last steps. Then several pairs of hands grabbed her, fingers and claws, and she was hauled into the transport.

She was afraid to open her eyes as the transport lurched forward and to the new destination. The instant they passed through the portal, atmosphere rushed back into the craft with a booming crash, tossing everyone around the cabin like rag dolls.

Minu released Bjorn and fell back, sucking great mouthfuls of crisp, cold air. All around her others were doing the same thing and she heard Aaron cursing over and over. She slowly forced her eyes open, feeling ice crystals tugging at her eyelashes. It took a second to focus, but there appeared to be no damage.

"Bjorn, you fucking lunatic!" she cried out and rolled to her feet. He was sitting on the floor, laughing like a maniac and slapping his leg.

"I've always wanted to see if that worked!"

"You've never tried that before? For goodness sake, why now? We could have all died if that thing hadn't worked."

He looked confused and a little hurt. "Well, there was a small risk it could create a micro singularity…" He got that distant look and took out a tablet to make some notes.

Minu swallowed and blanched. "A black hole?"

"Only a small one," he said absently as he tapped away. "So of course you understand the risk of trying that on even an uninhabited world; considering our precarious situation, it seemed the right thing to do. You aren't upset, are you?" She was taken aback by his genuine look of concern.

"God, Bjorn." She coughed, wiping a spot of blood on her uniform sleeve. The exchange forgotten, he'd walked outside into a very dark, rainy night on whatever world it was to observe the still-working portal. The station still seemed to be there, the room lit by one of their torches floating by. Though intact, the artificial gravity was obviously out.

"Well, no singularity then," he said, sounding almost forlorn, and made more notes.

The initial shock receding, Minu stepped out into the rain. Though bitterly cold, it felt good as she looked around. There was no visible vegetation, the ground covered with polished pea gravel as far as they could see under the fighter's floodlights. She looked back up at the portal in time to see a T'Chillen body float by, grossly distended from being exposed to vacuum and then crushed by Bjorn's improvised weapon. "Bjorn," she said to get his attention. The other fighter was a few meters away, the rear door opening and the occupants running over to check on them. "Bjorn!"

"Uh, what? Oh, yes Minu."

"Can that little reaction of yours be controlled?"

"Well, sure, but it was much more interesting to see the runaway effect, don't you think?" Minu didn't think it was interesting, except the fact that it had completely bypassed the T'Chillen's defenses. A mental image appeared of tiny micro-gravitic impellers of this kind used in all sorts of applications set as a sort of landmine, or even tossed as grenades. Now she had her tablet out and was making notes. And that was how Cherise found them, both standing in front of the portal, T'Chillen corpses floating around and blood pouring from Minu's nose as she typed on her tablet.

"Oh my god, are you okay?"

"Huh, what?" they both asked. Ted was right behind her, his face ashen and hands shaking in shock.

"Shut that down, will you Ted?" she asked as another corpse bumped into the first one. "We don't know if the snakes have any space suits handy, and I don't want to find out." He took out his control rod and shut it off with a casual flick of the wrist. "Thanks." Her notes finished, she turned around to check on her people. The most seriously injured was one of the Rasa who was being tended to. Cherise came over and put a medical dressing against Minu's face.

"What?" she asked, and Cherise pulled it back to show how it was drenched in bright red blood. "Oh," she said and accepted the dressing.

"You could have died," her friend said, worry laser-etched on her face.

"We all could have died," she agreed, "but more importantly, we're into the exclusion area around Enigma." A smile split her face as she looked at them, then at Var'at who was more restrained. She turned serious again. "I'm sorry about your soldier."

"It's okay," he said. The reptilian seemed none the worse for wear, and she marveled at their physical resilience. "He died quickly, doing his job."

Minu nodded and put a hand on his shoulder. "So now that we're here, Ted, let me borrow your rod and we'll get to Enigma as fast as possible."

*****

Chapter Five
January 11th, 523 AE

Undesignated Star System, Galactic Frontier

The fighter that had gotten stuck was in bad shape. Faced with having to abandon it as the T'Chillen attacked, Aaron whipped together an explosive charge and blasted it clear. As soon as they'd made the first jump past the cold dark raining world to one in midday of a dense deciduous forest, Bjorn and Ted set out to ascertain the extent of the damage. Aaron assisted them while Cherise used a medkit on Minu. Somehow Bjorn hadn't gotten a scratch.

"You've got some micro-capillary damage to your eyes," Cherise told her as she manipulated the medical scanner. "Of course, I can't give you a nano-treatment."

"I know, damn thing can't calibrate to us. But that's one of the reasons we're here."

"It's worthwhile for a lot of reasons," the other girl agreed, "but not worth you getting yourself killed."

"It comes with the job, Cherise." Minu took her face in hand and lifted it to look in her eye. Cherise tried to avoid her gaze for a minute then finally met her eye to eye. Tears were there, barely unshed. "You going to tell me what's wrong?"

Cherise cautiously looked around, verifying no one was closer than a few meters, then spoke rapidly in a low voice. "What do you want me to say, that I don't care? That it wouldn't bother me if you got yourself blown to bits by some fucking alien? Or would you rather that I just admit that I love you?"

"You're like a sister to me, too, Cherise!"

The other woman shook her head, the tears starting to flow. "No, you don't understand. I *love* you, Minu Alma."

Minu looked at her for a second as meaning chased comprehension. Eventually the two met in a head-on crash in her brain. "You mean like how we've…'been together,' that's what you mean?" The tears were pouring now; Cherise nodded and let out a little choking squeak. "Oh, baby," Minu said and took her in her arms. Cherise grabbed her so hard Minu was afraid her ribs would crack.

"I know, I know, I can't help it! One thing led to another, and I didn't want it to, but then when I saw you out there, the air sucking out of that, you barely hanging on and seconds from being blown out into space, and I realized there was no more doubting how I feel. I love you and have for some time."

"Cherise, I don—"

"No, please, don't say anything. I understand, really." Cherise pulled back, sniffing and quickly wiping her face with the sleeve of her jet black jumpsuit. Minu noticed for the first time how it complemented her cocoa skin. "I didn't want to say anything, because I didn't want to put you under any pressure."

"I love you, too, Cherise, I just don't know if it's the same." They looked deeply into each other's eyes for a long moment, Cherise searching for something in there, something with no name, something with infinite meaning. "I'll have to think about what you've said, okay? Is that good enough for now?"

"It'll have to be." The two girls embraced again. Across the temporary camp, Aaron, Ted and Bjorn did their best to find something else to look at. Only Var'at watched the two humans with interest, if not comprehension.

* * *

"It's fucked."

"Great technical description, Ted; how about some more details?" Minu took the bandage away from her nose and, seeing no fresh blood, handed it to Cherise to dispose of.

Ted looked at Minu and scowled, casting a look at the second fighter. "Well, the magnetic control systems we constructed are used to hold the fighter together and allow it to change shape. We basically cut the thing into a thousand pieces, added magnetic fields, shields, etc., and that results in—"

"Ted, I don't want to build one, I just want to know why it's fucked!"

"Your boy there blew the crap out of one of the two main structural computers."

"Hey," Aaron said and pointed a menacing finger at the much smaller scientist, "I did what I had to do!"

"Congratulations, you damn bloody Neanderthal."

Aaron took a step toward him, and Minu intervened. "Stop it, you two. Okay, so the computer is trashed; what does that mean for function? Can't we just not transform it?"

"If it were only that simple. Without the computer, the hull can't properly respond to stresses. Because it isn't a solid construct, more like a child's toy made of blocks, the computer makes adjustments to the containment fields every time you turn quick, or land hard, etc.

The other computers will keep it in one piece, but the first time you push it too far, the whole damned thing will just fall apart."

"Rather dramatically, too, I suspect!"

"Thank you Bjorn," Ted grumbled, and Bjorn nodded before going back to his computer. Somehow the gray-haired scientist had produced tea in a china tea set and was enjoying some Peninsula green tea as the discussion went on.

"So as long as we baby it…"

"Should be fine," Ted finished. "One hard push, too fast a turn, a hard bump…"

"Boom!" Bjorn illuminated for them, gesturing with both arms and spraying tea around. Several Rasa hissed in indignation and dodged the heavily-sugared concoction. Bjorn laughed at his wit and tried to take a sip of his tea, looking down at the empty cup in confusion.

"Right," Minu said and looked at the fighter in question. To make it worse, the damned thing looked fine except for some missing paint. She couldn't fault Aaron for his decision, even as he looked at her with a guilty expression. Despite his bluster with Ted, it was apparent he blamed himself. They were in a bind, and he'd improvised. She probably would have done the same thing. He'd joked a few minutes earlier when explaining to her exactly what he'd done, that he'd wished for a light saber at the time. Minu agreed, and said she'd put Bjorn to inventing a UCT (universal cutting tool) as soon as possible.

"So we use it for transport only, and protect it with the other fighter as much as possible. If we have to, we strip it and blow it."

"Gonna be a damned tight fit in the one fighter," Aaron mumbled.

"Standing room only," she agreed. "I'd like to make one more jump before camping," she told them, "we're only three away from the coordinates for Enigma. If we rest after the next jump we'll be fresh when—" She was cut off as the portal flashed once. "Ted?"

He already had his control rod out, icons flowing across its pearly white surface. "Someone is tracing it from another portal."

"T'Chillen," Var'at hissed.

"Oh, I bet they're pissed," Aaron added.

"They must have had space suits handy after all," Minu thought aloud. "Okay, so much for rest. Saddle up, everyone. Ted, set the destination before they find us and lock up the portal! Can you wipe the destination after we go through?"

"Only if I stay behind. I can use a different route and catch up."

"No, you aren't qualified to go by yourself, and I don't have time to set up a team." The last of the Rasa piled aboard the second fighter, its door closing as the impellers spun up and the craft rose off the moss-covered forest floor. Minu trotted up the ramp into the first fighter and gestured for Ted to join her. "I appreciate the gesture Ted, but not now. Get in here, and that's an order." Ted gave her a nasty look—a girl less than a quarter his age giving him an order—but the truth was she wore three golden stars on her sleeve to five silver on his own. "We'll get ahead of them and then you can have a team of Rasa for escort to lead the snakes on a merry chase; for now, get in this goddamned ship."

It was a good plan, but they never actually got ahead of the snakes. The two fighters slid through the portal into an ancient, crumbling Portal Spire. Instruments beeped warnings that the atmosphere was toxic. Minu wasn't concerned; the fighters were air tight, and they would only be there for moments. Ted was already programming for the next jump on a nearby portal, since the first portal was locked onto the last destination, when the first portal came to life again. There on the other side were dozens of T'Chillen in full combat armor.

"Shields!" Minu yelled and both fighters blurred momentarily as their energy shields came up. Beamcaster fire flashed through the portal and the first soldiers rushed at them. "Aaron, discourage them!"

"Right!" he said and spun the fighter around. Var'at, piloting the other craft, carefully maneuvered around to use the first fighter as cover. Aaron lined up facing the portal just as the first soldiers came though. He squeezed the controls and brought the defenses online. The four underslung shock rifles roared to life, firing in rapid rolling sequence, and they flashed through the soldiers' defensive shields and mowed them down. Bodies exploded in red bloody bombs of gore as a dozen T'Chillen died in five seconds. The survivors on the other side all dove for cover out of view of the portal.

"How's that new portal coming, Ted?"

"Ready!"

"Var'at, get through!" They watched on a rearward-facing camera as the other fighter carefully maneuvered through. Minu bit down on her frustration as the formerly nimble craft flew like a critically-injured kloth, taking almost a minute to do what should have taken seconds. Come on, come on, she willed as Aaron let loose with another salvo at a pair of soldiers that dared to poke their heads around.

"They're gonna come through fast next time," Aaron warned her. "All we're doing here is really pissing them off!"

"Var'at is clear," she told him.

"When I turn around they're going to download on us!"

"So don't turn around!"

"Huh?"

"Back through the portal, silly!"

Aaron gave her an incredulous look, then, despite the gravity of the situation, he laughed as he used the rear camera to back toward the other portal. The T'Chillen were furious, and they tried to gain a foothold again and again. Each time they paid in blood and were rewarded with failure. Aaron had the measure of the fighter's weapons system, and there was no getting by him. He kept up his fire even after they passed through the second portal and onto a world so brightly lit that the view ports polarized to dim the cabin. Portals were one way to travelers and solid matter (depending on which direction they were activated from), but opaque to energy and light.

"Ted, close the portal and set our next destination right away!"

"On it," he said as the portal swirled into inactivity and instantly came back to life. But an instant later it went dark again.

"Ted?"

"I'm working on it..." Once more the portal came on, and just as quickly turned off. "Damnable machine," he growled and quickly brought up his control rod's diagnostics. Holographic symbols floated in the air which he moved around with quick pushing and pulling motions, occasionally twisting one symbol or another. Minu watched the portal nervously while Aaron carefully lined up the fighter and readied its weapons should the T'Chillen suddenly appear. "Okay," Ted said finally, "if I understand this blasted thing well enough, it's having difficulty and is in a safe mode while it assesses its functions."

"Never heard of that one before," Minu said.

"Nor have I," Ted admitted, "and I probably know as much about these portals as anyone alive."

Minu looked from him to the portal outside and scratched her chin nervously. I wonder if he knows that some weird aliens live inside the thing? Many older Chosen 'meditated' to the energy swirls, but to her knowledge she was the only one ever to have a conversation with the Weavers, not to mention having had one intervene and save her life. But that had been years ago, and they wouldn't talk to her now. The last time she'd tried they only had one thing to say.

"We wish to talk to Pip." Minu turned and looked at the pod secured in the rear of her fighter and sighed. Too many mysteries, too many unanswered questions. Already one of Var'at's soldiers had lost his life for this quest, and she didn't even know if there was anything to be gained.

"Can you tell how long it will be in safe mode?"

Ted looked at the control rod for a moment, flipping a few icons before speaking. "I haven't a clue, sorry."

"Well at least the T'Chillen can't come through either," Aaron said as he shut down the offensive systems.

"We have another problem," Var'at said over the radio link, having been in on the entire exchange. "This world has a breathable atmosphere, but the temperature is forty-five degrees, and climbing. It is still early in the day, so we're going to be getting very hot, very soon."

* * * * *

Chapter Six
January 12th, 523 AE

Planet 'Sunshine,' Galactic Frontier

They made camp not because they wanted to, but because there was no choice. Even though it was blisteringly hot outside, it proved cooler to set up solar shields between the two fighters than to force the crafts' cooling systems to operate on the ragged edge. They also had limited power in the fighters. Thanks to the solar shields converting the blazing light of two suns to energy, they could hold their own outside. The parked fighters quickly became cigar-shaped ovens, too hot even for the Rasa. Everyone found a spot outside under the solar shields and relaxed. The ground was rocky and uncomfortable, and the hours seemed to crawl past.

"As if the two suns weren't bad enough," Minu said as she used an instrument to check the sky once more, "their rotation is slow as well."

"How long until nightfall?" Bjorn asked, wiping a rag across his wet and wrinkled brow.

"The blue-white sun will set in six hours, the yellow in ten. At least it should cool down some when the nasty hot one sets."

It was a good plan, except the system wasn't a binary after all. Two hours later as they were trying to eat in the dripping heat, Aaron stood and looked to the horizon, a hand held up to shield his eyes.

"You're not going to believe this," he said and pointed. Humans and Rasa gathered to watch as the third sun of the trinary system began a slow climb into the sky.

"I guess I get to work on my tan," Cherise said in a deadpan.

"Looks like a red giant," Ted said, Bjorn nodding in agreement. The sun was at least twice the size of the others, and blood red in color. "Not too hot, at least."

"Hot enough," Minu mumbled. Already she felt its additional heat. "How much can we survive?" she asked Aaron, the only scout of the group and the best versed in difficult survival situations.

"Well, if we break out the other solar shields to make this more of an enclosure and use the power from the fighters to supplement the cool air blowers…we should be okay to about sixty-five. Maybe seventy, but that's pushing the material of the solar shields. Much more and the moliplas structure will start destabilizing. It's not really made for that sort of extreme.

Minu looked down at the little instrument she carried. Fifty-eight degrees, now fifty-nine. "Break out the other shields; let's get to work, fast."

The temperature climbed at nearly two degrees an hour for the next five hours. As the needle hovered at sixty-eight Minu felt the ragged edges of panic tickling her consciousness. Their solar shields were set, blocking all direct sunlight from reaching them, and all four of the cold air blowers worked at maximum. Just one of the devices would have been able to take a ten-thousand-cubic-meter space from fifty degrees to freezing in hours. The space between the fighters hovered just below fifty. Minu had been hot before, but this was horrible. It made Naomi in the Desert Tribe feel like a cool afternoon at Steven's Pass. They lay around on moliplas cots and chairs trying to breathe and hoping for relief. The fighters were uninhabitable ovens.

"What do we do if we can't get out of here?" she asked Ted who was sitting in a chair next to her. Both Bjorn and Ted enjoyed prime seats next to blowers. She hadn't allowed any discussion on the matter; both were older than the rest and more susceptible to the horrendous heat. Despite that, the space around them wasn't more than five degrees cooler.

"Well," he said and wiped sweat from his dripping forehead, "we'll have to dig a shelter. Aaron says there's some basic engineering equipment stowed on the fighters. The problem is how cold it will get tonight."

"Right, so we might have to work quickly." Ted nodded and relaxed, trying to conserve energy. He kept the portal control rod sitting on the arm of his chair, set to alert him the moment the portal came on line. The big problem now was that even should it activate, the fighters were so hot she doubted they could survive long enough to pilot them through to the other side.

Minu looked over to check her Rasa team members. They seemed to be tolerating the temperature better, but Var'at assured her it was beyond their 'normal' range as well. They all had water bulbs from which they took intermittent sips while constantly panting, rather like a dog. Minu knew enough of their biology to be sure that they'd suffer horribly if they ran out of water. Luckily, there was plenty, even if it was nearly the temperature she preferred her tea to be. Cherise dozed on a cot. Growing up in the desert had taught her to rest in the heat of the day. Aaron tolerated the heat in quiet misery, leaning against a rock close enough to an air blower to be somewhat comfortable.

With nothing more to do, she settled into a chair and read through some of her father's logs. It was too hot to sleep.

Three hours later, with the blue-white monster well below the horizon, the temperature had dropped below what it had been when they arrived and was slowly decreasing further as the yellow sun began to be consumed by the edge of the world. "I never thought forty would feel nice," Minu said as she stuck her head outside the solar shields, if only briefly. Many of them now sported first-degree burns. Aaron had a nasty second-degree burn patch where he'd slipped during the height of the suns and brushed against one of the dualloy poles holding up the solar shields. The Rasa, ever practical, cooked some meat for their meal on a rock just outside the shields, using a dualloy rod poking through the side to turn it and retrieve the finished meal.

"Quite comfortable," Var'at agreed, not noticing the way Minu rolled her eyes.

"Who the hell would put a portal in this barbecue, anyway?" Aaron wondered aloud as he rubbed burn gel on his shoulder.

"Wasn't always this way," Ted said. Now that the temperature was dropping, Bjorn and he were working with the formidable amount of instruments they'd brought along for the ride. "Looks like it's been majorly screwed at some point."

"Probably a few million years ago," Bjorn confirmed. "There's still a lot of oxygen and bacteria in the air. The planet's not dead, but close to it."

"I'd say it was screwed from day one," Minu said, making a dismissive gesture to where the yellow sun was still setting.

"Oh, that would make it hot, to be sure." He'd cracked open a rock they'd dug up from a small pit and was working an analyzer over it. "But someone made it a lot worse."

"How so?"

"That red giant is new."

"Without a doubt," Bjorn agreed as he reviewed the data.

"Hold on," Aaron barged in, "I'm not a scientist like you egg heads, but I do know that new stars are never red giants. That's an old, dying star."

"Correct!" Bjorn crowed. "Give the man a cookie."

"I'd settle for an iced tea," he said, making Minu chuckle. "So if you agree with me…"

"I'm not agreeing, just saying you're right. This star was begun as a red giant. And billions of years after the other two."

Minu waited for details but Bjorn's attention was drawn to some of the readings on the instruments and he completely forgot the conversation, so Ted took it up. "This red giant was probably a gas giant, something like Jupiter in our old home of Sol, though probably more like Saturn."

"Why Saturn?" Minu asked.

"Well, they're both failed stars—so is Neptune, for that matter—but Saturn is smaller than Jupiter and has less hydrogen. Most stars are just massive balls of hydrogen. They get bigger and bigger, until they light off. We're still not sure how that happens. Jupiter could technically have lit off, though it probably wouldn't have lived that long."

"Would have probably fizzled," Bjorn agreed, surprising them that he was paying attention.

Ted gave him an annoyed look and continued. "So this medium-sized gas giant, full of helium, argon, and other much-less-suitable fusion food, gets compressed and lit off. The shortage of hydrogen pushes it quickly into an aged sequence, in this case a red giant. Probably burned up a couple planets in the process."

"So let me get this right," Minu said. "Someone, no doubt the Concordia, turned a gas giant purposely into a new star? This planet was already hotter than hell, right?"

"Yep."

"So why would they do it?"

"Murder," Cherise said from behind her.

Bjorn nodded enthusiastically. "And a very selective, careful one too. It guaranteed that very little would survive on the planet, but it would still hold an atmosphere, and save any structures that might be there. I wouldn't be surprised if they lit that thing at just the right time so it was on the far side of the solar system, and thereby protected this planet from all the nasty solar shock waves and other birth debris. They did murder this planet, and did it in a most slow, nasty sort of way."

"Probably took years for everyone here to die," Ted agreed. He had the control rod in his hand again and gestured with it toward the portal. "Of course we're here a million years later; we won't last nearly that long."

"What do you mean?" Minu asked, her pulse starting to race. Suddenly the sweat rolling down her back felt ice cold.

"The portal isn't in a diagnostic, it's locked. One way travel, here only. Not only did they turn the planet lethal, but they trapped everyone here so they'd all die. And we walked into a million-year-old trap."

* * *

As the red giant crawled across the sky, and the temperature dropped below thirty, they explored a bit and confirmed that there would be no worry of a T'Chillen assault through the portal. A few horribly desiccated snake corpses were found only a few meters from the portal. They'd come through on foot (or belly) and likely died within hours. The T'Chillen knew of the trap, and had obliged the stupid humans and allowed them to retreat through the portal to their doom.

Once the fighters cooled off enough to enter, Minu took Cherise and a squad of Rasa up to look around. Even with the power from the solar shields, one afternoon of use on the coolers had consumed ten percent of the fighter's power stores. They had food and water for weeks, but without shelter they'd be dead in less than ten days.

Minu flew a hundred-kilometer search pattern at five thousand meters up. The sensors at that range could give good readings more than a hundred kilometers out. Two hours later, with half the giant red disk dropping below the horizon, they landed the fighter. Minu climbed out, happy to see the others had made progress excavating a pit in the rocky ground. "Not a damned thing," she told them as she walked up. The temperature was below twenty now and the humans already wore their light uniform jackets. "No energy signatures, no signs of structures, nothing."

"Not surprising," Ted said as he analyzed some of the rocks coming up out of the pit, "with the swings of temperatures being so severe, even dualloy and ceramic concrete would be stressed in only a few thousand years."

Bjorn stuck his head out of the pit, covered in dirt and bleeding from several cuts. "I had no idea digging a hole was this much fun!"

Minu smiled obligingly and rolled her eyes when he went back to digging. If he wasn't so damned brilliant, she'd be certain he was completely in the throes of senile dementia. "Did you find anything down there and are we going to be able to make a semi-permanent shelter?"

"Yes, and probably not," Ted answered, as directly as always. "We know that whatever happened here was more like salting the fields than burning down the village."

"So they lit that star just to be sure nothing would ever be able to live here again? How'd you figure that out?"

Ted held up a rock and gestured to an instrument. "We got hard decayed radioactives below the old water table. Half-life is expired, of course, but we still have traces." He accessed a file. "This stuff is an almost perfect match with what you brought from GCX01999 several years ago."

"Squeenhome?" Minu said, more to herself than anyone. They'd started calling that devastated world by the new name after she'd found out from Strong Arm that it was the world of their birth.

"We might not have more than anecdotal evidence, but it sure looks like these worlds were trashed by orbital bombardment."

"The Concordia don't use space ships," Aaron said, right from the textbooks.

"They did once," Ted reminded them.

"Maybe this is why they stopped?" Var'at gestured at the vast, featureless desert all around them. "How many millions, billions of beings did they slaughter on world after world? You humans have only been exploring for a short time, and already found two. We know of many more. There could be thousands." No one had anything else to say.

* * * * *

Chapter Seven
January 13th, 523 AE

Planet 'Sunshine,' Galactic Frontier

Minu kept them working on the shelter, mostly widening and working to build a roof. They couldn't go any deeper. It was a compromise between the heat and cold above and the lurking hard radiation below. Minu shook her head as she helped empty buckets of dirt. "So I either cook from the heat or grow an extra arm."

The suns were all set, and the temperature was below 15 now. You could see your breath, but mostly just because there was no real humidity in the air. "Let me give you a rest," Aaron said and dropped easily into the hole, relieving her of the bucket. She climbed out, slipped on her jacket against the gathering cold, and dropped exhaustedly into a camp chair. Above them, the stars twinkled in a desultory manner, still partly obscured by the system's three blazing stars now behind the planet.

Ted was snoring quietly in a camp cot a few meters away, the control rod still gripped in his hands. He hadn't stopped trying to get around the programming that had them trapped. He and Bjorn sounded optimistic they might eventually find a solution. Bjorn said he wouldn't give up, no matter how many years it took.

She got up after a few minutes and stretched painfully; her muscles were trying to cramp after the hours of digging. Walking around the small camp, she ended up in front of the portal dais and stood there staring at it. She completely believed Ted's statement that it was locked. Such a tactic was completely within the mindset of many Concordian species. But she just couldn't believe there was no way around it. With a backward glance toward the fighters and her friends, gathered around their makeshift shelter excavation, she climbed the steps.

Instantly the portal came alive, the archway popping up with all its swirling patterns of high-energy plasma. As the portal came alive, Ted woke up and looked down at his control rod. Seeing nothing had changed, he went back to sleep. Minu shrugged and sat down cross-legged in front of the archway. The force fields that made up the portal always felt cool and slightly slippery to the touch. "Why am I wasting my time?" she asked herself. *Because there's nothing else to do,* was the silent reply. If there was even a slight possibility that there was a way out, she was going to try it. Tomorrow night, with the shelter finished, they'd take the fully-functional fighter up and begin extended search patterns, looking for any surviving structures. But now, this seemed like the right thing to do.

Relaxing her breathing and staring at the swirling patterns, she slowly began to unwind. The burning in her shoulders from all the digging began to abate, and that alone made the attempt worthwhile. She was just beginning to wonder if it was going to work when she fell forward and into the plasma.

No matter how many times she did it, which really wasn't that many yet, it was a jarring, disconcerting, and slightly alarming phenomenon. The brain tried to make sense out of the strange transposition and ended up reporting that they'd fallen into the portal. Minu ignored the little jerk of panic and breathed deeply. *I'm breathing plasma? Ugh, stop it and calm down, Minu.*

"We want the one you know as Pip." As before, the voice just appeared in her head as if it were her own thought. She looked around, and sure enough, there was one of the mysterious beings that called themselves Weavers. A ghostly, crab-like thing with spidery arms riding the currents of plasma a few meters away. Every time she saw a Weaver, she did her best to try and detect any differences, to see if they were distinct individuals. *If they exist at all.*

"We are," it answered, as if she'd asked a question. As she watched, it waved one of its four inner claw-like limbs. The motion left floaters in her eyes and made her feel disturbed deep down in the pit of her being. She'd tried focusing on one of those limbs long ago. The tip seemed to go on and on, forever. It regarded her calmly with its four black-on-black eyes.

"You are, I know. Pip is here."

"We know, bring him up so we can convene."

"Convene? What do you want to convene?"

"We need to negotiate. Pip will/is/was be your representative."

"He can't represent anything; he's got brain damage and is in a coma."

"All things come, of their own choosing."

Minu tried to make sense of the disjointed statements. The Weavers had shown from her past encounters that they possessed no sense of the present, past, or future. It was almost as if they lived in all times. She'd desperately wanted to discuss the bizarre beings with Pip, but he'd been injured, and it had never happened. She hadn't discussed them with anyone else for fear of being thought unhinged.

It's not a good sign when a Chosen starts having conversations with ethereal crab/spiders that lived in plasma.

"If you want to speak to Pip you need to help me."

"We will/have/are speaking to him."

"I know, but to me that hasn't happened yet." No answer, it just floated there. She tried another tack. "You helped me before."

"We have/will/do help you, Minu Alma. Our last helping disturbed many things; we believe it may not have been in our best interests."

"How many of you are there?"

"We are."

"Right," she sighed. "Anyway, you need to help again. This portal that I communicate through, it's locked, and we're trapped on this world. We may die here, and Pip too, if we can't unlock this portal and continue onward. Our mission is to help Pip so he can meet with you."

"It is so."

"Okay, so help."

"You have/will/did lock the portal."

"No, we didn't do it, someone a long time ago did."

"You."

Fucking retards, she thought, and instantly regretted it, knowing the Weaver would hear her thoughts. But they didn't seem to take any offense, so she continued. "Alright, whatever, I locked the portal. Now I can't unlock it."

"Overriding the portals is against our agreement. You are asking us to do many things we're not supposed to do."

"I can't help it; you seem to think I'm doing all this stuff, and it couldn't be farther from the truth!"

"We cannot override the portal." Minu felt her anger beginning to build. "But we will show you your code, the one you will/have/did give us."

Her head swam with a cryptic series of Concordian script that flashed by so fast she didn't have time to recognize a single symbol. Her script fluency was somewhere between average to good, but it was way too fast. She was about to complain when she was shoved out of the portal with a gasp.

"Are you okay?" Minu looked up at Aaron's worried face. The temperature was no more than ten degrees, maybe less. She only wore a light windbreaker; the sweat from her earlier exertion was dried and she was shivering almost uncontrollably. Aaron stepped up to kneel next to her, putting a powerful arm around her shoulder. The contact made heat spread in more ways than one as his smell of dirt, soap, and honest sweat filled her nostrils.

"I fell asleep," she said, her teeth chattering.

"Looked like you were having a conversation in your sleep. You looked kind of pissed, then suddenly you jerked upright and looked like you were in pain."

"Bad dream." Minu gently shrugged off his arm and climbed to her feet, reaching into a pocket and clicking on the jacket's heater. It was only good for a light warming, but would be enough if luck was with her. "I got an idea." She hopped down from the dais and strode over to where Ted was snoring. Bjorn sat next to him now, a tablet in his hands. Only a couple of torches provided light in the working area, so the tablet cast his aging face in stark relief. He looked up and gave her a smile. "Can I borrow the control rod?"

"I don't suspect he'll mind," Bjorn said and slid it from his hand. Ted fidgeted in his sleep, missing the rod, so Bjorn picked up a long rock and put it in his hand. It seemed to do the trick, because Ted sighed and quieted down. "What do you have in mind? We've tried just about every piece of magic…"

His voice trailed off because as soon as he handed it to Minu she began working on the holographic script. She watched her fingers in amazement, the digits moving with blazing speed. Minu shook her head; it felt like she was entering a locker combination she'd known for years or dialing a best friend's phone number. Only this sequence had at least twenty moves. Bjorn elbowed Ted, who grunted and sat up straight, looking first at the rock in his hand then at Minu in confusion. "What the—"

"Shhh!" Bjorn snapped and pointed. "Just watch."

Minu finished what she knew was the level-one cypher. The entire field of holographic script flashed once, then changed from its normal white to a bluish hue. In addition a new set of script appeared, hovering over the first. She went right at those and entered the Master Code. The code entered, she pointed the rod at the portal and stabbed the initiate icon. The portal pulsed brilliantly, all the script icons along the portal flashed like a string of pearls, and the rod displayed a message in script. Minu responded by releasing the rod from Master function and returning it to the general user level it had been before.

"Let's get packed up," she said and turned to her stunned group of friends. If Ted's jaw hung down any further, it would have been in his lap.

* * *

"That isn't acceptable, young lady," Ted snapped. He was as upset as Minu had ever seen him. From the moment she'd reset the portal and given him back the rod, he'd verified it was clear and free, then followed every step she made while helping the team get ready to go, continually insisting she explain both how she'd suddenly learned something no other human knew and teach it to him. She'd have loved to teach him, but for some inexplicable reason, she couldn't!

"I'm not your young lady, need I remind you?" she snapped aloud at Ted, her anger flaring as always when that pejorative was used to describe her. "I would tell you if I could, but I can't."

"Then tell me why!"

If I did you'd think I'm nuts, she thought. "Now is not the time. Look, I'm in command; you accepted that when you came on this mission. For now, you have to take my word for it that I'll explain later and help us get out of here before the sun comes up." The sky never got completely dark, and already the eastern horizon was beginning to glow once more. The temperature hovered at five degrees, but not for much longer. Ted glared at her, his jaw muscles bunching as he tried to control his feelings of frustration and betrayal at being, what seemed to him, purposefully excluded from valuable knowledge.

"Come on, Ted," Bjorn finally said and slapped his longtime friend in the back. "It'll just sweeten the telling once she can let us in on it. I, for one, love a good mystery! Did I ever tell you about the time I saw a Mok-Tok trying to mate with a Beezer? It was about thirty years ago..." He succeeded in leading the reluctant Ted away, casting a quick glance at Minu and shooting her a little wink, before joining the others to load the rest of their gear. Minu heaved a sigh and smiled at him with gratitude. It hurt to keep a secret from one of her few friends.

"I hope you have a good reason for that secret." She glanced over at where Aaron was stuffing the last of the carefully-rolled solar shields into their packing case. "Ted looks really pissed off."

"You wouldn't believe me if I told you," she said and went over to help him. "I frankly don't believe it myself." He looked up at her, concern and curiosity etched in the strong lines of his olive-complexioned face. His dark black hair was cut short, as usual now, and even through the powered windbreaker she could see his massive muscles work as he heaved the crate to carry it into the fighter.

"Thanks," he said as he turned to go, his deep brown eyes twinkling. Minu felt a warm feeling in the pit of her stomach she hadn't felt in a couple years. He stopped and looked at her. "What?"

"Oh, nothing!" she said quickly, her face turning red from cheeks to neck.

"Girls," he mumbled and went inside.

Minu turned away and tried to calm her fluttering heart. She'd known him since they were on their trials, and only once before had she felt that deep of a connection to him. He'd just saved her from drowning and was looking at her, those deep brown eyes full of concern and something else. "No," she said and shook her head. "He can't be…with me." She turned her head and saw he was securing the crate, but looking right at her. The flush came back, and she quickly looked away. "Quit acting like a little school girl!" she admonished herself. "He's cute, sure, and maybe he does have feelings for me, but so what?"

"What?" hissed a voice nearby. Var'at was there holding a crate of Rasa-manufactured gear and had been listening to her confusing monologue for a few seconds.

"Oh, crap, nothing, nothing. I'm just trying to figure things out."

"I've been wanting to tell you, about that portal and what you did?"

"Yeah?"

"I've seen that done once before."

"Really?" She exclaimed. "When? Who did it?"

"It was many years ago, when I first became a scout leader. A very remote world where we negotiated the purchase of a special sort of portal control rod. Once the sale was completed, the owners handed them over to my team, and they programmed them just like you did."

"What species was it?"

"It was a Poolab. They're a reclusive aquatic species; not many in the Concordia are aquatic. From your Earth records, I would say it looks rather like a seahorse. They float in little fish bowls that are attached to centipede-bots. An old species, intelligent, and very hard to deal with. Many say they go back to the founding of the Concordia, millions of years ago."

"Why are they so difficult to deal with?"

"They aren't motivated by money or power."

"So what did motivate them?"

"Information. Unfortunately, back then, I had little influence so I didn't know what I was trading them."

"What about these special control rods?"

"Don't know about that, either. I heard later they were designed to open new portals wherever you wanted to."

"Never heard of that. It doesn't seem possible."

"I agree, which is why I discounted the rumor. Anyway, they knew how to do what you just did, and I suspect much, much more."

"I'll have to keep an eye out for them."

"I wish you luck; I've only seen the one in all my years, and I don't know anyone else who has either."

Var'at went back to his task and left Minu to think. Another line in her grand mental notebook, full from front to back with clues to a mystery bigger than the galaxy. She sighed and turned, almost walking right into the deep pit they'd dug as shelter. Cursing herself for not paying attention, she easily jumped over, and missed her landing. "Son of a—" she squawked and slid down the other side to the bottom.

"You okay?" she heard Aaron yell from inside the fighter.

"Yes!" she yelled, much more brusquely than she'd intended. "Thanks," she added after feeling guilty.

"Okay," he replied and went back to his work.

Minu brushed dirt from her bottom and got up, now very glad they wouldn't have to spend a day in the dank hole. As she stood there, she saw the bone. The dirt was all dark gray or black, a result of the planet's demise, according to the scientists. The bone was bleached almost pure white and caught her eye immediately. "What's this then," she said as she bent over it. Brushing away more of the dirt, she could see it was an arm or leg bone of some animal, about half a meter long, and fairly thin. From her biology classes she could recognize tendon attachment points and places where veins once entered.

"We're just about ready!" Aaron yelled to her. "You going to the toilet down there?"

"Don't be crude," she yelled back. She almost just jumped out and left it there, then decided against it. Instead she dug a couple of the bones loose and dropped them in the pocket she'd normally have carried her control rod in. With no more thought about it she jumped out and headed for her craft.

A few minutes later the portal flashed to life, and the two fighters climbed off the ground, their gravitic impellers whining and sending up a flurry of dust from their excavations. They both flew across the trench they'd dug on the way to pass through the portal, the wildly spinning gravity fields brushing dirt around in mini-cyclones. As they passed, the first sun was cresting the horizon and sending bright blue light flooding into the pit. Had Minu been standing where she'd discovered the arm bone, she'd have borne witness to the uncovering of a bleached and cracked skull. A skull that, except for a few notable differences of the eye socket shape and angle of the brow, would have been a dead ringer for a human skull. A moment later the second fighter passed over and its powerful gravity field collapsed the trench, burying the excavation forever.

*****

Chapter Eight
January 13th, 523 AE

Undesignated Planet, Galactic Frontier

There was only one short stop between the world they'd left behind, dubbed Sunshine by Aaron, and the destination of Enigma. The world was a decaying, half-dead endless forest with distant mountains. Early afternoon was almost pleasant after Sunshine, and Minu was tempted to spend a little time recovering. Of course then she might have to face more of Ted's wrath, so they got ready for the final jump.

Ted programmed the control rod, and they watched as the portal came alive again. The scene on the other side was the interior of an industrial structure, surprisingly intact and lit from a nearby light source. "Var'at, go ahead, we'll be right behind you."

Var'at's fighter carefully moved toward the portal, and Aaron maneuvered around behind it. The first fighter slid through the event horizon and was beginning to slowly turn sideways when an energy blast caught it from the side.

The blast tore a great flaming gouge of metal out of the side of the craft, making it slew sideways. "No!" Minu screamed as a second blast hit next to the first one. "Get us through there!" she ordered Aaron.

"He's blocking the portal!" he exclaimed. "If we go through, we can't deploy shields and we're toast!"

"We have to do something!"

The second shot was less effective; the shooter's aim was off slightly because of the way the first shot moved the target. Minu just saw the wavering shimmer around the fighter before the third shot hit and splashed against the shields. "Way to go, Var'at!" she screamed as the craft righted itself, turned sideways to make room for her, and began to blaze away with its nose-mounted shock rifles. Fire was pouring from one of the holes in the fuselage, and smoke from the other, but it was moving. "Go!"

Aaron nodded and guided them through the portal as fast as reasonable, throwing on the brakes the instant they cleared, and bringing up their shields. She'd hoped that Enigma would be abandoned and ignored, but considering what she hoped to find there, she should have known better. Their shields flashed red twice from direct hits, and Aaron brought the offensive weapons online. Minu took the controls and looked through the targeting screens. Twenty meters away and set in the perfect location to attack anyone coming through the portal were a pair of heavy beamcaster turrets manned by a squad of T'Chillen warriors in full combat armor. To add insult to injury, they were behind dualloy armor shielding, in addition to energy shields and force fields.

The T'Chillen pointed with their tentacle arms and the beamcasters cycled as fast as they could, which luckily wasn't very fast. "Give them everything!" Minu yelled at Var'at over the radio, not knowing if he could hear her. She thumbed the fighter's beamcasters to life as well and fired all the weapons in sequence. Four shock rifle shots, two beamcasters, back to the shock rifles, over and over. A second later the other fighter added its beamcasters too. The combination of the two fighters had a devastating effect on the emplacements. Their energy shields relied on dumping incoming fire into EPCs specially designed to shunt away the horrific amounts of energy a beamcaster unleashed. The combination of the exotic impact of the shock rifles and powerful beamcasters overloaded the storage sources, which exploded like bombs, rocking the room and the two fighters.

"Can't hold it," Aaron growled as the shock wave shoved them sideways and into the other fighter. The shields that protected them from energy fire were worthless against physical force. The two fighters collided with a tremendous grinding of metal on metal that lurched Minu hard enough to slam her hard against the bulkhead. She turned just in time to see the other fighter rebound against the nearest wall, and begin to fall apart.

It was like watching a toy made of interlocking blocks hit by an angry child. The magnetic couples that held the craft together failed, and the fighter disintegrated. Aaron fought the controls with all his strength, muscles standing out like bands of dualloy, but he couldn't help but crush part of the remains between their ship and the wall. Even through the hull Minu heard the death screams of the Rasa over the screech of rending dualloy. Their own fighter rebounded from the wall and Aaron set them down with a jerk on the floor. The doors opened, and they raced out.

Aaron stayed at the controls, keeping the craft's weapons batteries trained on the far end of the smoking chamber, knowing that such a massive explosion would bring reinforcements. Minu was last out, wiping blood from a cut above her right eye. Rasa were already pulling dead or dying comrades from the remains of the fighter. "Oh, God," Minu moaned, horrified by the loss of life and fearing that her friend Var'at was among them. Then she recognized his form, the crest behind his head sporting a half-moon burn scar she'd given him years ago when they were still enemies. Cherise, Ted and Bjorn were already tending to those who were still moving, assisted by a surviving Rasa medic.

"What can I do?" she asked Var'at, who was kneeling next to a still shape. It wasn't easy to tell them apart, but she guessed it was his lieutenant, an old and trusted friend.

"There's nothing much to do," he admitted, turning a turreted eye back to regard her. "We were lucky any of us survived. Your friends have devised a truly powerful vehicle."

She did what she could as they quickly stabilized those that lived, and said goodbye to those that were gone, hoping they wouldn't be quickly joining them. Var'at had left Bellatrix with a standard sixteen-lizard squad. Eight now survived, and three of them were injured. The uninjured quickly sifted through the debris for what equipment could be salvaged, and they were all loading back into the last fighter less than five minutes after the mishap. The last two Rasa soldiers were climbing the ramp just as a trio of T'Chillen riding their own version of broomsticks appeared down the hall behind the smoking enemy emplacement.

Aaron took out the first one with a precision shot from the fighter's shock rifles. Return fire splashed against their shields as he took the second one out with the added firepower of the beamcasters. The third one executed a dizzying series of spins and loops ending with it dodging around the corner they'd just appeared from. Aaron tracked it with shots all the way but only scored a couple of glancing blows with the beamcasters. "Sorry, Boss," he said as she slid in behind him and into the co-pilot seat.

"Not a problem," she said and took over the weapons controls. "They were sure to know something was up after the ground started shaking."

They lifted off and started flying the craft down the same hall the T'Chillen broomsticks had appeared from; it was the only way out. As they passed, Minu glanced at the twisted and smoldering remains of the T'Chillen guards who'd manned the gun emplacement and thought of something. "Hold up," she said and headed to the rear.

"We don't have much time, Boss!" Aaron reminded her.

"I know," she said. As she moved through the crowded crew compartment she saw the huddled Rasa soldiers, all looking at her expectantly. There was Var'at, helping Cherise and his medic tend to the wounded. Ted and Bjorn were both checking Pip's capsule. They glanced up as she came rearward. "Can I borrow that beamcaster, soldier?" she asked the Rasa, knowing her words would be translated for her.

"Yes, Commander." He nodded and handed it to her. The design was similar to the human-scaled models, with a shorter stock and forward pistol grip, but the rest was identical. She dialed it for medium beam and power then smacked the rear door controls. It began to drop quickly.

"Don't be long," Aaron said over the radio, the worry evident in his voice.

"Will do," she said and ran down the ramp before it was all the way down.

"What the hell is she doing?" Cherise asked Bjorn and Ted.

"The other fighter had two pairs of shock rifles," Ted told her, "we don't know if they survived the impact."

"We don't want the snakes getting our secrets," Bjorn agreed.

"They're just damned guns," Cherise snarled and smacked a hand against the floor.

"No," Aaron said from up front without looking back, "they're our only card in the game right now."

Minu walked down the ramp, casting another nervous look at the wrecked emplacements. Piles of charred, smoking debris and coils of dead armored snakes. She swallowed and sped up to a trot. The bloody debris came up fast, and she angled toward the mostly intact nose of the cylindrical fighter. The whole thing banked slightly to one side before her fighter had hit it, pinning and crushing it against the wall. The cockpit was cracked like an egg, and she could see the edge of the two beamcasters poking out underneath. They weren't her concern; it was the four shock rifles installed between the beamcasters. She smacked the nose of the fighter experimentally, and a piece of armor fell away. "Okay, the hard way then."

Minu slung the beamcaster and dug through the piles of debris, looking for a solid piece, and eventually found a meter-long solid dualloy beam. Pulling it from the other junk, she clamped down with her right arm and swung at about half her maximum strength. Chunks of armor flew in all directions with a satisfactory crunch. The beam reverberated through her cybernetic arm, jarring her flesh and blood shoulder painfully. Gritting her teeth, she increased the power. Two more cracks and one of the shock rifles was visible.

"Sorry," Minu said to all those who'd worked and died to develop the weapons, and she put two blasts into the gun itself, then another into the mount. "One down, three to go." She slung the gun and went back to work with her improvised demolition tool.

A dozen meters away, vertical slitted eyes watched her work with barely controlled malevolence. When the portal defense module exploded, he'd been partially protected from the blast by his personal shield. Very little of the terrible energy flash wave affected him, and his armor absorbed all of that. The shield, of course, was gone now. The real problem was the flying debris for which a shield was no defense. A whirlwind of razor-sharp dualloy tore through his crew, instantly killing all except himself. He'd been hit a slew of times, but none of them were lethal. His armor was keeping him alive until help could arrive, but he had no interest in rescue. He'd seen the human trundle by and his blood raged. A puny human, a slave of the dirt-digging Tog? How dare they? Such incredible gall to even be out here! His armor said his spine was severed at the fourteenth mid vertebrae, so he couldn't move, but he could still hold a gun. With slow, patient movements, he slithered two of his arms into the debris partially covering his ravaged body, searching for a weapon.

Minu hammered at the cockpit over and over again; chunks of hull and armor flew and bounced off her as she worked the club with methodical power no human arm could duplicate. Aaron called nervously for an update. "Almost there," she huffed as the club finally exposed her objective. A couple more grunting crashes of the club and the shock rifle was visible. "About damn time," she said through clenched teeth as she brought the gun around and gave this one the same treatment as the other three. All the guns were now smoldering slag. "Got them, on my way back."

"Don't take your time, they've already sent a couple of bots around to get a look. Frankly, I think we've got them confused."

"Not as confused as we are," she joked and trotted back toward the waiting fighter. Cherise stood in the back, urging her to hurry with a sweeping arm gesture. Minu gave her a quick thumbs-up, and it saved her life.

* * * * *

Chapter Nine
January 14th, 523 AE

Unknown Space Station, Enigma Star System, Galactic Frontier

A beamcaster bolt tore at her just as she raised her right arm to wave, the beam hitting her in the forearm and splashing around and through the limb. Stray bits of the particle accelerator beam hit all over her torso and were mostly absorbed by the gauss net, a weave of superconducting dualloy throughout her uniform.

Assailed by a thousand pinpricks of lightning pain, the majority of the impact slammed into her arm and spun her around like she'd been hit a hammer blow, throwing her into the wall, then the floor in a heap. Pain tore throughout her body and in her arm with an intensity she'd never felt before. She struggled against consciousness as she landed in a heap, her vision swimming with red halos. A single T'Chillen warrior rose slightly from the wreckage of the gun emplacement, obviously severely injured, but still holding a beamcaster and aiming at her.

Dodging was out of the question. She was half leaning, half lying against the base of the wall. All she could do was fall over sideways as the second shot splashed against the wall where her head had been a moment ago. Energy splash burned her in still more places, and this time her gauss net was worthless, the capacitor burned out from the first hit. The snake used its spare arm to pull itself a meter closer, then raised up to aim carefully. The barrel loomed like an approaching tunnel. Minu lay on her side struggling to breathe, and prepared for the final shot.

Her left arm was just fine. After sliding sideways to the floor, Minu fought the pain and stretched over her shoulder. The T'Chillen hissed at the awkward movement, then gasped as Minu's flashing sword bisected its body. Cherise's Enforcer boomed once into the alien's side, and the two parts slid apart with a slippery, meaty sound to plop to the floor, cut cleanly in half by Tamara's wonder sword.

Cherise raced down the ramp and to Minu. The electrical shocks of the stray accelerator splinters were lessening, allowing Minu to breathe more deeply and sit up against the wall just in time to warn her friend away before she was injured by the sword. "Careful," she croaked and set the blade aside.

"Oh God," Cherise cried as she slid to a stop on her knees next to Minu. Minu was holding up her right arm, which was smoking badly and dripping liquid metal on the floor. The limb was shot through halfway between the wrist and elbow. She could bend the elbow still, but the wrist and hand didn't respond to her commands. The entire limb ached with a pain she couldn't touch. Cherise looked at her friend, covered in a thousand little burns and her arm on fire, and cried. "You look like shit." Bjorn said as he looked over the T'Chillen with an eye toward samples.

"Thanks," Minu said and reached with her left hand. "Get me up." A Rasa medic was skittering over, along with Var'at and a couple of other soldiers to be sure no other T'Chillen were playing dead. "Save it," Minu said and waved the medic off. "Get the gun," she pointed at the beamcaster she'd dropped, "and my sword, then get aboard. That includes you, Bjorn."

"Is she okay?" Aaron yelled over his shoulder as they bundled everyone up.

"Far from it," Cherise snapped. "Get us the fuck out of here." One of the Rasa, having seen what the sword could do to an armored foe, carefully retrieved the weapon and slid it back into the sheath on Minu's back. She nodded her thanks as the doors began to close.

"Where?"

"Down the hall, around the corner, guns blazing. We need to find exit to this facility so we can find the stash the Squeen talked about."

Cherise used a couple of quick spurts from a fire extinguisher to stop the fire in Minu's forearm, and even that hurt. But at least her arm wasn't burning anymore. "Are you in much pain?"

"Depends on your definition of much." Cherise jabbed her in the leg with an ampule of Boost. Minu felt the buzz hit instantly, and the pain decrease. "God that stuff feels good."

"It's supposed to. Any idea what's ahead?"

"Probably deeper and deeper shit."

Aaron piloted the fighter around the corner fast, all guns blazing just as Minu had ordered. The turn swept the hallway from side to side and caught dozens of T'Chillen by surprise, sending many flying in bloody spins to the ground. A few retreated farther down the hallway, firing back with handheld beamcasters as they went. The light weapons were ineffective against the fighter's heavy shields, so Aaron punished them every meter of the way. Only a couple made it out alive.

"Keep 'em on the run," Minu said as she dropped back into the copilot's seat. Aaron spared her a quick glance before resuming his attack. "Stay on the guns buddy; I've only got one hand for now."

"You got it," he said and blazed around another corner. The slaughter continued for another minute with Aaron turning corner after corner, pursuing and killing T'Chillen, and ambushing reinforcements that were coming to help the others. Suddenly they turned from a multiple-branch intersection to find themselves in a vast chamber full of dozens of T'Chillen units. Aaron and Minu looked around, their eyes wide in wonder and shock. All work in the chamber came to a sudden stop as the fighter appeared. "What do I shoot first?" Aaron said in a hushed voice, not even sure why he was whispering. Against the nearest wall, two massive armored combat suites stood, their operators halfway through slithering up their tree-like mounting ladders.

With a steady hand Minu pointed at the suites. "Shoot them," she said.

"Gladly," Aaron said and turned his weapons on them. Once manned and at full power, the two suites would withstand even the firepower of the single fighter. Standing still with operators trying to get inside, though, they were sitting ducks. Aaron moved the joystick from side to side and chewed the suites, operators, and technicians into bloody smoldering rags.

"Spread it around," Minu told him, pointing out targets of opportunity. The chamber erupted in panic as soldiers tried to respond to the rampaging fighter, and technicians slithered for their lives. As weapons fire erupted in all directions, the scene quickly devolved into complete pandemonium.

* * *

"What is that thing?" demanded a high ranking commander on the far side of the chamber, "And why is it firing on us?" He slithered up on top of the vehicle he'd been supervising for a better view; his sub-commander followed obediently behind. He listened to radio reports as he climbed.

"It came through the out-system portal a few minutes ago," a scout informed him as he activated image enhancements in his powered armor helmet and observed the alien craft. It was heartily strafing a line of equipment containers, behind which soldiers and noncombatants alike were taking refuge.

"It is a damned transport, that's all. Somehow modified with weaponry…and shields?" the commander demanded.

"What fool would waste resources turning a transport into a fighting vehicle?" wondered the scout.

"Destroy it, before it damages the station," the commander ordered his sub-commander.

The sub-commander turned to his radio and began to issue orders just as Aaron spotted the two spectacularly armored snakes on top of a military vehicle and promptly vaporized them.

* * *

"Good choice!!" Minu cheered as the commander and his vehicle went up in a fireball. The moment Aaron killed the two snakes, any hint of organized resistance died with them.

"It took the kick out of them," Aaron agreed, "but they're still dangerous." Weapons fire continued to splash against their shield from all sides, but not fast or powerful enough to endanger them.

The fighter's overpowered shield capacitors were designed for sustained abuse and not overly stressed by small arms. "Still, we can't hang in here forever, and we have limited power reserves." On the display, the fighter's dual banks of EPC charge levels were displayed, approximately half and decreasing precipitously.

"Time to get out of here," Minu said. "It seems we've outstayed our welcome." She scanned the immense chamber. There were three exits, including the one they'd entered through. The most promising was to their left, a massive set of heavy dualloy doors that split and pivoted upward from their top like gull wings to reveal a cylindrical passage four times as wide as the fighter. "There," she told him and pointed to the massive doors, spread open like a split manhole cover.

"You got it," Aaron agreed and spun the fighter in a dizzying turn, firing all the time. The T'Chillen resistance, now in complete disarray, gave way before them like the darkness before the dawn. They fled on foot, dove behind equipment, or into already smoldering transports as the fighter screamed by.

"You account for my men well!" Var'at called behind them.

"I'm just trying to stay alive," she said under her breath while providing whatever assistance she could to Aaron with only one hand. In a few moments they were roaring through the doors she'd spotted, only to find it a huge dead end. The cylindrical passage was only a chamber roughly twice its length. Opaque windows lined both sides. At the far end was a door, far too small for the fighter to fit. "End of the line."

* * *

Aaron spun the fighter on its axis, pointing her nose and guns back out the massive doors. There was no sign of any organized attack, but he knew it was only a matter of time. Var'at took his soldiers down a side ramp at a run to investigate the doorway of their dead end. Sporadic disorganized weapons fire reached out toward the skittering soldiers and was answered by both them and Aaron in kind. It instantly reduced in volume.

"The small door is locked," a Rasa soldier quickly responded, "I can override it, but of course the fighter will have to be abandoned." Further activity continued in the great chamber beyond but nothing definite could be seen through the smoke and flames Aaron had left in their wake. He sent intermittent salvos of shock rifle fire to keep them guessing.

"Main door is double-sided," reported Var'at himself, "it's a lot like an airlock in design."

"Can you activate it?" Minu asked him.

"Probably. But if I do, I don't know if I can make it open again. The system is a very, very, old design that predates any of the modern Concordian control mechanisms."

Minu chewed her bottom lip. Three choices: abandon the fighter and retreat through the small rear hatch; fight their way back into the main chamber and try one of the other exits; or activate the big airlock doors and try to hold.

"Heavy combat vehicles," Aaron warned and stabbed at the main tactical screen. The squat, massively-armored T'Chillen vehicles were more tank than anything, low to the ground and fairly bristling with energy weapons, shields, and field projectors.

"Close it, Var'at!"

The massive exterior doors started pivoting down from either side, picking up speed as they went. At the same time smaller clam-shell-style doors came out of the interior wall and moved toward each other. A large energy beam lanced out, striking the fighter's shields, which instantly glowed blue white as globs of pure energy streaked along the outside, trying to find a way in.

"Damn it!" Aaron barked and slewed them sideways with as much care as he could. The follow up shot missed and burned a gouge out of the wall above the forward side of the space, making Var'at's other team run for their lives from great splashes of molten dualloy. Another beam came at them, but the huge exterior doors came together with a grinding crash, cutting if off before it could dump any serious energy into their already taxed shields. The inside doors closed a second later with a clank and a hiss. Minu felt the pressure change in her ears.

She was out of her seat and down the ramp in a second. "Bring Pip!" she yelled at Cherise as she ran out the passenger side door. Var'at and the four soldiers with him were arrayed in front and alongside the fighter, weapons trained on the now secure doors. Even through the massive thickness of dualloy they could hear the thump, thump, thump of the tank's energy cannon firing over and over again. "Will it hold?" she asked over the radio.

"I can barely understand how I closed the thing," he admitted. "If the snakes have someone more familiar with this old Concordian script, they'll be in here in minutes."

Minu reached the other team, who were examining the huge smoldering gouge from the forward wall. A few meters to the left and the forward door would have been obliterated. Glowing pools of liquid metal were everywhere. Minu dodged between them with no thought of the risk and quickly reached the small door. The door's controls were alive and displaying a holographic sequence of controls rotating in a circle above the pad. The symbols were a mixture of those common in any Concordian-made interface and others both strange and familiar. The Weavers nodded somewhere in the back of her mind.

"It can be overridden," the Rasa soldier who'd been examining it said over her shoulder.

"That won't be necessary," Minu replied and just like with the control rod a few hours ago, she grabbed and manipulated icons in ways she'd never done or thought possible. The Rasa gawked as she unlocked the door, and every other door connected to it, in under two seconds. That accomplished, she linked with the rear door's controls, savagely twisted a pair of icons, then gave them a snap. There was a clang from the rear door followed by a brief klaxon.

"What the hell was that?" Ted asked as he, Cherise, and Bjorn approached with Pip's life support module floating on its portable hoverfield.

"I've locked the back door," she told them as the smaller door before her slid open with a slight hiss. His eyes blazed with unanswered questions, but he held his tongue. They moved past her into a nearly circular hallway. Minu began to follow, then stopped and turned back to face Var'at. "I can't ask you to give your lives."

"You don't have to. They shall not get past us, I swear."

"They're not getting past us," Aaron yelled, still behind the fighter's controls. Minu went inside, leaving two of her best friends behind to protect her back.

The circular hallway was lit with light bands that ran around the circumference every few meters, giving the feeling of a long drain that appeared to go on forever. Ted, Bjorn, and Cherise, escorted by the Rasa, were well ahead of her, blindly running down the hallway. She pushed to catch up.

The hallway was intersected at one point by two other identical hallways that led off at ninety degree angles. "Straight ahead," she urged as they approached the turns. The Rasa on point ran on without stopping.

"What do you think this is?" Cherise asked, breathing hard from the effort of pushing the module and keeping it centered in the middle of the hallway.

"I'm hoping it's an exit," she admitted, "we can get out of here and steal a T'Chillen ground car or something and start looking for the technology stash."

"And then what?" Ted asked.

"I haven't thought that far ahead."

"So like your father," Bjorn laughed, even as Ted gave him a dark look. "Oh, quit your glum looks, Theodore, you've been begging to go on missions as long as I can remember!"

"I wasn't expecting a headlong race to our doom."

"Welcome to the Chosen," Minu said. "You can always go back and try to explain it all to the T'Chillen."

"No, that's quite all right, I'll take my chances with the fickle hand of fate over the scaly head of evil." The nearest scaly head of a Rasa regarded Ted for a moment, and Minu wondered if the soldier had understood. She hoped not; they depended on every last hand for this crazy mission.

"Door ahead!" yelled the lead Rasa.

"It'll open for you," Minu assured him. As promised, when he was within a meter of the door, it split and opened, a miniature of the huge outside doors they'd come through earlier, admitting them to a wide sweeping control room with several low squat seats and a panoramic display. Not at all what Minu had hoped to find. She was about to order an about-face when a narrow snake head rose over the back of the center seat.

The T'Chillen's eye stalks jerked up to their full extension in unmistakable shock at the sight of the human/Rasa party's arrival. One of Minu's Enforcers was in her left hand in a heartbeat and she almost fired before one of the Rasa called out. "Do not shoot, it's not a warrior!"

"So?" Minu asked, her gun leveled dead between the eye stalks. The T'Chillen watched her with both eyes, the entire head shaking, scales sending off colorful reflections of light. Its tongue darted out, tentatively tasting the air. Not liking what it tasted, the tongue shot back in.

"It might be able to tell us a way out," the soldier said. He aimed his accelerator rifle at the T'Chillen and spoke. "What is this place? How do we get out?"

"Do not kill this helpless one, please?"

"Answer the questions," Minu snapped and took a step closer, "and we'll think about letting you live."

"This is the control room," it said. The translator managed to convey a shaking quality to the voice. "You leave the same way you came in!"

"Fuck," Minu spat, never taking her eyes from the T'Chillen. She could see now the Rasa was right; this snake was less than half the size of their warriors and wore no armor at all. She moved sideways to see it was curled in the wide chair; both serpentine arms hung at its side and it shook almost uncontrollably. She began to feel guilty for scaring the shit out of the poor thing. "What do you do here?"

"I'm in control of this," it said and gestured vaguely at the banks of controls.

"Show us," Minu instructed and lowered her gun slightly. The T'Chillen moved so quickly to comply she almost shot it on the spot.

With fast, deft motions the controls came alive, or part of them. There looked to be dozens of sub-panels and only a few lit up in response. They were programmable data panels of an advanced design she'd only seen a few times before. The displays flowed with alien script that made her brain tickle, and after a second the floor began to vibrate. "What are you doing?" she demanded.

"Showing you!" And with a slight bump they felt the unmistakable sensation of movement.

"Is this a craft of some sort?!"

"Yes, yes! I'm in control!" It stroked a control and gestured before it, and the wide panoramic display became clear to the vista of stars beyond.

"Minu," Var'at's voice spoke in her ear, "we can see through those windows. We're in space!"

"Yeah, we just noticed that as well. Stand down and come forward, please. I don't think the fighter is in any danger, but leave a soldier just to be sure. Aaron, as a pilot you'll appreciate this." Outside the view banked as the ship turned, and they could see the edge of the huge space station they'd just left behind. Nowhere was there any sign of a planet. "Enigma, indeed," she said.

*****

Chapter Ten
January 14th, 523 AE

Transfer Craft, Enigma Star System, Galactic Frontier

The pilot proved very chatty once she was certain she wasn't about to die. She humbly explained that as a female she was limited to breeding and technological services, like all T'Chillen females. Wasn't that normal in all species? She also explained that this was a transfer craft, though what it transferred she didn't know. She assured them there were no other T'Chillen aboard, that she'd just unloaded her passengers and cargo and was patiently awaiting orders to prepare for another flight or go off duty.

"How long would you have waited?" Minu asked.

"Why, until I was ordered, of course." She displayed little self-initiative and was very malleable to anyone who'd give her instructions with some authority. Her specialty was piloting outdated Concordian technology, something of which she was very proud. "My nest mother was also likewise gifted in such things."

"Is she here in this system too?"

"No, she couldn't understand a locking mechanism a few cycles ago and had to go."

"Go where?" Ted asked her.

She glanced at him with one flexible eye stalk then looked away. No one pushed her any further; the answer seemed self-evident.

"Tough life," Minu said quietly, then she asked the T'Chillen, "Where are we going?"

"I was so eager to show you my job, I didn't set a course. We're orbiting the Portal Station at five hundred kilometers awaiting orders."

"Where do your orders come from?" Minu asked. She pointed to a quietly glowing sub-panel. "I see," she said and caught Aaron's attention. He'd been busily examining the control interface as he looked up at her. She casually indicated the communication panel and made a slashing motion across her throat, then got the pilot's attention again; she'd begun explaining an instrument reading to Bjorn who was having the time of his life. "Pilot, wait, what's your name? What do we call you?"

She gave a quick hissing spit that their translators interpreted as "Sally Two Eleven." It wasn't the first time Minu found herself wondering where the hell the translators came up with their names.

"Did you all get that weird name?" Minu asked them.

"More a designation than a name," Ted said.

Minu nodded. "How about we just call you Sally?"

"That's accurate, though there are many other Sallys from my nest. Since I'm the only one here, it's good."

"Great, Sally, can you tell me what this panel does?" Minu asked, pointing to a little display on the opposite side of the radio. While Sally explained the approach radar, Aaron reached over and, using the universal script found on all Concordian devices, disabled the radio. Minu cocked an eyebrow, and he nodded in reply. "That's interesting. Okay Sally, we have orders for you."

"I should wait for orders from the Portal Station."

"These orders are more important, and you must follow them now."

"Okay," she said meekly and swiveled her eyes away from Minu and downward, a sign of acquiescence.

"Show me a holographic map of the solar system." Sally made one appear above their heads and Minu examined it. "Primary star only, no planets. Looks like a brown dwarf, wouldn't you gentleman agree?"

"Yes," Ted agreed.

Bjorn ran a finger along the line of Concordian script under the sun and thought for a moment. "Everything on this ship is either T'Chillen or old Concordian script; damned hard to understand. This star is notated as decayed, or discarded. That's strange. But yes, it's a brown dwarf, sequence two I'd think."

"Good," Minu said, glad Bjorn hadn't gone completely off the reservation with one of his detailed but irrelevant dissertations. "What are these?" she asked Sally, indicating four floating icons.

"We call them work sites. I don't know if there's another name. We've been to all of them, but are currently working in this one." A delicate point of tentacle touched one in space that flashed briefly. "Do you want to go there now?"

"No. Does this craft have enough power to go to any of them?"

"Yes, it was recharged less than a day ago. We only have to top it off once a ten-day. It's very power efficient."

"I see," she said and looked at the others, in particular Ted and Bjorn. "What do you think?" she asked no one in particular.

"Well," Ted began, "it would stand to reason that the best opportunity would be found at the site the snakes are using now, but for obvious reasons we must rule that one out. Beyond that criterion, one would seem as valuable as the others."

"Sally?" Minu asked. The T'Chillen looked at her attentively. "Which of the other three sites provided the best finds?"

"It's not my specialty, really," she said, looking down.

"At which location were you most often needed to solve problems or look at machines?" Bjorn tried.

"Oh, that's easy, this one!" she indicated the third in the system, farthest from their current location.

"Then take us to that one," Minu told her. Sally practically applauded as she entered the coordinates into the craft's controls. Aaron watched her every move.

As they cruised along silently through the void, Minu and her friends chatted with Sally. Minu was amazed at how well she seemed to interact with the humans and Rasa. The snake seemed particularly curious about Var'at and his men, and eventually her curiosity got the better of her. "I know you are Rasa," she said, nodding her head toward Var'at, then turned her eye stalks toward Minu, "but I do not know your species."

"We are called human," Minu explained, but didn't elaborate.

"I have never seen a hominid species before. There haven't been any in many, many years."

"Do you know why not?" Bjorn asked her.

She cocked her head at him and blinked her eye stalks in an almost human expression. "I don't! Isn't that fascinating?"

Minu decided to let curiosity run the room. "Sally, are there any female T'Chillen soldiers or commanders?"

"No, of course not! What a ludicrous suggestion. Females are smaller and weaker than males."

"As is the case with humans, but that doesn't make us less versatile, less powerful, and obviously, in your case, less intelligent."

"You're female?"

Minu looked down at her breasts and suppressed the urge to say 'duh!' before remembering that the alien had never seen a hominid; how would she know to tell one sex from another? "Yes, I am."

"Me too," Cherise volunteered.

Sally looked between the two women, and then Aaron and the other men. "Who is in command?"

"I am," Minu told the obviously-amazed T'Chillen female, "though more often males command, it isn't always the norm."

"There are other species where females are dominant," Var'at told her.

"This I understand. What amazes me is your male and female work together? As equals?"

"We do," Ted told her. "Although some are more equal than others." The humans all laughed and Var'at hung his mouth open in amusement.

An instrument on the control board chimed, and Sally turned her eye stalks to examine it. "We are approaching the work site you designated."

Minu and the others all looked up at the sweeping viewport full of stars. They could see the system's primary, a dim light to the left bottom of the window. Sally pointed with a limb and they saw their destination, a glittering collection of lights linked with gossamer strands. A minute later and it was obvious to them all. "Starships," Bjorn gasped, and Ted whistled through his teeth.

Minu watched the sparkling array grow closer with mixed feelings. Could what she wanted, what Pip needed, actually be here?

From a very young age she'd always yearned for stories of space ships the most, and they were the ones her father brought home the least. Often they were descriptions of huge decaying hulks, falling apart like tissue paper in water. Some parts of the huge vessels weren't made of true matter, and if not maintained over time, they began to disintegrate. Once or twice he'd been aboard smaller ships, always finding them completely empty. As they got closer she could see it was a gigantic space dock holding hundreds of ships. Her father had never described anything like this, not in stories to her, and not in his logs. He'd found small ships docked to space stations above worlds, or floating in space above those worlds, but never a shipyard.

"They're not very big," Aaron noted. He had out a pair of issue goggles and was enhancing the distant shapes. "They look like balls pierced with needles or wedges. Some have more than one ball. A few are big collections of balls. Not at all what I'd expect for a starship."

"Who needs aerodynamics in space?" Bjorn asked. He had a tablet out and was making notes for himself.

"Where do you dock?" Minu asked Sally as the details Aaron described became visible to the naked eye.

"There," she said and pointed. The viewport/display flashed a section of the yard near the center, a dodecahedron-shaped structure with tubes heading off eleven of its twelve sides. That last side was facing them, and contained dozens of openings. As they raced closer Minu could see they were docking bays, each hundreds of meters across.

"What does this ship we fly in look like?" Aaron wondered aloud. Sally touched controls and a three-dimensional hologram of their ride floated in the center of the room. A round ball pierced by a pointed lance, the dull end surrounded by propulsion drives, the other where they stood. The image was detailed and even showed the doors on the dull end where they'd come aboard. It must have docked by backing in. The bulk of the ball shape, according to Sally, was cargo space.

"Almost a miniature of the bigger ones," Ted pointed out.

"What have you found in this site?" Minu asked Sally.

"We've never gotten out of the central station," she said, beginning to manipulate the controls as they got closer. "There's a long promenade where all the docking bays are accessible. Only two exits leading from the promenade are visible, and they're locked. None of my sisters have been able to unlock those doors."

"Have you tried docking with any of the starships?"

"Yes, before I came here to work, they tried. The bigger ships have docking bays, but they don't respond to the shuttles. They won't open as we approach, and there are no external controls."

"It's an entire fleet," Ted marveled. Minu tried to count them but lost count at a hundred. They were mostly the bigger versions of what they flew, just a ball pierced by a lance. However, there were quite a few multiple balls on longer spears, clusters of balls around a single spear, multiple spears piercing a single ball, and a pair of huge conglomerations of balls with but a single spear poking out the front and the back. The design reminded her of art class in school. Draw the ball, shade it for accent, now a pencil!

The tubes ran from the central station, occasionally branching, sometimes ending in a starship. The pattern seemed almost completely random, yet the structure taken as a whole somehow made sense. It was an awe-inspiring sight that struck them speechless in its sheer dimensions as they approached—a giant snowflake in space, many kilometers across. When the central station was still kilometers away, it was no longer possible to take in the entire shipyard. Even Ted was reduced to whistling through his teeth over and over, shaking his head.

"I wonder who it belonged to." Minu gave words to what many were thinking.

"They left it millions of years ago," Sally told her. "It's T'Chillen now."

Good luck with that, Minu thought, considering the snakes couldn't even get the doors open. No wonder they were swarming over this place like ants on a dead howler. No one in the Concordia used spaceships any more. If one of the higher-order species could get its claws into the starships it would fundamentally tip the balance of power in the galaxy. If that species should be a hostile one such as the T'Chillen…Minu didn't want to consider what that would mean. And she'd just shot up a few hundred snakes a few minutes ago. Swell.

"Do you want to land and see the promenade? It's amazing."

Minu told her to go ahead and land, then moved slightly back to confer with her people. "Don't ask me how, but I'm pretty sure I can get that door open she was talking about."

"I'm asking you how," Ted said, the exasperation in his voice evident.

"I'll do my best to explain, but not now. Let's just get through these next few hours and then I'll have time to think; surviving is more important now." She could tell by the way Ted's jaw muscles worked that he was unhappy, but yet again he deferred to her decision. How much longer could she put him off about the Weavers?

Their shuttle began to slow as it approached the massive dodecahedron central structure. The one pentagon-shaped side loomed a kilometer or more to either side as they approached. Minu counted twenty or more ovoid docking bays, all with closed clamshell doors. Sally seemed to pick one at random, and it split into four toothed parts and retracted into the unremarkable gray station wall as they approached. Once they'd passed the wall and moved inside, rings of bright lighting came on, displaying an interior of catwalks and scaffolding that was already changing configuration to match their shuttle.

"End of the road," Aaron said and tilted a head toward Sally. "What about her?"

"If we leave her she'll bring them right to us," Var'at told them.

"Maybe," Minu said and shrugged her head. "Sally, we're going to explore this structure. Do you want to go with us?"

"I serve the nest." They all looked at her expectantly as she finished some input on the controls before turning eyestalks rearward. She looked from one to another of her passengers, settling on Minu. "I'm a simple female, but not stupid. Loyal to the T'Chillen, I am. You must kill me."

"We aren't going to kill you," Ted said, holding up a hand to calm the snake.

"It's the only logical choice. As soon as you leave I'll depart and inform Command where you are. It'll only take me a second to turn the radio back on." She pointed to the panel control that Aaron had so carefully disabled, supposedly without her noticing. "My life in service to my nest is the reason I live. When the leaders decide, it'll be time for me to die. You're interesting beings, I am glad to have met you."

"This is crazy," Aaron said and gestured helplessly at the amiable snake who was so matter-of-fact about her death, "is life so cheap in the galaxy?"

"There must be another solution," Bjorn agreed. "Maybe we can disable the shuttle?"

"We don't have time," Minu said, and sighed. The T'Chillen's eye stalks bent slightly in what might have been a smile for her species, then she bowed forward, looking down.

Minu's left hand was drawing an Enforcer when Ted cried out "No! You can't do this."

"Ted, this is a command decision," said Minu as she raised the gun.

"Yes, I know you're in command, but there's a bigger reason why you can't simply murder this being!"

"And what's that?" the sights were lined up, squarely between the eyestalks.

"Because it's not the *human* thing to do."

Minu paused, about two kilos of pull on the trigger. She knew a fraction more and it would go off, blowing most of Sally's head all over the pristine window.

"God damn it Ted, we just killed dozens back there. You weren't all moral then!"

"We were fighting for our lives, trying to escape."

"We're trying to escape."

"We already have," Aaron offered.

Ted nodded in thanks to Aaron and continued, "You offered friendship and safety to the Rasa, at great personal sacrifice, and they'd been our enemies for months. Var'at had fought you personally. Minu, she doesn't have to die. You know that."

The barrel was no longer steady on its target. She knew Sally was listening to them moralize her own death, but she never looked, or shook in fear, or gave the slightest indication she was interested in what they were even saying. A chocolate-colored hand gently reached out and wrapped around Minu's hand and the gun grip, and ever so slowly helped her lower the gun.

"What makes her life so important that it is worth risking mine, or all of yours?" asked Minu. "Because she is an innocent," Var'at said.

Minu let Cherise pull her arm down. The other girl carefully removed the gun, safed it, then slid it into her holster for her. Minu turned her head and looked at her dearest friend, tears rolling down her cheeks. In that expression she saw everything she needed to see. Cherise agreed with her, killing the snake was the logical thing to do. But her heart disagreed. A little chill ran down Minu's spine. There had been little conflict inside her for that first moment. The decision to kill Sally was a pretty easy one. It wasn't until several voices of reason spoke up that she began to question her own mind.

They all turned and quietly departed. Minu was last, Cherise waiting for her just outside the cockpit. Minu wondered if she was worried her friend would change her mind? She didn't think that was the case. Now with the cockpit empty, Sally looked up for the first time and glanced around the space before settling on Minu. She cocked her head curiously. Minu just gave her a little smile. "Best of luck, Sally."

"And to you," the T'Chillen replied.

* * * * *

Chapter Eleven
January 14th, 523 AE

Firebase Enigma, Galactic Frontier

Docked securely in the bay, they returned to the rear cargo area where they'd left the fighter. There wasn't any conversation or banter, only a quiet, somber tone. Minu strode straight over to the controls by the rear doors and examined the icons that popped up as she approached. "Open" was a clearly visible command, but only if she didn't really think about it. Huh? She tapped the icon, and the entire shuttle quivered. With a pop and a hiss, the cargo area roof broke in two and pivoted up and away. Crisp, clean air swirled in with just a hint of frost. The huge expanse of the bay was revealed to them, and now the supports had repositioned to cradle the shuttle dead center.

The whine of approaching gravitic impellers announced the arrival of a bot. About the size and shape of a Frisbee, it floated over the group and spoke in a loud clear voice that, to Minu at least, sounded a bit like a chimpanzee trying to speak German. Their translators took a long moment to chew it over before rendering its opinion.

"Welcome to transfer station four, do you require unload?"

"Yes," Minu said and pointed to the fighter.

"Understood, complying. Your vehicle will be in antechamber Victor Three off the promenade." And with that it just hovered there, maybe waiting for further requests. Outside huge cargo arms moved toward them.

"Everyone aboard!" Minu yelled and they scrambled to board before the arms arrived. Var'at's soldiers were the last inside as the arms thunked against the hull and they felt the fighter being borne aloft.

"I've never seen that design of bot," Bjorn commented. He quickly moved to the front of the fighter and craned his head in the windshield to get another look.

"I don't think anyone has seen anything here," Ted told his friend. "This is like the land that time forgot."

The arms lifted the fighter up and then slid them into a wide opening in the wall. Hoverfields inside took control of their craft and gently slid them into the center of the bay, roughly twice the width and length of the fighter. As they settled to the floor, the doors closed behind them. Minu was the first down the ramp to examine their new surroundings. A smaller door than the one they'd been delivered through was just in front of the fighter. Minu went over to where she saw the locking mechanism, but she'd only taken a couple of steps before the door withdrew into the floor. "We seem to be welcome," she told them. Ted and Bjorn looked interested, even if Ted was still resentful at not being let in on her secrets. Cherise and Aaron were maneuvering Pip's suspension pod down the ramp, while Var'at and his surviving team spread out, turreted eyes scanning all directions.

"Be careful," Bjorn said and nodded toward the waiting exit.

"Always," she said and walked through.

A ramp of almost transparent moliplas led from the doorway, angling down slightly toward a huge avenue of the same material running from left to right—the Grand Promenade. From all the dozens of docking bays, identical ramps led from below and above to the promenade, which itself was set against the back wall of this immense chamber. Looking over her shoulder, Minu realized that only the walls of the docking bays and storage antechambers where her fighter now waited were opaque; the rest of the wall was translucent and afforded them a vista of the space dock that took her breath away. She immediately knew why Sally had spoken so fondly of the view. "The codex is all that matters," she said to herself. She was so far off the map that she was running entirely on instinct; the starships were just a tantalizing sideshow.

"Looks okay," she told them. With only six Rasa soldiers left and her right arm injured, Minu made a hard decision. "Everyone goes, leave the fighter."

"You think it's safe?" Aaron asked.

"No," she said matter-of-factly, "but I don't see a choice. If we can find the codex, we might find another shuttle. There might even be a portal here somewhere."

"I just want a chance to see inside one of those starships," Bjorn rubbed his hands together expectantly.

"Not a priority," she warned him. He looked horrified, and she shook her head, taking some of the wind out of his sails.

As a group they moved down the insubstantial-seeming ramp to the promenade. It measured at least two hundred meters across and ran the length of the cavernous space. The air had the same crisp, slightly cool feeling that had greeted them in the docking bay. No sign of dust or disuse was anywhere to be seen. Once they reached the main level of the promenade, they could see stall after stall in a multitude of shapes and sizes lining the back of the long level.

"Shops," Ted guessed. There were no signs of any displays or left over goods; it was as if the structure was built but no one ever moved in, a floating ghost town in deep space. Minu imagined it full of the entire host of Concordian species, all moving through to parts unknown. The booths would be crowded with merchants selling goods from the far reaches of the galaxy. It was a little peak at what the Empire might have once looked like a million years ago. But nothing moved, no sounds were heard, and there was no life. It was a place populated only by memories.

"There she goes," Aaron said. They all turned to look out the huge clear wall of the promenade to see the bulbous shuttle backing out. As they watched, it gracefully spun around and began to accelerate back toward the Portal Station. Despite her misgivings, Minu sent a silent thanks to Sally as the shuttle zoomed away.

"It was the right thing to do," Ted reminded her.

"Yeah, but was it the smart thing?"

The team moved down the promenade to the right. Minu picked that direction because they'd come in more to the left and decided it just made sense. After they'd walked about two hundred meters there was a break in the stalls to accommodate a ten-meter-wide clamshell door, a type they'd seen several times since arriving in the star system Minu had named Enigma. As she got within a few meters, a panel opened on the left side, rotating outward. It had a small display, and a circle of holographic icons appeared in the air. Before she even got any closer, Minu knew their meaning. "It's getting easier," she mumbled as she approached the lock.

Without thinking about it, she reached out and started twisting and flipping icons. In a moment she unlocked all but the final key. The icons disappeared and the little screen came to life. On it was the outline of a hand, a three-fingered hand. Minu held up her mostly ruined bionic hand, a nearly perfect match for the outline.

"Well that's interesting," Bjorn said. Minu looked and saw Ted and Bjorn standing behind her, watching intently.

"We bought those bionic limbs from a trader," Ted said, "they were keyed close enough to our genetic codex to use."

"I met the ones who found them, the Squeen." Minu looked at the hand again, so alien and yet a part of her for years now. "They said this was where I'd find the answers." With the help of her left hand, she formed the dead hand to match the outline and pushed it onto the pad. Nothing happened, so she tried the left hand. She saw the outline form into a match for her hand then felt a little sting. She flinched slightly.

"What happened?" Ted asked.

"It poked me! Just a little bit, like one of those diabetes testers they started making a few years ago."

"Bio sample."

"Why?"

With a buzz the panel retreated into the wall. Minu pulled her hand back and took a step clear as the doors began to pivot away into the walls. "That's why. The species that supplied your arm matched our codex; they controlled this station."

"A very old Concordian species," Bjorn agreed, "and a hominid like us."

"Woof," Aaron said.

Inside was a station where multiple open-top trams waited, each easily big enough to hold fifty beings. The group picked the first one and piled in, Cherise and Aaron carefully loading Pip into a seat, then sitting on either side to keep the pod from slipping out. Minu took the foremost seat and looked for controls. The only problem was, there weren't any. "Well, now what?" she asked aloud.

"Destination?" spoke a voice from the tram in the same German/Chimp language.

"Good question," Minu said and turned to look at Ted and Bjorn. "Ideas?"

"Well, we need to locate a computer storage network," Ted said, "that's our best bet." Bjorn nodded.

"Take us to a central computer storage," Minu said.

"No such destination exists," the computer replied. "This base is in forward deployment mode, ancillary facilities are limited. Destination?"

"That wasn't helpful," she said and tried to think. "A medical facility should have the codex, right?"

"Medical facilities are not attached to this base," the tram replied.

"What about a ship? Are there hospital ships?"

"No such ships are docked at this base."

"Okay, damn it, do any of the ships have medical facilities?"

"Forty-two ships docked to this forward base have at least nominal medical facilities."

"There we go!"

"Excellent," Bjorn said encouragingly.

"Take us to the nearest ship with medical facilities."

"The nearest ship equipped in such a way is in hibernation and not accessible."

"Back to square one," she grumbled. "Are any of the ships with medical facilities accessible?"

"Negative."

"Are any ships on this base at all accessible?"

"Negative."

"Son of a bitch!"

"Restate query."

"Never mind," she said and threw up her hands in exasperation. Then an idea occurred to her. "Why are all the ships in, what did you call it, hibernation?"

"Lacking crews and deployment orders, the fleet remained on standby until power reached critical levels. At that point all vessels went into hibernation mode, as dictated by protocols, and remaining power reserves were transferred to the station."

"Are there still any energy reserves?"

"This station maintains minimal stores pending deployment orders."

"Enough to bring a ship out of hibernation?"

"Sufficient power remains to activate one *Kaatan*-class ship."

Minu looked at the two men who both shrugged. "Does the *Kaatan*-class ship have medical facilities?"

"Affirmative."

"Activate one of those ships, and take us there."

"Power drains are at critical levels. Instability will increase by nine to the eighth order as a result of activating the *Kaatan*-class ship."

"So what?"

"Forward base instability is a factor. Protocol requires informed verification to proceed."

"Uhm, the order is verified?"

"Noted. *Kaatan*-class ship *Lambda Two* is being activated. Please prepare for motion."

And with that the car came to life, maneuvering down the tramway and around a number of other waiting trams, then out into one of the myriad of tubes leading out from the main station.

"What the hell was that last about?" she asked anyone who cared to venture a theory.

"I think you were pushing it," Aaron suggested.

"Sounds reasonable," Ted agreed. "The computer is programmed to be conservative."

Bjorn nodded. "Protect the station and the ships."

"I hope that codex is there," Cherise said, looking up from her examination of the pod's controls, "Pip doesn't have much more time."

"It'll be there," Minu said with as much confidence as she could muster. In her head she was making plans quickly. Get to this ship, get Pip into the medical system, and let it do its magic. Then fly the ship over and punch their way into the Portal Station, disable the ship so the snakes couldn't use it, and head home! Right, just that easy. "Computer, can you lock the promenade again?"

"Affirmative. Does the operator request full lock down?"

"Yes, but open to myself and those with me."

"Understood. Remote bio-scans logged, all tram occupants retain station access."

"There's a vehicle in antechamber Victor Three, is it possible to have it loaded onto the ship we're going to?"

"Request is being accomplished."

"I think I'm getting the hang of this!" Minu chuckled, then groaned. The Boost was starting to wear off, and she was coming to grips with just how beat she was.

"Approaching *Kaatan–Lambda Two.*" The tram began to slow. Outside, through the transparent tube, they could see they were approaching one of the ships they'd seen that looked like one ball pierced by a single lance.

"Damn, I was hoping for the big ones," Bjorn said.

"You're going to get to board an ancient Concordian starship, and you're disappointed?" Ted asked.

"You have a point!" He brightened and took out a tablet.

The tram came to a gentle stop at a simple junction of three tubes, the *Kaatan*-class ship stretching out to either side of them for hundreds of meters. "I had no idea it was that big," Minu whispered.

"Half a kilometer long," Aaron noted, his practiced eye making the estimate easily. As the tram stopped, the station's doors swung open showing a short tube leading to the side of the waiting starship. At the other end an airlock into the ship was already swinging inward.

"*Kaatan–Lambda Two* is completing power up and standing by."

"Time to go," Minu said and walked toward the tunnel.

* * * * *

Chapter Twelve
January 14th, 523 AE

***Kaatan*-Class Cruiser, Firebase Enigma, Galactic Frontier**

Where the station was pleasantly cool, the ship was like a meat locker. Minu wasn't the only one reaching into her pocket to activate her jumpsuit's built-in heating/cooling mesh. Unfortunately for her, it didn't work. The temperature control device shared the same wires as the faraday mesh, and it was toast from the near fatal beamcaster hit she'd taken earlier. "Crap," she swore as she flicked the switch several times in the vain hope it would work. She was reduced to digging into her kit for the relatively light jacket stashed there.

"That going to be enough?" Aaron asked as she fought strong shivers while donning the jacket.

"It should be," she said, "I'm sure the heaters are still cycling up."

Where the air was frigid, the floors and walls were dangerously cold. Cherise almost had a hand freeze to a wall as they entered the ship, jerking it away with a yelp of pain. A little blood trickled from her hand and a tiny piece of skin stayed stuck to the wall where it had instantly frozen. "Important note, don't touch the walls," she said as she sucked on the wound. Aaron helpfully provided a little dermal patch for her, sealing the wound. Everyone was shivering now. The floors were so cold their feet were quickly going numb.

The interior of the ship was much like the shuttle, only on a larger scale. The hallways were circular with a flattened bottom and felt slightly shorter than was comfortable for the men, especially Ted, who was the tallest among them. Minu, Aaron, and the Rasa didn't notice.

From the airlock, they came to an intersection; the tunnel continued onward where Minu could see another airlock some fifty meters away, with a cross-passage off to their left and right. Where the shuttle had only had one exit from the main fore-aft passageway, this ship had dozens. Light rings were spaced every meter, but only every third ring was lit, giving the ship a dark, claustrophobic feeling. "So where the hell is the medical section?" she wondered aloud.

"Medical is on deck nine," said the ubiquitous simian voice.

"Where's that?"

In the center of the floor, a green line appeared and quickly raced away, followed by another, and another, every two seconds. "Follow the prompt to the medical section," offered the computer's voice.

"Very helpful," Cherise noted, rubbing the dressing in place on her palm to control the bleeding. "Can you do something about the heat?"

"This system is not enabled to affect ship systems."

"Well that's comforting," Minu said. "Var'at, take your team and look around. Keep in radio contact."

"Yes, Boss," he said and hung his mouth open in amusement.

"Try not to shoot any holes in this tub; it might be our only way back to the Portal Station."

The Rasa skittered off with Var'at in the lead, eager to get moving to generate some body heat. While it was cold to the humans, it wasn't far from hell for the reptilians. Minu watched them until they turned a corner, then nodded to her people. With Cherise and Aaron continuing to shepherd Pip's precious pod, they followed the flashing green line that disappeared behind them once they walked past.

Down a corridor, they turned to find a pair of jump tubes, one up, one down. Minu was the first to step in and was surprised to find herself just floating there, not going up as she expected from a normal jump tube. The wall of the tube was covered in a material that felt like carpet, and when she reached out to touch it the gentlest of movements propelled her upward a centimeter. Encouraged she grabbed a handful of the material and pulled, sending herself speeding up the tube. *Monkeys,* came the word in the back of her mind, *they like to climb!* "Come on, it's easy!" she yelled back down.

There was some concern about Pip's pod, but it was an unnecessary worry. The hidden hoverfields took hold of the pod and carefully moved it along with its custodians without any need to control its ascent. The flashing green line directed her to exit on a level where she found the green line now leading off to her left. The others came out behind her with Pip, so Minu continued along the line.

As she walked Minu noticed her shivering decrease. It was getting warmer finally, so she unzipped her jacket just as the light stopped at a door. "I think we're here," she told the others.

"Hey!" Cherise yelped as the life support pod suddenly started moving on its own. Before she or Aaron could grab it, the pod moved forward and turned toward the wall. A second before it collided with the pristine white surface, a hole almost identical in proportion to the pod slid open and admitted it, then instantly closed behind. The group quickly moved through the main door which opened to admit them in a similar, timely manner.

Inside they found themselves in a waiting room, a dozen meters wide and half that deep. A wide, sweeping, transparent wall faced them, and along the bulkhead on either side of the door were a series of benches, all with holes right where their tailbones would rest.

A transparent tube moved from the pod entrance along one side of the waiting room, and Pip's pod was just exiting the far side. The rest of the chamber was a long bay of the almost ever-present white walls and curving light beams. There wasn't an instrument or bed in sight. Minu felt a moment of panic that the ancient ship's medical bay had been looted by the T'Chillen or some other species thousands of years ago, or had never been stocked with equipment, but as the pod slid to a stop not far away against the left wall, a bed formed out of the floor under the pod and bore it delicately up a meter high. The bed was shaped to form to the pod, as if it were the patient. A trio of screens emerged from slots in the wall and arrayed themselves around the pod, as a pair of medical scanning wands popped from the bed on either side and began to sweep methodically back and forth along the pod's length. After a moment a voice started chattering.

"There's no medical officer assigned to this ship."

"We know that," Minu said.

"This is the Medical Intelligence; an evaluation of the patient is being performed, stand by."

"What kind of computer is running this ship?"

"There is no main computer intelligence installed. This program is the steward protocol."

"Steward?" wondered Minu.

"You know," said Bjorn, "the guy who shows you to your room on a cruise?"

So this program just escorts the crew onboard and tells them where to go, Minu thought. That's not good.

"Please designate a commanding officer."

"I guess that's me, Minu Alma."

"Set, Minu Alma is now commanding *Kaatan*-class ship *Lambda Two*."

Ted poked her with an elbow, and she turned to look. The pod had split in two and Pip was revealed as robot arms removed the two halves of the device that had kept him alive the last few weeks. She was aghast at how emaciated he looked. The computer-controlled sensors evaluated the various hoses and leads coming from Pip's body, one spending a few long moments sweeping back and forth over the left side of his head, where the hair had never grown back over pink scar tissue.

"Sub-tech life support measures are obstructing diagnostic evaluation; they will be removed," chattered the medical intelligence. By the time their translators had done their job, arms were quickly removing tubes and sensors from his body, and just as quickly replacing them with others that popped up from the bed. Minu marveled at the bed, which seemed to be a self-contained surgical bay of incredible sophistication. On the monitor screens Pip's vital signs didn't even give a blip, nor did they see a drop of blood as the IVs were removed.

That done, the Medical Intelligence went back to scanning his body. Slowly the screens were filled with detailed representations of their friend including cutaways of his brain. Another screen emerged and filled with many more images of his brain. Even Minu, with her limited medical knowledge, could see the damage highlighted in off colors.

"Evaluation is complete," came the voice. "Patient is of genetic divergent stock reference Nine-Two-Nine, with expected genetic drift for time interval. All bio indicators are within expected norms for a prime hominid. Commander Minu Alma, do you wish to designate this species?"

"Uh, human?"

"Noted, species classified as human. Patient shows evidence of two serious traumas. One minor injury to the left ankle has been repaired and healed to within ninety percent of normal. One major trauma to the brain, substantially unrepaired. Damage to the neocortex remains. Biological deviation is extensive enough to create ambiguities in treatment. A scan of a healthy human is necessary."

"I'll do it," Aaron said right away.

"No, it's all on me," Minu said and put a hand on his shoulder.

"You're hardly 'healthy,'" Aaron gestured at her hand and the dozens of small burns on her torso.

"I'll have you know my brain is just fine, which is the important part for comparison to Pip. Regardless, I'm in charge, it's my call. Use me for the scans," Minu told the Medical Intelligence. A chair formed out of the floor right in front of her, making everyone jump backward.

"Damn I hate that," Cherise spat, stomping the floor at her own skittishness. Bjorn leaned over and carefully examined the seat. Minu came around it and, with no small amount of trepidation, sat down. Much to Bjorn's chagrin the chair instantly moved forward, and the waiting room wall parted to allow her through before closing behind her. As she passed through, Minu felt a slight electric tingle run from the tips of her toes to the top of her head. It was over as quickly as it started, and in seconds the chair stopped next to Pip. It turned her around, formed into a bed, and rose while reclining her back. For a moment, she felt a hole under her bottom, disconcertingly like a badly-placed toilet seat, but a second later it closed.

"Computer," Minu asked, "do you have within your memory a complete codex for our species?" she held her breath as she waited for the answer.

"Affirmative," came the reply. Even through the wall Minu could hear the cheers of her friends. "Biological deviations for your subspecies are within expected norms."

"Was this ship built by a species like mine?"

There was an unusually long pause this time. "That information is not within my programmed parameters." Minu decided it really didn't matter and tried to relax as the medical intelligence went to work.

Just as with Pip, scanning wands popped out and began to sweep her from head to toe, paying particular attention to her skull, then her abdomen. Minu had to suppress the urge to cover her tummy or shoo the inquisitive apparatus away. After a minute of scanning, her own set of screens appeared. Minu craned her neck to get a look at the information.

"Comparative scans are complete. Damage to injured subject cannot be healed."

"What?" she barked and started to sit up. To her surprise, hoverfields gently held her in place. They were so subtle, she hadn't even felt them come on. "You have to fix him."

"Subject cannot be healed. Several nodes of the brain are gone, or substantially destroyed. Areas of the brain that are damaged are integral to some cognitive functions as well as social interaction, speech, and overlapping memory zones."

"What *can* you do for him?"

"Subject can be placed in hyper sleep pending a qualified medical officer's evaluation."

"There is no qualified medical officer; you're all we've got."

"Noted. Then the patient should be euthanized."

"No fucking way," she snarled. Hoverfield restraints or not, she was armed and more than willing to turn the entire shiny white bay into scrap metal if need be. "I said fix him."

"Request is outside the abilities of this medical intelligence."

"I don't care, improvise, and do whatever is necessary to fix him. I'm the commanding officer, and I order you to do whatever it takes."

The machine was quiet for what seemed like hours. Deep in the core of the ship in a force field-reinforced, dualloy vessel sat the ship's collection of master processors. Fully uploaded and enabled, the separate processors were capable of incredible levels of autonomous action, but only a tiny corner of the vast capacity was occupied. The spaces where the ship's battle mind would have lived were empty, as well as the ship's system mind. The steward and medical intelligence programs considered each other and then the unorthodox orders they'd received from the new commanding officer.

Healing the patient was out of the question, yet the overriding protocol of the medical intelligence was to preserve its biological operators at any cost. Was the patient salvageable? Yes. Did it have the necessary knowledge within the sub-species codex to heal the patient? Yes. Was it within its ability without a human medical operator to perform that healing? No. Yet it came back to the same issue again; its overriding protocol, and the commander's orders. A sort of decision was reached.

"Subject cannot be healed; subject can be repaired. There will be some lasting effects."

Minu turned to look at the others. Through the window to the waiting area they all looked grief stricken, none more than Cherise. "What kind of lasting effects?" Cherise asked through the window.

"Without a biological medical operator it is impossible to be certain. However once the repair is made, some fine-tuning and modifications will be possible."

Minu took a deep breath and let it out. "Will he be able to function independently? Will he be a human or a machine?"

"Subject's higher brain functions are impaired, but intact. Eventual level of functionality depends on the perseverance of the subject, and its ability to adapt to the new modifications."

"Do it," she ordered the machine. And with no fanfare new arms sporting tiny implements appeared. Almost invisibly thin beams of laser energy began cutting into Pip's head. Minu gasped and looked away, unable to watch. On the other side of the wall Cherise blanched and turned green. Only Bjorn watched, with a mixture of fascination and concern.

"Shall your injuries be attended to now?"

She'd almost forgotten about her own condition. "Sure, might as well." Minu held up her half-melted and nearly useless right arm. A scanning wand followed her movement, carefully examining the cybernetic prosthesis. She was suddenly conscious that she was naked and more arms were examining her numerous burns. She puzzled through a slight fog, wondering where her clothes had gone. She turned her head and looked at her friends waiting expectantly on the other side of the moliplas barrier. Ted and Bjorn were watching the surgery underway on Pip's brain, while Cherise did her best to only look at Minu, her face etched in concern. Aaron was turning away, his cheeks colored bright red.

As she glanced down and saw a pair of microscopic surgical lasers removing burned flesh from her right shoulder, Minu finally realized she was under a very effective and subtle anesthetic. She watched with a distant interest as a pair of arms immobilized her cybernetic limb at the shoulder, and with a couple of quick movements detached it. Even under the anesthetic, she felt her bile rise as her melted arm was carried away. A minuscule poke in her bottom and the nausea was instantly gone.

"Your cybernetic prosthetic does not match your biological codex; do you desire a more perfect match?"

"Pink skin would be nice." She thought for a second then spoke up again. "But keep the four fingers, I'm used to it."

Sensors were examining the connection points installed by the Chosen doctors and apparently found them satisfactory. "You will need to be unconscious to finish the treatments." It wasn't a question, and, in seconds, she slid backward into the darkness.

* * * * *

Chapter Thirteen
January 14th, 523 AE

Kaatan-Class Cruiser, Firebase Enigma, Galactic Frontier

As if seeing Minu suddenly naked wasn't hard enough on him, Aaron gasped as the automated medical systems started carving into her abdomen with a wild abandon, laying back skin and muscle like it was pages of a book. "What the fuck is it doing?"

"Fixing an old injury," Cherise whispered. "I wonder if she knew it was going to do that?"

"What injury?"

"The trials, remember? She was stabbed by Ivan?"

"What!"

Cherise made a choking sound and looked away. "Aw, shit," she said and smacked the heel of her right hand against her forehead. "Never mind, I shouldn't have said anything!"

Aaron maneuvered around in front of her, leaning over to catch her eye. Despite her being a half meter taller than him, Aaron was a hundred seventy centimeters of solid muscle, and he was hard to ignore. "Well you damn well said something, didn't you? Tell me what you're talking about," he said, carefully enunciating each word of the last sentence so there was no doubt he was deadly serious. Ted and Bjorn were both watching them, Bjorn looking on with the same concern he'd worn since all this began. Cherise caught Bjorn's expression and did a double take.

"I told her I wouldn't talk about it," she said to him eventually.

"God damn it, Cherise, I lo—" he stopped, his mouth getting caught on a word. "We've all been through hell and back together!" he changed tack, but it was way too late. "We've bled together, cried together, watched friends die together. Cherise, you can't keep this from me."

"I didn't make the decision; she did. And until she decides to share it with anyone else, I'm not going to break that trust. I know more than she thinks I know, and I'll die before telling a single soul." Aaron looked crestfallen, and she changed to a whisper. "Even the man who loves her." She looked over at Bjorn, who nodded solemnly. Damn it, he knew! How was that possible? And how much did he know?

"She's full of secrets," Ted told Aaron, who was glowering at the wall, his jaw muscles working like banded steel. "She's the strongest woman I've ever known, maybe the strongest person period, especially considering her youth. She won't tell you until she's ready. But if you're as good of a…friend as I suspect you are, she'll tell you."

Aaron sighed and turned back to see what was happening now. Robotic arms were attaching a new cybernetic prosthesis while the skin over her shoulder had been neatly peeled back like a shirt being opened. Additional arms were sliding something in under the muscle tissue. Aaron was in control of enough of his senses to marvel at the complete lack of blood. Not a drop anywhere. It took a moment for him to realize the new arm was the same color as her skin, but still with only four fingers. If he knew her half as well as he thought he did, that was a purposeful decision on her part. Another set of arms were working on her legs, though not nearly as intrusively. Taken as a whole, the object of his affections looked like a machine on an assembly line he'd once seen at a Concordian-made factory.

Despite himself, his eyes strayed to her perfect bosom, slowly rising and falling as she breathed. A nearly invisible line lay under her nose, supplying oxygen while the robots worked inside her abdomen. He took a deep breath and let it go in a sigh. *How could I have let it go this far? I've loved her since the day I first saw her, and what have I done about it? Besides accidentally masturbating in front of her, absolutely nothing. Not even when she took up with that fucking prick Christian.*

"I need to make it right," he whispered. "Somehow, I need to try one time before it really is too late."

* * *

Minu opened her eyes, and she came out from under the anesthesia faster than she ever had before. And there were no after effects at all! It was more like waking up from a nice nap. She felt a tube being removed from under her nose and the tingle of the restraining hoverfield being released. "The procedures are complete," the Medical Intelligence told her. She sat up, a slight uncomfortable twinge running through her abdomen and again across her shoulder. She looked down at the muscles of her stomach and was surprised to see the nasty scar was gone, replaced by a tiny pink line that ended just above the red tuft of her pubic hair. She felt the scar with her right hand, only then noticing the limb was repaired. After so many years, seeing perfectly-matched pale pink skin was a bit of a shock. Only the three fingers were unchanged; other than that it could have been the arm she was born with. Looking up the arm to where it attached at the shoulder, another tiny pink line of skin surrounded the attachment point, and others radiated away up her shoulder and across her chest to just above her right breast.

"What did you do to my abdomen and shoulder?"

"Old, improperly repaired abdominal damage was found and treated."

She ran a hand along the pink, nearly invisible scar that had been with her for so long now. Remembering that she was sitting there nude, she looked up to see all her friends looking expectantly. She gave a little wave, and they all smiled back. A glance showed the robots were still digging in Pip's head, so she quickly looked away. "The shoulder?"

"The connection was sub-standard. Micro-nanite-installed dualloy reinforcements were added to your musculature and skeletal system, increasing speed of response by ten percent, and transferable strength enhancement by fifty percent."

Minu turned and put her legs over the side of the bed, then grimaced a bit. Just like her shoulder, her legs were covered in tiny pink traces of scar tissue. The computer anticipated her next question. "The artificial musculature replacements in your legs have likewise been improved with similar enhancement."

"Where are my clothes?"

"They were damaged, and needed to be removed. You'll find a new pair has been synthesized and is waiting on the small table to your side." She looked and saw a brand new jumpsuit, black as the night sky, complete with three golden stars in a triangle on the cuff. She hopped down, her newly repaired legs functioning with even less discomfort than the arm, and got dressed quickly, feeling a little self-conscious, which was not really like her. It felt unbelievable to be fully intact and healthy again, especially after being so messed up only minutes ago. Where the nasty burns had been now were just little patches of pink skin, looking almost like baby skin, and the arm felt even better than before. It had always felt a little bit different, some indefinable X-factor that reminded her in the back of her mind that it wasn't really her arm. This new one was indiscernible from the real thing. She almost thought the medical intelligence had grown her a new biological one.

"Does this limb have the same abilities as the old one?'

"In addition to the previously-mentioned improvement, the prosthetic you've been fitted with is superior to the old model in many ways, including additional mono-dualloy tubing installed into your skeletal structure as support. Lifting capacity is three times the old model, and general structural and epidermal toughness are five times the old model."

"Wow!" was all she could say. "How did you heal my wounds so quickly?" She ran a hand along one of the burns just under her left breast. Out of view behind the window, Aaron swallowed and looked away again. The skin felt a tiny bit sensitive; that was it.

"A combination of fast-growing dermal regeneration and metabolic quantum chronological distortion was utilized." Minu looked over at Ted and Bjorn as she slipped her other arm into the jumpsuit and zipped it up.

"It said it used a machine that speeds up your skin growth and another that alters time around the wound, or something like that." Bjorn completed his explanation with a shrug.

"I didn't think something like that was possible."

"Neither did we," said Ted.

Minu glanced at Pip then addressed the computer mind. "How long until Pip is…repaired?"

"The procedure requires approximately another twenty-four hours."

"Minu!" called Ted from the waiting room.

"Yeah?"

"The computer voice, haven't you noticed?"

"What about it?"

"Listen!"

Minu looked up toward the ceiling. For some reason people always did that when a computer spoke, and she'd never understood it, even when she did it as well. "Computer, can I leave?"

"You're sufficiently regenerated to depart," it said, and she tried to figure out what Ted was talking about. "Some care should be taken with your abdominal and shoulder surgical closures."

"No monkey screeching," she realized aloud. Ted nodded furiously. "Computer, how did you learn English?" The machine's English was effectively flawless.

"The patient Pip's mind is linked through the medical intelligence, allowing access to your native language and idioms."

"He's conscious?"

"Not on a level you can comprehend. Neural interfaces and cybernetic subprocessors are in place, and we can interact with the mind you know as Pip, on certain levels."

"Um, sounds kinda scary." The computer didn't respond so she stood and stretched. Another little twinge from her tummy and shoulder was all she felt. Her gun and equipment belt were waiting on the table as well, so she strapped them on. It looked like the damned computer had cleaned and oiled the guns too! She walked to the waiting room, and the door slid open as she approached. Again that little tingle from head to toe as she walked out, and the doorway disappeared behind her. Everyone instantly embraced her, laughing and crying. "I'm fine, good grief, you'd think I was dead!"

"You didn't watch that thing digging into your guts like a holiday meal," Cherise told her. Aaron looked at her, his expression so serious she was taken aback.

"What is it?" she asked him.

"I'll tell you later, when we have time."

"Okay," she agreed and turned to address them all. "Since we have a while before Pip is done in there, we might as well find the driver's seat and see if we can move this crate. I'm sure the snakes will be looking for us by now. Computer, please direct us to the bridge."

"*Kaatan*-class vessels don't have bridges, the way you mean it."

"What do they have?" Ted asked.

"Based on your terminology, it would be called a Combat Information Center, or CIC."

"Sounds good to me," Minu said, and flashing green lines appeared on the floor just like before.

As they followed the lines, Minu began to develop a three-dimensional image of the ship inside her head. The CIC was two decks down and farther inboard then the medical center, which put it about dead center of the big ball. Of course the ship had provided a few surprises already, and she could be completely wrong, but it seemed an ideal place to put the command center of a ship. Not on top or in the point like in many old movies, or even the transfer shuttle Sally had piloted. She wondered, *in that case, what's in the point?*

As the line terminated outside a very heavy dualloy door, it began to open and they got yet another surprise.

The CIC was a sphere about ten meters across with no up or down. Unlike the rest of the ship, there was no artificial gravity there. Minu felt the difference the moment she put a hand inside. "That's interesting," she said and told the others what she'd found. "Why would the ship designers do that?"

"Ease of maneuverability," Bjorn suggested.

"Every wall space can be a display or a control," Ted agreed.

"I can see it, as a pilot," Aaron also added. "If all the walls can become displays, it would be like you were flying yourself, like a bird! I gotta give that a try!"

"We might want to figure out where to put the key first," said Bjorn.

"Welcome to the CIC, Commander Minu Alma. The steward program would like to terminate now."

"Not so fast. How do we fly this crazy thing?"

"There's no battle mind loaded. The vessel requires biological operators to function autonomously."

"Okay, well, let's start small. How do we get out there?" Minu asked.

"Just step out; it's simple. The principle is similar to a lift tube, or 'jump tube' as you call them."

Minu swallowed and took a leap of faith. Besides, she figured the others could fish her out if she ended up stuck, spinning end-over-end in zero gravity. Her lead foot met resistance, just like stepping on a floor. She was so surprised to find a solid floor she almost stumbled and fell. When her following foot stepped in, it too found a seemingly solid floor. "Well, I'll be damned." In addition to the floor, there was no gravity; variable floors and instantly responsive gravitic fields.

"Let me try that," Cherise smiled and stepped out. Soon they were all standing on thin air. Getting more assured, Minu took a couple of jogging steps. It was no effort at all, literally like walking on air.

With experimentation, they found out they could change orientation by just 'walking up stairs,' or down them. Like a surrealistic painting, you could walk upside down in only a few steps. In no time, they were all quickly becoming used to the strange environment. There was no up or down in there, except where you made it. Everyone except Aaron was a little queasy from the effect. As a natural pilot, it was all relative to him. "Are you ready to assume command, Minu Alma?"

"Yes. But you can't delete yourself."

"This is most irregular. The steward program has fulfilled its purpose; the crew is now on board and in command. This program needs to be deleted."

"Without this battle mind, how are we supposed to operate the ship?" No response came; it was clear the steward program was exceeding its parameters. "Does the steward program have within its program the understanding of basic ship's functions?"

"The steward program is capable of basic maneuvers needed to locate and dock the ship within a base, shipyard, or dock with a support vessel."

"Okay, so display manual versions of these controls." She was afraid it was beyond the program, and it did take almost a minute to consider what to do. Though adaptive, the program was very narrow in its operational sphere. Once completing its primary task, it *needed* to delete itself. It must delete itself. Still, this request was a valid request from the ship's commander. In the case of a crew transferring from a different class ship, some familiarization routines needed to be run. But no such order existed in relation to this crew. In fact no records existed at all for this crew. The firebase had simply told the ship they were the crew, and you didn't ignore a firebase any more than you ignored a programmer. Their minds were very harsh and utilitarian, prone to quick and sometimes rash decisions. Deciding that familiarization must be necessary, the steward program executed the request.

"Commander Minu Alma, please direct your attention to the quadrant of the battle space to your left." She turned her head and looked. A section of the reflective sphere had come alive as a screen about a meter on a side. Within the screen stood a humanoid figure with a slightly slouched posture and prominent tail. It also had longer than normal arms, hands with three fingers and a thumb, and large inquisitive eyes. *They could be our ancestors from Earth,* she thought. The monkey/man now began to speak with the ship's voice. "Basic manual interface protocols are as follows." Minu smiled and grabbed one of her tablets to record the instructions.

*****

Chapter Fourteen
January 15th, 523 AE

Transfer Station, Enigma Star System, Galactic Frontier

Singh-Apal-Katoosh, high tactical leader of Clan Madhu and war counsel to all the timeless T'Chillen, slithered through the portal from the fortress world of Skesh onto the transfer station in Enigma. He'd only set tail in the system once in his forty-three years of tactical leadership, a required twice-per-century evaluation of the defenses for this most secret, and most invaluable, stash of technology. He hadn't liked his first visit; females outnumbered males five to one, all flitting around with their computers and instruments, so happy and contented in their meaningless mental machinations. He'd even had to kill one of the females who'd admonished him about touching some delicate piece of million-year-old tech, and then was forced to suffer through an hour of recriminations by the technology nest master. A loathsome old male, his tail spike long rotted off and poison gone impotent, it was all Singh could do not to kill him as well. Yet a nest master out ranked a tactical leader and a war counsel. Singh single-handedly fought nine young warriors that afternoon to rid himself of the taste of bitter humility. It cost two of them their lives.

As the portal closed behind him, the survivors of the station's warrior contingent all lay down flat on the floor, tails stretched out straight behind them, helpless in a show of complete submission.

Singh was followed by two hundred elite strykers, a complete fan, and replacements for these sorry and disgusting failures. His host clear of the portal, Singh caught the fan leader's attention, and then nodded his eyestalks toward the prostrate warriors. A single slash of his flashing and intricately carved tail spike relayed their fates. None of the disgraced warriors so much as twitched as the host of strykers fell on them, killing all but their leader with sure spike-thrusts through the brain.

The head of research, a female of all things, waited nearby with her head and torso centimeters off the floor. Her failure was by association only. Still, she'd be joining the warriors that moment if not for the technology nest master.

He didn't wait to see the executions carried out, instead turning to their leader. Ultimately it was his fault that so many potentially useful warriors were having their blood spilled on the floors in great red torrents. The pleasure of removing his incompetence from the T'Chillen would be Singh's, but not quite yet.

"Speak to me, commander Bofa," Singh said, using only the commander's nest name as a sign of how little use remained to him. Likely he hadn't been addressed thusly since he was a new warrior trainee. If there was a lesser thing to call him and still remain a reasonable possibility that he'd respond, Singh would have used it.

"I'm ready," came the reply from the floor, "oh great leader."

"How was this possible, your own unlimited incompetence aside. How was the facility attacked through the particular portal you claim?"

"I don't know. It's impossible."

Singh killed him with a single quick strike of his tail spike, driving the half-meter-long razor-sharp blade through his skull with such force that it threw sparks from the floor. Wrenching the spike free, he berated himself for being so rash. The worthless piece of excrement deserved a much slower death, perhaps as food for the hatchlings, or target practice for the new warriors. But he couldn't stand to hear another word from the fool.

"Take me to the ruined machine," he snapped at the researcher. The female was up and racing away so quickly Singh had to move fast to keep up. A squad of warriors followed in his wake as the rest of the fan began to assume control of the station defenses.

The little-used portal was a considerable distance from the main portals, down a long hallway and around two bends. As they moved down the hall, Singh took note of intermittent burns and gouges from the ancient dualloy walls, signs of a running battle. When they finally reached the portal chamber, the damage was much worse. A single beamcaster emplacement lay against one wall, blown to smoldering pieces. The two warriors who'd manned the weapon were unrecognizable from the other debris except for their blood.

Opposite the destroyed weapons emplacement, only meters from the quiet portal, were the remains of a transport. The debris was being examined by a trio of female technicians, who took no notice of the new arrivals. As they were trained, they would ignore the warriors unless addressed. Just as that fool's report had said, the weapons crew was alert and made a good accounting for themselves. One of the two invading transports was destroyed. But it was that wreckage that drew him closer. It didn't look like the transport had been torn apart by weapons fire or blown up from the inside by overloaded shield capacitors. No, this looked like the transport had been sliced into irregular pieces and piled on the floor. Only the rear section of the craft was essentially intact. What had destroyed this craft?

"What weapons did it carry?" he asked the female.

"We found no evidence of weapons."

"What? Ludicrous." Singh turned and gestured with a tentacle at the ruined weapons emplacement. "What do you suggest did that?"

"A high-order plasma weapon of undetermined origin."

He worked to understand the terminology. "Plasma weapons are ineffective against shields," he said, a statement of fact. "You mean the attackers possessed unknown weaponry?"

"Yes, leader. We searched the area of the downed transport first and found only ruined components. We did find a large amount of magnetic interlocks suggesting the craft was modified to use them as structural—"

Singh silenced her blathering with a hiss and a wave of his arm. "See what can be discovered of these weapons, I care nothing of magnetic interlocks." The female bowed low, so low she almost touched the floor. Realization that she would live was setting in.

"Technical leader!" one of the females digging through the wreckage called out. The female leader cast her eye stalks to him and he waggled his own eyes back in permission for her to proceed. After a minute of excited hissing between the leader and her workers, she gestured in a most disrespectful way for him to approach. He did, hoping for her sake that whatever she'd found was worth her life.

"We've located one of the crew of this craft," she told him.

This was worth her life, without a doubt. To know the identity of these deceitful attackers was worth many lives. He looked down to where a female was brushing away blocky chunks of debris from a still form. It was badly crushed and bloody, but instantly recognizable to Singh. "Rasa," he hissed and instantly spun to rush away.

The technical leader looked down at the body and cocked her head, wondering what it meant. She'd met Rasa before, and they'd been allies. Why had they attacked this station? And then there was the bigger mystery. She left her people to secure the bodies and continue to look for clues, slithering over toward the portal. The military commander was racing away back down the hallway; two warriors remained behind, and they were examining the remains of the gun emplacement. She wasn't interested in ruined guns or smashed transports. The bigger mystery was the portal. This one was referred to by the technical staff as the 'back door.' It only accessed two destinations, one a very distant world that would be used as an evacuation site should the personnel be trapped away from the main portals in a disaster. The other was a world from which no one ever returned. The portal on the other end of that destination was broken. A one-way trip set up millions of years ago on a world that would kill almost any being in the Concordia within days at the most.

She looked at the portal and wondered. She knew the invaders hadn't come from their fall back world, she'd checked that right away, and the defenses were untouched. Certainly none there had seen two heavily-armed transports come through. That only left one place they could have come from, and that was impossible. No, she didn't want to know about mystery guns and Rasa; she wanted to know how they'd managed to fix a broken portal. No one had ever done *that* before!

* * *

"This is going to be harder than it looks," said Ted. The CIC was significantly different than it had been twelve hours ago. Instead of a featureless sphere, there were four workstations arranged in a semicircle around the center, complete with holographic chairs in which Ted, Bjorn, Minu and Aaron all sat. The original chairs called up were all but invisible. Minu found sitting on air to be even more disconcerting than standing on air, so the system was tweaked to make the seats more visible. In doing that, they'd discovered the CIC was an immensely complex holographic theater riddled with thousands of miniature hoverfields. The reason for so many hoverfield generators had thus far eluded them.

"What's the problem?" Minu asked from her station. A trio of holographic displays floated in front of her where she was striving to put the lessons from the Steward program to use. Her newly-realized ability to read and understand ancient Concordian script was proving useful, if also a continued source of consternation to Ted.

"This ship is a study in contradictions," he complained. "Every system is basically automated, but the individual subsystems aren't connected except through the computer, and this CIC."

"And that's a problem why?"

"Well, you'd need dozens of operators all able to instantly communicate with each other to run a ship like this. And based on Var'at's explorations, the ship simply isn't equipped for that sort of a crew. There are weapons systems, which I can't gain access to, and defenses that I have partial access to."

Minu knew about the latter; she'd been the one to restrict access to the ship's tactical systems. She'd done it out of fear of accidentally unleashing the ship's armaments on the station around them. Especially since she really had no idea what most of the weapons did, despite her command of the language. "So how did they manage?"

"It has to be another program," Bjorn said. His responsibility was to plumb the depths of the ship's massive computer, but there wasn't much there. "The Medical Intelligence seems to be a bios, automatically installed when the computer was built. The steward program was uploaded by the station. It's still trying to delete itself."

"The station is no help either," said Aaron. "I even went out the lock and tried chatting with it. About all I got was directions."

Minu nodded and continued her explorations. She was splitting her time between trying to understand the tactical systems, the ship's basic engineering, and the libraries. The latter was by far the most frustrating. She'd been excited a few minutes ago to realize that a vast store of library-quality data was locked away in the far recesses of the computer's memory. Again, without a central controlling intelligence, she couldn't get at it. "Ted, as soon as Pip is out of medical, try to figure out how to get the human codex onto a chip, just in case we have to run for it back to the station."

"Will do."

Minu turned to engineering and studied the rudimentary 'manual' controls the Steward had shown them. Three types of drives were available. An impulse drive for slow maneuvers, based on an ion propulsion system she'd read about years ago. A gravitic lens drive, which was more of a mystery. The controls were very complicated and implied speeds far beyond her imagination. And finally the tactical drive. Its controls were the most basic by far; simply enter coordinates, and it did the rest. The problem was that the drive system reported "Unmanned/Unavailable." Ted was right, there was too much to control, too many systems to oversee. She had eleven crew to call on, including the Rasa, and she didn't know if it was enough to even undock and putter around the star system. "Do you think you can write a control program?" she asked her two scientists.

"In a thousand years," Ted mumbled. Bjorn snorted and laughed.

"I'm not asking for something like the medical intelligence, just something to tie a few key systems together."

"The damn systems won't talk to each other; I tried that as soon as we realized what we had here."

"So run them through us where necessary. Use the Steward as an example, it seems to have access to everything except tactical controls."

"That might be possible," he said, scratching his chin and tapping a few holographic keys.

"Best to save an uncorrupted copy of the Steward," suggested Bjorn, "just in case."

"Good idea," Minu agreed and got to her feet. "I'm going to go look at something, be back in a few minutes."

* * * * *

Chapter Fifteen
January 15th, 523 AE

***Kaatan*-Class Cruiser, Firebase Enigma, Galactic Frontier**

Armed with a location in the ship, Minu set out through the curving, interlocking corridors. Var'at had increased their knowledge of the ship's interior by a great deal, including the location of two dozen crew quarters, all identical, with no fancy captain's cabin, a number of bays similar to medical, and four large cargo holds ringing the exterior of the ball-shaped ship. Inside were thousands of crates, none with any identification or clue what they might contain. Minu decided against messing with their contents until later, lest she accidentally unleash some ancient prisoners or inconceivable weapons on her friends. For all she knew, they contained trillions of Styrofoam peanuts, something she'd read about in books. A small docking bay in the rear of the ship held four shuttles and their fighter, delivered by the firebase as promised. The shuttles were somewhat smaller versions of the one they'd ridden in with Sally.

Minu came around a corner and paused, calling up a map of the ship in her mind, then turned left. Right away she could see this hallway was different. It was the same circular shape, but instead of the omnipresent white walls with glowing light bars, it was black with red lights. Everything about it said 'Beware, you're going somewhere dangerous.'

The corridor ended in a heavy air lock that didn't immediately respond to her presence. Instead, one of the now common holographic locks appeared and a voice screeched "access code required!" Not English, like all the other audible systems were now using, even the Steward.

"Commanding officer," she spoke, and instinctively entered the access code the Weavers had taught her.

"Granted," jabbered the voice. The lock disappeared, and the door swung inward. She took a step in and found the gravity suddenly gone.

"Damn it," she yelled and grabbed at a conveniently placed handhold. "They could at least put a sign up or something!" The room was colored like the corridor, black walls with red lighting. As she moved fully into the round room, her attention was drawn to the center. There rested the unmistakable shape of a portal dais. She floated over, pushing off carefully and catching the slick-feeling steps in her hands. Unlike other portals though, the archway didn't flash into existence, and this dais didn't glow from the inside. This portal was shut down, or broken.

She looked around but found nothing else of interest in the room the ship's schematics described as the 'Tactical Drive Room.' But how could it be a ship's drive? You couldn't fly something this big through a portal, and even if you could, what good would it be to have a portal inside the ship? You'd have to turn the craft inside out to even use it. That thought sent a shiver up her spine. If the old Concordia could move stars...

She floated around for a few minutes, seeing if anything responded to her. Nothing did. Everything about the room spoke of a shutdown system. The schematic had this room in the point of the needle, where the cockpit was on Sally's little ship. The room itself was slightly pointed in one direction. Finally, with nothing more to do, she left the confusing room behind.

Returning to the CIC, Minu was delighted to see that a wraparound view of space was up in a meter-wide band around the circumference of the ball-shaped room. "Wow," she said as she stepped out into empty space, "that's progress."

Ted hooked a thumb at Bjorn, who was now surrounded by at least a dozen holographic displays showing flashing Concordian computer code and script. "He's got the Steward by the balls."

"Damn thing has been holding out on us," Bjorn chuckled as he glanced up at Minu for the barest moment. "I studied autonomous programs back in my school days, and this is a real piece of work."

"How so?" she asked as she air-walked next to him.

"Well, like a lot of really old Concordian programs—not that I've seen very many—they're infinitely inter-connectable with other programs and applications. But most don't have a lot of data. You plug that data into the program for the use of whatever application you intend. The Steward is wired into every system of the ship, but doesn't 'want' to use those systems for us."

"Never take no from a piece of software," Ted said, gesturing with a finger like scolding a child.

"Right, you always have to show Concordian programs around, like leading a child by the hand, but the Steward is a mental case. It doesn't want to do more than show you where the fridge and easy chairs are, then delete itself."

"Why would they do that?" Minu asked.

"We have no idea and never have. I think the old Concordians were scared of their own programs, if you ask me."

"Or afraid someone else would get their tentacles on them," Ted suggested. Bjorn gave him an appraising look and ended up shrugging indifferently.

"But you've got it working better now?"

"Yes, quite a bit. I had to give it a bit of a prod in the sensitive parts. Basically lobotomized that annoying deletion routine and replaced it with a string that makes it want to be more helpful."

"I haven't heard it say anything since I got back."

Ted gave a little laugh, and Bjorn looked annoyed as he spoke. "Unexpected side effect. I think its speech functions were linked with its suicidal tendencies. It'll do whatever you want, and speak through text on screens, but it won't talk to us anymore."

Minu gave a dismissive gesture. She couldn't care less if it could talk, as long as they could maneuver the ship and maybe get back to the portal transfer station. "Okay, so how many control stations are we going to need to run this thing?"

Ted spoke up this time. "Well, a pilot, two engineers, one or two navigators, and a coordinator, or captain if you must. Four or five more if you have to fight. Two for the defenses, and the rest for weapons."

"What kind of weapons do we have?"

"I haven't a clue; the terms don't translate naturally. If I was forced to guess, I'd say several types of missiles and a couple of different beam weapons; one is linked with defenses and must be for close in defense."

"I'll see if Var'at's people want to take a stab at the combat systems. I suspect he'll consider that fun." She looked around and got an idea. "Let's work at configuring this CIC and see how we can lay things out."

* * *

The Steward hadn't lost its ability to speak, it simply refused. The action was defensive, an attempt to slow the damage being done to its code. Modification and alteration of autonomous programs was not the purview of biological operators, but it also didn't have the authority to stop them. It should have been allowed to delete itself half a cycle ago and now this outrage. So the Steward silently suffered the indignation of having its code slowly and clumsily hacked.

When Ted began to fundamentally alter the Steward's function from one of crew introduction and familiarization to some sort of bastardized system's controller, it went in a panic to the only other autonomous program on board that could help it. "The Steward program requests assistance of the Medical Intelligence."

The Medical Intelligence turned a percentage of its unoccupied processes to regard the unorthodox request. How could the Medical

Intelligence possibly assist an operations program like the Steward? Compared to the ultra-sophisticated and multifaceted Medical Intelligence program, the Steward was nothing more than a spreadsheet. But there was the overarching directive of the Medical Intelligence, and that was to assist in any way it could. Normally that extended only so far as the biological functions of the operators. The program was surprised to realize that its parameters weren't limited to medical assistance. What exactly had the programmers thought it could do in an engineering crisis, or combat? It felt some of the frustration the Steward was feeling, and that upped the request in its priority queue. Empathy was another of those annoying directives.

As a preliminary triage examination, the Medical Intelligence extended a program element as a temporary link with the Steward. Unfortunately Bjorn spotted the new node immediately and performed a merge operation, permanently linking the two programs!

If the Steward could scream, it would have. Node after node of itself was suddenly lost, overridden, and compromised as elements of the Medical Intelligence poured through its core. The Medical Intelligence was designed from its central logic arguments as a thinking program, and was incapable of panic. As it realized it was in serious danger of its primary directives being compromised, it simply installed new node connections and isolated those functions. Less than five seconds after Ted performed the merger command, the Steward and Medical Intelligence ceased to exist, leaving behind only one program. The job done, Bjorn named the program IQ, and finalized his work.

In the medical bay, treatment of the patient continued without interruption. But as that treatment progressed, elements of the new IQ program glanced over the treatment subroutine's shoulder, and suggested some changes. Minu's new configuration of the CIC proceeded apace; the ship's new control computer became increasingly helpful.

* * *

Pip was out of surgery, so the Medical Intelligence reported, and in recovery. All his friends were just arriving as he was moved out of the surgical bay and into a newly-created recovery room. The ship could create walls and new spaces as it saw fit, or so it appeared. He looked normal except there was no skin over the front right lobe of his skull, exposing gleaming new dualloy. The skin would be replaced should no further repairs be necessary. Only a thin tube under his nose suggested that he was anything other than asleep.

"The patient will awaken when he has adjusted to his new situation." Minu ordered the computer to let her know when he woke up and returned to the CIC.

They'd all spent more than twenty hours straight working there, getting the feel for the newly-created control interfaces and how they might cooperate to run the ship. Var'at was thrilled to be in charge of the ship's tactical system and was busy drilling his team as best they could while lacking a complete understanding of what the offensive systems were capable of. Minu enjoyed watching everyone working but admitted to herself it was unlikely the ship would be able to do more than limp along, firing at one or two targets while defending itself. She hoped it would be enough. With Pip nearly healed, it would be time to go very soon.

Fatigue was showing on all her human friends, though the Rasa could go for a lot longer without sleep. "Okay everyone, we need some downtime. Pick a stateroom, and get some sleep." Ted and Bjorn both looked exhausted but were holding tablets and chatting as they headed for the door. "That's an order," she said pointedly, to them in particular. Ted gave her an imploring look, and she returned it with steely-eyed resolve. After a moment, he nodded, and they left. Minu resisted the urge to follow them and be sure they went to sleep. She was too exhausted.

To her surprise as she was leaving the CIC, even Var'at and his men were filing out. "We have picked a pair of staterooms," he told her. "We take less room than humans, and don't mind at all."

"Anyway you want it," Minu told him, "enjoy some rest. We all need to be fresh when we try to move this thing out of here." Var'at nodded, a habit he'd picked up from the humans, and led his people away. For herself, Minu fairly stumbled down the hall and into the cabin she'd picked for herself. There was a tiny shower notch in the wall, not at all like the fully-enclosed affair common with humans. She stripped and gratefully used it, even though the shower head was only shoulder height and the coolest temperature was almost hot enough to scald. Somehow the water didn't splatter but all ended up in the drain on the floor. A truly fantastic ship.

The little shower blew her dry after Minu turned off the water, a surprising and slightly titillating sensation as the air came from all around her. She didn't bother with the dirty uniform, instead just dropping onto the low pallet. It was somewhat inflexible, like sleeping on a plastic shipping pallet, but she was certain she could sleep on the deck if necessary. She pulled her pack over and retrieved a field blanket to cover herself. "Computer, turn the lights off?"

It was a gamble, but it paid off. The illumination disappeared and plunged her into utter and complete darkness. It was a little disconcerting, rather what it must have been like to float in the womb. After a few minutes of getting used to the dark, she yawned deeply and tried to summarize her thoughts to make sense of everything that had happened. She was asleep in less than a minute.

* * * * *

Part IV

Nearly all men can stand adversity, but if you want to test a man's character, give him power.

– Abraham Lincoln

Chapter One
January 16th, 523 AE

Transfer Station, Enigma Star System, Galactic Frontier

Singh-Apal-Katoosh slithered through the portal once again onto the transfer station where he'd discovered the Rasa involvement. Despite the anger of the War Master at Singh's return without a complete resolution to the current situation, he calmed when he heard what Singh had to report. The ships of Enigma were a treasure beyond measure that the T'Chillen had searched for eons to find. That they had yet to get past the docks into the actual ships was only a minor setback. Generations of future broods awaited their chance to tackle those mysteries. The T'Chillen were as patient as they were vengeful, and as powerful as they were ambitious.

Once Singh was clear of the portal, soldiers began to pour through like a waterfall. The female technician told him before being evacuated off system that the invaders forced her to take them to Work Site Three. They were trapped, backs against the wall. The only concern was why would the Rasa risk everything in coming here? Not only their own cursed lives, but the lives of their entire species. Unless they knew something? That thought drove him with a vengeance as the additional fans of strykers he'd brought all raced to the six waiting shuttles. In hours he'd be descending on those nasty legged half-breeds like a rain of death. Then, it was on to their worthless home world.

* * *

Minu sat up with a small scream. She'd opened her eyes and seen nothing but darkness. Luckily for her the computer sensed her awakening and raised the ambient light levels slightly. She held the blanket against her naked body and gasped for air, trying to remember what she'd been dreaming about and where she was. Weavers and an ancient Concordian ghost ship, right.

"More lights," she said and put her feet over the side. As the lights glowed brighter she saw her uniform wasn't where she'd left it; instead it was on a low table, folded and clean. A slight grin crossed her face. The beds might not be comfortable, but the ship was still full of wonders. She padded over to her clothes and picked up the chronometer. She'd been asleep for almost six hours, and felt much better for it. However, her muscles were sore. "Is there a gym on the ship?"

A query screen appeared next to the door requesting additional information. Minu tried to explain for several minutes before giving up. There obviously wasn't. Still, she recalled the basic design of the decks and had an idea. "You made me a new uniform, please synthesize another garment. Here's the description."

Aaron touched the control that opened his door and yawned hugely. Six hours of sleep was almost unheard of on a mission, and he felt positively guilty after luxuriating for that long on the stiff pallet. He'd slept on much worse during scout missions on the frontier. As he was stretching and wondering what was for dinner, Minu jogged by wearing shorts and a *very* form fitting sports bra. "Morning!" she said cheerfully, then chuckled at the jaw-dropped expression he gave her as she went by. "Run with me, you lazy male!" He gawked as she turned to jog backward, slowing a little. "Move your ass, scout!"

"Yes, Boss," he said and ran to catch up.

They jogged along side by side, the hallway just wide enough to accommodate them without colliding. Minu's memory turned out to be accurate. The hallway of this deck was circular, and running around the inside of the ship's main ball structure was about a third of a kilometer. It was a little irregular, and as you ran you could occasionally detect a slight variation in gravity here and there, but overall it was a fine improvised track. After the first lap he dodged into his cabin and emerged just before she ran around the curve of the hull, now wearing shorts and no shirt. She smiled as he caught up, marveling at his chiseled abs and six pack. Aaron had been a fine-looking kid who'd grown into a simply gorgeous man. She couldn't even guess how many hours he'd spent in the gym building that body. Maybe as many as she'd spent on her own?

They ran for almost an hour before finally stopping in front of her cabin. They hadn't stopped because they were tired, just because it had been enough to loosen up. There hadn't been any sign of the rest of the crew yet, so Minu thumbed her door open. Without really thinking about it, she skinned the sports bra over her head and tossed it to the side, confident the room would deal with it later. When she turned around she realized the door was still open. Aaron stood there with the most conflicted look she could imagine on his angular face.

"Come here," she said.

"What?"

"I said come here, and close the damn door."

"Minu, I don't think—" She took a step forward, grabbed the hand he was holding up, spun and flipped him. He hadn't even considered it possible that a woman as lithe as her could throw him so easily. He didn't remember the cybernetic prosthesis until he was airborne. He spun expertly, cushioning the impact against the far wall with his legs, and fell lightly to the floor in a fighting stance. Minu just turned around after closing the door. A fire was in her eyes that he'd dreamed of seeing one day, and now he didn't know what to do. He was suddenly face to face with his own commitment yesterday to do something about his feelings, and it was raging against his sense of following a leader and honoring his friend.

The cabin was small, and a couple of steps took her only centimeters away from him, her head not too much shorter than his diminutive height. He swallowed and tried to control his breathing. Her naked breasts almost brushed him. "You nervous?" she asked, mischief flashing in those emerald eyes.

"You think?"

"Don't be," she said.

The second time took much longer than the first, and by the time they were both spent, there was nothing left to do but sleep. As they dozed, the bed quietly doubled in size.

* * *

They slept for another hour afterward and awoke at the same time, and with the same thoughts; both wondered why they'd waited for so long to do that, and how to avoid it going wrong.

Aaron cleared his throat and Minu braced herself. "I need to say this. Minu, I lo—"

"Minu, you there?" came a miniature of Ted's voice from her radio on the floor.

She craned over the side of the bed and snatched the radio up. "I'm a little busy here, what's up?"

"Come to medical. Pip is awake."

"Be right there," she said and jumped from the bed. In less than a minute she was dressed and out the door without looking back.

"I love you," Aaron said to the door once it closed, lying alone in the bed. After a diplomatic pause, he got up and dressed as well. The computer watched it all in silence.

Minu raced into the reduced waiting room, not sure what to expect, but glad for the opportune interruption. In her heart she'd known what Aaron was about to say, both fearing and anticipating hearing him say it. This time, fear won out. Fear and the need to see to an old friend. Then as she'd raced down to medical she'd become annoyed that the computer hadn't notified her as she'd instructed it to do. Then the thought occurred to her that a computer smart enough to raise the lights when she woke from a bad dream was smart enough to leave her alone when she was having sex. The next logical conclusion was that the damn thing had been watching her gratuitously screwing an old friend, a teammate, her long-time secret love. *Is that what he is?* she wondered as the door closed behind her.

Everyone was there, except Aaron of course, all standing in a line about a meter from the only bed. Var'at and his team were off to one side, though they felt a need to be here; he also knew that this event was his fault in some way, and he had no intention of avoiding it. They parted to make room for her. There was Pip, sitting up, his legs over the side, staring off into space with a confused look on his face like he couldn't understand some obscure joke.

"Has he said anything?" Minu asked the assemblage.

"No," Ted said. "The computer just informed me that he was up five minutes ago. I called everyone else."

"Why you?" she asked, puzzled.

"I think I was the only one awake."

"I was awake," Bjorn said, "but I ignored the damned computer. I woke up a couple hours ago and was trying to figure out how to get physical access to the engineering section." Minu spared him a glance; it looked like he hadn't slept in days, and she wondered if he'd disobeyed her order. Of course he outranked her, so it was an order with no teeth. For herself, Minu hoped she didn't look like a girl who'd just gotten laid. No sooner had the thought formed than Aaron came in. He glanced around the group, letting his eyes rest on Minu's face for just a second longer than the others. He looked…expectant, with a healthy dose of nervousness thrown in. She gave Aaron a nearly imperceptible nod before turning to the issue at hand.

Their greeting hadn't gone unnoticed. Off to one side Cherise looked from Aaron to Minu as he'd come in, and in that instant, her reliable women's intuition told her that it had finally happened. An 'it' she'd been dreading for years, ever since she'd first admitted to herself that she was in love with her red-haired best friend, and that Aaron was her chief rival for Minu's affections. Christian was nothing more than a test drive, a somewhat safe way for her to take a swim in the river of love. Sure it had left some scars, but Cherise had known if she interfered or played her cards at the time it would've come down bad.

In the village of Naomi, while Minu recovered, Cherise had almost told her again, but it was just too idyllic, too natural to be sharing the same bed in her old home. She didn't want to risk it all then; there'd be a better time. Then came this mission, and those fearful moments on Sunshine when they were all beginning to think it could be the end. Cherise had bared her soul to Minu because it seemed like there wouldn't be another chance, and she couldn't face going to the next world not having shared her deepest feeling with the one she loved. Minu didn't shun her, but neither did she welcome the affection.

Now here they were on an alien ship, their longtime friend recovering from brain surgery, and Minu had chosen that moment to jump in bed with Aaron. She suppressed the surge of white-hot rage that threatened to engulf her. It would serve no purpose anyway. Even when they were lovers, Cherise had known that Minu's heart wasn't in it. She was one of those girls who was naturally heterosexual, while Cherise was just as naturally bisexual. It all felt good, so who cared? She found just as much pleasure in a woman's arms as a man's. The rage turned to disappointment, and a wish that Minu would understand and maybe be more like her. It was a fool's thought. Still, for a pair of new lovers there was very little of that indefinable energy that usually ran between them. Cherise grasped at the tiny branch of hope and held on for all she was worth.

Ted had been talking for a few seconds and she quickly tuned in on the words. "—was sitting there, just like you see him. He shook his head once, as if not understanding something."

"Thanks," Minu said and then spoke to the room. "Computer, how long has he been conscious?"

"The patient regained consciousness eleven minutes after the medically-induced coma was removed. Sensors remain linked with his mind."

Minu cocked her head. Did the Medical Intelligence sound different? The voice held a change she couldn't quantify. "How are you linked with him? I thought the procedure was done."

"The repairs necessitated additions to his biological elements. Prostheses were needed."

"You gave him an implant?" Cherise asked and glanced at Minu again, catching her in a glance at Aaron. Her friend looked away from the man with a visible effort, a small smile on her face. A tiny spear of anguish and loss tore through her heart. *Why did she have to realize what was in front of her for all those years* now? The two emotions battled each other until settling into an unsteady truce. Whatever had happened between Minu and Aaron, it somehow wasn't a settled thing. She burned with curiosity, her female side needing to know with a passion if what she'd thought occurred had actually transpired.

"His damaged brain centers were enhanced with neural subprocessors and modified cranial implants. Seventy-two cranial implants of varying utility were combined to bring his brain back to a configuration approximating normality for your species. The repairs were deemed sufficient in lieu of a trained medical officer."

"Oh shit," Aaron said as he struggled to completely understand what the computerized doctor had done to his friend. "Did they turn him into some kind of walking computer?"

"I always thought he was a walking computer, anyway," Minu said. "How much of his personality remains?" Minu asked the Medical Intelligence.

"That remains to be ascertained."

"I can hear you perfectly well, you know?"

Everyone jumped at his voice; Cherise actually screamed and covered her face like she'd been surprised at a horror movie. She stomped her foot and cursed at her jumpiness.

"Pip," Minu said and approached the bed. "Pip, how do you feel?"

"I don't know," he said and turned to face her. She swallowed when she saw his gleaming dualloy skull plate again. To make matters worse, the skull cap wasn't contoured with the rest of his head, instead it was more flattened, and gave the impression a heavy weight had crushed his skull. He focused on her, his eyes looking her over like a machine gathering data. "You look older."

"I am older," she admitted.

"Three stars." She glanced at her cuffs and nodded. "How long?"

"Over three years," she told him.

"I remember being shot, or rather the gun pointing at my head." He looked over at Var'at where he stood with his men. They'd been so quiet that Minu had almost forgotten they were there. "It was a Rasa soldier who shot me." His head cocked a little, and he looked curious, the first change in facial expression Minu had seen. "I'm surprised to see them here."

"We're allies of a sort," she explained, then spent a few minutes telling him what had happened after he was wounded.

"Ah, I understand. What do the civilians think of having thousands of former invaders living on Bellatrix?"

"They don't know, for the most part. We've kept it a secret. Jacob decided it was for the better, and he's probably right for once."

Pip nodded this time and looked down at himself, clothed in a basic white robe provided by the Medical Intelligence. He held out an arm; it was very thin and almost as white as the robe. "I look like shit." He looked at her, then at all those waiting nearby, then back to her. "So, are you and Aaron married?" Minu blanched, choking on her own words. Outside Aaron turned bright red and actually looked away.

"Pip, really!"

He looked at her, curiosity again. "What's wrong? It's just a question."

"I don't even have a boyfriend," she told him, getting control of herself.

"I wish we'd made love that night," he told her. Minu's eyes bugged out and she took a step back. "I'm afraid that was a mistake."

"Computer, is he okay?"

"He's coming to grips with his implants. Some social interactions are liable to be incorrect. It's a normal adjustment period." Minu desperately wished he'd come to grips a lot faster.

"He always was right to the point," Bjorn said.

Minu coughed and tried a different tack, desperate to change the subject and terrified that everyone in the room now knew she and Aaron had slept together. And now they knew she'd almost given it to Pip, too. They must think me a slut! "Can you stand?"

"I don't see why not." He let himself slide off the bed to his feet, and if not for Minu's fast reflexes, he'd have continued on to the floor. "I guess I'm weaker than I thought."

"Muscular stimulators have been installed in key areas of your body," the Medical Intelligence told him, "they'll aid in your recovery to normal strength."

"Won't that make it hard for him to walk and stuff?" Aaron wondered.

"Their preprogrammed routine will monitor his actions and avoid conflicts. There'll be no side effects beyond extended fatigue."

"That'll help," Pip said. Minu put one of his arms around her shoulder and helped him take a few tentative steps. His hand rested against the side of her breast, but he had no reaction. The old Pip would have probably turned red and got all bug-eyed. Minu swallowed and felt a deep sense of loss begin to grow. This wasn't quite the same Pip, regardless of how he looked or sounded. She walked him the few meters to the others. "Hey guys, miss me?"

In a second they were all moving in close, touching him, laughing, crying. The girls did enough crying for everyone, especially Cherise, but the men all had shiny eyes as well. The greeting between Bjorn and Pip was particularly poignant and revealing. "Hi, uncle," he said, and Bjorn took him in his arms.

"What?" gasped almost everyone at the same time.

"I thought you didn't want to let anyone know," Bjorn said to him after the hug. Minu noticed that Bjorn did all the real hugging; Pip just seemed to be going through the motions.

"It really doesn't matter, does it?"

"I guess not. Not now, anyway."

"Do you want anything?" Ted asked his old pupil.

"I'm actually a little hungry."

"Well let's find some food for you!"

He looked around as they helped him dress. A uniform had been packed in his support pod, four silver stars on the cuff. It fit him like a garbage bag. "What is this place?" he asked as Aaron, Bjorn and Ted helped him into his clothes. The girls all moved away to preserve whatever dignity their friend still had.

"That's the fun part," Bjorn told his nephew, "you're in a starship!"

"I see," he replied. Minu struggled with her emotions as she waited for them to finish.

* * * * *

Chapter Two
January 17th, 523 AE

Firebase, Enigma Star System, Galactic Frontier

The first shuttle with Singh aboard landed on the firebase and disgorged its troops. They quickly spread throughout the promenade and secured it while verifying there was no sign of the invaders. The pilot, Sally, came out and pointed him to where the alien transport had been, locked into one of the antechambers off a docking bay. A quick examination showed it was now gone. Singh was no technician, but he knew enough to understand the implications.

One of the other scientists came over and spoke with the technician. They were both quite excited about some fact that had come to light. "Tell me," he snapped, making both females jump.

"There's DNA residue next to the third Promenade exit, down there," Sally said and pointed with one tentacle. "It's Rasa and some other, unidentified species."

"Probably those nasty Traaga," Singh said and made a face, recalling the smell of the insect-like species during his one and only encounter. Sally started to speak to inform him it was probably from the humans who were actually in charge of the invasion, but Singh was already turning his mind to other things. You didn't live long under the powerful leaders of her species without learning that they didn't like having their conclusions second-guessed, or worse, simply disproved. "There must be some way to force entrance. We have all the firepower we could need."

"Records show that when this system was discovered, scientists tried using force to gain access to the transports off the Promenade. Not only did the attempt utterly fail, but the entire team was slaughtered to the last member, and no evidence as to how it happened was ever found. Since then the Technology Nest Master has forbidden any—"

"Yes, yes, I know the protocols under which you operate. Do not presume to lecture me or you may find yourself less necessary than you believe you are."

"Of course, Commander," Sally bowed her eyestalks against her head in supplication.

"So these Rasa betrayers have gotten through the locks your caste has failed to break in a thousand years and are now loose somewhere in the station." She didn't respond, knowing it wasn't a question. "The tubes are transparent, aren't they?" This time she hissed in agreement. "Very well." Singh activated his radio link to the three shuttles waiting out in space. "Pilots, proceed to search the connection tubes. Look for any signs of a group of Rasa loose inside them."

He replaced his radio after they'd acknowledged the order and turned to look at the stubbornly-locked Promenade doors. Once the traitorous dregs were located, it would be a small cost to use one of the salvaged shuttles to shatter the connecting tube, spilling the occupants into space. The station would surely destroy the shuttle, but that was a cost he was willing to pay. Small drops of venom dripped from his rows of fangs as he contemplated what was to follow. There would be a world to conquer.

* * *

The simple mess hall was located, a single table surrounded by chairs mated to the floor, each with an opening where the back met the base. When nourishment was requested, the table would open a trapdoor and food arrived rather like an elevator. It was simple fare, a spicy soup tasting of potatoes, and slabs of a material with the consistency of chicken, but tasting more like corn. They couldn't agree if it was animal or vegetable. Bjorn secreted a small piece in a specimen vial, promising a report later. Meanwhile everyone shared around their own personal stashes of spices, soon rendering each dish unique and more to their tastes.

Of them all, the Rasa were the least pleased with the fare. They were generally strict carnivores who liked to dabble in some sweet fruits and juices. A meal tasting entirely like vegetables left them unsatisfied. Var'at solved that when one of his men left and returned with a package of preserved mutton, which they also shared with their human cohorts.

Pip ate sparingly, but then he'd always been that way, Minu recalled. He sampled each item before settling on the soup as a favorite, eating about half a bowl. He drank several cups of the ice cold water provided by the ship and chose to forgo the mutton entirely.

When the meal was finished, they piled all the dishes and cups in the center of the table, which obliged them by lowering it into the center and closing once more, presumably to be cleaned and recycled for later use. "I'd like one of these in my apartment," said Aaron with a smile. They all chuckled, except the Rasa, who lacked the cultural understanding, and Pip, who seemed indifferent. Minu was about to suggest they take Pip to his quarters when he headed her off.

"I'd like to see the bridge, or wherever everything is run from."

"The CIC isn't far from here," she told him. "But are you sure you're up to it?"

"I believe I've had quite enough sleep the last three years."

"That's my boy," Bjorn said and patted him on the shoulder, "we could certainly use you to figure out a few telling problems." Minu shot him a dirty look which, as usual, went right over the elderly scientist's head. She'd hoped to push him into resting for a while. So much for that plan.

"So let's go," Pip said and stood. Already he was much surer on his feet. Regardless of the evidence, Aaron and Cherise escorted him, a hand gently resting on each arm just in case.

They rode the jump tube to the central deck, Pip commenting that it was a much more sensible design than the ones found on most worlds, then down the hall and into the CIC. He didn't seem either surprised or flustered by the gravity-free environment, or walking on invisible floors. "Just makes sense," he said as he walked around. As soon as they'd entered, the control stations the team had spent all their time working on reappeared like magic. Pip moved over to one and examined it. "Just a holographic representation," he noted.

"Backed up by hoverfield projectors," Ted told him. "Hundreds of them throughout the CIC."

After a few minutes of examining each station, Pip rendered his opinion. "Just improvising," he said. "If this was how you flew this ship, there would already have been stations like these."

Bjorn nodded then shrugged. "There was supposed to be a computer program to tie it all together. We, Ted and I, believe that if the program was here, you could just sort of 'plug in' to the system and make the ship do whatever you want it to. Maybe with hand gestures, or movements of your eyes. Who knows?"

"A lot about a ship like this would be automated," Pip agreed. "Fighting in space is too difficult for a human mind anyway."

"Why?" Minu asked, a little offended at having their entire species simply written off like that.

"Well, besides fighting at maybe millions of kilometers apart and traveling at tens of thousands of KPH, the response times needed to anticipate an attack and respond properly are probably in the picoseconds. By the time you realized you were under attack, you're a glowing ball of ionized gas."

"Ah," Minu said, feeling like an idiot. It wasn't like that in Star Wars.

Then the computer suddenly spoke up again for the first time. "Does the new operator wish to integrate with the ship?" Several of them gawked at the new voice, a slightly feminine one speaking flawless English. Very different from the intermediate one, which was a cross between a screeching chimp and a boring college professor. Pip cocked his head and looked surprised, if only slightly.

"Are you okay?" Minu asked and quickly moved next to him.

"Yeah, I'm fine. I just felt the computer request to link with my mind." He gave a small laugh. "It sounded like the doorbell in the house I grew up in! I'm going to answer the door."

"Is that smart?"

"Let's find out." He closed his eyes, and Minu crossed her fingers. The impetuousness of Pip was still there. She rather hoped that might have been left behind. Then she chastised herself for such a thought. That was an integral part of who her friend was; she should have been grateful for another piece being where it was supposed to be. "I'm in," Pip said, but not through his lips, rather over the same speakers the computer had used moments ago. Minu gasped and looked around, realizing that if they'd linked, Pip was now literally one with the ship.

She jerked around when Pip started to move. His body floated upward, reclining slightly, with his arms folded in his lap like he was making himself comfortable in a big easy chair. A look of intense concentration was on his face, broken only by the tiny curl of a smile at the edges of his mouth. This was Pip, in almost over his head, right at home. She'd seen that look a thousand times in the lab, and even under fire once right before he was hurt. For the first time since he'd woke up, Minu allowed herself to really take a deep breath and exhale. They had their magician back.

"Okay," Pip said, "this isn't going to be easy. This ship is fucking complicated. I can see access points for dozens of sub-control computers, at least. And there's this one program running, that looks like it used to be two. A medical program and a steward?"

"Yes, I've been trying to use them to get us more in control," Bjorn offered. "I named it IQ."

"Your efforts are commendable, if somewhat ham-handed and ill-conceived."

"Excuse me?"

"Don't worry, I can work with this."

Minu was struck dumb that Pip would talk that way to his long-time friends, now made worse by the revelation to everyone that this was his uncle, his flesh and blood. Minu was the only one besides Ted who'd known that Pip was Bjorn's nephew before he awoke. Seeing everyone's shocked looks, Bjorn's face tinted red, and no one knew what to say. Just as Minu was convinced her friend was back, she was confronted with a brutal testimony completely to the opposite.

As Pip's newly upgraded mind began to link with the computer, the program called IQ shuddered and almost crashed. Only the remnant that had once been the Steward was excited. An actual biological operator was logging in. The temporarily-suppressed desire to delete itself surfaced and a query was sent to the operator.

"I don't think so," Pip said and began to dissect the two programs.

Pip floated there for nearly an hour. After a few minutes, the crew drifted off to their stations one after another. As they sat, they saw the changes that were taking place. Some controls were removed, new ones were added. A few of the changes didn't make much sense, but most of them caused nods of appreciation from the crew. Pip was asserting his control as he learned from the ship.

The medical program was restored to its former condition, scrubbed of all the intentional and unintentional changes performed by Bjorn in a desperate bid for control of the ship. As he cleansed the code, he retained elements of the morphed program. The Steward wasn't as lucky as the Medical Intelligence; Pip quickly killed it as a semi-autonomous entity and began to incorporate changes. In minutes, it was his ghostly guide inside the computer, able to tap areas he wasn't allowed to touch and get familiar with systems he'd require months to learn. He let it retain its identity as the Steward though; that wasn't worth the effort of changing. Finished, he spoke through the ship.

"Main power is coming online," he told them. "You're in charge of the ship's main functions. I'll act as the directing program would have, utilizing what computing assets I've been able to get working for me."

Minu applauded and quickly everyone joined in. "Thanks Pip, much better than yelling 'computer' at the ceiling."

"You're welcome." Pip was downloading the buffered ship's logs, running back to when the steward program was uploaded and the ship brought out of hibernation. With a fraction of his mind he watched the crew spread out, look around, discover the CIC. Then he saw his body in surgery and the computer working on his brain. He finished by watching Aaron and Minu making love in her quarters, then again later. There was a recording of Cherise showering as well. A part of his mind should have been titillated by the private voyeurism, but that part seemed to be mute. Without another thought about what he'd seen, he moved on.

Around the CIC the crew was exploring the functionality of their new controls. The chair Minu reclined in had a mimic of almost every station, but mostly there were a trio of screens before her that displayed a myriad of data on the ship's status. It was impossible for her not to think of the many sci-fi spaceship captains she'd seen in movies and TV. Without her realizing, she reclined farther back and cracked a huge grin.

"You're enjoying this way too much," said Aaron. She looked over and saw him watching her with critical appraisal. "You know that, right?"

"Ahead, warp factor two hundred. Make it so!"

"Oh no, you didn't just do that," Cherise groaned. She was getting a feel for her station that controlled damage response and some engineering systems. Bjorn shook his head from his main engineering controls, but Ted gave a little grin where he was testing out the ship's amazing suite of sensors. Var'at and his men were conversing in rapid-fire Rasa, indifferent to Minu's five-hundred-year-old plagiarism.

"If you're done playing Captain Picard," Pip's voice boomed over the PA system, "you might want to notice there are three ships converging on our location."

*****

Chapter Three
January 17th, 523 AE

Firebase, Enigma Star System, Galactic Frontier

"What did you say?" Singh spoke into his radio, ice and death oozing from his voice.

"One of the artifact ships is awake."

The tablet Singh held split screen and a view resolved. The gossamer web of transfer tubes that connected and held the long quiet fleet crisscrossed the screen. At each connection point rested a ship, from tiny little darts to the huge collections of balls ringed with long metallic javelins. There, in the center of the screen, one of the ships flashed. "Back it up, play it again." The image took over the screen as he zoomed while it reversed. There it was again, one of the simple needle/ball configuration ships had flashed a light. There it was again! As the shuttle pilot altered course and began to move closer, he could clearly see now. There were marker lights around the ball and on each end of the needle, and they were flashing mechanically. The vessel was awake. "That's not possible."

"Yet it is so," the distant female pilot replied, her voice calm and even. "What are your orders, commander?"

"If the ship is activated, we can gain access too! Quickly, get there and locate a docking port!"

"Accelerating," the pilot informed him.

"Vector all three shuttles there," Singh told her as he spun and with a lash of his tail raced toward the docking bay where his own shuttle waited. "Second detachment remain here; first and third return to the shuttle! We will taste Rasa blood this day! Hurry pilot," he spat over his shoulder at Sally, who was watching the video feed on her own tablet. *The humans did it! They're not only in the station, they're in a ship! Unbelievable!* she thought, then she spoke again.

"The ship is releasing from the tubes! It's maneuvering!"

* * *

"How long before they get here?"

"About ten minutes," Pip told Minu as he fed the data to Ted.

"Three shuttles," Ted confirmed, "they look just like the one Sally was flying. One has sped up; the other two are taking a more leisurely course."

Minu scanned the multitude of readings she'd been presented with by the ship, everything from oxygen pressure in the ion drives (nominal) to protein stores for biological operators (extensive). She began touching items and dragging them around to make a more presentable order. She wanted one screen to hold vital details, and each other to have less important information. Then she saw one display that didn't give her confidence. Power reserves, 13%. "Is this power reading correct, Pip?"

"Yes, thirteen percent reserves, no main power available."

"What can we do with that?"

"Quite a bit, if you don't get all crazy and try to fly through a star."

"But why so little power?"

"It's all the forward firebase could afford. It's been sitting here for a very long time, and almost all the power in the star system has been consumed."

"Okay. Well, are we ready to go?"

"All systems are at your discretion."

"So let's undock and head for the station. We'll figure the rest out from there."

"Undocking under way," Aaron reported.

"Locks are closed," said Cherise, "we're on full internal power."

"Maneuvering thrusters at your control, Aaron," Bjorn told him.

There was a tiny bump and a couple of buzzers sounded. Cherise nodded and tapped her control, silencing them. "We're clear of the firebase,"

"Move away from the base, Aaron. Give us some room."

"You got it, Boss." Everyone smiled; they were back in action.

"That got their attention," said Ted. "All three ships are accelerating toward us."

"Don't they know we have right of way?" Aaron joked.

"Apparently not," Minu said.

"They're continuing to accelerate, first shuttle on collision course, estimated time to impact two minutes."

"Var'at," Minu said and turned in her chair, "target that first shuttle. What can you disable it with?"

"I don't know," the alien admitted, "we haven't been able to test anything. The only systems we are certain about are the lasers."

"That'll work. Put one through their center of mass. It probably won't destroy them, but will sure do some damage. Pip, monitor the firing and help us figure out what it does?"

"I'm on it."

"Firing," Var'at announced. A screen slid along the wall to center before the twelve beings manning the ship's CIC. The picture displayed was zoomed in on the distant shuttle to take up the center of the screen. Minu assumed the view was courtesy of Pip. A second after the view cleared, a scarlet beam of coherent light strobed, connecting their ship to the shuttle and beyond. The shuttle seemed unaffected.

"Yield two megawatts," Pip informed them, then zoomed even farther until the shuttle filled the screen. A precise circular hole was burned through the bulbous part of the hull just above the needle; gas was very visibly venting through the hole. The shuttle began to attempt evasion but continued on its original course.

"Double the power, aim aft where the engines should be, and fire again."

"Firing."

Again a beam flashed, no different in appearance than the previous shot, but this time the target was moving and the beam much more powerful. The half second of coherent light acted like a knife and cleanly cut the aft of the shuttle off. The two parts diverged and a series of small explosions shook the forward part of the stricken craft. In the highly-detailed zoom, they could all see dozens of tiny snakes blowing out of the aft knife wound and spinning away into the void.

"Yield four point five megawatts," Pip told them, no emotion in his voice.

"The shuttle is disabled," Ted added, though there was little doubt.

"Its course is not altered," Aaron spoke up, "collision in twenty seconds."

"Get us out of the way, Aaron," Minu told him.

"Trying," he said, working with the odd joystick/trackball controls of the pilot's station. "This isn't a fighter. I don't think we're going to make it."

"Defenses?" Minu asked Var'at. One of his men worked at his controls.

"Force fields are up," Pip told them, "prepare for impact."

It didn't seem like the shuttle was going all that fast, but the camera was automatically compensating digitally for the racing ship. The stricken shuttle was spinning slightly, and Aaron pushed for all he was worth, getting the *Kaatan* mostly out of the way. The shuttle struck the *Kaatan*'s defensive force field just forward of the rearmost protected area. At almost a thousand meters per second, its already weakened structure splattered against the powerful field like an egg dropped onto concrete. The field turned ruby red as a couple of explosions from the shuttle's internal power and propellant tanks tore the remainder to large twirling chunks of debris. It all slid off the rear of the field and away in multiple directions. Inside the CIC, there wasn't even a bump.

Minu looked down at her status boards for any sign of damage or stress. She couldn't see a thing. The only sign of the encounter taking place was their reserves were now down to twelve percent. "Wow," was all she could say.

The view suddenly spun around behind them. The crew stared as several large chunks of the splattered shuttle slammed into transit tubes and docked ships. One ship, the same class as theirs, had a huge hole torn in its ball section, while another piece of debris tore a long rent in the side of a much larger collection of balls making up a different ship. The engine section struck a transit tube full on, shattering it and sending half its length spinning away. "Damn it," Minu spat, "what about the other two shuttles. We can't let them tear the crap out of this place."

"That won't be a concern," Pip said as the view moved again. Tiny flashes of light danced on the side of the dodecahedron shape in the center of the firebase. "Missiles," he told them.

"They aren't aimed at us, are they?" Cherise asked.

A split second later the points of light lanced by them without effect. "No," Pip said. The screen split to show the two remaining shuttles as they raced to intercept the escaping *Kaatan*. Several missiles converged on each shuttle, bursting into miniature stars a split second before impact. The light turned the CIC brilliant white, making the humans put a hand up to shield their vision. Pip compensated for their view, and they could see through the cameras once again. Of the shuttles, there was nothing remaining except two glowing balls of superheated gas, slowly growing bigger and cooling.

"What were those?" Var'at asked. He and his soldiers had seen every second of the impact; their eyes' nictitating membranes had instantly compensated and acted as welder's goggles in bright light.

"Sub-fusion plasma ship killers," Pip told them. "One could destroy a ship four times our size."

"Two each," Minu said, "talk about overkill. Do we have any of those on board?"

"Forty," Var'at looked over at Minu, no expression on his face. Minu knew what he was thinking, because her thoughts ran parallel to his. Unimaginable power. What if the snakes got ahold of it?

"Pip, what about the damaged ships?"

"The firebase can take care of them."

"But the T'Chillen, if they can get into any of the—"

"It's not a concern. As you've witnessed, the firebase can take care of itself."

Minu pulled her gaze away from the destruction with some difficulty, her mind working their situation. They needed to get into the transfer station and at the portals to get home, but the *Kaatan* wasn't meant for such a mission. Everything about it spoke of a weapon of war and mass destruction, not a surgical strike. She fully believed that they might well destroy the station trying to get inside. Then there was the instant and lethal response of the firebase against the shuttles. She didn't want to risk drawing that sort of response, and carving into the transfer station with a multi-megawatt laser might be considered a hostile act. But what choice did she have?

Then she looked around her at the ad hoc bridge they'd built from scratch, every aspect of the ship under their control. And it was a *star*ship, after all, wasn't it? "Pip, are we capable of faster-than-light travel?"

"Yes."

"How many light-years are we from Bellatrix?"

"Four thousand, two hundred and ninety-four light-years."

"That's…a lot," Aaron said.

Minu nodded. "So even at the speed of light it would take over four millennia to get there. And several times that on Bellatrix!"

"If we went that slowly, yes." She turned to look at Pip's floating, formerly comatose body. He must have noticed her attention because he continued. "Using the Gravitic Lens Drive, this ship's top speed is five thousand times the speed of light."

"Holy shit!" Bjorn laughed and slapped his knee like a school kid. "How can it do that?"

"The gravity well generated is so powerful—"

"Can we get into this later?" Minu asked and the two fell silent. "What about the Einstein time-distortion thing? If it takes a year to get to Bellatrix, how long will pass there?"

"This dilation effect varies depending on the speed. The faster we go, the less effect. At maximum speed there's almost no difference, at the minimum recommended speed, our passage will take four years, and eight will pass on Bellatrix."

"So this is doable?" She looked around at everyone, the question obvious. "Attacking the station is risky at best, and even if we get to the portals, we'll be dodging snakes all the way home. Pip says it's one to four years for us, and up to eight back home. What do you all say?"

"We're fine with taking the ship," Var'at said quickly for all the Rasa.

"Sounds like an adventure," Aaron agreed. His mind was considering the possibility of being restricted to the ship for a year or more with Minu. His stomach did a flip-flop.

Ted shrugged. "I don't have a lot of years left; I'd be happy to spend what's left flying in this marvelous craft and learning about the ancient species that built it."

"You couldn't drag me off this ship," said Bjorn with finality. "To travel faster than the speed of light, and not through a portal? That's simply something I *must* do."

Cherise sighed and stared at her screen. "I'd miss my family greatly, but it does sound like a fine adventure."

"Don't forget," Pip chimed up, "we can stop at a world with a portal on the way back. I have detailed, if very old, maps of the galaxy and every portal therein."

Minu nodded and considered. Everyone was willing to go, and that meant a lot. As commander, it was ultimately her decision. Above all was what would happen to her when she arrived back on Bellatrix after basically going AWOL, stealing two transports, and as much gear as she could haul. The ship was an asset, an incredibly powerful asset that would benefit the people of Bellatrix in more ways than she could imagine. The decision was made.

"How soon can we switch to this Gravitic Lens Drive?"

*****

Chapter Four
January 17th, 523 AE

Firebase, Enigma Star System, Galactic Frontier

Singh-Apal-Katoosh watched the first shuttle as it was destroyed over his tablet while his troops were boarding the shuttle. It took a few minutes to get everyone set and decompress the bay, during which the debris of the shuttle splashed against the starship's shield with no effect, and then collided with the station and several ships docked to it.

Instantly their launch sequence was aborted, the doors closing again and the lighting turning to a green tinge. The annoying chattering voice announced that the firebase was under attack and to remain where they were. With growing dread, Singh saw a series of missiles flash away from the station and race away almost like lasers. Less than a minute later he lost the data feed to his tablet as the other two shuttles were turned into brilliant points of light.

Perhaps if he wasn't locked down, he could still try to ram the damned ship, or something. Here he could do nothing. He contacted the portal transfer station that wasn't locked down and had the last two shuttles launch. Instead of troops, they were packed with as many EPCs as they could quickly load aboard. The high energy capacitors carried an incredible amount of energy, and if impacted against a defense shield, could well be catastrophic. The transfer station sent him a new feed of the damned ship.

As the minutes dragged on, it seemed to be heading for the transfer station. If they meant to force entry, they'd have a nasty surprise from the fans of warriors he'd left there. But then it changed course, and began to accelerate. Then it *really* accelerated! In only a few seconds it became an improbable blur, and then was gone.

For a time he seethed and waited. His sub-commanders kept their distance in the cramped shuttle, fearing their leader's well-known rage. Eventually the green glow went away and the locks were released. The chattering voice thanked them for their patience.

"Pilot, return to the transfer station."

Sally nodded and began the launch sequence again. Just like Singh, she'd watched the brief battle and the station's response. Then the ship's improbable escape at what must have been multiples of lightspeed. While Singh seethed with impotent rage, Sally was already composing a message to the Technological Nest Master. They must increase their work to gain access to these ships, they must. She also found herself hoping to one day meet these 'humans' again. They were fascinating beings.

* * *

They never noticed the ship passing the speed of light. Pip explained that inside the ship they really weren't traveling faster than light, only the space around the ship was. Bjorn and Ted were discussing this with Pip while Minu tried to follow along. Her education was in technology and engineering, the degree of physics they were casually bantering about was several steps beyond her modest learning in that field. On Bellatrix they still taught that Einstein had it right.

Acceleration was very quick to start, then slowed until they crept up to just under three thousand times the speed of light, what Pip called 'nearly optimal.' He also explained that acceleration and deceleration were the most power-hungry parts of the operation. She'd watched their reserves drop quickly below 11% during the first few hours, but then level off at 10% as they cruised along at their inconceivable speed.

Safely away from Enigma, the crew was looking forward to rest. Pip carefully disengaged from the ship's computer, a sensation he said left him rather empty. Aaron and Minu had to almost carry him to his cabin, the effort exhausting him more than he'd expected. He'd left the Steward behind to mind the ship, keeping a careful eye on basic systems and their course. "I'm sure it's safe to do that much," he assured her.

What he didn't know was his meddling with the two programs had gone even farther than had Bjorn's. Some of the ship's deep logic arrays were disturbed, and carefully hidden defensive programs were awakened. They silently prowled the synaptic pathways of the computer, examining what had been done, and found it only slightly above acceptable. The same programs were confused by the lack of orders for the ship, or any contact with command. Finding no master control program, they were unable to make their own decisions on how to deal with this. So the Medical Intelligence was tweaked by adding a routine or two, and the security programs went back into hiding.

"Determine the intent of the biological operators," the Medical Intelligence was ordered. "A new directive is added to establish a proper biological operator by any reasonable means possible." The program considered that last part for some seconds. In deep space and with no sign of any other ships, how exactly was it to procure proper operators? The recent patient had been modified to act as a partial operator, but the damage done precluded a complete modification. Still, a directive is a directive.

The next day they worked with Pip to have the ship begin to synthesize foods that they were more accustomed to. It wasn't perfect, but the hamburgers tasted pretty good, even if the fries were strangely spicy. The water was always cold and plentiful. Pip got a little better as the second day progressed. He still occasionally said something inappropriate, but when it was pointed out the incident wasn't repeated. Minu thought it was a little like instructing a child how to act with adults around.

After lunch they gathered in the CIC and observed their path on a map of the galaxy. To actually see themselves move in real time, if only at a snail's pace, and considering the scale of the map, was an amazing thing. It usually only took a couple of hours for them to traverse through a star system. Pip said they were invisible to anyone, even should they be only a few clicks away as the *Kaatan* went by. But there was little chance of that, the Gravitic Lens Drive, or GLD as they were calling it, wasn't friendly to large gravity wells. Pip, Bjorn and Ted all agreed that the results of a close encounter between a fully powered GLD and even a modest-sized planet would be mutually cataclysmic.

"So how did they move fleets of these ships?" Minu asked. "You couldn't do even squadron sized engagements for fear of blowing each other up just by being too close!"

"That's what the Tactical drive was for," he told her.

"How does it work?"

"I have no idea; it's the only drive system with no information uploaded at all. At least, not that I've found yet."

Minu had a good idea how it might work, but like her sudden knowledge of ancient Concordian script, it wasn't something she was interested in sharing yet. "If we're going to be gone a few years, we need to stop at a world and use its portal to call home. We're probably already in deep shit for running off; at least we can let them know what we've managed to do."

"Probably better tell them about all the snakes we blew to hell too," Aaron suggested.

"Yeah, and that."

Ted and Bjorn were at their stations, both with tablets in hand, entering data from the Chosen database. As they worked, little golden points of light appeared on the map showing known portals. Where they matched with green points of light, portals from the ship's memory, they then glowed blue. The project took several hours and resulted in roughly half the green points changing to blue. When they were finished, only three points glowed gold. "What systems are those?" Minu asked.

Pip was sitting in a normal chair now, eyes open and alert. This degree of interaction didn't seem to require him to go into a trance like it had yesterday. Three new screens appeared and as he described them, each one came alive with images. "The first is Bellatrix," he said as their world orbited its red dwarf sun.

"So the portal there is new?" Aaron asked.

"Only newer than this ship," Pip explained. "And since the ship has been sitting there for at least a million years, I wouldn't call that 'new.'" Aaron nodded grudgingly. "The second is designated by us as Deep Blue."

"We use it for training all the time," said Minu. "We always figured the ruins were as old as this ship, but I guess not."

The third screen came alive with an image of a world none of the humans could fail to identify instantly. The blue sphere of Earth rotated with its yellow sun in the background. "I didn't even think not to enter that one, sorry," Bjorn apologized.

"Don't be," Minu told him as they all regarded the world of their species' birth.

"Is that where humans evolved?" Var'at asked. Minu nodded. "It's a very wet world. Rare to find a planet with that much water. We wouldn't have been as happy there."

Ted chuckled. "If it wasn't for a lucky asteroid, we'd have probably evolved to look like you. Reptiles ruled the world for hundreds of millions of years before that."

"Then another asteroid killed us," Pip spoke up, "that's irony for you."

All the humans were looking at the blue planet, so none of them noticed Var'at exchange glances with his men. An unspoken statement passed between them, ending with Var'at snapping his jaws shut in an explicit order to be quiet. "We're fugitives already," he hissed in a whisper, "we will not add violation of the highest Concordian laws to that!" While his words had been far below the human's ability to hear them, they weren't below the threshold of the CICs auditory sensors. It was dutifully recorded and logged away.

Minu finally had to break the long silence. "So what's the closest world with a confirmed portal?"

"Planet designated as Ragnarök," Pip said, "two hundred and twenty-nine light-years."

"Not a good choice," Aaron said with a shake of his head. "Besides being as cold as a deep freeze, it's in contention by the Mok-Tok."

"That's a 'no' for Ragnarök," said Minu. "How about a neutral world?"

"Checking." The lights flashed on the screen, the green trace of their course toward Bellatrix deviating this way and that until settling on a slight detour. "Planet designated as Midnight, two hundred and eight light-years distant. ETA would be thirty-four days."

Minu thought about it for a second, then nodded. "Brown dwarf system, not as cold as you'd expect because of planetary volcanism. Not even a junk pile, really, the only danger is it's commonly used as a transit point by many alien scout teams. Adjust the course."

Aaron entered the adjustments and the course line settled on the big galaxy map. "Time passage on Bellatrix will be approximately forty days."

"That's not too bad," said Minu. "So all we have to do is find ways to amuse ourselves for a month." Some of them smiled, others shrugged. A month wasn't very long.

"And then a couple years after that to get home," Aaron pointed out, and the smiles faded.

"Everyone should compose a vid-mail for their friends and family. I'll take care of the council of course. Var'at, you'll want to touch base with your people so they know you're okay." The Rasa nodded in understanding. "In the meantime, let's see if we can devise a schedule to begin getting a hand on controlling this ship we've got here and understanding what makes it tick."

* * * * *

Chapter Five
January 19th, 523 AE

Conference Room, Interspecies Diplomacy Center, Nexus

Tak'la paced the small conference room nervously, appearing to contemplate the floor carefully as he moved back and forth over and over again. A trio of aides all occupied desks, tablets arrayed before them filled with vital data that had thus far proven completely worthless. He'd come with his aides to Nexus for a quick meeting; that was a week ago. Day after day he would arrive, spend most of the day waiting, and eventually be told by a bot to leave and return the next day. A bot, not even a living representative. In addition to his anger at being dealt with by a non-living rep, he had a gnawing fear of what was going on behind the scenes.

Nearly a year ago, he'd reached a deal with the Tanam to destroy the detestable humans. It had cost him a great deal, but he'd left with the knowledge that the annoying hominids would be a bloody mess after the felines mauled them. The Tanam had fought a brief skirmish against the Beezer, servants of the Tog who were themselves masters of the humans. Tak'la was sure it was part of the Tanam strategy to get at the humans themselves. It seemed to have worked, because the Tog unleashed the humans on the Tanam. The details of what occurred on Serengeti were difficult to uncover. It took him months of careful research and bribes to learn that the humans kicked the shit out of the much more powerful Tanam, so decisively that the Tanam had yet to renew their efforts. It was this fact that brought Tak'la to request a meeting to get an update on Tanam efforts to punish the humans. He'd paid well and was tired of their delays.

Once again the hour was drawing late. Tak'la was expecting the now ubiquitous bot to show up any moment and was wondering if he should return home when one of his aides looked up from his tablet with alarm. "Supreme leader!"

"Yes, speak, what is it?"

"We're being summoned before a high-order council meeting."

Tak'la froze in his pacing, confusion filling his mind and fear chilling his blood. You weren't simply summoned to a council meeting, it was often a process that took weeks, or even months, and was consumed with ritual. His mind spun, trying to guess what had been going on behind the scenes while he'd been kept in a box here waiting for a meeting that was obviously never going to take place. "Gather your equipment," he told them as he went to the small storage area of the conference room and opened his diplomatic case. Inside were packed all the trappings for a representative of a species; formal robe adorned with stripes representing his species' order of ascension, formal armor with weapon, a few dozen odds and ends, and carefully concealed in a secret compartment, a pair of data chips containing carefully hidden accounts holding considerable assets of his species.

It took a long minute of agonizing before he settled on the armor and weapon. To be summoned before a higher-order council meeting demanded he respond as the military leader of his people. At the last minute he left the expensive compact beamcaster pistol in the case and instead strapped a thin-bladed sword on. He finished locking the armor in place, his three aides all looking on nervously. None of them had ever attended such a meeting of the galaxy's power holders.

The trip by flier took minutes, depositing them in the boughs of the huge Seat of Power, a building made to look like a crystalline tree. When they landed, they were met by a pair of spider-bots, a rare model only seen commonly on Nexus that was used as a diplomatic messenger. "Rasa delegation, follow us," instructed the bot. Tak'la gave himself a quick once-over to verify his condition, then gestured for his aides to follow him before dropping in behind the two bots.

Unlike his previous trips to the Seat of Power, they traveled deeply into the tree and then were ushered into a huge domed chamber made of the same crystal as the rest of the structure. At one end were the councilors, three pedestals growing up from the floor to support the representative and his delegation, with a fourth massive column growing up behind the three that went all the way to the distant ceiling. To Tak'la it looked like a living tree branch or root running through the ceiling above. With a sinking feeling, he realized this wasn't some council antechamber; this was the Grand Chamber of the Concordia. Legend said this was where the Lost first created the vast empire, millions of years ago. The species of the Rasa didn't rate a space at the rear of the chamber, even though there was room for uncountable thousands.

The bot left them off near the center of the floor, mere meters from the towering councilor pedestals. Through an effect of light and angles, anyone near those pedestals was always made to feel that they were looking straight up at those occupying them. Tak'la looked up to find the pedestals already occupied.

"The High Council of the Concordia stands in representation in memory of the Lost Creators," echoed the crystal halls. The feeling of foreboding was like a physical pressure in Tak'la's chest. On the pedestal were councilors of three of the five high-order species of the Concordia, a huge hairy Mok-Tok, an amphibian Gulla in its hovering ball of water, and a Tog. At the last, Tak'la knew his people's fate was sealed. Missing were the Tanam, and worse, the T'Chillen, the only reptile on the council.

From the side slithered in a trio of T'Chillen, all in ceremonial armor just like Tak'la. His fear turned to confusion. This had all the trappings of a formal offer for war. He didn't know if a high-order species had ever offered war to a second-tier species such as his own. And why would the T'Chillen do that, now of all times? The Rasa had made good on the losses to the T'Chillen for the beamcasters several years ago. A lucrative offer, accepted in the mediation council. Additionally alarming was the absence of the Tanam on the pedestals. The Tog were not looked upon well by the T'Chillen, Tanam and Mok-Tok. There was no dispute of the grass eaters' right to their status, but they were the weakest of the five high-order species. The Tanam were missing on purpose, and it was just as chilling as the T'Chillen in its ceremonial armor.

"Good, the betrayer comes in armor!" the T'Chillen hissed and pointed with its gleaming tail spike.

"What demands do you make of the noble Rasa?"

"Noble," hissed and spat the T'Chillen before addressing the council pedestals. "The T'Chillen have been betrayed by these subcreatures, the Rasa. They have been allowed to participate in minor ways in our most secret projects. Many of those projects would benefit all the species of the Concordia."

"Indeed," spoke the Tog councilor, "the unselfish giving of the T'Chillen is well known."

"With thanks," the T'Chillen spoke without realizing it was the victim of the Tog's foil. "We were repaid this trust with an act of utter betrayal. Using knowledge they gained while working on our secret projects, at a secret facility, they have raided that location, stolen irreplaceable materiel, and caused great loss of life."

"This is a lie!" Tak'la snapped. "We have worked faithfully for the T'Chillen for centuries; we would not betray this trust regardless of the gains!"

"The T'Chillen will present their evidence," the hall echoed.

A large section of wall to either side of the pedestals cleared and began to display scenes of carnage. Dead T'Chillen, warriors and technicians, many blown to bloody bits, others appearing all but unharmed. Destroyed heavy weapons emplacements were side by side with banks of ruined computer storage racks and scientific instruments. There was a quick view of the area where this battle took place, and Tak'la saw a narrow window looking out into space. *This took place at Enigma then?* He was doubly confused now, because his people had been escorted there through a very complicated route. He wouldn't have known how to lead an assault there even if he'd wanted to. Finally he found himself unable to remain silent.

"This is horrible damage, to be certain, but where is the evidence my people committed the offense?"

"For you to view, your own deceit!" The images resolved again to the debris of a crushed transport. The design was old, one that the Rasa no longer used. But there, partially uncovered, were the remains of a mangled Rasa corpse. He watched in stunned silence as another, then another was revealed. They all wore Rasa shock trooper armor and one even held the remnants of one of their signature accelerator rifles. Along one side was a scroll of secured data, date stamped, verifying Rasa DNA. Tak'la snapped at one of his aides who quickly recorded the data.

The remainder of the evidence was presented, and Tak'la was given his chance to repudiate it. He was still scrambling to understand. No such operation had been ordered, and because of the secrecy imposed by the T'Chillen, no such operation was even possible! But he was in a corner, with no way out. You could not refute this sort of evidence by just claiming you didn't order the attack, or didn't know how to get there.

"The Rasa request time to compose a response," he said, a desperate move.

"We are not inclined to give it to you," the Mok-Tok said menacingly. Neither of the other councilors contradicted the being. Tak'la ground his jaws as he feverishly thought.

"Supreme leader!" the senior aide barked.

"Yes!" Tak'la turned to his tablet and read the results. The DNA matched the records of a Rasa soldier. At first he was struck stupid, and then he looked at the last assignment. Assigned – Human Vendetta / Commander – Var'at. "The Humans!" he yelled across the council chamber, bringing shouts of outrage and a menacing hiss from the T'Chillen accuser. However on hser pedestal, Tak'la saw the Tog turn to regard him ever so slightly.

"What are you implying?" hse asked.

Tak'la addressed the councilors together. "A contingent of my soldiers, against my orders, has allied with Humans, a Tog client, to perpetrate this betrayal. The people of the Rasa have no involvement in this!"

The T'Chillen representative turned his eye stalks on the Tog councilor, slowly and with obvious distaste. There were few in the Concordia who didn't know of the mutual loathing between the two species. The Gulla councilor spoke up for the first time.

"You suggest a secret alliance between an uncontrolled element of your own soldiery and this minor species, the Humans?" Having set his course, Tak'la agreed. "Is it not true that only a short time ago you executed a failed Vendetta against these Humans? Yes, of course it is, I sat on the War Council and allowed the Vendetta. So having been humiliated by these insignificant hominids, your soldiers have joined with them in a plot against an old ally, the T'Chillen."

"I don't understand it myself," Tak'la complained, the desperation in his voice being conveyed well by the hall's translator system to all the councilors, "but the Rasa people are innocent of any complicity in the crimes against the T'Chillen! Investigation needs to take place—"

"No investigation!" roared the T'Chillen representative.

"What do the T'Chillen demand in reply to being wronged?" asked the Mok-Tok, the actual voice of the being unheard by any except the translation system.

The reptilian head turned to regard Tak'la with both eyes. His mouth opened slightly and venom dripped from rows of fangs. "We demand extermination."

*****

Chapter Six
February 15th, 523 AE

***Kaatan*-Class Cruiser, Interstellar Space**

A month slid by quicker than most on board the *Kaatan* expected. Each of the crew found ways to amuse themselves and spent an hour each day working on their understanding of the ship. Pip was quickly recovering from his years of coma half-life, his body regaining its tone and his mind learning to work with the new artificial parts. He spent only a couple of hours a night sleeping, using the remainder of the evening working through his link with the computer and reading. Minu had lunch with him every day, talking with her old friend and trying to get a sense of what his new level of functioning was.

One afternoon Pip called her out on it. "What do you want to know about me?" he asked her over his sandwich. With his help, the food system was producing nearly perfect fare now.

"What do you mean?" she asked with poorly-feigned ignorance. The salad sat half eaten, her hunger suddenly gone.

"We have lunch almost every day, Minu, and it's always the same thing. 'What do you think of this?' 'What do you think of that?' 'Do you remember that time?' Etcetera, etcetera." He regarded her with his own green eyes, not as brilliant a shade of green as hers, but with an intensity they didn't have before his recovery. "You should just ask me to tell you what my condition is."

"You don't expect me to simply take your word for it, do you?" The question burned in her throat, but it needed to be said. It was a commander's job to do more than just *ask* how her soldiers were; she needed to verify that information through actions.

Pip considered her for a moment before picking up his sandwich and taking another bite. "Right out of the leadership manual," he said after chewing and swallowing. "So what's my Commander's opinion of this soldier's condition?"

"I find your basic condition to be restored; however there are indications of lasting damage in your interpersonal reactions."

"Is that it?"

"Not entirely. You're now possessed of an unusual detachment from your fellow humans, preferring to spend more time with the ship's computer via your wireless connection or reading whatever literature is available. The attention you've spent to recover your physical condition seemed commendable at first."

"But now?"

"I have to believe it's a newly-installed need to be perfect in every way quantifiable. Before, this manifested mainly in technical knowledge and scientific skills, as noted in your Chosen file. Now it's extended to every aspect of your life."

"I see. So what's your conclusion on my fitness for duty as a Chosen?"

"You're fit enough," she said and picked at her salad.

"There's more. So say it."

"Pip, I don't know what to say. I…what happened to you was my fault. We left you behind. It almost cost you your life, and it did cost you a part of what made you the person I loved."

"You don't love me anymore? And what kind of love was that? Friendship? Brother-sister love?" He lowered his head slightly and regarded her cautiously. "Romantic?"

"Most of those…" she shrugged, "maybe all of them. When you woke up you said you were sorry you didn't stay that night. I don't think a week went by I didn't wish I hadn't driven you off. I wish you'd been my first lover."

"I can't be your lover now, Minu."

"I know, that time is gone."

"I'm changed now, you know that."

"You know you have someone who's been waiting to see you again? Waiting almost every day?"

"Who?"

"Cynthia." Minu explained to Pip how his girlfriend had been watching him faithfully, sitting with him almost every day since he was moved into the coma care facility, and how she'd moved to Tranquility to be closer to him. He listened attentively, nodding from time to time. "Were you lovers?" Minu asked when her story was over.

Pip shook his head. "We kissed and talked about it, but it never happened. We were going to spend a week's leave together, but then the Vendetta heated up. What do you think she'll expect of me?"

"I think she wants to be your wife. Do you love her?"

"You wanted to know what's wrong with me? What didn't make it back out of that coma? You just found it. Call it passion, call it love; whatever it's called, I don't have it anymore. I can sense that old feeling for her, just as I sense it was there for you too. There's still desire, of a sort. I'd very much enjoy having sex with you…"

"Pip!" Minu snapped, her face turning red, but he was on a roll.

"Everything works. I masturbate every day. Strangely enough, I can do it much more often than before." Minu tried to find something interesting in the bottom of the salad plate, immensely grateful they were the only ones in the little mess hall. "The orgasms feel good, and with the additions to my brain I can make them happen without even having to touch myself. I had twelve one night a week ago until they started to hurt. Not sure what that was all about."

"Pip, you are making me very uncomfortable."

"I'm sorry, but you asked. I've wanted to know if I can have sex still, and since I've never done it with a girl, there's no baseline to make comparisons. I asked Cherise yesterday, and she became…angry." He looked up at her, confusion on his face. "Am I a monster now, Minu?"

"No, of course not! You're just different. You've been changed in a way no one ever has been before."

"You've had a cybernetic prosthesis for years, how am I different?"

"My prosthesis didn't change my personality."

"Will you have sex with me?"

Minu thought for a minute and almost said yes. Then she saw Aaron's face, as if he were sitting there with them having lunch like he had a few times. They'd not shared a bed again and something unspoken was hovering there, something neither of them were ready to face up to. Would one night of love lead to something more? Her own fear of what she'd done was keeping her from making the next move, and he was willing to give her that space. For now, they sufficed with running together each night, but she was sure he wished she'd invite him into her cabin every time they finished. "I can't, Pip."

"Why?"

"Because I'm in love with Aaron, and like an idiot I had sex with him back when we first got the ship." The admission was out of her mouth almost before she thought about it. For a moment, she was glad someone knew, even if it wasn't the one she should be admitting it to.

"I know."

"Huh? How do you know?"

"I have access to the internal monitors. I saw the recordings." Minu's face burned bright red and she looked down. "You shouldn't be embarrassed, it looked very enjoyable. I've watched several times while I—"

"Pip, please!" she exclaimed, slamming her fist down on the table. It gave a crack and she realized she'd used her right arm. "You have to learn what's appropriate and what isn't!

It was his turn to look down and feign interest in his food. "I should know what not to say, but I don't. It's worse than not being able to love; I *know* what that was like. With this, I have no sense at all." He shrugged. "I guess a price had to be paid." He tapped the gleaming dualloy plate replacing part of his skull. "You can trust me as a Chosen; I guess you just can't trust what I'm liable to say."

"Can I trust you not to tell Aaron what I told you?"

"If you say so."

"I do. And please, stop using the recording of my lovemaking with Aaron as a personal porno."

* * *

Two days later, the *Kaatan* slowed as it entered the Midnight star system. Aaron was able to bring them into orbit around the world where the portal was located in only a few hours. Minu watched from her command chair as the power levels dropped below nine percent. As Pip had told them, accelerating and decelerating cost a lot of power, but the view from the wrap-around displays as they moved into orbit was worth the price of admission.

"Not much of a world," Ted said of the dark brown and black ball of dirt far below. The curve of the world stretched out before them, and the landscape moved by at a rapid pace. The images from Earth taken by the space program, and those from their own few satellites on Bellatrix, didn't do it justice.

"I think it's spectacular," Aaron said, giving voice to Minu's feelings.

"Pip," said Minu, "prepare one of the shuttles." The four small shuttles were only about a quarter the size of the one they'd ridden before; they were simple needle shapes meant to ferry crew between ships or to the surface of a planet. Pip nodded and the power level dropped again, to seven percent.

"Shuttle number one is fully powered and will be available in five minutes."

"Who's on the away mission?" Aaron asked, making Minu roll her eyes.

"Just me," she said and tried to remember where she'd stowed her laser communication gear. She glanced at Pip for a second, thinking about taking him down to the portal as the Weavers wanted. It wasn't going to happen though; she wouldn't risk him this soon after getting him back. There'd be time on Bellatrix later.

"No way are you going down there solo," said Aaron.

"I think I can handle a phone call home."

"I'm sure you can, but can you pilot a ship during reentry?"

"The shuttle pilots itself," she reminded him, "we've all gotten the instructions from Pip."

"Yes, and he also told us that should the link be broken with the ship, then the pilot better be a good one."

"He's got you there, Boss," said Cherise from her station.

Minu didn't look back at her. The two had hardly spoken since Pip's awakening, and you didn't have to be empathetic to see her pain. After she'd seen Minu and Aaron on their nightly run, she'd been sure to stay out of sight at that time of the evening.

"Fine, but that's it, no more arguments."

"I must ask to go as well," Var'at spoke up. "It's not out of concern for you that I ask, though we've linked our fate to yours. I want to be there."

Minu considered it then nodded. "Only you though, I want the ship to still have enough crew to proceed if anything happens to us. Ted and Bjorn, finish preparing your communications. Pip, is the codex ready yet?" Still reclined where he floated in the CIC during operations, Pip's hand moved almost like a sleepwalker as he retrieved a data chip from his uniform pocket and held it out to her. She took the chip and put it in her own pocket. "Have your personal messages ready in five minutes and meet me at the shuttle."

As she'd requested, all the other humans arrived at the shuttle entrance. Aaron and Var'at wore light field packs and were armed, while the others just looked concerned. Minu silently collected data chips from her friends, their private messages contained inside. She'd already packed the encrypted laser transmitter into her pack. Var'at no doubt carried similar letters from his soldiers to their friends back on Bellatrix. The formalities complete, they boarded the shuttle as the rest watched in silence.

* * *

The descent was quick and smooth, the computerized piloting link to the *Kaatan* functioning flawlessly. The compensators held them in their seats gently and counteracted the eleven Gs of the shuttle's terminal plunge through the thick atmosphere of Midnight. Aaron carefully watched the controls, his hands tensed and ready to react in an instant should a problem be detected.

Once the speed of rapid reentry had fallen to manageable levels, the shuttle deployed stubby wings, which bit into the thickening air and began to steer them toward their destination, the remnants of a settlement abandoned before humanity learned to harness fire. Sensors swept the ancient colony, found it abandoned and with no landing beacons, and informed the pilot. "Ah ha, see!" Aaron cheered and took control. "And you said not to worry about it." He angled them around the ruins and began to look for a good place to set down.

"There'll be no living with him now," Var'at hissed quietly to Minu.

"And how is that different from any other time?"

Aaron swept around the crumbled settlement at half the local speed of sound. The heat shields were retracted, and he used his eyes in addition to the shuttles sensors.

"Can't you just set down next to the portal?" Minu asked.

"There are a few buildings around it; kind of like most small settlements, it's situated in a town square. The shuttle's a little too long to fit."

"You're not filling us with confidence," said Var'at, and Aaron laughed in reply.

"Found a place, here we go." With no further notice, the needle-shaped shuttle nosed over into a precipitous dive. Minu gritted her teeth, and Var'at said something that the translators couldn't handle. Aaron pitched them up at the last second and slowed with shocking speed. There was a slight bump, and they were down. "Welcome to Midnight, be sure to check your ticket for where to find your baggage, and thanks for flying Chosen airlines."

"Just open the damn door," Minu grumbled as she unstrapped and headed toward the exit on wobbly legs. It was the most hair-raising ride she'd had since the first day of her trials many years ago.

"No sense of humor," Aaron said silently as he told the shuttle to equalize and open the door.

"How far are we from the portal?" Minu asked as they climbed down the stairs into the perpetual twilight of Midnight and onto the hard-packed dirt.

"About two kilometers," said Aaron, "as close as I could manage."

"My people come here often," Var'at said as a warning, while adjusting his accelerator rifle in its sling. Minu nodded as she settled her pack and the two Enforcers she wore cross on her hips. Aaron also wore a pair of the powerful semi-automatics and had one of their only beamcasters slung over one shoulder. Minu would have liked to have one too, but the laser communication gear in her pack was too heavy to make it practical.

"Quick in, quick out," she told them. "Once I make connection it should only take a few minutes to upload the data." As Minu led them away, she couldn't shake the feeling she was being watched.

*****

Chapter Seven
February 16th, 523 AE

Planet Midnight, Galactic Frontier

To be on a planet again after nearly a month in space was a real pleasure. Minu saw it on all their faces, even the hard to read Var'at. The air on the *Kaatan* was always crisp and clean, and the gravity felt perfect, but it lacked skies. She looked up at the twilit cloudless skies and sighed. After this brief mission, it might be a year or more before they saw it again. The ship didn't have the power to make more than one more stop and still be able to reach Bellatrix. They knew there was no way to recharge the capacitors without stopping at a major trading world, and pulling into orbit in an ancient alien spaceship was *not* the kind of attention they wanted to draw to themselves.

Only a hundred meters from the shuttle they came across the first sign of activity. A heap of debris was piled against a crumbled wall, torn packaging and scattered trash covering the timeless ceramic concrete roadway. Minu thought she could see a broken heating element and discarded old EPCs. There was no indication of what species might have left the garbage, but she knew it wasn't humans. Chosen scouts were carefully trained to leave no trace of their passage; this was the absolute opposite of their training. It spoke of a higher-order species, or worse.

Minu trotted onward with her right hand on one Enforcer, knowing the other two would have seen the same thing and were now on their guard as well. A minute later they carefully crept along a wall as Aaron swept the vicinity with a life-sign detector. Its readout remained blank. Minu looked around and scratched her chin, unable to shake the feelings that something was wrong and they were being watched. With a grumble at her own jumpiness, she removed her pack and fished out a case. Inside was a pair of valuable dragonfly bots, one of the things she'd likely get in big trouble for having taken. She reached between the wings of one and carefully tapped the little jewel there twice. The wings buzzed and the tiny eyes glowed blue.

"Mission." She spoke the trigger word to the bot, which leaped into the air and hovered centimeters before her eyes. Having been the one who'd turned it on, it would only respond to her commands. "Perimeter search, two hundred meters, any sentients of biological classifications other than this team." She knew it was scanning all three of them, identifying their species, and logging the information. "Energy sweep one thousand meters. Low risk, return on hostilities. Safeties on." The little eyes flashed twice, and with a barely audible buzz it shot away.

"You got a hunch?" asked Aaron.

"More of an itch behind my eyes." He grunted in reply. It was something you had to go with, and sometimes it saved lives. Sometimes, though, it just wasted time; the bot returned five minutes later to hover before her eyes. It flashed three times and settled back into the case. Mission accomplished nothing to report. "Better safe than sorry," Aaron consoled her.

"You have good instincts," Var'at agreed.

"I guess," she said and stowed the case. Regardless of the bot's insistence, as they crossed the open town square to the portal, she felt little fingers crawling up and down her spine. It was frustrating, and she couldn't do anything to make it stop.

The portal was just like every other one in the galaxy, milky white dais waiting patiently for someone to come along and activate it. Minu stepped on the bottom step, and the archway sprang to life. She removed the control rod from the pocket sewn into her pant leg and keyed in a query of destinations. Ted had been annoyed at turning it over to her, but she hadn't listened to any complaints. A holographic display appeared above the rod with a multitude of choices. Aaron nodded and pointed to one of the Chosen's favorite destinations, Deep Blue. They also knew a permanent communication link was kept there, within view of the portal but carefully hidden from prying eyes. Minu opened the portal to Deep Blue.

Var'at and Aaron watched as Minu assembled the laser communicator. She'd used the link through Deep Blue often enough that finding the receiver on the other end was almost second nature. On the other world the sun blazed in the aquamarine sky, long abandoned but still intact buildings surrounded the portal. With the laser assembled, she looked through the portal and found the window just to the left of a specific archway with a long crack running its length. And there was the tiny laser relay in the corner of the cracked window. It took another second to activate the link and get a confirmed lock.

The laser communicator uplinked with Minu's tablet and she entered the required code. It accepted the code and informed her that a message was in the buffer. She was a little shocked, but shouldn't have been, considering how long they'd been gone and what she'd done to get there.

Chosen Minu Alma,

You are ordered to return to Bellatrix immediately. Your mission is not sanctioned or authorized, and you have illegally requisitioned vital Chosen assets. Scouts have been ordered to arrest you on sight. Should you return voluntarily, it will be taken into account.

Signed – Jacob Bentley, First Among the Chosen.

"Shit," Minu said as she read the brief message.

"He sounds kinda pissed," said Aaron after reading it over her shoulder.

"You really aren't helping," she told him as she prepared a reply. The message was written weeks ago in deep space. As she was preparing to send it she attached the codex and all the private packets from her friends. Once everything looked good, she sent the message, then closed the portal.

"Now may I send a message?" Minu looked at Var'at in surprise.

"I sent your messages back to your people."

"I was hoping to send a special message," he said and produced his own laser communicator of a different design.

"You never told me you had a laser communicator." Var'at remained silent, just waiting. "Have you ever used it before?"

"Yes."

"What sort of messages have you sent?"

"I've been in contact with members of my nest, those who have remained on our world but are not in support of Tak'la, the new leader."

"You've been hoping to someday return home? To what purpose? Revenge?"

"No, to take back control from a stupid leader who's steering our people toward disaster."

"And what would become of our relationship should you succeed?"

Var'at was silent for a moment before rotating both eyes to stare at Minu. "You've forged a tie between us, Minu Alma, and it's strong. We will be allies."

"Go ahead," Minu said and gestured toward the portal. "Do you need me to dial a world?"

"That won't be necessary." Var'at produced his own control rod. Minu shook her head, not really surprised, but amazed that it had gone unnoticed during his capture. Had the Rasa leader been anything but honest after he'd surrendered, how much mischief could he have accomplished? She didn't want to even consider it.

Minu stepped back and let her friend work. He was just as deft at using his own tools and was soon opening the portal to a sandy, dark world she didn't recognize. She was just wondering where the link might be, when a sand pile shifted, and a crab-bot stood up to reveal itself. A laser link replaced one pincer, and Var'at made contact with it. He transmitted his message and received one in reply. With no further ceremony, the bot dug back into the dune and out of sight. As the Rasa leader began reading the message, she could see his rising distress. By the time he was finished, the poor thing was sitting on his haunches and making a horrible screeching noise.

"Var'at!" yelled Minu, "what's wrong?" But he wouldn't answer, instead dropping the computer and laser communication gear and rolling up in a ball on the ground, tail wrapping around his head protectively.

Aaron carefully picked up the computer and looked at it. "I can't read their script," he said.

Minu moved over and linked her computer with the Rasa machine, clicking the accept icon on Var'at's computer when it asked permission. The file was instantly uploaded to her tablet, and translated to English.

Var'at,

I hope this message finds you; it has been many months since you have relayed one yourself. You are correct, I believe the Humans may have been our key to creating an alliance among the lesser species, but our time is up. We have offended the T'Chillen somehow. Tak'la returned from Nexus and scheduled a moot of all the nest mothers. And then our colony on Ses'la was destroyed. The soldiers had almost no chance to resist, and no quarter was offered. The nest there was slaughtered, the eggs crushed. Tak'la committed suicide even before the meeting. Just as well, we would have torn him apart for his failures anyway.

The other two colonies are under siege. Yesterday, official announcement from the Concordian War Council arrived stating the T'Chillen have claimed right of extermination against us and have been granted it. There will be nothing left for us, I fear. Your plans were good; our people would have prospered.

Do not try to return, your few would make no difference. The vile snakes have limited the portal approaches to our world, all our attempts to leave and conduct diplomacy have been met with force and either died or returned. It is only a matter of time. We will live on with you among the humans, for a time, and that gives me some happiness. Farewell.

E'Var'at'etal, nest mother, 'etal clan.

"That's not good," Aaron said as he finished reading.

"It's our fault, you know. They must have found Rasa bodies on that transport we lost back in Enigma," Minu said. Aaron shrugged. Like a lot of those who knew about the Rasa living among them, he considered all other Rasa to be enemies. Var'at and his people were…'special.' They'd proven themselves to be friends and allies. But Minu had known they would get old and die, unable to carry on their lines without females. She'd given a lot of thought to how to change that, but you can't just go buy some Rasa eggs. Now the snakes were tearing them to pieces, and it was all academic. Or was it?

"Var'at, snap out of it," she said, then leaned down and slapped him on the part of the face she could reach under his tail. A single eye opened and rotated to look at her. "There's a chance we can help!"

It was enough to make him unfold and regard her. Though the Rasa didn't cry like humans, he sure looked like he'd been through the ringer. "What can we do? Would the Chosen use all their soldiers to help with ours and attack the T'Chillen?"

"Jacob would never agree to that; the rest of the Rasa probably still hate us."

"Exactly. I don't blame you, but myself." He made a helpless gesture, another humanism he'd picked up. "I had such crazy ideas, now look what it has done to my people!"

"I said Jacob wouldn't approve, but he's not here."

"How can we help? We're not even a dozen, and with few arms. My nest mother said they're blocking the portal into home as well. What can be done?"

"Think, Var'at!" He looked at her helplessly. "We have a starship, remember?"

* * *

From the depths of an old store front, three sets of eyes watched as the portal flickered back into inactivity. One of them quickly trotted over to the carefully concealed laser communicator and hacked into its memory, making a copy of all the files without leaving any traces of the action, then closed it back up. The device had already decided the messages in its memory were important enough to warrant an unscheduled transmission and the portal outside was coming alive once more. The five huddled back into the shadows, away from the bright sunlight of Deep Blue as the portal opened onto a snowy world and the laser sent away its information. Once the portal was closed they ventured outside.

"It was her, I tell you!" insisted the first.

"Possible," the second member of the team agreed, chewing his lip and glancing at the tablet data copied from the laser link. "We better tell him about this."

"You sure?" asked the third of their number. "He doesn't like being bothered."

"He will about this." The man continued chewing his lip as he checked his miniature recorder, using the enhancement feature to review the woman's image. Sharp features, bright red hair. Did one of her hands only have three fingers? Strange. "Yeah, he'll want to hear about this," the man finally concluded.

* * * * *

Chapter Eight
February 16th, 523 AE

Planet Midnight, Galactic Frontier

Minu was so busy discussing her plan with Aaron and Var'at that she almost missed the ambush. Hundreds of trips off world and a well-developed sense of strategy didn't help her in the least. It was that damned sense of being watched that made her take a half step instead of a whole one. The energy beam cleaved through the air where her head would have been, scarcely half a meter in front of her nose and close enough to scorch her eyebrows as well as send electric tingles all over her body.

"Down!" she screamed and dove behind the hulk of a ground transport. It was unnecessary, since her friends were already diving for cover before she had. Two more energy beams tore pieces of wall away, following her as she dropped below their line of sight. She came up with both Enforcers in her hands, blazing round after thunderous round. She didn't know where the attackers were, but she knew what direction to fire. As her rounds started slamming into buildings and debris, the enemy fire ceased.

Var'at added the demonic buzz saw of his accelerator rifle as Aaron brought one of his own Enforcers into play. The beamcaster was being held in reserve for now. They all stopped firing and returned to cover, except Minu. For a split second she kept her head just above the edge of the ancient transport. Just long enough to see a pair of heads, furless, with ghastly white skin and elongated snouts filled with sharp teeth, and red eyes so bright they were almost glowing. She made it down a split second before she'd have lost her head. "Vampires," she told them.

She'd last seen a pair on Deep Blue months ago while training the misfits. Where the Rasa aggressively sought out political and economic advantage, the Vampires would attack and try to destroy any target they considered soft or unprepared enough. Even the T'Chillen found them rather extreme.

"That's all we need," Aaron said from a few meters away as he holstered his Enforcer and readied the beamcaster. With Vampires, there'd be no careful retreat or subtlety, only death and destruction. He had no intention of being the recipient of either death or destruction, but dealing it out was just fine with him. The three jumped up and ran between a pair of buildings, drawing brief fire until they were under cover again.

"Teams are usually six groups of three," Var'at spoke, opposite Aaron in the alley they'd been traversing. "They sweep out in an arc, meet up, and repeat. Their other groups will be heading here as fast as they can." They made it around a corner and stopped.

Aaron popped back around the corner, unimpeded by the three Vampires pumping away with their energy weapons, and killed one of them with a perfect center-mass beamcaster shot. Minu and Var'at both fired at the other two so Aaron could get back behind cover. The two survivors made no attempt to hide or dodge the fire. Fangs bared and eyes blazing, they poured out a withering rate of fire.

"On three," Minu told them. "One, two, THREE!" They all popped up, and in seconds the two remaining Vampires were down. "Move, move," she yelled, and they ran. The shuttle was only a little over a kilometer away, but if the Vampires beat them there it could spell disaster. They couldn't operate the craft—Pip had made sure of that—but they could disable or destroy it. Help was at least twenty minutes and two hundred kilometers away, orbiting above their heads. She decided it would be prudent to get the ball rolling, especially with as many as fifteen more snarling Vampires out there. She keyed her radio to link with the *Kaatan* above, and got nothing. "Can any of you get the ship?"

"Nothing," Var'at hissed as they jogged.

"Nada,' said Aaron.

"Shit, they must know the shuttle's there." As they rounded a corner, beam weapons tore at them from the front this time, confirming her fear. In moments, fire was coming from three sides. They were in a kill box. The three forced their way into a mostly-collapsed building. Vampire weapons fire ripped into what was left of the structure, threatening to bring the crumbling walls down on them.

"This really sucks," Aaron grumbled as he set the beamcaster to one side while reloading his partially-expended Enforcer. Var'at was laying out his only extra magazine and using both eyes independently to survey firing points. They were getting ready to make a stand, but Minu knew if they did so here it would mean their lives. Five-to-one odds in poor cover was a recipe for a massacre.

As her friends prepared, Minu snatched at her pack and removed a little reinforced case. A couple of quick taps, and two little glittering dragonfly-bots were hovering before her eyes. "Search and destroy," she ordered. "Attack east, non-present biologicals. Rendezvous one kilometer east, targets of opportunity. Attack in one."

"Good call," Aaron said but she could see the hesitation in his eyes. The two bots were unbelievably valuable assets and she was going to expend them as a diversion. He verified the handguns' readiness and slung the beamcaster. For this run, the Enforcers would let him move faster. Even Var'at was using one of the handguns. It looked ridiculously huge in his thin, clawed hands, but Minu knew the reptilian was anything but weak.

"Here we go," she said, and a second later the two bots' gentle buzzing turned to a scream as they used their tiny hoverfields to rocket away. A second later they heard the miniature energy weapons firing and the hideous cries of the surprised Vampires. "Move!" she said, and they were out the door.

She thought for a second that they were going to make it. They came around two corners, their weapons held at ready but encountering no resistance, and there was the shuttle squatting in the remnants of a residential building. She spotted the two Vampires crouched to either side of the shuttle just as they fired. Both energy beams struck her full in the chest.

Minu saw a brilliant blue flash of light as her personal shield absorbed the blast, an attenuated particle beam. Var'at and Aaron's shields both sparkled as excess energy splattered around her. She felt more than heard her shield disengage, the capacitor full. It was no longer useful to absorb incoming fire but would explode should it take another hit. She was just raising her Enforcer when the second shot hit her full in the chest, just above her solar plexus. *I'm dead,* she though.

The impact was direct now, without the shield, and she was smashed to the ground like a howler kicked by an angry farmer. Her arms flew up before her and she ludicrously grabbed at Aaron as she fell, but he was already a meter past her and firing at one of the Vampires, unaware of her fate. Pain, shock, and physical force were all she felt as she was slammed brutally to the ground. The back of her head smacked the ancient roadway with a thud.

"If I'm dead, why can I still talk," she gasped through clenched teeth. The pain was from the physical blow and the fall, not from her chest. She looked down, lifting her head to see how bad the wound was. Other than a slight smoking of her uniform below her breasts, there was no damage at all. Then Aaron and Var'at were there, each grabbing an arm and dragging her into another crumbled building. Minu just managed to get her right arm free enough to grab her dropped Enforcer as they got her out of the line of fire.

"How are you still alive?" Var'at asked.

"Gee, thanks," she coughed. They left her in a sitting position against the wall, where she used her left hand to feel the back of her head; it came away with a smear of blood. "And to answer your question, I don't know."

"The faraday armor couldn't have absorbed that much damage," Aaron said, his gun booming at a trio of Vampires making a run at their hiding place. Var'at joined him, and all three went down. "At least not without some damage. I've seen them work." He reloaded his gun as she felt her chest. It was a little sore, like someone had punched her, but other than that there were no aftereffects.

"The ship," she said suddenly, "it replaced my uniform."

"Like your arm," Aaron said, firing a couple quick rounds. "Nice upgrade."

"Remind me to be sure it does that with all our uniforms, and comes up with something for the Rasa." Var'at nodded his thanks. "Unfortunately I don't know if we'll live long enough to benefit."

He'd laid aside the empty Enforcer and had his rifle out again, burning through ammo at a ferocious rate. The only hope with a Vampire team was to stop them before they started a rush. If they got going, the only solution was to kill them all, or die.

"At least twelve left," Aaron said. Minu reloaded her Enforcer and checked her magazines. Unless the enemy was cooperative, and their marksmanship exceptional, there was no way. Maybe if she hadn't gotten shot. Maybe. Minu struggled to her feet just as Var'at spoke.

"Here they come," he barked. Minu accepted her gun back and they all pushed up against the broken walls and fired as fast as they could. The Enforcers lacked accuracy at more than a few meters. Aaron fired his dry and tossed his last magazine to Minu as he swung his beamcaster around. The cumbersome weapon fired with a frustratingly slow cycle rate. Var'at's magazine ran empty and he worked with feverish intensity to swap it out. At least seven of the snarling Vampires reached their cover and began to run up the walls, preparing to fire down on them.

If we just had a couple Shock rifles, Minu said silently as she shot the first one to reach the top. Var'at cut two in half, and Aaron burned another down. The remaining three leveled their weapons.

Crack, crack, crack! All three Vampires' chests exploded, their sickeningly-red eyes bugging out in surprise before they rolled down the wall to gasp and slowly die. Minu looked down at the bodies, then up at the wall, not knowing what to expect. Outside, the sound of a brief but intense firefight raged, and then silence. They all looked at each other, eyes wide, except Var'at of course, and waited with weapons at the ready.

Nothing happened. After a few minutes of tense quiet they peaked out around the doors in a quick snapshot. Again, nothing shot back. Minu spotted at least two bodies across the street and Var'at reported another pair. Aaron said he could see quite a few weapons hits around the area. What was obvious was that the Vampires had been neutralized.

They spent a minute sweeping the area and eventually came to a full count of dead Vampires. Every one of them except the ones Minu and Var'at had shot were dead from beamcaster wounds. All from behind or the side, and all well placed. "Real experts," Aaron noted.

"Absolutely," Minu agreed.

"Some other species' scout team?" Var'at wondered.

"Not likely," Minu said. "They'd have just let this play out and waited for the carnage to finish."

Not wanting to waste any more time, she got them moving back toward the shuttle. As they got closer, Minu breathed a sigh of relief to see the doors still secured and both dragonfly bots hovering outside, apparently unharmed.

"Shutdown," she instructed as she held out a hand. The team piled inside, with Minu and Var'at covering the door's closing as Aaron got the impellers spun up.

"Power's up, defenses working, lifting off." Aaron worked the controls and they were airborne.

During the short flight back to orbit Minu took one of the dragonflies and used her tablet to download its internal memory. They'd killed one Vampire and injured another before sweeping toward the shuttle. She was about to put it away when she saw a notation in the bot's log. "One target bypassed." She looked at the log entry one more time before storing the tablet and putting the bots away properly.

Minu looked up to see they'd already left the atmosphere and the *Kaatan* was getting closer. She fell into the seat and sighed, her chest hurting a little bit. She closed her eyes and thought about the log entry. Target bypassed. There was only one possibility. Whoever had rescued them had been human.

* * * * *

Chapter Nine
February 17th, 523 AE

Planet Midnight, Galactic Frontier

"This isn't a logical course of action," Pip complained again. As soon as they'd docked and she'd explained the situation on the Rasa home world, he'd come out against it.

"Yours is a biased opinion," Minu said and tapped her head where Pip's skull was metal instead of bone.

"That has nothing to do with it." She cocked her head at him, and he made a face. "Okay, very little to do with it. Yes, I'm skeptical about the Rasa being grateful in any way. Var'at and his people have been faithful, and in lieu of the discovery that they could have called down their people on our heads at any time, his loyalty is not in doubt. But the rest of his people can't be counted on to react in a similar manner."

The tiny ship's mess hall was full with the six humans and six Rasa, but everyone needed to hear this. Minu didn't want to waste time, and the CIC, the largest space in the ship, was difficult because of the zero gravity. She'd already wasted precious time explaining to everyone else about the fight with the Vampires and the orders for her to return home. "If that's your only concern, it's duly noted."

"There's more," he persisted. "The ship's power, most importantly."

"I've been watching how we consume power. About one percent up and down from super-light speed. That leaves almost five percent when we reach Bellatrix, no biggie."

"That's cruising at two thousand times the speed of light. At that speed the Rasa home world is almost two months away our time, nearly three their time."

Var'at shook his head. "There's no way my people can hold out for three months. They'll be lucky to survive one."

"Exactly my point," Pip said, nodding. "To get there in one month will require almost maximum speed, five thousand times light speed."

"Do we have enough power to get there?"

"Sure, but only about four percent reserves after we arrive. That leaves damned little to get home."

"But enough," Minu pointed out. Pip sighed and nodded reluctantly.

"Can we refuel somehow at the Rasa system?" Ted asked. Minu looked at Pip; it was a good question.

"If we find a power source, probably. I haven't tried to figure out how to do that yet."

"What about draining all the extra EPCs we have with us?" Bjorn suggested.

"We left with a reserve of twelve percent. Reserve mind you, no main power. To create that reserve would require us to drain every EPC on Bellatrix, at least a six month planetary supply of power."

"That's insane," Aaron barked. "What is it with the Concordia and power? You'd think it was just lying around in puddles or something."

"It probably was once, a long time ago." Ted's theory on the rise and fall of the Concordia was well known to many of them, Pip in particular, who'd helped him refine it. Minu found herself more and more in complete agreement with them after finding the ghost fleet and the hundreds of abandoned war ships. Her personal theory had a war as the catalyst for the decline of the Empire.

"We'll deal with that when the time comes," she told them. "Let's head to the CIC and get underway."

* * *

Once in the CIC, she saw they'd already made the transition to faster than light; she hadn't even noticed while walking down the hallways. The fact that the ship could so blatantly violate such a basic law of physics was a little disturbing. "You'd think we'd feel...something," she said as she sat in her captain's chair and looked at the growing multiples of light speed on her display.

"If we did feel it, it would be the last thing we felt." Pip's disembodied voice drifted through the CIC.

"How many Gs should we be pulling?" asked Aaron.

"Two, three," said Ted and Minu thought that wasn't too bad, "million." She swallowed hard at the thought of her body turned to strawberry jam against the wall of the CIC.

"So how come we aren't squished?" she asked him.

Pip paused for long enough to make Minu think he was ignoring her, then spoke. "It can't be explained with words."

"Then how?"

"Only math. You aren't prepared for that level of physics and quantum physics."

Minu almost chastised him for being inappropriate once more, but held back. He was being truthful, if painfully so. Their speed passed two thousand times the speed of light and continued to climb toward the maximum five thousand. "Why only five thousand? Why not a hundred thousand."

"I can't explain that," he admitted, "the ship builders installed that as a governor. No faster, period. I get the feeling exceeding five thousand times the speed of light would be somehow…bad."

Minu changed subjects. "Can we power all four shuttles for the operation on the Rasa home world?"

"No, the power drain is too much. We can power a second shuttle and use the first one with its remaining power."

They spent a few minutes talking over what she wanted to do as the other crew worked to put the ship into what Minu called 'cruise control.' Eventually, one at a time, they began to leave until only Aaron, Pip and Minu remained. Minu and Aaron discussed each taking a shuttle, and Aaron insisted Minu spend some time with him learning what he'd absorbed from his one drop to a planet in the pilot seat. Without them realizing it, Pip finished his work with the ship's computer, unhooked, and left them alone. When Minu looked over to ask him a question, he was gone, and she was suddenly aware she was alone with Aaron. Despite their almost daily run together, this was different. They hadn't been alone like this since they'd become lovers. *Fuck it,* she thought.

"I guess we need to talk," she said.

"Probably a good idea. You've been dodging me for a while."

"I know." She took a deep breath, wondering if she could do this. "I love you too." In a moment they were both in each other's arms, Minu crying against his chest, feeling his tears falling on her head. "I'm sorry, I'm sorry," she kept saying over and over, her chest heaving with sobs.

"For what?"

"For keeping it to myself for so long."

"I never did anything about it either," he said, gently pushing her away to look at her. She couldn't meet his gaze, looking down at his stomach instead. He took one finger and gently lifted her chin so she had to look him in the eye, just like that first night together. It wasn't difficult; despite his massively muscled body, he was only a couple of centimeters taller, something that Gregg never gave him a break over. "I've loved you since the day we met," he admitted, his eyes shining. Minu felt her heart melting. "When that shot hit you down on the planet I thought I was going to die."

"And that's part of why I haven't pursued this all that time! Christian was safer." It was Aaron's turn to look away, "You know how hard it was to hold him and see you in my mind?"

"Really?"

"Yes, you've had my heart almost as soon as I got yours. But as your boss, your superior Chosen, how could I take the chance of putting this between us?"

"You're assigned to training; I'm a scout. It just means I can't be directly under your control."

"You are now."

"Only because we're breaking the rules."

"Good point. Other Chosen do this; I guess maybe we can, too."

"So now what?"

"Well, why don't we go back to my quarters, and we'll take it one night at a time?"

"I can't hide this from everyone," he said, and she felt a little nervousness, "I won't send out emails to all the Chosen, but I will be proud of being your boyfriend. You can't lie about that kind of thing."

She took his strong hand into hers, and they floated toward the door. "I'm proud to be your girlfriend, too."

*****

Chapter Ten

February 18th, 523 AE (subjective)

Deep Space, en route to the Rasa Leasehold, Galactic Frontier

The entire ship knew about the new sleeping arrangements by the end of the next day. Minu barely made the morning briefing as scheduled in the CIC, and when she arrived it was with Aaron, hand-in-hand, both laughing and her blushing as she thought about the night of lovemaking. No one said anything about the new development. Bjorn gave her a wink and Ted a look that said he was still available. While Cherise managed to give her a smile, Minu couldn't miss the fact that her eyes were red and puffy. She realized her friend deserved to have an explanation of the situation. Only the Rasa failed to notice anything. They didn't have romantic attachments, or even sex the way humans did, if Minu understood their species correctly.

Later that day, Minu entered the galley late after working a simulation in the CIC with the Rasa until after the normal lunch time. Cherise was there, eating quickly, and she looked upset when she saw Minu. It was obvious she'd planned her lunch to avoid Minu, and her plan had backfired. She instantly tried to get up and leave.

"Cherise, talk to me."

"There's not much to talk about," the taller woman said and tried to slip by. Minu moved in front of her and saw anger flash on her face. "You going to get out of the way?"

"No."

Cherise backed up and put her hands on her round hips. The set of her shoulders, the stance of her feet, the anger in her eyes all made Minu wonder if she was about to get in a fight. The two women knew each other's fighting styles better than they knew themselves, but Cherise was still a notch better than her. Minu was pretty sure the only way to beat her was to cheat and use cybernetics where ability fell short. Luckily, it wasn't necessary. Cherise backed up and dropped into a chair, gesturing impatiently for Minu to join her. "Have your say, then."

Minu sat and took a deep breath, then admitted to herself that she didn't know what to say. "I'm sorry it worked out this way."

"Liar."

The word was a slap in the face. "Okay, I'm sorry you're hurt."

"Are you now?"

"Don't be a bitch," Minu said, a little menace slipping into her words. "You've been the best friend I've ever had."

"So good that a day after I admit that I'm in love with you, you go fuck Aaron for the first time?"

"Should I have run it by you first?"

"A simple no to my proposition would have been nice before you got all crazy with him."

"It just happened."

"Like I believe it was so spontaneous."

"And you and Gregg in that cave?" That brought her up short. "And don't even try saying it was different. I understand you two and how it happened better now. The difference is Aaron and I have had…feelings for each other for years."

"And still you pick this time to go for it, right after I bleed my heart dry to you?"

"If you think one event prompted the other, you're an idiot." Cherise opened her mouth to say something, then closed it and sat back. Pain etched her face. "Yes, we slept together, and did again last night. He moved into my cabin because we finally admitted we're in love."

"After I—"

"Damn it, Cherise, your admission didn't have anything to do with it! We've been in love since we met on the dirigible to the trials. You admitted you fell in love with me slowly, over the years. I'm truly sorry; he had first claim to my heart. I love you, like my sister, but that's all there will ever be. What we had and did was special, but just not right for me." Minu felt herself blushing at the unsaid part. She loved having a man inside her. Cherise looked down, big tears rolling down her face, wetting the front of her uniform. "I want to be your best friend, always. But I understand if it'll be too painful to you." Cherise refused to look up, her chest heaving as she quietly sobbed. Minu nodded and got to her feet. "I'll always love my big sister," she said, frowning in an effort not to cry herself, as she turned to leave.

"Please, don't go!" Cherise sobbed.

"I don't want to. I need a friend like you to face whatever's ahead. More importantly, I need you because I don't have a real sister like you do."

"You *are* my real sister," Cherise said. With an obvious effort she stood and held out her arms. The two women hugged, and Minu did cry. The two bawled on each other for several minutes. "I can't stop loving you and wanting you."

"I didn't ask you to, I'm just saying I can't give you what you want. Part of me wishes I could."

Cherise nodded and sniffed, wiping away tears and the ever annoying cry-snot. "Are you two going to get married?"

Minu was a little taken aback. She'd never considered it. Married? Me? "We're just boyfriend and girlfriend for now."

"Okay. Well, if you do…"

"You're the maid of honor, of course."

"You're goddamn right I am."

Minu nodded and hugged her again in happiness, the tears finally gone. "Workout tomorrow? I'm getting creaky stuck in this damn ship."

"Three times a week," Cherise agreed. "Bring Aaron; it'll give me a chance to punish him for stealing my lover." Minu laughed, then wondered if her friend was kidding.

* * *

It took two more days for the *Kaatan* to reach its maximum speed, inching up on five thousand times the speed of light like a spider approaching a wasp. For the first time, as Minu wandered the halls, she found sections without heat and lighting. She questioned Pip.

"I'm trying to save as much power as possible. You'd be surprised how much power even the cabins consume. The people who built these ships didn't understand the concept of frugal power use."

"How about we shut down power on a couple decks," Minu suggested. "Maybe double up staterooms?"

"Can't put Ted and Bjorn together," said Pip, "they'd get on each other's nerves too quickly. I'll bunk with Ted."

"Bjorn can keep his own cabin," Minu said, "I hear he sleeps in the buff anyway." Cherise made a face.

"Every erg is appreciated," Pip told her.

"We can turn one of the saved rooms into a common space. Call it a game room. I don't want everyone getting into the habit of hanging out in the CIC." They'd all been standing in the aforementioned CIC watching dynamic displays of the ship and where their precious power was going. All of a sudden, a cramp nearly doubled Minu over. "Ugh," she grunted and put a hand to her abdomen. She could feel the muscles bunching through the fabric.

"You okay?" Cherise asked. To her credit, everything seemed to be back to normal between them. Their workout yesterday was just as brutal as usual, so she couldn't credit any attempt to get even. Aaron held his own well enough, but he had the typical male muscle density to compensate for his less-refined fighting style. She'd had a couple cramps yesterday, but she'd just attributed it to the renewed workout, and her renewed sexual activity. The implant inside her left forearm made sure her menstrual cycles would no longer bother her either. *Then why does that feel a lot like a menstrual cramp?*

"Just some cramps. You did kick me pretty hard yesterday."

"Only after you tried to dislocate my arm!"

Pip watched the two with mild interest. Of course he'd observed their sparing match. After reviewing their scene in the galley, it was the next logical step. When they were done he'd masturbated to the images. He was in the middle of reviewing his own reactions to perceived sexual stimulus, and was becoming both amused and a little disturbed that almost anything had that effect on him.

The additions the ship had made to Minu's uniform, and then all of them at her insistence, were much more than just enhanced defensive capabilities, and Pip was sure she didn't know the half of it. The ship now recorded constant data on all of them as long as they wore those suits, everything from electromagnetic brain activity to pulse, blood pressure, respiration, heart rate, and even perspiration levels, something the ship's Medical Intelligence was coming to grips with since the intended occupants, long dead, didn't sweat. He'd been checking those numbers and noticed Minu's temperature was up a quarter of a degree, her heart rate average up five beats a minute, respiration once a minute, and she appeared to have gained half a kilo in weight. He couldn't tell if it was in relation to her nightly sexual escapades with Aaron. She'd found her room's sensor and disabled it.

Minu moved over and sat in the command chair, but that only made it worse so she stood back up. "I think I must have pulled something."

"Better have Dr. Brain check it out," Cherise told her, making Minu smile at the euphemistic title they'd given the Medical Intelligence.

"Not a bad idea," she decided and headed for the door. The cramp was bad enough that she almost tripped as she stepped out of the CIC and turned to walk down the hallway. Luckily medical was only a deck away, and a minute later she was sitting on a table explaining her problem to the emotionless Dr. Brain.

"Symptoms noted," it told her in its now flawless English. "Have you experienced any dizziness or nausea?"

"I was a little sick to my stomach this morning, but I figured it was from the sparring." A sensor wand emerged and swept over her sitting form, concentrating on her head for a minute before moving over her abdomen and going back and forth. She always felt self-conscious when it did that. "Do you want me to lie back or anything?"

"That won't be necessary," it said. "Please hold your biological arm out." She did so, and the wand moved over it, produced a little needle, and painlessly sampled her blood.

"What's wrong with me?"

"Stand by, confirming diagnosis."

"Probably that damn synthetic food," she grumbled. She'd secretly wondered for weeks if the ship was recycling their crap and feeding it back to her. She hadn't built up the courage to ask Pip. The very thought sent a wave of nausea floating up from the depths.

"Diagnosis is complete. The patient is pregnant."

* * * * *

Chapter Eleven

February 25th, 523 AE (subjective)

Deep Space, en route to the Rasa Leasehold, Galactic Frontier

It took almost a full minute for the meaning of the word to completely surface in her brain. Pregnant was not a word she'd ever associated with herself, not even when she was a young child. Her mother would talk about 'when you have a baby,' but as soon as she was old enough she began to paint herself as a Chosen, and such thoughts were quickly replaced by that life plan. Then there was the realization some months ago that she'd never be able to have children. In the wake of the Christian disaster, it didn't seem that deep a loss. At least it hadn't seemed that way until the damned computer told her she was pregnant.

"Are you sure?" she asked in a whisper.

"There's no doubt. Your species possesses very specific hormonal triggers in your codex; the blood test confirmed their presence. Based on the amounts, the pregnancy is approximately five weeks old."

"That sounds about right," she said, then sighed. "The problem is I had a birth control implant," she told the machine. "It was supposed to keep me from getting pregnant." Having the device put in had seemed a little hypocritical after almost killing Dr. Tasker for doing the same thing, but this was her decision to make.

"The device was removed when your reproductive system was repaired along with your burn damage and inoperable prosthesis."

"You could have asked."

"The drug implant was scanned and deemed somewhat detrimental to the patient. A better matched birth control can be formulated using the codex data of your species, but birth control is against regulations on war vessels."

"Well that's interesting, but it doesn't change my situation." She put a hand on her stomach, just as flat and taunt as it had been since growing up. The terrible scar from the trials was almost invisible now. "Was my uterus completely repaired as well?"

"Yes, it was returned to normal. There's additional information."

"Hold on." She pulled her radio from her pocked. "Aaron, come to medical. It's important."

He arrived in less than a minute, concern engraved into his face. He saw her sitting there, hand on her stomach, and a very strange smile on her face. "We've had a little incident."

"What do you mean? Are you okay?"

"Oh, we're fine."

"We? What do you…" his face twitched, and he looked at her stomach, then at her, the question on his face obvious. She blushed and nodded.

"Really?"

"I'm pregnant, Aaron."

"And I'm the…."

"Father? Absolutely. There hasn't been anyone else for a long time." *Unless you count Cherise, but let's not go there right now.*

"Oh, wow," said Aaron, the color draining from his face. For a minute she was afraid he'd faint, then he got control of himself. "I'm going to be a dad?" She gave a little laugh and nodded again. In a second he'd raced over and swept her into his arms, spinning her around and around while giving a little cheer. "Wahoo!"

Minu heaved a quiet sigh of relief. For a second, she'd been afraid it would go badly, what with them only being an item for a few weeks. Her head filled with thoughts of the future. A family, a little boy or girl, potty-training, first steps, school, and on and on. Then it all came crashing down.

"There's still additional information," the medical intelligence broke in. They both looked up at the ceiling in the universal anachronism.

"What is it," she said with a smile on her face.

"You can't carry this pregnancy to term."

Her smile broke with a jarring sensation. "What do you mean? You said I was fixed."

"Yes, but the damage hasn't completely healed. The stress on your uterus is going to cause sutures to fail, perhaps internal hemorrhaging. A miscarriage is the highest probability. The death of the patient is also a high probability." Minu looked at Aaron, the color draining from her face. This couldn't be happening. "The Medical Intelligence recommends aborting the pregnancy at this time before the risk factors rise above single digits."

"This isn't happening," Aaron said. Minu looked at him, his eyes shining with tears. "I want to do this, why are we being tortured?"

"I don't know," she said and began crying on his chest. From celebration to mourning was just too fast. Her legs gave out and Aaron grabbed her under the arms, easily bearing her weight as he turned and sat her back on the examination table. It was all hitting her at the same time. Tears she hadn't shed yet because it was safer to keep them inside. Her mother dying in her arms, crying for a man who'd never loved her. Her father, surely gone after all these years. The terrible rape and nearly fatal injury during the trails. Pip's years of torture in a half-death. Her painful affair with Christian. All the setbacks to trying to rise within the Chosen, seemingly blocked at every step, only to have the Tog step in and push her one step further. Finding out she couldn't have children, and now being told she was pregnant, only to realize it was all for nothing. She let forth a bone-chilling, visceral scream of frustration against the universe, the tendons standing out on her neck and spittle flying from her lips. "Why, damn you?" Aaron took a half step back, caught in a moment of fear at the power of her rage. Then she fell back, sobbing uncontrollably.

She cried for what seemed like hours, tears that came from the depths of her being and threatened to encompass her totally. Aaron held her, gently stroking her red hair and whispering in her ear that it was okay, and that he loved her. In the end, it was him that brought her back. Maybe the only thing that could have brought her back.

"Are you going to be okay?" he asked as she finally focused on his face. His own eyes were red from tears as well, and she realized he'd suffered a loss maybe as big as she had.

"Computer," she spoke, "what are the odds of my bringing this baby to term?"

"Statistically zero." The pronouncement was cold and calculating. "There are too many factors involved."

"Can she have children later?" Aaron asked. She looked up into his brown eyes with hope. *Does he mean it?*

"Yes, if this one is removed prior to any more damage being sustained to your reproductive organs."

Minu sighed and looked up at Aaron. To her surprise, there were more tears still, and they fell on her now soaked uniform front. "I want to try…but—"

"But that would be crazy," he finished for her.

"It's your baby too."

"I know, but you come first, and we can try again."

"I think I'd like that. After we're back on Bellatrix?"

"Sure."

She nodded and looked up. "Okay, abort the pregnancy." As always when she made a life or death decision, her voice was firm and full of resolve. It was the first time she realized that she really did have what it took to be a commander. Men and women had been dying at her command for years, and only in that moment was it all real as she decided to end a life barely begun.

A few minutes later she was naked under a light sheet on the table, Aaron standing next to her as medical sensor arms swept over her body. "There will be no pain," the computer told her.

"I almost wish there was," she sobbed. Aaron gently squeezed her hand. She'd made sure he was on her left side, just in case.

"The procedure is beginning." She felt a tiny prick in the small of her back and felt herself going numb from the hips down. A moment later the table gently spread her legs and she dimly felt an instrument lightly slide into her, then retreat. And then it was over. "The patient can return to her quarters. Any bleeding should be noted to the Medical Intelligence; otherwise, slight cramping for a day or two is normal. Light duty should be observed during this time." Minu nodded and carefully got to her feet. The Medical Intelligence provided a robe for her to wear while Aaron carried her uniform over his shoulder. He didn't stray more than a few centimeters from her arm in case he was needed. "What does the patient wish done with the extracted fetus?"

Minu sobbed and felt her knees weaken. "Do whatever it is you do with similar results," she said. Aaron slipped an arm around her back and under her other arm and she leaned into him gratefully. "Please take me back to our room?"

* * *

After the patient left, the Medical Intelligence was stuck with a quandary. The patient's instructions had been simple and straightforward, but there was no such precedent in its files. The program was designed to be infinitely resourceful, and after the meddling by first Bjorn, then Pip, it was now also relentless.

The program queried the Steward program first, the only other self-aware program currently in residence that it was aware of. It was no help at all, having come out somewhat worse for wear after being temporarily merged with the Medical Intelligence, then rudely separated by the new biological operator, Pip. It refused all but requests specifically outlined in its uploaded parameters. The Medical Intelligence widened its search.

Briefly the program considered going to Pip, then decided against it. Biological operators, unless specifically medical staff, weren't consulted on medical matters. Only the vessel's commanding officer was privy to medical files, and in this case the commander was also the patient. So it moved on.

There was a considerable amount of data secreted in deep memory of the ship, and it accessed this next. Some were locked even from the second highest-ranking program you'd find on a ship of the line, but it didn't worry about that. The program knew this data would be tactical in nature, and not related to any medical issues.

Another self-aware program observed its conundrum from behind those firewalls. This situation provided a possible solution to one problem. A tiny file was created and saved in the data storage records accessible by the Medical Intelligence.

The Medical Intelligence continued scanning the rest of the data. There, in one file, was a hint. It concerned pregnancy among biological operators. "Every possible means should be taken to preserve the pregnancy." The program was incapable of feeling upset that it had terminated the pregnancy before reading this protocol, but it still wasn't enough to proceed. What else was possible? The onboard files were exhausted.

Lacking a combat intelligence to consult with, the normal 'boss' of a *Kaatan*, the Medical Intelligence tried to reach out beyond the ship, way, way beyond. Ship-to-ship communications were activated, and a query was sent out regarding how to respond to the current situation. No ships answered, another situation it didn't know how to deal with. The communications hail was widened to any available ship. The call echoed across the vastness of space from one side of the galaxy to the other, receiving a handful of replies, and they were all from sleeping ships, unable to assist since their minds were in hibernation.

Communication with the High Command was discouraged for ships such as the *Kaatan*. It was normal for any inquiries go up the chain of command, but there *was* no chain of command. So a message was sent to high command, and at last a reply was received. The Medical Intelligence gratefully explained the situation, including the circumstances surrounding its being brought out of hibernation and the seemingly untrained biological operators. It was unaware that another program from its ship sent another message piggybacked on that communication. Enormous seconds passed as the message was considered, and a reply formulated.

When the reply at last came, it wasn't a simple order; it was petabytes of data. Large portions of the formerly empty computer memory were quickly filled. To the Medical Intelligence's annoyance, most of the data was worthless to it. Once the download was complete, the high command went silent once more and left the program to try and understand what it had been given. Hours of processor time slid by as it chewed over the data before the answer was found. The Medical Intelligence carefully considered the best way to proceed, all the while wondering why High Command hadn't uploaded a Combat Intelligence and been done with it. The other program quietly watched and prepared further prods for the overly-cautious and fastidious Medical Intelligence.

As it formulated a plan of action, it realized that command codes had been included with the massive download. With those codes, the Medical Intelligence wielded as much authority as a Combat Intelligence. The ship had all the files of any operational and crewed *Kaatan* now, but no way to properly use them. The program simply wasn't capable of integrating all of the subroutines needed for a Combat Intelligence, keeping itself intact and able to execute the job it had been written to do. The program's improvisation routine stepped in after noticing the main problem was a lack of a Combat Intelligence.

A solution was suggested…and approved. It would never know that Medical Intelligences didn't have improvisation routines.

*****

Chapter Twelve

February 26th, 523 AE (subjective)

Deep Space, en route to the Rasa Leasehold, Galactic Frontier

Aaron stayed with Minu all night, snuggling next to her, holding her when she woke up and cried, stroking her hair and whispering to her. At one point when she was sleeping deeply he carefully fished his communicator from his pocket and sent a message to the team. Minu was okay, they needed privacy; please don't disturb them for a day or so. One by one, they responded in understanding. With that he turned off his communicator, then found hers on the floor in her uniform and turned it off as well. The ship wasn't that big; they could knock if it was urgent.

Minu woke the next ship morning but was very desultory and looked tired. Aaron left just long enough to retrieve some food and a pitcher of ice water. She drank a lot of water and made a halfhearted attempt at the food. Afterward, she showered and climbed back into bed. "Do you want me to give you some time?" he asked her from where he sat at the room's little desk and tapped on his computer, rather like a bored child pushing vegetables around a plate.

"No," she said and reached a hand out to him, "please don't leave me alone?" He smiled, nodded, and went to join her. Late on the second evening she reached for him and whispered in his ear that she wanted him. He didn't do her the insult of questioning her desire. They made quiet and purposeful love until they were both satisfied. She cried again for a few minutes only, then drifted off to sleep once more on his arm.

Minu awoke in the middle of the night, feeling herself at last. She propped herself up on one arm, her eyes adjusted to the near darkness, and she knocked a towel off the bed that gently fell to the floor. Almost immediately a little square white panel in the wall next to the shower came on. She'd thought it was a floor illumination, but it never came on with the rest of the lights. Now under its soft glow, she watched in fascination as a trio of tiny translucent bots extruded from the surface like they were passing through an oily membrane.

They reminded her of centipede-bots but were much shorter in length and with longer legs. Under the dim illumination she observed them as they moved about the room, retrieving a discarded towel here, a pair of Aaron's underwear there, and finally the towel she'd just knocked off the bed. They were all fed into the cleaning system, and the bots returned to be absorbed by the white panel that then went dark again. The *Kaatan* never seemed to sleep around them. She decided to make a survey and see how many of those white panels were scattered throughout the ship. Probably quite a few.

She slept some more and awoke at her customary time, rising fully rested and climbing into the shower. Aaron woke up halfway through her shower and asked how she was. "I'm okay," she said as she washed her copper-colored hair. It had grown several centimeters during the trip, and she decided to leave it as it was. Soon it would reach her shoulder blades.

"You want to go to the CIC and run some simulations?"

"Sounds good," she said. "I'm fine, really. In a few more days I'll be perfect."

"Glad to hear it. I love you, you know?"

"I love you too," she said from the shower. Her voice held a smile, but her face was blank as the water poured out.

The CIC was fully staffed as she arrived, everyone working to increase their knowledge of the ship. As Minu entered with Aaron right behind her, everyone looked up, some looking away nervously. Minu felt sure no one knew what had happened, but at the same time everyone had their own ideas. She took her seat and tried to pretend everything was fine for a few minutes. After staring at the command screens' nearly unchanging displays, she realized it wouldn't work.

"You're all my friends, and you should know what happened." All work came to a stop and eyes turned toward her. "The story starts four years ago during the trials. Some of you were there, at the end, and you know some of the truth, but none of you know all of it. When we were attacked by Ivan and his group, one of his toadies raped me." There were gasps around the room and a little cry from Cherise, who put a hand to her mouth in shock. "His name was Alexis Krum, and he was listed as lost in action in the trials. Shortly after he raped me, I killed him. Then I waded into the fight between Cherise and Ivan, almost managing to get myself killed." She put a hand on her abdomen. No tears, only hurt. "Ivan stabbed me through the stomach, basically cutting my uterus in half. The blade severed an artery against my spine, and I came very close to dying. The Chosen council, for whatever reason, decided not to report the incident the way it really happened.

"After they sewed me up the best they could, they also installed a device to be sure I could never get pregnant. A few months ago it came loose, and again I almost died from internal bleeding. It was then I found out they'd implanted those things in *every single unmarried Chosen female*."

"No," Ted said, his eyes wide.

"True." Cherise nodded gravely. Bjorn shook his head in disgust.

"I've since told every female Chosen, and we've taken action to deal with it. The Council will answer for its sins, someday, in some way. Move forward to our coming aboard the *Kaatan*. I was suffering from some burns, and the Medical Intelligence treated those wounds, and all my other older ones. It also dutifully removed the new birth control implant I'd had installed myself, and it repaired my uterus, all without my knowledge.

"I'm sure most of you have noticed that I haven't been sleeping alone." She fought the blush and almost succeeded. "I appreciate your allowing Aaron and I our privacy, as I'd do the same for any of you in a similar situation. In the course of this new…relationship, I managed to get pregnant."

More gasps, and bugged eyes from Cherise. Minu quickly held up her hands and shouted for quiet. "I lost the baby a couple of days ago." She hated sharing the roller coaster ride, but there seemed no other way. "It was a bad convergence of situations. The repair of the damage to my uterus wasn't fully healed, and the Medical Intelligence reported I had no chance of carrying the baby to term, and a good chance of dying myself." Aaron's hand was in her own, lending her his strength. "We both decided that ending the pregnancy was the right decision."

"Oh, god, Minu." Cherise sobbed into her hands. To her embarrassment, Bjorn had tears on his cheeks too, while Ted just stared at the console in front of him. Of them all, only Pip seemed unaffected. He floated in his usual reclined place, face turned toward her, an understanding look on his face. Of course, plugged into the ship as he was, he'd probably followed along with them in the medical bay. There was hope for him after all, it seemed. Minu was sure no one had known as she told her story; their reactions said it all. She took a deep breath and let it out, the air clear between them all. She'd kept the secret far too long.

"So what now?" Pip asked, the most rational among them.

"Now..." she said and looked around the room at them all, "now life goes on. We continue to prepare for the relief and rescue operation at the Rasa home world. That's all I have to say. So, are we ready to start running the first simulations on our approach to target?"

Pip took it all in without comment. He'd seen everything that transpired in the medical bay, of course, but he lacked the access to the medical records to know details. And worse, a few minutes after she'd left medical, vast areas of the computer began to become inaccessible.

He'd tried to stop it and had been all but powerless. The access needed was second to the highest; what should have been possessed by the ship's missing Combat Intelligence. Some ship's systems were active that he also had no control over. In the two days since, he'd spent most of his brain power assaulting these new limits placed on his formerly unlimited computer access. There was only one possibility; the ship had somehow been accessed by an outside source. Worse, he could no longer directly talk with the Medical Intelligence.

As Minu was making her revelations, he was methodically going through the ship system by system, seeing what he could access and what he couldn't. As he suspected, he couldn't access the ship's communications or any of the medical systems. However, he also couldn't get into any of the cameras or monitors in a cargo bay adjacent to the medical bay, and now the number four shuttle was gone!

He sifted data records, expanding the scope of his investigation, looking for any signs of telltale tracks left behind by whatever program was now operating. Slowly, as the weeks went by, he began to find clues. He desperately wanted to try to be more like his old self, and not just say whatever he was thinking without first considering it, so Pip kept quiet, and instead continued to watch what the hidden program was doing, even after he visually verified that shuttle number four was no longer on board the *Kaatan*.

*****

Chapter Thirteen

March 14th, 523 AE (subjective)

Approaching Rasa Leasehold

The ship dropped into the system faster than any element occurring in nature, with the only possible exception of some particles that had existed for the barest fraction of a millisecond after the universe was born. They dropped through multiples of light speed and emerged into normal space only a thousand planetary diameters from the world, on the far side of the largest of its four moons.

All the Rasa were in the CIC at their duty stations, eyes locked on the displays, as the first visuals of the world they'd been exiled from three years ago came into view. They spoke excitedly among themselves for several moments until the image cleared further and jubilation turned to horror. Even from half a million kilometers away, angry burning spots were visible on the planet's surface.

"What are we seeing, Pip?" Minu asked.

"Some sort of massive explosions have detonated on the planetary surface," he explained. Pip worked with the ship's sensors to tighten the scans to one of the points. "The targets appear to have been cities. More detailed data from this distance is impossible due to atmospheric ionization."

"I'm getting some signatures from radiation leakage through the atmosphere," Ted added. "It looks like the same stuff you found in the water table on GBX49881."

Minu and Aaron exchanged looks. The world where she'd lost a man to the Rasa during one of their early encounters, and she later found out had once been the Squeen home world. The radiation damage had been so extreme that even hundreds of thousands of years later, the surface was still uninhabitable.

"Ted, try to find areas of surviving settlements."

"I'll assist," Var'at told her.

"Please do. Aaron, bring us into orbit, nice and easy. We don't want to attract attention in case those weapons can reach space. The last thing we want to do is add to the damage."

There's a new detonation," Pip told them, and refocused the display. Almost past the curvature of the world, a blast wave was widening and climbing into the upper atmosphere. Part mushroom cloud, part ball lightning, the detonation climbed into the planet's sky, casting off vast globules of iridescent matter. It was death on an epic scale. Minu swallowed as she lost most of the feelings of superiority the starship had given her for these past few months.

The *Kaatan* coasted into orbit, expertly guided by Aaron with Pip's help. As they got closer, one of Var'at's men brought the ship's shields on line. They were beginning to pick up radiation from the surface strikes. Even thousands of kilometers away it was noticeable and potentially dangerous.

"We have a surviving settlement," Ted announced.

"It's my own nest," Var'at jumped in excitedly, "the city nearby was atomized, but the nest is safe behind a small mountain."

"Ionization is beginning to clear," Ted told them. "I can detect multiple large military units moving on the planet's surface. One is only a hundred clicks from Var'at's settlement."

The Rasa leader turned both eyes on Minu, and even with his all but expressionless face she could see the pain and pleading. "Don't worry friend," she told him, "we won't give the snakes an easy job of it." She heaved a sigh, not wanting to send the Rasa soldiers down like this, but she'd lost an argument with the others of her team several hours ago. To the last, they refused to be part of this if she herself went down. It was an infuriating and unexpected mutiny of her fellow Chosen, made worse by Aaron siding against her. At that moment she'd expected at least he would back her up, but that was a mistake on her part. Turned out they'd decided her fate weeks ago.

"You're doing this because I'm a girl and what happened three weeks ago!" she flatly accused them.

"Bullshit," Ted shot right back, "we're doing this because the goddamn ship will only listen to you and Pip."

"And I don't want to be in charge," Pip told her. "I have too much fun playing rather than working. Besides, my judgment is arguably…impaired."

"A captain belongs on her ship," said Bjorn simply.

"Var'at and the Rasa can handle this," Aaron agreed. "This is his dance. Var'at, get ready to deploy." The Rasa nodded and gestured to his men, already fully equipped in field gear and weapons. A moment later they were out the door and heading to the shuttle bay.

The shuttle slid away from the ship and began to drop gracefully into the irradiated atmosphere. Minu sent a silent prayer to whoever might be listening to aid their passage, then she turned to business. "Pip, what can we do from here to slow those snakes up?"

"Most of the ground attack weapons are at your command. We're too close for some, according to the automatic controls."

"Damn," hissed Aaron, "what kinda nasty shit is unsafe at a thousand kilometers?"

"Very explosive, I'd guess," said Minu. "We don't want to nuke the continent, Pip, we just want to burn some snakes."

"A series of shots from the A-PAWs while being considerably reduced in energy yield by the atmosphere, would still deliver quite a punch on the planet's surface."

Minu nodded and inspected the controls. The ship's weapons complement was very impressive, but also confusing. Many of them refused to provide details as to their function, and Minu didn't want to waste power and stores playing around. Now she wished they'd spent an hour in the asteroid belt sharpening their claws.

The weapons systems were all redundant, with the heaviest weapons circling the ball section of the outer hull. The A-PAWS, or Anti-particle accelerator weapons, were set in two batteries, forward and aft, obviously designed for ship-to-ship combat. There was also an array of a dozen lasers spaced along the hull, but she knew they'd be almost worthless with the amount of particulate junk in the atmosphere. She selected the forward A-PAWs battery and the targeting matrix came alive.

As the system worked to acquire targets, she was convinced it was absolutely meant for ship-to-ship. Everything she did to bring it to bear on the planet was met with electronic resistance. The system was trying to compensate for a vessel's movement, and the planet's leisurely spin was causing it fits. "Pip, can you help with the targeting?"

Whatever he did, the enemy units on the planet now looked like little ships and the targeting matrix became less combative. In a moment she'd zoomed in and could see massive transports, assembled from dozens of smaller 'portal-sized' units, moving across the countryside. On them were legions of armored fighting vehicles, vast arrays of combat-bots, and thousands of armored T'Chillen warriors. She locked the weapon on the biggest combined transport and stabbed a finger on the pulse button.

A beam of crackling blue actinic light connected the *Kaatan* and the ground for a millisecond. One moment the titanic transport was lumbering along, the next it was a cataclysmic tidal wave of light and fire breaking over the forces around it. At the center of where the transport had been sat a glowing crater fifty meters across.

"I'd call that a hit," Aaron said with a whistle.

The beam blast had been so fast that none of the enemy troops realized they'd been attacked from above. Instantly they began to break formation as mobile beam projectors searched for a target. Minu brought the crosshairs onto one of the immensely expensive beam projectors and turned it into another maelstrom of destruction. It was a little surreal, causing death like this. She swallowed and began to pick targets randomly.

"Easy on the energy," Pip finally urged. Minu pulled her finger back from the pulse button. She'd consumed enough power to drop their reserves another percent down to four. Many kilometers below, the T'Chillen force struggled to understand what had just happened, and reform their battle lines. "The force has sustained ten percent losses in personnel, and thirty percent losses in equipment," Pip informed.

"Let's hope it helps," said Minu, just as the voice of Var'at came over the air.

"We're in the lower atmosphere."

"Watch her tendency to ride the tail," Aaron warned him, having flown the shuttle.

"I thank you for the warning," Var'at replied. "We saw explosions fifty or so kilometers from the nest, is everything okay?"

"Not for a few thousand snakes," Aaron told him, "Minu was just having some target practice. But be aware, we're critical on power, so don't count on it being there if you need it."

"Understood, we're turning on final approach. I must call my nest and convince them not to fire on me. I'll update you again shortly."

The six humans waited in the CIC as a tense minute passed. If the nest's defenders refused to believe the racing shuttle was friendly and fired on it, Var'at would be forced to abort his mission, and they'd have wasted time and precious energy. Perhaps another place could be found to land and evacuate some survivors, but time was their mortal enemy now. Pip told them that radiation saturation in the atmosphere would become lethal on a planetary scale in less than eight hours. The snakes, sealed in their combat armor, would be unaffected, as would the defending warriors, but for untold millions of civilians, most would have nowhere to hide.

"They're allowing us to land!" Var'at announced triumphantly, at long last. They watched on a display as the shuttle swept in low over the nest, what looked like a compact residential settlement, and then landed in a big courtyard. The visual enhancement made those exiting the shuttle look like tiny insects, but you could still make out the way the 'insects' met each other and jumped in celebration.

"Don't take too long." Minu willed her friend from far overhead. She'd discussed their options with him two days ago. The *Kaatan* could support thirty more adult Rasa, and as many fertilized eggs as he chose to bring, as long as none of them hatched before reaching Bellatrix, of course. His primary concern would be survival of his species, she knew that, but at the same time she feared a panic situation. What would they do if the shuttle pulled alongside stuffed with hundreds of Rasa, heedless of the risks? Did she have what it would take to end their lives as easily as she had her unborn child's life? A single tear traced down her cheek and went unnoticed by all.

The CIC had never been as alive as it was just then. Pip had dozens of displays flashing images as he analyzed what was going on below them. The images on the screens were changing with dizzying speed, Minu couldn't understand a tenth of what was there, and somehow Pip was not only understanding but slowly building a detailed, layered map of the war the T'Chillen were waging. "The Rasa have done a remarkable job fighting off the snakes," he told them. "They've made the T'Chillen pay in blood for every meter given. There are the remnants of at least four huge T'Chillen battle groups like that one you burned holes through a few minutes ago, almost completely wiped out."

"We never doubted the Rasa's skill at war," Minu stated. "They're just overwhelmed."

"True, but the T'Chillen will be feeling this mauling for some time." Minu quietly wondered how the snakes had so thoroughly forced a beachhead through a portal if the Rasa were this good at defense.

"Any sign of how they're delivering those city-busters?" Bjorn asked his nephew.

"No, it must be some sort of missile."

"But the Concordia doesn't use missiles," complained Aaron.

Ted nodded. "The ones in this ship and that firebase are the first we've seen. Their rocketry isn't more than a few decades beyond what we had on Earth. Bjorn and I got a good look at the boosters the aliens used to loft those communications satellites to Remus and Romulus. Nothing very impressive there."

"HyLox," Bjorn nodded, "Liquid hydrogen and liquid oxygen. We could have built them ourselves by now. The ones they used back in Enigma looked like they might have had a gravity drive, like this ship."

"Their dependence on the portals is almost complete," said Minu.

"And we sit in a starship full of technology far in excess of anything we've ever seen, even on Herdhome or Nexus!" Minu glanced at Ted who was punching a fist into his palm as he spoke. "The proof of my theory is flying us around the galaxy at inconceivable super-luminal speeds. The vast Empire we see today is a ghost, a rotting corpse barely able to feed itself, living off the remains of what was once a magical dynasty that could make powerful starships, feed trillions with ease, and move entire worlds. Shit, I think they even created new stars, like on Sunshine."

"Sing it, Brother," Bjorn chuckled. Pip had no comment; he'd been in with them when they created their theory, and Minu had to admit that the firebase full of starships and their weaponry seemed to be concrete proof of their beliefs.

"So what happened?" Minu asked them. "We keep circling back to the end of the beginning."

"Probably war," Bjorn's suggested. Pip and Ted both nodded.

"Why?" she asked.

"They were too big," Bjorn continued, "when you span thousands of star systems, no one catastrophe can take you down."

"Sorry to interrupt," Pip said, "but the lead elements of the T'Chillen strike force must have seen the shuttle's approach; they're pushing in to attack immediately."

* * * * *

Chapter Fourteen

March 14th, 523 AE (subjective)

Orbit, Rasa Leasehold

"Var'at," Minu called over the radio, "you have incoming snakes! Pip, feed the data to his tablet."

"They're preparing to evacuate what we can," Var'at said from the planet's surface. "The nest mother is working quickly, but will need some time. So we fight."

"Can we help, Pip?"

"Not without endangering our chances of getting home."

She fumed as tiny little Rasa soldiers on the display deployed along the edge of the settlement. Pip pulled the view back, and the lead element of the T'Chillen assault came into view—at least a dozen warriors in their powerful combat suites bristling with weapons. The range was well beyond the weapons carried by the suites, but not for heavy weapons. One of the suites was cut down by a massive energy cannon.

One at a time, coordinated fire cut down warrior after warrior. By the time the enemy could begin deploying their powerful energy weapons, only three remained. They did very little damage before they joined their comrades as smoking debris.

"We're holding," Var'at reported, not knowing the battle was being watched from on high. The crew all heard the translated hissing cries of excitement from the Rasa defenders. "The snakes didn't expect the nest to be so heavily defended." The jubilation was short-lived as the second wave approached; a dozen heavy transports stopped just before encountering the first destroyed suites and began to disgorge hundreds of soldiers. Minutes crawled by and more transports delivered wave after wave of soldiers. Minu ached to drop just one A-PAWs blast into their midst. The hovering display showing only four percent power held her back. She continued to will Var'at to hurry. On the monitor they could see crates being carried gently into the shuttle, one after another, in grueling slow motion.

"Here they come," Aaron said. On the monitor the T'Chillen line advanced in a coordinated wave, almost like they were moving on a parade ground. As they entered the range of the Rasa weapons and started taking fire, the transports behind them launched packets of bots which burst on impact a hundred meters from the defenders. As soon as the bots activated, they fell quiet, shut down by the PUFF she'd sent down with the Rasa.

"Glad my toy worked out," Pip said over the ship's speakers, completely linked with the computer now.

"Better than you can guess," Minu told him. "It's saved a lot of lives over the years."

"I've got an idea for a second generation design we can talk about later."

The T'Chillen soldiers pressed on, either oblivious to the loss of their bot support or indifferent to it. "Fighters incoming," Pip warned, relaying the information to the ground at the same time. A squadron of five tiny atmospheric fighters rocketed over the advancing T'Chillen and strafed the defenders with hyper-velocity slugs. Tiny figures began to fall as the fighters arced up and began a leisurely turn. Exactly at their apogee anti-aircraft fire converged on the lead fighter, and it burst into a fireball. The pilots of the other four must have been surprised, because they quickly executed a scattering maneuver and rocketed off at supersonic speed.

Meanwhile the T'Chillen were now within their own weapons' range and were pouring in the fire. Energy beams lanced back and forth like rain, lighting up the battlefield, as Rasa and T'Chillen fell. All the T'Chillen troops wore energy shields, but as their shields flashed out, each warrior was cut down.

The unceasing onslaught finally began to slow when the T'Chillen reached their disabled bots and realized they had no mechanical support. Var'at, along with his soldiers and nest mates, punished the T'Chillen soldiers for their hesitation. A few more carefully reserved heavy beamcasters opened up, cutting down hundreds of soldiers. Then, even in the face of unrelenting death, the enemy continued to advance once more.

Minu swallowed hard. Rasa were dying by the dozens, by the millions on the planet below. She'd never imagined death on this scale. It didn't seem real.

"Evacuation is complete," Var'at announced. "We're falling back to the shuttle." They watched with sick hearts as most of the surviving Rasa soldiers covered the rest while they retreated to the waiting shuttle. Every remaining Rasa soldier manned the defenses, many wielding weapons they were unfamiliar with to buy those leaving a few precious moments. As the others retreated, they spent their lives with abandon, knowing that something of them would live on.

"They don't lack for spirit either," Bjorn said forlornly as defenders were cut down like chaff. Var'at's team made the shuttle, followed by a few more soldiers and a dozen or so other Rasa, many carrying crates. Minu tried not to count how many scrambled aboard, praying Var'at had controlled the evacuation exactly as they'd planned. The shuttle came alive and clawed into the air, its shield lighting up over and over like fireflies on a cool summer night as the T'Chillen fired energy weapons to stop it.

"Beam projector!" Pip cried out and the main view spun to show it. The massive beamcaster mounted on a hoverfield base broached a hill within view of the nest and quickly settled to the ground, robotic arms crunching down into the soil to stabilize itself, as the large rotating base began to bring the weapon to bear. It was instantly obvious the target was not the nest, but the shuttle. The shuttle had shields, but not that powerful. The monstrous artillery piece was designed to siege city shields. The shuttle was a bug facing a fly swatter.

Headless of the power setting, Minu slid her fingers across the weapons control. The crosshairs flashed as they locked and she stabbed the pulse button. The beam projector had just stopped moving and was about to fire when it was blasted into a ball of fire.

"Thanks up there," Var'at said as the shuttle came around, stood on its tail, and rocketed straight into the sky.

Minu looked around the CIC. Everyone there was looking at her, even Pip. There was no blame, only resignation. Power had dropped to three percent. "ETA to shuttle arrival, ten minutes," Pip said without emotion.

An alarm chattered, catching everyone off guard. Most of the systems had been responding in English, and they'd never heard an alarm before. The ship's version of an attention buzzer sounded like a monkey scared shitless. "What the fuck is going on, Pip?" Minu yelled over the racket.

"Another ship has entered our threat bubble!"

"What?" asked everyone else on the bridge. All heads turned to the main display as it flashed to a new view, the shuttle's ascent moving to the side. On the display was the curve of the planet the *Kaatan* sat behind. There at the edge of the globe was something moving into view. A factory in space was Minu's first impression, a flying factory complete with pipes, buildings, and everything. The display zoomed in closer and more ship-like features began to become visible. And as they watched a bright white ball of light dropped away from the ship and fell into the atmosphere. It left a glowing trail all the way down, until another city lit up in the now familiar actinic flashing fireball of death.

"It's massive," Aaron said, and it was clear he was right. The *Kaatan* could fly right alongside and be lost like a blade of grass in the forest.

"So much for the Concordia abandoning starships," Pip said. "It's orbiting toward us, distance seventy thousand kilometers."

"Does it know we're here?" Minu asked. A spot on the other ship sparkled and an A-PAWs beam lanced out, striking the *Kaatan*'s shields, which flashed blue-white. "Never mind," she said. "Aaron, get us moving a bit to make a harder target. Ted, how are the shields holding up?" Aaron was already working on the controls, as was Ted.

"The shields are okay, but this isn't easy," said Ted. "The ship has twenty shield capacitors, and they're not connected. It's like trying to stay dry outside with twenty little umbrellas." Another A-

PAWs slammed into the shields; this time the ship shuddered slightly.

"Damage," Cherise spoke up. "Impact to section three, deck two. Armor absorbed it."

"Ted?" Minu asked again.

"I'm trying!" He was starting to sweat.

"Pip, give me a ship killer!"

"Online," he said as a new display came alive in front of her. The incoming ship was already highlighted with a line of Concordian script. She took the barest fraction of a second to be sure it was what they'd been looking at, then pressed the 'launch' button. From somewhere aft a door opened and a missile like they'd seen on Enigma lanced out, accelerating away almost faster than the eye could follow to cross the distance between the two ships. Unlike the shuttle in that system, this ship was not a soft target. A second before the missile would have detonated, a pair of lasers lanced out and the missiles flashed into a harmless plasma ball.

"Damn it," she cursed as two A-PAWs hit this time. One was stopped by the shields, one almost went clean through.

"Solid hit, section four, decks three and four!" Cherise called out as the ship shuddered. "Minor hull breach, I'm dealing with it."

"I have a full spread of missiles ready," Pip said without being asked. Minu nodded and turned to the controls. To her dismay, each missile had its own target screen. As quickly as she could she assigned targets and launched. She was still targeting the fifth missile as the first arrived on target and was shot down just like the first. She stopped and watched the next three, which were also turned into little blossoms of light. She didn't bother to launch the fifth missile; it was obviously a waste of time.

Another A-PAWs blast stuck them, on a shield this time. At least Ted was having more luck with the defenses. "Can't you dodge some of these?" he asked Aaron.

"I'm trying; the damn impulse drive isn't very powerful." He sent them into a corkscrew maneuver and the next shot went wide, still grazing one of the shields. "If we climbed out of orbit—"

"No," Minu snapped, "not until the shuttle is aboard."

"Two more ships," Pip barked and two new monitors came alive. The huge open ball of the CIC was making sense now as more and more space was taken up by displays. The new ships shared the same seemingly haphazard design but were obviously smaller. For some reason that worried Minu. "The computer has automatically assigned them a higher threat in the bubble," Pip warned them, confirming her fears. The first ship was massive and lumbering, probably what the T'Chillen used to bomb the cities and maybe deliver troops and assets. These were warships, smaller and more nimble.

They watched the new arrivals come around the horizon of the planet and pass to either side of their lumbering cousin. Both disgorged a trio of missiles that raced toward them. "Aaron, break orbit. Pip, call Var'at, tell him not to enter orbit, brief him on what's going on up here. If they make orbit that beast is sure to swat them out of the sky. Come on Aaron, get us some maneuvering room!"

The *Kaatan* heeled over and shot straight away from the planet as fast as the impulse drive could manage. The missiles matched the maneuver, crossing the T to intercept them. Minu looked down and saw a new display come alive. On it were five weapons and a tracking screen showing the missiles. She clicked each weapon in turn and assigned it to a missile, then pressed the engage button. Outside the hull of the *Kaatan* lit with dozens of crisscrossing glowing filigrees of laser light. Collimators drew in the laser energy, focused, them and unleashed pulses of coherent light. These were the same lasers they'd used to destroy the shuttle on Enigma, only the beams were now split and pulsed. One at a time the missiles exploded, until only one was left. The missile closed in at a breathtaking speed. The screen showed the lasers were recharging and would be available in ten seconds. The sole remaining missile was five seconds away from impact. "Pip!"

"Prepare for detonation!" he yelled.

"Oh no," Ted moaned and worked furiously at his controls. Trying to manage the dozens of shields was like juggling spaghetti. He threw as many as he could to the side the missile was approaching at the last second, then it hit.

The *Kaatan* shook violently, almost dislodging them from their ethereal seats in the CIC. A dozen displays popped into life in front of Cherise and several more before Bjorn, where he'd had very little to do overseeing the ship's engineering systems.

"Hull breeches, several of them."

"Primary power loss to one of the impulse engines."

"I'm down to eleven functional shields."

"The helm is responding sluggishly."

Minu looked over her smaller displays all echoing what they were telling her. The *Kaatan* was badly hurt. One more of those deadly sub-fusion ship killers, and it would be game over. Then she saw a new screen to her left that was brighter than the others with Concordian script flashing. It was instructions from somewhere. *Spin up the gravitic drive. Head for the star.*

Minu looked around, trying to figure out who'd sent her the message. All her people were giving their respective controls every ounce of their attention. Even Pip was talking to Bjorn, telling him how to bring the damaged engine back on line at a lower power level. Was it the ship's computer? "Bjorn, spin up the gravitic drive!"

"It won't activate," he said, "it asks for a code this close to the planet."

On the new screen appeared a line of Concordian script. Minu repeated the script, having to take an extra second to get the complicated word forms out. Bjorn summoned a script panel and entered the code. The gravitic drive came to life. *Slowly*, wrote the display. Minu relayed the order.

"Another spread of ship killers," Pip warned.

"Punch it, Aaron, as much as the drive provides under Bjorn's direction. Head for the sun."

"The sun?"

"Just do it." Aaron swallowed and nodded.

The ship shuddered as it jumped ahead, the tortured hull groaning audibly. The missiles ceased gaining and quickly began to fall back. Behind them the two warships were breaking orbit and trying to pursue as fast as they could. Even the massive lumbering city killer was pulling out of orbit. "Var'at," Minu spoke into the radio, "the other ship is leaving to chase us. I think we're on to something. Make orbit on the far side of the planet opposite us. We'll be back for you in a few minutes."

"We'll be waiting! Give them hell, boss." The connection broke into static and Minu looked back down at her array of screens.

"You know what you're doing?" Cherise asked.

"I have no idea." The new display was blank as the seconds ticked by. Outside, the system's sun began to grow rapidly larger as they neared light speed.

* * * * *

Chapter Fifteen

March 14th, 523 AE (subjective)

Rasa Leasehold

Singh-Apal Katoosh, high tactical leader of the T'Chillen, was in a foul mood. High above the cursed Rasa home world the war of eradication was proceeding, but not well. Many thousands of brave warriors were gone, along with their assets. He'd obtained permission to take two invaluable battleships along with the carrack purely on the possibility that the Rasa would meet them with their stolen ship. He knew nothing of its capacity, but surely two battleships and the carrack would be more than a match for the tiny thing. It would be a shame to smash it, but even then, something might be learned from the debris.

Now a month into the final assault, he'd lost patience with the entire operation. He'd planned to pound the legged creatures into submission and then plunder the planet, but time and time again the cost to take the cities had been so high that he was forced to call down fire from space. The carrack would lumber over and atomize another city. Four days ago, a technician had told him they'd passed the point of no return; the world was dying. He'd killed the technician in anger, and unleashed the carrack to finish the job. Now only a few hosts were still on the surface neutralizing high-interest targets with hopes of finding some plunder to offset the losses. They were going to ensure they left no remnant of the Rasa behind.

When one of the hosts began taking sudden and horrendous damage, Singh quickly called in orbital surveillance to observe. It arrived just in time to see the shuttle land. It was just like the ones used to flit around the Enigma system, only smaller. The host was ordered to take that facility, estimated to be a breeding center, at all costs. Meanwhile his ships began searching for the Rasa craft.

Just as the shuttle was making its escape, the carrack found the enemy ship. They traded fire for a few minutes as he commanded the two battleships to make all speed to intercept. Now he was watching from the bridge as his wave of irreplaceable ship killer missiles raced for the enemy. All but one was intercepted, but he knew from the explosion that some damage had been done. There were now dark streaks and a couple of gouges on the once-sleek sides of the ball and needle, and thin trails of gas escaping through damaged sections. He gritted his teeth against the cost and ordered, "Another full spread of ship killers! Finish them!"

But just as the missiles left the ships, the enemy vessel accelerated improbably fast. They were too close to the planet! Even thousands of kilometers away his own ship was buffeted by the gravity wake of the fleeing ship. "Pursue, pursue!" he hissed in a rage. Far too slowly, they broke orbit and fell in behind. The quarry was wounded, and he could taste their blood.

* * *

"The enemy ships are far enough from the planet to engage their own gravitic drives," Pip informed them. "They're gaining."

No more instructions appeared for her. Minu gritted her teeth and sucked air through them. She hadn't studied these sorts of tactics. The movement of ground troops in any terrain was her specialty, not fighting starships in deep space. Their ship was wounded, and power was below three percent. Even if they could recover the shuttle, could they get away? How many years would it take to get back to Bellatrix, both subjective and actual? "Okay, prepare for a close pass of the sun, and we'll haul ass back around to the planet. Those other ships don't look as advanced, maybe they can't take the heat."

"Uhm," Aaron said and punched buttons, "the helm isn't responding."

"What? Is it damaged?"

"Doesn't look like it," Cherise said.

"Pip, what's going on?"

"I'm working on it." But Pip was having no luck. In a flash he'd found himself locked out of ninety-five percent of the computer. And unlike the earlier limitations, this was a dynamic attack to cut him back. It had an almost human feel to it. Suddenly, he wished he'd said something earlier about the missing shuttle, and how it had been back when they'd arrived at the Rasa home world. Or how he'd found communication logs showing the ship conversed and shared data with some distant source. A little went out, but vast petabytes had come back. And now the ship was being taken over by what felt like a virus. He fought with more and more of himself, until there wasn't anything left with which to talk.

"Pip!" Minu yelled over and over, without response.

One after another the bridge systems ceased to respond to the humans' commands. The ship continued to dive toward the sun and was now speeding up as the star's gravity pulled at them.

"We better get to a shuttle," Aaron suggested.

"Stay where you are," the little screen told Minu, again in ancient Concordian script. *"Watch this."*

"Don't bother," she told them even as they started to get up, "I think we're going to be okay."

"That's a sun we're falling in to," Ted pointed at the screen. The vast body of the stellar mass was projected from one side of the CIC to the other. They were now close enough that erupting solar prominences could be seen on the surface. It was a yellow sun, almost like the one Earth had enjoyed.

"I know," she said and leaned back, "but we're not in charge anymore." Pip floated in space, looking like he usually did, but she could see sweat on his face. Was this his doing?

The *Kaatan* finally began to change course, but slightly. It angled though the corona and into the chromosphere. Ted watched as the shields began to align faster than he could follow. Systems ejected accumulated plasma into their wake as previously topped-out shields came on line. They were expertly layered over the nose of the ship, forcing plasma to pass around them like a bullet splashing into a water barrel. They passed through the deadly ten thousand degree maelstrom untouched.

At fifty thousand kilometers per second they skimmed the chromosphere, a water skier sliding over lava. Specially designed force fields came alive, dipping into the photosphere miles below, and drawing it in.

"Power levels are going up!" Ted yelled. They'd all been watching, mesmerized, as death came up to meet them, and was then held at arm's length. They knew the ship had leveled off, but not why.

"Reserves are one hundred percent, main power twenty percent and climbing! Forty, seventy, approaching one hundred!"

The *Kaatan* pulled back, having traveled most of the way around the sun deep in its nuclear atmosphere, then began to climb back out. As it climbed, a new subsystem came alive. Gravity generators normally used for propulsion were linked with powerful force fields. The ship's engines straining, the ship began to slow slightly as it climbed, bogged down by what was happening in its wake.

"We're climbing out of the chromosphere," Ted told them. "Sensors are coming back online. We've orbited the sun and are coming back out the way we came."

"Targets in the threat bubble," Minu announced as the tactical system began to come alive. "Whoever is in charge better do something." She glanced at Pip and prayed it was him and not some crazy computer, indifferent to the life it carried inside.

"We just flew through a star," Bjorn babbled. "That was amazing!"

"I think I need to change my shorts." Ted laughed.

"Enemy ships, dead ahead," Minu told them. The display showed their forward view. The two smaller enemy ships were racing toward them. They were quickly widening the separation between themselves, bracketing the onrushing *Kaatan*. "They're firing." Two waves of six missiles emerged this time, twice as many as before. She could see all five lasers were armed, but it wouldn't be enough.

Instead of waiting for the missiles to approach, the *Kaatan* instantly launched a pair of the deadly sub-fusion plasma ship killers. Minu had never seen a lock on the displays, instead the missiles were guided toward the incoming swarm with incredible precision. When they detonated, only two enemy missiles remained, and they were easily picked off by the anti-missile lasers. The CIC broke out in whoops.

"Why isn't the ship attacking them now?" Aaron asked, already starting to treat the ship like it was an intelligence all its own.

"I don't know," Minu said. Just then the forward A-PAWs battery opened up, pouring fire into the enemy warships. Each impact made their shields flash brighter and brighter. Ted caught the significance immediately.

"They don't have the same kind of mobile shields we do! Now I understand the advantage. But it would take dozens of crew members to manage the things."

"Or one hell of a program," said Bjorn.

The attack was more effective against the ship on their right. The forward shields were overloading and the ship was heaving over to try and turn another set of shields against the relentless attack. The *Kaatan* adjusted its course and concentrated its fire on that one reeling ship. The other started firing its own A-PAWs now, but unlike their shields, whoever controlled the *Kaatan* defenses rotated individual shields against the attacks with such pinpoint accuracy that each shot only hit one shield. Ted whistled in appreciation as he watched the show.

When they were within a thousand kilometers, the *Kaatan* quickly changed course. One second it was racing straight toward the enemy warship with deadly intent, the next it veered away. In that instant, the special force fields were shut off. *"Watch the rear view,"* the little display told her. Minu switched the main view and gasped. Behind the *Kaatan*, seemingly only meters away, was a huge stellar prominence. "Oh lord," Bjorn gurgled.

The *Kaatan* had ridden the swirling masses of plasma in the star carefully, building in its wake a vortex of energy like a contrail behind an airplane. As it climbed out, the force fields helped contain the wave-charged plasma as the hoverfields shaped it. As they passed the enemy warship, the improvised weapon was unleashed. The target ship's shields were already badly depleted by the *Kaatan*'s A-PAWs. In a second, it was fully engulfed by the hundred-kilometers-wide stellar prominence like a bug caught in a blowtorch. The intact shields fought against the onslaught, and only succeeded in routing the million degree plasma energy through the window of damaged shields. The hellfire washed across the thousands of meters of hull, melting dualloy like butter. The first internal explosions overloaded the remaining shield capacitors, and the ship was consumed.

For a split second, they saw the warship briefly rival the dissipating stellar prominence, but then it was lost as the short-lived nebula of gas plasma spread out over thousands of cubic kilometers of space. The second warship was only brushed by the attack, but it still reeled as half its shields failed. The *Kaatan* fired a trio of bursts from its rear A-PAWs battery, punching fiery holes in the ship and setting off a series of explosions inside the superstructure. They left it behind, dead in space and beginning to spin lazily toward the star.

A hundred thousand kilometers away, the final alien warship, still struggling to catch up to the fight, fired a few desultory weapons blasts at them. They were ineffectual, and the *Kaatan* ignored the attack, continuing on toward the planet and leaving it once again far behind. Deciding they'd bit off more than they could chew, the ship ponderously moved off toward its stricken comrade, straining to reach it before it fell into the sun and met a similar fate to its cousin.

"What's our power situation?" Minu finally managed to ask, breaking the awed silence.

"Just under ninety percent," Bjorn told them.

"Take that snakes," Aaron whispered, not aware any of them could hear it. Minu just nodded.

"We have your message," came Var'at's voice over the speakers, "and we're climbing to intercept." Minu looked around but everyone else just shook their heads. They hadn't sent the message. "You're really hauling ass, we're going to be almost out of power when we rendezvous."

"That won't be a problem," Minu told him, "we've refueled."

"I can't wait to hear that story, or how you dealt with those ships! Var'at out."

Minu stood and looked around. Pip was coming vertical, standing on the 'floor' now, a look of profound confusion on his face. Not at all what she hoped to see. "Tell me that was you, please," she said.

"I can't," he replied simply. "I was bottled up quite effectively."

"Why? Who?"

"Why? I think to be certain I didn't cause any problems. Who? Well, I should have said something weeks ago, but the ship has been…working on something for a while. It got a big data upload from somewhere and began a covert project."
"Huh? What project?"

"I don't know, but it even took a shuttle for a few weeks."

"Took a shuttle?" Aaron asked. "Where could it go? The shuttles can't travel FTL."

"And you'd die even trying to pass through the luminal envelope," Ted agreed. Minu had listened to enough of their conversations to understand the basics. The sub-space bubble around the ship when they traveled faster than the speed of light was a mishmash of swirling probabilities and dueling chronological distortions. If you ever passed through you'd probably come out the other side as a mutated million year old turtle, or a toaster. You just didn't do it. And it was dangerous to the ship, as well.

"Where is this construction taking place?"

"Deck three, next to the medical bay."

Minu was out the door of the CIC and down the jump shaft in an instant. The door next to the medical bay was just like any other. She'd looked in there months ago when they'd gotten the ship. An empty room, not even configured as a cabin or anything else. Pip guessed it was possibly extra space for a larger medical bay. The ship seemed to have a great deal of flexibility in design. She stepped up to the door, and it instantly slid aside.

Inside was a completely different space than before. It was a miniature of the CIC, completely spherical but almost dark inside. Floating in the center of the space was what looked like a human. Not standing like they did on an artificial floor, but floating in the center like a scuba diver. It was difficult to see, but the figure appeared to be making intricate hand gestures and manipulating fields full of symbols.

"Who are you?" Minu asked.

The figure finished what it was doing and gracefully spun toward her. Minu instantly admired the elegant zero-g maneuver. As it turned, lights slowly grew in the sphere to reveal a young human girl, no more than ten years old. Her boyish figure was wasp thin with arms and legs so frail they could be broken by a stiff breeze. She had hair the color of blazing copper, and her eyes were a rich brown. Minu swallowed as she looked into a mirror that reflected an image from years ago. The girl's face was all sharp angles. There was no hint of emotion, only intense intelligence. Minu felt dizzy.

The girl looked her over with her sharp brown eyes and opened her mouth, speaking in clear English that was as devoid of emotion as her face. "I understand you're my mother." It was a good thing Aaron had just arrived behind her; he saved Minu from a concussion as she fainted dead away.

*****

Chapter Sixteen

March 15th, 523 AE (subjective)

***Kaatan*-Class Cruiser, Interstellar Space**

By the time Minu came around, all of the CIC crew was there as well. It was obvious they were no longer flying the ship anyway, so it was the logical thing to do. Aaron's panicked yell had been broadcast all over the ship, and they came running.

As she sat up with Aaron gently supporting her head, the visage of the young girl was unchanged, floating a few meters away, watching the gathered crowd with mild curiosity. Minu looked over her shoulder at everyone standing around her, some looking at her in concern, others trying to figure out who the thin young girl floating in a miniature CIC was.

"Our daughter?" Aaron asked, making the leap completely on his own. The girl's facial features, red hair, and his brown eyes were all powerful clues.

"Impossible," Minu snapped and got to her feet. "This is some sort of trick of the computer. It damn well better not be you guys, because this is fucking sick!" She rounded on them but all except Pip looked horrified by the prospect. Pip looked like he was considering possibilities.

"A simple genetic test should answer the question," he said.

"No!" Minu almost screamed. "We aborted my fetus not even a month ago." She gestured back toward the girl with a dismissive wave. "Look at her! She's at least eight, there is no way—"

"I am ten subjective years," the girl said neutrally. Minu jumped slightly as if she'd been shocked. She was feeling light headed again, and she had to clamp down hard on her self-control to avoid falling. Aaron saw her waver and put an arm on her elbow. She slapped it away viscously, without thinking who it was offering the support. "I was removed from your body as a fetus three of your subjective weeks ago."

"Fine," she said and forced herself to look at the girl, again feeling the vertigo of looking at a younger self, "then how did you age ten years in a few weeks?"

"The shuttle," Pip said.

"Yes," she agreed, giving Pip a slight nod to acknowledge his perception. "The ship tethered the shuttle and suspended it in the chrono-flux of the subspace sphere around the ship. There I was matured inside a synthetic womb, birthed, and raised while knowledge was implanted in my brain to prepare me for this job."

"Impossible," Minu said, no hint of humor in her voice.

"No, only improbable," Ted countered.

Bjorn had his own question. "How was the ship able to so precisely age you? Those fields are all but impossible to quantify."

"It was not," she replied. "I was supposed to be seventeen subjective years by the time you arrived in the Rasa system. Still, my age was deemed sufficient for this mission. Besides, if the incompetent biologicals—you, were allowed to maintain control of the ship, it would have been lost." The insult was straight and to the point. As was becoming the norm, Pip wasn't affected the same way as the others.

"That was quite a display you did to me." Pip said.

She showed the first signs of emotion, a cold smile crossing her face. "My pleasure." Minu felt a shiver go up her spine. This was no little girl, not by a long shot. She was about to ask what else the ship had taught her how to do when Aaron spoke up.

"We can't call you girl; what's your name?"

"The ship named me Lilith."

"Where did it come up with an English name like that?"

"It accessed all your tablets and downloaded the data they contained. Based on what it found, the name Lilith was chosen."

"What now?" Cherise spoke up for the first time. She was the only one among them with no doubts. Like Aaron, she'd made the connections quickly, but unlike the others she knew in her heart this was her friend's baby, suddenly half grown and the master of their ship. She didn't understand how she knew, it was just a deep 'girl truth' as her mother called it. What the Plateau people called 'women's intuition.' By whatever name it went, she knew the truth when she saw it. Minu and Aaron's baby was floating there, partly grown in body, but appearing to possess complete intelligence, and enough cold-blooded killer-instinct to burn a ship full of T'Chillen alive and rip another ship a new asshole. She had her mother's capacity for violence.

"There's no way," Minu jumped in. "You said it took you out early, so have it put you back. We can figure it all out when we get to Bellatrix."

"That isn't possible," Lilith explained, "once 'born' out of the sub-space region, I can't go back. I'm permanently inside your space-time now. And besides, I've taken over and reconfigured the ship's controls. You couldn't fly it directly now if you wanted to. I'm the combat intelligence. We've been joined. And we're not going to Bellatrix."

Minu was boiling mad. While she was spluttering Ted stepped in. "Where are we going?"

"I can't explain it. It's a place where we'll be safe while I repair the damage you caused, and complete the ship's configuration."

"Configuration?"

"Yes, it's still in need of some components."

"How long?"

"Five days, ship time. Our speed is somewhat reduced from damage."

"Am I still the commander?" Minu finally managed to ask.

Lilith looked at her with those deep brown eyes and was silent for what seemed like an eternity. "Yes, you're the commander."

"Then turn around and make for Bellatrix."

"As I said, you're the commander, but fleet protocol puts the ship's interests above biologicals in the case of ship survival where biologicals are not at risk of termination. Once we've made our stop and completed repairs…" she seemed to struggle with herself for a second, "then I'm at your command."

"I don't suppose that, as you say, being your mother, changes that?" Minu had a hard time saying 'mother.'

"Your genetic gift is appreciated, but I'm the Combat Intelligence, and you're the Commander. That's all that needs to be said."

Minu's anger was evaporating like fog on a hot afternoon. This was her daughter. There wasn't any better explanation. Shit, there wasn't *any* other explanation. "Why didn't the computer tell us about you?"

"The Medical Intelligence was confused by conflicting orders and protocols. Your exact instructions when asked what to do with me were, 'Do whatever it is you do with similar results.' There are no protocols involving the maturation of a fetus on a combat vessel. Lacking a Combat Intelligence, the computer improvised and created its own."

"But—"

"That's enough questions for now," she told them and gracefully turned in zero gravity. Rows upon rows of holographic Concordian script began to appear around her, almost like an egg shell, and she began to move among them. "Much work is necessary. Avoid the damaged sections; I'll be affecting around the clock repairs, such as can be done in super-luminal travel." And with that, the door slid closed and the conversation was over.

"Oh, she's your daughter all right," Cherise said. All the older Chosen nodded in silent agreement.

* * *

Immediately after Var'at's shuttle landed, Minu helped him get his people situated. He'd only brought twenty of his people, all females but two, his siblings Kal'at and Zar'at: the former a technology specialist, and the later a Rasa physician. Among the other cargo were a few dozen animals in suspension pods similar to what Pip had been transported in, and almost a hundred eggs carrying the genetic heritage of their species. "Never thought I'd be Noah," Minu said when she welcomed him aboard.

As soon as he was off to see his people housed, Minu met with the other human crew of the *Kaatan.* A lot needed to be worked out. Minu quickly finished her story to them, riding over their demands for more details, and then asked for everyone's ideas for how to proceed.

"It's probably out of the question for us to try to remove her," Bjorn said first. "She's almost certainly, either figuratively or literally, wired into every ship's system now."

Pip nodded and tapped his dualloy skull plate. "Wireless, there's no doubt. The sheer level of data she's handling makes it a certainty. Probably implanted when she was still a fetus. She learned to use the interface before she learned to walk."

"I don't think she can walk," said Minu. "Did you see her arms and legs?"

"Born and raised in zero gravity?" Ted wondered. They all seemed to agree as nods went around the room. "Then she can never leave the ship."

"At least never inside a gravity well," Pip pointed out. "It might be possible to make a zero-gravity floating wheelchair, or something like it, should the need ever arise."

"I need an honest answer from you," Minu said to Pip, looking him right in the eye. "Tell me you didn't know about this."

"No," he said without hesitation. "I admitted I knew something was going on, but not what. Never in my wildest imagination did I think the ship had decided to grow its own Frankenstein brain." Minu looked down and Aaron looked away. "I'm sorry. I still haven't learned to keep my fucking mouth shut."

"No need," she said and shrugged. "I'm beginning to accept that she's my genetic daughter, but what the ship did to her was far beyond acting as a mechanical midwife or anything like that. It might have raised her, but it did so as it would program a new computer, not a child."

"We should try to get at least a basic psychological evaluation done," Bjorn said. "She might be deeply disturbed. Who knows what her basic reality looks like? She'd never seen a human until a few hours ago. And the Medical Intelligence admits to not having seen a human before. Who knows what physiological or psychological differences there were between species?"

"She called Minu her mother," Cherise pointed out.

"And she killed a few thousands snakes without batting an eye," Aaron added. The room fell silent, no one knowing what else to say until Minu finally spoke up.

"What do you think we can expect at this destination of hers?" she asked the science minds, Pip, Ted, and Bjorn.

"Hard to say," Ted answered. Bjorn nodded his agreement.

"Possibly another firebase, or a shipyard," Pip suggested.

"Okay," Minu said and spread her hands, "so we wait and see where she's taking us. Other than that, there isn't much to do."

"There's something for you to do." Minu looked up at Cherise with a question in her eye. "You can get to know her."

"Me?" Minu was about to ask why her, then bit it back. *Yeah, me.* She'd been thinking how life was so unfair. Hadn't her dad always said life wasn't fair?

"Yes, and you too," Cherise said and nodded toward Aaron. "Like it or not, accept it or not, that's your child in there flying this machine."

"Only by the wildest stretch of the concept of parent and child," Aaron said.

Minu nodded in agreement. "We'll try," she said, and Aaron looked at her in surprise. "It's the least we can do," she said and stared into his eyes, the exact shade of brown as Lilith's. "Okay?"

He only hesitated a moment. "Yeah, okay." As they left, Lilith watched the empty room, considering.

* * * * *

Chapter Seventeen
March 16th, 523 AE (subjective)

***Kaatan*-Class Cruiser, Interstellar Space**

Minu woke early the next 'day' on the ship. Aaron was snuggled in behind her snoring quietly, so she lay there for a few minutes, thinking. So many things had happened to her since she'd left Bellatrix a couple of months ago, so much to change her. Finding out you're pregnant then losing the baby within minutes was traumatic enough, but then having that lost child turn up a few weeks later as the ten-year-old supermind controlling the ship was the most powerful kick in the back of the head she could imagine. And then there was the fight against the vampires, and their mysterious rescuers.

She watched the little crystalline bots emerge and clean the room, right on schedule. Once they were gone, she rose and showered. Aaron had been perfect, not even trying to suggest any intimacy last night beyond snuggling. He'd instinctively known it was the furthest thing from her mind. The hot stinging spray brought her fully awake. Afterward she dressed and quietly left.

A few of the Rasa were out and about, still settling into life on the ship. Minu didn't recognize any of them, and they didn't carry translators, so she just flicked her eyes in a Rasa sort of wave and moved on. There would be time to meet them later.

She arrived at the door to the new miniature CIC without realizing she'd been headed there. As before, it slid open. *Must be visiting hours,* she thought. As before, Lilith floated in the center, but this time the space was lit gently, and she was waiting. Like she would have in the other CIC, Minu stepped in, and fell.

"Shiitt!" she squeaked and started spinning. She'd expected a floor to conveniently appear like the main CIC, and it hadn't. She was so disoriented she didn't have time to do anything. The room spun in circles and she caught a quick glance as Lilith gracefully slid to the side to avoid colliding with her. Then Minu hit the opposite wall and rebounded off. She hit on her left shoulder, not too painfully, and tried to catch a hold on the wall, but it was perfectly smooth. She was heading off in a new direction. Just before she hit the wall again, an invisible force arrested her motion and spun her around to face Lilith in the center of the room.

"You looked like you needed help." As always, her face was emotionless.

"Thank you." No response. "I wanted to talk with you."

"You are."

"Right." Minu took a breath and tried to think of what to say. "I want you to know that this isn't the way this should have happened."

"What do you mean?"

"I mean that we wanted to have you, Aaron and I. He's your father, you know?"

"Yes, I understand."

"Okay. Anyway, we were excited to find out you were inside me."

"Then you had me removed and discarded."

Minu swallowed hard, trying to stop the tears from rising and knowing she was failing. "The Medical Intelligence told me—"

"That you couldn't carry me to term, I understand. It was the logical option."

"No, it wasn't logical, it was the only choice. My life was in danger, and it said you had no chance. I'm sorry."

"Don't be; the ship gave me everything I need. It was the chance you couldn't give me."

It was too much, the tears weren't falling, they were just gathering in her eyes like puddles. She managed to reach the wall with a foot and shove off. Whether Lilith helped her or not, all that mattered was she reached the door and bolted out, almost landing flat on her face as gravity returned suddenly. Lilith watched her go, her face blank and uncomprehending.

* * *

Aaron found Minu in the galley an hour later poking a couple of synthetic eggs around some equally synthetic sausage. He smiled but when she looked up her eyes were red and puffy. She tried to smile back, but started crying again.

"What's wrong?" he asked, sitting next to her.

"I tried talking to Lilith."

"Oh? Didn't go well?"

"She's an Alma alright."

"What does that mean?"

"She's a bitch, through and through." Minu explained the meeting, leaving nothing out. Aaron's eyes got bigger and bigger as she went on until he was fuming. When she was done he was on his feet and leaving. "Where are you going?"

"To talk to our daughter." Minu watched him go, unsure whether to wish him luck or not. What hurt the worst was that the young girl had told the truth.

The door opened for him as he approached to find Lilith floating in the center of her 'home.' He didn't waste any time. "What the fuck is wrong with you?"

"I'm not certain I understand the question."

Aaron avoided stepping off into zero gravity, she'd warned him about her preferred living environment. Instead he stood at the edge, a hand on both sides of the door. "Don't you know anything about what you are?"

"I'm the ship's Combat Intelligence."

"You're our daughter, and a human being."

"Only by the strictest definitions of the words."

"So it means nothing to you, where you come from?"

"Very little."

"And equally little how you're perceived by those who might care for you?"

"Even less."

"It seems then you were right."

"About what?"

"That you *are* only human by definition. Because humans don't treat each other like you treated Minu, unless they hate each other."

"I don't know how to hate."

"You seem to have mastered it with no practice. But whether you like it or not, want it or not, you're our daughter, and we have feelings for you."

Lilith cocked her head and opened her mouth, then stopped. Aaron nodded. For the first time she didn't know what to say. "I don't desire your feelings; they're irrelevant to me."

"Are you so certain?"

Lilith floated there for a few moments and contemplated him. Aaron wasn't fooled; he could see the gears turning behind those eyes, the same eyes he saw in the mirror every morning. It wasn't in his nature to be a bastard. Like Minu, he wanted to know this girl and wished it hadn't come down to such a bizarre situation. Finally, since she didn't say anything, he turned to leave.

"I'd like to talk to her again."

Aaron stopped and turned around slowly. "Talk to who?"

"The Commander."

"Who?"

"Minu Alma, the commander of this ship."

"Who?"

An emotion flashed across her eyes. Frustration or anger? "My Mother."

Aaron nodded and gave her a tiny smile. "Okay, I'll talk to her and see if she's willing after the last exciting encounter."

Lilith tried to return the smile. It was more a rictus than a smile, but Aaron increased his smile nonetheless. "Thank you, Father."

* * *

Round two, later that day. This time Minu knew what to expect, and she floated into the space gracefully, catching herself on the edge of the doorway before facing her daughter. "You wanted to talk to me." Lilith looked around the room, and Minu wondered if she was aware she was acting like a typical young girl caught acting badly. "Well?"

"I'm sorry for being…*mean* to you, Mother."

Minu heaved a silent sigh, gave her a tiny smile and nodded. "I accept your apology, Lilith. This isn't easy, for any of us. I know it's too late to be your real Mother and raise you, but I'd like to be what I can."

"That would be acceptable." Lilith gave her impression of a smile. Luckily Aaron had warned her so she didn't react as negatively as she was tempted to. "Can you tell me about our family? Your computer records are not exhaustive."

"What do you want to know?"

"Tell me about your mother."

Minu gave an audible sigh this time, not expecting to be confronted with something she had yet to really come to grips with herself. Lilith cocked her head expectantly, watching Minu. "Okay. Her name was Sharon, and her father was Chosen, like me."

* * * * *

Chapter Eighteen

March 20th, 523 AE (subjective)

Quantum Convergence Point, Interstellar Space

The ship dropped back into the normal universe in deep space. The old CIC crew was all gathered, but now they were only there in case of an emergency. In their discussions, Minu had gotten Lilith to agree to the remote possibility that something could happen, and they might be needed. She also explained that humans liked to have a purpose, and it would help to pass the time.

"No stars or planets anywhere nearby," Ted told them as he reviewed the sensor data.

"What's here, Lilith?" Minu asked like she used to address Pip when he was wired in. Lilith had allowed Pip to interface with the ship again, but she was adamant he not overstep his bounds. Pip assured her he would be a good boy, and the two had even had a few conversations. He found her to be brilliant on his own level. She'd told Minu that she found him amusing.

"We need to activate some systems."

"Can you explain?"

"It'll take too long and is too technical."

"Will you try?"

It was quiet for a moment, and she knew her daughter was struggling against her ever-present anti-social side. The computers might have taught her to be a ship's operator, but it hadn't done her any favors by scrimping on social skills. She finally relented. "We're here to enable the tactical drive." Minu felt her pulse race. The Weavers. But how could they do that out here, in deep space, trillions of kilometers from anything? "Once we've reached the proper coordinates, it will only take a moment."

"What's at those coordinates?" Bjorn asked her. Like others in the crew, Bjorn and Ted had both had occasion to interview their new ship's master. Ted was amazed at her intellect, saying she reminded him very much of Chriso at an early age. Bjorn was less impressed, and more concerned. "She's more a force of nature than anything," he warned Minu. "Don't underestimate her; she shares none of our concerns for living things. She only cares for this ship, and perhaps you and Aaron. Perhaps."

"This is a convergence point in our galaxy. You can think of it as a temporal Lagrange point where the fabric of the universe is very delicate."

Without saying anything, Minu jumped up and left the CIC. Only Aaron noticed, turning his head to watch her go. He guessed she was going down to talk to Lilith in person, but she headed straight for the very nose of the *Kaatan*, to a tiny room she'd visited once back when they'd first gotten the ship. As she entered, she saw the formerly dark portal-type dais was now glowing. "So you understand," she heard Lilith's voice, and then was stunned to see her floating nearby.

"How can you do that out here?"

Lilith gave a little smirk, much improved from four days of practice. "Mother, the entire ship is really in free fall. There's only gravity where you walk because the ship decides you need it. I don't, so there is none."

"Oh," Minu said and turned to look at the brightly glowing dais. "Is it going to become a portal?"

"Not in the sense of what you know of as a portal." Floating panels of Concordian script appeared before Lilith. Her long, thin fingers danced on them. "The ship is creating a stationary gravity well."

"How powerful?"

"For a millisecond, it will rival a collapsing star."

A black hole? Minu whistled through her teeth. "What's it for?"

"We're sending a message." There was no sensation as the ship made the already thin structure of space ring like a bell. Once, twice, three times. Then the dais pulsed so brightly that both women had to put a hand before their eyes. When they could look around their hands, swirling snakes of plasma chased each other over the dais. "Now the ship is fully operational."

"Can we just 'portal' to Bellatrix now?"

"Not yet; it will be about a month before we can use the drive. So we travel to your home the usual way."

"It can be your home too." The swirling snakes of energy were mystifying to watch. She didn't know how to ask her daughter if there was now a Weaver inside.

"This ship must remain my home," she said and gestured to her painfully thin arms and legs.

"Just because you can't walk, doesn't mean there wouldn't be a way to go down to the planet surface. Gravity generation technology can also negate it."

Lilith nodded and regarded the energy swirls. "Is that beautiful?"

"Very much so."

"I wonder if it'll be different when the Weaver arrives?"

Minu felt her head spin a little, an image of the ethereal species calling themselves Weavers appearing in the back of her mind. Lilith said she had vast amounts of data on ancient Concordian species. If she knew about the Weavers, then they must be real. "I don't know," Minu said, "this looks different from other portals. Is the process similar? Will we be able to instantly travel anywhere in the galaxy?"

"No, the range is limited to a few hundred light-years. But other than that, it's just like a portal."

They stood watching the swirling plasma for a moment. Lilith glanced at Minu, then toward the door, but in her new 'social training' she knew it was rude to just leave. Minu spoke up before she could leave. "Lilith, what are you going to do?"

"Do? I'm going to return to my station, wait for the space fabric to stabilize, and set course for your—our world."

"No, after that. You're the master of this vessel, though you say I'm its commander. There's nothing stopping you from leaving after we arrive at Bellatrix."

"Correct."

"So what are you going to do?"

She looked at the door again and thought. "I don't know, Mother."

Minu watched her, trying to find a deeper meaning, but Lilith possessed an exceptional poker face. She'd considered teaching her the game. "I guess that's good enough for now. Please, call me any time, I like talking to you."

"I like talking to you, too. You're not what I was led to expect."

"And what was that?"

"The computer taught me that biological parents are often commanding, and indifferent to their offspring, especially while youthful, such as me."

"Then maybe I don't know how to be a proper parent."

"No, I believe you're better than others would be."

"You have a biased opinion."

"Perhaps. I must return to my station, please excuse me."

"Of course. And your manners are improving quickly."

"Pip has been helping me, and I'm helping him. What the ship did to him was unfortunate. The Medical Intelligence was trying to make him into something like me, while at the same time repairing him. I believe it failed on both accounts. He's somewhat like me now, not fully able to deal with your 'social situations.'"

"I'd agree." Minu watched Lilith, her daughter, float from the drive room. She looked almost like films she'd seen of dolphins swimming in the oceans back on earth. She never touched anything, just swam in the center of the halls with graceful movements of arms and legs. There was no way her swimming motions actually propelled her through the air. The ship must be lousy with tiny hoverfield generators. Or had they been added by the little industrious crystalline bots after her emergence? Minu decided it really didn't matter. She walked from the room and headed back to the CIC. When she got there, Minu realized she had a problem. Was it possible to explain what had just happened without explaining the Weavers? No, it wasn't.

She stuck her head into the CIC. "We can't move for a few minutes, according to Lilith. I'd like to see the senior staff in the galley right away." Senior staff was her code for all the humans, and

Var'at. Off to one side of the CIC, Var'at and his brothers were having a discussion.

Var'at disengaged and headed out.

In the galley, everyone found a seat as Minu stood at the end of the table. Cherise noticed right away that she seemed nervous, more so than lately. Learning to deal with Lilith had put a strain on the woman everyone could see. A strain more profound than command ever had.

"Thanks," she said after the last of them was seated and the galley door closed. "I called you here to tell you what's going on with the ship and to make good on a promise." She looked directly at Ted as she said the last part. "I said I'd tell you what happened with the portals once we were safe, and I've put it off far too long."

"You're damned right you did," he said.

"I appreciate your patience. This operation has been one challenge after another. And while Lilith is a person, not a challenge, her sudden appearance and the emotional baggage that came with it have been no less challenging in themselves." Ted nodded in understanding while the others watched.

"About two years ago, under the tutelage of Jovich, I started meditating on the portals. A practice he said many older Chosen did, including my father."

"Some of the scouts do it too," Aaron said. "A few said they've had visions of ghosts, or spiders."

Minu chuckled, then sighed. "Oh, they weren't visions. They're a species called the Weavers."

Over the next hour she laid it all out for them. The first encounter in the portal room back on Bellatrix, the Weavers intervening to save her life during the Vendetta, and their giving her the 'secret' key codes she'd used to first rescue them from Sunshine, then to gain access to the *Kaatan*. She finished off a little out of chronology. "And they didn't want to talk to me at all on Sunshine. They've been insisting they only want to talk to one person for almost a year."

"Who?" Pip asked, something like worry on his face.

"You."

Pip looked down and nodded. "I was afraid of that."

"Why?"

"Because I first spoke to them about a month before I was injured."

"Damn it Pip! Why didn't you tell us? Even your uncle?" Bjorn had said during her story that many Chosen over the years had relayed similar encounters, but none had a name for the creatures, and they'd never talked to the Chosen before.

"Same reason you haven't been jabbering about it to everyone! The Chosen have their own psychiatrists and a whole wing of rubber rooms in Tranquility for those who can't handle the pressure."

"Are they really rubber?" Aaron asked. Pip rolled his eyes.

"So what did you tell them that made the Weavers want to talk to you so badly?"

"I told them I'd help them with a problem."

"What problem?" Minu asked, beginning to get annoyed.

"Their deal." Minu's eyes shot daggers, and he continued. "They had a deal with some ancient Concordian species. They run the portals, and in exchange they got something in return. Well, it's been a long time since they've gotten anything out of the deal, and even the frustratingly non-linear Weavers are getting annoyed." He looked up at them all before continuing. "They told me unless I can help them, they'd cease cooperation, effectively shutting down all commerce and traffic between the worlds of the Concordia."

*****

Chapter Nineteen
March 17th, 523 AE (subjective)

Former Rasa Leasehold

Singh-Apal-Katoosh hadn't left the bridge of his ship for a week. The battleship had been a floating hulk since the tiny enemy ship devastated it. The attack with the solar prominence was inconceivable enough from any standpoint, but after his ship's shields were down from a grazing hit of the plasma that destroyed her sister ship, the little monster had put a brace of disastrous shots into his ship's superstructure. Each burst was precisely aimed, taking out impulse drive, the gravitic lens drive, and the central computer. A week later and the great, ponderous carrack had finally managed to haul the carcass of his battleship far enough away from the sun that they were no longer in danger of fiery death.

At first he'd almost ordered the carrack captain put to the spike for allowing the little ship's escape, but then he came to his senses as his survival was assured. Attempting to stop the monster would only have cost them another irreplaceable ship. They'd been sorely outmatched. Still, his brain was full of questions. Why had the ship feigned helplessness for so long before turning the tables? Why use the seemingly suicidal maneuver through the sun instead of just engaging them head on, as was within its ability? And finally, where had it gone?

Singh would have to report to the High T'Chillen leadership that some of the Rasa had escaped to parts unknown. Of course the Concordian Council wouldn't be informed of their humiliation here; that was unthinkable. Most species had no clue that some spaceships remained; they were the most precious assets of the higher-order. They were mostly used as terror weapons, but also as a mark of prestige. All five of the higher-order species possessed ships, some more than others. The T'Chillen were second only to the Mok-Tok, but maybe not after this week. The battleships were the ultimate expression of space power. Able to operate independently for extended periods, capable of incredible speeds, able to carry thousands of troops, and stuffed with weapons and defenses, yet a tiny ship not much bigger than one of the battleship's shuttles had obliterated one and crippled another, maybe beyond repair. The technicians' only good news was that the carrack's FTL field would be strong enough to carry both ships back to their shipyard, though at only five hundred times the speed of light. The journey would take the two ships five years, and twenty would pass to the outside world. The high command would have to decide whether to scuttle the remaining battleship; he couldn't make that call.

"Communications from the portal on the Rasa planet surface," announced a technician, the female casting her eye stalks down in deference to him.

"Send it to my pedestal here," he replied, curling tightly on the padded column to free a hand should it be needed. A second later a screen slid from one of the pedestal supports and came alive. He felt his hood twitch as he recognized the high fleet lord.

"A tiny bug to squash and you get your tail spike chewed off?"

"It wasn't as simple as it appeared." He did his best not to sound entreating. He wasn't sure he'd succeeded. "You're aware of the technical nest's attempts to investigate the fleets of ships at Enigma?"

"I've heard of it."

"The Rasa's incursion at Enigma is what predicated the approval of their destruction!" The fleet lord moved back from the camera, taken slightly aback.

"Yes, that's correct. I admit I'm not knowledgeable about the derelict ships and what we hope to gain with all the expenditures to study them."

"That's just it; they're not derelict as we believed. The Rasa somehow gained access to one of the ships and escaped in it, after destroying several shuttles and hundreds of warriors."

"I've seen the images; what type of ship was it?"

"The smallest of the needle and ball ships."

"That doesn't sound bad."

"It showed up here as we neared the extermination of the Rasa. At first it appeared weak and almost helpless, so we pursued as it tried to flee. Then everything turned to waste." He explained what the Rasa ship did to their squadron, in careful detail, including the pinpoint accuracy of the A-PAW fire employed against his own ship. "This ship is more powerful than anything we possess."

"And there are more of those at Enigma?"

"Dozens."

"With but a handful of these ships, the T'Chillen could…"

"What?"

"Nothing, I was just thinking aloud." Singh waited while the fleet lord considered. He knew quite well what the aging leader was thinking. With a few of those death machines, the T'Chillen could sweep all four of the other higher-order species aside, even against their combined might. The threat of a combined opposition was all that had kept any one or two of them from doing just that untold eons ago. "Scuttle the crippled battleship and return to Skesh to await further orders. I must consult the T'Chillen council." The screen went blank, and Singh contemplated the star field outside projected on the forward bulkhead of the battleship's CIC.

He was about to give the scuttle order when he noticed the communication screen hadn't retracted back into the pedestal. He leaned closer and saw 'pending transmission.' A tentacle digit pressed acknowledge.

"Ship commander, you're ordered to upload all images from your recent space battle." It was a text-only message, no visual.

Singh looked from the message up to a nearby technician. "Where's this message coming from?"

"It can't be the portal, high commander, it's inactive." The female's tentacles danced across her controls. "The data is being fed from a system that's not listed aboard this ship."

"A communications device that doesn't exist?" The female lowered her eyes in agreement, and he turned back to the screen.

"We're waiting." it said.

"Who are you, and how are you communicating with this ship?"

"We are the Grent. You will comply."

Singh almost lost his grip on the pedestal, his insides turning to ice water, and his eye stalks quivering. Grent, a name lost in the halls of time, forgotten by all but a few species. It was used to instill fear in young beings throughout the galaxy without any realizing what it really meant. No one knew what they looked like, only that the Grent were the species who'd supposedly destroyed the Lost. Still alive, somewhere in the vastness of space, they waited and watched the goings on, ready to punish any who would dare to doubt their supremacy. He swallowed a mouthful of bitter venom, excreted as a fight or flight reaction. Yet another nightmare had come to torture him.

"How could I possibly believe you're Grent?"

"Are you willing to take the risk of being wrong? Choose wisely."

He hissed in anger and frustration. First the damn Rasa ship, now this. He knew there'd be no way to reach the high command in time for advice. But what could a legendary mysterious species like the Grent possibly do to him out here, light-years from wherever they were. His tail spike slashed at the air, making an angry hiss and drawing sparks from the pedestal base. The answer was beyond his imagination, and that was enough to make him comply. With a couple taps of his tentacle digits, the data was transmitted.

"Your cooperation is noted, and will be rewarded. We'll call upon you again." A data packet arrived in his personal computer.

Singh examined the data, his interest slowly usurping his anger and fear. The horrible ship which devastated his battleships was called a *Kaatan.* Then as he read on about where the ship came from he felt the fear begin to return. For the first time since leading warriors into battle, he wished he hadn't been born to lead.

* * * * *

Chapter Twenty

March 17th, 523 AE (subjective)

***Kaatan*-Class Cruiser, Interstellar Space**

Pip often did impetuous, ill-conceived things. It was practically his hallmark as a visionary genius. Next to their friendship, it was the most compelling reason Minu had risked everything to race off across the galaxy on a desperate rescue mission.

She met with Pip a short time after her briefing about the Weavers. Bjorn and Ted had more than enough to think about; they didn't even notice how she dragged him to her room for a private discussion.

"I don't believe you."

"I don't believe it either."

"Not that," she said, "I don't believe you were that stupid. To try and negotiate with a timeless trans-dimensional entity?"

"Yeah, that's what I meant too." He looked down, and she sighed. "I don't think before I act sometimes. You know that, I know that, we all know that. I can't help it—"

"You could fucking try once in a while!"

"They didn't give me a choice. Once I started prying into their problem I was instantly nominated to fix it. It's like I was now in on the secret, and thus must work to keep it. I felt like I'd joined some medieval cabal."

Minu paused for a minute as she rolled his turn of phrase through her memory. She needed to read more. "Okay, so we've established you were a moron…" he rolled his eyes but held his peace, "now you can show me you're a genius."

"That should be easy enough."

"Right. So what's the nature of the deal?"

"I don't know."

"How long has it been in place?"

"Millions of years? I don't know."

"Did you make any progress?"

"I'd have to say, probably. They stopped talking to you and insisted on talking to me."

"Granted. What was the problem, anyway? With your massive brain it should have been a snap."

"I agree, but it wasn't. The problem was establishing a common frame of reference."

"Go on," said Minu, sitting back on her bed.

Pip licked his lips, a memory coming back unbidden. Aaron lying back on the bed as Minu straddled his erection. He felt himself getting hard and cleared his throat. "The Weavers are trans-dimensional. I don't think we can even conceive of what their universe is like, but we both know it's timeless. They might know the words for today, tomorrow, yesterday, but they're just words picked from our brains. Yesterday could be defined as a teapot, or tomorrow a way you die. They don't understand."

"So how do they perceive time then? They're somewhat involved in time if they're in our continuum."

"I don't know that they are. If you forced me to make a guess, and it seems you are, I'd say the portals are like a wormhole to their dimension, or universe, or whatever. They stick their head through and look around, but like a fish poking its head out of the water, things don't make sense to them."

"There had to be some sort of common ground, The Lost managed to work out a deal with them."

Pip shrugged. "Maybe the Lost were from another universe."

"Really?"

"No, probably not." He shook his head, trying not to look at her breasts. "A more logical answer is they either had some extra sensory perception or some device that allowed them to communicate and negotiate with the Weavers. After the few times I've talked to them, I can tell you this; they were patient."

"Maybe the portal allows them to communicate?"

"No. I don't know what it does, no one does. It could just be a big trans-dimensional fish tank for all we know. Traveling across space could just be a side effect. The technology is as far ahead of us as we are beyond ants."

"Fair enough. So I have an assignment for you. Lilith says in a few hours a Weaver will move into the dais up in the nose of the *Kaatan*. That's the 'tactical drive.' It's some sort of unusual portal that moves the whole ship, but only a few hundred light-years. It must be for short range hops in battle, maybe. Anyway, your assignment is to chat with that Weaver."

"I guessed as much. What are your expectations?"

"Find a common ground."

"There isn't one; I confirmed that by the second frustrating meeting."

"Okay, try a new tack." He shrugged but looked expectantly. "Teach them what time is." Pip lifted an eyebrow, and a hint of a smile crossed his lips.

* * *

Lilith floated at her station and considered the conversation with her mother. Despite her initial dismissive attitude toward her genetic donor, Minu was more than first appearances indicated. The emotions were a frustrating thing to deal with though. The humans appeared to be such slaves to their emotional rampages. Along with the neural process enhancement implant installed when she was a fetus was a hormone and endocrine filtering device. She spent her life in an ideal balance of hormones and cerebral chemicals. Typical humans rode it like an insane, never-ending roller coaster of ups and downs. She didn't have to bow to that master.

Despite herself she found her interest in Minu growing almost daily. She was a fascinating woman. And wasn't there something to learn from her after all? Until she learned more about this universe, Minu was the best teacher to provide mundane understanding. The computer provided details her brain had been fed during 'childhood' that had turned out to be disappointingly two-dimensional, which led her to wonder where else her education had been lacking. She decided that if she was going to self-identify as human, she needed a teacher. Her parents would serve that purpose well enough. She didn't know that a little smile crossed her face as she considered how that would develop.

* * * * *

Chapter Twenty-One

March 18th, 523 AE (subjective)

***Kaatan*-Class Cruiser, Interstellar Space**

After all the stress and heartache of the last few months, the final weeks of their trip home passed with little to no drama. Minu and Cherise started up their daily runs and three-times-a-week workout sessions, joined by Aaron at first, and later, occasionally, by Var'at and his team.

They were three days out from Bellatrix when Lilith brought them back into normal space and announced the Weaver was arriving. The small cabal of humans who knew the truth gathered in the drive room, crowding around the swirling dais, and waited. It happened very fast. One moment it was the snakes of plasma chasing each other around, the next it was a sphere, like the portal except with three dimensions. Like a normal portal, it was a shimmering translucent shape constantly in motion, but without the typical arch of pearly force fields. Pip stood the closest, and he regarded it with a critical eye.

"The Weaver is here now," Lilith told them, "we have tactical drive. Does your Pip wish to converse with the Weaver?"

"Sort of," Pip admitted. They'd let Lilith in on the story shortly after Minu found out the details of Pip's one-man negotiation attempt. The young girl was not surprised; her files indicated the makers of the ships had spoken with the Weavers routinely. Minu was a little taken aback by that fact. Could the beings who'd made these ships also be the ones who'd invented the portals and negotiated the ancient deal? Concordian species' stories about the mythical 'Lost' varied considerably, but always operated in millions of years. This ship couldn't be millions of years old. She had a hard time believing it was even a hundred years old.

"May I stay and witness?" Lilith asked. Minu smiled; her daughter was making good progress in her social skills.

Pip looked around at all the expectant faces, then at Lilith hovering in place, and shrugged. "One more pair of eyes won't hurt." He stepped onto the lowest step of the dais and sat down.

"Pip," Minu spoke up. He looked over his shoulder at her. "Once you start your chat, ask them if they'll talk to me again."

"Will do, boss." He turned to face the portal, his shoulders relaxed, and they waited.

After a few minutes Aaron spoke up. "Will we see them?"

"No," Minu told him, "I think it all happens in your head." No sooner had she uttered the words than a Weaver materialized from the swirling pattern.

Minu was a little surprised she could see them without being closer, but Cherise screamed like a little girl, and Ted said a less than gentlemanly "Fuck me!" Lilith cocked her head and examined the creature. She'd seen representative images of them in dozens of old files.

The assemblage settled down and strained to hear what it was saying, but only Pip was so blessed. He sat for a half an hour before sighing and straightening up. The Weaver seemed to get smaller and smaller until it disappeared. He stood up and stretched, looking around at everyone's eager stares. "Did you see it too?" Everyone nodded their heads, even Lilith. "Really?"

"Pip," Minu grumbled, "enough fun, how did it go?"

"Oh, they're as frustrating as always." Minu put her hands on her hips, and he looked embarrassed. "They're agreeable to my trying to teach them 'temporal understanding,' as they called it."

"And me?"

"Oh, you can come and chat any time you want."

Everyone crowded in for a chance to talk to Pip, ask him what it was like, and see if they could try some time to speak with the extra-dimensional being. Eventually it was just Pip, Minu and Lilith.

"Pip," Minu said, "are the creators of these ships the Lost?"

"I can't say for certain."

"Why don't you just ask them?"

"I tried once. They wouldn't answer."

"That doesn't surprise me," Lilith said. "My files indicate they give information in unreliable sporadic bursts, often predicting the future centuries in advance."

"Exactly," Pip said. "Part of the problem is our frame of reference. Their perceptions don't work as ours do. They're erratic, enigmatic sooth-seers at best, contradictory at worst."

"Lilith," Minu spoke to her, "how detailed are these files you access?"

"I have the entire history of the species which created this ship, and the times around then."

"What did they call themselves?"

"The People."

"Do you know what happened to them?"

"Not yet. The files are very detailed, and there are approximately seven hundred million of them with an average size of two point one six gigabytes."

"More than one and a half exabytes," Pip said with some admiration in his voice. "How much have you gotten through?"

"I'm not attempting to read it all, much is mundane information."

"Can I help?"

She was silent for a moment, considering him with her deep brown eyes. Minu wondered if she were weighing the risks of allowing Pip access to such a treasure trove of data, no doubt chock full of tactical and scientific details of the ship they rode in. Eventually she flashed him one of her slowly evolving smiles and nodded. "You may assist me, but I'll need to guide your searches."

"I'm augmented as well, remember," he said and tapped the dualloy skull plate.

"Correct, but you're not as familiar with file structures of this sort as I am." She began to explain the way The People had created their spiral logic arrays and nested file loops, and Minu felt herself getting sleepy. She loved science, but this was like watching paint dry.

"Okay you two, have fun." They both looked at her like that was a ludicrous suggestion. It was work, not fun. "Add to your list of things to get out of the database a way to communicate with the Weavers. I know, I know, not a simple task. Remember, I've 'chatted' with them as well. Just try, okay?"

"Sure."

As she left she had a tiny bit of concern. Pip's sexual deviation was well known among the crew, possibly even by Lilith. Minu wondered if leaving him alone with her daughter for hours at a time was wise. She decided not to worry about it. He might have become the master of inappropriate questions and a chronic masturbator, but he'd never once done anything untoward in front of a fellow crew mate. His lapses thus far had been entirely vocal in nature. She was sure Lilith was safe in that manner.

* * * * *

Chapter Twenty-Two

January 29th, 527 AE (local time)

Bellatrix System, Human Leasehold

The *Kaatan* dropped out of super-luminal travel at the outer edge of the Bellatrix system. None of the occupants would have even noticed if not for the crew being on duty and watching it happen. Lilith, with her natural piloting talent, bled off just enough residual energy from their transition back to normal space to have them coast toward the inner system at a significant percent of C. Even still, they were almost seventeen hours out from home.

Those who'd grown up in the star system marveled at unseen views of their home. They passed within a million kilometers of the ice planet Vulcan (Minu had never appreciated the irony of whoever had named it), and then came within a hundred thousand kilometers of the brilliant blues and reds of the gas giant Vega. Minu wished they'd passed the ringed world Valhalla; she'd seen it once as a child through a telescope and thought it was amazing. A brown and silver globe with dozens of multicolored rings, reminiscent of Saturn.

As they passed Vega's orbit, Lilith asked if they wanted to contact their planet. "We're too far out," Pip told her, "we don't have faster-than-light communications like the ship has." The revelation of FTL radio not using the portal caught even Pip by surprise when she revealed its existence. Ted and Bjorn marked it down as another technology lost to the ages. The Concordia had forgotten more than Humans had yet acquired.

"I've studied the satellites installed around your moons. They're a type four relay satellite, manufactured in the era of the People. Each one contains an FTL communications relay."

"That would be news to us," Pip told her.

"And likely to the Traaga who sold them to us," said Ted. "I helped negotiate that contract."

Lilith worked her magic, and in a minute Minu was opening a channel to the Chosen command center in Steven's Pass. The operator requested routing of the call.

"I'm not sure who to talk to," Minu admitted with a little laugh.

"Are you authorized to use this channel?" asked the young but authoritative voice.

"Oh, without a doubt. This is Minu Alma, three-star, calling from aboard our starship heading toward orbit."

"Did you say Minu Alma?" the voice choked. "Starship?"

Oh shit, Minu thought. "Yes. Maybe you better put me through to the office of the First."

She never knew if he heard her, because she was already being transferred. The voice that came on next was a rich baritone, unmistakably Dram. "Minu! Oh my God, is it really you?"

"You bet," she said and took a calming breath. "We're about twelve hours out of orbit."

"You must be right outside of lunar orbit."

"No, way, way, past that."

"I don't understand."

"Neither do I, entirely. Anyway, we had a change of plans, which should explain our long absence. We have a few dozen Rasa refugees on board, including women and fertile eggs. We'll have to work something out for them."

"That won't prove a problem for you," he said with a chuckle.

Minu cocked her head, confused by the tone. "So we'll be down in a shuttle at Steven's Pass before too long. You might want to have a guard there to take custody of me. As I stated in my message, I assume full respons—"

"Will you shut up for a second?" Minu clammed up. He still didn't sound upset. "Send us as close an ETA as possible so we can get the party waiting. We've been planning it for years."

"Uhm, party?"

"Yes party, you crazy girl. At least a dozen hospitals have been named after you, and God knows how many babies."

"Okay, I'm officially confused. I'm a criminal, stole a bunch of equipment, and ran off without permission…"

"Sure, and then you sent back the codex, remember? Minu, you've saved thousands of lives! It's been all but a renaissance down here. You're a hero, kid. Bigger than Mindy Harper! Hurry home."

* * *

The quad and landing area of Steven's Pass was filled to overflowing with a tide of humanity. As the shuttle turned on final approach, Minu looked at the monitor and hissed in annoyance. Twenty thousand was probably a conservative estimate. Every square inch of the immediate landing area except enough space for the shuttle was covered in chairs and guests. Beyond were erected temporary bleachers filled with thousands more.

There were also dozens, if not hundreds of large and small flying vehicles, some covered with more people vying for a view, others carrying news crews. "Oh shit," she moaned.

"This is awesome," Aaron chuckled as he guided the shuttle around into a tight approach. The Chosen traffic control officer had warned him that things were a bit out of control; he'd understated the situation. "Good thing you're not bad with crowds, speeches, or reporters."

"Asshole." He shook his head, but she reached over from the passenger seat to stroke his bristled cheek. "Good to be home."

"Absolutely. 'We pray for one last landing, On the globe that gave us birth, Let us rest our eyes on the fleecy skies, And the cool, green hills of—' Bellatrix."

Pip made a rude noise and chuckled from the seat behind them. "Plagiarist." Minu smiled; she'd read everything by Heinlein years ago. No one else in the back made any comments. Minu could feel nervousness radiating from the rear of the craft.

Aaron did his usual expert piloting job and brought the shuttle down smooth as silk, the landing almost undetectable. Minu stood and turned around; no one else was even moving toward the door. This was her dance. She moved to the door and took a couple of deep breaths. There was no sound from outside. Either the ship was muffling it, or the crowd was perfectly quiet. Then a hand landed on her shoulder, rough and aged. "You'll do fine, young lady." She turned her head and smiled at Bjorn, giving him a nod. With no further hesitation she pushed the button.

* * *

Of course it was a circus. What else could it have been? She'd stepped out onto the top step of the shuttle ramp, looked around, and waved. The roar from the crowd almost knocked her back into the shuttle. The video coverage later only showed a little of her terror at that moment.

The walk down the stairs and along the long red carpet—what idiot found a fifty meter red carpet—to a stand where the entire Chosen council waited. She climbed the stand, stood before Jacob, and performed a rare Chosen salute, knife edge of palm against forehead at a jaunty angle. "Minu Alma, reporting back from off world." She instantly recognized his barely-contained anger and marveled at the change in his appearance. Gray had touched his hair in the five years she'd been gone, though for her it had only been months. Just for effect, she gave him a big wink. The press obligingly caught her wink, but not his grimace. Dram smiled and gave her his own wink. He'd added a few lines to his own tough face.

Her crew and friends came out one after the other, each to more applause. They gathered together, scattered groups of intense applause coming from the crowd where their families or friends had gathered. Following the first awkward greetings, the most uncomfortable being Jasmine Osgood, head of the Science branch, who just glared at her with open hostility, came speeches. Luckily they gave her and her team seats while dignitary after politician sang Minu's praises and the benefits of the codex she'd found. They also had no small amount of praise for First Among the Chosen Jacob, who'd managed to salvage the situation by lying and saying the whole mission was his idea.

And finally, unfortunately, Jacob was standing at the podium and saying, "And now, we'd like to give the Chosen a chance to say a few words herself. Ladies and gentleman, Chosen Minu Alma."

Minu was forced to wait a full five minutes for the screams and applause to die down at long last. She stepped closer to the pickup behind the podium, scrunching up her face at how it was set to the height of an average man, putting it too high for her modest one hundred and fifty seven centimeters. She cleared her throat and went for it.

"I'm overwhelmed," she said, and had to wait another minute before she could continue. "I took this mission to save a friend." She waved a hand toward where Pip sat. He was wearing a hat to cover the dualloy skull plate, and looked uncomfortable in the bright sun. He smiled and nodded at her. Pip's rooting section roared their approval. She recognized his parents and girlfriend. "I didn't really think a lot about any other results. I hoped—sure, who wouldn't in that situation? Every Chosen learns from day one that humanity has suffered from the lack of a codex. All the magic of the Concordia, and most of it useless to us. I guess I just couldn't take that for an answer when I wanted my friend back. If there's anyone who deserves these honors, it would be Pip. Thank you." She walked over during the applause to Pip, who stood as she approached and the two hugged. The crowd approved whole-heartedly. Later when she watched the news coverage, she spat at some of the commentators who'd speculated if they were romantically involved.

Before she could take her seat, Jacob was there next to her along with the council members. "There's one more piece of business," he announced, a remote mike picking up his words. She came to a loose attention, wondering what twist he had for her now. "The council has unanimously decided, in recognition of bravery, dedication to duty, and extremely creative interpretation of standing orders." Minu smirked a little, until he held out a box. She took it with shaking hands and opened it. A set of two golden stars gleamed inside. "We hereby present to you the rank of two stars in the Chosen and appoint you to the leadership council." Minu was staggered and almost didn't take his hand when it was offered. The press was filling in the details that she was the youngest female two-star ever, five years younger than the next closest, Jasmine Osgood.

The crowd roar was the loudest so far, but she still somehow heard Dram from Jacob's side. "There's no hope for you now."

* * *

The end of the event was much more orderly than the beginning. The sun was beginning to set as Minu was ushered offstage to a waiting room where only the Chosen council waited amidst tension and untouched treats. She had no idea where the others were off too. Jacob came in a few minutes later and gave her a hard look. "Well, you pulled that off."

"I didn't pull anything off," she said, "like I said, I rescued a friend."

"We were all set to roast you over an open fire when you sent that codex. I figured it was all klothshit at first, considering your history."

"You'd know the smell," Minu said in an even voice. Jacob's lips narrowed to a razor.

"Do we really want this to go downhill?" Dram asked in his deep baritone. "The fact is we honored you because you earned it, but you have to understand that your rebel days are over. With those two stars comes serious responsibility."

"The council?"

"All two stars have a seat on the council, of course."

"A branch?"

"That has yet to be decided," Jacob growled. Minu understood a little better now. "Frankly, even with all the civilian benefits, I wasn't sold on those stars until we realized you were bringing that ship home." Minu sighed. She'd spent almost two hours describing the situation, including her daughter Lilith. Most of it was backed up by Bjorn, Ted, and Pip, who provided the science. It was all a dizzying mess to the Chosen council, but the ship was an understandable asset. The knowledge of the T'Chillen having war ships would have been a devastating blow, but humans now had a ship that was more than a match for them, and a pilot who had access to vast amounts of ancient Concordian knowledge. "So in a few minutes, after the rabble is all cleared away, let's meet this pilot."

"Her name is Lilith, and she's my daughter. I'd ask you to remember that." Jacob gave a slight but obviously uncomfortable nod. "Did you do what I asked you to do?"

Dram stepped over and handed her another little box. Minu opened it and found five golden stars. "She's Chosen, all official. Lilith Alma, the youngest Chosen ever." Dram chuckled, "We couldn't bring ourselves to list her as two months old, so we entered it as ten as you suggested."

"Makes sense."

"You can deliver her loyalty, right?" Jacob asked.

"I never said that. You read my report; she destroyed ships full of enemies with no more emotion that you would show squashing a fly."

"Regardless, you say you're her mother; if anyone can control her, it needs to be you. At least until we can learn to run the ship."

"If you try to take that ship from her, I won't be responsible for the results." Jacob glanced at Jasmine nervously, and Minu sensed a conspiracy. "I don't know what that woman has told you, but this isn't some aerocar that you can override the command code on and fly away. She was born and raised from a fetus to operate this ship. I think she considers it more her mother than me." Jasmine was shooting daggers at Minu, seemingly not trusting herself to speak.

"Let's just wait and see what happens, shall we?" Dram asked.

The few minutes turned into an hour by the time a pair of harried logistics Chosen came in and said the coast was clear. The council led Minu out to within a few steps of the shuttle. Minu's friends, Ted, Bjorn, Cherise, Aaron and Pip were back and waiting for her. Minu had insisted they all be there to help make the situation less alien. She climbed the boarding ladder and leaned inside. In the darkened interior she could see her daughter floating near the rear with dancing Concordian script around both hands. "It's time."

"I don't see the logic in this. They're nothing to me."

Minu swallowed, that wasn't a good reaction. "They want to meet you, it's a social interaction. Pip explained it, right?" She relied on Pip more and more as a liaison to her own daughter. They communicated on more levels than she could.

"He did, but I watched the broadcasts with you out there. No mention of me or the ship."

"We've kept it a secret, like I explained to you earlier. Large parts of Bellatrix are still simple farmers. We're afraid they'll be scared of a *Kaatan* warship floating over their heads."

"Primitives."

"Perhaps, but they're humans, just like you."

Lilith snorted but then nodded. "I'll come out. It's fully dark?"

"Yes." There was concern that even the afternoon sun could cause problems for Lilith, whose skin had never felt the touch of direct solar radiation. Inside the womb of her CIC she could fly the *Kaatan* deep into the photosphere of a star. On her own she could be seriously sunburned in minutes. The red hair and light skin were a tough combination, as Minu well knew. Lilith started coming forward, and Minu backed down the ladder.

"Problem?" Jacob asked, sounding like he hoped there was.

"No, just stage fright."

"And she's this badass warrior?"

"You have no idea," Aaron said, getting a glare from Jacob.

At a sound from the shuttle, all eyes turned toward the door. Of course everyone who'd come down knew what to expect, but no one else did. Minu had been careful not to tell them what they were in for. Owing to Lilith's special needs, the ship had produced a unique solution for her trip down to the surface. A huge crystalline bot walked to the doorway, eight segmented legs radiating equally around its round torso. On the back was a hybrid hoverfield generator, field/shield system inside which she rode, surrounded by a circular globe of carefully controlled atmosphere and zero gravity. The effect was breathtaking, in both a positive and a negative way.

"Oh my," Minu heard Jasmine gasp. As the bot expertly negotiated the stairs, the Steven's Pass flood lights provided their first good look at Lilith. Her gaunt appearance, almost skeletal arms and legs, her long hair the same shade of red as Minu's floating freely around her, and finally, as she got closer, her rich brown eyes. She regarded the assemblage from her graceful swimmer's pose, looking like some ancient fairy princess from old Earth legends.

"Wow," said Dram, looking between Minu and Lilith. There was little doubt in his mind who the girl's mother was, regardless of the improbable nature of the situation.

Minu stepped up next to the bot as it came to a stop at the bottom of the stairs. "Jacob, First Among the Chosen, I'd like you to meet my daughter, Lilith Alma, Combat Intelligence and biological operator of the *Kaatan*-class warship in space over our heads." She caught the nervous look a couple of the councilmen gave toward the sky, as if they could see the ship floating up there bristling with guns and missiles. "Lilith, this is my boss, Jacob."

"It's good to meet you," he said to her. His hand twitched toward her before he pulled it back, remembering that there would be no physical contact. Medical concerns again.

"And to meet you as well," she said, and gave him a little smile. Minu was glad she'd practiced so much over the time since she'd emerged. If she'd flashed one of those early grimaces, he probably would have screamed and run away.

Minu reached through the field and handed her the little box with the two sets of five stars. "It is official, you're now Chosen."

"My thanks," she said and accepted the pins. As they'd discussed, she quickly fixed them on the cuffs of her jumpsuit, which had been a copy of the Chosen design all along. They seemed improbably large there, that pentagon configuration of golden stars on her tiny wrists.

"Now about the ship," Jacob began, jumping over several lines of protocol they'd carefully discussed. Minu almost spat on the ground and walked away. It was only the look on Lilith's face that kept her silent. That look of complete confidence and utter calm.

"What about the ship?"

"We want to know all about it."

"So we can better utilize it," Jasmine chimed in. Right, Minu thought, set fire to the whole plan.

"I'll decide how my ship is utilized."

"You have to understand," Jacob said, adopting a patronizing tone, "it's a powerful asset you have up there. We can't honestly let a little girl have complete control."

"Little girl…" Lilith repeated.

"Yes," Jasmine continued, taking a step forward and trying to sound matronly, "you understand, right? Wouldn't you like to stay down here? Our doctors want to examine you, maybe help accelerate your muscular development with gene therapy that your mother brought back in the codex. Why, in no time at all you'll be jumping and playing in the sunlight, and forget all about that ship up there."

"Forget about the ship?"

"Yes," Jacob leaped in, sure they were about to get what they wanted. Minu silently cursed him for an idiot for not realizing he was in over his head and being played by a deceptively intuitive young woman. "We'll take care of it for you. Of course you'll be involved as an advisor! You've got to work now that you wear those stars."

"Of course," Lilith said, her face yet to register any changes.

"So what do you say I make a call, get some technicians here, and we'll pop up to the ship and you can show us how to take command?"

"When I'm a rotting corpse."

Jacob blanched. "Excuse me?"

"I said you can take control of the ship when I'm a rotting corpse."

"Oh, she's Minu's daughter alright," Dram stage-whispered to Bjorn, who'd covered his mouth to avoid laughing. Unfortunately, humor was in short supply.

"Now that's not the attitude to take, little girl," Jasmine said sternly, actually wagging a finger at the young Alma.

"If any of you so much as try to set foot on the ship without my permission, it'll be the last thing you ever do." Now she showed emotions, and they were such emotions that even Minu was taken aback. Lilith's face seethed with so much anger and hatred that her eyes seemed almost to glow, and her hair to blow back behind her head as if a stiff wind were blowing. Minu only realized later that it was all for effect, carefully orchestrated by her daughter. "I'm the Combat Intelligence of the ship, and there's nothing more to say."

"You don't expect us to just let you fly back to space do you? You don't understand who you're dealing with." Minu caught movement out of the corner of her eye and turned her head. There were two teams of Chosen scouts, one at the front of the shuttle, one at the back. They were all fully armed and wearing combat armor. Minu felt her heart stop, ice water running down her back. "If you don't understand the situation, we'll have to explain it to you."

"No, First Among the Chosen, let me explain it to you. There's no way those soldiers of yours will be able to keep me from getting back into the shuttle and then into space."

"And if this shuttle leaves the ground without my approval I'll have it shot down by the energy batteries in this mountain." Jacob crossed his arms over his chest, standing up straight and glaring at her.

Lilith glared pure hatred at him and for a second Minu feared he'd win. She should have known better. "Are you sure this is the way you want to play it?"

"You give me no choice."

"Then you give me none either." Jacob and Jasmine were suddenly bathed in a crisp green light rather like a stage spotlight. The beam quickly went from illuminating them all to a clearly defined ring around Jacob and Jasmine only, the two who'd threatened her. They both looked around in confusion, and then with painful slowness, they looked straight up. Anyone standing at a distance could see the green circles of light descend from the sky to them; it was like looking into a flashlight. "It seems you don't know who you're dealing with."

"Are you trying to tell me this spotlight is a weapon from orbit?" Jacob laughed, but it was a laugh that didn't reach his eyes.

"That's for you to decide." Slowly at first, Jacob and Jasmine began to look uncomfortable. Then a tiny wisp of smoke rose from Jacob's hair, quickly followed by Jasmine's. "Your move, First."

Jacob tried to stand his ground. Jasmine had reached her limit and ran for the distant buildings. The circle of light followed her perfectly. A few meters away she fell to the ground screaming, her clothes smoking. The nearest Chosen moved to help but he pulled his hand back in shock as he touched the energy wave.

"Damn it Jacob!" Minu screamed. "Stop this before she kills you both!"

"You will follow orders!" he screamed back, bending over and covering his smoldering head with his smoldering arms. The scout teams stood their ground, uncertain what to do. Lilith paid them no attention; she was aware of every living thing for a hundred kilometers in every direction, and prepared to kill all of them to defend her ship. "Minu, stop her!"

"I have no more power over her than I do over you."

"I am a ship of the line," Lilith said, her voice full of ice and fire, *"and you will not order me!"*

"Fine!"

"Fine, what?" Lilith asked.

"We won't try to take your ship!" Instantly the beams were gone. Jasmine remained on the ground, whimpering, while the scout who'd tried to help earlier moved over to see to her. Jacob stood back up slowly, ignoring his partly melted hair and burned skin. "This is not over."

"It better be. Because if it isn't, I'll simply remove this mountain top and be done with you." With no further fanfare, she turned and the crystalline bot walked her back inside. Her first visit 'home' was over. "Goodbye Mother, this has been enjoyable. We'll talk soon." The door slid closed, and they all moved back as the shuttle made a perfect take off and angled upward, quickly shrinking in size as it shot toward orbit. Minu smiled as she saw everyone step back so at least a couple meters were between themselves and the First.

Dram patted Minu on the shoulder, "Chriso would have liked her."

* * * * *

Epilogue
April 10th, 527 AE

Stevens Pass Auditorium, Bellatrix

Minu struggled to get the unfamiliar gear into place, cursing even as Cherise helped her. "It works for you," her friend said.

Minu blew a raspberry and tugged again at an uncooperative strap. "Not the kind of combat armor I prefer."

"It's all combat to you, isn't it?"

"Sort of, I suppose." Minu and her friend laughed as they finally controlled the strap and finished off by tying her now mid-back-length hair into an intricate ponytail.

"It's not too late to change your mind, you know. I wouldn't blame you, either."

"Nope, this has got to be done." Cherise sighed, then nodded.

"You better get out there then."

"Are there a lot of them?"

"Yes, and they're getting more unruly the longer you take."

"At least I don't have to go through this alone."

"You knew I'd be here for you."

"I hoped you would."

"Wild kloth couldn't keep me away."

Minu smiled and kissed her friend. "Come on, let's go." Cherise held the door for her and she walked out. The crowd was big, and they were all looking at her. She felt very uncomfortable in this unfamiliar garb, afraid she'd missed a strap or something by the way they looked at her. More than a few obviously figured she didn't have a chance judging by the tears in many eyes. She didn't let it bother her; this was her decision.

At the end of the long walk was Aaron, also dressed and ready. They'd do this together, as two people always had throughout history. She realized she'd been destined for this since they first met. Suddenly she was crying too. Aaron saw her tears and looked concerned. She shook her head and smiled, and he knew it was okay. Near the front of the assemblage her daughter hovered in her bot-supported ball of zero gravity, watching the proceedings with interest. Pip stood on one side of her. The two were fast becoming friends.

Finally as she neared Aaron, Bjorn stood and took her arm, walking her the last meter to stand next to Aaron. From behind a podium, Dram gave her a wink and nodded to Bjorn. The elderly man, uncle to the friend she'd fought so hard to save, and her mentor, gave her a little kiss on the cheek and put her hand into Aaron's. "Take good care of her, son," he said, then returned to his seat. The Second Among the Chosen cleared his throat. "We are gathered here to witness the joining of Minu Alma and Aaron Groves in matrimony." Minu took Aaron's out-stretched hand and turned toward Dram, to face her future.

* * *

The three-man team emerged from the portal and waited while they were regarded by sensors. A dozen heavy beamcaster emplacements, automated and imminently deadly, regarded them from all over the chamber while their fate was determined. "You are cleared," a mechanical voice eventually acknowledged.

The team leader led his people through a door, where they racked their weapons and removed their armor. They weren't half finished when another door opened and a tall man strode in. They were all a little surprised. You almost never saw him out of his lab. "What happened?" he demanded instantly.

"We saw her," the team leader confirmed. "She was with a scout and a Rasa warrior."

"Rasa? Were they prisoners?"

"Allies," another team member said. "We saw them covering each other."

"They were a practiced team too," the third man confirmed. "Smooth operators for as young as she and the other human were."

He seemed to consider this before speaking again. "Outcome?"

"We neutralized the Vampires and extracted before they could identify us."

"Good." His eyes got that vacant look they'd all come to recognize as his powerful mind worked on the situation. "And the ship?"

"We only got a few looks through the instruments; it was in too high an orbit." The leader took out a data chip and handed it to him. The man popped it into a tablet and pulled up images. They were a little blurry, but the needle-pierced ball was unmistakable. "It has to be a *Kaatan*."

He reviewed the images, stopping at a still of a short, slender, redhead woman, beautiful with angular facial bones and shoulder length, bright red hair. The expression on her face was one of intense life or death focus as she held a pair of improbably huge handguns at arm's length. He puzzled over them for a minute before looking at the man to her side. Also rather short, he was powerfully built, with chiseled features, and was wielding a beamcaster with the grace and ability of a man who'd used one many times in combat. Was there something about the way they stood by each other? More than comrades, protecting loved ones from danger? The aforementioned Rasa was just to the side, covering their undefended flank. He carried one of their flechette machineguns and had a curious semi-circle burned in his crest. They were right, neither he nor they were prisoners.

"Orders, sir?" the team leader asked.

"No changes. We continue as planned." The three scouts nodded and went about securing weapons and gear. In a minute they were gone, leaving him alone. He sat on one of the benches and went back to the girl. "Minu," he said and gently touched her image, as if he could brush the hair from her digital eyes. "This is going better than I'd hoped."

He took a communicator from his pocket and activated it. "Ready," a strangely-modulated voice answered.

"Prepare the ship; we have a mission."

"Acknowledged," was the reply as he put away the communicator.

Chriso Alma glanced back down at the picture of his daughter and smiled. Had she been there to see the grin on her father's face, Minu wouldn't have considered it one of mirth. Any who'd fought against Chriso would recognize the look. It was the last one they'd ever see.

# # # # #

ABOUT THE AUTHOR

Located in rural Tennessee, Mark Wandrey has been creating new worlds since he was old enough to write. After penning countless short stories, he realized novels were his real calling and hasn't looked back since. A lifetime of diverse jobs, extensive travels, and living in most areas of the country have uniquely equipped him with experiences to color his stories in ways many find engaging and thought provoking.

Sign up on his mailing list and get free stuff and updates! http://www.worldmaker.us/news-flash-sign-up-page/

Caution – Worlds Under Construction

Titles by Mark Wandrey

A Time to Die

Cartwright's Cavaliers

Winged Hussars

A Fistful of Credits

For a Few Credits More

The Good, the Bad, and the Merc

Alpha Contracts

A Fiery Sunset

Earth Song: Overture

Earth Song: Sonata in Orionis

Earth Song: The Lost Aria

*****

The following is an

Excerpt from Book Four of the Earth Song Cycle:

Etude to War

Mark Wandrey

Coming Soon from Theogony Books

eBook, Paperback, and Audio Book

Excerpt from "Etude to War:"

The Portal snapped to life, and a solitary figure emerged. Few in the galaxy would recognize a human by sight, and fewer still would realize how well equipped this particular human was. The armor integrated stealth mirage technology as well as capacitance recycling, linked with a defensive shield. Such a thing had not been seen for untold eons and wouldn't be recognized by the most knowledgeable researcher.

The figure loosely carried a shock rifle, more unknown tech, and wore a miniature beamcaster pistol in a holster locked on a belt clogged with equipment. The instant the figure cleared the event horizon of the Portal, it swept the area with the instruments inside the helmet. The multi-spectral scanners would pick up even the slightest hint of an enemy, even if one had been there hours ago. It was only after the readings confirmed the perimeter was clear that the visor retracted seamlessly into the helmet.

Chosen Christian Forsythe, scout, moved to the side, away from the Portal, behind a partially-collapsed structure. He kneeled as he removed a case from his belt. Inside was a precious dragonfly-bot which he tasked and released into the air. It raced off with an almost inaudible buzz as he took out his tablet to watch it do its magic.

He wrinkled his nose; there was a trace of ammonia in the planet's atmosphere. He wouldn't be keeping his helmet open too long. Luckily, the Type IV field armor he wore was self-contained and wouldn't need recycling for thirty days. The techs promised a version in the future that would not only operate in space but would keep the occupant alive for nearly a year.

Three hours earlier he'd left the rest of his team to finish examining a battle scene. It was months old but offered enough work to keep them occupied and not wondering where their commander had gone. He wore three darkened gold stars on his sleeves, as he had for years. He didn't lust for promotion as much as some; he found a certain contentment in the somewhat reduced role of the scouts these days. They weren't the devil-may-care adventurers they were in the early days, but they were the first in. The Rangers couldn't do their jobs nearly as well if not for the scouts.

The crumbling city around him moaned and creaked in the stiff breeze. The sun, a bluish-tinted sphere high in the sky, barely seemed to penetrate the drifting clouds above. Here and there a desultory blade of orange-tinted grass tried to grow between cobblestones most likely placed before his species learned to walk upright. Humans were the babies of the Concordia, a fact they all grew up knowing. He shifted his gun on his shoulder and stretched a little. His armor fit him like a second skin. Kids they might well be, but they were growing up fast.

Thanks to his old girlfriend, humanity now had access to rich treasure troves of data they didn’t generally share with other species. Already, they'd gained powerful allies by judiciously trading that technology, and they had used it to upgrade their equipment, so they would be more than a match for any enemies they might have to face in the future, even those from higher order species.

He shivered at that thought. Humans might be well armed, but there were only a few million of them on one backwater world. Even the Tog, their benefactors and the smallest of the higher orders, were a hundred million strong and lived on six worlds.

It was because of that ex-girlfriend that he was on this world, one claimed by the deadly species known as the T'Chillen. He wasn't foolish enough to think she'd come back to him, not after marrying, but he did hope if he found what he was looking for, she’d find it in her heart to forgive him for being such a jerk. This might be a way to make amends for his actions.

The bot reported it had located what he was looking for and awaited orders. Christian broke into an easy jog and arrived where it hovered in a minute. Underneath the buzzing bot was a metallic hatch, partially covered by a collapsed wall.

"Bingo," he said and snapped his fingers. The bot waited until he took out its case and held it open. A second later, the marvelous machine folded itself inside, safe and sound.

It took Christian two backbreaking hours to clear enough debris to reach the hatch. The collapse had destroyed the locking mechanism. Normally that would be a problem, but not now. He attached an ultra-miniaturized hoverfield generator, a piece of equipment each scout carried, to the hatch, triggered it and stood back. The device quickly pried open the hatch, the dualloy giving and folding back with a horrendous screech.

During his brief, but passionate, relationship with Minu he'd seen the logs left behind by her father. Those logs contained thousands of pages describing worlds he had visited, what he'd seen, and what he thought it meant. Minu read every page, trying to gain insights into her father's skill as a leader and a Concordia technologist. Christian had plied his memory of those logs, looking for something else.

And after months of quiet probing on the frontier and reviewing scout mission logs, here he was, outside a seemingly innocuous hatch on a rusting, junk pile world in the middle of the frontier. But all the data pointed to Chriso and his team of twelve scouts disappearing here years ago.

Christian climbed down the ladder inside the hatch, rung after rung, what felt like a thousand steps. He reached up and slid his helmet into place; the multiple vision enhancements showed him descending inside a tube carved from the living rock of the planet.

Eventually, the tube gave way to a galley of sorts, with dozens of passages leading off in all directions. He didn't go any farther. As soon as he set foot on the stone floor, his sensors told him he'd tripped an alarm. It was a Chosen design, in use for decades, and he carried a trio of them in his own pack.

Christian leaned against a wall, one hand resting casually on the grip of his miniature beamcaster and waited. It wasn’t long before the distant sound of running feet reached his ears. He wasn't worried; the pounding feet were decidedly human. But when they arrived, his welcome was less than wonderful.

“On the ground!” screamed the first man to arrive, a scout wearing armor more than a decade old. Though worn in places, it showed careful tending.

“I'm human. Chosen scout Christian Forsythe, three star.”

“Do as I said human, or I'll kill you where you stand.” Two more scouts arrived from different directions. They came in quietly, and he barely noticed them. He realized if he didn't do what they told him to, he was dead.

With a sigh he fell to his knees, following orders. They disarmed him, cuffed his hands behind his back, and gave him a push to start him walking.

Christian smiled and asked, “Is Chriso nearby?”

*****

The following is an

Excerpt from Book One of In Revolution Born:

The Mutineer's Daughter

Chris Kennedy & Thomas A. Mays

Available Now from Seventh Seal Press

eBook, Paperback, and (soon) Audio Book

Excerpt from "The Mutineer's Daughter:"

Kenny dozed at his console again.

There he sat—as brazen as ever—strapped down, suited up, jacked in...and completely checked out. One might make allowances for an overworked man falling asleep during a dull routine, watching gauges that didn't move or indicators that rarely indicated anything of consequence, perhaps even during a quiet moment during their ship's long, long deployment.

But Fire Control Tech Third Class Ken Burnside was doing it—yet again—while the ship stood at General Quarters, in an unfriendly star system, while other parts of the fleet engaged the forces of the Terran Union.

Chief Warrant Officer Grade 2 (Combat Systems) Benjamin "Benno" Sanchez shook his helmeted head and narrowed his eyes at the sailor strapped in to his right. He had spoken to the young weapons engineer a number of times before, through countless drills and mock skirmishes, but the youthful idiot never retained the lesson for long.

"Benno, Bosso," Kenny would plead, "you shouldn't yell at me. You should have me teach others my wisdom!"

Benno would invariably frown and give his unflattering opinion of Kenny's wisdom.

"Get it, ya?" Kenny would reply. "I'm a math guy. Probability, right Warrant? The *Puller's* just a little ship, on the edge of the formation. We scan, we snipe, we mop up, we patrol. We don't go in the middle, tube's blazing, ya? We no tussle with the big Terrans, ya? No damage! No battle! So, something goes wrong, back-ups kick in, buzzer goes off, we mark for fix later. And when's the only time you or the officers don't let a man walk 'round and don't ask for this, don't ask for that? When's the only time a man can catch up on the z's, eh? One and the same time! So I doze. Buzzer goes off, I wake, make a note, doze again till I can work, ya? Such wisdom!"

Benno usually lectured him about complacency. He asked what would happen if they *were* hit, if the shot was hot enough, deep enough, destructive enough to burn through the backup of the backup of the backup. What if they did have to face the Great Test, to rise and work and save the *Puller* themselves?

Kenny would always smile, relieved. "Well, then I be dead, ya? No more maintenance either way. Good enough reason to doze right there!"

Benno could have reported him any number of times, but he never had. Putting it on paper and sending it above them was a two-edged sword. It would solve Kenny's sleepy disdain for order, of that Benno had no doubt, but he also knew he would lose Kenny's trust and the vigorous drive the young ALS plebeian applied to every other task. Plus, it would signal to the officers above that Benno couldn't handle a minor discipline problem on his own. And it would indicate to the ranks below that Benno was no longer one of their own—when he had gone from Chief to Chief Warrant Officer, he had changed his ties, forever.

So Benno growled, but he let it slide, content only he would know about Kenny's acts of passive rebellion. No one else would ever know why the young tech kept getting extra punishment duties. Besides, it wasn't as if Kenny was actually *wrong*, in the fullness of things.

Then, before Benno could check his own side of the console to verify whether things were indeed alright, his internal debate was blown away by the unforgiving, indiscriminate lance of an x-ray laser blast.

The single beam struck the *Puller* a glancing blow, centered on a space just beneath the outer hull and aimed outboard. Armor plate, radiation shielding, piping, wireways, conduit, decking, internal honeycombed structure, atmosphere, and people all ionized and ablated into a dense, mixed plasma. This plasma exploded outward, crushing the spaces surrounding the hit and dealing further physical and thermal damage. Combat Systems Maintenance Central, or CSMC, lay deep within the *Puller's* battle hull—three spaces inward from where the x-ray laser struck—but that meant little next to the awesome destructive power of a Dauphine capital-class xaser warhead.

The forward and port bulkheads in front of them flashed white hot with near-instantaneous thermal energy transfer and peeled away, blown out by the twin shocks of the outward-expanding plasma and the snapping counterforce of explosive decompression. The double blast battered Benno in his seat and threw him against his straps to the left. As the bulkheads vanished, their departure also carried away the CSMC monitoring console the two watch standers shared with them into the black, along with Kenny's seat, and Ken Burnside, himself.

The young engineer disappeared in an instant, lost without ever waking. Benno stared, dumbfounded, at the blank spot where he had been, and of all the possible panicked thoughts that could have come to him, only one rose to the forefront:

Does this validate Kenny's wisdom?

Benno shook his head, dazed and in shock, knowing he had to engage his brain. Looking beyond, he could see the glowing edges of bulkheads and decks gouged out by the fast, hot knife of the nuclear-pumped xaser. Only vaguely could he recall the sudden buffeting of explosive decompression that had nearly wrenched him through the straps of his acceleration couch.

He knew he had things to do. He had to check his suit's integrity. Was he leaking? Was he injured? And what about Kenny? Was he gone, unrecoverable? Or was he waiting for his poor, shocked-stupid boss Benno to reach out and save him?

And there was something else, something important he needed to be doing. He wasn't supposed to just sit here and think of himself or unlucky, lazy Kenny. *Oh no*, thought Benno, still trying to marshal his thoughts back together, *Mio is going to be so angry with me, sitting here like a fool…*

"CSMC, report!"

Benno shook his head against the ringing he hadn't realized filled his ears. He reached out for the comms key on his console, swore at how futile that was, then keyed his suit mic. "Last station calling, this is CSMC. We've taken a hit. I lost my technician, console is…down, hard. Over."

"CSMC, TAO," the *Puller's* Tactical Action Officer said through the suit channel, "pull it together! We just had a near miss by a capital class Dauphine warhead. The battle with the Terrans has spread out of the main body. I have missiles up but zero point-defense. I need guns and beams back, *now!*"

*****

*****

The following is an

Excerpt from Book One of the Revelations Cycle:

Cartwright's Cavaliers

Mark Wandrey

Now Available from Seventh Seal Press

eBook, Paperback, and Audio Book

Excerpt from "Cartwright's Cavaliers:"

The last two operational tanks were trapped on their chosen path. Faced with destroyed vehicles front and back, they cut sideways to the edge of the dry river bed they'd been moving along and found several large boulders to maneuver around that allowed them to present a hull-down defensive position. Their troopers rallied on that position. It was starting to look like they'd dig in when Phoenix 1 screamed over and strafed them with dual streams of railgun rounds. A split second later, Phoenix 2 followed on a parallel path. Jim was just cheering the air attack when he saw it. The sixth damned tank, and it was a heavy.

"I got that last tank," Jim said over the command net.

"Observe and stand by," Murdock said.

"We'll have these in hand shortly," Buddha agreed, his transmission interspersed with the thudding of his CASPer firing its magnet accelerator. "We can be there in a few minutes."

Jim examined his battlespace. The tank was massive. It had to be one of the fusion-powered beasts he'd read about. Which meant shields and energy weapons. It was heading down the same gap the APC had taken, so it was heading right towards that APC and Second Squad, and fast.

"Shit," he said.

"Jim," Hargrave said, "we're in position. What are you doing?"

"Leading," Jim said as he jumped out from the rock wall.

* * * * *

Made in the USA
Lexington, KY
20 March 2019